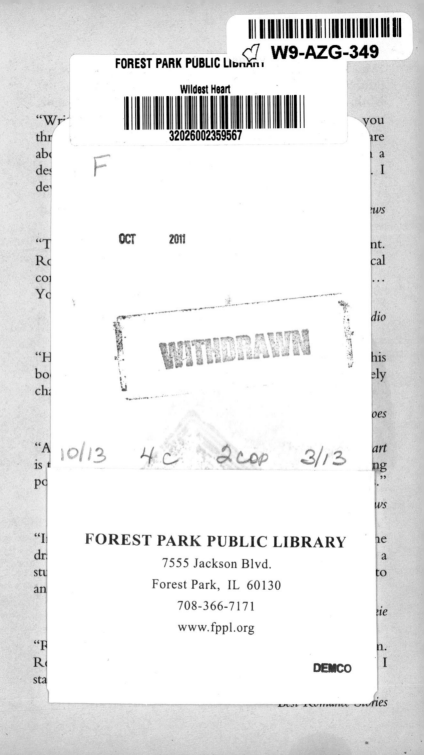

W9-AZG-349

FOREST PARK PUBLIC LIBRARY

Wildest Heart

32026002359567

F

OCT   2011

WITHDRAWN

10/13   4 c   2 cop   3/13

FOREST PARK PUBLIC LIBRARY

7555 Jackson Blvd.

Forest Park, IL 60130

708-366-7171

www.fppl.org

DEMCO

"Wri... you
thr... are
abo... a
des... I
dev...

...ws

"T... nt.
Ro... cal
con... ...
Yo...

...dio

"H... his
bo... ely
cha...

...oes

"A... art
is ... ng
po... ."

...ws

"I... he
dr... a
stu... to
an...

...ie

"R... n.
Ro... I
sta...

Best Romance Stories

"Ms. Rogers has crafted an epic novel. The plot twists and turns and has so many surprises you won't be able to put this work down until you've reached the climatic end. I highly recommend this wonderful work."

—*Night Owl Romance, Reviewer Top Pick*

"Exceedingly well written, detailed, and rich in character with vivid descriptions of the landscapes from India to the wild west of New Mexico. A complex romance… filled with mystery, intrigue, love, and betrayal."

—*Rundpinne*

"Plenty of drama, adventure, and romance… the kind of book you can really sink your teeth into."

—*The Bookworm 07*

"Timeless in its appeal. Rosemary Rogers is a storyteller who knows how to weave story lines… I think this reprint will find a whole new generation of Rosemary Rogers fans."

—*Found Not Lost*

"Strong characters that will keep you captivated all the way to the last page! A very erotic and true romantic read."

—*My Overstuffed Bookshelf*

"A great story of revenge, mystery, searching for the truth, belonging, and romance. There are twists and turns, it is fast paced with disappointments and intrigue… the characters leave you spellbound."

—*My Book Addiction and More*

"A sweeping, beautiful epic historical romance… Be prepared to be captivated through the entire book… Just beautiful."

—*Revenge of the Book Nerds*

"The perfect romance... historical, full of tension, with a really compelling story and strong characters."

—*Books Like Breathing*

"An epic saga... Be prepared to be consumed by gun-slinging, hijacking fun with some captivating fire-and-rain romance thrown in!"

—*The Burton Review*

FOREST PARK PUBLIC LIBRARY

OCT   2011

FOREST PARK, IL.

The WILDEST HEART

ROSEMARY ROGERS

Copyright © 1974, 2009, 2011 by Rosemary Rogers
Cover and internal design © 2011 by Sourcebooks, Inc.
Cover design by Dawn Pope/Sourcebooks
Cover photos © Shirley Green; © Corbis

Sourcebooks and the colophon are registered trademarks of Sourcebooks, Inc.

All rights reserved. No part of this book may be reproduced in any form or by any electronic or mechanical means including information storage and retrieval systems—except in the case of brief quotations embodied in critical articles or reviews—without permission in writing from its publisher, Sourcebooks, Inc.

The characters and events portrayed in this book are fictitious or are used fictitiously. Any similarity to real persons, living or dead, is purely coincidental and not intended by the author.

Published by Sourcebooks Casablanca, an imprint of Sourcebooks, Inc.
P.O. Box 4410, Naperville, Illinois 60567–4410
(630) 961–3900
FAX: (630) 961–2168
www.sourcebooks.com

Originally published in 1974 by Avon Books

Cataloging-in-Publication Data is on file with the publisher.

Printed and bound in Canada
WC 10 9 8 7 6 5 4 3 2 1

For Shirlee, with thanks.

Contents

✣

PROLOGUE

i

INDIA—1872

"WILD BLOOD! IT'S A TAINT IN THE BLOOD. I'VE HEARD IT SAID that every generation of Dangerfields produces one of them. They call it the Dangerfield devil."

Mrs. Leacock, beginning to fan herself vigorously, continued, "All those generations of inbreeding... what do they expect? They call Melchester 'the Eccentric Earl' behind his back, but at least he hasn't done anything too outrageous yet... but I think it's a positive outrage that he lets Rowena go her own way! That girl will come to a bad end one day—I can feel it. That temper... do you remember the time she half whipped a groom to death because he had forgotten to rub down her horse? And she's the only white woman in the province of Jhanpur who has ever witnessed a public execution. The colonel told me he was stunned to see her there in the first place, and that she didn't turn a hair, either!"

"Something," Mrs. Leacock pronounced awfully, "must be done! You know how my dear husband hates to interfere, but I shall ask him to speak to the governor. We cannot have a scandal here, and especially one involving a young Englishwoman and a native prince!"

It was the custom of the Englishwomen who had followed their husbands to the small province of Jhanpur to gather together for tea every afternoon. When Mrs. Leacock, who was the bishop's wife, or Mrs. O'Bannion, whose husband commanded the small English garrison, presided at such gatherings they became tea parties, with the rules of protocol and etiquette strictly adhered to. Dainty iced cakes, sweet fruits, and thin sandwiches cut into pretty shapes by a well-trained cook were graciously served. Either of the two ladies sat graciously behind a silver tea service, making a pretty ceremony of pouring.

On this particular afternoon, Mrs. Leacock was the hostess, and as she served the last steaming cup of tea she leaned forward, lowering her voice slightly.

"Speaking of discipline," she continued, "I must confess that the natives are not alone in their lack of it! I tell you, my dears, that girl's behavior grows more outrageous every day!"

Ever since the Earl of Melchester, who was British governor of Jhanpur, had brought his granddaughter to live with him, Rowena Dangerfield had been a source of speculation and comment among the small British community.

"Oh, heavens!" Mrs. O'Bannion said, sitting up straight, "are the rumors true?"

"I learned from our groom, Mohammed Khan, that she has taken to meeting the young prince on her rides. And if you'll remember we were talking about him only last week, about how glad the maharajah must be that his son has stayed so long on a visit."

"Oh, dear! You think *this* is why he's stayed?" Little Mrs. Loving, whose husband was a very junior subaltern, opened, her blue eyes very wide.

Mrs. Leacock smiled graciously to show that she forgave the interruption.

"Everyone knows that the Shiv Jhanpur is far fonder of the fleshpots of Bombay and Delhi than he is of the province he'll rule one day. He was educated at Oxford, like his father, but that doesn't really make too much difference to these native princes—they follow their old ways as soon as they return here!"

"But, Marion!" Mrs. O'Bannion looked visibly agitated. "Surely—what I mean is, is the governor aware of this? As—as peculiar as some of his ideas are, I do not think…"

"You know as well as I do, Amy, that he allows that

girl to run wild! Allowing her to visit the palace, and even to—to visit the women's quarters! It's unchristian, positively heathenish that these Indian princes should be allowed to continue with their old custom of having so many wives! Why, even the prince has five, at least. He was married to the first of them when they were both no more than infants!"

"Oh!" Mrs. Loving breathed, and the older women gave her understanding looks.

"You haven't been here long enough, my dear, to understand how very primitive these people can be!" Mrs. O'Bannion smiled knowingly.

"Of course not!" added Mrs. Leacock. "And you haven't met the governor yet, have you? My husband, who is a dear, sweet, *charitable* man has reached the point of despair. I mean, one expects the governor to set an example, but he hasn't been to church for years, and neither has that hoydenish, arrogant granddaughter of his. I mentioned it to him myself, I said, 'It would be so pleasant to see dear Rowena in church some Sundays; after all we *do* live in a country of heathens, and if children are not taught their own religion while they're still young enough to be influenced…' and then, my dear, he cut me off! He wouldn't let me say another word, merely frowned down at me in that bushy-browed way and said curtly that *he* did not wish his granddaughter's mind to be cluttered up by dogma! I can tell you, *that* left me speechless! I sometimes doubt if he's a Christian himself."

"But you were telling us about Rowena," Mrs. O'Bannion persisted, and her friend gave a long-suffering sigh.

"Yes, of course. Well, to my mind it's all part and parcel of the way she's been brought up. She's never been to school, and when I mentioned once that my own dear Marcia would be going to an excellently recommended boarding school in England, all he did was raise one eyebrow and growl 'Is that so, madam? Well, I'll not have my granddaughter's mind ruined by pianoforte lessons and watercolors. She'll get her education from *me*.' He had boxes and boxes of books brought here—some of them from France and Germany. And if the girl isn't out riding, or on a tiger shoot, she has her nose in those books—some of them, I'm sure, hardly suitable reading material for a child her age."

Mrs. Leacock's pause was purely rhetorical, but Mrs. Loving, knitting her fair brows, said softly: "Oh! I didn't know she was still a child. I thought—I mean I'm almost certain I heard someone say she was almost eighteen…"

"Rowena Dangerfield is seventeen, but you would never think it to look at her. She cares not in the least how she dresses, and some of her riding habits have grown far too tight and far too short. She goes out riding during the hottest part of the day, bareheaded if you please, and it's a wonder she hasn't caught sunstroke yet! My Marcia always wore a hat and carried a parasol, and it was only with the aid of my buttermilk and cucumber lotions that we managed to keep her complexion so fair and pretty. Rowena is positively sunburned, and with that mane of black hair I'm sure she hardly bothers to comb, she could easily pass for an Indian herself. It—I hate to sound uncharitable, but it's positively shocking, and a terrible example to the natives. And now, this!"

"Deplorable," Mrs. Carter murmured, shaking her head. She cast an almost pitying glance at Mrs. Loving, who had not been in Jhanpur long enough to hear all the gossip, and added, "But of course, when one considers her *background*—that terrible scandal—it's no wonder the governor brought her back here, and hasn't been back to England himself!"

Mrs. Loving's eyes widened with a mixture of horror and pleasurable anticipation.

"Scandal?" she murmured softly.

"My dear child, where *have* you been?" Mrs. O'Bannion asked incredulously. "They were whispering of nothing else in London, some years back."

"It was fifteen years, to be exact, and Rowena was still no more than a baby when *he* brought her here." Mrs. Leacock shook her head ominously. "Such a shocking affair! But then, Guy Dangerfield was always a ne'er-do-well. The younger son— spoiled by his mother, of course. He was sent down from Oxford twice for the mischief he got into. Then, to make matters worse, he ran off to America, to make his fortune, he said."

"And then, some years later, he was back again, like a bad penny! You see, William, who was the heir, was killed in a hunting accident, and that left only Guy to inherit the title. I suppose the earl sent for him. But suddenly, after people had almost forgotten him, there he was, and engaged to be married of all things! Fanny Tolliver—a pretty little thing, she was only seventeen and barely out of the schoolroom. Good enough family, though not very much money, of course. We were back home on leave at the time, and I remember reading the announcement in the *Times,* and telling the colonel, 'You mark my words, I've a feeling that no good will come of *that* match.' And I was right, of course." The lady paused to draw a breath and her friend interposed quickly:

"Amy's quite right, nothing good did come of it. Fanny Dangerfield was a flighty little thing, and not at all ready to settle down. They say she threw hysterics when she found she was to have a child. She persuaded Guy to let her live in London with her aunt after that, while *he* stayed down in the country at Melchester with the baby. The best thing I can say for him was that he positively doted on his daughter and neglected his wife. He should have gone to London and taken her back with him the minute she started kicking up her heels. Letting other men escort her everywhere in public—all those soirees given by the wrong set—and when he *did* go, she talked him into staying. No good came of that either. Took to gambling and drinking hard; visiting those dens of vice in Soho. And then…" Mrs. Leacock paused dramatically for effect.

"And *then*," she repeated triumphantly, "he shot and killed a man over a game of cards! I hear that in America men carry pistols around with them, but in this case it turned out to be all the worse for Guy Dangerfield. Not only did he kill that French gambler, but he also shot a constable who tried to arrest him. No one knows how he managed to escape and catch a ship that sailed to America that very night, but I can tell you it caused quite a furor!"

"Oh, my!" Mrs. Loving sighed, her small hands clasped together.

"Later, to make matters worse, Fanny Dangerfield actually *divorced* her husband. And after that she went away to France and came back married to that scoundrel, Sir Edgar Cardon. A baronet—but his money was made from trade, of course. A man with a notorious reputation. You see *now* why the Governor was so anxious to get his granddaughter away?"

Mrs. Leacock would have been even more perturbed if she had known that at that very moment Rowena Dangerfield, unescorted by a groom, was perched on a broken wall of an ancient ruin, talking to the prince.

"Shiv," she was saying in her soft, calm voice, "you are being silly! Why should I want to marry you and join your collection of women?"

"But I've already promised you I would give them all up!" the slender young man said urgently, brushing back a lock of his dark hair. "I will have no other wife but you, and you will come everywhere with me in public. You will help me to govern my people. I will do anything you ask but turn Christian!"

"Heavens!" she replied calmly, "sometimes I'm not sure that I'm one myself! But that's not the point. I can't possibly marry you, Shiv, even if I wanted to, and I do not. I don't think that I shall ever marry. Why should I? To become some man's domestic pet, to be treated like a child with no mind of my own, to—to have all my movements, yes, even my money, controlled! Why, I'd rather be dead!"

"Rowena! How can you talk that way? Women are meant to be married, to have children, to make their husbands happy. And not only in my country, but yours as well. Don't you like me at all?"

"If I didn't like you I wouldn't be here. I enjoy talking to you Shiv, and you understand horses…"

"Horses!" He clapped a hand to his brow and groaned dramatically. "I talk of marriage, of love, and you speak of horses! I've had my fill of horsy English misses. None of them interested me, even when I was in England. You're the first truly intelligent woman I have ever met—the only one I could talk to. And…" his voice dropped meaningfully as he gave her a long melting look from his brown eyes, "you are also very beautiful, even if you try to hide it. You're the only Englishwoman I've seen who could wear a sari as gracefully as an Indian woman, and your skin has turned to gold under our Indian sun. When your hair is loose, as it was the day beside the lotus pool, and you wear gold ornaments at your ears and around your bare ankles…"

"Shiv, stop it! You had no right to come barging in that day! I dressed up that way only to please your—your wives, and then you had to come striding in and stare like an idiot!"

He burst out laughing. "But, little lotus blossom, why should I not visit the women of my household when I have just returned from a long trip? I shall never forget how I made you blush—the color turning your cheeks to dusky rose. It was then that the thought came to me like lightning, 'This is the woman who must be my true wife! I would like to clasp the gold marriage *thali* around her neck and make her mine forever!'"

"You should have been a poet instead of a prince," Rowena said drily. "Don't remind me of my embarrassment, please! And I wish you would stop talking of marriage between us, for I can tell you again that it is completely out of the question!"

His face darkened. "Is it because I am Indian and you are a member of the British nobility?"

"You should know me better than that!" Blue eyes so dark that they appeared violet flashed into his, and in spite of his hurt and disappointment the young man could not keep his eyes from lingering on her wistfully. How lovely she was, even if she herself did not fully comprehend it, and often called herself plain. She looked like a young goddess, wild and untamed, with her mane of black hair and her slim body, hard-muscled from constant riding. She rode free and untrammeled as a goddess, too, her tiny waist owing nothing to corsets. Her eyes, even when they flashed angrily as they did now, were her most beautiful feature, large and widely spaced, fringed with thick lashes. And her face—it would have been oval, if not for the small, squared-off chin that somehow added character to it. When she smiled her mouth was full and generous, a sensual, woman's mouth.

He had been studying her slowly and almost caressingly, but Rowena's irritated voice brought him back to earth.

"Shiv! What on earth is the matter with you? Surely you aren't going to sulk because I won't marry you? You really ought to feel relieved that you've had a lucky escape, for I would never make any man a dutiful, obedient wife, I fear!"

"You have not been awakened yet. In some ways, you are still so young! Perhaps, someday, I'll be able to make you fall in love with me, and then you will never leave India. I will make you realize that you belong here, and you will belong to me."

"I'll belong to no man, Shiv Jhanpur!" Rowena's voice merely took on an inflexible tone as her straight black brows drew together. "Never! And if you want to remain my friend, you had better remember that."

"We'll see!" he said teasingly, and then in a persuasive voice, "But I want to be your friend, of course. Who else can I talk to around here? My father is of an older generation and talks of nothing but duty. The Englishmen I meet are all such bores, and so conscious of the superiority their white skins confer, even though they try to hide it. But your grandfather is different, of course, just as you are different." He seized her hands for a moment and said passionately, "My family goes back as far as yours does—perhaps farther. Jhanpur is small, but its maharajahs come from a long line of kings and princes. Rowena, if you should change your mind, I feel sure that your grandfather, at least, will place no objections in our way. Please think about it."

The young crown prince of Jhanpur was a handsome, arrogant young man in his impeccably cut riding clothes that had been tailored in Savile Row. The girl who now stood facing him, shaking her head stubbornly, was just as arrogant in her way, even though she might have been taken for a gypsy in her shabby, old-fashioned riding habit. A distant ancestor of hers had run off with a gypsy girl once and made her his countess. Rowena had heard the story countless times.

But she was not thinking at this moment of her appearance. She seldom did. She shook her head at Shiv because he annoyed her with his persistence, but without her knowing it, or him knowing it, he had nevertheless planted a tiny seed in her mind—the beginning of consciousness that she was a woman.

"We had better go now," Rowena said quietly, and this time he made no objection, not wishing to frighten her off.

Later, he thought to himself, as he helped her to mount the big black stallion she had named Devil. *I spoke too soon, of course. Like all Englishwomen of her age and background she is still a shy, half-wild creature. Yes, in spite of all her book learning and her intellect, she is still virginal, and afraid of men. But the time will come when she is ready....*

Rowena, feeling oddly relieved that Shiv had reverted to the role of her friend again, kicked her heels against Devil's sides as she urged the big stallion into a gallop.

"Both walls, and then the old fence!" she called to Shiv over her shoulder, the sound of her clear young voice almost drowned by the drumming of racing hoofbeats. "I'll race you as far as the palace and see myself home!"

ii

LONDON—1873

"EDGAR! HOW *CAN* YOU ACT SO UNCONCERNED? READ THIS—
here!" Lady Fanny Cardon's voice, normally slightly queru-
lous, had risen to a wail. "It was bad enough to hear that
Melchester is dead, and Guy, of all people, if he's still alive,
is the new earl. But now, to cap it off that wretched child
has—has disappeared!"

Lady Fanny, still in her pink silk negligee, sat before her
mirrored dressing table holding a lacy square of cambric
dramatically to her eyes as she held out several sheets of closely
written pages to her husband.

"Well, then, if she's vanished, that ends all our troubles,
doesn't it? Gad, Fan! Why fuss so? Didn't want a daughter
foisted on you at this late stage, did you?"

"Edgar!" Lady Fanny's voice cracked with approaching
hysteria, and her husband, shrugging, took the letter from
her hand.

"Oh, very well! Just to oblige you, m'dear, but I don't see…"

"You will understand when you read it! Good heavens—
the scandal with Guy was bad enough, but people have started
to forget it. And then this! Guy always doted on Rowena—he
wanted a child, not I, and it almost killed me, as you very
well know. Why must *I* have her? And why couldn't she be
like any other well-brought-up child? Running away—all
by herself, in that wild, savage country. Just read what Mrs.
Leacock has to say!"

"I will, if you'll just stop talking, my love."

Sir Edgar, a heavy-featured, robust-looking man who affected the muttonchop whiskers so fashionable in England, stood with his back to the fireplace, his hard gray eyes contradicting the mildness of his voice as he raised them to his wife's distraught face.

Lady Fanny, who had begun to twist the tiny handkerchief between her fingers, caught his look and gave a small sob.

"Sometimes I think you're heartless! What on earth am I to do?"

Ignoring her outburst, Sir Edgar lowered his eyes once more to the letter he was reading, one hand going up every now and then to tug at his whiskers.

"So she's gone to find peace and the right frame of mind in an—what in blazes is this word? An *ashram?* Ah yes, here we are; this Mrs. Leacock had the goodness to explain. Some kind of Hindu retreat. I must say, Fan, the girl sounds just as eccentric as her grandfather was! Queer in the attic, if you ask me. What's an Englishwoman doing alone in a place like that?"

"You know very well what Mrs. Leacock told us in her last letter! Rowena has been allowed to grow up as wild as a—a gypsy! Completely undisciplined. She's had no formal schooling, and she refused to make friends with children her own age. Mrs. Leacock says it was a scandal! And there was that Indian prince she used to see constantly, until the bishop put a stop to it. Edgar!"

He had begun to smile. "Only thinking that perhaps the chit takes after you, after all, Fan! Still pretty, if you'd stop your frowning and your crying. Indian prince, eh? Maybe that's the solution. Get her married off."

"What can you be thinking of? She cannot marry an Indian, a—a native! Oh, Edgar, I don't think I can stand another scandal! And besides, Rowena's still a child!"

"Child? The gal's eighteen, isn't she? That's hardly a child. *You* were married long before then." Sir Edgar's voice became bluff. "Now look, Fan, no use going into a dither. This Leacock woman, who seems to know everything, says the chit has not much money of her own; and they're scouring the countryside for her. Says they'll pack her back here as soon as they find her. She's under age, isn't she? Have to do as she's told, like it or not, and you're her guardian, unless Guy turns up. And we both know why he daren't, don't we?" He gave his wife a significant look.

"But…"

"Now look here, Fan, like it or not, we're going to have to take her in, *if* she arrives, if only to stop the gossip. Can't turn her out, can we, since you're her mother? It's plain to see she needs discipline. We'll send her off to a finishing school, and then get her married. Provide a dowry myself, if I have to."

"But we don't know what she's like!" Lady Fanny's voice quivered with emotion. "He's turned her against me. I *know* he has. He was such a horrid, hard old man. I was always terrified of him!"

"He's gone. And the girl will come to heel, once she's learned *I'm* not going to stand any nonsense. You'll see."

Presently Sir Edgar went off to his club, and Lady Fanny recovered herself sufficiently to order the carriage so that she might go shopping.

She left the letter, in her usual careless fashion, lying on top of a welter of spilled powder and half-empty perfume bottles on top of her dressing table.

"Will you look at this, Mrs. Jenks?" Adams, who was Lady Fanny's personal maid and had attended her for ten years, was the only servant who considered herself an equal of the rather austere housekeeper, who had been in Sir Edgar's service for even longer—before he married, as she was fond of reminding the other members of the staff belowstairs.

"Another letter from India—and about the same thing, I'll be bound. That daughter of hers. My lady was crying, when I came up to dress her hair. And it's no wonder she's upset! Fancy having a child you never wanted turning up after all these years—and grown up into a regular hoyden, from all accounts. If you ask *me*," and Adams dropped her voice conspiratorially, "the girl's no good. Just like her father. It's in the blood, I heard her say to Sir Edgar when that last letter arrived. *All* the Dangerfields were a little bit mad, she said, and this daughter, this Miss Rowena…"

"It's *Lady* Rowena now, and you'd better not go forgetting it, hoyden or not," Mrs. Jenks said sourly, as she picked up the letter.

She was fortunate in being able to read, Adams thought enviously as she watched the housekeeper's sharp black eyes scan the crumpled sheets of paper.

"Well, do tell!" she said at last, and Mrs. Jenks's mouth pursed itself tightly.

"She's run away. By herself."

"She has?"

"But they've sent soldiers to fetch her back, and this lady who wrote the letter says they'll put her on a ship bound for England as soon as they find her."

"No!" Adams breathed. "Poor Lady Fanny. What will she do with her, a daughter like that? So wild!"

"Sir Edgar will tame her. *He* won't stand any nonsense, I can tell you that."

"What else does it say? Surely that can't be all, such a long letter like that?"

Unwillingly, Mrs. Jenks produced a pair of spectacles from her pocket and put them on. The truth was that she was just as curious as Adams was. The last letter from India, breaking the news of the old earl's death and his granddaughter's waywardness had sent Lady Fanny into hysterics for days. *This* one seemed just as startling.

Run away indeed! Mrs. Jenks thought to herself. A likely story. A girl so used to gallivanting all by herself around the Indian countryside, and consorting with natives. Mrs. Leacock was a bishop's wife, and very likely was only trying to spare Lady Fanny the worst of the story, although she had seemed to go into some detail regarding the girl's behavior at the beginning. English-born or not, it was clear that Lady Rowena had been brought up just like a foreigner, or worse, if one read between the lines.

"Well, do go on, Mrs. Jenks!" Adams leaned over the housekeeper's shoulder, breathing heavily. "It surely can't be that bad—can it?" Her voice sounded hopeful, and Mrs. Jenks gave her a cold look.

"It says she's a hard, arrogant girl who won't listen to what anyone has to say. Mrs. Leacock says she was rude to anyone who tried to advise her, even when they all went around to the house to comfort her. Told them to—" here Mrs. Jenkins paused to lick her lips, "told them to go to the devil, is what she did! And in a house of mourning, too. Told them they were all a bunch of narrow-minded hypocrites, that her grandfather had never liked them, and she didn't either. Shocked them all by producing a letter that said he wanted to be cremated, just like one of them heathen Hindus!" When Mrs. Jenks was agitated her grammar tended to slip.

"Lord have mercy!" Adams said in a shocked voice. "Well, the bishop wouldn't have it, of course. How could he allow such a thing after all?"

"And then?"

"She didn't turn up for the funeral. Ran away, taking only her big black horse with her, and left a rude, nasty note. They thought she might have run off with that native prince, or whatever he calls himself, but *he* didn't know where she'd gone either."

"She might have been murdered by those savages over there, and heaven knows what else! My poor lady!"

"Well, it's not as if Lady Fanny really *knew* her, is it?" Unknowingly, Mrs. Jenks paraphrased Sir Edgar's parting words to his wife. "We'll just have to wait and see what happens, I suppose."

In a subdued voice, Adams murmured, "Call me heartless, if you like, but I can't help thinking it'll be a blessing if she doesn't turn up."

Mrs. Jenks put the letter back carefully, exactly as she had found it.

"I've been thinking the same thing myself, and I'll not deny it," she admitted. "We've got enough to keep us all busy without having to worry about some young foreign-brought-up female with wild ways disrupting the whole household!"

Only Mary, the youngest parlormaid, ventured to speak

up on behalf of the young woman whose imminent arrival formed the topic of discussion belowstairs that night.

"I don't understand their ways," she sniffed to Alice, who shared her bed in their poky little attic room. "Fancy a mother not wanting her own daughter to live with her, and letting them say all those wicked things about her too."

"You'll never understand the gentry, so don't even try," Alice said wisely.

"Well, I hope she *does* come, after all," Mary persisted. "Be like a breath of fresh air, I'll be bound!"

"Yes, or a gale!" said Alice. "I've heard tell them foreigners treat *their* servants worse than slaves—and didn't you hear what Mrs. Jenks was telling cook, about this Lady Rowena being a hard little creature with no heart? Better count your blessings, my girl. Now turn over, do, and stop tossing so. Remember we have to be up by five to light the fires!"

The subject of Lady Fanny's errant daughter was soon dropped as a topic of conversation when there were no more letters from India and no more hysterics on the part of Lady Fanny herself. Cardon House settled back into its usual routine, and Sir Edgar was heard to mention a holiday in Paris in the near future.

And then, one late spring morning, the clanging summons of the front doorbell hurried Briggs the butler into his dark jacket, grumbling as he waved aside the new footman who was busy polishing the large brass urn that stood in the hallway.

"Never you mind. I'll get it, since I'm dressed already. And you had best disappear into the kitchen, my lad, and put on your jacket, in case it's someone important."

The bell clanged again imperatively, causing Briggs's features to settle into lines of doleful severity.

"Now, who could that be so early in the morning? The racket will wake *them* if it's kept up!"

Still grumbling, Briggs hurried down the long, imposing hallway to the front door. Whoever it was was mighty impatient!

"I knew right away it could be nothing but bad news—or trouble!" he reported later in the servants' hall.

But words could hardly describe Briggs's emotions as he

opened the door and saw the apparition who stood there, small, booted foot tapping impatiently on the step. His usually impeccable poise deserted him; his mouth dropped open.

"I hope this is Cardon House?"

The accents were unmistakably those of a lady, clear and self-possessed; but the appearance of the young person who had spoken certainly did not fit such a description.

She wore a shabby black velvet riding habit, the skirt shockingly ripped on one side, exposing a slim, booted ankle. A hat that reminded the stunned butler of a man's bowler hat was perched on her head, and from beneath it strands of black hair straggled untidily. There was even what looked like a smudge on the young person's cheek—Briggs could think of no other way to describe her.

Realizing that he was being eyed questioningly from under frowning dark brows, Briggs drew himself up and pronounced in his most forbidding accents:

"I beg your pardon?"

"I asked you if this was Cardon House. Good heavens, why does everyone I have so far met in England make me repeat the questions I ask?"

The young woman pulled the bowler hat impatiently off her head as she spoke, and her hair, which had been untidily stuffed beneath it came tumbling over her shoulders.

"This is Sir Edgar Cardon's residence when he is in London, miss, but I do not think…"

"Good." She cut him off impatiently. "Then the directions I received were correct, after all. If you will see that my horse is taken around to the stables and fed, I think I can manage to carry my portmanteau inside myself."

The clear voice held an imperious ring that made Briggs's eyes bulge.

"Your—horse?" he repeated faintly.

"Certainly. Did you imagine I walked here? I took a carriage as far as I could, and then, because I found I was running out of money, I rented a horse to bring me the rest of the way. I promised he would be returned tomorrow. Sir Edgar does keep a stable, I hope?"

The horse, a sorry-looking nag, stood with its reins carelessly looped over the polished railings.

"Sir Edgar…" Awful suspicions were beginning to flit through Briggs's mind. Surely this shabby-looking young person could not be one of his master's flirts? What was he expected to do about her?

It was with unutterable relief that Briggs suddenly caught sight of Constable Parsons sauntering up, his eyes curious under his shiny helmet. "Any trouble here, Mr. Briggs?" The girl turned her arrogant blue gaze on the florid-faced policeman.

"Certainly not. I am Rowena Dangerfield, and I am here because my mother and my stepfather insisted I must come."

"You could have knocked me over with a feather!" Briggs reported with relish later on. "There she stood, giving orders as cool as you please, and you should have seen Parsons's face when she said who she was! Come all the way from Tilbury, she had. And rode all the way through town on a horse—by herself!"

Adams took up the story. "My lady's still lying in her bed with a headache, and Mrs. Mellyn's with her. Prostrated she is, poor thing, and small wonder! Fancy having her own daughter, whom she hasn't seen in years, walk in like that, with never a word sent in advance to say she was coming! No baggage—she'd left it all on the dock. Just that shabby little bag with only a change of clothes. And she just up and walked away from those kind people that took charge of her and brought her all the way from India. I heard her say, as cool as a cucumber, that she did not like them and could not stand another moment of their company!"

"Wonder how she'll get on here. Ooh… I expect Sir Edgar was in a fine rage! I could hear his shouting all the way to the scullery, I could." Mary's mouth was as round as her eyes, and Mrs. Jenks gave her a crushing look. "That's as it may be, but the doings upstairs are none of our concern, and you'd be wise to remember that, my girl!"

Subdued, Mary relapsed into silence, although she longed to hear what Mrs. Jenks and that snooty Adams had begun to talk about in low, hushed tones.

Strangely enough, the calmest and most self-possessed person in the whole household was the subject of all the heated discussion that swirled both above- and belowstairs that afternoon.

Her dripping wet hair still wrapped in a towel, Rowena Dangerfield sat before a small fire in the room that had been given to her, a book on her lap. But she was not reading. Her narrowed eyes gazed into the orange and blue flames as her mind went over the confrontation she had had with her mother and stepfather earlier.

It had been an angry scene, with Lady Fanny weeping that she had disgraced them all, and Sir Edgar, red in the face, shouting that she had better learn at the very start that she would no longer do exactly as she pleased.

Rowena, her eyes demurely cast down to hide their expression, had listened in silence, her face unmoved.

At last, when his wife had collapsed into a chair with her handkerchief and vinaigrette held to her nose, Sir Edgar bellowed, "And what do you have to say for yourself now, miss?"

Rowena raised expressionless blue eyes to his face. "What do you wish me to say?" she replied quite equably, taking him so much aback that he could do nothing but stare at her in speechless fury for a moment. He had expected tears, remorse, a quailing before his declaration of authority. Instead, the irresponsible chit with her sun-browned face had the impudence to look him in the eye quite calmly, with one eyebrow slightly raised.

"By God!" he said at last. "Have you understood nothing of what your mother and I have been saying? Do you have no conception of the upset and turmoil your outrageous behavior has caused? I tell you, miss, that you will learn some discipline while you're under my roof! You'll learn some polite manners, and to act like a lady! And you'll do exactly as you're told, by God, or…"

"There is no need to raise your voice in order to make yourself understood, sir," Rowena retorted in her calm, cold voice, eliciting a gasp from her mother. "Indeed, I had already realized that since I was offered no other choice but to come here to live under your guardianship, I would have to accept whatever restrictions you might insist upon until I come of age. But…" and her eyes narrowed a fraction, "I see no reason to pretend, do you, that either of us is happy with the present arrangement? I do not want to be here any more than you want me here yourselves. But I suppose we'll have to make the best of it!"

Lady Fanny's sobs had risen to an almost hysterical pitch, and Sir Edgar had ranted and raved even louder than before. But in the end, when Rowena had thought he came almost close to striking her, he turned and stamped out of the room, ordering his wife to have her ungrateful child sent upstairs to be made presentable.

How calmness had the power to discompose some people! Rowena shook her hair loose, still staring into the flames, and began absentmindedly to towel her hair dry as she sorted out her impressions.

She had not expected to like her mother, and had found her to be even sillier and too determinedly youthful than she had imagined. Poor Lady Fanny, with her gold hair too elaborately arranged for morning, and her pretty silk gown with rows of ribbon and lace at the neck in an attempt to hide the telltale wrinkles. *Thank God I don't look like her*, Rowena thought, with a shudder of distaste. Sir Edgar, with his curly muttonchop whiskers and protuberant gray eyes had come closer to being the way she had pictured him.

Sir Edgar had left the house to take refuge in his club. And Lady Fanny, declaring she had one of her terrible migraines, now lay in her darkened room with her old nurse, Mellyn, to soothe her.

"You was always a difficult child, and a trial to my poor dear baby!" Mellyn had sniffed disapprovingly at Rowena, and had then left her to the ministrations of a disapproving lady's maid with steely eyes, who had announced that her name was Adams. And even that poker-faced female had closed her eyes in horror when she saw the crumpled cotton gown that Rowena produced so carelessly from the bottom of her battered portmanteau.

"But miss—I mean, my lady—you cannot possibly go down to luncheon wearing that—garment!"

"Oh? But you see, it is all I have, except for the riding habit I was wearing when I arrived here. All the rest of my clothes were packed in my trunk, and that, for all I know, may still be at Tilbury!"

Cool as a cucumber, Adams thought angrily. *Doesn't care a fig for all the trouble she's caused.*

Aloud she said firmly: "If you'll give me the gown, Lady Rowena, I shall have one of the maids press it and starch it for you. But it's hardly the type of garment you could wear in this climate, when it turns cold at night."

"It was eminently suited for the climate of India, and I had no time to buy other clothes before I left," Rowena said coolly. With a shrug, she accepted the serviceable-looking wool wrapper that Adams handed her, wondering whose castoff it had been. "Perhaps I could have my luncheon brought up here? Something very light, please, I am not particularly hungry."

Adams had departed with a stiff bob of her head, and here Rowena sat before the fire, with only a book to keep her company.

Perhaps they will contrive to forget I am here if I keep out of their way, she thought hopefully, but the very next morning she was summoned to her mother's room and informed that her measurements would be taken by Jenks, so that some suitable gowns and underwear could be procured for her immediately.

Lady Fanny, sitting up in bed, appeared a trifle calmer this morning, although her pale blue eyes were still red-rimmed and slightly swollen.

She sighed as she looked at her daughter. Those dark blue eyes, so like Guy's, with their cold and arrogant look. That wild black hair, also his. There is nothing of me in her, Fanny thought; nothing at all. She is his child, just as she was from the very beginning, even before she was born.

"All right, all right! So we've both made a mistake. But it's too late to rectify that—we're married. But give me a child,

Fanny, give me my son, and you may go your way. Have all the fun you whine about, do as you please, I'll not care. We'll make a bargain."

They had made the bargain after all, and she had given him a daughter instead of a son, almost dying in the process. And Guy had kept his word, except that she'd met Edgar, and become careless. The Dangerfields cared more for their precious honor than they did for people and human feelings. And it was this same concept of "honor" that had undone Guy in the end, when he played into their hands.

I mustn't think about that! Fanny thought now, almost feverishly. *But why did she have to come? Why must I be saddled with her?* Duty, Edgar had said. People would think it strange and unnatural if they did not take her in. *But I don't want to have a daughter eighteen years old! When I've been telling my friends for years I'm younger than I am.*

"My lady, about the clothes for Lady Rowena..." Mrs. Jenk's brisk voice brought Fanny Cardon back to earth. Her daughter still stood in the center of the room, staring at her with those cold eyes that gave nothing away.

With an effort at composure Lady Fanny said lightly, "Do you have any preferences as to color and style, Rowena? Bustles are all the rage now, of course, but if you—"

"Dark colors, please," the girl said in her infuriatingly cool voice. "I am still in mourning for my grandfather, you know. And as for bustles, I have never cared for them—they look so ugly and unnatural. If I may, I would rather wear simpler clothes—nothing too elaborate or tight-fitting, for I won't wear stays or corsets."

Mrs. Jenks looked scandalized, and Lady Fanny helpless. If only Edgar were here!

"But, Rowena!" Lady Fanny protested faintly. "Every young woman wears them, if she wants to cut a pretty figure. You'll be going out in public. I cannot have you looking dowdy!"

She sounds as if dowdiness is the worst sin in the world, Rowena thought viciously. She made her voice sound subdued.

"But I can hardly be expected to make public appearances

while I am still in mourning, can I? Even in India, we heard how strongly the Queen feels about a decent period of mourning following a bereavement. My grandfather and I were very close, and I would much rather stay quietly in the house and read, if I will not be in the way, of course."

"Well, I—I just don't know!" Lady Fanny shrugged helplessly, looking at Jenks for support. The austere housekeeper merely pursed her thin lips. What was *she* expected to say?

Later she told Adams, "False meekness, that's what it was! And Lady Fanny far too kindhearted to see through her. Mourning indeed! If you ask me, that young woman hasn't enough feeling in her to mourn for anyone. Cold-hearted—you can see it a mile off!"

It became the consensus of opinion belowstairs, as the days passed. Lady Rowena Dangerfield was a cold-hearted, arrogant little creature, even though she dressed plainly and dowdily.

"Like one of them popish nuns, dressed all in black, and wearin' those ugly bonnets with thick veils that she chose herself," the under-footman said.

"More like a Salvation Army lady!" Alice giggled.

"Ah, but she's got all the haughty airs and graces of a grand lady, even though she's got no money of her own—nothing! I heard the master say the Earl of Melchester owned nothing but his title—spent everything he earned living in grand style out in India. Left her nothing but a few pounds, and she soon spent that, didn't she?"

Adams and Jenks exchanged significant looks. Neither of them liked Rowena, who persisted in giving them orders in exactly the same tone she used to the other servants. "She'll get her comeuppance one of these days, just you mark my words!" Briggs said, determined not to be left out of the conversation. "I can tell the master's getting tired of having her moping around the house." He lowered his voice, so that the parlormaids, sitting at the other end of the long kitchen table, would not hear him. "The other night when the Wilkinsons from Yorkshire came for dinner—you mind when the gentlemen retired to the library for their port?"

Adams sniffed.

"*She* said she had a headache and went upstairs to bed. It made my lady terribly upset, I can tell you!"

Alice, who was allowed to wait on table occasionally, chimed in pertly. "I can tell you what they were talking about at dinner! Mr. Thomas was asking her about India, and she hardly answered him, except to use all kinds of big words I'd never heard of before, and about the Hindu religion being older and wiser than any other, and..." her eyes widened, "the Wilkinsons are *chapel*!"

They were all struck dumb by this shocking pronouncement, except for Briggs, who shook his head in grim disapprobation.

"That's what comes of being brought up in a land of heathens! But I have a feeling Lady Rowena will be brought to heel yet. Sir Edgar's too clever not to see through her, and I can tell you, in the strictest confidence of course," here he frowned at Alice and the giggling Mary, "that he has *plans*!"

Even Cook looked up from her knitting.

"Do tell, Mr. Briggs!"

"Heard him talking to Mr. Wilkinson senior. And the young Mr. Wilkinson, from the way he sat there grinning, didn't seem to mind what he was suggesting too much. Lady Rowena has a title, and Sir Edgar isn't a man to be stingy with his money. Offered a dowry to go with her, he did. And it's my prediction there'll be wedding bells before long, and Lady Airs-and-Graces, like it or not, will be packed off to Yorkshire with a husband!"

The Journals of Rowena Elaine Dangerfield

1873–1876

PART I:

THE MARBLE GODDESS

One

I sit at my window looking out at the hot sunlight reflecting off the sunbaked, pink brick of my patio, and try to imagine myself back in London, and eighteen years old again. Somehow I find that calling up the distant past is less painful than recalling events that happened only a few months ago.

Suddenly I have a compulsion to write—to chronicle everything that happened to me since I arrived, so unwillingly, on the doorstep of my stepfather's house in London. Perhaps I am only seeking excuses to escape into the past as a barrier against the present. Or perhaps I will understand better the whole train of events that led me here, once I set them down and can see them in perspective.

Only a few years have passed since that time, and I am still a young woman. But so much has happened since then, and I have lost a great deal of the arrogance and self-assurance that they used to complain of. "They" were my mother and stepfather, and their large, anonymous household staff.

The opinions of the servants didn't concern me, for I was too occupied with my own thoughts and plans. I took care to stay out of the way of my mother and stepfather, and in all honesty, they were rather kind to me in those early days.

With surprisingly mature logic I came to realize that I had, in effect, been forced upon my mother. I was unwanted. I was not a child of love, but the child of a man she had been compelled to marry. Mellyn, whom my mother still called

Nanny, spoke bluntly to me on the subject. "Barely out of the schoolroom, my precious lamb was at the time," she grumbled. "But they decided that she was ready to be married. He was much older than she was, had money, and the prospect of being an earl some day. I remember how she cried, her eyes turning all red and swollen. 'I'm not ready to be married yet, Nanny, and he's so old,' she said to me. 'I want to have fun first, to come out in style and go to parties and balls...' but her feelings were never even taken into account! Guy Dangerfield met her at a house party, and as pretty as she was, he was taken by her, I suppose. He was looking for a wife, to please his father, and she was the one he chose."

According to Nanny, my father had had nothing to recommend him beyond the money he had made in the gold fields of America. He was a dark, gloomy man, she said, who preferred the country to the city, and would have made a recluse of his wife if he could.

"I suppose he didn't want me to be born either?" I questioned.

"Don't you talk like that, miss! You don't know the whole of it, and that's for sure! Your grandfather turned you against her, I'll be bound, and for all that he'd have nothing to do with Mr. Guy after it all happened. He had a great notion that the Dangerfields were better than anyone else. My poor baby was no more than a child herself when you were born. I ask you, why couldn't he have waited awhile? Why couldn't he have taken her to live in London for a while? But no—he liked the country, he said, and he wanted a child. And he had his way. When you were born, it was just as if my poor Miss Fanny didn't exist for him any longer. He fair doted on you, he did—had your nursery moved into the room next to his, and it was he got up at nights when you began to cry. 'You take care of your baby, Mellyn,' he'd tell me, 'and I'll look after mine.' Unnatural, I called it. It was no wonder my lady pined and pined, and finally went off to London by herself. Who can blame her?"

A few new clothes were purchased for me—all in somber colors, in deference to the fact that I was still in mourning. I refused to have my hair done up in tortured coils and ringlets and preferred more severe styles, and on the few occasions when I was dragged out to teas and small evening gatherings I always managed to find myself sitting with the older ladies present, who complimented me on my "old-fashioned looks." I had none of the accomplishments that young ladies of my status in life were supposed to have. I could not play the pianoforte and I refused to sing; I could not paint a passable watercolor, and I could not dance.

I always scared away the bolder and more persistent young men by showing myself to be intellectual, and better educated than they were. I know that I gained the reputation, in a short while, of being a dowdy bluestocking—a born spinster. My mother despaired of me. Her friends commiserated with her, sometimes in tones loud enough for me to hear.

I do not know how long matters might have gone on the way they were if Sir Edgar hadn't suddenly decided that I must be married off. I had hardly spoken to him since that first day, but I'm sure my mother must have complained to him how recalcitrant I was, and how embarrassed I had made her feel on several occasions. Edgar Cardon had never liked my father, and I'm sure that my presence in his house was a living reminder to him of Guy Dangerfield.

Several months had passed since I had arrived in England, and the dull routine of my days had almost become a habit, when Tom Wilkinson came calling on me one afternoon.

We were already into autumn, and the servants had begun lighting fires every afternoon. I was in the library, desultorily searching through the shelves for a book I had not yet read, as he was announced.

"Mr. Wilkinson, to see Lady Rowena."

I turned around in some annoyance when Briggs announced him, and then quickly withdrew. I did not like Tom Wilkinson, especially since he was the most persistent of my so-called suitors. "A stout Yorkshire lad," Sir Edgar had stated bluffly when he introduced us, and indeed Tom was not only stout but short and squat as well—a dark-featured, bumptious young man who was always boasting of his fortune, his father's mills, and the grand house he had built for his future family.

Of all the young men I had met, Tom Wilkinson was so conceited and so full of himself that he ignored—or pretended to ignore—the fact that I had no time, and hardly any conversation to offer him. He implied, in fact, that my quiet demeanor and dowdy way of dressing actually appealed to him. I was obviously not the kind of woman who might give him cause for jealousy, and my reserve and coldness of manner seemed to attract him, instead of putting him off.

On the last occasion we had met I'd hardly said two words to him, and had thought, thankfully, that I'd seen the last of him—and now here he was, intruding into my privacy, with that annoying, everlasting grin still on his face.

"No need to look at me so haughty-like, Lady Rowena. I've your stepfather's permission to call on you this afternoon. 'You'll find her in the library,' he said. 'Just get Briggs to announce you.' And so here I am!"

He looked at me, grinning and licking his thick lips. "Come, lass—no need to pretend you're not glad to see me, eh? They told me you've a habit of hiding yourself in here, but that's a waste! You're a lady, and I know that, but I'm here with the consent of your stepfather—aye, and your mother too. There's no more need to act so priggish and standoffish with me. I've come to offer for you—and I hope you aren't going to be missish and act surprised, for I'm sure you've known what I've had in mind. I may be a blunt Yorkshireman, but I'm proud of it, and I've made up my mind! You're not going to act coy, now, are you? I think you're a sensible lass, with no fuss or frills about you—and that's why I chose you."

All the time he was talking he kept stalking me around the room, forcing me to retreat, and quite ignoring my angry protests. "Come, now," he said coaxingly, his pop-eyes looking paler than ever in the diffused light, "I ain't going to hurt you, you know! Haven't I just proposed marriage? All I'm asking is a kiss to seal the bargain. Now, you ain't too shy for that, are you?"

"Mr. Wilkinson—Tom—I do wish you'd stop making a ridiculous fool of yourself!" I protested angrily, but my denial of his suddenly declared passion only seemed to make him more ardent.

I moved backward, and he moved forward. I passed by the window, blinking in the light let in by the partially drawn blinds, and I saw him give a start of amazement.

"You're not wearing those spectacles today! I'll be damned if you don't have pretty eyes, after all. In fact, you'd make a handsome woman, once you're dressed right and proper—damned if you won't! And I'll have the last laugh on all those others, won't I?"

By now I was as much annoyed with myself as I was with him. I stopped running from him and with my hand on the back of a chair, said forbiddingly, "Mr. Wilkinson, you are taking far too much for granted!"

But I think he mistook my annoyance for an attempt to play coy, and shook a finger at me. "Come, come, Lady Rowena—or may I call you Rowena? Surely—yes, we cannot stand on formality now! I respect your shyness and your modesty, but after all, since we are to be engaged, a little kiss at least will not be out of order, would it?"

At any other time I might have found some humor in the situation I now found myself in, but the expression on Tom Wilkinson's face as he followed me around the room made me almost apprehensive.

I retreated. He followed, still grinning, as if we were playing some kind of game.

"Mr. Wilkinson," I said firmly, "I hardly think it proper for us to be here alone. I've no desire to give rise to belowstairs gossip, and I've nothing to say to you. I'm afraid I must ask you to leave."

"Ah, but I'm not ready to leave yet, and I'm sure you don't want me to—not till I've said what I came here to say! Come, what's the harm in a little kiss, eh? After all, we are to become engaged."

"I would not marry you, Mr. Wilkinson, if you were the last man on earth!" I said forcibly.

"Want to play hard to get, don't you? There's no need for all that. I've made up my mind, you see!"

Without warning he made a grab for me, and I found myself clutched in a man's arms for the first time in my life, while he planted wet, repulsive kisses on my averted face and neck.

"Give us a kiss, then, lass! Eh, will you stop struggling? I'll be wanting more than just kisses when we're wed, you know!"

"Will you stop it?"

Forgetting all my coolness I pushed violently against his chest with my hands, and when he still wouldn't let me go, but kept muttering how pretty I was with my hair coming loose and my eyes not shielded by those ugly spectacles, I slapped his face as hard as I could.

He released me and stumbled backward with an expression of shock and bewilderment on his face. I seized this respite to escape to the doorway. I was panting. I hadn't realized until this moment how disgusted and how afraid I had been.

With an effort, I managed to force some semblance of coldness into my voice as I told him I hoped he would manage to find his way out.

His mouth twisted in an ugly fashion. "You bitch! By God, you'll be sorry for what you just did!"

I walked out of the room, and left him standing there, still mouthing threats at me. I heard his voice call after me as I began to ascend the staircase, forcing myself to walk slowly, and not to run from the sound of his words.

"Think you'll ever get yourself a husband, an ugly creature like you?" he shouted thickly. "Why, I'd never have offered for you in a thousand years if Sir Edgar and my da' hadn't cooked it all up between them! Offered to pay off all my gambling debts, they did. No wonder they're anxious to get rid of you!"

I found myself wondering where the servants were—hiding in doorways and broom closets, no doubt, the better to enjoy such a juicy little scene! I wanted to flee from that ugly, sneering voice, but I would not let myself; I was a Dangerfield, and the likes of Tom Wilkinson with his loud, vulgar voice, were beneath my attention.

At last I had reached the head of the stairs, with my hands

wet and sweaty, and my back stiff—and at last I heard the distant slam of a door somewhere below me.

When I reached the safety of my room I was shaking. That ugly, vulgar, repulsive little man! How dare they send him to me, deeming him good enough for me? And even he had had to be bribed to make an offer for me!

Ugly—dowdy—frumpish—a born spinster—was there really something wrong with me? Was I some kind of freak, set apart from other females?

For the first time in my life, as I leaned against the door of my room and fought to control my emotions, I was conscious of a feeling of rebellion, of almost overpowering rage and humiliation. I had been brought up to believe that birth and education were enough, that I needed nothing else to make a success of my life. But—and the thought came insidiously, cracking the foundations of all my beliefs—had my grandfather been wrong? Had he deliberately turned me into an introverted bluestocking to protect me from the devil that was said to taint the Dangerfield blood?

"I'm a woman—a woman!" I raged inwardly, and my fingers began to tear viciously at my ugly, constricting clothes. Perspiration had begun to pour from my body, trickling down the back of my neck, down my thighs and between my breasts.

Still panting, hardly conscious of what I was doing, I found myself standing unashamedly naked before my mirror, my clothes strewn haphazardly around the room. My hair hung down about my shoulders and tickled the back of my waist, and my eyes looked enormous in the whiteness of my face. Was this the real Rowena? What had happened to the laughing girl who had worn a sari and an exotic black caste mark between her brows? The same girl who might have married a prince? "Do you think you're living in a fairy tale?" I had chided myself then, proud of my own good sense and practical turn of mind. But I should have married Shiv. I should have stayed in India! I was a stranger among strangers here.

Suddenly, I saw myself as I had been then, viewing my reflection in a polished silver mirror. Perhaps if I wished hard enough Shiv would appear behind me, as he had on that day, striding in with his high, polished boots and fawn jodhpurs, the white silk turban he wore giving him an air of barbaric splendor. Dear Shiv—my brightest memory!

The sari, carefully packed away in layers of tissue paper, emerged like a jeweled treasure from the bottom of my small, battered trunk. It was made of gossamer sheer silk that shimmered when the light caught it—a deep blue-violet shade that Shiv had told me matched my eyes. A design worked in gold covered the material like an intricate spider web, and the *pallau*—the section that was meant to be draped around its wearer's head—was even more resplendent with gold than the rest of the sari.

A garment fit for a queen—the gift of an Indian prince. What was I thinking of as I slowly wound it around my body as the women had taught me? Did I imagine that I would be magically transformed into a princess? I cannot remember what thoughts went through my head, but when I put it on I shook my hair loose so that its straight, fine strands hung about my face, giving it a shadowed, mysterious look.

Beneath the thin material my pale flesh seemed to take on an amber glow as I saw myself outlined against the fire—all subtle shadings of hollows and curves. Seized by a strange, trancelike feeling, I stared at myself, and it was like looking at the shadowy portrait of a stranger. Was that exotic creature in the mirror really me? All the features I had so despised in my face seemed to take on a new, softer look. I felt like Narcissus discovering his own beauty in a pool of water, and could not stop staring at myself.

I think I was a little mad that afternoon. Not only did I look like a stranger, but even my thoughts were not my own. I remember putting my hand up to touch my face, as if I could not believe it was mine, and the gesture had a strangely sensuous grace I had never possessed before. I was a woman, discovering her own beauty before a mirror—an Indian princess, carefully cloistered from men, and yet born to please them… and then, with a shattering force, the spell was broken.

I hadn't heard the door open until it slammed shut behind

him, and I whirled around with an involuntary, gasping cry of fear.

"What in hell do you mean, treating Tom that way? I tell you, girl, once and for all…"

He had begun to shout at me in his loud, blustering voice, and I smelled the liquor on his breath as he came closer. And then his words trailed away as his jaw dropped, and I saw the look in his eyes as they slowly widened and then became narrow.

"Good God!" he said, very slowly, and I saw the look of rage on his face replaced by something else. "Are you really the shy little spinster we all took you for? Is this what you've been hiding away all these months under those ugly clothes you wear? For what lover are you guarding those treasures I see, little Rowena?"

For those few moments, while he was talking to me in that strange, thick voice, while his eyes were moving greedily over my body, I remained as frozen as a marble statue, incapable of motion, or of coherent thought.

And then Sir Edgar began to laugh, and his arms reached for me.

"To think—to think you had me fooled—all these months, and right under my own roof too. Why, you're a raving beauty, girl! The prettiest body—"

"No!" I remember saying. Had I already, without any experience to warn me, sensed his purpose? I had meant to scream the word, but it came out as a choking whisper from my dry throat.

And then, when he put his hands on me, it was too late. My pride would not let me cry out aloud and beg him for mercy, and nor, I think, would it have done any good, for he had become a man possessed by lust.

I struggled—I beat at him with my fists and kept on struggling until I was half-swooning with exhaustion. Somehow he had dragged me over to the bed, ripping my lovely sari off my body with his greedy, grasping fingers. His face loomed over mine and I heard him mutter hoarsely.

"God, you're a lovely thing! I've got to have you, don't you

understand that? You've no right to hide such beauty away—
no right to wear any clothes at all with a body like yours…"

He kissed me, his mouth covering mine, stifling me so that
now I panted and gasped for breath and heard the strange,
whimpering noises that came from the back of my throat.

The weight of his body pressed me down until I felt my
back must surely break. But that pain was forgotten when a
worse one took its place—a terrible searing agony like a knife
thrust between my thighs. I would have screamed, then, if his
mouth had not been pressed over mine. I remember that my
body arched with shock as he gasped, groaned, and shuddered
against me.

It was over. He still leaned heavily above me, his sweat
dripping onto my still body, but the terrible pain I had felt was
gone, succeeded by a sticky wetness that I knew was blood.

Of course. It's normal for a virgin to bleed when she first
lies with a man. I remember lying there, feeling as if every
bone in my body had turned to water. I was no longer a
virgin. I had been raped by my own stepfather. I watched his
face change, its muscles growing slack as the taut expression
of lust was wiped out by the gradual realization of what he
had done.

He suddenly rolled away from me with a groan, and I
lay there watching him as he staggered to his feet, fingers
fumbling with his clothing.

"Dear God, Rowena! I didn't know. Girl, just seeing you
the way you were, half-naked—so lovely—I don't know what
got into me!"

"It's too late to feel guilty now, isn't it?"

Was that my own voice I heard, sounding so calm, so dead?
Suddenly I felt a sickening feeling of distaste for the soiled,
stained sheets I was lying on. Without looking at Sir Edgar,
who still stood there watching me, I used the corner of the
sheet to wipe the blood from my thighs fastidiously, and then
I stood up, and brushed past him, to walk to the mirror.

I think I wanted to see if I had changed in any way—if my
face would carry the marks of my experience, but it looked
unchanged. Pale, still a stranger's face, with black hair lying

in tangles around it. "It shows in the eyes, when a maiden becomes a woman." Where had I heard that? But my eyes showed nothing, except a kind of blankness.

Without knowing why I did it, I seized my silver-backed brush off the dressing table and began to brush my hair, with long, viciously tugging strokes. Perhaps I was suffering from shock, perhaps my strange action was due to my instinct of self-preservation that fought to keep me sane by forcing me to concentrate on some small, ordinary task.

Strange as it seems, I had almost forgotten Sir Edgar's presence as I stood there at my mirror, with not a stitch of clothing to cover my nakedness. And then he came up behind me. I saw him in the glass, his eyes gleaming with a strange light, his mouth twisted in a smile.

"Damnation, but you're a lovely creature! First virgin I ever took without paying for it. Only one who didn't cry afterwards. You're a strange girl, aren't you?"

He put a hand on my bare shoulder, and although I stiffened, I didn't flinch away from him. He gave a small, satisfied chuckle.

"You're sensible. I like that. So cold, so lovely—" his voice dropped, and I heard him say softly, "You're the kind of woman who can carry off diamonds, you know. With that dark hair and your eyes—yes, by God, you're a diamond girl, all right! And I want to make it up to you. See here, Rowena, I'm not a brute, I'm a fair man, and I can be generous too."

He quickly left the room and I remained standing, trance-like, before the mirror.

I saw something sparkling in his hand as he returned and my arms dropped to my sides, very slowly, as I felt him lift the heavy mass of my hair—felt a coldness like ice around my throat.

"There!" he said triumphantly. "There, now. Look at yourself in the glass, girl! You should not wear anything else. Diamonds—and maybe sapphires on some occasions, to match your eyes. What do you say, eh? I'd be kind to you—wouldn't hurt you again for all the world. Dress you in jewels."

His hands, with the reddish brown hairs on the back of

his fingers, slid slowly down my shoulders, and still I did not move, but my eyes met his levelly in the glass.

"What exactly are you suggesting to me, Sir Edgar? Are you attempting to bribe me not to tell anyone what you have done, or are you proposing I become your mistress?"

I felt his fingers tighten about my arms for an instant, and then he swung me around to face him.

"Will you always be so cold? There's flame burning under the iciness of a diamond, Rowena. I'd like to uncover the fire in you!"

I stood passively in his crushing embrace, and watched his eyes search my body greedily. I felt nothing, except for a slight soreness between my thighs. Was that all there was to the act of love between a man and a woman? Love, lust. I suppose the two were inextricable.

"Rowena—Rowena! Now that I've discovered you for myself, I'll not let you go."

When his mouth had lifted itself from mine I twisted from his grasp and went back to brushing my hair. If I had a thought at that moment it was, strangely, that I hated my mother even more than I despised her husband. This was the man she had left my father for—this man who had so little self-control that he had taken her own daughter by force only moments before, and now proposed to make her his mistress! This same man, who had seemed so arrogant and overbearing at the beginning, but now pleaded with me for warmth and a response to his bestial embraces. He could have overpowered me again by sheer brute strength, but no. He wanted more. He wanted response—the feigned passion of a whore! Was that the only way a woman could dominate a man? How easy it would be to exploit this man. Yes, and to make my mother suffer too! If I wanted to...

"For God's sake, girl, aren't you going to say anything to me?" He was pleading again, eyes almost haggard now. "What's done is done. I would have preferred it to have happened differently, but I had had too much to drink at the club, and when Tom came storming in—"

For the first time since Sir Edgar had entered my room, a

spark of anger pierced my defensive shell of reserve. "Don't speak to me of Tom Wilkinson! To think you sent him to me, knowing I'd be alone—to think you considered him good enough for me!"

"No, girl, no! But how was I to know! By God, I think I'd kill that young pup if I thought he'd touched you! Didn't I just say I'd make it all up to you, for everything? Listen—" his voice became feverish, his hands touched my shoulders again as if he could not help himself—"listen, you shall have everything, anything you want, do you hear? Fine, fashionable clothes, jewels—would you like your own horse to ride in the park? A small carriage? I'm a rich man."

"And how will you explain your sudden generosity to— your wife?"

Deliberately I hesitated before my choice of a word, and he flushed dully.

"Don't turn hard, girl. Fanny—well, you don't know her, do you? She—she's not the same. Always those headaches, dragging me off to dull dinners."

"Don't you mean that my mother is no longer young—and I am?"

He could find nothing to say to refute my blunt statement, and I moved away from him.

"Please, I'm rather tired now. I think I would like a bath."

I was trying my power over him already, and we both knew it.

He looked at me, at my body, and I saw his shoulders sag.

"I'll—I'll send Jenks in to you. She won't talk—owes me too much. I'll have her move you to the blue room. It's larger, and has a view of the park. And—we'll talk tomorrow?"

"Perhaps," I said coldly. And for the moment, that was the end of it. He left my room and I was alone again. Automatically, I took my one, ugly flannel dressing gown from the wardrobe and draped it around myself.

"Vanity, Rowena! It was your own vanity that caused this to happen."

Why did I suddenly imagine I could hear my grandfather's voice? Deliberately I shut it out. He had educated my mind, but taught me nothing about the world as it was. I had realized, in the space of an afternoon, that I was ignorant in many other ways. All of my education had not taught me to get along with other human beings, any more than my birth and breeding had protected me. For the first time, I realized that I was completely alone, with only myself to depend upon. And yet, somehow I would survive—and I would use any methods I could think of to do so.

Two

✣

How can one describe the passing of time? Light and shade—patterns seen through a kaleidoscope—

I blossomed forth, like a butterfly from a cocoon, taking, as one of my many later admirers said, all London by storm. I'm sure he exaggerated, although my sudden transformation from quiet, dowdy obscurity to flamboyant debutante was bound to give rise to some comment.

I shall never know what transpired between Sir Edgar and my mother—if anything did—but almost overnight I found myself no longer a retiring, unwanted poor relation. Suddenly I was the petted, spoiled daughter of the house, a pampered creature whose every wish must be indulged.

I was presented to Her Majesty. Like the rest of that year's debutantes, I was dressed in virginal white; my dark hair crowned with a diamond tiara. I was seen at all the fashionable functions with my doting parents.

My mother and I were still virtual strangers, but what did it matter? In public she was proud of me; in private, we had nothing to say to each other. And Edgar Cardon, as he promised, continued to be generous.

We traveled in Europe, and my knowledge of languages proved an asset, instead of the liability it had once been considered. An Italian prince dubbed me "the marble goddess" when I rejected his attempts at seduction, and the name followed me back to London. I was an acknowledged beauty now; I, who had always considered myself plain, who had been called ugly and frumpish. And when the prime minister said I had a mind as scintillatingly clear as one of the diamonds I constantly wore, my position in society became secure. The Earl of Beaconsfield had also added, in private, that I was as cold and as hard as the stones I seemed to admire, but this comment was never noised abroad. I put him off by protesting that he was a married man, but he was also a supremely intelligent individual, and my evasions did not fool him.

"I wonder if you are capable of loving?" he once asked me when we were alone. "I could almost understand your rejection of me if you were in love with poor Edgar Cardon, but I know that you're not. You are too intelligent to be a lady, and too much of a lady to be a little whore at heart. Have you ever asked yourself what you are searching for, Rowena?"

My eyes met his. His honesty appealed to me. "Why should I have to search for anything?" I said lightly. "If I'm not entirely satisfied with my way of life, I'm not too discontented either. I manage to fill up my days."

"With a man like Edgar Cardon? What do you have in common with him? I'll be frank. I've known my share of beautiful women, but in your case, it was your intelligence that appealed to me. You're wasting yourself."

I realized that I could be perfectly honest with him. I shrugged. "Would you have noticed me at all before? I was an ugly duckling before sheer chance, and Sir Edgar transformed me into a swan. I still had the same intelligence you say you admire, but who would have bothered to pay any attention to it then? No, my lord, it is you who are not being logical now. I discovered that in order to be recognized as an intelligent woman, I had first to be noticed as a woman. Would we have met at all if you had not been alarmed that the Prince of Wales might have formed a *tendre* for me?"

He laughed, and leaned forward to pat my hand.

"Touché, my lady! No, I must confess that it had not entered my head what a disadvantage it might be to be born a female—and an intelligent one, at that! May I wish you good fortune?"

He kissed my hands when we parted, and that was that. Sir Edgar was flattered that the prime minister had noticed me, and I never told him what had transpired between us.

There were other things to think about. I was almost twenty years old, and a grand birthday ball had been planned for me. Had I but known it, my whole life was to be changed again, drastically, following that special occasion.

It was truly an enchanted evening. I had danced every dance, consumed great quantities of champagne, and laughed and flirted the night away. The festivities continued until after six in the morning, when the last of our guests finally went home, fortified by an enormous breakfast.

When, at last, I climbed the stairs to my room, I was so weary that I had barely enough energy left to take off my shimmering satin ball gown. I dropped it on the floor next to my satin dancing slippers, and threw myself into bed.

I slept deeply, dreamlessly, waking only when my maid—or so I thought—drew apart the heavy velvet draperies that covered my window and brilliant sunlight suddenly streamed across my face.

"Did you have to open them all the way, Martine? What time is it? I promised I would go riding in the park this afternoon..."

"Perhaps you could postpone your riding until later. There is a certain individual you should see this afternoon, on a matter that might prove of vital concern to your future."

I sat up in bed with a jerk, my sleepy, swollen eyes widening with surprise. The last person I had expected to see, in my bedchamber of all places, was my mother.

"I'm sorry if I woke you up," she said in an expressionless voice. "But the news I have wouldn't keep. I told Martine she could leave, that I would see you had your hot chocolate. It's there on the table by your bed."

I looked at her, bunking to clear the last vestiges of sleep from my eyes. My mother—Lady Fanny. All these months we had existed like complete strangers, passing each other in the corridors of the house without any visible recognition. It was by her avoidance of me that I first sensed she knew very well what had caused my changed position in the house, but like an ostrich, she preferred not to see. I had hated her all the more for it, of course. My mother, the procuress! She had been Sir Edgar Cardon's mistress while she was still married to my father, and now, in my own twisted way, I was paying her back in her own coin, on my father's behalf.

We watched each other for a few moments, while I reached slowly for my cup of chocolate.

The morning light was cruel to her face, in spite of the carefully applied powder and rouge she always used. Perhaps she had been pretty once, but her plump blonde beauty was not the kind that lasts into middle age. I saw her suddenly, in the harsh light of the sun, as a fat, aging woman—an object of pity, if I had been capable of pitying her.

As if she could not bear to look upon my face for too long, my mother had walked impatiently over to my dresser, where she stood fiddling with my combs and brushes as she waited for me to finish my drink. All this time I had said not a word to her, but now at last I put my cup down and saw that she had picked up the necklace of sapphires and diamonds which had been Sir Edgar's birthday present to me.

"Do you like them?" I said idly. "I also have the bracelet and the earrings to match. But the necklace is a beautiful piece, don't you think?"

She dropped the necklace as if it had suddenly turned red-hot and looked at me with hatred and malice in her eyes. It was just as if a mask had dropped from her face.

"Perhaps you could soon be buying your own jewels, Rowena. That is—if you are sensible."

"Why don't you come right out with whatever it is you came here to say, Mother? I'm still too sleepy to find solutions to riddles."

I swung my legs off the bed, realizing I was naked only when I saw the expression on my mother's face.

I laughed, reaching for one of the sheer, lace-embroidered robes that Sir Edgar had surprised me with on one occasion. "Heavens! What strangers we are, to be sure! I had no idea that my nudity would appall you."

"It's not that..." she began, and then bit her words off

short. "Never mind," she went on quickly. "I did not come here to quarrel with you, but rather—rather to offer you a belated birthday present, you might say." The short, almost hysterical laugh she gave startled me into looking more closely at her, and indeed, her face bore an almost unnatural flush that underlay the rouge she had applied too heavily, and her plump, be-ringed fingers trembled as she nervously pleated and unpleated a fold of her skirt.

"It's a little late for recriminations between us, isn't it, Mother?" I said equably, and began to brush my hair. "Well?" I went on when she seemed to hesitate. "Aren't you going to tell me what my belated birthday present is?"

"It must be a secret between us," she said quickly. "Edgar—I do not want Edgar to know—not yet. He never did like your father, you know. Guy's name must not be mentioned."

My hand stopped in midstroke. "My father? What has he to do with it? You've never mentioned his name before!"

"Of course I haven't. Why should I? We are divorced, and all the unpleasantness he put me through… but that no longer matters," she said hurriedly, when I would have spoken. "The least you can do is to hear me out. It will not take long. Your father—you knew he went to America? When your grandfather died, the lawyers had a difficult time tracing him. No one had an address, and of course, it was out of the question that he should ever return here! Even so, there was the matter of the title. He is the Earl of Melchester now, murderer or not." A barely suppressed note of bitterness had crept into her voice, and I wondered whether she had begun to regret the fact that she might have been a countess, instead of the wife of a mere baronet.

I repeated, "Why should you suddenly speak of my father now? What are you trying to tell me?"

Suddenly there was a note of triumph in her voice.

"That he wants you to come to America to live with him! Yes—" she hurried on, seeing my expression, "it's true, the lawyers found him. He had not known that his father was dead, or that you were here with us. I was contacted by the solicitor who is acting for him, and he wishes to meet you, to discuss various arrangements that will have to be made. You will go, will you not, Rowena?" In the face of my stunned silence, her voice became almost desperate. How much she wanted to be rid of me! I had not realized.

"He's a rich man, Rowena! I cannot imagine it. Guy, who was always such a spendthrift, a man who never cared for money, except to get rid of it as quickly as possible. But Mr. Braithwaite tells me he's a millionaire, and it will all be yours! You'll be an heiress! The minute you sign those papers and I give my consent for you to go to him, you'll have fifty thousand pounds settled on you outright. Do you understand what that means? You'll be rich—and completely independent, of course. Well, what do you say?"

I had received a shock—and if I managed to keep my face expressionless, I know it must have showed in the unusual brilliance of my eyes. I looked at my mother, who was biting her lip as she tried to search for some answer in my face.

"Well?" she said again, her tone a mixture of impatience and fear.

"I need time to—to think about all this, of course," I said slowly. "My father—do you not think it strange that he should have waited so long to try and contact me?"

"I wrote to him!" she burst out defiantly. "Well, why not?" she went on, her voice rising slightly. "Do you think I wanted you here? Especially after—after—"

"Why are you so reluctant to say it?" I broke in coldly. "You surely mean that after your husband had raped me, he was weak enough to become infatuated with me. You are afraid you'll lose him to me completely, are you not? Is that why you've decided not to bury your head in the sand any longer, but to get rid of me instead?"

"You are a cold, calculating little hussy, Rowena!" she whispered, and by now I had regained enough composure to give her a scornful smile.

"Certainly, I must take after you in some ways, I suppose. Are we going to indulge in recriminations at this late stage?"

I could see her trying desperately to pull herself together, torn between her desire to pour out all the accumulated resentment and hatred she felt for me, and the need to placate me.

In the end, she said abruptly, "Will you go with me to visit Mr. Braithwaite or not? Once you have spoken to him and he has explained everything to you in detail, I doubt that there will be any need for us to converse further."

"Quite so. At all costs, let us not become hypocrites." I turned away from her once more and continued brushing my hair. "If you will send Martine to me, Mother, I should be ready to accompany you in less than an hour."

The drive to Lincolns Inn Fields, where Mr. Braithwaite maintained his offices, was accomplished in stony silence. And indeed, once we had been politely ushered into the cozy office of the senior partner of the august firm of Braithwaite, Matthews and Braithwaite, my mother quickly informed that gentleman that I was possessed of an intelligent mind and had a will of my own, so that *her* part in this matter would be merely that of an interested observer.

I shot her a somewhat sardonic glance, but she had settled back in her chair with her hands primly folded in her lap, and would not meet my eyes.

"Well, Lady Rowena." Mr. Braithwaite said briskly from behind his paper-cluttered desk, and I looked up to meet his blue, twinkling gaze, which was remarkably shrewd in spite of his advanced years. He surprised me by saying suddenly, "You look like your father, y'know! Hmm—too bad things turned out the way they did. Guy—but you're not here to listen to an old man reminisce, are you? Shall we get down to business right away, then, or would you ladies like a cup of tea first?"

Both my mother and I declined the offer of tea, and, nodding his head in a satisfied manner, Mr. Braithwaite made a small pyramid of his fingers, gazing over their tips at me like a benevolent gnome.

"Very well, business it shall be, then. You'll stop me at any time you do not understand something I am saying, or need clarification of any point, Lady Rowena?"

I nodded, and he inclined his head to me, in a courtly fashion.

"Good!" he exclaimed, and then picking up a sheaf of papers that lay in front of him, his voice became businesslike as he began to read to me—first a lengthy letter of instructions from my father, and then a copy of his will, listing all his assets.

To say I was slightly stunned at the end of Mr. Braithwaite's recital would be an understatement. I had made some study of the law, among other things, mainly because I knew Latin and wanted to practice it as much as possible, but my father's will and his instructions were simply, yet concisely, drawn up, leaving no loopholes.

"Whoever Guy's attorney in Boston is—this Judge Fleming—he's a good man. Makes everything clear, does he not? Do you have any questions now, Lady Rowena?"

I was amazed, even slightly dazed, by the sudden change in my fortunes, and my somewhat ambiguous status. Because I was used to thinking before I spoke, I was silent for a few moments after Mr. Braithwaite had spoken, and he repeated his question, giving me an understanding smile.

"It's something of a shock, eh? Not surprising. I understand you believed your father to have dropped completely out of sight, or to have forgotten your existence? Well, the letter explains it all, of course. Your grandfather"—he sighed— "well, in his way he was a hard man. Unforgiving. You understand everything now, do you not? Guy Dangerfield— the Earl of Melchester, I should say—is a sick man. No, let us be frank, he's a dying man, and he knows it. That is why there is a reason for haste. He wishes very much to see you before he dies. I don't wish to press you, of course, for I realize what a shock this must all be to you, but—" I heard my mother's sharply indrawn breath and knew she was watching me, her eagerness to hear my answer almost a palpable thing.

But I already knew what my answer would be. I had known it when I agreed to come here—even before I discovered the extent of my suddenly acquired fortune. I was free! Amazingly, unexpectedly, I had been set free, granted independence. From now on I need belong to no one, answer to no one but myself.

I leaned forward and heard my own voice say in level, perfectly composed tones, "But of course I agree, Mr. Braithwaite. To all the conditions outlined in the will and my father's letter, as well as to the need for haste. I shall be ready to leave England as soon as you can make the arrangements."

"We will not say anything of this to Edgar," my mother said flatly when we were in the carriage again. She had signed all the necessary papers relinquishing her guardianship of me, and now she met my eyes coldly, as if she had already said her good-byes to me. "Mr. Braithwaite said it would take about a week. It was fortunate that he had the forethought to reserve a passage for you on that American ship, just in case you agreed to go. There's no need for—for any unpleasantness before you leave. Best to do it this way."

I shrugged wearily, still occupied with my thoughts. "As you please," I said indifferently. "I shall leave it to your ingenuity to get Sir Edgar out of the way on the day I'm supposed to depart. And you'll have a week to think of some explanation to give him."

"That will be my affair," she said harshly, and we conversed no more for the rest of the journey back.

I had much to think about. Not only was I to start off upon a journey that would take me to a whole new life, but I had a father at last, and he actually wanted me! I remembered Nanny's words—"He fair doted upon you, he did"—and found myself wondering, for the first time, how my father had got on after his return to America. Forced to leave England under a cloud, leaving both wife and daughter behind, denied all communication with me afterwards—it had been fair to neither of us, but of course, my grandfather had believed he was doing what was best for me.

I would not waste time on regrets for what was past and done with; that much, at least, I had learned. And I did not think that anyone but Sir Edgar would regret my departure. I know that the servants whispered about me, even Mrs. Jenks, who positively fawned upon me in the hopes I'd recommend her devotion to Sir Edgar. And Mellyn, who was bluntly outspoken because of her age and privileged position, had been pensioned off at Sir Edgar's insistence, because he was afraid she would "kick up an ugly fuss" as he put it, when she discovered what was going on under her "poor baby's" very nose. Well, Nanny could come back now, and no doubt, after his first rage was over, Edgar would play the dutiful and loving husband again, keeping his mistresses in the discreet little apartment off Curzon Square.

Everything would settle down to normal again, just as it had been before I arrived; and I—but things would be different for me this time, I vowed to myself. I had learned my lessons in survival as diligently as I had once studied my books that taught me of abstracts. Soon, when I was on my own, I would have the chance to see how well I remembered these lessons.

There was nothing to do now, but to wait. The carriage pulled up before Sir Edgar's imposing town house, and my mother and I, incongruous co-conspirators, alighted in silence without glancing at each other.

Upstairs in my room, Martine was waiting for me.

"We have been shopping, but I did not see anything that I wanted," I told her casually, and dismissed her on the pretext that I was tired and would rest again before dinner. Poor Martine. What would she do when I was gone? I told myself that I must leave her an excellent letter of recommendation, and perhaps a bonus of fifty pounds to take care of her until she found another position. It would be more than she would earn in two years, but what did fifty pounds matter to me now? In my reticule I carried a packet of carefully folded bank notes, amounting to well over five hundred pounds—money for "incidentals," Mr. Braithwaite had called it. My father, it seemed, had been insistent that I must lack for nothing. I had also been given a letter that authorized me to draw as much money as I needed out of my father's banks in Boston and New York. I was really an heiress, after all!

I sat at my small Chippendale desk—another gift from Sir Edgar, who had allowed me to refurnish my room according to my own tastes—and carefully opened the sealed envelope I had taken out of my reticule. The writing on the front was in black ink—a rather spidery, unfamiliar scrawl. "To my Daughter, Rowena Elaine Dangerfield." Now, at last, I would learn something about my father, from himself.

My fingers trembled as I drew out the stiff, crackling sheets of paper. My father. Strange that I, who had so carefully taught myself to suppress all outward show of emotion, should suddenly feel almost moved. Strange too, that even before I began to read, I should feel a sense of familiarity, even of closeness.

> *My Dearest Daughter,*
>
> *It must surely seem as strange to you to read this letter from me as it seems for me to be writing to you at last, knowing that you will be reading this letter. And yet we are hardly strangers. I do not refer only to the tie of blood that binds us, but to the fact that you have never been far from me in my thoughts. Whatever you have been told about me, I hope you will believe this much at least; that I love you, as I loved you ever since I first held you as a tiny, squalling scrap of humanity, your eyes tightly screwed shut, and on your head a thatch of black hair that had to come to you from me. My daughter!*
>
> *I felt closer to you, in that moment, than I have ever felt to any other human being…*

My eyes moved down the closely written pages, reading more slowly than was my wont. My father had not wasted too much space in explanations, or reasons for our long separation, except to tell me that it had not been of his own will or doing. He had kept journals, which I would be able to read someday. They would explain everything.

> *I have tried to envision New Mexico through your eyes—as I saw it first. A savage, beautiful land of contrasts. Perhaps, since you have lived in India, the transition will not prove too difficult. You see, I am already taking it for granted that you will come here. I have begun to hope again, to make plans….*

Further down he had written,

I have spoken to Todd of my plans. He does not believe that you will want to live here. He does not understand. How can he? I feel that I know you, in spite of everything; it is more instinct that tells me this than anything else. But to satisfy Todd, I have included certain stipulations in the will I have drawn up. Whether you decide to make your home in New Mexico or not, you will be amply provided for, as I am sure Samuel Braithwaite will have made very clear to you. If, before a year is up, you decide you would rather make your home elsewhere, the SD Ranch will be all Todd's—but even now, when I have been forced to realize that I am a dying man, I have hopes that I will live long enough to see you again, to talk to you, and explain all that you will have to face when I am gone. I have certain requests to make of you—they are requests only. I think, when you have read my journals, you will understand why I make them. But I would make another request of you, my daughter, and that is that you read my journals in sequence…

I was to get in touch with a man named Elmer Bragg when I arrived in Boston. "An ex-Pinkerton man," my father called him. "A frontier lawyer with the soul of a scholar—or perhaps a prophet. Elmer chooses his clients since he had retired, but he is one of my closest friends, and if I am unable to meet you, it is my wish that you will contact him."

The letter was signed "Your loving Father, Guy Dangerfield."

I thought about my mother, whom I had known these past two years, and for whom I could feel nothing but a vague kind of dislike. I had hated her at times, but I was beyond that violent emotion now. She was a poor, wily woman, the product of her environment and upbringing. I was more my father's daughter than I was hers, and she, oddly enough, had realized it first.

I had passed the time for looking back! The thought came to me with a kind of violence, bringing me to my feet, and to the mirror again, where I looked at my reflection with a feeling of wonderment, remembering myself when I had first come here. It was a different Rowena Dangerfield who would be traveling to America—not a girl, but a woman.

"It is better this way," my mother said, as she rode opposite me in the carriage. It was our first real conversation since we had spoken of my new life a week ago, and now we were on our way to the docks. "You'll get on in America, I'm sure," she went on, her eyes flickering over me. "Guy should have been allowed to have you, of course. I see that now. But at the time your grandfather was insistent, and I had no choice in the matter. I was forced to go abroad for a while. The scandal was really terrible. I wasn't prepared for any of it—then."

"I'm sure Sir Edgar went with you," I said idly, and saw her eyes narrow.

"Yes, he did! But then, it is not something you would understand. You have never felt deeply about anything, or anyone, have you? Oh, I see you raise your eyebrows. I know what you think about me. But you have never loved. I wonder if you are capable of it! I might have—I might have felt something for you, even if it was only pity, if I hadn't recognized how hard you are, under that indifferent surface!"

"What is the point of saying this to me now?"

She leaned forward, and her mouth, usually soft and pouting, was hard. "It has to be said! I know you never loved Edgar. You never felt anything for him, did you? And perhaps it was for that very reason that he became so—besotted—obsessed! You saw him merely as a man you had maneuvered into an awkward position, and then you used him, did you not? But I love him. Yes, look at me any way you want to. You may think me a silly, stupid woman, but at least I'm capable of feeling! He had his mistresses when we first met, and he had them afterwards, but he married me. It didn't matter until you came. Guy's daughter—Guy's revenge!"

I said coldly, "How unfortunate that you had me at all! And how awkward of my grandfather to die so soon."

"Oh, yes," my mother said a trifle wildly. It seemed as if she was suddenly determined to have her say. "Yes," she added, in a lower voice. "You would not understand, but I was only seventeen. What did I know of love or marriage at the time? It was all arranged. I was to be married to Guy Dangerfield, who was so much older than I was, a man I had met only twice before. It was what I had been brought up for, after all. To make an advantageous marriage. No one thought to consult my feelings in the matter! I was married in order to produce more Dangerfields. Thank God that after I had you I was allowed some respite!"

A tiny shiver of anger shook me as I looked at her flushed face. "You hated my father. And you hated me from the moment I was born. I'm a product of your hate, Mother dear. Why blame me for being stronger than you were?"

"Why? Because you are hard. It's not strength, but hardness—a lack of feeling in you."

"It's hardly important now."

"No, I suppose not. But the blame wasn't all mine! I was prepared to be a good wife. If your father had loved me more and despised me less, something might have come of it. But he too married to please others. There was another woman. I never knew who she was or what she was to him, but he would mutter her name sometimes, in his sleep. 'Elena—' he would say—'Elena!' And he called you Rowena Elaine. No, he never loved me! Is it any wonder that I sought love?"

For an instant I saw her as she must have looked twenty years ago, before she became overly plump and the fine lines etched themselves in her face. Poor Fanny. Product of her environment. But as selfish in her own way as she accused me of being. Whatever her reasons for her sudden outburst, we were past the point of understanding each other, or, for that matter, of any genuine communication.

So I looked back at her, saying nothing, and after a while, shrugging, she seemed to regain her composure.

"Ah, well. Perhaps it's a good thing we need not indulge in the conventional strain of farewells. There were things that I felt had to be said, and they are behind us now."

We did not kiss when the time for final parting came. A footman lifted my trunks from the carriage and set them down for the swarming porters to carry. Nor did I turn my head when the carriage drove off. Within a few hours I would be leaving the past behind me and embarking on a new life. I remembered my last journey, and could almost have smiled with pity for the miserable, frightened, and resentful creature I had been then. Could it have been only two years ago? This time, at least, I knew what I was going to.

I had reached the water's edge, and as I lifted my head I felt the tangy, salty kiss of the wind on my face, felt it ruffle my skirts and tug at my bonnet.

"Journeys end in lover's meetings." Now, why had that ridiculous piece of nonsense suddenly sprung into my mind? I had no lover to meet me—indeed, I had already made up my mind that I would never have, if I could help it. I would never be controlled by anyone again. I would be my own mistress from now on.

Hadn't I learned about love? A ridiculous, fumbling thing that made an animal of a man and required from a woman only a certain degree of compliance: At least animals didn't try to rationalize their expressions of lust or attempt to prettify it by calling it love.

"We'll be sailing with the tide," I heard a sailor call to another, and the same wind that touched me made little dancing ripples in the water. A fine, sunny day. A good day to begin a journey.

Three

꒰

THE VESSEL ON WHICH I SAILED WAS AN AMERICAN ONE, AND I
was soon to get used to hearing the strange, nasal accents of my
fellow passengers. These Americans were all more friendly and
outgoing than the English, and although I kept to myself they
persisted in being friendly and curious. Strangely enough, the
fact that I was possessed of a title excited the most comment.
For all that they prided themselves on their form of democracy,
most of the friendly Americans I met could hardly hide the fact
that they were impressed at meeting the daughter of an earl.

We stopped for over three days at Le Havre to pick up
passengers from Paris, and I had the chance to visit Paris again
myself, but under vastly different circumstances from all the
other times I had been there. I saw none of Sir Edgar Cardon's
friends this time, but spent my time in shopping, completely
on my own, which in itself gave me an exhilarated feeling.

Still, I was impatient for my journey to be over, and for the
time when I would meet my father at last. My mother, who
should have known, had said we were alike, Guy Dangerfield
and I. I thought we would understand each other, for we were
both travelers.

I had come halfway across the world and as I looked out for
the first time at Boston harbor, I found myself wondering what
my father's impressions must have been when he first landed
here. He must have been around the same age that I was now.
Would he be here to meet me, or was he too ill to travel?

As I left the rail and made my way to my stateroom, the echo of my mother's bitter voice suddenly came back to me.

"You are hard, Rowena… it is not strength, but hardness. I wonder if you are capable of any emotion…"

Well, at least I wasn't weak. I remembered the diamonds that Edgar Cardon had presented me with—hard, scintillating stones, each one burning with its own tiny fires. How often he had compared me to a diamond. I had a cutting tongue, he had complained, and he had never been able to arouse in me the warmth and passion he had hoped to find. But I could not pity him. We had used each other—each for our own separate reasons—and now, at last I was free. I would never let myself be used again by anyone.

"Lady Rowena—" the steward's voice broke into my thoughts, and I turned away from snapping the lock on my last trunk.

"Pardon me, Lady Rowena, but you have visitors. The other passengers have already begun to disembark, but your friends are on board to escort you personally to shore."

"Thank you."

I had not been sure whether there would be someone to meet me. We had been delayed by bad weather, and I had noticed that Boston, although basking in watery sunshine, had been thinly blanketed by an early snowfall. Still, I had been expected, and there were "friends" to meet me. Not my father, then. I wondered who his friends were.

When I went up on deck, they were standing there rather uncertainly, amid all the bustle of visitors and disembarking passengers. Mrs. Katherine Shannon was obviously a widow—a rather formidable-looking lady dressed in black. She was the sister-in-law of Mr. Todd Shannon, who was my father's partner, and was accompanied by her niece and her husband, a pleasant young couple with friendly, if rather sober, manners.

I was soon to learn why they had taken the trouble to come on shipboard to meet me, and why Corinne Davidson, who was normally a vivacious, bubbling young woman, appeared so subdued on our first meeting. "The telegram arrived only a week ago," Mrs. Shannon said in her quiet voice. "My dear, we are all so terribly sorry! It is not precisely the way your father would have wished you to be greeted upon your arrival in America. But you had to be told, of course." She said again, "I'm so very sorry…" and I saw that Corinne Davidson's eyes had filled with tears. My father was dead. I would never see him now. I could not cry. I suppose I felt numb, and I knew that my face had gone stiff, betraying no emotion.

It was a relief to be taken charge of for the moment, with Jack Davidson, a quietly competent young man, seeing to the disposition of my luggage.

They were tactful, understanding people, who seemed to take my silence for shock, and did not press me with any further displays of sympathy.

"Jack and I live in New York, but we're visiting Aunt Katherine," Corinne Davidson said softly. "Of course you will stay with her too. Isn't that right, Aunt Katherine?"

Mrs. Shannon insisted that I must do so—a room had already been made ready for me, and I needed to rest, and to feel that I had arrived among friends.

"If you feel like talking later, I hope you will not feel reluctant to do so," Mrs. Shannon said kindly, adding that my father had been a frequent visitor to her home in the past, before he had become so ill.

But in the end it was Corinne Davidson, with her natural, open manner, who broke through the shell of reserve I had learned to erect around myself, and became my first friend in America.

She came up to my room that first night, and her soft, hesitant tapping at the door turned me away from the window, where I had been standing looking out at the snow.

"Will you promise to tell me you'd rather be alone if that is how you honestly feel?" she burst out, almost as soon as she had closed the door behind her. She bit her lip, before rushing on, "Jack tells me that I have no tact at all, and that I talk far too much, but I know how I would feel in your place, and I—we were all so fond of Uncle Guy, you know! I just think it's so terribly sad and tragic that you didn't get to know him.

He was a wonderful person. So quiet that people wouldn't notice him unless he wanted them to, and yet he cared about people! I remember that he came all the way to Boston to see us after my papa died, and he took me out to dinner and to the opera, and that was how I met Jack..."

She clapped her hand suddenly over her mouth, a dismayed look appearing in her eyes. "Oh, heavens, there I go again! I do keep rattling on, don't I? And I really came up to see if you wanted to talk."

It was impossible not to like Corinne, although I had never been close to other females of my own age. She openly admitted that she loved to gossip, but there was no guile in her, and she had a habit of saying exactly what she thought, even though it often proved embarrassing later.

I suppose I needed a friend during the weeks that followed. I had never had one before, and although Corinne and I were complete opposites as far as personalities went, we complemented each other in a way; and she had a quick, intelligent mind, for all her madcap ways. Certainly it was Corinne who helped me most during those first difficult days, when I had to adjust to the fact that I had lost my father before I found him again, and that now I was really alone, with no one but myself to depend on.

I was rich, of course, and that would help. And I was no longer naive, for Edgar Cardon had seen to that. It did not shock me, therefore, when Corinne proceeded to drag out what she laughingly referred to as the family skeletons.

"Well, of course someone has to tell you," she pointed out reasonably, "and Aunt Katherine never would! So it had better be me. Even Jack agrees with me that you should be prepared for what you'll find when you go to New Mexico."

"Good heavens, you make it all sound alarming!" I teased her, but she insisted, for once, that she would be serious.

"For instance," she said dramatically, perching herself on the end of my bed, "how much have you been told about Todd Shannon?"

I admitted that I knew only that he had been my father's partner, who owned a joint interest in the vast SD Ranch.

"Just as I thought!" Corinne pursed her lips in an unusual expression of gravity. "And of course he's Aunt Katherine's brother-in-law, although I'm sure she never became too friendly with him, even while Uncle James was alive. You see, my Uncle James had come to America many years before his brother Todd turned up suddenly. He was a serious young man, who had been given an education, and while he studied law here in Boston he went to work for my grandfather, who was Aunt Katherine's papa, of course, and…" Here Corinne stopped to draw in a long breath, and catching my slight smile grinned mischievously back at me. "I know what you're thinking! They say that all of us Bostonians are related in some way, and I don't doubt that it's true! But Rowena, you must listen to me, for I'm trying to be serious for a change. What was I saying?"

"You were going to tell me something about this man Todd Shannon," I said helpfully, and she nodded her head sagely.

"Yes, of course! Well, it was rather embarrassing for my poor aunt and uncle when he turned up in Boston, for he'd been a kind of black sheep, you know! They said that as young as he was he had been mixed up in some kind of revolutionary activities in Ireland. They're always fighting the British, are they not? Well, anyhow, he had to leave in a hurry, so he came here."

"Is that how he met my father?" I asked curiously, and Corinne gave a small shrug.

"I'm not sure, for it was all before my time, of course. But I think I remember hearing someone mention that they had met on the ship coming over here, and decided to seek their fortune together. It sounds very romantic and exciting, doesn't it? They went west together, for in those days the frontiers were still expanding, and it was before the war with Mexico. The Spaniards still owned most of the Southwest, and California as well."

I had made a point of studying American history, so that I nodded, and Corinne, with one of her quick flashes of intuition, seemed to understand that I was becoming impatient for her to come to the point of her recital.

"Oh dear!" she said ruefully, "there I go again. Rambling! You don't want to hear about history, but about Todd Shannon—and your father, of course, for he played a large part in what happened as well." She giggled suddenly. "How I loved to listen to the grown-ups talk when I was a child! I would stay very quiet, and pretend to be reading, or busy with my embroidery. But you know, to me, the whole story was quite fascinating, and more exciting, than anything I had read in a book."

"Go on," I said. "Now you have me quite fascinated. What happened?"

"Well, as I was saying, your father and Uncle Todd—I'm supposed to call him that, but somehow he always frightened me a little bit—went west and they had all kinds of adventures; sometimes together and sometimes not, for they were both very independent men. But then, just before the war with Mexico, Uncle Todd fell in love. They said she was very beautiful, a young Spanish girl of good family, who was under the guardianship of her brother. She had been meant for a convent, but instead she met Uncle Todd and fell in love with him too. They eloped, ran away to Texas, and left her brother vowing vengeance. There!" Corinne looked at me triumphantly. "Now isn't that an exciting and romantic tale so far?"

"Isn't there more?" I asked pointedly.

"Oh, Rowena! Sometimes, I vow you prefer tragedy to romance! Well, there is one involved here. You see, after the Mexicans were forced to cede their lands in the Southwest to the United States, Todd Shannon brought his bride back to New Mexico, and filed claim to her family's lands."

I frowned. "But what of that revengeful brother of hers?"

"Alejandro Kordes? Oh, he had been one of the few hotheads who refused to acknowledge their new American government. They say he took off into the mountains along with some others like him—and later on there were rumors that he had joined up with a band of *comancheros*. At least, that's what they call themselves, but I've heard Uncle Todd say that they're nothing but a crew of renegade cutthroats who trade with the Indians and sell them guns to use against the white men. Alejandro had become an outlaw, but he still hated Todd Shannon."

Once she got down to it, Corinne proved a good story-teller, with a gift for evoking atmosphere, so that it was easy for me to picture the terrible, tragic events that had led to a family feud that, Corinne warned me, was still in existence. At the time, it was my father's part in those events that intrigued me the most.

He had made some money in the gold fields of California, and when his old partner had written to say he needed capital, he had traveled to New Mexico. He and Todd Shannon had become partners again, in an enormous cattle ranch they called the SD—Shannon-Dangerfield. They had been prospering when tragedy struck.

"It was the time of the great silver rush in that part of the world, and Uncle Todd and your father went prospecting together. Alma, Todd Shannon's wife, had given birth to a son, and had not regained her strength, so they had left her behind with a young cousin of Alma's who had suddenly appeared on the scene, confessing she had run away from the Apache Indians. Elena, her name was, and she was the result of union between a captured Spanish girl, Alma's aunt, and her captor, an Apache chieftain. Although she was half Apache, Elena had said she had been intrigued by her mother's tales of 'civilization,' and wanted to live as a white woman, not as an Indian squaw."

"Elena?"

The name struck a chord in my memory. I heard it again, repeated in my mother's spiteful voice.

"Elena! Sometimes he called the name in his sleep. And you were called Rowena Elaine."

"Corinne—what was she like? Did anyone ever describe her?"

"Why, not exactly," she said slowly, as if trying to remember. "She—I believe she was very young—only fifteen or sixteen—and very pretty, in a wild sort of way."

"Did—did my father ever speak of her?" Something impelled me to ask the question, and Corinne gave me a rather puzzled stare.

"I—I can't remember! But he must have been fond of her, for I know he taught her to read and write, and of course, later, he saved her life."

She was tactful enough not to ask why I questioned her as she went on with the story in a hushed voice.

My father and Todd Shannon had returned from their expedition within a matter of weeks, only to find that while they had been away, the Indians had attacked. Their house was burned, their cattle stampeded, and worst tragedy of all, both Alma and her son were dead.

"One of the *vaqueros* survived long enough to tell what had happened. He said that Alejandro Kordes and some of his *comancheros* had taken part in the attack. Perhaps he didn't know that his sister had been left behind. The house had begun to burn and she ran outside, carrying her child. An Indian arrow killed them both."

"Oh, no!"

"The old *vaquero* said that before he became unconscious he saw Alejandro Kordes run forward, shouting like a madman. He said he wept as he knelt by his sister's body."

"And then? What of Elena? Was she killed too?"

Corinne shook her head, her small face unusually grim.

"That is what really started the feud. Just before Uncle Todd left, he'd had some kind of disagreement with her. He never liked Indians, you see, and he hadn't wanted Elena there at all. A few days after he left, she had run away without a word. Later, he blamed her. He said she had called her people down on the ranch, as her revenge."

"But my father?"

"You must understand, Rowena, that Uncle Todd was like a wild animal, crazed with grief and hatred. He would have gone after the Indians and his brother-in-law alone, if your father had not stopped him. And then, to make matters worse, a few days later, Elena came back. It—it appeared—" Corinne lowered her voice conspiratorially, giving me rather an embarrassed look. "It appeared that she was—well, expecting a child. They always hushed their voices when they started talking about that part of the story, and I was ordered out of the room, but my mama told me later, when I was old enough, that Elena had been in love with Uncle Todd, and that the child she was expecting was his."

"Oh, God. What did he do when she turned up?"

"He almost killed her, that's what! He would have, if Uncle Guy had not dragged him off, after he started beating her. She lost her child, and it was Uncle Guy, your father, who nursed her back to health. But as soon as she was well enough, she ran away again, back to her people."

"That couldn't have been the end of it. How did the feud you were talking about begin?"

Corinne sighed.

"Oh, Rowena, that was the worst part of it! It wasn't long before Elena had run off that the rumors began filtering back. She married Alejandro Kordes, of all people! Don't you see how it must have looked to Uncle Todd? He felt it proved that Elena and Alejandro had been in league all the time!"

There was more to the story, of course, but Corinne had been too young at the time to remember too many details. I was to hear it told again later, in all its facets, some of it related in my father's meticulously kept journals and some of it from the protagonists themselves. But I am going too fast—for many things were to happen before I was to know the whole of the truth.

First of all, I was to meet the strange and rather enigmatic Mr. Elmer Bragg, the ex-Pinkerton man to whom my father had referred in his last letter to me. It was my father's legal adviser, Judge Fleming, who reminded me to seek him out.

"He is—well, a rather *rough* man, who puts on a show of illiteracy, although he's self-educated, one of those men who are referred to in the west as 'frontier lawyers.' He was an excellent detective, though, and I know that my friend Allan Pinkerton was sorry to lose him when he insisted upon retirement. You know the saying—'Old soldiers never die'? Mr. Bragg is a living example of it. He has officially retired, but he is not the kind of man who likes to remain idle. He takes on cases from time to time. Your father and he were friends, and

I have the impression that he is in Boston at this moment for the particular purpose of meeting you."

"He hasn't attempted to meet me."

Judge Fleming nodded in a self-satisfied manner.

"Of course not. That is not Elmer Bragg's way. He knows of your father's letter to you, and I think he is waiting for you to contact him." He gave me a rather apologetic smile. "I've warned you, my dear, that Elmer Bragg is a rather eccentric man. This is typical of his way of going about things. I suppose he thinks that if you need his help or advice you will make some effort to seek him out."

In the end, I did exactly this—partly because my father had advised me to do so, and partly because I was intrigued by Judge Fleming's rather evasive comments about this Mr. Elmer Bragg.

I had decided to remain in Boston for a while until certain legal technicalities had been settled, so I had time on my hands. Besides, I wasn't anxious to travel to New Mexico until I knew more about what I would have to face. It occurred to me that this mysterious Mr. Bragg, being a Westerner himself, would be just the person to give me the advice I needed. And I was right in this assumption, for our very first meeting proved informative.

Four

~

"You're a sensible, self-possessed young lady, I see," Mr. Bragg complimented me in his gruff, rather grumbling manner. His eyes, shrewd under bushy, grizzled brows, swept over me quickly, and then he gave an almost imperceptible, satisfied nod. "Yes," he continued, as if there had been no pause in his speech, "I must say that you're a pleasant surprise! Didn't know what I'd have to deal with, if you'll excuse my blunt manner of speech. After all, even Guy knew nothing very much about you, except that the old earl, his father, was determined to bring you up according to his notions. And you're a highly educated young lady, too, I understand. That would have made your pa happy, for he set great store on education. What makes me happy is that you seem sensible as well as being pretty. Unusual combination in a female!"

I didn't know whether I should laugh or be angry with his abrupt manner, but I managed to retain enough composure to return Mr. Bragg's curious stare with a long, measuring look of my own. Then he began to smile, tugging at his large, untidy moustache.

"Huh! You don't say much either, do you? Sizing me up, I guess, and that's a good sign too. You're going to be meeting a lot of new people who are strangers to you, and if you don't mind a bit of advice from an old man, you'll do best to carry on as you're doing right now. Watch, listen, and say as little as possible."

He paused for an instant and then shot at me, "Do you have a mind of your own, Lady Rowena?" If his sudden question had been designed to take me on guard, it did not succeed in doing so.

"Certainly I've a mind of my own, Mr. Bragg! I should hardly be here if I did not. But I do realize that there is a lot I'm going to have to learn before I travel to New Mexico, and that is why I've come to you. My father wrote of you, and I understand from Judge Fleming that you are one of the few persons who is eminently qualified to advise me."

He chuckled at that. "So the judge recommended me, did he? Well, it's true that I know more about Guy and Guy's way of thinking than most others, including his partner, Todd Shannon. And so you think I might be able to give you some useful advice, eh?" He tugged at his moustache again, eyeing me thoughtfully. "That could be. Yes, it might be real interesting to see how you get on, at that. Did you have a business proposition in mind, then, Lady Rowena? You willing to hire my services?"

"If you are willing, of course," I said smoothly, and could not resist adding, "You might even find it a challenge, don't you think? Or is your retirement permanent?"

He snorted at that. "Permanent? Permanent hell, if you'll pardon me for using the expression. And that old fox Fleming knows it too. No doubt he told you that when he advised you to see me. Retired, huh!" He grunted again. "Your father sent for me just before he died. That's what took me so long gettin' up here. And I've been keeping tabs on everything that's been going on down there, as a kind of mental exercise, you might say. You'd be surprised at how much I know. For instance, did you know that Todd Shannon tried to contest your pa's will? The part where he left you a half-share in the SD?"

I intercepted the sharp, sly look he gave me and nodded in assent.

"Yes. Judge Fleming informed me of it. But surely—"

"Ah!" Elmer Bragg waved his hand impatiently as if to brush aside what I had been about to say. "That's what I meant earlier, when I said I knew more than some people realize. Shannon knew he didn't have a chance. It was more a gesture of—well, let's say he was registering a public, formal protest! He'd always taken it for granted that Guy would leave him the whole ranch, free and clear. And then, almost out of the blue, you turn up. What does he know about you, eh? A titled young Englishwoman, brought up as a fine lady. And what did Guy really know about you, except that you were his daughter? Believe me, if Todd had known when you were to arrive he'd have had his lawyer-nephew, young Mark, meet you right here in Boston with a very generous cash offer in return for your rights to the ranch. And no doubt he'd have instructed Mark to persuade you not to go down to New Mexico at all. It's rough, rugged country there. Lots of violence, very little law except for the jungle kind. Survival of the strongest and the sneakiest. You understand?"

I couldn't help frowning, but his words had made me thoughtful, and I said slowly, "You mean that Todd Shannon resents my inheriting a share in the ranch? But why just that? Surely, as vast as I understand it is, the ranch is the least valuable of all the joint interests my father held with him. What about their shares in that silver mine? And the railroad shares? Does he feel that I have no right to any of those either?"

"You've hit the nail right on the head!" Mr. Bragg exclaimed. "No, Todd Shannon's not a petty, greedy man by any means, although he can hate hard. He's an Irishman, big on family ties. He doesn't grudge you the money, even though the cattle business is booming right now and he's making money hand over fist, enough so they're calling him a cattle baron. No, the point is that he feels the SD is his. You take my meaning? Your pa put in the money to get it started, it's true, but Shannon built the SD into an empire with his fists and his guts and his guns. It's a symbol to him now, the symbol of the first piece of land he ever owned in his life, the symbol of his power. And in some ways, the SD is like a memorial to his wife. His first wife. Only woman he ever really loved. You've heard the story?"

Slowly I nodded, already puzzled by the complexity of Todd Shannon's character. What kind of man was he really?

My father had thought enough of him to become his partner. Corinne had told me that he had always frightened her a little, with his loud voice and the force of his personality. Judge Fleming had spoken of him with admiration, as a strong, stubborn man who had refused to admit defeat. Patently, he was a man capable of deep love, and capable of hating just as hard. A man who seemed to be haunted by tragedy. Corinne had told me that Todd Shannon had married again after my father had left for England to marry my mother. She was the widow of a schoolteacher who had been murdered by Indians, a woman with a young daughter, whom he had adopted as his own child. But this second wife too had died, in childbirth, and Todd Shannon had never married again.

"He's a big, handsome man," Corinne had told me. "A blond giant of an Irishman, the kind no woman can resist. But there's something hard about him too. My mother used to say he was the kind of man who is only capable of loving once in his life."

For all my self-confidence, I found myself wondering how such a man would react to my sudden arrival on the scene. No doubt he would resent me, and, in a way, I could hardly blame him for it.

I had been aware, while I was thinking all this, of Mr. Bragg's eyes upon me as he sat in silence chewing on the end of his cigar.

I caught his eye, and spoke aloud. "But, knowing all this, why did my father insist on leaving me his share in the ranch? He was a rich man without it, and certainly I don't need more money than I find myself with now. He must have had a reason."

"So you've asked yourself that too?" Elmer Bragg's shrewd eyes seemed to twinkle approvingly at me for a moment. "Well, I did too. I asked Guy about it. 'Why leave her trouble?' I said. 'Why insist she has to live in New Mexico for a whole year before she can inherit the ranch free and clear, in any case?'"

"So he did have a reason?"

"Your pa was a thinking man. After he came back from

England, he was never quite the same again. And towards the end, he lived like a recluse. Reading. Writing in his journals. Yes, he had a reason for giving you a half-interest in the ranch. A challenge, he called it. 'I think, Elmer—no, I feel that my daughter will grow up to be the kind of woman my mother was. Strong. Compassionate. I'm hoping, once she understands everything, that she'll be the one to end this senseless feud.' I'm an ex-lawman, Lady Rowena, and I've a good memory. Many's the time I've had to depend upon it. That, and my instincts. Some instinct tells me you're going to do what your pa wanted. You've already made up your mind to go to New Mexico, haven't you?"

I could not help smiling at his air of assurance.

"It's my turn to compliment you, Mr. Bragg. You're a very discerning man. My father has left me enough money to satisfy all my material needs, but I think I've inherited some of his curiosity about people. Perhaps what I really need is a challenge of some kind. Yes, I think I will go to New Mexico, if only to discover what kind of man this Todd Shannon really is."

"So it's Todd Shannon who's the challenge, Lady Rowena?" He saw my look and waved his hand impatiently. "Oh, come! Best get used to my rough manners and blunt speech. I'm going to help you, remember? Before you meet Todd Shannon, you have to understand him better. Tell me—" he paused to relight his cigar, "how much do you know of the rest of the story? I mean, what happened while your father was away in England, and after that."

"That ridiculous feud started up again," I said quickly, wondering what he was getting at.

"Ridiculous, you call it?" Elmer Bragg's voice had hardened. "It's hardly that, I'm afraid. If you're determined to go to New Mexico, it's something you'll have to live with. Every moment of every day. Todd Shannon is a man who has hated a long time, and that hate has eaten into him. While your father lived, he prevented really bad trouble, because he had earned the respect of the Kordes clan too. But now he's gone you'll be the one caught in the middle, Lady Rowena.

You, a little English gal who knows nothing of our Western ways. Gently brought up, too, from the look of you and your clothes. Maybe you're intrigued by all the stories you've been hearing, but that's not enough. Do you know what you'll be getting into?"

"Mr. Bragg!" He had finally succeeded in making me angry, and I could not help letting some of my annoyance show. "I may not know exactly what I'm getting into, as you put it, but that is exactly why I have come to you. And, although I may not look it, the life I have led before I came here has not exactly been sheltered." In a more controlled voice, I continued, "I was brought up in India, and we had our troubles there too. Not only from the wild hill tribes, but from the elements as well. And I have had the opportunity to study people, too. Perhaps there is more of my father in me than you think, Mr. Bragg, and you might as well learn that I can be stubborn!"

To my surprise, he had begun to chuckle, and pull at his moustache again. "So you have a temper as well! Good, good. I was beginning to wonder if you were all cool composure. But you know what, Lady Rowena? I think you'll do. Yep! I think that maybe Todd Shannon will find he's met his match in you!" His chuckle became a laugh. "By God, I'd like to see his face when he meets up with you and realizes he has no milk-and-water English miss to contend with, but a fighter! And you are that, aren't you?"

It would be some time before I would meet Todd Shannon, and then under circumstances that were hardly conducive to his thinking of me as an adversary worthy of his notice. But in the meantime, I had made two friends in America, Corinne Davidson and Elmer Bragg, for our strange association had grown into a grudging kind of friendship by the time we parted again, he to go his way on some mysterious errand he would tell me nothing about, and I on my way to New Mexico to claim the rest of my inheritance.

Neither Corinne nor her aunt, Mrs. Shannon, approved of my determination to travel alone and unchaperoned.

"I do wish you would wait until my son gets here,"

Katherine Shannon said in her quiet voice. "Mark would know what to do. And I'm sure my brother-in-law would never approve of my having let you travel alone, through that awful, Indian-infested country!"

"But I'm quite determined to do so," I said gently but firmly. "Please, Mrs. Shannon, I beg you not to worry yourself on my account. I'm quite used to traveling by myself, and I'm sure that there will be other people traveling with me, so that I will never be totally alone."

Corinne, however, was more outspoken than her aunt, and especially when she discovered how I meant to travel. "Rowena, I think you're out of your mind!" she said frankly, when I told her of my plan. "You're rich enough to travel in style, which is what I should do if I were you. I really cannot imagine why you should want to disguise yourself in those perfectly horrible, ugly clothes! And besides," she added, "my Uncle Todd despises plain women! I've heard him say so a dozen times at least. Oh, and I was so hoping that you would be the one woman to give him a set-down! He's such an arrogant, overbearing man—exactly the type you cannot abide. I've often thought that he imagines women were put on earth purely to serve men. To be their playthings. I remember how sorry I used to feel for Flo. She's his stepdaughter, you know. But of course, that was before I knew her!"

Corinne wrinkled up her nose, diverted, for the moment, from her purpose. "I was prepared to like her when Uncle Todd packed her back here to school, you know. I'd hear them all whisper about the terrible scandal, and I really did feel sorry for her, knowing how stern Uncle Todd can be. We used to ask her out to tea, and Aunt Katherine would have her spend weekends with her."

"And—" I prompted, more to get Corinne's mind off my plans than from any real curiosity.

"And I discovered what she was like!" Corinne's pretty face became flushed with emotion. "You can't imagine what a snob she is! And a flirt. I swear, all she could think about was men, and all she could talk about was how rich Uncle Todd is, and how she had her own horses to ride, and all the men in the territory were mad for her. I could almost feel sorry for that poor young Indian boy who was almost hanged because of her. And then she met Derek Jeffords, who is much older than she is, and because he's so rich, even Uncle Todd approved. Or maybe he was just anxious to get her married off. Anyhow, she married poor Mr. Jeffords, and she led him a dance from the very beginning. That was when we all started feeling sorry for Mr. Jeffords instead. She never loved him. I don't think she's loved anyone but herself, ever! She went after Mark too, for a while, and then, all of a sudden, she decided she was going back to New Mexico, to visit her pa, she said. I don't know what she told Uncle Todd, but he let her stay. So you'll have her to contend with too. And Flo doesn't like competition!"

"Well, if I travel in my 'disguise,' as you call it, she could hardly consider me competition, could she?" I objected reasonably, but Corinne was not to be mollified.

"But I want you to go as yourself!" she wailed. "I want you to show her up! And I want Uncle Todd to like you. It will be so much easier for you if you can win him over!"

"I don't intend to try to win Todd Shannon over. He'll have to accept me as I am, or as I appear to be. You must understand, Corinne, that I have a reason for doing what I plan. I want to discover people as they really are. Let Todd Shannon and his daughter see me as a dowdy, inconspicuous female. There was a time when I was exactly that. Perhaps, if they don't take too much notice of me, I'll see them as they really are."

"I still think you're making a mistake," Corinne said, but she did not sound as convinced as she had some moments ago.

In any case I had already made up my mind, and Elmer Bragg had set out on some errand of his own, telling me that he would meet me in New Mexico.

"I'll let you handle those first meetings yourself," he'd told me. "I got my own fish to fry. Just a notion, of course, but it might work out. We'll see."

I'd had to be content with that from him, but in the meantime, I was making my own plans. On the long journey to

New Mexico I had plenty of time to think about the rest of the story Mr. Bragg had related to me.

"Elena and Alejandro Kordes had three sons. Two of them were raised by the Apaches, because Elena wanted to travel with Alejandro and his *comancheros*. Liked the free, wandering life, I guess. But they left the third boy, Ramon, with the Jesuit fathers in Mexico City."

"But why?"

"How should anyone know? Perhaps because they happened to be there when Ramon was born."

"And the other two, the older sons?"

"Ah, that is how this feud stayed alive! Julio, the second son, was all Apache. Refused to leave the tribe, his grandfather's people. He has an Apache wife now. He doesn't care for the land the way the others do. Why should he? The Apaches are a nomadic people, warriors by profession. But Lucas, the oldest boy, was closest to his folks, I guess. To his ma, particularly. He went with them, and started to ride with the *comancheros,* just like his pa, when he was only twelve or thirteen. Killed a grown man when he was sixteen, outdrew a professional gunslinger."

I remembered that I had leaned forward in my chair with a slight stirring of interest.

"Why didn't they hang him?"

Mr. Bragg made a short, disgusted sound at my ignorance. "Heck, you have to remember this is the West. It was a fair fight, they said. Luke Cord, even then, was lightning fast with a gun."

"But I thought their name was Kordes."

"It was, still is, legally, but they anglicized the name later, when Alejandro laid claim to what he claimed were his lands. Don't think that he really wanted any more trouble, but Elena had become the stronger of the two by then, and she hated Todd Shannon. Luke, well, he kind of took it up, on his family's behalf. The law said Alejandro was an outlaw, but they made formal claim, all the same, on behalf of his heirs, they said. Case was thrown out of court, of course, although your pa spoke up on their behalf. And then Alejandro was found dead one day, killed from ambush on SD land. Bushwhacked, they call it in those parts. There were rumors, naturally. Some said that Todd Shannon had put a bounty on Alejandro's hide. And then Luke, who can read sign like the injuns who raised him, took the law into his own hands. Rode into Las Cruces, and called out two SD men. He was only seventeen or so then, but like I've said, he was fast with a gun, and he killed them both."

Mr. Bragg's story had taken on special interest for me, because of my curiosity about my father. It seemed that my father had been in Las Cruces that day, and had witnessed the gun battle. And he had gone against his own partner by championing Luke Cord, by giving evidence in court, stating that it had been a fair gunfight. Was it because this Lucas Cord was Elena's son? And had my father continued to love the woman even then?

It might have gone badly for Luke Cord, who was half Indian and considered a renegade, if not for my father's intervention. The judge had paroled Elena Kordes's hotheaded young son to my father.

"He accepted this?"

"The Spaniards, and even some Indians, have an almost fanatical sense of honor," Mr. Bragg had explained to me. "Luke Cord owed your father a debt, for they'd have lynched him for sure. He stayed with your pa."

"And the rest of his family?"

"Stayed on in the secret valley in the mountains. Where they still hide out. Apache country, but of course the Apaches wouldn't touch them because they're kin."

"It all sounds like something out of the pages of a novel!"

"You'd be better off sticking to your original simile," Mr. Bragg had told me dryly. "A Greek tragedy."

As I had listened to him, I found myself imagining how it must have been. My father, a lonely, bitter man. Rake turned scholar. Almost a recluse, until the fates, and his own sense of justice, had saddled him with the guardianship of a sullen young killer, part Indian, and unable to read or write. But in spite of all this, my father must have managed to win Luke

Cord's respect. He had even neglected his journals for a while, to turn teacher, and during this time the partners had not been on speaking terms. Todd Shannon had called my father a traitor and a turncoat and bitterly resented what he termed was his "softhearted interference."

It might all have turned out differently. The wild, dangerous streak in Luke Cord might have been subdued or channeled in other directions if not for Flo. Flo Shannon, she had been then. The same young woman that Corinne had so disliked.

She had been only fifteen years old then. Blonde, full-figured, and an inveterate flirt, with half the young men in the territory, including the SD cowboys, vying for her attention. But with all of them to pick from, she had deliberately chosen to practice her wiles on the one man who was forbidden to her, Lucas Cord. Part Indian, ex-outlaw, a man who had killed grown men, he was far older than his actual years in worldly experience.

Who could understand what had prompted the girl? Perhaps she had not realized that she was flirting with a man, hardly one of the callow, calf-eyed youths she was used to playing with. And in this case, Flo Shannon had found herself playing with fire.

Even Mr. Bragg had admitted, grudgingly, that no one was sure of what had really taken place the day that everything came to a head.

It appeared that Flo used to play her suitors one against the other, and had developed a habit of promising to meet a certain young man in a certain place, and then not show up; pleading some excuse afterwards. Her stepfather was a busy and somewhat remote man, and her mother was dead. Flo had her own horses and was allowed to ride whenever she pleased, her constant absences from home merely shrugged at.

"They used to meet in an abandoned line shack. No one knew for sure how long it had been going on, although Flo swore afterwards it was the first time that there had been anything but talk and a few kisses between them. They might have gotten away with it too, if some of her other admirers hadn't started to become suspicious about the way she'd suddenly started to put them off. Seems that a bunch of them, all SD hands, got to comparing notes one night, and the next time Flo went out riding they followed her."

"And then?"

Mr. Bragg raised his shoulders in a kind of shrug, and I had the impression that he was disgruntled because for once he could not quote me facts.

"There were six of them. They saw the horses tethered outside the cabin, and they said they heard Flo screaming. Certainly, and this much I know for sure, she was hysterical afterwards."

My imagination made it easy for me to picture the scene that must have followed. Flo Shannon, weeping with fear and hysteria, the six SD cowboys, in spite of their anger, must have been unable to keep their eyes off her half-naked body. Rape was an ugly word anywhere, and especially when the woman involved was white, and the man half Indian.

The cowboys had become careless, or perhaps they had not expected that Luke Cord, still on parole, would be carrying a forbidden gun. He had killed two of Flo's rescuers before making his escape, but then, instead of riding into the hills, Luke had done something that surprised everyone. He had gone instead to Guy Dangerfield. My father had persuaded him to give himself up, riding into town with him himself and staying in town to make sure there would be no lynching.

"If Todd Shannon had had his way, there wouldn't have been a trial," Mr. Bragg said grimly. "But your pa stood up to him. I guess he was about the only man who wasn't afraid of Shannon, even when Todd got in a rage. I wasn't present when they met, but your pa sent for me afterwards, to keep an eye on things, he said. There were two of us Pinkerton men, and we organized a twenty-four-hour watch on the jail. That's how I first got to know Luke Cord."

I interrupted him then, my curiosity getting the better of me. "What was he like? And why did my father continue to believe in him?" I wondered, even as I spoke, if it had been because of Elena, if my father had continued to love her.

"Luke Cord? Even then, when he was a young man, it was difficult to know what he was thinking. An' he never did say

much to me. I remember he spent most of the time in that
Socorro jail just sittin', or staring out the window. Didn't act
scared, although he knew damned well that most of the folks
in the territory were out for his blood. A sullen, bitter young
man. And even in those days it was hard to think of him as no
more'n a boy. He seemed more Injun than white, the way he
kept things inside hisself; never lettin' too much show on the
surface. Even at the trial…"

Mr. Bragg had been at the trial, and so had my father. In his
anxiety to make sure that Luke Cord had a fair trial, my father
had insisted that a federal judge be brought in all the way from
Taos. He had even paid handsomely for the services of a clever
attorney from San Francisco. Of all the protagonists, only Flo
Shannon had not been present. Her stepfather had packed her
off to school in Boston, but her sworn, witnessed deposition
had been read at the trial, sealing Luke Cord's fate.

"She said she hadn't understood what kind of man he was.
She liked to flirt, an' she liked to think there wasn't a man
she couldn't have at her feet. Well, she'd been forbidden to
ride over to the Dangerfield house as long as he was there,
but they met accidentally one day when her horse had lost a
shoe. She admitted he intrigued her, because he was different
from the other young men she was used to. He didn't pay
her much mind, treated her like she was a kid. At first, that
is. Later, well, she swore she hadn't led him on. Said she'd
grown frightened by the way he acted around her, that she'd
tried to end it, but he forced her to meet him one more time,
by tellin' her he'd see her pa found out if she didn't. And
then, she said, he'd called her names, told her she was a tease
an' was asking for it, and tried to force himself on her. And
then, luckily for her, but not for them, those cowboys bust in
the cabin."

Lucas Cord, surly-faced and tight-lipped, had denied that
Flo had screamed for help. "Only time she got scared and
started to scream was when those cowboys came bustin' in."

"Then you deny that you tried to force your attentions on
this innocent young girl? You dare to try and blame her?" the
prosecutor had thundered.

"Not tryin' to pin the blame anywhere. That's your job, ain't it? I guess she said what she felt she had to say."

He had refused to say more about his association with Flo Shannon, and the attorney for the defense had quickly objected that his client was being tried for murder, not for rape.

Luke said that he had killed the men only in self-defense. They had boasted that they were going to beat him to death and make the girl watch. Two of them had held his arms while the others began to use their fists on him.

"And in spite of that you managed to get free? And pulled your hidden gun?"

The judge himself had asked the question, leaning forward in his dark robes.

"I let them think I'd passed out," Luke Cord's eyes, coldly defiant in his bruised face, had met those of the judge boldly. "An' I wasn't carryin' a gun. Took Charlie Dales's gun off him."

The prosecutor had jumped to his feet, face scornful, finger pointing.

"Are we to understand that in spite of being beaten half-unconscious you managed to steal a man's gun from him, kill two men with it, and wound two others?"

And Luke Cord, some of the leashed anger in him showing through his tightly controlled guard, had said bitingly, "I ain't beggin' you to believe nothin'! I'm tellin' what happened."

Mr. Bragg's voice, as he told me the story, held almost a grudging respect.

"Wouldn't budge from his story, no matter how they tried to get under his skin with all the taunts and the innuendos about his being part Indian, out to prove somethin' with a white woman. He all but told them to their faces they'd have to take his story or leave it, though I think he knew by then that the crowd in the courtroom was out for blood. They'd been hoping he'd show up scared and begging for his life, and they didn't like his attitude. Only thing saved him from a hangrope, I think, was that your pa was so well thought of in the territory, and although he didn't flaunt his powerful connections and his wealth like Todd Shannon, he did have a reputation for bein' both fair and honest. God knows both commodities are only too rare in New Mexico!"

"So?"

"Your pa was a friend of the territorial governor, and the judge didn't exactly want to go up against him, 'specially when he gave evidence that Luke Cord could have gotten away if he'd wanted to, that he'd given himself up willingly, to prove his innocence. But you see, Lady Rowena, there were those other killings, too, and Todd Shannon sitting there glowering. The jury came back with a guilty verdict. They were all local men, farmers and ranchers and merchants, none of them daring to go against Todd Shannon, even if they'd wanted to. Luke Cord is half Apache, brought up by them, and not a man but didn't hate the Injuns.

"Your pa hoped for an acquittal, and Todd Shannon wanted a hanging. The judge compromised. He sentenced Luke Cord to imprisonment for life, and I guess that to a young man used to the freedom of the mountains, that must have been worse than hanging. Men have been known to go berserk, hearin' a sentence like that passed on them. I remember that everyone in that courtroom was watchin' his face, hoping he'd crack. But he went as still as stone, not a muscle moving to show what he was really feeling inside."

"So he did go to jail? But I thought…"

"You've heard he's loose now?" Mr. Bragg nodded sagely. "Yes, that's right, he is. They sent him to Alcatraz federal prison, in California, an island hellhole. But then, a year or so after, the War Between the States broke out. And that's how Luke Cord got out of jail. He was a free man, pardoned on condition he'd act as scout for the Union armies in the Southwest. The irony of it all was that Todd Shannon had joined Terry's Rangers, and was fightin' for the South, while your father managed the SD."

I had felt myself caught up in all the violence and action of the past, a past that I had to understand if I was to cope with the present. Todd Shannon had intrigued me, and now I found myself wondering about Lucas Cord. A wild young man, a murderer, and perhaps a rapist as well. But my father had believed in him, and I found myself wondering why. Because he was Elena's son, or because my father had actually felt that Lucas was the victim of injustice?

It was easy to ask myself questions, but I would find no answers until I took possession of my new home. What would I find when I arrived there? Not too much of a welcome, I was sure, for Todd Shannon, who was now forced into partnership with me, resented my intrusion even before he had met me. Mark Shannon, his nephew, the son of the same Mrs. Shannon who had been so kind to me during my sojourn in Boston, was an unknown quantity. But what of Flo Jeffords, formerly Flo Shannon, who had left her rich old husband to return to New Mexico? What kind of woman had she turned out to be, and how would she react to my presence?

I was intrigued. Challenged, if you will. All these people that I had heard so much about, their lives inextricably bound together. Would my coming act as a catalyst? Was that what my father had hoped for?

Five

AS OCCUPIED BY MY THOUGHTS AND PLANS AS I WAS, THE journey to New Mexico still seemed to take an almost interminable time. I was fortunate enough to travel by rail as far as Colorado, but from there the journey became rough, for I had to travel by stagecoach. At that point, I was glad that I had chosen to travel in what Corinne had despairingly called my "disguise," for the shabby clothes I had chosen to wear were far better suited for this kind of travel than my expensive garments would have been. The trunks containing my finery were to follow me later. For the moment I had only one trunk and a portmanteau, a fact for which I was thankful when I realized how many stops we would have to make, and how many times I would have to change coaches.

We arrived in Santa Rita just before noon, and by this time my black traveling dress felt uncomfortably damp. High-necked and long-sleeved, it seemed hardly suited to this hot climate, although I reminded myself that I had dressed just so in India, where it had been even hotter and more humid.

The fact remained that I had been traveling since early morning, and I suppose I looked just as wilted as I felt. The tinted spectacles I wore protected my eyes from the blinding glare, but made me look almost as I had done on that day I had arrived in England. The only change was within myself.

A fat drummer, who had been sitting opposite me all the way from Santa Fe, and had eyed me curiously from time to time, thought to help me out of the coach. As I waited with the others for my trunk to be unloaded, I had the opportunity to look around.

Santa Rita was a small, rowdy mining town, much like others I had passed through. The streets were dusty and unpaved, the buildings either wooden, false-fronted structures or made from adobe, Spanish-style. I saw nothing to recommend either it or the usual crowd of hangers-on who waited for the arrival of the stage.

I noticed as many Mexicans as there were white men, a few soldiers in their blue uniforms, and even some Indians, with blankets around their shoulders.

It was only when I heard one of my fellow passengers mutter to another, "Hey, will you lookit that welcoming committee? Darned if that ain't Todd Shannon hisself," that I realized that Mrs. Shannon must have done as she had threatened and telegraphed her son.

I had the advantage, though, of being able to study them before they discovered who I was.

I thought I recognized Mark Shannon, a blond, handsome young man who had his mother's nose and coloring. Beside him, in the buckboard, sat an extremely pretty blonde woman, holding a parasol over her head. Flo Jeffords? She had a voluptuously curved figure which her gown showed off to advantage, but her mouth had a petulant droop to it. Obviously, she was not happy at being forced to sit here, waiting in the blazing sunlight. I saw her turn to a man who sat on horseback beside the buggy and say something, her face looking sulkier than ever.

But once my eyes had found him, it was this man who held my attention. He was the kind of man who would have held anyone's attention. What had Corinne called him? "A big, blond giant of a man."

Yes, but I had imagined he would be different, after all the years that had passed. He had been my father's partner, yet he looked so untouched by time that he still appeared a comparatively young man! His reddish blond hair was only slightly touched by gray at the temples. He had harsh, craggy features and a wide, thin-lipped mouth under an arrogant beak of a nose. I could understand, unwillingly, why Corinne had once told me her uncle was the kind of man women would turn around in the street to look at a second time. He had a certain assurance of manner, an arrogance that I resented, even while I could not help admiring it. So this was the man who was my partner!

Todd Shannon's gun belt hung low on his hip, and he wore plain range clothes. I saw his narrow lips curve under his drooping blond moustache as he turned his head to speak to his nephew. Predictably, he had a voice that carried, too.

"Thought you said she'd be here for sure, Mark! What in hell are we waiting for? Gettin' mighty tired of meeting these damn stagecoaches, too!"

Mark Shannon, poor young man, looked embarrassed. "Now, Uncle Todd! All Mama said was that Lady Rowena had left Boston and expected to arrive here around today. We don't know if she decided to stop off somewhere else."

"She could have let us know, couldn't she?"

"Pa, couldn't we get out of the sun now? We've watched everyone get out…"

I decided that Flo Jeffords was a female who was used to getting her way.

It was at that moment that the driver, a grizzled, obliging man who swore quite ferociously as the coach slewed around curves, handed me down my trunk.

"Here you are, miss. But you're gonna need some help with that. Want me to find someone who'll carry it to the hotel for you?"

I had already observed that most of these rough-looking Western men were almost excruciatingly polite to women, which was more than I could say for Mr. Todd Shannon!

The driver's kind offer drew Shannon's attention to me, but I saw his eyes rest on me for only an instant, before sliding away with a kind of contemptuous disregard.

"Thank you," I said clearly to the man, "but I believe that I am supposed to be met, even though I did not have the forethought to send a telegram first."

My English accent must have given me away, for I saw three pairs of eyes fasten on me at that moment, registering various shades of shock.

Todd Shannon's mouth curled derisively under his moustache, Flo Jeffords put a hand up before her mouth as if to stifle a giggle or a gasp, and only Mark Shannon retained enough composure to leap from the buggy and come towards me, tipping his derby as he came.

"Excuse me, but we are here to meet Lady Rowena Dangerfield. By any chance…"

I put my hand out coolly. "How nice of you! You must be Mark Shannon? Your mother has spoken of you often."

I felt an almost vindictive satisfaction in seeing Todd Shannon's face change, his strange, greeny-blue eyes going frosty.

He didn't move his horse forward, but sat on it looking at me. "You're Guy's daughter?"

I gave a deliberately affected laugh. "Well! I should certainly hope so. I would hardly be here if I was not, would I?"

"Let me take your trunk and your portmanteau. I'm certainly sorry we didn't recognize you earlier…"

Mark Shannon tried hard to be tactful, but Todd Shannon whose lips had tightened, spoke abruptly.

"You don't look like Guy," he said frowningly, "and you don't dress like I'd have expected." His frosty eyes swept over me. "Thought Guy had arranged for you to have some money."

"Uncle Todd!"

As I heard Mark Shannon's dismayed exclamation, I realized that telltale, furious color had flared to my cheeks. "Mr. Shannon, if you have any doubts about my identity I shall be glad to resolve them when we get off this street! But in the meantime, I should like to make it plain that you are far more uncouth and—and rude than I had been given to expect!"

I heard Flo Jeffords gasp, her blue eyes widening, but Todd Shannon merely grunted. "Got a temper, huh? Well, you're right on one point, this ain't no place to discuss private matters. Mark, if you'll escort the lady to the hotel, I'll go ahead and make arrangements. Ma'am…"

He touched his hat brim with deliberate casualness and wheeled his horse around, while I fought to control the rage that shook me, rendering me incapable of speech for some seconds.

I was only half-aware of Mark Shannon's embarrassed attempts at an apology as he handed me into the buggy. I acknowledged his introduction to Flo Jeffords with a stiff inclination of my head, while she made no efforts to hide the fact that she was studying me curiously.

"You mustn't mind Pa! It's just his way. He always says what he's thinkin' and it makes people mad." She giggled nervously. "But goodness' sakes! We'd been imagining you to be so different! You know—"

Mark Shannon broke in smoothly. "What Flo is trying to say is that she's read too many romances! I've warned her that all Englishwomen do not go around wearing tiaras in their hair and carrying lorgnettes. But I do apologize for my uncle's unwarranted rudeness. I think there are times when he deliberately tries to shock people, just to see how they react."

I think that Todd Shannon and I had already declared war. My long hours of travel in the intense heat had set my nerves on edge, and I was in no mood to back down when he continued to provoke me during the confrontation that followed.

I found, when we reached the hotel, that Mr. Shannon had hired a small private room, obviously a bedroom at one time, but now converted into a place where businessmen could confer in private.

He hadn't even troubled to stay in the lobby until we arrived. I ascended the stairs with Mark Shannon and his cousin with an air, I hoped, of cool composure, but when I entered the room to find my new partner seated at a table with a bottle of whiskey and a half-filled glass before him, and he did not even rise but merely nodded, I felt my composure crack.

I ignored him and turned to Mark, who was looking extremely uncomfortable. "Is he always so mannerless? Or does he think to drive me away by this deliberate show of boorishness?"

"I—I really don't—" Mark stammered awkwardly, only to be interrupted by a deliberate snort.

"Huh! Why don't you ask her if she makes a habit of travelin' looking like an old-fashioned schoolmarm, in clothes that couldn't have cost more'n a few dollars apiece when they were new? What's the matter, miss?" This time he eased his big body around in his chair so that he faced me, his eyes narrow. "We Western folk not good enough to be treated to a sight of your fine English gowns?"

I looked back at him steadily. This was definitely a man I should be careful of. Obviously Todd Shannon was far from being a fool!

"I don't see that it is any of your business what kind of garments I choose to travel in, Mr. Shannon! But let us, by all means, get a few things straight at the very beginning." I accepted the chair that Mark hastily dragged out for me, noticing that Flo Jeffords had made herself inconspicuous in a corner of the room, where she sat biting her lower lip, and gazing in an almost nervous fashion at her stepfather.

Todd Shannon continued to study me through narrow eyes, and there was something almost contemptuously insolent in his look that made me draw in a deep breath to keep my voice from shaking with rage.

"Well?" he drawled.

"Well—" I said, and deliberately leaned back in my chair, looking back at him in much the same fashion as he looked at me. He didn't like it, and I pressed home this slight advantage.

"I'm afraid, Mr. Shannon, that you might as well get used to the fact that I have a mind of my own, and that I intend to dress as I please, and act as I think fit. My grandfather, who brought me up, believed in educating a woman's mind and thus forming her character, Mr. Shannon. He taught me not to rely only on pretty clothes and primping before a mirror to gain my way. And as for spending all the money my father left me on pretty clothes and jewelry, why, I think that is a ridiculous idea! Why should I waste it? I'm sure I'll find better ways to spend my fortune—ways that will help other, less fortunate people. But in the meantime, I must warn you not to underestimate me, for I happen to be able to think for myself."

During my speech he had begun to stare at me in a

stunned, almost disbelieving way. Now he swore, banging a fist down on the table and making the bottle jump. "By God! A do-gooder! Damned if Guy's daughter don't turn out to be a missionary!" He gave a short, ugly laugh and looked at Mark. "Hear that? She'll be wantin' to convert those poor dogs of Injuns next. And this—" he banged his fist again for emphasis, "this is the partner I get myself saddled with! Well I'll tell you straight, miss, we'd damn well better come to an understanding on a few things! I run the SD, and I built it up into what it is today, and there ain't no female gonna interfere with the way I run things! Now, if you want to spend your own money on helpin' the folks I suggest you build a church or somethin'—the preacher in town might need some help— but don't you go gettin' no notions…"

"Don't shout at me, Todd Shannon!" I said icily. "And I'm well aware of my legal rights. All of them. They don't include letting myself be badgered and bullied by you. Why," I added sweetly and reasonably, "don't you go back to court and try contesting my father's will again? Not that I think you'll be more successful than you were the last time, but the people of this territory who knew my father might not take too kindly to the spectacle of seeing his heir deliberately harassed by his own partner. There are some advantages to being a female, as I've discovered."

"Got a tongue like vinegar too, ain't you?"

"You might find that I'm more than a match for you when it comes to an argument, even if my voice isn't quite as loud, Mr. Shannon," I retorted.

Mark, who had been listening silently all this time, leaned over the table, his voice urgent. "Now look, Uncle Todd! Lady Rowena's right, you know! And since you are partners, like it or not, why not try to come to some compromise? You two start feuding, and it'll mean the end of the SD. You'll find half the wolves in the territory trying to get a piece of the action, as well as certain other interested parties." he added with heavy significance.

"Well, but damn it," Todd Shannon grumbled. I had seen, however, that Mark's warning had made him thoughtful.

"Mr. Shannon, I don't like you any more than you like me. I'm willing to be practical, but if you insist on quarreling with me merely because my father left something which was entirely his to give to his only child, then I'm afraid I shall despise you as well for being a petty, greedy man. You shall have war, if you want it, and I think you'll discover that I'm not to be frightened off."

"So that's your game!" He had pushed his chair back and was regarding me from beneath lowering brows. Suddenly he gave a harsh laugh. "You're pretty smart, for all that you look like a missionary or a schoolmarm. You can fight me, but I can't afford to let it get around that Todd Shannon's battlin' his own partner, the daughter of my best friend. Yes, and Guy was that, for all that we had our disagreements. So—" he frowned at me, "I guess we're stuck with each other for a while, eh? I don't for a moment think you're gonna like it out here, but for the moment…"

"I was raised in India." I said flatly. "The climate there is worse, the conditions even more primitive, and those Indians just as savage as the ones you are supposed to have here. But at least our laws of hospitality there were obviously far more gracious than yours."

He had the grace to flush at last. "By God, but you have a sharp tongue! But I guess I asked for that. Might as well be honest with you, I didn't want no female partner. And as for you, miss, being Guy's daughter, an' him thinking the world of you all these years, I didn't cotton to the fact you didn't write or nothin'."

"I was taken away to India when I was a baby, Mr. Shannon, and when I returned to England I had no idea of my father's whereabouts, or that he even remembered my existence! I was greeted in Boston by the news that he had died before I could see him again, and then you did your best to show me I was unwelcome. However, a plain woman has one advantage over a pretty one. She becomes used to using her head and fighting her own battles."

I saw him squinting at me. "You're a feisty one, I'll say that much for you! An' the first woman I've heard say right out she's plain. Makes me wonder…" he leaned his head to one side studying me critically. "Got real purty eyes, now you've taken off them eyeglasses. Long eyelashes, too, an' a nice skin."

"Oh, please, Mr. Shannon! I beg that you will not disappoint me by resorting to blatant flattery, for I know very well how I look. No, I would rather have honesty, and it would make me happy if you would learn to appreciate the fact that I have a mind, rather than keep reminding me that I'm a female!"

"Ah, Jesus!" Todd Shannon gave me a disgusted look. "A man tries to be polite and gets told off for it! Well, miss, have it your own way. I'll try to forget you're a female, and believe me, if you're going to keep dressin' the way you are in this climate, it ain't gonna be too hard!"

"Well, I'm sorry you don't care for the way I'm dressed, Mr. Shannon, but you'll just have to put up with it, won't you?" I made my voice sound prim, to hide the satisfaction I felt at annoying him. At the time, I did not try to analyze my emotions, nor my reactions to this annoyingly arrogant, irritating man.

We finally parted, after a formal and uncomfortable meal in the hotel's rather small and shabby dining room, I to travel to my new home, escorted by Mark Shannon and some of the SD cowboys who had ridden into town with their boss, and Todd Shannon, relieved at being rid of me for a while, I'm sure, to return to his house.

He had halfheartedly attempted to persuade me to accept his hospitality, but I turned his offer down firmly. I needed room to think and to be alone for a while.

"I would rather be left on my own for a week or so," I stated bluntly. "All the traveling I've done has left me exhausted, and I intend to be lazy for a while. Besides, I'd like some time to read my father's journals in privacy, and to form my own impressions of life on a New Mexican ranch."

"You just take all the time you want, miss! Longer the better!"

I only shrugged at his deliberate rudeness. There would be time later to make him regret it. And a time when he would not be able to avoid me. Todd Shannon might be a clever man, a resourceful, arrogant, overbearing man. But he was only a man, after all.

It's amazing now, when I look back, to remember how sure I was of myself. In my way, I was just as arrogant as Todd Shannon!

PART II:

THE INHERITANCE

Six

❧

THE NEXT TWO WEEKS WERE THE QUIETEST, AND YET IN SOME way the most rewarding, period of my life until then. A peaceful interlude, like a bridge spanning the two halves of my life.

I did nothing very constructive. I read. I lazed. I ate when I pleased and went to bed when I felt like it, even if it was for an afternoon siesta. Very occasionally I rode, having chosen a high-stepping little mare of mixed Arabian stock for myself, but I never rode very far, for Marta, who had been my father's housekeeper, had already warned me of the dangers I might encounter. I did not want trouble. I needed only to relax and be myself.

This part of New Mexico reminded me of certain parts of India. It was not too hard to adjust myself all over again to hot days and cool nights, nor to the brilliant, blazing sunlight that assaulted my eyes when I stepped outdoors.

My father's house was built from the earth, just as the houses of the old Spaniards who had first settled this land had been. Sun-browned adobe, whitewashed on the outside to reflect the rays of the sun, with great, massive beams to hold the structure together, and protruding out from the walls. There were two bedrooms, one leading out onto an enclosed courtyard. There I spent most of my time. My father had developed an irrigation system by channeling water from the stream that flowed down a steep canyon a few miles away.

The water flowed through a crevice in one of the thick walls that enclosed my retreat, and formed a small, ornamental pool in the courtyard. It was shaded by two willow trees, vines sprawled over the walls on all sides, and in one corner there was a collection of miniature cacti.

If I tired of sunbathing in the patio there was always the flat roof, protected by a low wall about three feet high, and reached through a trapdoor in my bedroom.

Marta informed me, with an apologetic bob of her head, that she hoped I would not find the house too small. It was not even one-tenth the size of the *palacio* of the señor patron, but my father had wanted it so.

"It's charming, and just right," I assured her, and saw her anxious face break into a smile.

Marta was a brown-skinned *mestiza,* married to Jules, a black ex-cavalryman. Jules had been wounded during the war, and Marta had nursed him back to health. My father had hired them both when Jules found he could get no other work.

"Where would we go? My people are just across the border. I visit them every year. Jules could not take me any other place, for ours would be considered a mixed marriage. And we both wanted to stay on here."

It was clear that they had both been devoted to my father, and were prepared to become just as devoted to me when I assured them that I meant to make no changes except, perhaps, to hire a girl to help Marta in the kitchen, if she thought it necessary.

"Perhaps later on," Marta smiled. Her eyes touched me shyly. "When the señorita feels like entertaining? There are bound to be many callers."

I smiled back at her.

"We'll see," I said.

To tell the truth, I didn't want to think too far into the future. It was such a new and delicious feeling to live entirely in the present, to exist like one of the lizards that sometimes sunned themselves on the patio walls.

I almost didn't want to think, and it was for this reason that I had been slow in starting to read my father's journals.

Instead, I questioned Marta and Jules, gleaning some of their impressions of this land and the people I would have to deal with, and picked up the local Spanish dialect in the process. My precise Castilian Spanish would never do here, for hardly anybody would understand me! I don't think they resented my questions. Jules was a quiet soft-spoken man with prematurely graying hair, but Marta, plump and smiling, enjoyed gossiping and would often stand in my room, flicking a dustcloth, while she chattered enthusiastically.

I had Marta make me some brightly patterned skirts and peasant blouses such as she wore and it was these garments I preferred to wear during the day, when I took the sun in the privacy of my patio.

"Ah, but the señorita must be careful of the sun!" Marta reproved. "It can be dangerous to have too much—and oh, what a pity, if the señorita's lovely, milk-white skin should turn as brown as mine!"

"I wouldn't mind that at all!" I laughed, but I was careful to expose myself fully to the sun only very early in the morning and late in the evening. 'Mad dogs and Englishmen!' I told myself as I became tanned in spite of all my precautions. Marta clucked and made me special lotions she concocted out of buttermilk, but my tan remained as a faint golden glow that seemed to underlie my usually pale skin.

How pleasant it was not to be bothered by anyone, or by anything that had to be done, I thought. I could go on like this forever! No one would miss me, nor I them.

Todd Shannon would certainly be relieved, and as nice as Mark appeared to be, I had even told him, quite firmly, that I needed time to be on my own.

"I won't press you, of course," he said gently, his eyes searching mine. "But I hope it will not be too long before you care to receive visitors. You cannot believe how boring it can be here, with nothing to exercise one's mind!"

Poor young man. No doubt he missed Boston and its amusements. For no doubt that his uncle was a hard task-master. And maybe Flo Jeffords, who called him her cousin but was no blood relation at all, provided some stimulation for this very polite, proper-seeming young man. He seemed anxious to see me again, but how much of his anxiety was due to the fact that I was an heiress and part owner of the SD? No sooner had I thought this than I chided myself. Hadn't I already vowed that I would no longer make snap judgments about people? No, I'd give poor Mark Shannon a chance. After all, his mother had been more than kind to me.

So, even as I continued to hibernate, I was more than half expecting Mark to call. I would not see him, of course. I had already given Marta instructions that any visitor except Mr. Bragg, whom I was expecting, was to be turned away. But what kind of man would Mark Shannon show himself to be if he did not at least make some token attempt to see me?

I had almost lost track of time. How long had it been, a week? Two, perhaps? My tan went from pale gold to a deeper shade, almost apricot, and I had taken to wearing my hair in two braids, like a Mexican peasant woman. What did I care what I looked like? There was no one here to see me.

And then one day, completely unexpectedly, there was.

It was late afternoon, and I had been reading one of my father's journals, in which he described his early life and his first meeting with Todd Shannon. Somehow, I could not reconcile the virile, handsome young man he described with the boorish giant that I remembered, and I put the leather-bound book down with an annoyed exclamation. I would rather not spoil my evening by thinking of Shannon.

I had barely closed my eyes, lifting my face to the warmth of the sun, when I heard his voice. Loud, arrogant, angry— drowning out my poor Marta's protests.

"Won't see anyone, you say? Out of my way, woman, and stop your damned sniveling! She'll see me, I tell you!"

Before I could say a word, or do anything but leap angrily to my feet, he had burst into the patio, filling it with his presence. And he had had the audacity to stride through my bedroom to get here!

"So there you are!" he said menacingly, but after one icy glance I looked beyond him at Marta, who was wringing her hands.

"It's all right, Marta. You may go now. I will deal with this—this unwelcome intrusion."

"Intrusion, is it? Well let me tell you Lady Rowena Dangerfield, that I refuse to hide away from facts, or to pretend to be what I ain't, either!" He glared at me, and jerked his head contemptuously, taking me in from the soles of my bare feet to my braided waist-length hair. "Look at you! Sure, an' it's like a Mexican peasant woman you look in that getup! Didn't know what to believe when some of the boys said they'd seen you out ridin' with your hair flyin' and a tan a your face. An' then Mark had this letter from his ma in Boston, and they was all ravin' about what a bloody beauty you were, and your fine, fancy clothes made by some Frenchman, and your jewels."

"Will you stop shouting at me?" I'm ashamed to confess that I lost my temper at that moment, and was now as angry as he was. "How dare you burst into my house like this and begin to abuse me? How dare you question me? I'll remind you, Mr. Shannon, of something I told you before. You may own one-half of the SD and you may own your stepdaughter and your nephew too, but you don't own me! Don't ever presume to criticize the way I choose to dress, or anything I choose to do!"

I saw angry red color suffuse his face, and for a moment I even thought he might strike me, and I stood my ground with my chin up daring him to do so.

"You—now look, miss, I won't be spoken to that way by any little chit of a girl, partner or not, you hear?"

"How can I help hearing when you don't have sufficient self-control to lower your voice?"

I looked him contemptuously in the eye, and deliberately planted my hands on my hips, peasant-style. "I wonder if you realize how ridiculous you look? Standing there like a thundercloud and shouting. What on earth do you hope to achieve? Do you imagine that loud noises frighten me? You are such a silly, petty man, Mr. Shannon! Under any other circumstances, your cheap blustering would merely amuse me."

"So I amuse you, huh?" He said it between his teeth, his head lowered like that of an angry bull. "Well, let me tell you, you knife-tongued little bitch, this is a man's world you're livin' in out here, and like it or not, you're gonna need a man to help you out!"

"And you call yourself a man merely because you are bigger than I am and have a louder voice?"

Knife-tongued, was I? If I had my way, I'd flay this brute of a man alive!

"I don't need any reminders I'm a man, missy! But I got some real doubts whether you've ever learned to be a woman yet. By God, with that tongue of yours an' the way you talk down to a man, there's no doubt you'll end up a dried-up, bitter old maid!"

"Better that than being tied to some oafish man who'll imagine he can make a slave of me," I flashed back at him.

I had forgotten my dignity, forgotten my resolutions to remain composed. All I knew was that my fingers itched to slap Todd Shannon's face, and I might have done so if he hadn't forestalled me.

"So you'd be pretendin' you don't like men, eh?" he muttered at me, the Irish brogue slipping back into his voice as it did when he was angry. He took me in his arms as if he wished to punish me, and for the first time I raged helplessly against the sheer strength of the man. "We'll see, shall we?" I heard him sneer, and then his lips, those same thin, cruel lips I had hated, came down over mine.

His arms, holding me so closely pinioned against his body that I could hardly breathe, were as immovable as rock. And, damn him, he took his time about kissing me, too. I think he enjoyed my useless struggles, and my choked, furious gasps of outrage. This was his way of teaching me how helpless I really was, and I hated him for it; hated him more because his kisses, as expert as they were, had actually begun to stir up some dormant, unrecognizable feeling in me. I had endured Sir Edgar's kisses and felt nothing at all except a faint annoyance.

But Todd Shannon—oh, God, the man was diabolically clever! His kisses went from anger to passion and then to feigned tenderness. I think he knew how he made me feel and took a delight in it.

Sheer desperation made me clever and I pretended to relax in his arms, hearing him chuckle deep in his throat. I closed my eyes and pressed closer to him, and his arms loosened slightly.

"Damned if there wasn't a woman hidin' under all that ice, after all," he whispered, and a jolt of sheer, unadulterated rage swept me at his crowing conceit.

I freed an arm and raked at his face with my nails, exulting in the stunned, stupid look I surprised in his eyes for a moment.

"You big ape! Did you really imagine I enjoyed your kisses?"

"God damn you for a cheatin' bitch!"

He knocked my hand away, almost breaking my wrist with the force of his anger, and then as I brought both hands up he seized my wrists, forcing them behind me, so that he had me held closely against his chest.

"Like any little bitch, you need to be shown who's master," he snarled. "You've been provokin' me, and you've teased me deliberately, but by God, you're gonna pay off now!"

Every time I attempted to twist my head aside he would laugh and give my wrists a jerk I felt sure would shatter them, and forced a moan of pain through my stiff lips. In the end, as he had been sure I would, I yielded and let him kiss me for as long as he wanted to, until my lips felt swollen and bruised and opened of their own accord to accept his seeking tongue.

I saw scarlet sparks from the last strong rays of the rapidly setting sun reflected in his blue green eyes, when at last he lifted his head. But this time he did not laugh.

"Damned if you ain't the strangest woman I've ever met! An' Godalmighty stubborn as well. What am I gonna do with you?"

I had never felt more humiliated in my life as I did then, with tears of self-pity and rage prickling behind my eyelids. I could almost have endured a brutal rape better than I could the memory of his slow, deliberate kisses, his forcing of a response from me. For I had responded, and that was the worst humiliation of all.

"You might release me to begin with," I managed in a husky, low voice. "And after that, perhaps you'll leave, if you're sure the display of brute strength is over."

"Girl, why won't you learn to hold your tongue? We could get on together, you and I—"

I would not let him finish. "Because you feel you've got the best of me? Or because you imagine I might just be a convenient outlet for your moments of passion?"

"I ought to slap your face for that, by God!" he swore at me, and I gave a short, bitter laugh.

"Why not? You've done everything but rape me!"

"An' it seems to me like you're asking for more," he said slowly, his eyes traveling over me with an odd expression.

"Oh God, you're impossible! Why don't we put an end to this whole disgusting episode now?"

"It ain't over, Rowena, an' I think you know it. I came here mad, and I guess I made you mad. Maybe I shouldn't have done what I did. But, by God, it happened, and it's changed something between us. If you'll stop acting like a stubborn, spoiled brat, you'll admit it too!"

Of course I would admit nothing. How could I? I would never give him the satisfaction.

Todd Shannon finally left, angry again, when I retreated into sullen silence and refused to say anything. And as for myself, I spent a miserable night. There was a side to my character I had not known existed, and it frightened me. Was it possible that I had inherited some weakness of nature from my mother? It was frightening to be swept by a sensuality, a feeling of pure lust, that had nothing to do at all with my rational mind! No wonder Todd Shannon was so sure of himself. How pitiful my self-confidence, my avowals of hatred must have seemed to him! All he had to do was kiss me, and after a while I had begun to kiss him back. What was wrong with me?

Shannon's last, scathing words, repeated themselves over and over in my mind. "For God's sake, what are you runnin' from? When you stop hidin', you just send me word. Until then, gal, I'll leave you alone!"

How dared he? How dared he insinuate… I felt as if I had

barely fallen asleep when Marta brought me coffee the next morning, her round face concerned.

"El señor patron—ah, there is a man who is like a bull when he is enraged! His rages are something terrible, this I know. Only your padre, our good señor was not afraid! Alas, señorita—"

I wondered how much of our encounter she had witnessed. So she pitied me, did she? Even Marta, even Jules, who seemed to tiptoe around the house this morning. I was a "poor señorita." A helpless female, incapable of standing up to a man.

Well, if I could not conquer through force, I would try guile. Yes, Todd Shannon would realize I was no ordinary enemy, and that he had not scored a victory over me yet!

Todd Shannon had broken my peace, but he had also cracked my shell of lethargy. I began to take more notice of things that were going on around me. For instance, because of the enormous size of the SD ranch, there was a bunkhouse within two hundred yards of my house. Even closer was a small shack which Marta explained had been the foreman's cabin during the time when my father and Todd Shannon had hardly been on speaking terms. The main house itself, my house now, was shielded by a grove of trees, but I knew that Marta and Jules took it in turn to cook for the men. The horses were corralled a little further off, but it was Jules who always brought my mare around for me, saddled and ready to ride. I had had no formal contact yet with the men, who took their orders from Shannon; however, I planned to change that after a while. For the moment, I wanted to learn more about the ranch itself, and how it was run.

I began to wish that Mr. Bragg would arrive. I needed his advice now more than ever, and he continued to stay away! Why did he have to be so mysterious?

Well, with or without him, I'm going to teach Todd Shannon a lesson, I vowed to myself, and by a strange coincidence, I was helped in this objective by the belated arrival of my luggage from Boston. Mark Shannon drove over himself from the stage depot in a flatbed wagon, his manner diffident.

"I didn't know if you'd care for visitors or not, Lady Rowena. But I thought you might want the rest of your clothes. I don't mean to intrude."

His eyes were a clear, pale blue, and his blond hair gleamed in the sunlight. He was polite, a civilized, educated young man, who had treated me with respect, even if I had looked a fright the first time he had set eyes on me.

When he drove up, I was still wearing a peasant blouse and a full, brightly patterned skirt, but I wore sandals—*huaraches* Marta called them—on my feet, and my hair was loose over my shoulders, since I had just washed it.

I saw the way Mark's eyes rested on me, moved away in embarrassment when he caught me watching him, and then came back to me as if drawn by a magnet. Mark Shannon was no shy Western man. I knew, from Corinne's inveterate gossiping, that he had been quite the young man about town, one of Boston's eligible young bachelors and much sought after by the girls. I had become used to seeing men's eyes on me, just this way, but that had been in London, and Todd Shannon had told me scornfully I looked like a peasant woman only a few days ago.

I found myself deliberately smiling at Mark Shannon as I invited him to see my patio. "Jules will see to my trunks," I said casually. "It was very kind of you to come all this way. Please, I've grown lonely, recently."

He followed me with alacrity. Obviously Mark Shannon was used to women who flirted with him. We sat down together and Marta, smiling, brought out orange juice, *naranjada*. And we began to converse about Boston, and London, the theater and the opera, books we had both read. Mark, now that the first awkwardness was over, seemed more self-assured. Neither of us mentioned his uncle, nor his visit to me. We laughed and talked easily, and before Mark left we had almost become conspirators together.

He would come early tomorrow to take me riding.

"You can't possibly see all of the SD, of course, but I can show you enough so you can get a general idea. There's a map somewhere. I'll see if I can find it for you." His blue eyes flattered me. "I have a feeling you're going to make out just fine, and I'm glad. In fact—" he laughed, the corners of his eyes crinkling attractively, "I think you're going to be a great success. Wait until the governor sees you!"

"Oh?" I lifted my brows questioningly and he gave another rather boyish laugh.

"I was leading up to that! The territorial governor will be visiting Silver City soon. It's a lot bigger town than Santa Rita, and they're giving a big ball for him. I'd been hoping I'd get the opportunity to ask you, and now I've found it! Will you allow me to escort you there?"

"You're asking me now that my clothes have finally arrived?" I teased him, and he flushed.

"You know that's not so! I meant to ask you before, but I was waiting until you were ready, I guess." He gave me a rueful look. "I saw through your disguise, you know! Even in those drab clothes, you were beautiful. The bone structure of your face... I'm something of an amateur artist, you see! That same night, I sketched you without those disfiguring spectacles I was sure you had worn deliberately. And with your hair loose, as it is now. Will you forgive me?"

"How can I not forgive you?" It was my turn to shrug a trifle guiltily. "I had no idea my attempt at making myself inconspicuous would arouse such a hornets' nest! Your uncle..."

"Uncle Todd is a very unpredictable man. I'm afraid his shocking rudeness showed me up at a disadvantage. I had no idea what he was going to do, and when I saw how he was acting, I didn't know what I could say to you!"

I lifted my shoulders lightly. "It doesn't matter now. I think we have begun to understand each other."

"Then you will go with me to Silver City? I'll come for you the day before, of course, and reserve a room at the hotel."

"I'd love to go," I said smiling.

Seven

꙳

THE BALL AT SILVER CITY WAS STILL A MONTH OFF, BUT IN THE meantime, I rode almost daily with Mark Shannon, and watched him fall in love with me. I was vindictively glad that his uncle made no overt move to see me again, although I guessed that he knew of all the time his nephew spent with me.

Let Todd Shannon wonder. Let him think the worst of me, if that was what he chose! I made no effort to take over part of the management of the SD, although I learned a lot from Mark. The riding habits I wore now were my newer ones, and I made some effort to pin up my hair so that it looked becoming, although I always wore a hat, a flat-brimmed, flat-crowned Spanish-styled one that Mark had given to me. Once or twice Flo Jeffords accompanied us, but I don't think she was happy at the transformation in my looks and manners. As soon as she found she wasn't the center of attention, she made excuses to stay at home.

I could sense that she did not like me, and that she resented Mark's growing interest in me. She reminded me, in some indefinable way, of my mother, and so I couldn't like her either, although there were moments when I almost felt sorry for her.

Poor Flo! The scandal attached to her past, when she had been still a girl, seemed to keep her isolated. Why had she come back here? I began to realize that in spite of Mark's eagerness to tell me as much as he knew, he never mentioned the feud or the Kordes family. And nobody else had mentioned it either. Had Mr. Bragg been exaggerating? I had met some of the SD cowboys, and recognized some of them by sight now. They would touch their hats politely when they saw me and explain whatever tasks they were engaged in if Mark pressed them. But everything seemed so peaceful! And I hadn't yet seen any of the fierce Indians I had been warned about.

Sometimes I felt that I had gone back into the past and was back in Jhanpur again. The climate here was very much the same, and even the fierce mountains that loomed like a gigantic backdrop in the distance looked familiar. Inconceivable that peril could lurk there! I began to think that all the stories I had heard before I'd come here had been figments of someone's overactive imagination. Wildly improbable tales, designed to put me off coming here, no doubt!

I thought darkly that Todd Shannon himself had probably started the rumors of violence and Indian attacks. There was no longer any feud, of course. How could there be? Hadn't I seen for myself just how powerful a man Shannon was, and how carefully the SD was guarded? He had enough men to form a small army. It was ridiculous to think that a man like Todd Shannon would fear anyone, and unthinkable that any man, no matter how reckless and vengeful, would dare to stand up against the might of the SD.

I had read Todd Shannon's character. Now, as the days passed, and I was constantly in his nephew's company, I began to have the feeling that Todd Shannon was only biding his time, waiting for something to happen. He was a dangerous, devious man, and he hadn't finished with me, nor I with him. What would transpire at our next meeting? In some strange way, I found myself waiting. This time, at least, he wouldn't catch me off guard. I would be ready.

It was Mark, though, who indirectly precipitated matters. He had been helping me sort out some legal papers that my father kept in a battered tin box. Railroad share certificates, shares in mines both in New Mexico and California. IOUs from men I had never heard of. All were jumbled together, filling the box almost to bursting. I had no idea how many of these documents were valuable and how many were completely worthless.

Mark was helpful, and I discovered that he had an extremely sharp legal mind. He should have stayed in Boston to practice law. Indeed, whenever he talked of it, and some of the cases he had handled, his voice became quite wistful.

We had become friends by now. Impulsively, I put my hand on his arm.

"Mark, that's what you really want to do, isn't it? Why are you here, then, wasting your time?"

There was an unusual, bitter twist to his lips when he met my eyes. "Because my uncle decided to make me his heir. You don't understand, Rowena. My mother has money of her own, and my father was an able lawyer. He was appointed a judge before he died. I always wanted to choose the law as my profession. But you see, there is the family obligation. And the money, of course; I'm no Sir Galahad!"

"But you said…"

"My mother is comfortably off, better off than most, I suppose. And I was making quite a good income following my chosen profession. All the same, how can any of it compare to what my uncle's share of the SD alone is worth? Don't you see, Rowena? He has no heirs! Someone has to take over some day. Your father chose you, and my uncle chose me."

I wanted to burst out at him, tell him to follow his own inclinations, as long as they made him happy, but logic held me silent.

As he had pointed out, in a way we were both in the same predicament. Both here because it profited us to be.

"Will you have to live here always?" I asked Mark, and he gave a slight shrug, shaking his head.

"Not yet, thank God! No, I'm here to learn the ropes, and then I can go back to Boston. Maybe come back here for a few weeks of each year. You have the same alternative, of course. As long as you reside here for a whole year, your father's share of the ranch becomes yours with no further strings attached." His voice became wry. "I suppose you'll spend your time traveling in Europe and appoint a manager to see to your interests here."

We had both been sitting on the rug before the fireplace with the box of papers between us, and now I sat back on my heels.

"And why should you think that? I've already done my share of traveling in Europe. It's all too civilized there. This way of life is a challenge, don't you see? My father and your uncle were the groundbreakers, so to speak, but you and I, we'll be the ones to build something lasting. We'll watch a new century come in, if we're lucky enough!"

"You make me look at things so differently, do you know that! You should have been an orator, Rowena! And when you said 'you and I' just now, I—"

Suddenly, his eyes shining, he leaned forward to catch my hands, taking me off-balance, so that I half fell against him. "Oh, Rowena, I'm sorry. I never meant—but I cannot help the way I've come to feel about you! Why, for God's sake, do you have to be so darned rich?"

"Why? What has that got to do with it?"

I pulled away from him frowning. I had not wanted this to happen. Certainly not a declaration which I would have to turn down and, in so doing, ruin what might have been a good friendship between us. I had tried to avoid a situation that might lead to such a declaration. But what had Mark meant by saying I was too rich?

"Rowena!" He reached for my hands again and succeeded in capturing one. "I only meant—well, as much as I care for you, I wouldn't want anyone to think that I would propose marriage to you merely to gain control of your fortune. Surely you see that?"

He continued to hold my hand, pressing it imploringly while his eyes searched my face for some reaction. "Rowena…"

"I could never think that you, of all people, would ever propose marriage to me with the motive of controlling my money. What a ridiculous idea!" I said forcibly. "But as for marriage," I added quickly to forestall the words I saw forming themselves on his lips, "nothing could be further from my mind! I'm still in mourning for my father, even if I have ceased to dress the part, and I certainly think I should wait a few years before I commit myself to any such arrangement."

"Arrangement!" He was staring at me with dismay showing in his eyes. "But Rowena, surely you did not think I was suggesting a convenient arrangement in order to join the SD under one management? It might be the sort of thing that my uncle would think of as a practical suggestion, but I'm not made that way. It is exactly for that reason that I can't ask you to marry me!"

"Well, then…"

"You don't understand. Rowena, I'm afraid I've fallen in love with you. You surely must have suspected it! I've never met a woman quite like you! Beautiful, intelligent, oh, God, what a mess I'm making of this!"

"Don't, Mark! Please, don't say any more, or you'll spoil everything. Our friendship—"

Despair showed in his kind, handsome face as he shook his head at me. "Friendship! You'll always have that and anything else you ask of me. But I'd hoped, and yet, how could I be so presumptuous? You've lived among the aristocracy of England. I'm sure you've received innumerable proposals of marriage from men far richer and more eligible than I. Please forgive me."

"Mark! Will you please stop talking that way? It's not that at all. Only that I—I'm not ready for marriage yet. Or love, for that matter." I pulled my hand from his grasp and looked at him severely. "You're infatuated with me. You know as well as I do that I'm probably the only eligible female in these parts, and so, when we were thrown into each other's company…"

"How logical you make it all sound," he said bitterly. "And yet, in spite of all your logic, I think you're only avoiding the issue. I'm no green boy, you know, and I've had my share of affairs of the heart. Do you think I don't realize the real thing when I've found it? I've already told you that you were different from any woman I've ever met before. What did you think I meant?"

I think he noticed the growing dismay on my face, for his voice softened. "Don't look so upset! I wouldn't worry you for the world, nor do anything to spoil our relationship. I love you, Rowena. But I promise not to pester you with my declarations of love again unless you indicate to me that they may be welcome. And in the meantime, please remember that if you ever need anything, you have only to tell me."

"Thank you," I managed. But what on earth could I say more than that? I almost wished that I could have cared more for Mark. And yet, the very next day, I was angry with him.

He rode over in the morning, looking rather sheepish, to inform me that I had been invited to dinner at the big house—the *palacio,* as Marta had described it.

"Oh, so he's decided to acknowledge my existence, has he? Naturally I refuse!"

"Rowena, please. You and Uncle Todd can't just go on avoiding each other. I assure you that he's promised to be on his best behavior tonight. I wish you would agree to come, even if it's only to show my uncle that he hasn't frightened you with his exhibition of rudeness!"

I looked at Mark narrowly, but his face was bland, faintly smiling. Perhaps he, too, was cleverer than I thought! Certainly it seemed as if he were deliberately teasing me into accepting this sudden dinner invitation.

"Your uncle's probably up to something," I said bluntly.

"No doubt he is! But you might as well find out now as later, don't you think? I know Uncle Todd. Once his bluff is called he'll settle down, you'll see. I wish you'd come, Rowena. If you'll forgive my saying so, it's high time you learned more about your responsibilities as half owner of the SD."

His voice had become stern, almost brotherly. So he had got over his passion for me so quickly, had he? Still, Mark did have a point. I couldn't go on this way forever.

I sighed resignedly. "Very well, Mark. I'll come. But only if you promise to escort me there, and to bring me home whenever I want to leave."

I was suddenly intrigued. So Todd Shannon thought to summon me to the royal presence, did he? After a suitable period of ignoring me, of course. We'd see who came out the victor in this encounter!

It took me several hours, and Marta's help, to prepare myself. And then, as I looked at myself in the mirror and heard Marta's admiring gasp, I couldn't help smiling wickedly back at my reflection.

Thanks to the estimable Mr. Worth in Paris and Cartier in New York, I certainly looked the part of an English duchess this evening.

The gown I had chosen to wear was a deep, midnight blue velvet, cut low in front, with tiny strips of crisscross material to hold it up on my shoulders. Generous folds of the rich material were swathed tightly around my hips, ending in a fashionable bustle behind. I wore silver gloves that came just above my elbows, and silver kid shoes with tiny diamanté buttons.

And my jewels, of course, were diamonds. I had never forgotten what Sir Edgar had told me that night.

Marta, her hands clasped together, eyes wide, muttered in excitable Spanish that I looked like a *princesa* with the diamond stars in my elaborately coiffured hair. But I must be sure to wear a cloak, to protect my gown and cover my hair. She crossed herself as she murmured something about bandits.

"Nonsense! This is the American side of the border. And Señor Mark will be coming for me, no doubt with an escort of cowboys."

But I suddenly realized that I was seldom allowed to ride far from the house without an armed escort. Even Mark carried a handgun, and when I had teased him about it, he'd shrugged and told me that his uncle insisted upon it. And yet, I had never seen any of the Apache Indians they all seemed so afraid of, nor any strangers who might be outlaws.

"It will be dark when you return," Marta said ominously, as she brought me my long, sable-trimmed evening cloak. Standing back to inspect me after I had obligingly put it on, she suddenly broke into smiles again and shrugged philosophically. "The señorita is very beautiful. No doubt the señor will think so too. And they would not harm our patron's daughter. He was a man who was much loved, your father."

"They?" I turned from the mirror to look at her questioningly. "Surely, Marta, you don't really believe that any member of the Kordes family would dare show their faces on SD land?"

Her lips tightened. "They say that this land should be theirs. Your father knew this and he would have helped them regain it if he could. When the señor Lucas used to live here, they would talk of it for many hours. And once, not long before your father died, he came back here with his brother Ramon. It was at night of course, very late."

"Marta!" My eyes widened in shocked amazement. "But you've never talked about this before. You've never even mentioned…"

"The señorita did not ask me. I told myself, perhaps the señorita already knows of all this, or perhaps she will not want to know unpleasant things that have happened in the past."

My brows drew together as I stared at her.

"But I did want to find out all I could. I asked you questions—"

"Only about your padre, señorita! Why should I speak of other things? Jules told me I was not to become a gossipy old woman. 'The books that the patron used to write in will tell her everything,' he told me. 'She will understand matters without your interference, woman.'"

Her lips trembled slightly, as if she was sorry for having spoken at all and I spoke more gently.

"Oh Marta, I'm not angry with you! Of course I'm not But all this time… why did you speak out today?"

She looked around the room almost furtively, although we were alone, and lowered her voice.

"It was because… oh, señorita, you promise you will not tell anyone? And especially not the patron Shannon, for this kind of rumor always puts him in a terrible rage. But I've heard—that is, when Jules went to Santa Rita for supplies yesterday he swears that he saw the señor Lucas. He was different, he said, he looked much older and wore a beard, but Jules knew him, and he saw that Jules had recognized him."

"Do you think, because he was recognized, that he'll try to do you or Jules some harm?" I asked sharply, but she shook her head.

"Oh no, no, señorita! He would not harm us. It is the fact

that he is here. We asked ourselves, why does he take such risks? The señor Shannon, he has put a price on Lucas Cord's head. Dead or alive. It made your father very angry indeed, and he would have done something about it, I think, if he had not been so ill, so weak."

"Well, why do you think that this Luke Cord has suddenly decided to risk his neck?" I gave her a long, level look. "Marta, you've gone too far to stop now. I must know, don't you see? What do you think is the reason for his sudden reappearance?" My voice hardened. "Did you think he might attempt to rob me tonight? Is that why you warned me?"

"No. Please, señorita! It is not that. He would not hurt you because you are the daughter of Guy Dangerfield. But if they think that the señor Shannon has won you to his viewpoint, that you and he—"

Her words trailed off miserably, and she avoided my eyes, so I went to her, touching her shrinking shoulder.

"You saw what happened that afternoon?"

She nodded, wordless, unhappy.

"But then you saw too that I sent him away! I hate that man! But he is my partner, and we must come to some kind of understanding, don't you see that? And as for other people, I owe them no explanations! I intend to draw my own conclusions, and make my own decisions, Marta, and Mr. Shannon is not the only person who must understand this!"

I was angry, and puzzled too. Had Marta been trying to warn me of something? But what? I could get nothing more out of her, for she grew visibly upset when I pressed her. In the end, I decided that I would speak with her later, when she was calmer and I had more time. I would tell Todd Shannon nothing, of course, but I would find out why Luke Cord had so suddenly decided to show his face in the area again.

I was to get my wish sooner than I had expected. But in the meantime, Mark arrived, and I had time only to reassure Marta in a whisper that I would not mention our conversation to a soul.

Mark had also dressed for the occasion. He was elegantly attired in well-tailored evening clothes, a pearl stickpin in his gray silk cravat. He looked rather embarrassed when Jules showed him in.

"I guess I forgot to tell you it's to be a dress-up affair! My uncle didn't mention it until after I'd got back! If you'd like to change…"

"Oh, I don't think that will be necessary," I said sweetly. "I hate changing once I'm dressed, and I'm sure the gown I'm wearing will do, even if it isn't exactly new."

I was more certain than ever that Todd Shannon was planning to spring some kind of surprise on me. An unpleasant one, no doubt! And maybe Mark was in on it, and maybe he wasn't. I made sure that I stayed muffled in my cloak, even when he helped me into the light traveling carriage that his uncle had thoughtfully provided.

"Do you always dress for dinner?"

"Almost always, I'm afraid! But don't worry. I'm sure he's only trying to impress you with the style he lives in."

"How strange! Todd Shannon hardly strikes me as the kind of man who would pay much attention to elegant living!"

I thought I saw Mark hide a smile at my barbed tones, but then he apologized for having to leave me alone inside the carriage while he took the reins.

"Uncle Todd had this made to his order in London," he said proudly. "And the horses are matched high-steppers. I'm afraid he doesn't trust too many people to drive them, so the responsibility is mine tonight."

"How flattered you must be!"

Sitting bolt upright in the carriage so that I would not crush my gown too badly, I could not help but admire the way Mark drove. Through the windows I could see our inevitable escort of mounted SD men, some of them carrying rifles. Was this a normal precaution, or did Shannon actually anticipate trouble? I thought of Luke Cord again and frowned. Why had he visited my father again after so many years? What had he been doing in Santa Rita? Something was wrong, and I couldn't put a finger on it. Even Mark's manner had seemed rather stilted ever since our awkward conversation the other night.

But I resolved to put it all out of my mind. Tomorrow

I would go back to reading my father's journals again and, as Marta had reproachfully reminded me, they would make everything clear to me.

The drive took much longer than I had expected, and in spite of Mark's expert handling of the team I was beginning to feel stiff and uncomfortable from sitting erect. Still, under a half-moon that rode high in the deep blue night sky, the scenery looked changed. Even the huge clumps of cactus that we passed seemed like trees in an enchanted forest, and the dusty ground seemed to shimmer.

It really is beautiful, I found myself thinking. Infinite, undulating plains, coming up suddenly against the wall of the mountains that made up most of this territory. A country of contrasts. Cattle ranches and mining towns. Snow and desert. And to the south, the same mountain ranges I could see in the distance extended all the way into Mexico. I thought suddenly of the hidden valley where the Kordes family had a small ranch. How could a whole valley remain hidden? But then, I didn't know these mountains as the Apache Indians who had lived there for generations did.

I thought of something I had said to Mark. "They were the groundbreakers, but we will be the builders." What had made me say that? Did I really believe it?

The moonlit plains fell behind us, and suddenly I saw the lights that loomed up ahead. Outbuildings, a windmill tower, bunkhouses, even the unmistakable outlines of a smokehouse. Horses milled around in an enormous coral, and further back were the stables.

And then the carriage slowed down and we were passing through an archway, with a huge, weathered sign over it, and down a long driveway. I had no opportunity to notice much more because the outline of a huge, imposing house, every window lighted, stood boldly against the backdrop of the starlit sky. No wonder they called it the *palacio.* It was bigger than any house I had seen in this part of the world. I recognized the Spanish-style architecture so common in the Southwest, but this house could not have been built of adobe. At least two stories high, it looked more like a small castle.

The carriage pulled up, and two men came forward to hold the horses, while Mark jumped down off the seat to help me out.

"Well, Rowena, what do you think? It's built from stone quarried in the mountains and hauled down here in wagons. Wait until you see what it's like inside!"

"I can well imagine," I said dryly. "It looks like a small fortress!"

His voice dropped. "Perhaps it was originally meant to be one. You know the story. After Uncle Todd lost his wife and son he made himself a promise that the next house he built would be strong enough to hold off the whole Apache nation. And this one is. It won't burn down, either!"

I had no chance to say more, for he was leading me up a shallow flight of steps, and Todd Shannon's huge figure loomed up in the enormous hallway. Even here, I had an impression of opulence. An enormous chandelier hung overhead, and in the background I saw a carpeted staircase that branched off in two directions from a landing that looked like the musician's gallery of an English mansion.

What I had at first taken for a hallway was, in fact, a great reception room, with open, double doors leading off it on both sides.

"So you came, did you?"

"Did you hope I would not?"

Todd Shannon laughed, taking my hand.

"I knew you wouldn't be able to resist the chance to get in the last word," he said meaningfully, as if we had been alone. "Got unfinished business, ain't we?"

"I hardly think so," I said coldly, and he laughed again, his eyes narrowing suggestively as they took in every detail of my appearance.

"Mark! What in hell are you doin' just standin' there? Take her cloak. Rosa will put it away. Want the rest of my guests to meet my new partner."

"You didn't tell me you had invited other guests, Uncle Todd!" Mark said sharply, feeling me stiffen as his hands touched my shoulders. "Rowena, you must believe..."

"Hell, what are you fussing about? Wanted it to be a surprise party for Rowena here. Have all my friends meet her."

My cheeks burned with suppressed fury. So he'd hoped to show me up, had he? No doubt he'd hoped I'd turn up dressed like a Mexican peasant or a dowdy English spinster! And how dare he call me Rowena?

"What a kind thought, Uncle Todd!"

I caught his look and smiled even more sweetly up at him. "Oh, but you don't mind if I call you that, do you? After all, you were my papa's dearest friend!"

I thought I heard him mutter under his breath, "You little hellcat!" And then the cloak slipped off my shoulders, and he caught his breath for an instant, before he threw back his head and laughed.

"By God! So you were smart enough to outguess me! And since I'm an honest loser, I'll say this much. You're a lovely, lovely thing! Damned if I don't get even madder at you when I think of the way you were dressed when you got off that coach!"

"Uncle Todd, for heaven's sake!" Mark whispered urgently.

I stood there, still smiling, and he smiled too, but our eyes met and clashed. We understood each other.

He took my hand, suddenly formal. "Well, come on in. Got lots of people who want to meet you."

Deliberately I offered Mark my other arm. "But Mark was kind enough to escort me. Mustn't he come too?"

Todd Shannon's dangerous glance told me that I was trying him too far, but he led me forward without another word.

We walked through enormous doors into a high-ceilinged room decorated with barbaric splendor. An enormous fireplace took up almost half of one wall, two highly polished, silver-engraved Henry rifles were crossed over the fireplace, and the walls were hung with paintings depicting various Western scenes and brightly patterned Indian blankets.

I knew that Shannon watched my reactions. I lifted my eyes to his and whispered, "A robber-baron's castle!" and felt his fingers tighten over my elbow.

"You'll find out," he muttered, and then we were surrounded, it seemed, by people.

I was introduced to the territorial governor, Mr. Wallace,

a bearded man with a habit of blinking rather shortsight-edly, to "neighboring" ranchers who had traveled over two hundred miles to get here. A cavalry colonel from Fort Selden, immaculately dressed, bent gallantly over my hand. I was introduced to a federal judge, a congressman from California, several rich mine owners with their opulently dressed wives. The men were more casually dressed than the women, who had attempted to outshine each other. Flo Jeffords, her shining blonde hair falling in long curls to her shoulders, was wearing a crimson silk dress that caught the light when she moved. Rubies sparkled on her ears and at her throat. I saw her eyes flick over me and widen slightly.

"Well, my goodness, Lady Rowena, I wouldn't have recognized you!"

To my surprise, it was Todd Shannon who cut her off, his voice holding a casual kind of contempt that immediately made me feel sorry for her. "Flo, you go with Mark and see that everything's ready for dinner. An' have that lazy rascal Ben bring some wine up from the cellar. Rowena, you ever tasted our American whiskey? Or are you scared to drink anything stronger than wine?"

"Is it more potent than Russian vodka?"

Did he hope to get me drunk? I would disappoint him there, for Sir Edgar's friends had all been hard drinkers, and I had learned to handle what liquor I did consume.

"You get nervous without Mark to protect you?" Todd Shannon seemed to sense my thoughts.

I caught his wicked look and shrugged. "Why should I be nervous when you're with me, Uncle Todd?"

"Call me that just once more and you'll be sorry, gal!" he threatened grimly, and I widened my eyes at him.

"Oh, but why not? After all, you and my father..."

"You all excuse us for a few minutes, huh?" he said in a loud voice. "Promised to show Rowena the rest of the house. It's her first time here, you know!"

Willy-nilly, his fingers gripping me painfully, I found myself following him. He seemed to enjoy my discomfort. "This is the parlor, never use it much. The small dining room through here, but we don't use that too much either. These doors lead right out onto the patio. Ain't seen my patio yet, have you?"

"What do you think you're achieving by this show of force?" I whispered furiously. "You had better take me back before your friends."

"Shucks, my friends ain't gonna think a thing is wrong! Always show a pretty gal around the house."

"If you think to exercise *le droit de seigneur* with me, Todd Shannon…"

"Whatever that means, all I'm doin' is what I've wanted to do ever since I saw you walk in that door. An' you've been asking for it, too! Uncle, hell!"

He took me in his arms, ruthlessly holding me still in spite of my furious protests. "When are you gonna face up to facts, little gal? I want you. Have done even before I saw how you look all dolled up. You turned Mark down, didn't you? An' you've been needlin' me all evening. Better learn to pay up when your bluffs been called."

He bent his head to mine and I saw his thin, cruel lips curve in a smile of triumph. "We're two of a kind, and you know it," he said, before his lips claimed mine.

Eight

❧

"YOU ARE A ROBBER BARON. A CONSCIENCELESS PIRATE. AND you're old enough to be my father."

My voice sounded breathless. I felt as if he had choked the breath from my body.

I couldn't remember how long he had kissed me, out here in the moonlight, with the trickling sound of the small fountain in the background. When he finally raised his head, I think I might have fallen if his arms had not held me. I hated him.

"Damnation, woman, why don't you stop fightin' me? It was meant to be this way. Think your pa knew it too. You're going to marry me, you know that?"

"So that you'll have all the SD, and my money as well?"

I was fighting for my sanity, and I knew it.

"You know better than that, damn you! You kissed me back. Think I didn't know it? Why'd you think I lay low an' let you play around with Mark? He's not man enough for you, an' I knew you'd find that out for yourself. You're the kind of female that needs a strong hand on the reins. An' don't tire yourself strugglin,' because I ain't gonna let you go until I've had my say! You're the woman I've been waiting for. Why'd you think I haven't married again? A woman with guts, damn you, and yes, with a sharp tongue, too. A real woman, not a damn doormat who'd cry every time I yelled at her. I got a temper, an' you know that. But so have you. But you dressed up for me tonight, an' don't you think I don't know it!"

"Stop it, stop it! You're insane! I hate you, Todd Shannon!" I said the words out loud, but he only laughed.

"That's a good start! Closer to love than indifference! Gonna take you back now, an' you're going to act the cold, unapproachable lady, because that's the way you are. Cold on the surface, fire underneath. Mine. You hear that? Like it or not, you wear the SD brand now."

He took me back to his guests after that, and I found myself forced into the position of hostess, as he kept me at his side. I can't remember the thoughts that swirled through my head during those hours that seemed to drag by. I was determined not to show him how he had affected me.

We might have been in a London drawing room. There was the same exchange of surface politeness, the same inanities, the same pointless bursts of laughter.

We went in to dinner, and I discovered that Mark and Flo had been placed at the other end of the massive table. I sat on Todd Shannon's right, the governor's wife on his left. I responded mechanically to the questions and comments that I was besieged with. Mark avoided my eyes. How much had he told Todd? How much had Todd told him? Flo Jeffords was unusually silent, although I imagined that from time to time she shot resentful glances in my direction.

But what on earth was I going to do? When the evening was over I would have to face Todd Shannon again. I could no longer rely on Mark for support. Suddenly I wondered wildly if the whole thing had been carefully planned between them—Mark's proposal, the sudden invitation to dinner. I felt trapped.

"Dancin' after dinner," Todd announced unexpectedly. I caught his significant glance and looked away. He leaned closer to speak to me, his blue green eyes gleaming with deviltry.

"Same musicians gonna play at the big shindig at Silver City. Had it all arranged before I knew you'd be here."

"Oh, really? And if I hadn't agreed to come I suppose you would have had me kidnapped?"

"I was thinkin' about it," he said solemnly, and I turned away from him, fighting an impulse to slap his face.

Governor Wallace was telling me about the book he was writing, and I tried to pay attention, but I was overwhelmingly aware of Todd Shannon's presence at my side. I thought that dinner would never be over, and was hoping for some respite when the women retired, but unfortunately they did not have such civilized customs here.

"Time for dancing," Todd said, and dragged me off with him to begin it.

"Didn't think you'd be able to manage a fandango, so I told them to play a waltz first," he said, locking me in his arms.

"You're going too far!" I said between gritted teeth. "If you think you can force me into something…"

"Ain't gonna force you into nothin'. You're going to be willing, stubborn as you act! Give you two months, less, if you keep on rilin' me."

"I won't marry you, damn you!"

He laughed when he saw he had made me lose my temper. "We'll see! It's that, or be made a dishonest woman of. Won't look right." He sighed with mock regret. "No, much as I'd be tempted, I guess it had better be marriage."

"I will not! I'd rather…"

"You gonna run away back East? Give up?"

"No! You won't scare me away either, Todd Shannon!"

"What makes you think I'd let you go?"

It was impossible to reason with him. Even my sarcasm seemed to slip off his hide. I had never met a man so sure of himself, so sure of me.

In the end, I only escaped from his arms on the pretext that I had to freshen up.

"Flo will go with you to show you the way," he said, lifting one eyebrow in an infuriatingly amused fashion.

We went upstairs. My nerves felt like taut wires. I was too much on edge myself to be tactful.

"But don't you miss New York? Boston?"

Flo stared at me with open dislike. "You mean Derek? Well, why should I? He's old. Like Pa, only Pa doesn't show it as much, and Pa goes after what he wants."

We faced each other across the room, and she reminded

me suddenly of those gossipy old women in India, who had also sneered at me. Only this time, I had the advantage. The mirror told me that.

I touched my hair, pushing the diamond stars into place, and smiled at Flo. "You're afraid that he might want me?"

"I know he does. And you do too! Well, I don't care. There's been other women Pa thought he wanted, but the last one he married was my mother!"

"And what makes you imagine that I would want to marry him?"

"If Pa wanted to marry you, he would! But it won't come to that. You're young, see? And you own half the SD. You're a titled English girl. That's all Pa can see for now. Would you enjoy being my stepmother?"

I couldn't help laughing. "Heavens, no! If I was to be so foolish, I'm sure you'd do your best to make my life as miserable as I could make yours. Except that I'm a trifle cleverer and more subtle than you are!"

She gasped, her hands clenching into fists, and I said soothingly, "Why don't you grow up? Although I think you hate me at this moment, if you start thinking a little more clearly you should realize that you have more to gain by pretending, at least, to be my friend!"

"Oh! I thought at first that you were stupid. But you're horrible! You're hard—"

"Oh, goodness! Must you dramatize things so? I'm merely being realistic. Whether you realize it or not, I'm trying to help you." I looked her in the eye. "Your stepfather wants to marry me. Oh, yes, he's already suggested it. But I have no intention of doing so. I like my independence. If we cannot be friends, don't you think we might at least be allies, since we have a common cause?"

She stared at me, wide-eyed.

"I believe you're really serious! You mean you don't want to marry Pa?"

"Of course not," I said crossly. "Why should I? I don't want to be married to anyone, to tell you the truth."

"But you don't know my stepfather! If he wants something—"

"You've said that before," I reminded her. "He may think he wants me, but he's going to find out I'm not a plaything he can pick up at will. My father stood up to him, and I will too, if I have to."

Flo looked at me suspiciously. "Are you going to tell him what I said? Not that I care if you do, but…"

"*You're* the one who's afraid of him, not I!" I said reasonably. "Why can't we both be sensible about this? I'll admit your stepfather is a very dominating man, but I don't intend to go as far as marrying him. You don't want to see him with another wife either, do you? Perhaps there'll come a time when we need each other's help."

"Maybe." I could see she was half convinced, struggling between her dislike of me and her instinctive sense of self-preservation.

"Well?"

I shrugged at my reflection in the mirror. "Shall we go downstairs then?"

Downstairs, to my annoyance, Todd claimed me again for a dance.

"Shouldn't I dance with someone else?" I objected reasonably. "Your guests are going to think…"

"Let them think! They might as well get used to the idea." His eyes, more green than blue in the light of the chandeliers, seemed predatory as they looked into mine. I felt him trying to hypnotize me with all the force of his will. "An' who did *you* want to dance with?" he growled.

"Mark," I said quickly, seizing on the first name that came into my mind. "I think I should dance with Mark. He brought me here, did he not? And I don't like the way you try to bully me. I won't be dominated, you know. You're not going to manipulate me, as you do other people." I made my voice deliberately cold. "You build too many presumptions on a few stolen kisses, Todd Shannon!"

"You're a stubborn spitfire!"

"I won't be crowded and—and stifled!" I retorted. We glared at each other in silence for a few beats of the music, and then he shrugged his massive shoulders.

"I'll give you your head for a while longer, if that's what you need. Go dance with Mark, then. Want me to send him to you? Mark may imagine he's in love with you, but he ain't about to go up against *me!*"

The contemptuous way he could dismiss Mark, the way he spoke as if he was already sure of me, flicked me on the raw. I had come here with some idea of dazzling him, of putting him at a disadvantage, but he had contrived, in some fashion, to turn the tables on me, as he had done before. And in spite of all my protests, he persisted in treating me as if I was a pet kitten showing my claws, but already half tamed in spite of it.

"When your eyes get all narrow like that I can guess you're thinking up new ways to fight me!"

"How very discerning you are sometimes!" I snapped, and pulled away from him as the music stopped.

"When are you going to lay down an' start purring for me, little hellcat?" he asked softly as he led me back to where some of the ladies were sitting fanning themselves.

"For you? Never!" I whispered back emphatically.

He only raised a mocking eyebrow at me, and after bowing in an exaggeratedly polite fashion, he walked away whistling. He looked far too pleased with himself.

Mark asked me to dance after a while, but we were stiff with each other. I could not help wondering if his uncle had sent him to me, and I could not quite forgive him for letting Todd Shannon take over, without even a protest.

"Are you enjoying yourself, Rowena?"

I could not resist being sarcastic.

"Oh, but of course I am! How could I not? I dearly love surprises of this nature. To be asked to a quiet private dinner party and find myself presented to all the notables in the territory. It reminds me of my coming-out ball in London!"

Mark had the grace to flush, the dull red creeping up under his tan.

"I swear I knew nothing about it! He had me running fool's errands all day, until I had barely time to change. And *then* he announced that dinner was to be a formal affair. But believe me, I didn't know."

"You mean that your uncle didn't confide to you that he planned to have me brought here merely to put me on exhibition? I've no doubt he hoped that I would arrive looking a fright, so that I would be made to seem like a frumpish idiot among all his fine friends! *That* would have suited his purposes, I'm sure! Perhaps he wished I'd be embarrassed enough to turn tail and flee back East!"

"I'll admit that he has a rather crude sense of humor, but I don't think he wishes you to leave, Rowena. He's taken a liking to you."

"He has a strange way of showing it, then!" My eyes looked coldly into Mark's. "Or perhaps it's only this sense of humor you are so anxious to defend that persuaded him to propose marriage to me. Would you like having me for your aunt, Mark Shannon?"

I saw his lips tighten as a strange, shuttered look dropped over his face, making it appear harder and older. "I think you know that's the last thing on earth I would like," he said quietly. "But my Uncle Todd is a very forceful man, as you must already have discovered. People usually end up doing exactly as he wants them to do. I was hoping that you would turn out to be different, Rowena. But the choice, of course, is yours to make."

Why would I have to make a choice? I liked Mark. I had come to look on him as a brother I never had. And he had accepted my rejection of his half proposal like the gentleman he was. His uncle, on the other hand, was a different breed of man. A robber baron—determined, grasping. Used to reaching out and taking what he wanted. But he would not find me as easy as that!

Perhaps because it filled me with anger to find out that everyone, even Mark, believed I would give in to Todd Shannon in the end, on this occasion, I was driven by an almost desperate need to prove my independence. I said suddenly, "Mark, I would like to go home now. Will you take me?"

He looked startled, and, I thought, rather apprehensive.

"But, Rowena, it's past two in the morning! I thought my uncle had already mentioned it to you. All his guests are to spend the night. Believe me, it's the custom in this part of the world. I'm sure Marta and Jules will take it for granted that you…"

"If you're afraid, Mark, then I'll find someone else to take me," I said. "Your uncle thinks he can do anything he wants with people. But he shan't find me a pawn to be moved around and manipulated as he pleases!"

For the first time, I saw anger in Mark's eyes as he looked down at me. Anger, and a kind of baffled frustration.

"But you think *I'm* easily manipulated, don't you? I think you're using me to get back at Uncle Todd, Rowena, and I can't say that the idea pleases me."

His sudden perspicacity made me flush with annoyance and embarrassment. Was I running away from Todd Shannon? Would *he* think so?

I said, "I'm sorry, Mark. You're right, of course. But I don't like being bullied."

He gave a short, unhappy laugh. "I'm sure you won't allow yourself to be. You're a strong, self-contained person, almost as strong-willed as my uncle, I think. And I cannot honestly criticize you for thinking me weak in comparison to him." His fingers tightened over mine for an instant and he said in a low voice, "Until now, you see, I have never felt strongly enough about anything to take issue with him."

"You mean that you would stand up against him for me?" My eyes widened. I was seeing a new side to Mark this evening, and it made me feel ashamed to think I had been baiting him deliberately, venting my chagrin at his uncle on him.

"I would do anything for you," Mark said now, his blue eyes suddenly so piercingly bright that they reminded me of Todd's. "If I knew there was a chance I might win you in the end. Your respect, at least, if not your love."

The music ended, to my relief, before I could find words to answer him with. What could I have told him? I liked Mark, but I did not love him. I had found that in spite of my dislike for Todd Shannon, there was an odd physical attraction between us that I did not quite know how to cope with. It made me almost afraid.

If he had not swept me again into his arms soon after my dance with Mark ended, asking what we had been talking about with such solemn faces, I might have acted more sensibly. But Todd Shannon made me feel smothered, especially when he dared display signs of incipient jealousy.

"I asked Mark when he would be taking me home, and he informed me it was the custom in this part of the world that dinner guests should stay overnight. Did you order him not to tell me that before?"

It put me at a disadvantage, having to tilt my head far back in order to look into his face, and he made it even more difficult for me by holding me far too closely in his arms.

"You mistake me for a greenhorn if that's what you think, missy! I just took if for granted someone would tell you, I guess. You'd do the same if you were invited to have dinner with the Bradys, or the Kilkennys. It's just accepted around here that dinner guests spend the night." An unholy light danced in his eyes as he grinned mockingly down at me. "What did you think I had cooked up for you, eh? A nice little private seduction? When you get to know me better, you'll find I don't believe in sneakin' around. I'm gonna have you yet, girl, but when I do you're going to want it as much as I do."

"You're the most conceited, arrogant man I've yet had the misfortune to encounter! If you think that I…"

"At least I don't play games, little girl. Ain't the type to go pussyfootin' around, wastin' time on long courtships. When I find what I want, I go out and get it."

I controlled my rising temper with difficulty. "How flattering to me. But if I should ever decide to marry, I'll make my own choice, thank you!"

"You're like a little kitten, showing your claws! Well, that's all right. Wouldn't want you if you was a doormat. Just don't take too long, hear? I ain't a patient man."

He laughed down into my flushed, angry face and began to whirl me around until I was breathless, holding me tightly against him. He was determined to show me his strength and how puny and insignificant my efforts would be if I continued to fight him.

But I would show him! Yes, I would show him exactly how much he'd mistaken his woman!

Nine

‍‍‍‍‍‍✍

"HOW ARE YOU AND PA GETTING ON?" FLO JEFFORDS ASKED maliciously. "He sure seems mighty pleased with himself!"

Clad only in a thin, ribbon-trimmed chemise, she stretched her arms above her head like a lazy cat, but I saw how closely her eyes watched me in the mirror.

Sitting on the edge of her bed, I continued to brush my hair, shrugging casually. "I can't help that. He takes entirely too much for granted, of course, but that's his mistake."

"You gave in about staying the night, didn't you?"

"It would have made me appear ridiculous to have made a scene. And I could hardly find my way back home by myself."

"I know the way Pa goes about things. He's going to want you to stay on. First we'll all sleep in late, and then there'll be a big breakfast. He'll take you riding, and maybe ask if you want to see the books. He'll find reasons to keep you busy until it's dinnertime again."

"Oh?" I raised an eyebrow. "It sounds as if he does this often!"

"Are you jealous! Of course he's done it before. Pa's a man, and there have been women who have caught his eye. Don't think you're the only one. But I guess your being half owner of the SD makes it different."

"It makes no difference to me what his motives are," I stated calmly. "In any case, I intend to leave very early, before the rest of your stepfather's guests are up, if possible. Since you're no more anxious than I to have me stay, why don't you sheathe your claws long enough to wake me at about six or seven, shall we say? *He'll* sleep late too, I hope!"

She swung around to face me, her eyes suddenly gleaming.

"You mean that? You'd actually go against Pa that way? Oh, but he'll be fit to be tied! My goodness, *I'd* hate to face him after you did a thing like that!"

"I'm sure you'll contrive some way to fasten all the blame on me. Tell him I insisted, and you could do nothing to deter me. After all, I'm not his prisoner!"

Flo giggled spitefully. "It might just be worth getting him mad at me, just to see his face! You really mean it? *He* won't sleep late of course. He's always up at six like the rest of the men, no matter how late he stays up. But he'll ride out with them, and he won't be back before nine or ten. If you're really determined, I'll lend you a riding habit." She laughed again. "Maybe I'll even ride part of the way with you. I don't think I'd like to face either Pa or Mark, until they've both had a chance to cool down some."

"That's very kind of you. And you're welcome to ride all the way with me, if you'd like to. I daresay Marta can fix us an adequate breakfast." I stifled a yawn. "And now that that's settled, don't you think we ought to get some sleep while we can?"

"You're a cool one, I must say that much for you," Flo admitted grudgingly as she climbed into the wide bed beside me. She stretched again and yawned. "Heavens, I'm so *tired*. But I'll be sure and wake in time. I've done with much less sleep before, when I've had to."

I was tired too, and in spite of the fact that I was not used to sharing a bed with someone else I must have slept soundly, waking only when Flo shook me by the shoulder.

"It's past six! Pa rode out a little less than an hour ago, all fired up because one of the boys rode in to say someone cut one of the fences. That means we have a little more time. You still want to leave?"

I sat bolt upright, shaking the hair out of my eyes. "I certainly do!" Flo was dressed already, in a maroon riding habit with a divided skirt. She was almost friendly this morning.

"There's warm water in the pitcher, and I laid out my green habit for you to wear. You *do* ride astride, don't you?"

"I've done it before," I said grimly, remembering the shocked comments this had excited among the good British ladies of Jhanpur.

"Well, then, while you're dressing I'll go downstairs and have two horses saddled up. Better hurry, because when Pa finds out he's likely to come after us!"

I hurried, used to dressing fast if I had to. I had folded my velvet ball gown carefully before I went to bed, but I would have to leave it. Perhaps Mark would bring it back to me. I slipped the jewelry I'd worn into the pocket of Flo's riding habit, a garment which fit me adequately enough. Having no time to do much with my hair I merely combed it free of tangles and braided it, coiling the single, thick braid to form a loose knot at the back of my neck.

I had hardly done so when Flo sped back upstairs, closing the door behind her with exaggerated care. "Do come on, but you have to be very quiet. Mark's room is at the end of the hall, and I don't want him to hear us."

I was reminded of some schoolgirlish escapade—the kind of mischief I had never had an opportunity to indulge in.

For the first time I had an uneasy feeling—a kind of apprehension that I was behaving in a silly, spiteful fashion. But it was too late for regrets now, and if Todd Shannon thought I was running away from him, let him think it! For now, I should think only of escape.

A gangly young man who eyed us both curiously was holding the horses when Flo and I emerged from the house. She gave him a dazzling smile, which immediately made him blush and shuffle his feet.

"Ben, you are the nicest, kindest man! Remind me to tell you so again when we get back, hear?"

He stuttered, "Er—Miz Jeffords—you all ain't goin' to ride too far, are you? Mr. Shannon wouldn't like it if he thought— I mean—"

He was helping Flo to mount her mare, while I mounted my horse unaided, and I saw her pat his shoulder gently, an action which seemed to render him speechless.

"Now, Ben! You know I've lived here long enough to

be careful. And this lady is Mr. Dangerfield's daughter. She hasn't had a chance to see *our* part of the range yet. Isn't that right, Rowena?"

I felt sorry for poor, adoring Ben, but I had my own fish to fry, so I smiled at him just as guilefully as Flo had done and said we only meant to have a nice, healthful ride early in the morning, before the sun became too hot.

She began to laugh after we had cantered out of sight.

"Poor Ben! Did you see the calf eyes he made at me? He'd do anything I asked him to!"

I suddenly thought of Luke Cord, the young man who, they said, had almost raped Flo. Had he too been as enamored of her as Ben obviously was? And did she know that he had been seen in these parts? I was suddenly very curious about Flo Jeffords. She was a woman that most men would find attractive, and she was sure of her charms and power over men. What had she been like when she was only fifteen, and the belle of the countryside?

Flo was a good rider, and after a sidewise glance to make sure I was capable of keeping up with her, she urged her little mare to the gallop. I followed, easily enough. The horse that had been provided for me was of Arab extraction, though a trifle smaller and sturdier. It was a gelding, about four years old, and inclined to be a trifle frisky until he realized I would stand for no nonsense.

After a while I caught up with Flo, and we rode side by side, following a trail of faint depressions left by wagons and buckboards.

"No use winding our horses—it's quite a way yet," Flo said and I nodded, leaving the conversation, if we had any, up to her.

She didn't remain silent for too long. Pretty soon I saw her look towards me, her eyes shining. "Well? What do you think of the SD? Of the *palacìo* my father has built? Are you sure you wouldn't like to live there, after all? *Your* little house is hardly what you're used to, I expect!" She gave a mocking little laugh. "It's really odd that you've stayed so long. We expected you to go back to Boston within a week, at the most. Pa can't abide plain women around him, you know, and the way you looked when you first arrived here! Then, when my aunt's letter arrived, he was furious because he thought you were up to some kind of trickery. He wasn't even sure that you *were* Uncle Guy's daughter!"

"I expect he's convinced of that fact by now," I responded levelly. "Do you make a habit of being deliberately rude to other women? Or it is only because you don't like *me*?"

She was taken aback for a moment, and then her eyes began to sparkle maliciously. "Oh, my! So you can be rude, too, when it suits you. But in this case, you ought to thank me for being so direct. He's a difficult man to live with. He can be very hard. And sooner or later, he would get to you." She looked at me from under her lashes, as if gauging my reactions. "I don't think he's capable of really loving another woman, you know. Not since his first wife, Alma, died. But I expect you heard all about it when you were in Boston. Corinne Davidson is such a nasty little gossip!"

I didn't let her see that her slighting reference to Corinne had angered me. Instead I said coolly, "But he married your mother, did he not? And adopted you? He must have cared for her."

Flo's pretty face hardened.

"He only married her to get a housekeeper, and a hostess for all his guests. And to have sons, of course. My mother had been ill, but *he* didn't care! He only came to her bed when he was drunk. He spends most of his time in Alma's room!"

"But she's dead!" I burst out, startled in spite of myself.

"Not to him! She'll never be dead, as far as he's concerned. I guess they didn't live together long enough for him to tire of her. He had a room especially furnished with all the furniture they planned to buy together, when he made his money. And he had her portrait painted from an old photograph. I used to imagine, when I was younger, that I could hear him talking to her. I could almost imagine she answered him! Don't you see? The real reason my mother died was because she couldn't bear to live with the ghost of a dead woman any longer! She loved him, but he made her unhappy with his indifference and his moods. I think, at the end, when she lost the baby, she was afraid to live, and to face him with the knowledge that she had failed him. And that is what you would have to live with too, if you were fool enough to marry him!"

There was a note of haunted desperation in Flo's voice that moved me. She was a spoiled, vain creature, but she could not have been happy.

"He's kind to you, isn't he?" I said quietly.

"He adopted me as his daughter, which only makes me one of his possessions. Of course he gives me everything I want. Everything that his money can buy, that is!"

"Why did you come back here then, if you're unhappy here?"

"Because I couldn't stand to live with Derek any longer, that's why! *You* wouldn't understand. I married him to escape from that horrible school Pa put me into. It was worse than prison! And Aunt Katherine, and Mark, and that mealy-mouthed Corinne—all patronizing me, talking in whispers behind my back, looking at me as if I was a kind of leper! Derek had money, he said he loved me, he'd give me anything I wanted. But it wasn't enough! He's an old, flabby man with foul breath. Ugh! I thought I'd be sick every time I had to lie next to him in bed, every time he put his clammy hands on me! But *you* wouldn't know how that is, would you? I don't think there's any passion or feeling in you. You're always so calm, so controlled. 'A puritanical spinster' Pa called you after the first time we met. What would *you* know of anything but your safe, quiet little world?"

"It might benefit you to exercise some self-control occasionally," I said sharply, for her eyes had filled with tears of rage and frustration. "And to try to understand that other people, too, might have their share of unhappiness and bitter memories locked inside them, even though they may not wear their emotions on their sleeve!"

Flo bit her lip, tossing her head disdainfully. "Are you trying to tell me that *you* have had an unhappy love affair? Is that why you decided to leave the fleshpots of London?"

I could almost laugh at her sudden change of mood.

"I've never had a love affair, fortunately for me, I'm sure. Have you? Is that why you ran away from your husband?"

She shot me a narrow-eyed searching look.

"I *told* you why I left Derek!" she said sullenly. "I just couldn't stand to live with him another minute, that's all! So I just packed my bags and said I was coming to visit Pa, and once I arrived here, Pa couldn't very well send me away because it would have caused talk if he had. And for a while he even seemed glad to see me. Until *you* came," she added childishly. "*Now,* he's starting to ignore me. Maybe he thinks I'm in the way, that I'm going to interfere!"

"I think you're overdramatizing things," I told her simply. "I've no intentions of interfering in your affairs, nor in becoming your stepfather's third wife. He's never discussed you with me, and I'm sure he doesn't intend to."

"That's what you say!" she muttered sulkily, and then fell silent.

I was in no mood to indulge in further discussion with her, for I had enough to think of as it was, and I had already begun to yearn for the peace and tranquility of my own house. No one, and especially not Todd Shannon, was going to destroy that peace.

Flo rode with me for a considerable distance. She was quiet now, deep in thought.

When we had reached the top of a slight ridge, she pointed downward, telling me that I could not fail to find my way back now, and I thought I recognized certain landmarks from other rides I had taken with Mark.

"Are you sure you'd rather not come all the way with me?" I asked her politely. "Marta can give us breakfast, and I could ask Jules to ride with you as far as the ranch. Everybody keeps warning me it's not safe to ride out alone."

"For *you,* perhaps, but not for me! I know this country. I've ridden here since I was a child. And besides, I always carry a gun with me. See?"

She pulled up her skirt, revealing a small derringer strapped against her thigh. "So now you can see that I can take care of myself. I hope you can. Or are you afraid to go on alone?"

"Now that you've assured me how safe it is, why should I be?" I retorted, adding, "Thank you for bringing me this far."

"I only did it to get you away from Pa!" What a child she

was in some ways! Shrugging, I watched her whirl the mare around and touch her spurs to her side. She did not bother to look back.

Suddenly I found myself in no great hurry to be on my way. I was alone, this was *my* land. Why should I worry?

I sat on my horse, looking down the slope. There was no danger here. It suddenly seemed quite preposterous, and realizing this, I felt my spirits lift. It was time for me to cast off my feeling of lethargy and begin to learn more about my inheritance. I'd show Todd Shannon that I wasn't helpless.

A small puff of breeze fanned loose tendrils of hair against my face, bringing with it the faint smell of dust and aromatic brush, and just as I was about to guide my mount forward, something—some tiny movement at the corner of my eye—made me turn my head. Had I really been afraid for a moment? It was only a thin strip of red material fluttering from a cactus spine. Some unwary ranch hand had ridden too close to that enormous, Y-shaped cactus and had snagged his shirt, or perhaps his neckerchief. Whoever it was certainly had loud tastes! The red was so bright that the tiny piece of material showed up plainly against the dull green of the cactus.

Idly, as I rode past, I reached forward and tugged at it, frowning again. He had to be a tall man, whoever he was, for I'd had to reach upward. And the material was silk. A red silk shirt? I couldn't imagine a cowboy wearing either a silk neckerchief or a silk shirt. A woman, then? But who? And how had she managed to snag the material of her gown so high up?

In spite of the growing warmth of the day, I felt as if a chill wind had brushed me, and I was suddenly uneasy and anxious to be home. I pushed the little strip of cloth deep into the pocket of my borrowed riding skirt and tried to forget about it as I urged my horse forward.

If Jules and Marta were surprised to see me back so early, and alone, they hid it well enough, although Jules shook his head disapprovingly when I told him I hadn't bothered with an escort.

Remembering my manners, I sat down and wrote a short,

formal note to Todd Shannon, apologizing for leaving so abruptly. He would understand my real reasons of course, but I felt less guilty, now that the conventions had been observed. Jules would take the note himself, along with the horse I had borrowed. And Todd Shannon, with his guests to see to, could hardly come chasing after me, even if his pride allowed him to do so. He would be angry, but he would learn that I would do as I pleased.

I wouldn't let Shannon spoil the rest of my day! I picked out two of my father's journals and took them with me to the cool, book-lined room that had been his study, sitting in my favorite chair by the window that overlooked the patio. Marta, hovering nearby, asked me solicitously if I would care for something cool to drink.

"You've already overfed me with that wonderful breakfast," I said, smiling at her. Then, as a thought struck me, I pulled the tiny scrap of red silk from the pocket of my skirt.

"Marta, do you have any idea who this could belong to? I found it fluttering from that big saguaro cactus, where the trail forks. You know the place, don't you?"

I saw her face change, and grow quite pale. "Ah—*Madre de Dios!* After all these years! It was the signal they used…"

"Who? Marta, you're not talking sense! For goodness' sakes, you've done nothing but talk in riddles lately!" Her mouth was working, as she continued to stare at the piece of material I still held between my fingers. "He's back then. Ah, did I not say so? I knew it. She is here. It was the signal they used, so long ago, when they thought it was safe for them to meet. Did I not warn him of the danger? 'He'll end up killing you,' I said. 'Stick to your own kind.' But he wouldn't listen. 'We want each other,' he told me. 'One day, Marta, I'm going to take everything that Shannon calls his!' And then he would tease me into giving him a piece of my old red petticoat, the one the patron gave me when Jules and I were married."

I interrupted her sharply.

"Luke Cord! Is *that* who you mean? Look at me, Marta. I must know the truth. Do you mean that he left that piece of silk there as a signal to Flo Jeffords? That…"

Of course. Why need I ask? She had seen it, of course. That accounted for her sudden change of mood, her sudden decision to leave me. Silly, reckless Flo. But I blamed *him* even more. How dared he return and deliberately, defiantly, leave their old trysting signal on *my* land? Had she known all the time that he was back?

Marta was nodding, miserably.

"Si, señorita, there can be no other explanation. When she came back, I told Jules, 'No good can come of this.' She came here, asking if we had seen *him*. It was before you came. Jules and I, we both hoped…"

"No one is blaming *you*," I said, more gently. "But Marta, don't you see? I must know what is going on. If Mr. Shannon should ever find out, the whole ugly business could start up again. And what is more, I'd be involved in it too." My lips tightened. "Lucas Cord! I'd turn him over to the law myself, if I ever found him on my land!"

But Marta, it seemed, had a sneaking fondness for Luke. She looked at me with apprehension in her round face. "Señorita! Surely you would not? He is not all bad, that one. Wild, yes, but not evil. Your father used to say so. It was not all his fault. I remember when he would have nothing to do with her, that blonde one, and she would not leave him alone."

"It seems to be the other way around this time, doesn't it?" I said coldly.

I decided that I would have to speak to Flo. Whether she hated me all the more for it or not, I would say what I had to say. And as for Luke Cord, when Mr. Bragg finally decided to show up, *he* would know how to deal with the matter, I was sure.

Having shooed Marta back to the kitchen, I turned to my father's journals, frowning. How could he possibly have taken such a liking to such a wild and reckless person as this Luke Cord appeared to be? Apparently the years and his imprisonment hadn't changed him. It seemed to me that he deliberately courted trouble.

I was supposed to read the journals in order, but I flipped through the closely written pages, putting aside one volume

to take another from the desk until I found the entries I was
interested in.

> *Brought Lucas back to the house with me today. Elena's*
> *son, who might have been mine. It is difficult to commu-*
> *nicate with him, but I think he has begun to trust me. He*
> *knows that I loved his mother, and that alone forms a kind*
> *of bond between us. He adores her. The only times I have*
> *seen his face soften is when he speaks of her. He says she is*
> *still young-looking, still as beautiful as ever...*

So my father's quixotic action *had* been for this mysterious
Elena's sake, after all! I skimmed through various entries,
turning the pages quickly.

> *I have turned professor! We started by playing chess together,*
> *and now I am teaching Lucas the rudiments of reading*
> *and writing. I was horrified when I discovered he could do*
> *neither, but what, after all, should I have expected? He*
> *was brought up to be an Apache warrior. He tells me that*
> *he learned to draw and fire a gun accurately before he was*
> *ten years old. This knowledge, of course, came from his*
> *wanderings with the comancheros.*

A few pages further on, I read:

> *I had not realized how lonely I was before. It is good to have*
> *the companionship of someone young, and eager to learn;*
> *although I fear that Lucas's thirst for knowledge is in part*
> *motivated by his burning desire to be revenged, ultimately,*
> *upon my partner. He is all Apache in this respect, although*
> *he seems to want to adjust to living as a white man in a*
> *white man's world. Such stupid discrimination! If the color*
> *of one's skin was all that mattered, Lucas would not be*
> *taken for one-quarter Indian.*
>
> *I have tried to talk philosophy to Lucas, but he is not yet*
> *ready for abstractions.*
>
> *Lucas told me today that he fixed the shoe on Flo*

*Shannon's horse. She was almost thrown while riding. It
was on the tip of my tongue to warn him against seeing her
again, but I kept silent. He would have looked at me with
that cold, closed look that, thank God, he does not turn
on me as often any longer. He would have thought I had
spoken only because of his Indian blood...*

My eyes, skimming impatiently over yellowing entries,
stopped suddenly.

*I shall always blame myself for not having guessed what was
happening. Marta and Jules both knew, but they confessed
they were afraid to tell me. I was young once—why didn't
I think? Flo Shannon, for all of her youth, is an empty-
headed flirt. I have always thought so. Haven't I seen her
make calf eyes at my cowhands?*

*God help me—I could almost wish he had not come
back. But he has grown to trust me, and he had given his
word. He came to tell me the truth, he said. I could see from
the old, sullen look on his face that he knew what would
happen. "White man's justice!" he said bitterly to me, and
there was nothing I could say to refute it. Hate breeds hate.
I tried to tell Todd that, but his own hatred has made him
blind to everything else.*

*I have written to the commandant of Alcatraz prison.
Perhaps it will help. For the first time, I am glad of the
friends I have made through the years, and for the first time
I will try to use whatever influence I have. It was not justice,
but prejudice that sent Lucas Cord to jail for life...*

Abruptly, I closed the leather-covered book. I would read
no more for now. My father had believed in justice, he had
believed Luke Cord's story. But Luke Cord was no longer a
youth; he was a man. Bitter, hardened, and hating, no doubt,
as hard as Todd Shannon did. Had my father been prejudiced
in his favor merely because he was Elena's son? That small
piece of red silk had ruined my whole day, and thrown me
into the middle of an unpleasant, dangerous situation. My

instincts told me that he was using Flo as an instrument of his revenge, and she, poor fool, was too vain to see it.

I thought grimly that I would dearly like to meet this Luke Cord, face to face, and tell him what I thought of him.

Ten

I WENT TO BED EARLY THAT NIGHT, STILL FEELING CONFUSED and uneasy. Jules had returned from the *palacio* wearing a grim expression. He had handed my note personally to Todd Shannon, but the patron had barely glanced at it. From the subdued atmosphere and guarded faces of the SD hands, he had gathered that the patron was in an ugly mood. Had he said anything? Jules had shaken his grizzled head. Nothing at all. He had heard from one of the men that a fence had been cut and a few head of cattle were missing. No doubt that was what made everyone so preoccupied. Still, it sounded rather ominous, and I wondered if Luke Cord had had anything to do with the cut fence and the missing cattle. A ruse to keep Shannon and his men occupied while he kept a secret rendezvous with Flo?

I had half expected Mark to come, but even he stayed away, and in spite of my determination to have a talk with Flo I could hardly send Jules back to the big house again with a note for *her* this time. We were hardly friends, after all! In the end I realized that there was nothing I could do but to wait until the proper opportunity presented itself. And meanwhile, I was tired, both physically and mentally.

I ate at six, and by seven-thirty I was in bed, too tired and too lazy once I had pulled the covers up to climb out again and extinguish the small lamp I had left burning on my dressing table.

Never mind, I remember thinking drowsily, *there's not much oil left in it, and it will go out by itself...* and then I must have fallen asleep, too weary even to dream.

I could not remember, afterwards, what woke me, forcing my eyelids open. Some slight noise, perhaps? The brightness of light against my closed lids?

I remember thinking, still half-asleep, that the lamp had become brighter. But how could that be? It had been going out. How could it be that there was a strange man in my bedroom, leaning against the wall, watching me? It was he who had turned the lamp up.

He had seen my eyes open and widen, and he straightened unhurriedly, still watching me with a wary, brooding gaze. "No need to scream. I ain't here to do you no harm, but this was the only way I could get to see you alone. You awake enough to understand?"

He had a quiet, husky voice, with a note of urgency in it at the moment. Still blinking against the light, I thought irritably that he was not at all as I'd pictured him in my imagination.

I had not expected that he'd be tall, nor that his thick, dark hair would be shot through with bronze glints as it caught the light. I had thought his features would be flatter, darker, like the Mexican and Indian faces I had seen, but instead he had the straight nose of his Spanish ancestors, and a hard mouth that curved grimly, if rather mockingly, up at one corner when he became aware of my scrutiny.

"Well?" he said in the same husky voice, and I thought that secretly he was laughing at my stunned, stupefied expression.

I found my tongue at last. "Do I look like the screaming type?" I demanded tartly, sitting up in bed with the covers held closely against my shoulders.

"Not now," he said, the sun wrinkles creasing at the corners of surprisingly hazel eyes, as he noticed my instinctive movement.

"Well, since we have that out of the way, suppose you tell me what you're doing in my bedroom in the middle of the night, Lucas Cord?"

"You been studyin' my wanted posters? Either that, or you're a good guesser."

"I'm in no frame of mind to engage in pointless banter!" I exclaimed furiously. "I don't know how you got in here, but I'd thank you to say whatever you came to say and leave the same way!"

"Had the notion you might have somethin' you wanted to say to me."

The creases appeared again. A deep groove etched itself in one cheek when his lips curled in a mocking, one-sided smile that did not reach his eyes. I suddenly had a feeling that he did not smile often. There were green flecks in his eyes, like tiny fires, and I was being ridiculous, staring at him as if I had never seen a man before.

"How did you…"

In the same soft voice, he said, "I watched you take that little strip of red silk. Knew you'd probably ask Marta about it." He grimaced. "She has a long memory, that old woman! She told you, huh?"

He had been watching my face, and I suppose my expression gave me away. But his cool, impudent manner annoyed me, and I think he knew that, too. "I'm sorry," he said, suddenly, running his fingers through his long hair. For a moment, his guard slipped, and something almost boyishly apologetic showed in those strange eyes of his. "Your pa always used to tell me I ought to learn better manners. As it turned out, I didn't get the chance to. Shouldn't have busted in here this way, but I guessed you suspected somethin', and so I—"

"Suspected! Do you take me for a complete idiot?" The memory of his assignation with Flo made me angry enough to interrupt him, completely forgetting to choose my words carefully. "I've learned enough about you to know very well what you were up to! And if Flo Jeffords is fool enough to be taken in, let me assure you *I* am not! What could you be thinking of? Are you trying to punish her for something that happened long ago, or is it revenge on Todd Shannon, even if it's indirect, that you hope to get?"

His face had hardened, lips thinning. And when his eyes narrowed I could see why people had said he had a dangerous look. Right now he looked lethal. His words were cold, thrown like stones in my face, although his tone was just as quiet, "What's Flo to you? Thought she was exaggerating, just like she always did, when she told me Shannon was sweet on you, but maybe I was wrong. Maybe he *has* gotten to you after all. Was your concern for Flo for his sake, Miss Dangerfield?"

I said through gritted teeth, "I don't care how much you and Todd Shannon hate each other. Yes, and you can kill each other, for all I care! But don't use someone else as an instrument for your revenge! Flo's an unhappy, confused young woman, and she doesn't need you to complicate her life further!"

I thought I saw a flicker of surprise in his eyes. "Why do you bother about her? Why, she don't even like you!"

"That makes no difference!" I said heatedly. "Can't you see that? If you have a quarrel with Todd Shannon, why don't you find him and face him like a man? Get it over and then maybe everyone else around here can live in peace!"

"You think it could ever be as easy as that?" His voice sounded bitter. "Christ—how little you know! I'd have faced Todd Shannon before, if I could have gotten close enough to him, but that ain't his way of doin' things. He put a price on my head—bounty money—same as he did to my pa. Why should he dirty his bullets on an Indian? That's Shannon's way. Let someone else do his dirty work for him. He almost killed my mother and had my father killed from ambush, the same way he'd like to see me killed, if I don't get to him first!" Lucas Cord took a step towards the bed, and then, swearing under his breath, he stopped. I sat there silently, watching him pace like a caged animal to the far end of the room, and then back again to face me.

"Why don't you go away, then? You're young enough to make a new life for yourself, to make a new start. Why did you have to come back? In time Shannon would forget about you. He'd forget…"

"He ain't the type to forget anythin'!" Those hazel cat's eyes stared angrily into mine. "An' neither am I, come down to it. Shannon stole most of the lands he claims as SD property from my pa and by rights it should belong to my mother! But they said Alejandro Kordes was an outlaw, because he kept fightin' for somethin' he believed in. Said all the records, the grant deeds datin' all the way back to the Spanish king had been lost or destroyed in the war. Some people remembered that the Kordes family had called this land theirs for years and years before the goddamn Anglo came to steal it, an' Shannon got around that by sayin' he married a Kordes. That any claim to the land was hers, as passed through her to him. You askin' me to forget all that? Or the time I was railroaded to that hellhole island they called a jail? Or the times I bin shot at by Shannon's hired bounty killers?"

"You're as full of hate as *he* is!" I said accusingly. "You'd use any methods you can think of to get back at Todd Shannon, wouldn't you?"

"An' if I did, what's it to you?"

I tried to keep my voice even. "You're here to start a war. It *was* you who cut that fence, wasn't it? But why? Why now?"

"Maybe I wanted to get Shannon's mind off his new partner." The curiously husky quality of his voice was even more apparent when he lowered it.

I stared uncomprehendingly at him. "For heaven's sake! You didn't know anything about me. I can't see the point in any of your actions!"

"Seems to me, whether you realize it yet or not, that *you're* the key to settlin' things once an' for all. Your own pa saw it, only he didn't get the chance to talk to you, like he'd hoped."

"I?" My voice had risen, and I bit my lip. "I'm afraid you're talking in riddles. What have I got to do with any of this? I've been here less than a month and all I know about this feud that seems to be so important to all of you is that it began a very long time ago and should be over and forgotten by now. And what little I have been told came to me secondhand. How can you say that I can settle matters?"

He was rubbing the heel of his hand abstractedly over a beard-stubbled jaw while he studied me, and I had the impression that he was judging me in some way; trying to gauge my reactions to his next statement.

In that instant when we stared measuringly at each other,

I defiantly and he thoughtfully, I found myself comparing him to Todd Shannon. Lucas Cord wore faded jeans, with knee-high Indian moccasins. His shirt, which had once been blue was equally faded, and open at the throat. Instead of the string tie that Todd invariably wore, this man wore a carelessly knotted red bandanna. What gave him the right to sneak into my bedroom at night, like a thief? What had he meant when he said curtly that I was the key to ending the feud? Worst of all, it was ridiculous that I should be sitting here, with my bedcovers drawn up to my neck like a frightened virgin, actually conversing with the man!

I think he must have read something in my face that made him change his mind about what he had been going to say to me. "You ain't ready to listen yet, are you? Right now you're mad at me for bein' here."

He said it flatly, without expression, and I found myself wondering if *this* was what my father had meant when he referred to Luke's "sullen, closed look."

"You can hardly blame me for it, can you?" I said coldly, and saw him shrug.

"I guess not. But it was the only way I could think of to get to see you without Shannon's men findin' out." He gave me a twisted kind of smile. "Left my horse some distance off. Walked the rest of the way. I learned to walk an' run for whole days at a time when I lived with the Apaches. A man on foot, who knows where he's goin' and what he's doin' can hardly be spotted—especially not at night."

I looked at him haughtily, mostly to cover my self-consciousness at my state of dishabille. "You certainly have strange notions of the way to pay a call on a lady you don't even know!" I said scathingly, and again one corner of his mouth lifted in a mocking smile.

"Ain't hardly a gentleman, am I? Did you expect me to come callin' all formal like Mark Shannon does? Or send you an invitation to dinner like his uncle? My brother Ramon, now, he'd know how to go about it the right way. He's the educated one of the family. Me, I'm here partly because you cottoned onto that sign I left for Flo. Mostly because that Pinkerton man told me you was here, and I should talk to you."

"Mr. Bragg? What has Mr. Bragg got to do with your coming here?"

He shrugged again.

"Elmer Bragg is an old fox. But he ain't stupid-old yet. I was in Mexico when he tracked me down. You might say I was kinda anxious to leave, at the time." The cleft in his cheek deepened, and I had the impression he was laughing at himself. "Pinkerton man can be mighty persuasive when he holds all the aces. So here I am."

I eyed him narrowly. "You're talking riddles again. You came here to meet Flo."

"An' you're talkin' like the prosecutor at my trial. Already had me guilty an' hung before I got tried."

I found that I already disliked Lucas Cord immensely.

"But you left that signal for her. You saw her."

"Why not? We had things to talk about. Nothin' to do with you."

"You're insolent…"

"That mean I don't show the proper respect? I sure am sorry. From knowin' your pa, I expected a warm, generous woman. Thought you might take after him. He used to talk about you a lot, about how he hoped you'd grow up. But then, he was the kind of man who saw the good in everyone. It's a shame he didn't get to meet you."

He looked at me with as much dislike as I felt for him, and this made me angrier than ever.

"This discussion is getting us nowhere. I think you had better leave the way you came."

"Sure. An' if I were you I'd get it nailed up. Might have visitors who ain't as backward as I am, seein' you in bed an' all."

He was tall enough to reach the trapdoor leading to the roof that I had completely forgotten about.

It was only after he had gone, catlike and silent, that I remembered we had not settled anything at all. I had not even found out why he had come to see me.

Hardly thinking of what I was doing, I jumped out of bed,

seizing my robe from its peg on the door. He couldn't have gone far. I pushed open the door that led out onto the patio.

"Lucas? Luke Cord, where are you?" I hissed, and heard only silence.

I fumbled with the bolt that fastened the door leading from the patio to the cleared space outside. Where had he gone? Surely he couldn't have gone far, he had to get from the roof to the ground, and then—a grove of trees hid the bunkhouse. Not there! He had to have gone in the other direction.

I ran, stumbling over the hem of my robe, and risked calling his name out loud.

"Lucas? Oh, damn you! Where are you?"

Without warning an arm clamped around my waist and I found myself thrown to the ground with a force that knocked the breath from my body.

"What the hell are you up to now? Want to get them all down on us?"

"Us," he had said, as if I had already thrown in my lot with his. But for the moment I felt as if I was hunted myself, when I heard the voices of some of the occupants of the bunkhouse who were early risers.

"Did you hear something, Pete?"

"Ain't certain. Thought I heard someone call out…"

"Damn white robe of yours stands out like a signal flag. Can you crawl backwards? An' don't make a sound, if you can help it."

There was hardly a way I could crawl, with his body half covering mine. He dragged me backwards, and even through the thin material of my robe I felt the flesh skinned from my knees and elbows.

I felt his hand come over my mouth, stifling me.

"Lie still, hear?"

The robe was bunched up over my thighs by now. Hearing the hammering of my heartbeats in my ears, I had no choice but to lie still, feeling the clump of brush he had dragged me under pricking into my bare flesh.

"Shit! Ain't nothin' out here. You probably heard a coyote back in the hills."

Thankfully, I heard Marta's voice, scolding softly.

"What are you boys trying to do? Wake the patrona? You all hush now, or you won't get any breakfast. Shoo!"

I heard them straggle, grumbling, back to the bunkhouse.

Lucas Cord's breath was warm against the back of my neck. "Why'd you come after me?"

I moved my head angrily and heard him make a half-stifled sound that might have been a laugh as he moved his hand from over my mouth.

"Never mind. You got 'em all awake now. Better go on back to the house."

I whispered furiously, "You didn't tell me anything! Why Elmer Bragg sent you, or…"

"You didn't want to listen. Will you hold still? You're gonna be all scratched up come morning, if you don't."

"It already *is* morning! And you're despicable!"

"Sounds like you're swearin' at me. There—got you loose now." His fingers, brushing against my shrinking skin, had disengaged my trailing robe from the twigs that held it.

It was ridiculous that I should be lying out here in the dark, half-naked, with a man I knew to be a murderer and a violator of women. It was idiotic of me to have followed him. Still, here I was, and my curiosity wasn't yet satisfied.

"I want to know."

"Got no time to tell you anything now. And especially not out here."

"You'll answer my questions, Luke Cord, or I'll make such a noise that they'll all come out here, with their guns drawn!"

"Damned if you ain't threatenin' me!"

He put his hand on my shoulder, fingers pressing into my flesh, and involuntarily I shrank, remembering the way he had thrown me to the ground a few moments ago. With a movement just as sudden and as violent, he turned me from my bruised side onto my back.

I realized that my robe had fallen open down the front and I was conscious of the fact that somehow, his body still lay half-covering mine. My throat was unexpectedly dry, and I afraid.

I remember that all kinds of thoughts wove in and out of

my mind at that moment. He must be a good wrestler, the ease with which he throws my body around—and, oh God, now he's going to rape me, it'll be much worse than the last time, and I don't dare scream.

He put his hand on me, and I made a smothered sound, but all he did, impatiently, was pull the edges of my robe together.

"Now, look," he whispered, bringing his face close to mine, "why don't you just go back in the house an' try to forget you seen me? Ain't no point in us tryin' to talk out here anyhow."

"I want to know—"

I thought I caught the flash of white teeth in the blur that was his face as he grinned.

"Stubborn, ain't you?" His voice changed, subtly, from amusement to impatience. "But so am I. See you in Silver City, if you still got questions then."

I felt him ease his weight from me, and then he was gone, leaving me with my bruises and frustrated anger.

I fumbled my way back to the patio, and through it to my bedroom, aching in every bone. I had made a fool of myself, and I hated Lucas Cord all the more for his being the cause. See me in Silver City indeed! Would he actually have the daring to show himself there? And as for seeing him again, I had no desire to do so. I vowed to myself that when I saw Mr. Bragg again I would tell him, in no uncertain terms, what I thought of his peculiar sense of humor—if it had, indeed, been some kind of joke on his part.

My white robe was dirty and crumpled, and there was a long tear in the hem where it had caught on a twig. Even my embroidered linen nightgown looked crushed and had faint dirt stains on it. Marta would be upset and ask questions. I would have to tell her I couldn't sleep and had wandered out onto the patio before the sun came up, that I had tripped and fallen over the hem of my robe. That would account for my bruises too. I could not help grimacing at the thought that I was becoming an accomplished liar!

But why did I feel it necessary to lie? I lay across my bed, having turned down the lamp, and frowned into the darkness.

All I had to do was tell them what had happened. Better still, I could tell Todd Shannon! I pictured myself doing just that, quite casually.

"I had an unwelcome and unexpected visitor last night. He came through the trapdoor to the roof that I had quite forgotten about. Of course you know him! Lucas Cord."

Todd, of course, would fly into a fury. Oh, I could almost shiver at the thought! And I would say coolly, to his inevitable question, "Of *course* he did not touch me! Do you think I'd let him, a man like that? But he *did* say he'd see me in Silver City."

Of course. That would be all that was necessary. I was certain Todd would see to the rest. I would need to say nothing to Flo. With Lucas Cord out of the way, surely the feud would die a natural death!

And then, unaccountably, I shivered. A strange choice of words. What had he told me about the bounty killers that Todd had sent after him? Lucas was a man who lived with death, even as he had dealt it out. They would kill him. Darn him, why had he told me he'd see me in Silver City? Could I bear to have his—or any other human's—blood on my hands and my conscience?

I had all morning to think about it. Marta accepted my story of a fall on the patio with a rather doubtful look and comment that I should think about getting a dog.

"The boys said they heard something last night. I think maybe they disturbed you?"

I denied this, but promised her I would ask Mark to find a dog for me when I saw him next. And when I was alone in my father's study at last my thoughts went back, inevitably, to last night. What on earth was I going to do? I still hadn't come to a conclusion when Mark was announced.

I greeted him with an unusual amount of warmth, but his very first words set all my defenses bristling.

"Rowena, what made you do it? There was no need to run away, surely you realized that? The other guests asked questions, and my uncle was like a grizzly with a sore paw!"

"I hope *he* did not send you then," I said coldly. "I'm in no mood to listen to recriminations. And I was not running away." I had gone to the door to greet him, and now I turned from him, walking back to the window in order to hide my agitation.

Mark followed me, his face concerned. "Rowena, what is the matter? What I meant to say was that you did not seem to be your usual self last night, and then, when you left without a word, I thought——" he caught my shoulders, gently drawing me around to face him. "Did Flo say anything to upset you? Or was it what I said? It is not my uncle's mood that upsets me, but the thought that you might be displeased with me!"

When I said nothing, he began to study my face, a worried frown knitting his brows. "There is something wrong," he said quietly. "You cannot hide it from me. Is it my uncle? Something he said to upset you?" I tried to pull away from him and his fingers tightened on my bruised shoulders, making me gasp in pain. Immediately, his hands dropped to my upper arms; his face darkened.

"He hurt you? My God—this is too much to accept, even from my own uncle! No wonder you wanted to leave, and I let you down. But this time, I swear to you, I'll…"

"Mark, no!" I had to interrupt him. I suppose my agitation was clearly visible, for his face seemed to go white with anger.

"He shall not get away with it! All his life he has ridden roughshod over people and I've pretended not to see it. But when he dares hurt *you*…"

"He didn't hurt me! Mark, you don't understand. Your uncle and I argued, yes, but I—I left the house merely to prove my own independence; it was not because…"

I had underestimated the extent of Mark's anger—or was it his love for me? Without warning he pulled down the shoulder of my loose peasant blouse, revealing the livid bruises I had hoped to hide.

"Good God!" he said softly, and I thought I felt his hands tremble.

"Mark!" I said quickly, "you must listen to me! It was not your uncle, it was a fall! I couldn't sleep very well last night; I wandered out onto the patio, and it was dark. I was clumsy, careless! I tripped over the hem of my robe and fell against the wall. You see? It was really nothing to become so concerned about."

"I don't believe you." Mark had never used such a hard, tense tone when speaking to me before, and shock made me widen my eyes. Before I could speak he had caught me by the arms again, holding me firmly. "You are protecting him, aren't you? In spite of what he did, you still want to protect him! For God's sake, Rowena! Have you let him bewitch you too? I thought that you, of all people, would be the one to stand up to him."

"That's quite enough, Mark!" I was so angry that my voice was uneven. "Once and for all, Todd Shannon had nothing to do with the bruises you saw. Nothing, do you hear? Must I swear it to convince you that I'm telling the truth? What right have you to stand here and accuse me?"

"I'm in love with you, and you know it!" He almost shook in his frustration. "Do you think I can stand to see you hurt? To see the dark circles under your eyes and know that you haven't slept? Oh, Christ, Rowena! I haven't been able to rest either, for thinking about you and worrying about you, for wondering what he said or did to you to make you run so frantically from him! Don't you understand? I know you do not think me much of a man, but damnation, I'm enough of one to want to kill whoever dares touch you and make you unhappy!"

The unexpected violence of his speech took me so much aback that I didn't resist him when he pulled me against him. "Rowena! If you only knew, if you would only trust me enough to tell me..."

He rained hungry, desperate kisses on my temple, my face, my mouth, when I would have spoken. And then he buried his face against my shoulder, kissing the bruises. I had not expected such vehemence or such passion from him.

When he released me at last and lifted his head, I saw the hurt in his eyes. I had remained passive in his embrace, neither rejecting nor returning his kisses, while my mind raced. Now I gently disengaged myself from his hands and moved backward, to lean against my father's desk.

He gave me a pleading look.

"Rowena... my dearest girl..."

I made my voice deliberately flat and expressionless.

"Before—before you say anything more you must listen to me, Mark! I realize that I must tell you the truth, in all fairness to everyone concerned, but first you have to promise me that this will remain in the strictest confidence between us; and that you will not do anything about it. Is that clear?"

I saw his face begin to harden again and shook my head warningly at him. "I mean it, Mark. If you will not give me your word, then I will tell you nothing." I added cunningly, "If you really care for me, you'll give me the promise I've asked for. I need a friend, Mark, someone I can talk to frankly. Don't you understand?"

White tension lines appeared at the corners of his mouth, but he nodded grimly. "You know exactly the right words to use to bring me around to your will, don't you?" There was a note of bitterness in his voice before it softened somewhat. "But whatever it is you ask of me, you have only to ask. Tell me what happened. I'll try not to interrupt and I'll try to restrain my temper."

I smiled gratefully at him, although my body still felt stiff with strain. Could I trust Mark? But I would have to. I could see that now. I could not have him thinking the worst.

It was even more difficult to relate the events of last night than I had imagined, especially when I could watch the changing play of expressions on Mark's face. They ranged from apprehension to grim-lipped rage to concern back to rage again. Several times I thought he would interrupt me, but true to his word, he merely tightened his lips and desisted.

He was silent until I had come to the end of my rather difficult explanations, until I cried out almost accusingly, "So you see how wrong you were? And that I was not exactly lying when I told you I had a fall? It was my fault, of course, for running out after him like that, and he—Mark, don't look that way! Lucas Cord did nothing to me! He could have, if he had wanted to, I suppose, but he only said it was too late for talking and went away!"

"You call *this* nothing?" Mark's voice was oddly quiet as his hand reached out to touch my shoulder gently. "Rowena, when I think of the narrow escape you had, of what *might* have happened, I—dear Lord, the thought is enough to drive me insane! Lucas Cord is a wild animal. Oh, I'm not saying that my uncle's thirst for vengeance didn't have something to do with turning him into one, but the fact remains that he is dangerous. And whatever you may say, I believe he is completely unscrupulous as well! Look at the way he treated Flo and the way he managed to arrange a meeting with her again. Can't you see it's revenge he's after? And you—"

"But my father was fond of him! I've been reading his journals and he thought that Lucas had been unfairly treated, that there was some good in him!"

"Your father saw good in everyone. He was that kind of man! But *you* must not let pity blind you to facts."

Mark ran his fingers distractedly through his smooth, fair hair and began to pace about the room, setting my nerves on edge. Now he had begun to sound like a logical, pitiless lawyer. And the worst part of it was that I recognized the cold truth of everything he said.

Lucas Cord was an outlaw. It was a profession, if one could call it that, which he had chosen. Mark was right. He *was* unscrupulous, even though he might hold sufficient respect and affection for my father so that he had not actually harmed me.

"But what about the next time?" Mark demanded reasonably. "Obviously, his visit to you was designed to find out how much you knew of his assignation with Flo. Perhaps he wanted to know just how naive you were."

I protested, "But Mark!" and he waved me into silence.

"Of course he knew you must have read your father's journals! He hoped to make an ally of you, so he pretended to act the gentleman, until fear for his own life made him show his true colors! He knew he had excited your curiosity, and he deliberately encouraged it. Be practical, Rowena! You're a very rich young woman, and heir to half of the ranch. Don't you see what an excellent pawn you'd make in his hands? Didn't he hint that *you* were the key to ending the feud, and that your father had said so? Doesn't that show you how diabolically cunning he is? What a perfect way to get his revenge—the ultimate revenge he has wanted all his life—through *you*."

I could not keep silent any longer. "Mark, I think you're wrong. Oh, I'll admit that most of what you've said makes sense, and could very well be true, but he seemed genuinely anxious to explain something to me! And he was so bitter about what had been done to his mother and about the way your uncle had hounded the whole family. Killing his father, sending *him* to jail, and then putting a bounty on his head as if he was some hunted animal! It must be terrible to live like that!"

Why was I suddenly defending Lucas Cord? I could see that even Mark wondered at it, for he gave me a sharp look. "He's not worth your pity, Rowena, although I admire you more for possessing a sense of justice. No, believe me, I know something of Luke Cord! Even I felt sorry for him at one time, but his actions have hardly been that of an innocent, put-upon man! Will you get it through your head, once and for all, that he is dangerous? A renegade cutthroat! How much have you heard about the band of men who call themselves *comanchero*. Let me tell you something about them."

He went on and on, and I was forced to listen, feeling physically sick at the bald account of some of the atrocities these *comancheros* had committed. They traded in death and dishonor. Selling guns and liquor to the marauding Indians and sometimes disguising themselves as Indians in order to raid homesteads and small settlements; kidnapping white women to be sold as slaves across the border. It seemed there was no end to their evil.

I saw Lucas Cord as one of *them,* and I could not help shuddering. To think that he had been in my own bedroom! To think that he had touched me, that his body had lain so intimately close to mine!

Mark told me that Elena Kordes, for all her youth, had been a cold and calculating creature who had deliberately thrown herself at her cousin's husband while poor Alma was sick. I had blamed Todd Shannon completely, but now I heard another side of the story.

"He's a *man*! Must I elaborate on it? He had a man's virile appetites, and with his wife sick, well, Elena was always *there*, flaunting herself. Don't you see it? He told me that she threatened to tell Alma everything. She taunted him with the fact that Alma was sickly and she was strong and that she could give him many sons. And when he refused to be blackmailed and sent her away, she threatened him. She said she would get her revenge, that some day he would turn to her. Do you think he fastened the blame for that terrible massacre on her with no facts to go on? Why, even afterwards, when he was so stricken with terrible grief and she came back, it was to taunt him again, to tell him that it was she, now, who could give him the heir he so passionately wanted. My God—he's only human! And you must remember he was half-grazed by grief and rage at the time. He turned on her…"

"But my father! Are you trying to tell me he was such a poor judge of human nature—of people—that he…"

"Your father was in love with her! How could he see her for what she was? Oh, she was clever, all right! She paid *him* just enough attention to make him fall in love with her so that she would have someone to fall back on. She wanted power and to be accepted as someone in the white man's world. And she was the only available woman for miles around—quite lovely, in addition. In a way, she ruined your father's life too. And then, when she saw she could have neither of them, she married Alejandro Kordes, hoping that he would regain his inheritance. Lucas Cord is her son, Rowena! He's had hatred and revenge instilled in *him* with his mother's milk, until it became a way of life with him. For God's sake, try to understand that it's too late to change him. He's the son of both his parents and he's chosen their way."

By now I was so shaken, so uncertain of what I should believe, that I felt I had hardly the strength left to go on standing. I sank into a chair, still staring at Mark, and his face changed, becoming softer.

"If I could have spared you all this sordidness, Rowena, I

would have. But you had to be warned, and I won't allow you to be hurt!" He gave me a quizzical, slightly sad look. "And now I've made you almost pity my Uncle Todd, haven't I; I can see it in your eyes. Perhaps you won't hate him so much now; perhaps I've ruined my own chances with you! You see, I know that you could not help feeling attracted to him. He has that effect on women. And yet I love you enough to want your happiness above all else."

"Oh, Mark," I said wearily, resting my chin on my clasped hands, "I don't know what to think any longer! What should I do?" Remembering something, my voice became stronger. I felt almost relieved. "But there's Mr. Bragg! Elmer Bragg. Lucas Cord said Mr. Bragg had sent him to me! Why would he do such a thing if…"

Mark said grimly, "Don't you think it at all strange that Mr. Bragg has not shown up himself? Ask yourself. Is he the kind of man who would send a complete stranger, an outlaw, to see you without any warning at all?"

We looked at each other, and I could feel the blood drain from my face. It was at that moment, I think, that I became completely convinced of the truth of everything Mark had told me.

Eleven

᠊᠊ᢧ᠊᠊

MARK HAD PROMISED ME HE WOULD SAY NOTHING TO HIS uncle, or to Flo either, but his face had become very serious when he warned me to have Jules fix a bolt on the trapdoor. I thought Jules looked at me strangely when I gave the order, but he asked no questions, and I was relieved.

After Mark left, though, I was still restless. I was tired, but I could not indulge in a siesta today. I was more confused and upset than I had ever been in my life before. At least a half dozen times I went to the locked drawer that held my father's journals and just as many times I turned away. I could not read them now. Was my father really a weak man, deluded by his obsessive love for Elena Kordes? Was it that obsession that had driven my mother to seek love elsewhere? And above all, had Lucas Cord murdered Elmer Bragg? I could not think of Mr. Bragg dead! In spite of his age, with his twinkling eyes and dry sense of humor; he had seemed so alive, so sure of himself and his ability to seek out the truth. What kind of truth had he found? He had tried to be fair when he'd told me of the past and yet, hadn't he been uncertain about Lucas? Hadn't he cut himself off in mid-sentence when I had begun questioning him too closely?

"Don't press me too hard, Lady Rowena. I'm the kind of man who likes to produce facts, not assumptions or hearsay. Ain't been able to keep too many tabs on Luke Cord. Ain't had reason to. Been retired, see? An' he's been movin' around a lot. Has he been keeping on the right side of the law? I can't be certain. There have been rumors, but rumors ain't facts. However, now that you've hired my services, young lady, I'm going to search you out some facts."

Had he? Or had death found him instead?

Facts, as Mr. Bragg would have said, were facts. I could not escape from them. Why, then, couldn't I escape from the memory of Lucas Cord's words?

"You're like the prosecutor at my trial," he had said. "Already found me guilty and hung before I got tried."

But I had been trained to have a logical mind. Evidence and logic had to set me squarely against Lucas Cord.

The only question was, what would Mark Shannon and I do about it? We hadn't reached any conclusions. "I doubt if he'll dare to show his face in Silver City," Mark had said comfortingly. "Not with half the bigwigs in the territory there, including my uncle. I think he threw that hint out to disturb you. No, I'll watch Flo, and you watch yourself. And I'll ask Uncle Todd if you can have one of Frisky's pups. They're German shepherds—not a usual breed out here, but they're fierce—good watchdogs."

Todd Shannon, riding in a buckboard, brought the dog over to me the next afternoon. I had been sitting in the patio until Malta's urgent words alerted me to his arrival. "Señorita! It is the patron himself! And he does not look in a very good humor!"

I met him outside, my manner deliberately light. "My goodness, what a surprise! Or should I say an honor! I didn't think you'd be speaking to me."

"You don't deserve to be spoken to, an' well you know it, miss! But Mark told me you had your heart set on havin' a pet, and I happened to be passin' this way."

As usual, our eyes met and clashed. But I could not help feeling differently towards him today. Did I dare pity him?

I put on a demure look. "You're very kind. Would you care to step down for a moment?"

I saw him lift a shaggy eyebrow. "You sure you ain't sufferin' from a touch of the sun? Or is it some kind of game you're playin'?" I knew he was not as indifferent as he seemed because his Irish brogue became more pronounced.

"Please," I said, and his eyebrow shot higher.

"Well! You sure seem all soft an' kittenish today! But I've no doubt you've got your claws hidden away to use when you're good an' ready!" As usual, he seemed to know exactly the right way to make me angry.

"Suit yourself, then!" I said sharply, and saw him grin.

"That sounds more like you. Yeah—I'd be glad to get down and set a spell."

I had been prepared to like him, but his manners were as brash as ever, setting my nerves on edge.

"Well!" I saw him glance around the living room. "You ain't changed much, have you? Expected you to have everything moved around and new furniture and all."

"Why should you have expected any such thing?"

He decided to change the subject abruptly. "Why did you run away? Didn't expect you to act the coward. Run like a scared rabbit, didn't you? Without the guts to face me."

"You mistake your effect on me!" I was stung into retorting. "I didn't run, as I attempted to explain in the note I sent you. I merely wanted to come home. I dislike being given orders!"

"You sure that was all? I'd asked you to marry me, remember? Maybe you didn't think I was serious. Or did you want me to come chasin' you to prove I meant it?"

"As usual, Mr. Shannon, you think far too much of your influence upon me!"

"Thought you just might be woman enough to admit the way things are between us."

"Oh!" He had made me so tense and angry that I walked around the room. "Why can't you accept me the way I am? I can't be bullied, or ordered about or taken for granted! I'm not ready to be married off yet!"

"Well, then," his look was wicked, "maybe you ought to start thinking of some other alternative. Look, girl, you get all bristly when I try to assert myself. But what about you? Ain't you tryin' to make a puppet of me too? You talk about bein'

fair. I think you ought to start bein' honest with both of us.
I won't give in, an' you won't give in. But you know damn
well how things stand with us. How long you going to keep
hidin' from the truth?"

But he took me in his arms just then, and whatever I had
been going to say escaped me when he kissed me.

"You're damn well goin' to marry me!" he said forcefully
after it was over, and I was breathless.

"You're not being fair!" I wailed, resorting to femininity.
"I think I hate you. And I'll never give in to you! What's
more, I refuse to—to live with a ghost!"

"What in hell are you talkin' about?" But his tone was
almost tender. "Listen, you stubborn, bad-natured female!
When are you going to realize I want you? That I've been
waitin' God knows how many years for someone like you?
You can have all the time you want, just so you wake up to
the fact you're mine. And Goddammit, I mean to have you!"

He caught me in his arms again, hardly allowing me to think.

"You little tease! I know that forward nephew of mine asked
you to go to the festivities at Silver City. But I already told him
you're goin' with me. Hell, he and Flo can come along too, I
don't care! But we'll make the announcement then."

"Wait! For goodness' sake, I haven't said anything yet! You
haven't allowed me to! Todd Shannon, you are the most exasperating man I have ever had the bad fortune to encounter!
You twist my words around and you *announce* what we will
do. And all this time, ever since I've known you, in fact, I've
been trying, yes trying, to convince you that I will not be
pushed into anything! Is that perfectly clear?"

Infuriatingly, he smiled at me, pushing his hat back on his
head as he let his fingers trail across my mouth and down my
neck. "You've convinced me, sweetheart. Now look, I've got
things to do. Only meant to stop by for a minute. But I'll be
comin' by again soon. An' you just start planning what you're
goin' to wear to the ball in Silver City. Want you to knock
their eyes out!"

The ball at Silver City.

Even after Todd had left, the thought was sufficient to

depress me. What a strange, peculiar situation I found myself in! Todd was so sure of himself, so confident. But what would I do about Mark? And suppose in spite of all the risks he'd be taking, Lucas Cord showed up. Then what? I could only tell myself firmly that I wouldn't think about it; but my dreams turned into nightmares, as they had done the night before, and I tossed and turned uneasily. Mr. Bragg, my father, Lucas Cord with a hangman's noose around his neck, his mouth lifting in the bitter, half-mocking smile I remembered so well. They peopled my dreams like ghosts, and the dark rings under my eyes were enough to make Marta exclaim disapprovingly.

"You have not slept well since that night you went to the *palacio*. And when the patron visits, he always brings trouble!" Her lips pursed themselves sourly. I had already gathered that neither Marta nor her husband had any great love for Todd Shannon.

The question was, what did *I* feel about him? The story that Mark had told me had subtly altered my reaction to his arrogance and bluster. I began to see him as a lonely man who had deliberately isolated himself, covering his grief and lone-liness with a hard veneer. He had loved his first wife. Perhaps he had not loved his second wife, as Flo had stated bitterly. Still, she had been dead a long time, and I was sure he had had the opportunity to marry again if he had wanted to. Why, so suddenly, had he chosen me? And what was I going to say to him?

"So it's come to that," Mark said quietly. "I suppose I have known it from the beginning, but I had hoped—" he gave a bitter, self-deprecating laugh. "Well, I suppose Uncle Todd has always had a kind of charisma! He has a way of bending people to his will. Even I have to admit it. I can only hope that you will think very carefully first. Be sure it is really what *you* want, Rowena."

"For heaven's sake, Mark!" I know I sounded irritable, I could not help it. "All I said was that your uncle seems deter-mined to force my hand. I won't be pushed into marriage, and I told him so."

"But you have been thinking about it a great deal, haven't you? You don't have to answer me. I can tell. Perhaps it is because I love you that I seem to have developed a sensitivity for your moods, the expressions on your face. And I know that he keeps finding all kinds of excuses to keep *me* busy while he rides over here to visit you."

"I didn't know that." I looked at him seriously, at his dear, kind face, and wished that it could have been Mark whose kisses were capable of making me feel weak and helpless. If I married anyone, it should be Mark, who understood me, and loved me enough to be my friend.

"Oh, Mark! I'm sorry. I—I've never met anyone quite like him before, you know! I keep telling myself that he's old enough to be my father, that he wants to marry me only in order to possess the whole of the SD. I keep telling him that too, but he only laughs and won't listen. All the same, I won't marry him. I won't!"

"But does *he* know that?"

Our eyes met, and I shrugged helplessly. We were out riding, and to take our minds off Todd Shannon, I said quickly, "How is Flo these days? I haven't seen her since she came over last week—and *that,* I'm sure, was only for the purpose of telling me that a woman in my position should be careful of gossip! 'Everyone knows, after all, that both Mark and my father come here far too often for their visits to be perfectly innocent,' was exactly the way she put it!"

"Flo is a little cat!" Mark's face had darkened. "The trouble with her is that she's been spoiled rotten, and allowed to have far too much of her own way. It's what started all the trouble in the first place. And even now—well, you know what she's like! A child-woman. She thinks that all she needs to know is how to bat her eyes at some man and he'll give her everything."

"Has she…" I didn't know why I had to ask the question, but suddenly it had become a compulsion that I must know. And Mark, bless him, understood immediately what I meant, for his tone became serious.

"It's been worrying me too, because, you see, I just don't know! I told you my uncle has deliberately kept me very busy of late. Ever since that fence was cut we've posted extra guards at all the boundary fences, and I'm supposed to ride out early each morning to inspect them as well, so I'm afraid I have not been able to keep as close an eye on Flo as I promised you I would."

I frowned, wondering why the thought made me angry. "She could still be meeting him, then. And if she is, it means that he…"

"Might well be hiding out somewhere around here." Mark finished my sentence for me. "I've worried about that too. You're sure that trapdoor is kept bolted? And the dog is kept loose on the patio?"

I grimaced. "Devil is still a puppy, you know! But he does have a loud bark, and I daresay he'd warn me if he scented any intruders."

"Still, you promise you'll always be careful? Don't ride anywhere by yourself, please."

I promised him I would not. But Mark's concern meant, of course, that he thought Lucas Cord was a danger to me. Especially if he continued to meet Flo, for she would certainly have told him of her stepfather's frequent calls on me. Where would it all end? Or how?

We were to leave for Silver City a week early, and rooms had already been reserved for us all at the same hotel where Governor Wallace and the other dignitaries would be staying.

In spite of myself, I began to get caught up in the preparations for leaving, and even Marta, who had seemed exceptionally quiet of late, began to smile and chatter as she helped me pick out the gowns I would take with me, folding each one very carefully with layers of tissue paper between each fold as I had showed her.

I would be away for ten days. I told myself that I would not think beyond the actual preparations for my journey. It was unlike me. I could feel myself changing, growing less sure of myself; I hated the change in myself.

"If Mr. Bragg should arrive, will you tell him where I've gone?" I said to Marta. "Tell him it is most urgent that I should meet and talk to him." But even while I was giving her these instructions I felt in my heart of hearts that Mr. Bragg would not turn up. He was lying somewhere, in a nameless grave, murdered because he had tried to help me. Whenever I thought about him I felt a return of the sick, frightened feeling I had had when Mark said to me, "Don't you think it strange that Mr. Bragg has not shown up himself?"

Lucas Cord had come instead, using Mr. Bragg's name to gain my trust, using even the name of my dead father who had befriended him in order to excite my curiosity. "Out here we shoot rattlesnakes before they have a chance to bite," Mark had said with a note of grimness unusual for him. I knew what he wanted me to do, but I would not discuss it.

"He'll never turn up," I said. I repeated those same words during the last part of our long and tiring journey across the plains and mountains, past Santa Rita, and into Silver City which, as its name implied, was a prosperous mining town.

We had a cavalry escort from Fort Cummings for most of the journey, and when we stopped to rest at Santa Rita the SD men who had gone ahead of us with Todd Shannon took over.

I was surprised at their number, and the arsenal of weapons they seemed to carry.

"Pa's Texas gunslingers, that's who they are!" Flo Jeffords said with a sniff. With a look of contempt for me she added, "Did you think they were ordinary cowhands? You've only got to look closely at their clothes, and the way they wear their guns. Pa's own unofficial army!"

She gave a shrill laugh, and I wished, not for the first time, that I had not been forced to travel cooped up in this little carriage with her. Only when Mark, who preferred to ride outside, joined us occasionally did Flo fall silent, gazing sullenly out of the window and pretending that our conversation bored her. I wondered what she was thinking.

As we drew closer to Silver City, though, some of Flo's sullenness fell away and she displayed some animation, her eyes shining with excitement. "You've never seen a mining town? This one's bigger than most. The governor's here to help them celebrate finding the silver that gave the town its name. It's not exactly a *city,* of course, but for *this* dull part of the world it's got plenty of excitement to offer." She gave me a slanting, sideways look. "There are gunfights almost every day, of course. Mostly between cowboys and miners, or cowboys and homesteaders. You seen a gunfight yet?"

The shine in her eyes took on an almost unnatural brilliance, and it flashed through my mind that she had once seen two men killed in a fight over her. Was she remembering the same thing?

"I hope I never have to see grown men fight each other with guns!" I said firmly.

She giggled again. "Stay in Silver City long enough and you're bound to, like it or not!"

It was shortly after this that Mark and I had our conversation, for Flo declared she had to stretch her legs, as the motion of the carriage was making her quite dizzy. Mark offered to let her ride his horse for part of the way.

I noticed that he was frowning as he stretched his long legs before him.

"I don't like the way Flo's been acting," he said bluntly. "Did she strike you as being... well, overexcited?"

"I don't know her or her moods well enough to judge," I said cautiously.

"But I do, unfortunately! I have the feeling she's up to some kind of mischief." He rubbed at his clean-shaven jaw morosely. "Darn it, I wish I knew what to do! I don't dare drop a word of warning in my uncle's ear without betraying *your* confidence, and then he'd fly into one of his rages and we'd have a war on our hands."

"A war? All Todd's Texas gunmen against one man?" I don't know what made me say it, but I caught Mark's sharp look.

"Don't forget that as part owner of the SD your money helps pay their wages too," he reminded me.

"But why do we need a small army to protect us?" I was just as glad to get off the subject of Lucas Cord, and I'm sure Mark sensed it, for he gave me a reproachful glance as if he knew I was deliberately evading an issue.

"I thought you'd have realized by now that it's necessary. Why do you think even the Apaches hesitate to attack us? I've heard of other, smaller spreads being overrun and looted—if not by Indians, by the renegades this territory seems to attract."

"A show of force?" I said thoughtfully, and Mark gave a pleased nod.

"Exactly! And the money spent is worth it, in terms of safety."

"I think I see what you mean." I sighed, and gave Mark a level glance. "I think I can guess what you are thinking too," I said ruefully.

"Rowena, it's got to be faced! We have to be prepared, just in case. You do understand that, don't you?"

"I carry that little derringer you gave me in my purse at all times," I reminded him, and laughed. "I even sleep with it tucked under my pillow."

"You'll have a man guarding your door too!"

"And how will you explain that to your uncle?"

"He'll see to that himself, as a normal precaution. Silver City has a reputation for being a rough town."

"Well, then, we have nothing to worry about, have we?"

"You don't know what men like Cord are capable of! Never forget that he's spent most of his life on the run and he knows all the tricks! If he said he'd see you in Silver City, it'd probably turn into a point of pride with him to make good his boast."

"I don't think he was boasting, exactly," I said slowly. "It was more like a… well, a casual statement of fact!"

Mark leaned forward, his voice urgent. "Then you *do* think he's going to be there."

"I didn't say that! Perhaps he intended to, but I'm sure he will have changed his mind. He won't turn up. He won't dare!"

"He dared slip into your bedroom! He's taken worse risks before. Look at the risk he took merely in bluffing you into believing that Elmer Bragg had sent him?"

I felt my hands get clammy inside my cotton gloves.

"Oh, Mark, don't! I can't bear to think of that poor old man…"

"But you have to! You have to be practical and realistic!" He leaned back in his seat with a sigh. "I won't press you any further now, Rowena, but I beg you to think about it. If you will leave things in my hands I feel sure I can handle it. I'm acquainted with the town marshal and the judge."

"How will you handle it, Mark? By having him killed if he's found? By putting him jail to await lynching?"

"Rowena!" Mark sounded as shocked by my outburst as I was myself. "I don't understand you! I thought you trust my judgment. I thought you realized that we are dealing with a killer just as dangerous as those mad dogs in India you were telling me of. But you sound as if you actually feel sorry for him!"

"I just do not like the thought of violence, Mark! We can't be *certain* that Mr. Bragg is dead, or that Lucas Cord killed him. And if we took the law into our own hands, acting on an *assumption*, then we'd be just as guilty. Don't you understand? You're a lawyer."

"*You* should have been the lawyer, Rowena!" Mark shook his head at me gently, but his voice remained hard. "All right, but suppose he commits some violent act? And I've already dispatched some wires to various places, trying to trace Mr. Bragg's whereabouts. Suppose, when we arrive in Silver City, the marshal is able to confirm my worst suspicions?"

I said flatly, "Then, of course, I agree that he should be hunted down and killed like the wild animal you compared him to!"

Twelve

꒱

I HAD BEEN IN SILVER CITY FOR TWO DAYS, AND DURING THAT time everyone I was introduced to kept assuring me that it was not only bigger but friendlier than most of the other big mining towns. My attention was proudly drawn to the grand new opera house, where the ball to honor the governor's visit would be held, to the white-painted courthouse with a cellar-like jail forming its basement, the three churches.

I'm sure the good citizens of the town would have preferred me not to notice the innumerable saloons and gambling halls that lined the main street, nor the red lamp over the door of a tall, two-story building that sat a little way back off one end of the street.

Sir Edgar, in an effort to excite me out of my coldness, had once taken me on what he termed a grand tour of one of Paris's most exclusive bordellos. Everything I had witnessed there had left me faintly disgusted, but otherwise unmoved. So Silver City's house of ill repute did not arouse my curiosity, although Flo whispered to me, in an attempt to shock, that she would dearly like to see what went on in there.

"Personally," I murmured idly, my fingers playing with the cord that held apart the draperies of the room we shared, "I would much rather see what the inside of one of those saloons looks like! They must be delightfully sordid, don't you think?"

We had been forced into proximity once again because the one decent hotel that Silver City boasted of was filled to capacity. This particular afternoon was too hot to warrant our venturing outside, so we engaged in desultory conversation.

"I've heard what they are like!" Flo said. Too restless to sit still for long, she continued to walk about the room. "There would be a long bar, of course. Mahogany, in one of the better places. And a mirror behind it, so a man can see who comes up behind him. Sometimes there might even be a large picture of a naked woman hung there."

She glanced at me to see if I was shocked, and I raised an eyebrow. "Oh? And what else?"

"Well, there'd be tables for the card players, of course. And females to wait on them." She gave one of her high-pitched giggles. "I understand they don't wear very much! And of course there would be rooms upstairs, in case one of the men wanted to pay for female company after he had done his drinking!"

I grimaced. "Those poor women could hardly lead a very pleasant life!"

"Oh, I don't know! Of course *they* wouldn't, but I've heard that in big cities like San Francisco and New York—and in Europe, of course—some of the most beautiful and charming women one sees are courtesans! They change lovers as they please, and of course I expect they're simply showered with expensive gifts! It must be an interesting, exciting way to live—to have the power to make men your adoring slaves."

"I would think it was the other way around!" I said dryly. "Do you think those women give nothing in return?"

"Oh, well, how would *you* know?"

Flo turned away sulkily and began fiddling with the toilet things she had laid out on top of the dresser. Changing the subject with her usual abruptness, she said, "Oh, Lord, but I'm bored! I wish something would happen! To think that silly old ball is all of three days away. I might easily go mad with boredom before then!"

"Well, who knows? Perhaps you'll get your wish and there will be a gunfight or two," I murmured, deliberately keeping my voice expressionless. "And perhaps they might have some really vicious criminals locked up in the local jail!"

She swung around sharply, and I thought I saw her eyes widen a trifle.

"Do you think so?" And then, as if afraid she had given something away, she lifted her shoulders in an exaggerated shrug. "If there really *had* been, of course, we would have heard Pa and Mark talk about it. But all they seem to be able to talk about at mealtimes is business. Men are so dull when they all get together and begin talking. At least women find some interest in gossip!" Her look was slightly malicious and I gave her a sugary smile.

"I'm sure *you* do."

"And you, no doubt, are the kind of woman who would rather create gossip!" she flashed back at me, and I could not help laughing.

"Touché!"

She had another lightning change of mood. "It's even becoming a bore to stand here exchanging catty remarks with you!"

Still standing at the window, I said aimlessly, "It might be an interesting experience if we could persuade one of the gentlemen to take us on a tour of the courthouse—and the jail, of course. I wonder if the one they have here is anything like the dungeons I have seen in our English castles!"

"That is the first really clever idea you've had since we've been here!" Flo's voice sounded excited, and the gleam was back in her blue eyes. "Do you really think they would let us?"

It was Mark I asked, of course. Flo seemed to have her heart set on it, and to myself I had to confess a rather morbid curiosity.

"The jail? I can see your wanting to flatter the good townspeople by asking to see their courthouse, but…"

Todd Shannon was far more outspoken, when he discovered what Flo and I meant to do with our spare time. "You two females gone loco? Filthy hole in the ground. I can tell you what it looks like—yeah, and probably smells like, too! Ain't no place for ladies to visit." He lifted an eyebrow at me. "You happen to know any outlaws you want to visit in there?"

I felt guilty color stain my cheeks, and feigned anger. "Todd Shannon, you have an odd sense of humor! If you hadn't been a cattle baron, you'd probably have ended up as an outlaw yourself!"

He gave a roar of laughter. Why did all my attempts to cut him down to size seem to amuse him? "Aha! Miss has her claws out again, huh? Well, I'll tell you what, if you gals are really bored, you come over here and I'll teach you how to play poker after dinner, how's that?"

Flo pouted angrily. I merely shrugged. I had actually become cowardly enough to let Todd Shannon dictate to me occasionally just to keep the peace, although I was still determined that he would never talk me into marrying him.

The subject seemed closed for the moment and Flo continued to sulk, but the next morning, after we had finished breakfast, Mark made an opportunity to speak to me for a moment. His face was unusually serious.

"I have to speak to you in private, Rowena! What had you planned to do this morning?"

I looked at him thoughtfully. "Flo and I had planned to go back to the milliner's shop, to try on the new bonnets we ordered. But she's been in a particularly vile mood since yesterday, of course, and it's more than likely she'll change her mind."

"I'll meet you outside the store then—say in an hour's time," he said hurriedly. "If Flo's with you, then we'll just have to think up some other opportunity. Believe me, it is important!"

I went back upstairs feeling unaccountably tense and nervous. What on earth could have happened to make Mark look so stern?

Flo was sitting in a chair by the window, her eyes fixed on something that was happening down in the street. When she heard me come in she gave an almost guilty start, but grumbled immediately.

"Oh, it's you! You gave me a shock, coming in so quietly! And if you've come to ask me to go out, well, I've changed my mind. I have a terrible headache—all those cigars that Pa's friends smoke!"

"Suit yourself!"

I was in no mood to trade barbs with her this morning, and her reference to cigars, moreover, did not fail to remind me that Todd had certainly been keeping himself busy with his friends of late. I hardly saw him during the day, and at night we usually dined with several of the men he knew, and their wives. Except for giving me meaningful glances from time to time he had been, for *him,* remarkably discreet.

Ignoring my presence, Flo had turned back to the window, and I started to tidy my hair before the mirror.

It was strange how gazing at my own reflection in a glass always started me thinking backwards. How many other images of myself had I seen? A plain, suspicious-looking girl in unbecoming clothes, preparing to disembark in London. An Indian princess wrapped in a gold-encrusted sari. A naked whore with diamonds about her neck, feeling nothing, thinking nothing. And later, a coldly determined young woman, elegantly dressed, with a face that showed no emotion.

Now, my fingers fumbling with hairpins, I stared, searching at myself. I had not changed very much. The bone structure of my face remained the same, my mouth was still the mouth that men called sensuous. I had merely learned to dress my hair differently and wear clothes that suited me, and *voilà!* I had been transformed from ugly duckling into swan.

"I suppose you are admiring yourself!" Flo had sauntered over and stood behind me. She put her head on one side, tone deliberately critical. "Well, you are passable, I daresay, but black hair like yours is far too common in this part of the country to attract too much notice. And you must admit that *my* figure is better than yours!"

Adjusting my wide, flower-trimmed bonnet, I turned away with a mock curtsy in her direction. "In that case, let me leave you to admire yourself."

As I left the room I heard her laughingly begin to recite: "Mirror, mirror on the wall, who's the fairest one of all?" Her giggle followed me down the narrow passageway.

It made me uneasy, for some odd reason. Suddenly I had the strangest, most peculiar feeling that something terrible and ominous was about to happen, and the feeling was so strong that my heart began to beat faster, and my hands went cold.

The feeling persisted when I walked out of the hotel. One of the Texans lounging outside straightened up when he saw me, his hooded, insolent eyes flickering over me in a lightning glance.

"Want me to have the buggy brought around for you, ma'am?"

Forcing a smile, I shook my head, telling him that I intended to walk only a short distance, that Mr. Shannon would be meeting me.

"The boss is across the way, in the Silver Dollar saloon." Was he telling me that he disbelieved me? After a short, but deliberate, pause the man added, "I could tell him you're waiting. He wouldn't want to keep you waiting, I'm sure, ma'am."

"I'm to meet Mr. *Mark* Shannon," I said frostily. "After I finish my shopping." I walked past him, not looking back, my lace-trimmed parasol held over my head.

He was one of the men I'd noticed Flo flirting with which, no doubt, accounted for his insolent manners. I wondered if he thought I was Todd's mistress, and that accounted for his measuring glance. Perhaps Flo had told him so.

"A woman has to be very careful of her reputation here," she had said mendaciously. It was the day she had ridden over to "warn" me about allowing too many gentleman callers. "Men respect *nice* women, but if they think she's—well, *easygoing,* you'll see how fast their attitude changes!"

I had had to bite my lips in order not to make some comment about her rather unsavory past. But heavens, she was an aggravating baggage at times!

Deliberately, knowing that the gun-hung Texan was still watching me, I forced myself to walk slowly down the wooden sidewalk. It had already began to get quite hot, but the sidewalk seemed crowded, all the same. Miners in filthy clothes, some of them wearing only their red undershirts tucked into their pants, moved politely aside to let a woman pass. Cowboys strutted arrogantly, their enormous spurs jingling. I could see some young girls, giggling together, eye them covertly. Grim-looking homesteaders, trailed by their drab, work-worn wives and round-eyed children pretended to ignore the cowboys. I saw several serape-draped Mexicans, most of them sporting drooping moustaches, even one or two Chinese, who scurried along, trying to look unobtrusive. Even this remote frontier town was a good example of a statement I had heard, that America had become a melting pot of all the races.

I studied the faces I saw in the crowd, trying to take my mind off the uneasy feeling that persisted like a knot in the pit of my stomach. It was nothing, I chided myself. Only the mystery that Mark had created with his urgency, his secrecy. After I had talked with him, I would probably laugh at myself!

Nevertheless, I quickened my steps slightly.

A handsome, light-skinned Spaniard rode down the street within a few feet of me, just as I had reached the small shop with the lettering on the glass which read "Madame Fleur, Ladies' Milliner." I might not have noticed him at all if it had not been for his horse, a really magnificent specimen of a Morgan stallion. I knew enough about horses to recognize good bloodlines, and this one was a beauty. His rider, who must have noticed my admiring glance, controlled the dancing animal easily with one hand, and raised his flat-crowned hat with a gallant, sweepingly Latin gesture.

"You like my Conde, no? It is unusual to see a pretty señorita who can recognize good horseflesh!" His teeth gleamed whitely under a thin moustache.

He was a magnificent horseman, but far too bold! I inclined my head coldly and walked into the shop without glancing backward.

Madame Fleur, who was a true Frenchwoman, left another customer to come bustling forward to greet me, her face wreathed in smiles.

"Ah, the *anglais* milady! I have your order ready, of course."

"Please see to your other customer first. I shall enjoy looking around," I said politely, and she bowed, finally leaving me alone after making clucking noises with her tongue to indicate how exasperating it was that she had someone else to serve when *I* had deigned to visit her little establishment.

I walked between crowded counters, pretending to study

ribbons, feathers, and other pretty trims. I examined bolts of
material on the shelves that lined the walls. From the low-
voiced conversation I heard going on behind me I could guess
that I was being discussed, so I moved to the far end of the
tiny room, and began to leaf through the small collection of old
pattern books that madame had brought with her from France
some years ago, to judge from the rather outdated styles.

"The lovely señorita's smile lights up this dingy place like
sunshine in a dark cavern!" a low voice said beside me. Was
there no limit to Latin gallantry? The bold Spaniard who rode
a Morgan stallion had actually followed me in here.

I gave him a freezing look and turned back to the patterns.

Suddenly he said quietly, "Forgive me if I appear to force
an acquaintance with you, Lady Rowena, but it was a meeting
your own father planned before his death." I could no more
prevent my sharp intake of breath than I could help turning
my head to meet his brown eyes.

"I am so sorry!" he said quickly. "But I saw you and I had
to follow you in here. Please do not be angry at my abruptness. I am Ramon Kordes."

He gave his last name its correct Spanish pronunciation, but
at the time I was too stunned to notice. Kordes! What was *he*
doing here? Why had he followed me? And if *he* was here,
then his brother…

Shamefully my first impulse was to turn away from him and
run to safety. But the concerned expression in his light brown
eyes made me hesitate.

Ramon? This then was the youngest son of Elena and
Alejandro. The one who had been left with the Jesuits in
Mexico City. "He's the gentleman of the family, I guess!" Mr.
Bragg had told me once.

"Lady Rowena! Please tell me you are not angry?"

I said, through stiff lips, "But why go to all these lengths to
meet me? Why?"

He looked swiftly over his shoulder and lowered his voice,
speaking quietly but fluently in Castilian Spanish.

"It is as well that the two old women do not know what
we are saying, and I know that you speak Spanish." His voice

became slightly bitter, reminding me suddenly of his brother. "You ask why I chose this way? I think you know already. It does not matter to Mr. Todd Shannon that I am completely innocent of all he accuses my brother of—or that I have spent most of my life in Mexico. No, to him I am merely 'one of the Kordes bunch' and he would have me shot down like a dog if he knew I were here!"

"But you took a risk, then!"

"Not too much of a risk! You see, he does not know me by sight. My picture, my description, they appear on no wanted posters. So you see? As long as I tell no one my name or who I am, I'm safe enough."

Bluntly I asked what was suddenly uppermost in my mind.

"Your brother, Lucas, where is *he*?"

I thought he reddened.

"Lucas is here, somewhere. But he does not tell me anything of his plans. It has always been like that." Rather caustically he added, "To Lucas I'm afraid I'm still the baby of the family. I do not know why Lucas decided to be so foolish as to come here, and especially at this particular time, but I came to find you. To see you for myself."

So—Lucas had obviously described me! Angrily, I wondered what kind of description he had given.

"Now that you've seen me…" I said out loud, and Ramon Kordes shook his head as if to refute my next statement.

"Please—I must see you again! Talk to you."

"But that's impossible, and you know it! And especially not here, not now! I'm supposed to meet a friend. Outside. In a very few minutes."

"I will not keep you too long then. But I must know one thing. Tell me—had you not heard of me before? Your father left you no letter? No message of any kind?"

I met his long, searching look and was suddenly angry.

"What is all this mystery? Why will neither you nor your brother come right out in the open and tell me what you hint at? My father…" I had been about to say that my father had left me only his journals to read when I remembered all that Mark had told me about Lucas Cord. This was his brother, and innocent or not, I did not dare trust him. I said in a more controlled voice, "Mr. Kordes, I'm sure you must realize that this is neither the time nor the place to conduct a discussion of this nature. Perhaps another time."

He looked disconcerted and more than a little unhappy. "But how? I can see that I have angered you. I know very well that you are a well-brought-up lady and are hardly accustomed to being approached in such an unconventional manner. Believe me, if there were any other way…"

I looked him straight in the eye, the thought that had been hovering on the fringes of my mind suddenly crystallizing.

"Your brother found a way of meeting me. I've no doubt he can find a method of contacting me again. But tell him, if you please, that I will not talk to him or listen to anything he has to say until he can tell me the whereabouts of Mr. Elmer Bragg."

Ramon Kordes's face was a study of incomprehension.

"Mr.—Bragg you say? But I do not know of such a person! I…"

"Lady Rowena? Oh, but there you are! A thousand pardons for keeping you waiting so long, but that Mrs. Green—ah, such a one for the talk-talk!" Her sharp black eyes lingered on Ramon Kordes, standing stiff and ill at ease at my side, and she smiled—rather slyly, I thought.

"Ah, but I see you have met a friend! So!"

"The gentleman was merely asking me to help him choose a gift for his fiancée," I improvised coolly. "I told him, of course, that *you* would be much better qualified than I in such matters." Turning to Ramon, I gave him a brilliant smile. "Señor, I wish you luck and good fortune on your forthcoming marriage."

He drew himself up and bowed stiffly. "You are very gracious, señorita, and I thank you. I will wait, of course, until you have concluded your business with Madame."

"*Certainement!*" Madame gave a throaty chuckle. "I realize this is hardly the place where a young man will feel comfortable, but I assure you, when your fiancée sees what we have chosen for her she will be—how you say? Very happy!"

I could almost have felt sorry for him, but I was far too angry with Lucas Cord and far too worried about Mr. Bragg to waste time on pity, even though the references to my father and his plans for me still filled me with curiosity.

My business with Madame Fleur was quickly concluded, once I had exclaimed over her creations with enthusiasm. She bustled into a back room to pack the hats into bandboxes, and when I glanced over my shoulder, Ramon Kordes had left as quietly and unobtrusively as he had entered.

Thirteen

⁊

WHEN I FINALLY ESCAPED FROM THE SHOP AND MADAME'S
dismayed exclamations, when she found she had lost a
prospective customer, Mark was standing outside and looking
impatiently at his pocket watch. He stuffed it thankfully back
into his vest pocket when he saw me emerge and hurried
forward to take my arm.

"May I carry your packages for you? Good heavens,
Rowena, I had begun to wonder if you had not managed to
get rid of Flo after all! "

"I'm afraid it was Flo who seemed anxious to get rid of
me," I responded tartly. "And thank you for offering to carry
my hatboxes but no, dear Mark! Men always contrive to
look slightly ridiculous carrying such things." I looked at him
sideways, opening my parasol to shield my eyes from the glare,
and asked casually, "Did you see anyone come out of the shop
a few minutes ago?"

He was already beginning to propel me along the sidewalk,
and gave me a harried, rather absentminded look.

"No, I don't think so. Was there someone I should have
noticed?"

There must be another entrance of some kind, then, or
Mark had not been paying attention.

Indeed, he appeared to be so lost in his own thoughts, he
seemed hardly to be paying attention to me at the moment.

"We'll have to hurry, Rowena. Uncle Todd will be out

of his meeting with the Cattlemen's Association soon, and it would be better if he didn't see us together before we decide what we must do."

"Decide what? Mark, I've had quite enough mystery for one day! Where are you taking me?" He was walking so fast that I was breathless trying to keep up with his long strides and almost tripped over an uneven plank. "Mark, for goodness sake! Must we hurry along so?"

He slowed down then, and squeezed my arm apologetically.

"I'm sorry! I had so much to think of that I hadn't realized I was practically dragging you along."

"I'll forgive you this time if you tell me at once, where we are going!"

"To the marshal's office." His voice had suddenly become flat, almost harsh. "There is something you must know, Rowena, and it would sound more valid coming direct from the marshal himself. And once you have heard what he has to say, I think you will find it easier to make up your mind about a certain matter."

The strange, panicky feeling I had had all morning came back like a blow, making me stumble again. I found that I could not speak, that my face burned, and my hands were icy.

Silently, I let Mark hurry me along, and since his few terse words, he seemed as little inclined for further conversation as I was by now.

The federal marshal's office, with the large painted sign by the door, was a few doors down the same side of the street as the Silver Dollar Saloon, and we could see the imposing brick and adobe Territorial Hotel across the street quite clearly. I remember glancing up at the windows that faced the street and wondering if Flo was watching us. It was all to take on a strange significance later, but at that moment my thoughts were all racing confusion.

Mark was ushering me inside with an impatience quite foreign to his usual easygoing manner. A grizzled, fiercely moustached man of middle height rose hastily from the wooden chair behind his cluttered desk, and I had a vague impression of faded wanted posters tacked to the walls in such numbers that the walls seemed papered with them. There was a padlocked gun rack fastened to the wall behind the marshal's desk and two more uncomfortable-looking wooden chairs.

"Marshal Hayes, this is Lady Rowena Dangerfield, Guy Dangerfield's daughter. She had hired the services of Mr. Bragg in Boston some months ago on the advice of her father's lawyer, Judge Fleming. She's been quite worried about his nonappearance, of course, and it was her concern that led me to take the steps I've told you about."

"Please, what is this all about?" I glanced from one to the other and the marshal cleared his throat awkwardly, carefully placing the cigar he'd been smoking on the edge of his desk. The sight of it reminded me so vividly of poor Mr. Bragg that I must have blanched, for I felt Mark take my arm again and hold it firmly.

"Rowena! Are you sure you are all right? This heat…"

I brushed aside his concern. "You've had some news of Mr. Bragg? Marshal, whatever it is, I must know!"

"Well—" absent-mindedly he touched the large, circled star of his sagging vest, and I saw him glance at Mark, then back at me.

"Is he—is he alive?" I cried. "Tell me!"

"He's alive, all right, but I'm tellin' you ma'am, it's a miracle he is!" Gruffly the marshal chose to be blunt to cover his awkwardness at my presence. "Can't be moved of course, an' it's still touch an' go from what I heard. He's in a convent hospital in Mexico where nursin' nuns are taking care of him. He was able to mutter a few words when they found him, but they say he's still unconscious and can't be disturbed again right now."

I remember Mark taking my hatboxes from me and placing them on the dirty floor and that he made me sit in one of the rickety chairs, and fetched me a cup of steaming hot, bitter coffee.

I insisted on hearing the whole story, or as much as the marshal knew, and bit by bit, it all came out. Every bit of it was damning to one man.

Mr. Bragg's mysterious errand had been in Mexico. I

glanced at Mark, and he gave me a significant nod. Apparently he had tracked Lucas Cord to a small town in the province of Sonora; either that, or they had met there by chance. But the fact remained the Lucas Cord had got into some trouble there, and was in jail.

The marshal cleared his throat and looked at me apologetically. "Something to do with a woman and the illegal trading of guns. But Mr. Bragg arranged to speak with him, and they say he seemed angry and disturbed when he left the jail. Left town the same night and headed out across the desert towards the border, the Mex Rurales said. But then that same night, Cord busted loose from the jail." I forced myself to listen silently as the marshal told the rest of the story. Mr. Bragg had been found two days later by some peasants. He had apparently been shot from ambush and left for dead. Delirious, half out of his head with pain and thirst, he had somehow managed to crawl to the shade of a rock, and had survived.

"Those old-timers! Tough—full of guts!" The marshal said admiringly.

"But you said he managed to identify his attacker?" What had I hoped for? A denial? Confirmation of all my suspicions? I received what Mr. Bragg himself would have called "the plain, unvarnished facts."

The nuns at the convent he had been carried to understood some English. In his delirium he kept muttering a name. "Luke Cord… must find Cord…" and then, "must stop…" and my name. "Have to tell Rowena—have to warn her."

The marshal looked at me apologetically. "The nuns know some English, but not much, you understand, ma'am? By the time the Capitan of the Rurales arrived there, having received the telegraph messages we sent, Mr. Bragg had relapsed into unconsciousness. Still is, to tell the sad truth. But one of those nuns, she was a real smart woman. Sat by his bed, and wrote as much as she could understand of his mutterings. Just in case it might be important, she said. An' that's how we got the whole story." His face became grim, and his mouth was hard under the full moustache. I could suddenly understand why this grizzled, middle-aged man was a federal marshal. "Ma'am, no need to worry. Already got all the marshals in the territory alerted. Cord's been sly enough to stay just on the right side of the law since he got out of Alcatraz, but this time we got him dead to rights. We'll find him."

"Will it make any difference that the crime was committed in Mexico?" I asked, and got a look of grudging respect from Marshal Hayes.

"Bragg's an American citizen, ain't he? An' bushwhacking's bushwhacking. If the judge says we can't try Cord here, the Rurales will be glad to give him their kind of justice over there. We'll be real glad to extradite him, you bet!"

"Thank you, marshal!" Mark said firmly, and gave my fingers a warning kind of pressure before I could speak. "Rowena, I'm sorry you had to be faced with such terrible news, but I knew you would want to hear it."

"Of course I did! But oh, Mark!"

"I'm sure you'll need a little time to recover from the shock. I'll take you back to the hotel, and then—" he looked significantly at the marshal. "I might just have some further information to give you, Marshal Hayes. Nothing I am certain of just yet, but after I have talked to some people and clarified some questions in my mind. You won't let the news get out yet? I'd rather talk to my uncle first in case he thinks I've gone behind his back by not confiding in him first."

"Sure, sure Mr. Shannon! I understand! Glad to see you in here anytime."

Mark hadn't wanted me to say anything to the marshal yet, although my shock and anger were so great I would have blurted it all out, Lucas Cord's presence in this very town; the way his brother had approached me. But Mark was right, of course. This was something we should discuss together before we made up our minds as to what must be done.

We went outside, Mark's firm hand holding my arm, I still carrying hatboxes. I remember that we paused on the wooden sidewalk, to allow our eyes time to get used to the glare that reflected off the dirt-packed street. And then it happened.

I saw Todd come out of the saloon, towering head and

shoulders above the two men with him. He was laughing, his head thrown back.

I saw a flash and a puff of smoke from somewhere high up, across the street, and then the explosion of sound, reverberating in my ears. There was a crimson splotch of color on Todd's white shirtfront; widening under my horrified eyes, as very slowly he seemed to crumple and then fall.

Everything had gone very still, all motion suspended for an instant, and then everything was sound and confusion. Running feet and shouts, the marshal, running lightly and fast for a man his age, going past us. Mark's quiet "Oh my God!" and his fingers tightening around my arm.

And then I had pulled away from him, dropping the hatboxes so that they went scattering over the sidewalk, and I was running—running.

I could not see past the crowd of men who stood closely packed together, their shocked exclamations drowning out Marshal Hayes's shouted questions.

"Please!" I begged, "please let me through!"

I would have pushed and shoved if I had to, but my distraught face and manner made them give way for me.

I heard the murmuring and the muttering of voices all about me and I did not hear what was said. I had eyes, at that moment, only for Todd, whom I had fought and hated and been drawn to unwillingly. God, how still he lay, how unlike him it was, he who had always been so vital, so forceful that one could never be unaware of his presence.

A gray-haired man in a black frock coat was on his knees beside Todd. I heard him grumbling, "Will you keep the crowd back, for God's sake! Go get whoever did it, and leave me with my patient!"

Somehow, I pushed my way forward and the two cattlemen who had been with Todd moved aside to give me room.

I looked down at him, and his usually ruddy face was alarmingly pale; his eyes were closed. Someone had cut aside his jacket and shirt and the doctor's fingers were busy, probing into a bloody, terrible wound that made me collapse to my knees beside him.

"Todd!" I said. "Todd Shannon—don't you dare die!"

I thought I saw a muscle by his mouth twitch, miraculously and his eyelids moved slightly.

"Not… yet! Marry you… first…"

He spoke with difficulty, the words hardly more than a whisper, but I could feel the color rush back to my cheeks.

"Shut up, Shannon!" the doctor said with the familiarity of long-standing acquaintance. He cocked a bushy gray eyebrow at me.

"Better tell him yes, miss, or I won't answer for the consequences! Stubbornest, toughest, orneriest bastard in the world in case you didn't know it!"

With a trace of his old, bullying manner, Todd whispered, "Gonna… marry me! Always knew it… too. Didn't… you?"

"Oh, damn you. Shannon! I suppose I'll have to now!"

I could almost swear he gave a satisfied grin before his eyes closed again. And then, looking up, my eyes met Mark's. The sun was in his face, and I saw the strange and unfamiliar look of anger and frustration in his expression.

He came forward.

"Doctor?"

"He'll live! Bullet just missed the heart though. Deflected by a rib. He's gonna have to lie low."

"Thank God!" Mark said in a low voice.

And like a hammer-beat in my brain the thought kept repeating itself. *What have I done? What have I let myself in for?*

I found myself walking, like a woman in a dream, towards the hotel.

"Someone has to tell Flo. Are you sure you feel up to it?"

Mark's voice had sounded distracted. "I'm going with him, of course, and I'll have to talk to the marshal. But will you promise to stay in your room until I can come to you? You may be in danger too! Be careful," he said in a quiet, suppressed voice.

It meant nothing to me at the time, for I was still reacting to the shock I had had. But now, as I walked into the hotel lobby, my mind began to function again.

I let my legs carry me past the staring desk clerk and the small knot of men who leaned over the counter, talking excitedly.

My fingers clung to the rail as I walked up the staircase. Mark had sent me away, but the look in his eyes had held hidden meaning. I wondered if he too had seen the flash of orange light and the smoke, and if he too thought as I thought.

Thought? No, I knew it! I was certain that Lucas Cord had shot at his enemy through one of the windows of this very hotel, meaning to kill him, just as he had shot Elmer Bragg. And Ramon? Had he suspected, and tried to warn me?

It's my fault—oh God, if I had only listened to Mark—if I had warned Todd! Was it my own feeling of guilt that had made me tell Todd Shannon that I would marry him after all?

I had my hand on the door to our room when Flo came running down the passage in her robe, hair flying loose. She was panting; her eyes were large with shock and fear, shining with an unnatural brilliance.

"Is he dead? Tell me! Is Pa dead?"

I looked at her, and the terrible suspicion that had suddenly flashed into my mind became so intense that I was speechless. I pushed open the door and walked into the room, leaving her to follow me.

"He *is* dead then! I know it!"

I found myself staring at her, and I know that my eyes must have looked like stones in my cold, dead face.

"Where is he?"

She had stared towards me, but now she stopped as if struck.

"Have you gone crazy?" she whispered at last. "I don't know what you're talking about, I tell you I asked you about Pa."

"Your stepfather is very badly wounded, but he's still alive." I could hardly bear to look at her with her tangled blonde hair hanging loosely about her shoulders, full red lips half-open; lush curves of her body showing whitely through the thin silk of her wrapper.

"Do you make a habit of running down hotel corridors half-naked?"

She made an instinctive gesture of clutching the folds of silk together under her breasts, still staring at me.

"I had been sleeping!" she cried defensively. "And then I heard the shot and I ran! It was so close, so loud. I was afraid! I tell you, I knew something terrible had happened!"

"But you didn't run outside," I said with cold, pitiless logic. "You ran in the other direction, didn't you? If you had run towards the front of the building I would have seen you earlier. And it's been a good twenty minutes between the time of the shooting and *now*."

"What are you trying to say? Why are you questioning me this way? Do you think I did it? Oh God! That's almost funny! That's..."

"Be quiet!"

Something in my voice must have warned her, for her mouth dropped open.

"How did you know your stepfather had been shot at? You said you were sleeping, and then you ran. How far did you run?"

"I'm not on trial!" Angry spots of color flared in her cheeks.

"You might well be, if you don't come up with a more likely story. If you persist in protecting a criminal that makes you just as guilty as he is!"

"No! You've gone mad, that's what it is! You saw Pa shot and you've gone insane!"

She had flung her head back defiantly, but when I took a step towards her she shrank away.

"Don't come near me! How dare you talk to me this way?"

"How did you know that Todd had been shot at? I'm warning you, if you won't answer me, I'll fetch the marshal here and you can answer *his* questions."

"You'd do it too, wouldn't you? You've always hated me!" Catching the look in my eye she bit her lip, and spoke quietly.

"I ran to the window first. Isn't that the natural thing to do? When I saw—well, how can you blame me for being so upset? I grabbed my robe off the chair, and then I thought I heard footsteps, running! I was so afraid! So I grabbed up my robe and ran outside."

"Where to?"

"Why do I have to tell you? You aren't..."

"Go on," I pursued inexorably, and she dropped her head sulkily, bare toes tracing a pattern on the carpet.

"How can I remember? I was hysterical by then. I remember screaming, and then I was just running! Away from that horrible sight, I guess. Upstairs. To Mark's room, and I pounded at the door and screamed for him to come out until—until I remembered that I thought I saw him out there too. And afterwards, oh I just can't remember! I think I sat on the floor, all huddled up, and I cried." Her hate-filled look said to me, "Just try and prove anything different!"

"What clever lies you can dream up on the spur of the moment!" I murmured viciously, unable to help myself. Because she was lying, of course. I would have sensed it, even if I hadn't seen it on her face.

"Why don't you admit you don't *want* to believe me? You'd like to get me out of the way, wouldn't you? So you and Pa…"

"Do you really imagine I'd need to get you out of the way, as you put it, in order to do anything I please?"

Sick at her, and sick at myself for my lack of control I turned away and saw the bed with its rumpled damp sheets; covers kicked off onto the floor, pillows pushed to one side.

I walked towards it slowly, as if drawn by a magnet

Behind me, Flo's voice rose hysterically. "Well? What's wrong now? I was sleeping. I already told you that!"

God, but she sounded guilty!

The animal scent of their mating rose from the bed to assault my nostrils as I walked closer, bringing back ugly memories.

"Then tell me this. Did he fire that shot before or after? Did you watch him aim the rifle and squeeze the trigger?"

She put her hand up against her mouth, her eyes going from me to the bed and back.

"I—I don't…"

"Where did he go?"

"There you go again! Attacking me! Flinging accusations…"

I was suddenly so tired, so sick to my stomach that I had to sit down. Not on the bed. Like animals… the thought went round and round in my brain. No wonder she didn't want to go out with me this morning. She knew where he was and she knew he'd come, as soon as I was out of the way.

I sank down onto the small, plush-covered chair in front of the dressing table and rested my chin on my hand.

Thinking she had won some kind of victory, Flo's eyes began to glow with hysterical anger.

"Aren't you ashamed of yourself! You have a vicious, evil mind! Even with Pa lying hurt you have to try and get at me, don't you?"

"Oh, stop it, Flo!" My voice was quiet, but it stopped her in mid-sentence. "Do you take me for a nitwit?" I went on wearily. "I *know* what happened here in this room—on that bed. The whole room reeks of your lovemaking! How could you do it? How could you let him touch you? And especially after…"

"After what? After what? And you tell me something, you bitch, with your airs and your cold manners, how would you know what it's like?" She spat the words at me, coming closer, her eyes gleaming with hate. "Ah, but you gave yourself away, didn't you? Accusing *me* and pretending to be such a saint yourself when all the time…" She gave a peal of shrill laughter. "God! What a hypocrite! Wait till I tell Pa. Wait till I tell Mark! Or was it one of them? How many times has *your* bed looked this way and smelled this way, Lady Rowena?"

I looked back at her without expression. "At least I haven't fallen into bed with a murdering animal. Where is he, Flo? Did he fire that shot from this window?"

She glared at me defiantly, and with a shrug I rose to my feet and started towards the door. She came after me.

"Where are you going? Damn you!"

"To fetch the marshal. Better get dressed before I return with him."

"No! No you wouldn't dare! Because I'd tell…"

"Tell what, Flo Jeffords? I think it is I who will tell the story."

"No, wait!" Her fingers clutched at my sleeve. "Wait, I'll tell you, but only if you promise you won't tell them! You can't! Pa won't like it, anyhow! I think he'd rather die than have that old scandal dragged up."

I paused, leaning back against the door because I didn't want her to know that my knees were weak with tension.

"All right then, it *is* true, I've been seeing Luke. You'd already guessed that, hadn't you? He told me you'd found that red silk, and he said we had to be more careful."

"And today?"

She gave me a gleaming, resentful look. "Yes! He did come today! I knew he was going to be in town and I spoke to him but you weren't clever enough to guess *that,* were you? We arranged another signal, and soon after you left, he came to me." Her eyes taking on their old, wild brilliance she said, "He couldn't stay away from me, you know! If you only knew all the risks he took, just to see me again! And he's a *man,* do you hear me? *You* wouldn't know what it's like to have a real man, after having had to lie with a soft, potbellied slug with creeping hands and nothing much else!"

"I don't want to hear the sordid details! It's *today* that concerns me."

Flo shrugged sullenly. "I don't know! I was with Luke, but we had to hurry because *you* might come back. He left. And then later I heard that shot! I was telling the truth! I'd almost fallen asleep when I heard it, and I ran out, just as I told you!"

"You ran looking for *him,* didn't you?" I accused. "You saw what had happened and you knew he'd done it!"

"Maybe I did go looking for him. Maybe I didn't. You can guess till you're blue in the face, but that's all I know!"

She burst into a storm of hysterical weeping that seemed genuine enough.

I left the room, closing the door on the sound of her sobbing. And because I could think of nowhere else to go, I went upstairs to Mark's room, feeling the door push open easily when I twisted the knob. Another lie, then, but I was too strained and exhausted to think about it just then. I sat in the chair by the window and waited.

PART III:

THE VIOLENT PEACE

Fourteen

༄

WE RETURNED TO THE SD IN VERY DIFFERENT MOODS FROM THE ones in which we had left it. Mark kept telling me that I had changed. His face was concerned and sad when he attempted to talk me out of what he called my "frozen coldness."

I was impatient with him.

"But I haven't changed. Don't you see, Mark? I had let myself grow lazy. I let my emotions rule me, and I allowed things to happen that should not have. I should have listened to my reason."

"You're a woman, Rowena!"

"Must that inescapable physical fact also make me weak?"

No one would ever be able to accuse me of weakness again. I had let myself go in this warm climate; let myself be coddled into relaxing my guard against people. And look what it had done! Todd was hurt, still forced to lie in loudly complaining inactivity in Silver City. And I, who had procrastinated and sat dreaming in the sun, waiting for something to happen, was the new manager of the SD. It was Todd himself who had insisted upon it.

"Mark will help you. He knows enough about ranching to tell you what has to be done. But you might as well learn the ropes, gal. Ain't you always reminding me that you're a full partner? Gonna be that way after we're married too, except in the bedroom."

"You're in no condition to think about that *now,* Todd

Shannon!" I said severely, but he had only laughed; the laugh turning into a cough that had sent the doctor hurrying in, with a quizzical glance for me.

"Didn't I tell you this old goat was to be kept quiet? Look at him—laughing, with a bullet hole that grazed his lung! Out with you, miss. You two can talk over weddin' plans later."

Todd was jubilant, in a better mood than I had ever seen him in before, in spite of his wound. But I would not let myself think about a wedding yet. We would talk about that later, when Todd was well, and back at the SD. In the meantime, I would be able to show him how well I had managed. I was determined that nothing would go wrong.

I moved my things into the big house, although my father's house would always remain my own special home to which I could escape whenever I pleased. Jules and Marta would manage very well, as they had done before I came. I had to explain to them, though, how practical this new arrangement was. I must learn as much as I could about running a big ranch, and the *palacio* was the hub of all the routine and activity. If I displayed any weakness, it was in not telling Marta the whole truth about the events in Silver City. Sooner or later she would learn that her "señor Lucas" was a hunted outlaw again, the price on his head endorsed by the Territorial Governor himself.

Todd knew, of course. We could hardly have hidden it from him. Mark never told him that I had known Lucas Cord would be in Silver City. The story we told was that Flo had caught a glimpse of him and recognized him, but too late to result in his capture.

And as for Flo herself, although she had returned with us, traveling in unusual silence, she took pains to avoid me, just as I did to avoid remaining too long in the same room with her.

I moved into the largest of the guest bedrooms and spent the first few weeks in learning all I could. I visited every line-shack, inspected every boundary fence. And in the evenings I studied the books that Todd had so painstakingly kept.

The pattern of my days assumed some kind of routine. I rose early, had breakfast with Mark, and then rode out. Either Mark or the taciturn Chuck Daly went with me. I felt that the men were beginning to accept me, especially when they found that I never complained of tiredness or the heat and was genuinely interested in the tasks each one of them performed. Even the hard-bitten Texans had stopped giving me slow, insolent glances when they encountered me.

How quickly one routine can replace another! The only breaks from the sameness of my days occurred when I went back "home" to read occasional entries in my father's journals. But I went seldom—perhaps once or twice a week; and then only to stay for a short time. On those visits I sensed a kind of withdrawal in the way that Marta and Jules greeted me, and one day decided to question her about it.

"Something is the matter, and you might as well stop shaking your head at me in that stubborn fashion. Won't you tell me what's troubling you? I'm still the same person, you know, even though I'm living at the *palacio*."

She began to talk to me in her quick, colloquial Spanish, as she used to do.

"The patrona has changed! The patrona does not feel compassion, as she did before. Si, I will say this, even though the patrona has the power to cast me out."

"I wish you would stop calling me 'the patrona'!" I protested. "Really, Marta, I'm only doing what my father wished me to do. I'm learning to be a rancher. I ask you, would he have approved of my lying in the sun and doing nothing?"

Her face took on a rather stubborn look. "Your padre would have understood. He wanted only that you should be happy."

"And do I look as if I am unhappy? I tell you, Marta, I'm happier this way, when I'm doing something, learning something. I could not shut myself away from life forever. Surely you understand that?"

"I understand that the patrona is young. And soon the patrona will be married. What will happen then?"

I frowned. "What do you mean by that? My marriage will not change things. I have a feeling my father would have approved."

"It is not for me to say. The patrona must do as she wishes, of course."

Gentle reasoning was useless against the wall of Marta's peasant stubbornness. I gave up, in the end, and went back to my large, impersonal bedroom in the *palacio*.

The bolt still held the trapdoor closed fast in my old room. I would have no unexpected, unwelcome callers *here*. But why had he come? What had he tried to tell me? Lucas Cord was Flo's lover. Ramon Kordes had looked deeply into my eyes and hinted of some mystery. What kind of men were these seemingly opposite brothers? Ramon had been quiet and soft-spoken. Lucas was brash and rough. A murderer, blinded by his need for revenge. But why had he tried to kill Elmer Bragg?

I asked myself questions that had no answers, and was stern with myself when I was alone. Soon Todd would be well enough to come back, and then I would find the responsibilities I had assumed taken out of my hands. Did I want it that way?

Flo surprised me as I came out of my bedroom one day. Her manner was sullen, as it had been ever since we had left Silver City, missing the grand ball she had looked forward to.

"I guess Pa'll be well enough to come home soon, and you two won't want *me* around!"

I had had a tiring day, and I said wearily, "Oh, *really* Flo, are we back to that again?"

"You even sound like a stepmother already! My God! And don't give me that look. I'm a grown woman, and I'll swear if I want to!"

"Please feel free to do so then," I said politely, turning aside to pass her, but she stood in my way, her eyes glittering.

"I haven't said what I have to say yet."

"Very well. And that is?"

"I'm going back. To New York. To Derek. Even *he* looks better after these weeks of living like a prisoner! I tell you, I'm bored, and I'm sick of it! I'm sick of Mark's sanctimonious sermons, and I'm sick of looking at your face. You're even getting to *talk* like Pa, you know that? And I don't want to hear him shouting and lecturing at me either. So there you are!"

I returned her defiant look. "So I see! Have you spoken to Mark about your plans yet?"

"Why should I? You're the patrona, aren't you? You're the real boss around here ever since Pa said so, and even Mark realizes that. So why should I tell him anything? You can't stop me, anyhow. I'm over twenty-one; I'm a married woman, and Pa would be the first to say my place is back with my husband!"

I nodded coolly. "You're right, of course. Well, let me know when you're ready to leave, won't you. I'll arrange for some of the men to go with you as far as Santa Rita."

"I was planning to go on from El Paso. I have friends there—the Bartletts—Mark knows them, in case you don't want to believe me! I hate New Mexico. At least Texas is a state and the stages run regularly."

"El Paso is a considerable distance away. Have you thought of how you'll get there?"

"I can catch the stage at Deming or Las Cruces, can't I?"

I sighed. "We'll make some arrangement then, since you are determined to leave. But you will send a telegram to your husband?"

"You don't trust me, do you? Not that it's really any concern of yours, but I'll write out a message if you like, and *you* can have it sent to Derek. I've no doubt it'll make him so happy he'll go right out and make another couple of thousands on the stock market!"

She brushed past me then, as if to indicate that all communication between us had ended, and I went on my way downstairs, wondering what she was up to this time.

When I discussed the matter with him that evening, Mark seemed to think that Flo's departure would be the best possible thing for all of us.

"You know that her presence here has us all on edge," he reminded me gently. "Heavens, Rowena, it's just as well she leaves before Uncle Todd gets back, or there'll be the devil to pay. She has a knack of rubbing him the wrong way, and when he finds out how deeply she's been involved in all the unpleasantness that has taken place, well…" He raised his shoulders expressively, and I was forced to agree that he was right. Neither of us could have turned Flo out of what was, after all, her home. But she had been the first to suggest going back to her wifely duties.

Mark and I went along with Flo as far as Fort Selden, where we paid a courtesy call on the colonel who was in command of the cavalry unit there. The tall gentlemanly officer assured us she would have an escort of soldiers all the way into El Paso.

"It's not putting us out at all. There's been trouble with the Apaches lately, so all the coaches get an escort. Just to prevent anything, you understand? Show of force. Victorio and his bunch understand *that*."

I discovered that Colonel Poynter had known my father.

"Fine man. Best chess player it's been my good fortune to encounter."

He was also a frank man, as I was to find out

"Guy should have been alive today. But there was something eating at him inside. He'd keep things to himself. Even his best friends didn't know what he was really thinking. Poured it all out in those journals he kept. You've read them?"

I had to confess that I had not read them all.

"Ought to, if you want to understand him. But I can see where it would be difficult for you to feel close. You didn't have a chance to know him, and he didn't know you, although he'd talk, sometimes, after the brandy, of how you'd turn out to be a true Dangerfield."

"Did he tell you about the Dangerfield devil? Someone described it to me once as a taint in the blood. All stemming from an ancestor who was a real witch."

Colonel Poynter gave me a rather austere smile. "Ah, yes. But in your case, Lady Rowena, I think we can safely say the traditional devil has skipped a generation!"

I thanked him demurely and we went on to speak of other things. Mark came in, and Mrs. Poynter rose from the corner where she had sat silently, engrossed in her sewing, to announce that she was sure supper must be ready.

The stage left on time for El Paso, but Mark and I stayed another day before we returned to the ranch. I liked Colonel

Poynter and his quiet wife, and I was genuinely interested in hearing more about the Apache Indians I'd been told so much about.

"Let us hope you'll never meet any." Colonel Poynter said grimly. "Believe me, Lady Rowena, and I don't mean to try and frighten you, none of the stories you have heard are exaggerations. They are warriors by profession, they claim all this land as their own, and they bitterly resent not only Americans but the Spaniards and Mexicans as well. They are savage, magnificent fighters. Enemies to be respected and feared, Lady Rowena. Make no mistake about it."

"But you *are* trying to frighten me, colonel!"

He gave me a long, thoughtful look, as if measuring my courage. "Far from it. I'm merely encouraging caution at all times. The Apaches have not chosen to show themselves yet; perhaps it's because they're cautious too, in their way. But they are *there*. Don't make the mistake of underestimating them."

I returned to the ranch in a sober mood, although Mark tried to tease me out of it.

"The colonel's been a frontier soldier a long time. I think he sees Apaches behind every clump of mesquite."

"Mark, you know that's not quite true! Colonel Poynter is a *soldier*. He knows the Indians, and I'm convinced he knows what he's talking about. He didn't want to frighten me, only warn me."

"Oh what, for heaven's sake?"

"I'm not sure, Mark," I said slowly. "But as commander of one of the largest forts in the area, I'm sure Colonel Poynter is a well-informed man. And as you pointed out, he's been in the territory a long time. He knew my father, and he knows Todd. I'm sure he knows everything else as well. There was some reason for his warning, Mark, and it wasn't just because the Apaches have been giving him trouble recently."

He gave me a troubled look. "If Colonel Poynter had heard anything specific, he'd have given us a specific warning. You were thinking of Lucas Cord, weren't you? Rowena, he's miles away by now, hiding out somewhere! And now that Cousin Flo has decided to leave us and go back to being a respectable housewife, he has no ally in the enemy camp, has he?"

All the same, I thought, I could sense an underlying uneasiness in Mark as well, and I found myself wishing that Todd would be able to return soon.

Our relationship was now close to brother and sister, but both of us realized very well the infeasibility of living together in the same house without Flo's presence as a chaperon. I returned to my little house, and I thought Marta and Jules were glad to see me back, although Maria's manner remained more formal than it had been before.

The days went by, and I passed them much as I had been used to during the past weeks. It became hotter, although we sometimes saw thunderclouds gather behind the distant mountain peaks.

I was content to keep busy, and yet I was not content. I had the strangest feeling that I was waiting for something to happen, something to interrupt the dull routine I had fallen into.

Todd... I thought. Soon, he'll be back, and we will start to quarrel again. He will infuriate me, and then kiss me forcibly into a temporary truce.

But we were to be married. I had given my word; it had been publicly announced. Marriage was hardly a temporary affair. How often I'd promised myself that I would never marry, and yet, suddenly and inexplicably, I found myself committed. Did I love him? I respected his strength, and I grudgingly admired the force of his will. But *love*? Did I know what it was?

The letter from Flo shook me out of my self-concern. It arrived only a day before Todd was due to come back, as I'm sure she meant it to, and was addressed to Mark.

I am only sending this letter because I'm sure Derek will write to find out why I have not arrived yet. You may tell him, from me, that I have decided to live, for a change. God, how bored I was. How tired of being watched, and having all my days and hours planned for me! I know you are going to show this letter to Rowena, and I don't care!

If you're content with standing on the fringes and accepting second-best, I am not.

I'm tired of gentlemen; I need a man. Ask Rowena, she will know what I mean. Poor Mark. Pa thought once that I would do the convenient thing and marry you, did you know that? Then she came, and spoiled everything. But it makes no difference now.

I'm going with Lucas. Send those marshals after us and I'll swear in public that we were lovers, that he was with me when Pa was shot at. Think of what a juicy scandal that would make!

You're a clever attorney, Mark, and will think of some story that will satisfy everyone. But I want to be left alone. Don't bother me, and I won't bother you. That's rather clever, don't you think?

There were several pages of recriminations, mostly directed at me. But the gist of Flo's communication was clear.

And, as Mark and I had both feared, the effect on Todd was catastrophic. His face became red, and he began to shout at Mark and me. It was our fault for not watching her, and especially for letting her go! He'd hire men to go after her and bring her back; if the U.S. marshals in the territory couldn't do what they were supposed to, he'd hire his own killers to go after Luke Cord, men as dangerous and predatory as Cord was himself.

Mark tried to explain in his quiet, reasonable voice. I merely walked out of the room.

"Come back here, damn you!" Todd shouted behind me. "I ain't through with you yet!" Ignoring him, I kept walking, and was halfway across the courtyard before he caught up with me.

"Rowena! Where in hell do you think you're goin'? Told you I wasn't through talkin' to you yet."

He caught my arm. I turned my head and looked at him coldly.

"I told you once that I would not be shouted at. Talk to yourself, if you will. Shout at Mark. But remember one thing, Todd Shannon, you don't own me."

"You walked out on me, dammit! I'm not used to that."

"You were being totally unreasonable. I refuse to listen to loud, childish blusterings."

"By God! You dare tell me I'm bein' childish? An' you no more than a chit of a brat."

"In that case, I'm sure you won't want to marry me."

I tried to pull my arm free, and his grip tightened. He pulled me around to face him.

"Do you have to make a public exhibition of your brute strength?"

"Stop cuttin' at me with that sharp tongue of yours, girl! Can you blame me for being angry? Flo's made fools of us all by flauntin' her shamelessness under the noses of the whole territory. An' you expect me to sit back an' talk about it *reasonably*?"

"There's no reason that you can't talk *quietly,* is there? And to waste your breath trying to place blame is useless."

"Well, by God, I ain't gonna let it go! She's shamed *me* by runnin' off with that damn halfbreed who tried to kill me."

"I'm not making excuses for Flo, but you have to remember she's a grown woman."

"I'm remembering a lot," Todd said grimly.

But he had seen that I would not let myself be intimidated, and in the end, grumbling, he apologized for losing his temper at me.

The whole unpleasant business could not be pushed out of the way and forgotten as easily as that. Had I ever thought it could be? We heard news of Flo. She had been seen in San Antonio with Lucas Cord. Someone thought he recognized the two of them in Amarillo. Perhaps Lucas realized her presence only brought the bounty hunters snapping too closely at his heels, for he apparently abandoned her in one of the wild Kansas cow towns.

It was Mark who told me the story, hoping to forearm me before I heard it from Todd, who was almost beside himself with rage.

"It's an ugly business, Rowena! God knows why he encouraged her to run to him, unless he wanted to make a public spectacle of Todd Shannon's stepdaughter."

"You think it was only for revenge? All of this?"

"What else could it be? He used her and then discarded her as publicly as he could. I'm sorry, Rowena. It seems as if I am always the one to give you unpleasant news. He put her up for auction in a cheap saloon and lost her in a poker game to a professional gambler."

I could hardly believe such callousness, but the report had come from a detective of the Pinkerton Agency. And having got rid of Flo, who must have become an encumbrance, Lucas Cord vanished again.

"Couldn't the detective have done something?"

"He heard the whole story from a man who was present." Mark shook his head glumly. "By the time he started making a closer investigation, no one could tell him where she'd gone. They said she left town with the gambler."

Fifteen

ᴅᴜʀɪɴɢ ᴛʜᴇ ᴡᴇᴇᴋs ᴛʜᴀᴛ ꜰᴏʟʟᴏᴡᴇᴅ ᴛʜᴇ ɴᴇᴡs ᴏꜰ Fʟᴏ's sordid escapade Todd became like a man obsessed. Mark confided that he felt he had to walk around his uncle on tiptoe; I avoided visiting the *palacio* as much as possible.

I saw more of Mark than I did of Todd, and when I did see Todd he seemed preoccupied. In his present mood it was easy to avoid setting a date for our wedding. "After the matter has been settled... after the trail drive..."

"I'm gonna bring you back the finest wedding dress you ever did see," Todd said in one of his better moods. "An' diamonds for your ring and your hair."

"Oh, no," I protested involuntarily, "not diamonds!" Seeing his chagrined look, I added quickly, "I never have liked diamonds very much. But I do like sapphires, or emeralds."

"You'll have whatever you want, little girl. Just so you'll keep right on puttin' up with me."

I was swept into his arms, and talking stopped. It was always that way. And yet there were times, when I was alone, that I couldn't quite believe that I was actually to be married. "I won't be any man's slave!" I used to say bravely to myself. Was it possible that I had given in so meekly?

I saw less and less of Todd once the spring roundup had begun, although I did, on occasion, ride out before the sun came up to see what went on. It seemed hard, back-breaking work, this task of hunting out the cattle, branding calves, and sorting out what the men called "the gather." It seemed that preparations for the long trail drive to the nearest railhead could take months, depending on how far the cattle had strayed.

As a member of the newly formed Cattlemen's Association, Todd would not be making the drive alone. Because of constant problems with Indians and renegade rustlers, the cattlemen in the area would be making an enormous combined drive this year.

"Meant to have Mark go along with us," Todd said gruffly. "But I guess he'd be more useful stayin' here keepin' an eye on things."

I knew he was thinking of that time, long ago, when he had ridden out with my father to find silver, and had come back to find he had lost everything he had worked for and loved. But I could not help feeling sorry for Mark, who was, after all, a lawyer, not a rancher.

When I mentioned this to Todd, he merely snorted. "Mark knows where his bread's buttered! He's my heir and it's high time he learned the cattle business." And then he gave me an exaggerated wink. "That is, unless *you* change things, sweetheart. Give me a son, and Mark can go back to Boston and his law books."

"Todd Shannon, I am not a brood mare!"

"You're too pretty for that. An' you better stop botherin' about Mark or I'm liable to get jealous!"

"It's a trifle late for that, isn't it?" I responded pertly, but as usual he laughed, with the assurance of a man who had no doubts of his hold over me. Yes, Todd was sure of me now, but was I sure of myself? Of my own feelings? I had come here to find myself and to accept a challenge, but found no peace, only violence and confusion. Several times I reminded myself that I was a rich woman. Giving up the SD would mean nothing. I would still be rich enough to travel where I pleased, do as I pleased. But how could I leave now? There was Todd, whose strong, physical attraction for me I could not deny. It was an attraction of the senses alone, but did that matter? Was this what people called "love"?

And then there was the thought of my father, who had

made everything possible, who had loved and trusted me without even knowing me. He had been a man who saw good in everybody and everyone had respected him, or so it seemed. What had he wanted of me? Why had he made the stipulation that I lived in New Mexico for a year at least?

I tried not to think about the mysterious hints that Ramon Kordes had thrown out. Most of all, I tried not to think about his brother. But then the news came from New Orleans, bringing all the unpleasantness back to the surface again.

Flo was dead. Killed by a flying bullet in some barroom brawl. Poor Flo. So bored, so anxious to *live*!

"He killed her! Just as surely as if he'd put the bullet in her personally. Everything, everyone that belongs to me they've destroyed. But I swear to God that this time I'm goin' to wipe out that whole brood of rattlers!"

I had learned that it was useless trying to talk reason to Todd when he was in such a mood, so I went back home; to be haunted, in my dreams that night, by visions of Flo as I remembered her. Poor, silly Flo.

I went back to reading my father's journals, obediently starting with those that told of his early life. It was difficult at first to imagine him as a young man, filled with rebellion, ambition, hopes and dreams. How had he turned into a lonely old man who sought oblivion in a bottle of brandy? When had he stopped hoping? Too late... too late... that was what everyone said, looking at me. I had arrived too late, but was it my fault? What was expected of me?

Nothing, Mark said. My father would have been the last man to demand any sacrifices of me. "All he wanted was your happiness, and if you have found it Rowena, hang onto it. Stop torturing yourself with supposition! that you are failing him in some way."

"Oh, Mark, whatever would I do without you?"

"Very well, I'm sure!" His tone was wry. "Do you know what I admire most about you? Your strength and your character. Yes, I think you will always do very well. Your father would have been proud of you."

I was relieved that Mark had assumed the role of affectionate friend. That he seemed to accept the fact that I was to marry his uncle, after all. I can't imagine what I would have done without his companionship and calm common sense.

After Todd had left on the long trail drive, Mark and I spent as much time together as propriety would allow. I had almost forgotten, by this time, that he had ever declared his love for me, and it never occurred to me that our being thrown together so much might prove a strain on even *his* gentlemanly forbearance.

My first inkling came one night when I had invited him to my house for dinner, and had added carelessly that he might spend the night, since Marta would be sleeping in the house to observe the proper conventions.

We had been playing chess; he startled me when he rose from his chair so suddenly that the board tipped over, scattering the pieces all over the floor.

"Mark! What on earth is the matter with you? And I was just about to put your king in check!"

"You must know that I cannot possibly stay!" he said in a strangely suppressed tone of voice.

I stared at him in dismay.

"But why on earth not? What has got into you?"

"Rowena—dear God, do you take me for a man of steel? Or not as a man at all? Don't you realize what it means to see you every day, to be constantly with you, knowing that you are promised to my uncle and that I can never possess you?"

"I'm sorry, Mark. I hadn't thought—that is, I thought you had forgotten all about your infatuation for me."

"It was no infatuation, and I'm trying hard to be a gentleman, and the brother you seem to want. But don't make it harder on me by inviting me to spend the night under the same roof!" He added, still in the same, controlled tones, "If I thought you loved my uncle, it might have been easier. I'm not such a dolt that I couldn't accept the fact that you might love someone else. But you don't love him. I might as well say this, Rowena, for I've promised myself to be frank with you always. You're drawn to Uncle Todd, I can see that. You've never met a man quite like him before, with the same aura of power and ruthlessness, and he intrigues you, does he not? But you don't love him any more than you love me!"

I took a deep breath, and tried to smile. "Well! I may not like what you said, but I'm flattered that you were frank! Mark, I *am* sorry! I've been selfish. I haven't thought of your feelings, only how happy I am to have your friendship and your companionship. And as for what you said about my feelings for Todd, well, that is something I cannot discuss, not even with you. Can we still be friends?"

He had remained standing; now he sighed deeply, shoulders slumping. "We'll always be friends, I hope. And I apologize for the outburst. Just don't invite me to spend the night with you again, will you?"

I was sorry for my thoughtlessness after Mark left, and rather anxious the next day lest our relationship might be spoiled. But his manner was just the same as usual and his smile just as warm, so I put the whole thing out of my mind and let the days fall into their old familiar routine.

Nothing was changed, I told myself, *nothing*.

We rode together, played chess together, and went over the account books as usual, neither of us making any mention of that night. Because our association was an innocent one, I never gave a thought to what other people might think. It seemed as if I had flouted convention for so long, in almost everything I had done, that I had ceased to think of it. After all, we weren't living under the same roof and Todd had left us together. Mark was his nephew; I was his partner and his affianced bride. We were almost related!

And then…

It is easy to ask oneself afterwards, what if I had not done this? What if I had done thus instead? But as I recall it, I had gone to bed exceptionally early that night and had waked earlier than usual. In fact, while I breakfasted I reread the letter I had received from Mrs. Poynter, inviting me to spend a few days with her and the colonel at Fort Selden. She had heard that Todd was away, and I think she imagined I must be upset by the news of Flo's death, and lonely for female companionship. In any case she mentioned that she and Colonel Poynter would be visiting El Paso, and she thought I might enjoy visiting that famous border town myself.

I thought I might discuss it with Mark. He had said he would visit me at about noon, but if I left my house early enough, perhaps I might catch him before he left to watch the breaking in of the raw mustangs. Perhaps I could accompany him myself.

Marta shook her head disapprovingly when she realized I meant to ride out by myself. "It is not wise. Better take Jules with you."

"And then who would stay here with *you*? I know my way by now, and I think I'm capable of looking after myself." To allay her fears, I showed her the small derringer I would carry with me, slipped into the pocket of my riding skirt.

"I still think that you should wait for señor Mark."

"But I'm not going to! Don't frown at me, Marta, you know how stubborn I can be!"

I left to the accompaniment of dark mutterings in a Mexican dialect I found hard to understand, and many doleful shakes of her head; but I was lighthearted this morning and would not let Marta's forebodings spoil my ride.

It was exhilarating to ride alone, to feel the long, smooth stride of my own horse under me, and to feel that I, Rowena Dangerfield, owned all this savagely beautiful land I was riding through. A light breeze, blowing down from the mountains, whipped tendrils of hair about my face, and I reveled in the feeling of freedom that riding by myself always brought to me.

What did it matter if Mark had already left the house? I would let my horse rest in the stables, order another saddled and go out to meet him. Perhaps I'd have my noon meal at the chuck wagon, with the men. Even beans would taste good on a day like this!

I was lighthearted enough to ride past the tall saguaro cactus without the unpleasant feeling that seeing it usually gave me. Nothing must spoil my day. I topped the small ridge where Flo and I had rested our horses on that day that now seemed so long ago, and cantered my horse down the gentle slope on the other side. Not too far to go now.

And then I saw him. A tall rider, hat pushed back on his head, reining his mount around so that it blocked my way.

"Mornin,' ma'am! Sure is a nice mornin' for a ride, ain't it? But if you're lookin' for Mark, he's already gone. Left real early this morning."

"Mark?" I said haughtily, lifting an eyebrow and he chuckled.

"Yeah, that's what I call him. Why should I tack a mister onto his name? *He* ain't payin' my wages!"

He had forced me to rein my horse to a stop, and he made no effort to let me by.

I had disliked this man ever since that particular morning in Silver City, when he had stared me up and down so insolently. I disliked him even more now, but I didn't fear him. Not yet...

"I'm paying your wages, Gil Pardee," I said coldly. "And I'll thank you to move aside. I'm in a hurry!"

He put his head on one side and studied me openly, taking in every detail of my appearance, I was sure. "Well, now, lady boss, if that ain't right unfriendly of you! And here I thought I was bein' obligin,' tryin' to save you a trip to the house. But I guess you ain't used to our ways out here yet, are you?"

For the first time I had a feeling of impending trouble, and my lips tightened. Was he trying to frighten me? Or to test me? Whatever his motives were, I refused to show fear.

I returned his stare with an icy one of my own. "Mr. Pardee, you are in my way!"

"Well, now, is that right? Shucks, an' here I thought you might appreciate some company, you bein' all alone and all."

"You thought wrong then, and my patience is wearing thin."

"Guess you *are* in a hurry to see Mark. I've often said to myself, 'now there's one lucky feller!' Wouldn't mind bein' left home to look after a purty little lady like you myself." The meaning of his sneering words was beginning to penetrate, and I felt my knuckles turn white with the effort I was making to control my temper.

"Mr. Pardee, you may consider yourself fired. I neither like your attitude nor your manners. You can pick up your wages at the house."

He shook his head infuriatingly, grinning meanly.

"You ain't got that right, lady boss. Todd Shannon hired me. An' I don't guess he'll fire me either, if he hears what I could tell him about the way you and that lawyer nephew of his been carryin' on." His grin widened, showing tobacco-stained teeth. "But if you was to be as nice to me as you are to Mark, well, things might be different! I ain't a bad sort, once you get to know me. Always found it easy to be persuaded by a purty little gal."

In some ways the situation I now found myself in was almost laughable. But I had begun to be frightened, although I would not show it. "If Todd Shannon ever finds out what you have been saying to me he'd kill you," I said contemptuously. "You'd better start riding, Gil Pardee, and I'd ride fast, if I were you!"

His smile had been replaced by a tight-lipped leer.

"Think you're too good for me, huh? Mebbe you think I don't know enough to please a lady. But that little Flo gal didn't think so! Fact is, she was real happy at what I could give her. Came after me askin' for more. Now, what makes you think you'd be any different? You bin giving it to Mark so I guess you can spare some for me."

His sudden, lightning-swift movement took me off guard. All the time he was talking, he'd been edging his horse closer to mine, and now he grabbed for the reins I held so tightly.

Dancer reared, almost unseating me. And I felt his leg brush mine. He had hold of the reins and was trying to control both Dancer and his own horse. I heard him cursing loudly.

And then I shot him. God knows how I contrived to pull the small gun from my pocket. I think I did it quite by instinct. He was so close, and I have always been a good shot. I hardly realized what I had done until I saw him start to fall, his mouth open, his eyes staring wide with shock. There was blood all over his shirt. I had time to notice that before I let the gun drop, my hands full with trying to control my frightened horse.

I had killed a man. And I had never realized before how easy it was to kill. Mark said I was suffering from shock. He said that was why my body felt so rigid, my face and limbs so cold. And yet, shock or no, I had left Gil Pardee lying on his face in the dirt, with his blood slowly seeping out to form a puddle under him, and I had ridden on to find Mark.

"Does it make me a murderer? Should we send for the sheriff?"

In Todd's enormous study Mark forced me to drink brandy while he knelt by me, chafing my hands and saying soothing things that I scarcely heard. My voice sounded strangely cold in my own ears.

"I remember killing a charging wild buffalo once in India. I dropped onto one knee—there was scarcely time to take aim, you know. But my shot took him just where I had meant to, and dropped him only a few feet from me. My grandfather was very proud of me that day."

"Rowena, you must stop thinking about it. You did what your instincts made you do. What you had to do. My God!" His fingers tightened convulsively over mine. "When I think of what might have happened! If you had not killed him, I think I would have. And of the other men here. You mustn't go on blaming yourself."

"But I don't. And can't you see it, Mark? That is the worst part of all. I killed a man, and I feel nothing. Not even remorse. I think I hated him so much at that moment I wanted to kill him."

The sheriff came and went, his face grim and serious. His attitude was the same as Mark's. I had been defending my honor, my virtue. I had merely saved someone else the trouble of killing the brute. No one reproached me for having been out riding by myself, in spite of all the warnings I had received. No one doubted my story.

I was perfectly calm, perfectly composed. Only Mark knew what the man had actually told me. He was worried about me.

"Pardee was a sick animal. After what he said about Flo… Rowena, you know Uncle Todd would never have believed him! Promise me you won't keep brooding about this."

The brandy made me feel warm again and curiously light-headed, but I was still able to think clearly in spite of it.

"I think I must go away for a while. That invitation from Mrs. Poynter came at just the right time."

"You mustn't run away! Rowena, no one blames you."

"You mean they did not say so openly. But those other men—the Texans who were Pardee's friends. How do I know what they might not think?"

"You saw for yourself how angry they were! The man was a loner, they said. I don't think anyone liked him very well. He was a boaster."

"He was a human being, and I killed him."

"Rowena, don't!"

"I want to go away, Mark," I said stubbornly. "I need to get away for a while. I shall write to Mrs. Poynter tomorrow."

Nothing he could say was able to change my mind. Perhaps I was running away. Perhaps all I needed was a change. Too much had happened in too short a time, and a holiday would do me good.

Sixteen

A YOUNG SOLDIER FROM NEARBY FORT THORN BROUGHT ME Mrs. Poynter's reply, and within a week I was ready to leave.

Mark went with me as far as Rincon, where I boarded the stage that would take me to Fort Selden, a little less than a day's ride away. We had a small escort of soldiers from Fort Thorn.

Our small escort of soldiers was in high spirits. Most of them were young, except for an older man wearing sergeant's chevrons. There were four other passengers. Two men; one of them a small rancher, a young army wife, going to join her husband, and another woman, a rather hard-looking female of indeterminate age, who kept to herself, her big, flower-decked hat shielding her face.

Mark leaned forward and kissed my cheek, his unusual demonstrativeness surprising me.

"Come back soon, Rowena. And take care of yourself."

The driver cracked his whip meaningfully and spat a long stream of tobacco juice into the dust. A last-minute passenger, a short man with a round moon face, shouldered past Mark and climbed in, puffing noisily, slamming the door behind him. And then we were off.

I was fortunate enough to have a window seat, and I leaned forward, waving my gloved hand at Mark. The young woman seated next to me smiled shyly.

"It's hard to say good-byes, isn't it. Mama cried all night

before I left, and I couldn't sleep a wink myself, although I'd been so looking forward to seeing Johnny again."

"I'm not going to be away for long," I said. "I'm only going for a visit." I believed it then. How sure I was!

I had chosen to wear a discreet, dove-gray dress for traveling, its bustle not quite as pronounced as on some of my other, more fashionable gowns. Trimmed with blue, it had long, tightly fitted sleeves and a high neck, with tiny blue buttons down the front of the fitted basque.

I had coiled my dark hair at the back of my head, in the Spanish fashion, and the small, modish bonnet that matched my gown sat forward on my head, with wide blue ribbons down the back. I wore no jewelry except for tiny sapphire studs in my ears.

I saw the men eye me, and then turn their eyes away. I was Todd Shannon's woman and half owner of the huge SD ranch. I think everyone in the territory knew it by now. How many of them also knew that I had killed Gil Pardee?

The young woman next to me was friendly. The round-faced man fixed his eyes on the disinterested-looking woman with the large hat, who continued to stare steadily out of the window. The rancher, for the most part, stared down at his boots.

We were an ill-assorted collection of people, I suppose, but I had grown used to that, after all the traveling I had done already.

The young woman, who said her name was Emma Jensen, apologized for asking me so many questions. But once she learned that I had already visited Fort Selden before, she wanted to know as much as she could about it.

"Johnny warned me it wasn't goin' to be easy. I mean, the heat, and the Indians, an' being cooped up an' all. But I didn't care. Johnny and I hadn't been married long when he was transferred out here." She blushed. "I guess I miss him something terrible!"

The rancher lit a cigar, after asking politely if any of the ladies would object. The round-faced man, fixing his small eyes on the tall woman at the opposite window, asked if she was going as far as El Paso.

"Goin' there myself. Have lots of friends there. You know Dan Sutherland? Owns the Matador Saloon." I could not help admiring her self-possession. Taking her eyes from the scenery outside, she looked him over without seeming to, responding coldly that she didn't think so.

"I hardly think we'd have friends in common, mister. And I'm not making this trip to make new friends."

He scowled, deflated. I think he would have said something else if he hadn't noticed the unfriendly looks that Emma Jensen and I directed at him.

We traveled on in silence, while the sun grew hotter as it rose higher in the sky. There was a shotgun guard beside the driver because we carried silver on the coach. I could hear the voices of the soldiers calling to each other occasionally. I had traveled this road before and as it had been the first time, everything seemed peaceful. We were following roughly the course of the Rio Grande, the river that seemed to cut New Mexico Territory in two sections. This was cattle country too, the same kind of scenery I had grown accustomed to in our valley. I looked forward to arriving at the fort, to changing my clothes. I remember feeling thankful that I had not worn corsets in this heat. Why did women force themselves to put up with such discomfort in this climate? Perhaps I was fortunate that I was slim enough so that my figure did not actually need the tight constriction of whalebone and stays.

I remember thinking all these things while the sun rose higher overhead and even the swaying, jouncing motion of the coach seemed conducive to drowsiness.

One moment I had begun to nod, trying to ignore the perspiration which had already begun to bead my forehead. The next minute there was a loud thud against the side of the coach, which began to sway even more violently.

Almost simultaneously we heard shots and the shouts of the soldiers.

"What the hell!" the middle-aged rancher leaned forward to look out of the window, and I heard him give a strange choking sound. His body seemed to be flung backward, and Emma Jensen screamed, her mouth open. An arrow protruded from his throat, his eyes stared, and he continued to make those horrible, strangling noises for a few seconds longer.

"Better get down on the floor!" the older woman said and, hardly thinking, I dragged Emma off the seat, to crouch down as best we could in the cramped space.

The round-faced man was muttering to himself in a loud, wailing voice. "'Paches! Oh my God, my God!"

"No use prayin'—why don't you get your gun out and start shootin'?"

It seemed as if the only calm and practical person in the coach was the woman who had been so silent.

Emma was still screaming; in fact I think she would have attempted to throw herself from the coach, which was now creaking and jouncing from side to side quite alarmingly, if I had let her. I tried to keep her still by throwing my body over hers, and now the other woman practically reached over and slapped the poor girl's face.

"Only way to stop hysterics, and it ain't going to help us any, her screamin' her head off."

I felt dazed myself. Meeting her eyes, I saw her give a slight shake of her head.

"Feel how fast we're going? An' the sound of shots is droppin' back. Better brace yourself real good, because I think we ain't gonna make the next turn in the road."

"Woman, you don't know what you're talkin' about!" the fat man panted, his eyes round with terror. "We're gettin' away from them!"

The dead man rolled off the seat onto him, spewing blood, and he screamed with fear.

"God!"

I think his voice was the last thing I remembered clearly for some time. One wheel must have hit a rock, or some other obstruction on the trail, for suddenly we were all bounced into the air, rolled helplessly against each other, and the next moment the coach tilted alarmingly. There was a tremendous crash, and I felt myself falling, rolling, screams echoing in my ears. The horses? Emma? Or had they been my own screams? I was never to know.

When had I closed my eyes? Why did my head ache so? Why hadn't the screaming stopped? When I opened my eyes to a steady, monotonous screaming, I looked into a brown, expressionless face with painted stripes of black and white across it. I thought I was having a nightmare, and that if I closed my eyes again everything would disappear.

Someone said something in a deep, guttural voice, and even though I could not understand what he said I knew it was a command. And then there was another voice—female, urgent.

"For God's sake, wake up! And try to pull yourself together, or they'll kill you!"

I opened my eyes again and looked into the small black eyes of the Apache. His hair was black and lank, hanging to his shoulders. He wore a red headband. I noticed all this without taking my eyes from his face.

He said something to me and made a jerking movement of his head. I realized, even in my present dazed state, that he was telling me to get up. How many bones had I broken? I knew that I had fallen and had rolled for a long distance after the door of the coach burst open.

But I was alive. Why didn't Emma stop screaming?

"Get up!" It was that other woman again. Why did she sound so angry?

I struggled to my feet somehow, feeling my hair slip heavily down over my shoulders. Oh, God—now they would scalp me. The Apache made a grunting sound and grabbed at my arm. Had they scalped Emma already? Was that why… and then, turning my head, I saw that it was not Emma who screamed in that terrible, animal fashion. Poor little Emma Jensen would never see her Johnny again. They had left her lying where she had been thrown, with a broken neck. But I would not—could not—believe what they had done to the men, two of whom were not yet dead.

I was thrown onto a horse, the Apache warrior who claimed me as his prize holding me with one arm around my waist. He had tied my wrists in front of me and I could smell the rank smell of his sweat and the oil he had used on his body.

My skirts were torn and bedraggled, I had lost my hat, and there were great splotches of blood all over me. Jewel was as badly off as I was, and she had a long scratch down the side of her face.

Shock has a dulling effect on the senses. I had learned that before. I did not move, I did not cry out, and perhaps it saved my life. It was a long time before I was able to *feel* sufficiently to care. For the moment, I found my numb mind trying to fasten itself on small things. The direction in which we were going, doubling back for part of the way over the trail we had traveled. The still, scattered bodies of the laughing young soldiers who had been so alive this morning, looking like ungainly, broken puppets in their blue uniforms.

The sun was unbearably hot, but we were moving towards the mountains whose shadows seemed to reach out menacingly toward us. Jewel was as stiff and silent as I was.

The ride became a nightmare in itself. The Apaches appeared to feel neither heat, nor weariness, hunger nor thirst. The horses became lathered, their breathing labored, and still they made no attempt to stop and rest them. Their faces were blank and ugly looking. They did not talk, and their silence was all the more unnerving.

I knew only that we were riding through what appeared to be a desert of desolation. Later I was to learn that this was the Jornado del Muerto: journey of death, literally translated from the Spanish. Had I known it at the time it would have made no difference to me. Perhaps death would have seemed preferable to thinking of what might happen to us when the Apaches finally halted for the night.

We had reached the forbidding-looking San Andres mountains when the first horse dropped in its tracks, its rider skillfully flinging himself from its back before the unfortunate animal fell. Our captors butchered the animal immediately; some of them stuffing hunks of raw meat into their mouths, chewing it, and then spitting it out.

From here on we were supposed to walk. Jewel and I were roped together and dragged over the rough, stony terrain, not daring to stop or to complain. "They'll kill either one who couldn't go on," she warned me in a low voice, and their faces and attitude toward us led me to believe that they would indeed do so.

The surviving horses were also led, with the remains of the huge steaks the Indians had carved out of the dead animal wrapped in hide and draped across the light blankets which served as saddles.

I cannot remember how far we walked, or how often I stumbled; my captor turned around to scowl and mutter fiercely at me whenever this happened. My feet, in shoes hardly meant for walking, were blistered and swollen. Each step was agony, and still I knew that I had to go on. My lungs labored for breath, my hair hung in damp, straggly strands around my face. Nothing mattered except taking one more step forward, and then one more.

The trail we followed was tortuous and rocky, sometimes a deep cleft in the side of a mountain, and often a narrow indentation in a wild-looking, weirdly formed outcropping. There were times when we could not walk two abreast, and Jewel dropped behind me. I heard her breathing in great, heaving sobs.

We made camp for the night in a narrow, oddly shaped canyon with steep walls wider in the middle than at both ends. It was an easy place to defend, but who could possibly find us here? We had crossed a virtual desert, and these ancient volcanic mountains were composed mostly of rock and shale where the hoofs of the unshod ponies the Apaches rode would leave no tracks. No, both Jewel and I were lost, perhaps in more ways than one.

How could this have happened to me? How could I have been so unprepared for the violence that lurked beneath the surface of even the most beautiful morning?

Jewel and I had been made to understand, by gestures and guttural grunts, that we were to perform the duties of squaws. We were shown what kind of twigs to gather. When the small, smokeless fire was lit, we were given the horsemeat to cook. Jewel, half-crying, looked helpless. Thankfully I remembered how our cooks had prepared meals in India, when we had gone on tiger hunts. I had the strangest impression that my captor was rather proud of me when I showed Jewel how to sharpen a twig against a stone and skewer the meat on it.

The smell of cooking meat turned my stomach, and I had to bite down on my lip to keep from retching. It brought back the memory of the soldiers, skewered with arrows to hold them down, the terrible smell of burning human flesh. I knew that Jewel was thinking of the same thing, and we dared not look at each other.

The Indians ate, watching us covertly. I gathered that we would be allowed to eat what was left when they were through.

"We have to eat!" I whispered fiercely to Jewel. I was the stronger one now, I was younger, and she looked half-dead with exhaustion.

The horsemeat was tough and stringy, but not unpalatable, and the Indian who had taken me gave me a little water to drink from an old army canteen he carried slung around his neck. He was about to tie my wrists together again, but I made a staying gesture, and began to take off my shoes, feeling their eyes watching me. When that was done, with considerable pain and difficulty, for my blisters had burst and my stockings adhered to torn flesh, I looked him in the eyes and ran my fingers clumsily through my hair. They were all silent now, watching me closely as I begun to braid my hair in one long, single plait that hung down my back. I had to tear a strip of cloth off my already tattered skirt to tie at the end of my thick braid, something like a little girl's hair ribbon. Finally, and more as a gesture of defiance than anything else, I tied another, slightly wider piece of material around my forehead, Indian-fashion, with the ends trailing down past my ear.

The man who had captured me gave an unintelligible grunt—whether of approval or not I did not know. But Jewel, I'd noticed, had begun to follow my example, pulling her bright hair, which was slightly shorter than mine, back from her face and tying a knot of cloth around it. I had no idea what we looked like. We were probably dirty, disgusting spectacles. And perhaps even the Apaches were fussy about the women they took. At any rate, they had decided to leave us alone that night. We were roped together again, a dirty blanket flung over us, and then we had to try and sleep.

Early the next morning we were roughly shaken awake and were each handed a pair of hastily contrived moccasins that we had to keep on our feet by tying each one firmly around the ankles with strips of torn cloth. My feet were swollen and sore and they oozed blood, but at least the moccasins made walking more bearable than my boots would have done.

We walked again, until my mind was a dull void, stopping for a few minutes every two hours or so. This, I am sure, was more to rest *us* and the remaining horses, than because the Apaches themselves needed it.

Jewel and I were past making any attempts to talk to each other. When *they* stopped, *we* stopped, immediately falling onto the ground and staying there until we were dragged onto our feet again.

I don't know how many miles we covered, pushing our way deeper and deeper into the rocky depths of the mountains. It seemed as if nothing could grow here except a few hardy, twisted shrubs for which I had no name, and the occasional, inevitable cactus plants.

The Apaches, who apparently knew the uses of everything in this godforsaken country, would sometimes cut off the top of a cactus plant and scoop out the pulp, chewing it until they had extracted all the liquid from it and then spitting it out. I was thirsty enough not to care, and it wasn't, in the end, too unpleasant to taste.

We walked for hours, or was it for days? Is it possible to fall asleep on one's feet and still keep on walking? We were climbing now, and amazingly, as the sun began to die, we began to come across signs of vegetation, especially where water had collected in ancient craters and scooped-out hollows in the mountain.

Our captors quickened their pace and began to talk to each other in their strange language that sounded like a series of grunts in varying tones. The two horses that carried the silver also quickened their pace. *They* had been the only ones fed and watered. No doubt if they had collapsed Jewel and I would have been forced to carry the heavy sacks until we, in our turn, also dropped in our tracks.

I felt my heart sink when another Apache rose suddenly from behind a ridge, his rifle ready. We were waved on with more grunts, and I saw his expressionless eyes touch me and move on to Jewel. No doubt he was used to seeing captives and plunder brought in here! I had gathered that there must be a camp of some sort here, and as we worked our way upward through a rocky cleft the ground dropped sharply down again, forcing us to scramble to keep our balance. Below were trees, thickly clustered along a small stream. Small fires glowed before strangely shaped brush structures, and dogs snapped and growled, not daring to bark, it seemed.

Jewel and I were dragged into camp like chained captives at the chariot wheels of a Roman conqueror. It was dusk, with a half-light that was a glow in the sky. Women and children ran out of their brush wickiups, surrounded us, and I could see neither kindness nor pity in any of the faces that peered at us.

"Oh, God, what now?" Jewel whispered, and I licked dry lips, trying to carry my head high although my mind was already echoing her question. What now? Would they kill us? Torture us? Or was there worse to come?

I had heard tales of women staked out and raped by Apache warriors, of being beaten to death by their squaws. There was no worse fate for a white woman than to be taken captive by Apaches. Was it Colonel Poynter who had told me this, or had it been Todd? All this time I had been concentrating every ounce of my mind and will upon walking. Now, as Jewel swayed against me and some of the squaws began to prod at us viciously with long sticks, every frightening story I had ever heard came back into my mind. I think the women would have treated us worse if the Apache who had captured me, and who appeared to be a man of some importance, had not waved them away. We were not to be beaten to death by the women then.

Other men had come up, and I gathered that there was much boasting being done. We were pointed at; the saddlebags containing silver were pointed at. The warriors carried handguns and carbines belonging to some of the dead soldiers, and these drew many admiring glances and grunts.

Jewel and I stood mute in the circle of Indians that seemed to press closer. They seemed to have forgotten us for the moment in their admiration of the plunder that had been brought back to the camp, but the malicious, sidelong glances of some of the women warned us that it would not be for long.

It was then that I noticed a warrior taller than the others, wearing an old cavalry jacket for warmth. He sauntered up casually and the others made way for him. I saw his eyes rest on me for a casual moment, and they seemed lighter in color than the eyes of the others. His features too, were different from those of the other men, his nose was straighter, his mouth not as wide. There was a strange, nagging air of familiarity about him, and I think it was because my wits had suddenly been sharpened by both terror and despair that I began to wonder if it could be possible… yes, and why not? A chance in a hundred, perhaps, but words spoken to me what seemed ages ago flashed into my mind.

"Julio, the second son, stayed with the Apache. Took himself a wife."

I suddenly knew that this man reminded me of Ramon Kordes. A coincidence? Perhaps. But it was still possible, still worth taking a chance on. I did not dare speak yet, but almost unconsciously I had straightened, wiping the back of my torn sleeve across my face.

As I had hoped it would, the slight movement brought his attention to me. His eyes flickered over me, and boldly, I caught their glance with my own. I thought he frowned slightly, that he would have spoken if etiquette had not prevented his doing so. He spoke to the warrior who had captured me and they appeared to be bargaining or arguing back and forth. I could not help the sudden hope that sprang up in me, and stood even straighter, staring at him, willing him to look in my direction again. Instead, he spoke to a small boy who had been standing at his side. The child ran off, and my hand closed comfortingly around Jewel's wrist. She had helped me through those first difficult hours. I wanted to help her, to comfort her in some way, even though she appeared to have given up hope and stood drooping wearily at my side.

The talking began again, in a more restrained fashion, although from the glances that were thrown at me I was almost certain now that they *were* bargaining.

But for what? A share of the silver, or…

For the first time, I realized there were others in the camp who were not Indians. Two men, who had been blurred shapes before a fire, walked up. The one in the lead looked as if he had Mexican blood in him. He wore crossed bandoliers and sported a bandit's moustache. I did not care for the way he looked me over; his eyes going from me to Jewel, and back again.

He spoke to the tall warrior, and he spoke in Spanish I understood too clearly.

"So we were right in thinking there'd be plunder to bargain for. And the women—are they for sale too?"

"You think they are worth trading for? The one with the bright hair, perhaps. The other—I do not know if my friend will trade for her. She does not look like much but she is strong, he tells me." The warrior's voice took on a deeper, slightly contemptuous note. "I thought you came to trade for silver, and not for women, who are common enough."

In spite of the disdain in his words I thought that perhaps he did not like the idea that I might be sold to this other man, who was clearly an outsider of some kind. A *comanchero*? Almost at the same time that the thought came to me I saw the other man who came up, his thumbs thrust into his belt He came shrugging, as if reluctantly.

"Siquisn, I thought we would bargain across a fire, like men. What is the hurry?"

The Mexican who looked like a bandit turned with a laugh.

"But we have more than silver here, amigo, although I do not think your brother is eager to trade for the dark-haired one, eh?"

He looked at me then, and my mouth formed his name.

"Lucas Cord!" I think there was hate in my voice. He was here, trading for silver bought in blood. *Comanchero*. All the worst things I had heard and been forced to believe.

Perhaps he would not have recognized me if I had not spoken. I saw his eyes widen and then narrow, and then his mouth twitched in the beginnings of a smile. There was a stillness all around us. Even my captor looked taken aback. Julio, for it could be no one else, said slowly, "You know this woman, my brother?"

He had the insolence to speak to me.

"Are you sure we know each other? You do not look very much like the clean and sharp-tongued lady I remember. Let's see—it *was* in your bedroom, was it not?"

"Oh! Why, you're a... a..."

"Doesn't seem like you're in a position to get on your high horse. And now be quiet!"

His sudden harshness startled me into silence, and a realization of the position I was in.

I watched them argue. Lucas Cord had lapsed into Apache and his *comanchero* friend did not seem too happy about it.

The argument seemed first between Lucas and his brother, switching to cross-talk with the warrior whose captive I was. I did not think Apaches could smile, but some of the warriors seemed to be hiding their amusement behind their hands. What was he saying?

After a particularly sharp exchange, Lucas Cord turned on his heel and stalked off, his friend following him, grumbling in Spanish, "But the silver! We came to bargain for silver!"

"I leave that to you, 'Gado!" I heard him say.

"What is happening? Do you know one of them?" Jewel's frantic whisper roused me, and I squeezed her wrist again.

"I'm not sure." Julio looked darkly at me. Even when his brother came back, carrying a long case, he hardly turned his eyes away.

But Lucas did not glance once in my direction, as he opened the case to reveal a sleek, silver-ornamented rifle.

Julio Kordes turned on his heel and stalked away as the

bargaining came to an end. I had been bought, it appeared, for a new Henry rifle and several rounds of ammunition.

Seventeen

❧

At the time it happened, I understood very little of what was actually going on. I guessed, but was certain only when I saw the rifle change hands. Lucas Cord looked at me, and it was hard to read what was in his mind. The strange, greenish flickers in his eyes seemed intensified in the leaping firelight.

Strangely, he spoke to me in Spanish, his tone curt. *"Ven aqui."*

I supposed, clenching my jaws against my growing anger, that he wanted to make sure everyone knew I was now his property. Just as if I was a slave—a piece of merchandise to be bought and sold!

I hesitated, feeling Jewel clutch at me despairingly.

"What about her? She's a white woman. You're not going to leave her to *them?*"

"You forgotten I'm one of *them* too?" There was a cruel, note underlying his words. He took one step forward and, seizing the length of rope attached to my bound wrists, yanked me forward so that I stumbled against him.

I had no choice but to go with him, even though I could hear Jewel begin to sob hysterically behind me.

"You can't just leave her! Don't you have any decent feelings at all?" I even forced myself to plead. *"Please!"*

"She ain't none of my business."

He was taking such long, angry strides that I found myself panting as I tried to keep up with him.

I tried to pull back and found myself stumbling again. "You have to do something for her! Even if you don't care for the fact that she's a white woman, she is a woman! What will happen to her?"

"Now you listen here, and listen good, because I ain't goin' to say this again!" He stopped so suddenly that I fell against him and felt his arm go unwillingly around my waist. He was angry for some reason, the husky voice I remembered deliberately controlled.

"You listen…" he said again, and I had the impression he spoke between his teeth. "This ain't the SD and you ain't the lady boss. So don't go givin' me any more orders. You know what's good for you, you'll take mine, and no back talk either. Where in hell do you think you are?" He was so angry that he actually shook me. "Back someplace where all you have to do is tell 'em you're Todd Shannon's woman an' they start bowing?"

"When Todd finds out where I am he'll have every single Apache in this territory smoked out of hiding!" I was now as angry as he was, but my anger only seemed to provide him with a bitter amusement.

"An' how would Shannon, or anyone else, know where you are? My friends don't leave tracks like white men would. For all he'd know you might be dead already, an' buried where nobody would ever find you. Or sold down in Mexico, where a pretty white woman could fetch as much as fifty pesos."

The significance of his last words made the color drain from my face. Was that why the Indians had troubled to bring us all this way with them? Was that what that other man had meant when he talked of having more than silver to trade for?

A horrifying thought struck me, making me stumble forward in silence when Lucas Cord, his face set, began tugging me along with him again. He was a *comanchero*. Why had he taken the trouble to buy me?

We were going away from the firelight, toward the trees and an even worse thought had entered my mind. Instinctively I attempted to pull away from him, and my sudden movement took him by surprise. He had been holding onto my arm, and as I twisted away from him I heard my sleeve tear. I turned to run and tripped over a root instead. I felt myself fall and could do nothing to save myself.

It was the culmination of everything that had happened to me since that long-ago morning when I had so lightheartedly left my home, determined to go riding alone. I lay there, feeling the aching in every bone in my body, and for the first time in my life that I could remember I gave way to tears.

Once I had started, I could not stop. I felt rather than saw him bend over me, his hand rough on my shoulder.

I could not move. I felt that I would never move again.

"For God's sake, what in hell's the matter with you now?" His voice was impatient, even angry. "Come on!" Catching me by the upper arms he hauled me unfeelingly to my feet, and immediately, feeling the stabbing pain that shot up from my ankle, I gave a cry of sheer frustration.

He swore—softly, crudely. I felt myself picked up in his arms and carried along, helpless to prevent it.

He had erected a rough shelter of brush and hides, a little more than a lean-to with some blankets spread under it. Apparently, Lucas Cord and his *comanchero* friend had been sharing the scarcely adequate space, and using their saddles for pillows.

I found myself set down to lie across the blankets, none too gently.

"If you hadn't pulled such a damn fool trick," he muttered, hunkering down on his heels by me. "How far did you expect to get, anyhow?"

With a swiftly impersonal movement he pushed the hem of my gown upward, and began to loosen the moccasin on my left foot.

"Stop it! What…"

I tried to raise myself on one elbow, forgetting that my wrists were still bound, and fell back helplessly. In the dim light, his flickering upward glance at me looked almost evil, although his voice remained flatly impersonal, like the touch of his fingers, which now probed gently at my swelling ankle.

"Keep still. Done some horse doctorin' when I had to. But nothin' seems to be broke, anyhow."

"How convenient for you!" I managed, with a gasp of pain when the pressure of his fingers increased. It was ridiculous that I still had the overwhelming desire to keep on sobbing. In spite of my efforts to fight my own weakness, I suppose I sniffled, for he looked at me sharply.

"You hurtin', or just mad?"

My ankle throbbed sickeningly, but I wouldn't say so. I wouldn't let him think I was begging for pity!

Pressing my lips together I turned my head aside. I would not let him hear me cry out again. I would not whimper, I would not sob, I would not grovel. No matter what he did...

He had begun to loosen the other moccasin and to draw it off my foot. I could not help wondering, with the part of my mind which was not invaded by waves of pain and tiredness, what he was about now, but I would not look at him either.

"I guess you did some walkin'." His voice was ironic; I hated him for it. "Wait here. I'll be back in a while." I knew he had come to his feet with all the easy litheness of an animal, and that he stood watching me for a moment, but I pretended to keep my eyes closed and would not speak. Through my lashes, I saw him shrug and walk away silently.

"Wait here," he had said, as if I had been in any condition to move. Perhaps he hoped I'd attempt to run away again— how? By dragging myself painfully into the bushes?

I was in a trance of weariness by now, halfway between dozing and unconsciousness, too tired to go on thinking.

When I opened my eyes a small fire had been lit nearby, and I felt a cold, stinging sensation in my feet.

I must have moved involuntarily, for Lucas Cord's husky, impatient voice ordered me sharply to hold still. By this time I was exhausted and light-headed with hunger and thirst. It was the odor of cooked food nearby which had awakened me.

Did he intend to torture me? He was binding strips of cloth torn from my own petticoats about my feet and around my injured ankle, working silently and deftly. Even when he tore off another strip I was capable of only a small gasp of protest.

He straightened, his face expressionless. In the firelight I noticed all over again the bronze glints in the stubbled whiskers he'd allowed to grow.

He walked over to the fire and came back carrying a kind of gourd dish.

"Thought mebbe you might be feelin' hungry." He caught my look and a corner of his lips lifted a trifle as if he had almost smiled.

"Ain't horsemeat, if that's what you're thinking. Nor dog-meat either. It's venison. Shot an elk-deer this morning."

"Dog-meat!" I stared at him in horror and he shook his head in mock amazement.

"Didn't you know? It's considered a real delicacy. But I guess your stomach has gotta get accustomed to it."

In contrast to his earlier impatience, he seemed almost affable now, but I didn't trust him even though I discovered that he had untied my wrists.

"Better sit up against that saddle; you'll find it easier to eat." Before I could attempt the movement he leaned across me, his hands hard around my waist as he levered me upward.

From behind the saddle he produced a battered canteen which was half-full of cold water. I think I would have gulped it all down thirstily if he hadn't warned me, with exaggerated patience, to take only tiny sips at first, barely enough to wet the inside of my mouth.

"Drink too much an' you'll get cramps so bad you won't be able to eat."

It was the most delicious stew I had ever eaten, although I did not dare ask what else was in it beside venison. Anything would have tasted good to me, of course, after having been half-starved, forced to walk for miles and miles in the broiling sun! Even now I did not quite know how I had managed to survive.

Lucas Cord was watching me with a strange, narrow-eyed look that did not swerve even when I happened to glance up and caught him at it.

He said, in that husky, caustic voice of his I was beginning to know so well, "Don't expect this kind of service after tonight! My brother's wife did the cookin' and made that salve I put on your feet. But tomorrow you can start makin' yourself useful around camp. Little Bird will show you."

I lowered the dish and stared at him wildly.

"What do you mean? Around camp? But you're not going to *keep* me here, are you?"

He had been sitting cross-legged, like an Apache. Now he leaned forward, putting his face close to mine.

"You don't listen good, do you? I *bought* you, for a damn good Henry rifle that was worth a lot more than you seem to be. That means I get to use you any way I damn well please, an' you better get that through your head right now!"

I could feel the blood rushing to my face as the meaning of his blunt speech became clear. Sheer rage and indignation kept me speechless, and he sat back with a satisfied look that made me even more furious.

"That's better. As long as you do like you're told an' don't talk back maybe I won't have to beat you to prove what I been tellin' you."

Hunger or not, this was too much to bear. I threw the dish at him. He ducked with amazing ease, and I could have cried when I saw the remnants of that glorious stew spilled all over the ground.

From the look on his face when he slowly straightened up I thought he was going to kill me. Instead, astonishingly, he began to laugh.

"Well I'll be goddamned if she ain't got a temper! And enough spunk to waste all that food, too. An' that's too bad, because I might just make you go hungry tomorrow!"

I should have been warned by the change in his tone. Before I could prevent it, he moved with deceptive casualness, one hand snaking out to fasten around my wrists, pushing them above my head as his body came down over mine. Almost contemptuously, he looked down into my face, his weight holding me motionless.

"This once, because you've had a hard time of it and were

tough enough to survive, I'm gonna let you get away with it. After today, ain't gonna be no excuse that you're tired, or scared, or hysterical. You ever throw anythin' at me again an' I'll beat the tar outa you, an' that's a promise."

I squirmed under him, hoping my eyes reflected all the hate and disgust he filled me with. He gave that mocking twitch of his lips that passed for a smile.

"There's another thing you just got me to thinkin' of, with all that wigglin' around you're doing…" Deliberately suggestive, he let his words trial off. My body stiffened with revulsion. "Hard to tell, with a woman like you, exactly what you're thinkin'," he said softly. I felt his breath fan my hot cheeks. Had he been about to kiss me?

Twisting my head away I said through stiff lips: "You don't have to wonder then, because I'll tell you! I was thinking how much I hate you, how much I despise you, what a bestial animal you are! I'm only glad that my father didn't live to see what you turned into!"

I thought I heard his indrawn breath, and then with a brutal movement he caught my face by the chin and forced it around to his.

"So that's what you think?"

"That's what you are! A beast—a wild animal—a savage killer!"

I would have said more, for he had pushed me to it, but he didn't give me the chance. With a swift movement he eased his weight off me a trifle, and with both hands, ripped the tattered remnants of my gown down the front.

I cried out, and beat at him with my fists, but as weak and exhausted as I was, my puny strength was no match for his.

Even now, as I tell it, I can feel my face begin to burn. He stripped me naked, twisting my body this way and that in spite of all my struggles.

And then, when he had had his way and I lay under him again, held down by his body and all too conscious of the rough feel of his clothing against my bare flesh, he—just lay there! Looking down at my face as if he enjoyed reading the humiliation and hatred there.

"You can do what you please!" I panted viciously. "You've

proved you're much stronger than I. You've proved you're what I said you were! An animal! A beast who can only take a woman by force! It's a habit with you, isn't it?"

"You think I mean to rape you?" Amazingly his voice was quite calm. "You're wrong about that, like you are about a lot of other things. Better take a good look at yourself in a glass tomorrow before you go jumpin' to conclusions." He smiled cruelly. "You're quite a sight, Lady Rowena Dangerfield! The sun's made you almost as dark as I am, an' your nose is peelin'. To tell the truth, your face needs washin' too. You need washing all over! An' another thing, I've met your kind of woman before. All promise and prettiness on the outside, an' nothin' but cold inside."

"You...!"

"I ain't quite finished yet. Didn't take your clothes off because I wanted you, just to show you what I *could* do, if I'd a mind to! An' that gown you was wearin' was hardly suitable for a squaw. I'll get you some others tomorrow, an' you start learnin' your place."

He rolled away from me and stood up, all in one easy motion. With a short, disgusted exclamation he flung me a blanket.

"Keep that around you an' try to get some sleep. Ain't gonna tie you, because there's no place you can go. Adios for now."

I was left shivering with shock, clutching the blanket to my shaking body as I watched him stride away towards the other fires without a backward glance.

In spite of the bitterness of my emotions, I must have fallen asleep from sheer exhaustion. I was so weary that I only half-awoke when Lucas Cord came back to the crude little lean-to and lay beside me. I turned onto my stomach with a muffled exclamation, pulling the blanket more closely around myself, but he made no move to touch me and, shockingly, I slept again.

By the time I had spent two days in the Apache camp I had managed to regain some remnants of my pride and common sense. It was not as if I had any choice in the matter. I was a captive, a slave, but I was in a much better position than any of the other miserable wretches who had been taken prisoner by the Apache. I was neither continually beaten, nor left to sleep out in the open like one of the dogs. I was not literally worked to death, nor tormented by both the women and the children of the camp.

I wasn't Lucas Cord's wife, although he came to lie by me every night, in the small wickiup that Little Bird, his brother's wife, had helped me build. I was not his mistress, although I think that only he and I knew that. He had made it clear that as a woman I held no attraction for him. I learned soon enough that I was merely an instrument of his revenge against Todd Shannon, and that by becoming engaged to the man he hated, I had made myself his enemy too. I was to be a pawn of some kind, but he would tell me nothing beyond the mocking statement he had thrown out that first morning, when he woke me by flinging a blouse and skirt at me. They were typical of the garments that all the Apache women wore. And apparently that was all they wore!

"What do you mean to do with me?" I had demanded. "I have a right to know!"

I was sitting up, clutching the blanket closely around myself, and his eyes seemed to strip me of its protection.

"Guess that's up to you," he drawled, in his infuriatingly husky voice. "Got a few days' business left around here, an' then I'm going home to visit my family. Now *you*," and his voice had hardened, "can choose whether you're goin' as a guest, or a servant. Always did promise my mother a white woman for a servant. She thought a lot of your pa, same as I did, but seein' as you've let Todd Shannon convince you we're all thieves an' murderers…"

"My father saved your life!" I flung at him. "And he saved your mother's life! Doesn't that mean anything to you?"

"You beggin' me to let you go for Todd Shannon's sake, or your pa's, or your own? You remindin' me of a debt I owe? Well, I owed that debt to Mr. Guy Dangerfield. I thought his daughter would be more like him, but you ain't. You're whatever they made you—your grandfather, your ma—that fine London society. Came to New Mexico to visit, didn't you? See how the natives live. You didn't care to see under the surface they showed you..." He broke off, his face dark with suppressed anger. "Ah, shit! What's the point? You're lookin' at me, hatin' me, and you don't see any further than that. Well, you got your choice. We'll talk about the rest later."

He talked of offering me a choice, but for the time being, I *had* no choice. After that one occasion Lucas Cord hardly spoke to me, except to give some order. I felt he was only waiting for me to rebel, to disobey, or perhaps to throw something at him; I would not give him the satisfaction of having an excuse to beat me in front of the whole camp, nor to prove to me all over again how ambiguous my position here was. I compressed my lips and did what I was told, although I knew he realized I was being sarcastic on occasion.

Little Bird, who was Julio's wife and the daughter of a chief, was hardly communicative, although she spoke some Spanish. I suppose my position puzzled her too.

She showed me how a wickiup was built, and which roots and herbs to gather. I was taught how to tan a hide and how to light a fire, how to cook food their way. I learned, and I did as I was told.

The Apache society was an example of society in the Middle Ages. The men, all-powerful, were warriors; the women were subservient and did all the work. A warrior went out hunting or raiding, and saw to his weapons himself. His woman saw to everything else. As in every other primitive society, there were taboos. A man must not look on the face of his mother-in-law, or converse with her. A man usually lived with his wife's family. A woman never spoke out in the presence of males, unless she was asked for her opinion.

I saw Jewel on a couple of occasions, but at a distance. I learned that she had been bought by the *comanchero* Delgado. She still wore the ragged remnants of the garments she had worn when we were first captured, and she did not seem too unhappy, although she was subdued and silent, just as I was.

When Lucas went out on a hunting trip with the men on the second day, he dressed just as they did, in a breechclout with knee-high moccasins. I noticed that they carried a bow and arrows as well as rifles.

I hated him. What had he meant by saying I might be a guest or a servant when he went to visit his family? When would he leave the camp? There were times when I wondered what the reactions of my friends might have been, when they learned what had happened.

Poor Mark! How he must blame himself! And Mrs. Poynter and the colonel. Much worse, when Todd found out what had happened. He would blame everyone else, of course. But I lived in the present, because I had to. I would not speak unless I had to. I looked down whenever there were males present.

It was not too difficult to adapt; I had adapted before to more hostile environments. My put-on meekness of manner was exaggerated, and Lucas Cord knew it. When Little Bird was not present I saw his brother look at me, and I could sense that he still wanted me. Good, I thought. It might be another weapon I could use against Lucas Cord. Perhaps, for money, Julio would set me free.

Two weeks passed—and a third. Only the trained, controlled strength of my mind, my will, enabled me to remain submissive and calm on the surface. I would not be conquered. He had a reason for "rescuing" me. I would find it out and use it against him.

I found out we were to leave in the morning when Little Bird instructed me on preparations for the long journey. As usual, she would not say more than was necessary, but I received the impression that she was no more eager than I to embark on this particular trip. She and Julio and their two small children, a girl and a boy, still strapped to his cradleboard, would accompany us. We would have to cross the Jornado del Muerto again, I gathered, from the quantity of water we would have to carry with us. We would skirt the Canada de Alamosa, the centuries-old home of the Eastern Chiricahua Apaches, and travel from there to the Black Range.

Was that where this mysterious secret valley was located? She would not give me a direct answer, but turned her head away. I had the impression there was something she would have liked to tell me, but her respect for her husband and his brother prevented her from doing so.

We were to take mules as well as horses, the former loaded down with silver. The Apaches knew its value, I had learned, but only vaguely. They would trade the silver and gold they stole for rifles and ammunition, bolts of cloth and trinkets, cooking pots and tools, things of more tangible value to them. The *comancheros,* who knew the real value of the precious metal, would trade for it and sell it in Mexico.

I had my only chance to speak with Jewel just before we left, when the mules and the horses were already loaded. I thought she looked wistful, as she stood some distance behind her new owner, and with a defiant glance at Lucas I went up to her.

"Jewel! I'm sorry I didn't get the chance to talk with you before. Are you all right? Do they treat you kindly?"

She shrugged. "Guess you know as well as I do how it is! But 'Gado ain't unkind, and he seems to like me. 'Least, he's been talkin' like he don't aim to get rid of me down in Mexico right away. Who knows?" She gave me a philosophical look. "He's not as bad as some 'protectors' I've had. Don't beat on me an' give me to other men." She gave me a surreptitious, hasty embrace. "It's you I bin worryin' about. You didn't seem like the type… but then he's young, ain't he? An' not half bad-looking. Be sensible, Rowena. Only way a female can survive is by bein' smarter than a man, an' learnin' how to roll with the punches."

That was our farewell, for we had no chance to say any more to each other. Little Bird pulled me by the arm, and I caught Lucas Cord's strange, green-fired glance upon me. With the men leading the way, we left the small, concealed canyon on foot, leading the horses.

Eighteen

❧

WE TRAVELED VERY SLOWLY AND CAUTIOUSLY, SOMETIMES continuing our journey at night, although I could tell that Little Bird was terrified by this. Apaches would seldom travel at night, because they believed that evil spirits lurked abroad then, but Julio, in spite of all his Apache ways, was like his brother in scoffing at such superstition.

I learned that Little Bird was expecting another child, and although she never complained or fell back, it became clear to me that the long hours of walking with a baby strapped to her back were a strain on her. I offered to carry the child myself, and though she glanced at me gratefully, her look was strange. The little girl rode on one of the horses, her small face solemn and unsmiling. The baby, like most Apache infants, never cried.

His name was Coyote Walking, and he had round, curious black eyes and a fringe of straight black hair. I would think he was watching me sometimes, and wonder if he would grow up like his uncles. Still, he was an infant, and although I had never been able to feel anything more than awkwardness around children, I grew fond of him, and of the little girl too.

Sometimes I would feel Lucas Cord's eyes on me, never giving anything away, and sometimes Julio's. What had Lucas told him of me? What did he think? I would not, I had willed myself not to think. It was easier that way, when we had to trudge what seemed endless miles across burning white sands in order not to overtax the horses, and then set up camp at the end of it, while the men rested. It was easier to keep my mind a blank and my body rigid and unyielding when Lucas came to lie by me at night. We did not talk at such times, and invariably he turned his back on me. Sometimes I thought Little Bird looked at me in a puzzled and almost pitying way, although she never said anything. She was kind to me, and spoke enough Spanish to make herself understood. She tried to teach me the Apache words for various objects, although I found it difficult to master the guttural sounds they used.

Lucas Cord was still a stranger to me. There were times when I felt a stranger to myself. I was on an arduous, ridiculous journey—the hunted now, instead of being on the side of the hunter. I knew there had to be other people not too far away. White settlers, soldiers. Surely Todd would have had half the territory out searching for me? And yet we saw no one until we had reached the foothills that reached up hungrily, it seemed, toward those towering peaks and ridges that formed the Black Range, legendary hideout of the Apaches.

Little Bird seemed almost animated when we entered an Apache *ranchería*. Her father, who was a relative of Victorio himself, lived here. We were enveloped by her family. Only her mother, out of politeness, carefully hid herself from her son-in-law. I realized again that the Apaches loved children as little Coyote Walking and his sister were immediately surrounded by affectionate, admiring relatives. I received many veiled, curious glances, but with the innate politeness that the Apaches displayed to guests, no one asked any questions, nor did my presence meet with any disapproval. Little Bird, in her own environment, went out of her way to make me feel welcome, and the only awkward moment I had was when the medicine man of the tribe, an extremely old man with lank gray hair escaping from under his ceremonial headdress, fixed his eyes sharply upon me, where I sat discreetly in the shadows with the other women.

I know he asked Lucas something, and the answer he received made him look at me even more penetratingly, although he did not say a word to me at the time. We were to spend a night here, and I remember feeling relieved at the prospect. The site of the *ranchería* was beautiful. A tiny plateau, protected on three sides by steep cliffs, it was high enough to be richly green, shaded by pine and aspen trees. A small stream, gushing down like a miniature waterfall from the cliff, ran through the center of it. It had been the home of the Apaches for a long time, although Little Bird told me, in a moment of rare confidence, that they had to move away in the winter, the time they called Ghost Face. Still they had planted corn here, and other herbs and shrubs they used for food. It might have been a pleasant, peaceful place if I did not remember that the war chief Victorio had stayed here on occasion, and from here bloody raids had been made on stagecoaches and unsuspecting white settlers.

But I told myself firmly that I would not think of that. I was here as a guest of sorts, and the Apaches on their home grounds were a different people from the Apache warriors who went to war with painted faces.

The men had gone to the ceremonial sweat lodge—a kind of Turkish bath—and late in the evening some of the women, Little Bird and I among them, went to bathe in a secluded, tree-shaded portion of the stream. I could almost have imagined we were in the bathing pool of the maharajah's harem at Jhanpur, from the giggling and teasing chatter. The women washed their hair with a form of soap they made from the yucca cactus, and combed it through with makeshift combs fashioned from bone or cactus spines.

My hair, as always, hung sleek and heavy when it was wet. I combed it with the comb that Little Bird loaned me, her manner more friendly than usual, and let it hang loose until it was dry, tying a narrow strip of buckskin around my forehead to keep the loose strands out of my eyes.

"Look in the still water," Little Bird told me, and giggled. I had not looked in a mirror since I was captured, and my reflection in the small pool made me stare in disbelief. I could hardly recognize myself! I might have been an Apache woman, except for my blue eyes, and in the rapidly fading light even they looked dark. My skin had tanned in the sun and turned almost brown. I had stopped peeling from sunburn. In the high-necked, long-sleeved blouse of an Apache squaw, my hair parted in the center, I looked like a brown-skinned Amazon.

Where was the dowdy, frowning girl with spectacles tipped on her nose? Or the sophisticated woman with jewels sparkling around her throat and at her ears? I still wore my tiny sapphire ear studs, and somehow, taken with the rest of me, they looked incongruous. Impulsively I unscrewed them and handed them to Little Bird.

"A gift," I said in Spanish. "Because you have been kind."

For a moment she seemed confused, staring from the small, sparkling jewels I held in the palm of my hand, to my face. And then she took them, her face solemn and touched my hand.

"*Gracias,*" she said in Spanish, and then in Apache, in a softer voice, "*nidee,*" which I had learned meant sister. At that moment, we were close to being friends.

It was a pity that Lucas had to spoil the moment. He came striding towards us, his chest bare except for the small buckskin pouch that hung suspended from a rawhide cord around his neck—the medicine pouch that every Apache warrior carried with him. And why not, since he was obviously proud of his Apache blood? His wet hair glistened in the dim light, and his face was closed and unreadable. "The shaman wishes to speak with you." Little Bird had dropped back unobtrusively, and his fingers closed around my wrist.

"Show some respect. He is an old man, but very wise. "My—" and I wondered why he hesitated before he went on, "my grandfather."

"I have always respected those who have earned respect." I tilted my head back and my eyes met his. "Do you think I would embarrass you?"

"How do I know what to expect of you?" His words were almost muttered, with a kind of frustration underlying them. "You're a most unexpected woman!"

"I'm adaptable," I said coolly, moving my wrist from his grasp. "I'm patient too. And I know my place. Shouldn't I walk a few paces behind you? My head meekly bowed, of course. I know you would not want anyone to think you had allowed your slave any extra privileges!"

I had the satisfaction of seeing him scowl down at me, his eyes puzzled. But "Watch your tongue..." was all he said to me before he turned and walked ahead of me toward the largest wickiup in the encampment.

I was horribly nervous, although I would have died rather than show it. Why did the shaman wish to speak to me? I could not understand my nervousness either. I had been presented to the Queen of England and had sailed through the whole performance without a suggestion of butterflies in my stomach! But this was not England, and as preposterous as it would have seemed to me less than a month ago, I was the prisoner of a man I despised and distrusted.

"Don't speak first," Lucas instructed me before we entered the conical-shaped brush dwelling. "Try to sit quietly without fidgeting until you're spoken to."

I could not resist letting a flash of sarcasm show in my tone. "Thank you for instructing me in the proper etiquette! Your slave will try not to disgrace you."

He gave me one of his brooding, expressionless glances that seemed to warn me I was going too far, but he said nothing and, bending his head, he preceded me into the gloomy, firelit interior.

The old shaman seemed half asleep as we seated ourselves on either side of the doorway. For some time he neither moved nor acknowledged our presence. A fat woman who appeared to be much younger than he moved quietly about her duties in the background. His daughter? His wife? Were shamans allowed to marry? He had discarded the ceremonial buckskin headdress decorated with eagle and turkey feathers and now wore only the usual headband of an Apache warrior. His brown face seemed to be composed of seams and wrinkles, and he might have been a hundred years old. "My grandfather," Lucas Cord had said, with that odd, tiny hesitation. Was it possible that this was Elena Kordes's father? The Apache chief who had made a young Spanish woman captive his wife?

I studied the old man from beneath my lowered lashes, and

after a short time I received the distinct impression that he was doing the same thing.

"So—you are the one." The words, spoken in rusty Spanish, were uttered so suddenly that I almost jumped. The old fox! So he *had* been watching me after all. I raised my eyes to his half-open ones, but did not speak. He had made a statement; what was there to say?

We regarded each other, and after a few seconds had passed the old man's eyes opened fully. He looked at Lucas, I thought. It was difficult to tell, with the fire between us.

"Does she speak, or is she afraid to do so?"

I compressed my lips together as Lucas answered him, his tone caustic.

"She speaks too much sometimes, oh my grandfather. And I do not think she is afraid."

The old man was nodding, turning his eyes back to me. "That is good. You do not have the look of a woman who is afraid. Sometimes my grandson is not as wise as he thinks he is. When I first saw you, the thought came to me—this is one of the rare women who listens, and observes; and learns what from she sees. I have seen for myself how quickly you have learned our ways. I told myself, perhaps the mind and the heart of this woman are as open and honest as were those of her father, who came one day to this camp alone, with no fear, because, he said, he would understand the Apache." The old man nodded again, as if it pleased him to turn his thoughts backwards. "Your father was the only white man I have called *siqiàsn*—brother. And as long as he lived he was a true blood brother to the Apache." The old, rheumy eyes seemed to search my face. "You understand now why I have called you here?" I did not understand—not yet, not quite. But my father, blood brother to the same savage, merciless Indians who had attacked the stagecoach, murdered and tortured, and then had carried *me* off?

I could see that the shaman expected me to answer him. I could think of nothing to say except, shaking my head, "No, I am not certain if I understand or not. Did you know who I was then? From the beginning?"

"Ah, ah!" Sitting cross-legged, the old man began to rock very slightly back and forth, as if it helped him to think. "Now I have made you curious. That is good. Your curiosity will make you speak out and ask questions, where before you were doubtful, you wondered, why has this old man sent for me? What kind of things will he ask me? You are your father's daughter, his only child from across the great water. That is why you are here." He paused and I leaned forward, but he raised one hand in a somehow imperious gesture.

"I see many questions in your eyes, but you will ask them later, those that I have not already answered. You are wondering if the warriors who first brought you as a captive to their camp were sent to look for you. No. It was a raiding party. For many days the young men had watched the coach go by and they learned how many soldiers usually guarded it, how many guns they carried. Sometimes the tracks left by the wheels were deeper than on other days. They knew that on such days silver was carried in a box hidden at the back. My daughter, it was by chance you were on the coach our young warriors captured. Or perhaps it was one of those things that was meant to happen, who knows?" His eyes turned for a moment on Lucas, sitting silent and cross-legged; his face still without expression.

"Perhaps it was also meant to happen that on the very day you were brought into the camp where my other grandson is subchief, *this* one happened to be there, and knew who you were. He brought you here first, as I would have wanted him to."

First? They were all talking in riddles, Lucas and his brother Ramon—now this old man. I had not been told what was expected of me. Why it was necessary for me to be brought here under such humiliating conditions!

Etiquette or no, it was impossible for me to sit silently for a moment longer. I cast an angry glance at Lucas Cord, and I thought one eyebrow lifted a fraction, as though he warned me to silence, or challenged me to speak. Well, I would speak out, whether he liked it or not.

"You have something to say, and the words are bursting from your throat." Perhaps the shaman practiced mind reading.

"Yes!" I burst out, trying to keep some of the anger I had suppressed for so long out of my voice. "I would like to know why I was brought here, and where I am being taken. *He*," and I poured all the contempt I could muster into my voice, "would tell me nothing at all, except that I could choose being his mother's guest or her servant! And what is more, he's used me despicably, threatened me, made me slave for him—just as if I'd done him some injury, or my father hadn't saved his miserable life! *You* have just said my father was like a brother to you, and you've spoken to me as if I was a guest, but *he*…"

"That's enough!" Lucas Cord's bitter, angry voice slashed through my speech like a knife. "If you'd have tried guardin' your tongue in the first place…"

"And I say peace! You will both be silent."

The shaman's voice was soft and papery, the rustling voice of an old man. But the stern note of authority underlying it brought the silence he had requested. His eyes studied us both, and when he spoke again his voice was gentler. "I was thinking, as you two spoke angry words to each other, that there must be a reason for the hate that is between you. It is a pity, for your father would not have wished it to be so."

He had chosen to address me, and my lips tightened mutinously.

"Perhaps my father did not know him very well!"

"And you do?"

"I know, and have experienced all that I care to!"

"She's a stubborn, ill-natured female!"

I glared at Lucas. "And you are a cold-blooded murderer and a violator of women!"

The shaman raised his hand again, and I could almost imagine that he frowned.

"Is this true? You know our customs, and that I consider this woman as my daughter. You are also aware…"

"I'm aware of what Guy Dangerfield wanted, but *she* is not. And I swear to you that I did not touch her."

How could he lie so flatly, and in my presence?

Sheer fury made me bold. "Ask him if he did not tear the clothes from my body on that very first night, after reminding me crudely that as he had bought me I was now his property, to do with as he pleased! He threatened to beat me."

"And she deserved it. She was hungry and I brought her food. She threw it at me in a rage."

"How cleverly you twist things about! The things you said to put me in a rage—have you forgotten?"

Our eyes clashed, and even in the firelight I could see those dangerous, greenish glints in his, like tiny flames.

"You are like children who throw angry words at each other in a fit of rage. My daughter, did he violate you?"

Trapped by his question, I bit my lip. "He—he lay beside me every night. No doubt so that his friends would think he hadn't wasted such a wonderful rifle for nothing! But no, he did not do more than that."

The old man nodded. "You are honest. And I think you understand how the mind of a man will work."

"*This* man's mind, perhaps! He is…"

"You're repeating yourself now, Lady Rowena. Can't you think of anythin' new to say?"

I gave him an icy look and turned my head away. If he wanted to act like an angry, thwarted child, then let him.

Again it seemed as if the old shaman had read my mind. "You are still confused, are you not? You wonder why you are here, and why I have spoken of your father's wishes. Will you hear me now, until I have finished speaking?"

He took my silence for consent, and his voice seemed to rustle in the stillness. "Your father and I spoke of peace. It surprises you? The Apache are few, and every day there are more of the white-eyes who come to settle on our old hunting grounds. In a rage against this our young men raid and kill, but for every white man we kill, two or three more come, and more soldiers with more guns. I am an old man and I see what must happen in the end. If we cannot make peace with the white man, the day of the Apache is ended. And so your father, my brother, and I would speak of such things. He made many writings in books, which he said he would leave for you. He knew that his days were not long, but when his daughter came she would turn all the old wrongs and the old hates into right. You did not read his books?"

I thought I could feel Lucas Cord's scornful gaze upon me as I shook my head. "I started to read them. But before I came here, I had a letter from him requesting that I read them in order, from the beginning. I started to read, but I became lazy in the hot sun. And then so many things happened that I did not have time."

"You had time to spend with Shannon—and that nephew of his."

I refused to look towards Lucas.

"Todd Shannon was my father's partner. I was going to marry him."

The shaman's face was bland. "Shannon is an old man filled with hate. Your father saw this. Understand me, he did not hate his partner. He hoped that you would be allowed to live in peace. But he knew this man. For you he had other plans. A scheme to end old hatreds and end old injustice. It is a pity you did not read what he wrote."

"Everyone keeps telling me that! But..."

"Be patient, daughter, as your father was. I am shaman of my tribe. But your father was wiser even than I. He saw ahead. And he was a man who placed truth and justice above all else." His look was benign; I thought he was being patient with me, and it only made me impatient.

"Everyone talks to me in riddles! I am told of my father's wishes, but no one will tell me what they were."

"You are a woman with the strong, quick mind of a man. But nevertheless you must learn to wait, to listen." His head nodded again, and I noticed the swaying movement of his gaunt body.

"Your father once loved my own daughter. Perhaps he always did. My daughter turned from her people and sought the white man's ways. I let her go. She had the mind of a warrior—stubborn, independent, seeking. She too hates. And that is why your father knew that the only way to end the hate was the old way. It is our custom, and your custom. Your father's father was a chief. Your father married to please him.

Was this not true? He expected you to think the same way. His wish was that you would marry one of my daughter's sons."

"Not *him*!" I could not help the exclamation that burst from my lips.

"Don't have to worry about *that*! I like to do my own huntin' for my own kind of game."

"Are you sure you do not mean *prey*?"

The old man's voice was calm.

"So you will not have each other. And Julio has a wife already. That leaves Ramon. He is not Apache in his thoughts. But he is educated, and a gentleman. He will fit well into the white man's world. And yet he is my grandson too. He has seen you and spoken to you. He understands his duty, just as you must understand yours."

"No!" I sat upright. I could not let this farce continue a moment longer. "This is—it's not possible! You tell me I am supposed to marry a man I do not know? Because of some old feud that was started before I was born?"

"When you have had time to consider everything, and to know Ramon, you will not think such a marriage impossible. I have seen that you do not find it difficult to adapt yourself to a way of life that is different from yours, and in this case I think you will begin to understand why it is necessary. Is it not the custom in the country where you were born, too, that such alliances are made between families? The marriage between your father and your mother—was it not made for such reasons?"

"That may be so, but look what happened! They did not love each other. My father…"

"Your father was a wise man, and you are his daughter. You are here because he sent for you."

"To be married off to a stranger? To become a pawn?"

"You are a strong-willed woman. My daughter was such a one too. If she had married as I had wished her to—if I had not been weak with her because she had her mother's eyes… well, it is done, and past. But I will keep the word I gave to my brother." His eyes looked into mine, stilling the angry protests that leaped to my tongue. "You look defiant,

Nineteen

∂

I HAVE BEEN ACCUSED AT VARIOUS TIMES OF BEING COLD, ruthless, unfeeling, calculating. And perhaps I've been all these things. I remember the time, too, when I prided myself on the control I had over my emotions.

It has always made me furious to find myself caught up in a chain of circumstances over which I have no control, or to feel myself at another's mercy. I was so angry that evening when Lucas Cord turned and walked away from me that I could almost feel my rage choke me.

And yet, before the night was over I had managed to calm myself sufficiently to become rather curious about the valley I was to be taken to, and the people who lived there.

The idea that I might marry Ramon Kordes was still preposterous, but it appeared as though I would have no choice but to meet him again. Very well, then, I told myself firmly. If he's the gentleman they say he is, he will surely understand the awkwardness of the situation in which we have both been placed. When he realizes that I have no intention of being forced into a marriage of convenience, perhaps he will pave the way for my leaving. But what of Elena Kordes, of whom I'd heard so much? And what of Lucas?

He took pains to avoid me when the men took their evening meal. As usual *they* ate first, and the women waited patiently until the men had eaten their fill before they could begin.

I was surprised when just after we had eaten, the fat woman

my daughter. You will not be forced into such a marriage, or any marriage, you understand? But you must be given the time and the opportunity to know the man your father chose for you—perhaps to know both sides of a story. Go now, and think of what I have said to you."

I would have said more, cried out my angry protests, but I felt Lucas Cord's fingers close around my arm, bruising my flesh as he pulled me to my feet.

The old man looked at us through hooded, sleepy eyes. "She is your sister; you her brother. See that you respect and protect her. We will speak again before you leave for the valley."

I found myself outside, scarcely able to believe what I had just been told. Impossible!

I must have said aloud, "I won't!" for Lucas shook my arm, and I looked up to find him glowering down at me.

"You start hollerin' and makin' a scene an' I swear I'm goin' to beat you, sister or not!"

I gasped with frustration, and his lips twisted. "Better go back to your meek and mild act—it suited you a lot better. If you were my woman I'd cut your tongue out!"

I gathered my wits together and stood still, forcing myself to smile into his angry face. "But I am not. Perhaps you had best start remembering that fact."

He dropped my arm as if it burned his fingers, and it gave me pleasure to see the effort he made to control himself.

Without another word he turned on his heel and left me, leaving me to find my way back to the wickiup of Little Bird's relatives by myself.

who had been in the shaman's lodge came in and spoke in low tones to Little Bird's mother. It turned out that the old man had decided to make our relationship public. As the daughter of his blood brother he felt some sense of paternal obligation toward me, and I must therefore sleep in his lodge and consider it my home as long as I remained in the *ranchería*.

Little Bird whispered to me that I was being shown great honor, and even her formidable-looking mother gave me a look of grudging respect

The old shaman, who was already lying wrapped in his blankets before the coals, raised himself on an elbow and gave me a nod of welcome.

"It is the custom for our young, unmarried women to sleep in the lodge of an older relative," he said in his dry, papery voice. "Sleep well, my daughter." I understood that there was to be no more talking tonight. The fat squaw, whose name, I was to discover later, was Falling Leaf, could speak no Spanish. She signaled to me with motions of her hands that I should prepare myself for sleeping, and showed me a place against the wall where a blanket had already been laid out for me.

I wondered, as I lay down obediently, whether the old man was protecting my reputation, or whether he was showing his grandson, in this subtle way, that I was no longer to be treated as a captive, but as an Apache virgin. What *was* my real position here? What would it be when we left to journey to the hidden valley?

My whole life had changed so much within the space of a few weeks that I could hardly believe all this was really happening to me. Tonight I could not fall asleep from sheer tiredness, as I had done on the nights past. My mind was full of questions to which I had no answers, and when I finally did fall asleep my dreams were frightening. I dreamed of pursuit across a desert where my feet kept sinking deeply into the sand and I could hear the thundering hoofbeats of my pursuers close behind me. I knew both fear and despair when I found myself at the edge of a very tall cliff, looking down into nothingness; and I felt a hand clamp down on my shoulder, ready to push me over...

I started up, sweat streaming down my face, but it was only the old woman, waking me. For a moment, reality appeared unreal. I felt stiff in every limp, as if I'd actually been running, the blood pounding in my ears.

The shaman slept. He was an old man, and liked to sleep late into the day, Little Bird told me later, at the stream. Sometimes his dreams foretold certain events; sometimes they held warnings. I wondered if *my* dreams had been meant to warn me of the dangers I was going into.

The feeling of foreboding I had awakened with seemed to grow stronger and stronger as the day passed slowly by. I was kept busy. I had already learned that the women in an Apache camp were always kept occupied with one task or another while the men, when they were not on raiding or hunting trips, sat in front of their brush dwellings and saw to their weapons or gossiped among each other like men everywhere.

Little Bird took me with her to gather roots and wild berries to prepare into a kind of paste for the journey. As we followed the course of the small stream she pointed out different kinds of edible plants, and some whose leaves had medicinal properties. This morning I noticed that her manner was much less reserved, and she chattered to me as if we were truly friends. Every now and then she would call me *nidee,* sister, and look at me shyly. And then I noticed, in spite of my preoccupation, that on the few occasions she mentioned the journey that lay ahead of us she would say: "When you go to the valley…" or "When you start out tomorrow…"

"But you are coming too, are you not?"

She gave me a startled, somewhat puzzled look. "I thought you had already been told. My father is old, and he asked my husband if I could remain in his lodge for a few days longer, so that he can continue to take delight in our children. My husband was kind enough to agree."

It was my turn now to look startled. "But surely I'm not to be forced to travel alone with that man?"

"Oh, no!" Little Bird looked slightly reproachful. "My husband will be going too. It is a long time since he has seen his mother, and he says it is his duty. And three other warriors, for the hunting along the way. Two of them, who do not yet have children, will take their women along with them, to dress and cure the meat and pack the hides. You will not feel lonely, with two brothers to take care of you."

"Brothers?" I stared at her uncomprehendingly, and she put her hand over her mouth, giggling shyly behind it.

"My mother told me, and my aunt, who is a widow and looks after the shaman, told her what he said. She says she heard your father and my husband's grandfather talk of this long before you came to this land. Truly, *nidee,* if I had known you were to marry the younger brother of my husband, I would have made your arrival to the camp of our people a happier one. I am ashamed."

"But I..." I looked into her concerned face and could not say what I had almost burst out with. She would not have understood, and my defiance would only upset her. I would save the scathing speeches I had stored up all day for Lucas Cord, when I next confronted him.

But I did not see Lucas at all that day. The women found tasks to keep me busy, and with a semblance of meekness I followed their laughing directions, although I seethed with anger inside when I found that I was expected to prepare *his* food for the journey as well, and wash his trail-grimed clothes. I beat them against a flat rock by the stream, following the example of the other women; and I did it with a vicious fury, hoping they would shred into tatters.

"Not so hard!" Little Bird protested, half-laughing.

"But what about *me*? He tore my other clothes off my back, and *these* garments are all I have. They're filthy!"

She looked concerned. "I did not know, *nidee.* But your father the shaman will give you more. He is rich."

"It's not the same thing!" I protested.

That evening, however, the old man made a ceremonial presentation to me of the traditional Apache costume. "Our women now would rather wear garments of the white women than wear the buckskin garments that their mothers took such pride in wearing," he said in his dry voice. "These belonged to Carmelita, who was the mother of my daughter Elena. She wore them when I took her as my wife, before the whole tribe. It would please an old man's heart if you would accept them, my daughter."

The traditional Apache woman's costume consisted of a long skirt, reaching just above the ankles, richly embroidered with beads and quills. The high-necked overblouse was just as heavily embroidered and carefully fringed at the yoke and sleeves as the skirt had been.

"To please me, I would hope that you wear these garments when you reach the valley. Perhaps it will remind my daughter Elena that she is also an Apache."

"I'm proud that you would give these to me," I murmured. I could not help wondering if, perhaps, this old man with his seamed and wrinkled face had loved his young captive. And she—had she loved him in return? I was constantly being reminded, through old stories of other people's hates and sorrows and loves, of a past I'd had no share in. I was supposed to react, but how could I? Even my father was becoming more and more of a stranger to me. What had he really expected of me?

The shaman, my adopted father, seemed to take his duties seriously.

There were other gifts; moccasins, another full skirt of cotton with a yoked overblouse for traveling in.

It was the traveling itself, and my company, that I objected to most of all. I ventured to protest, and his face became closed.

"I had a dream last night. All this was meant. Your father, who should have been a shaman of his own people, saw it first."

"But he didn't even know where I was," I objected. "Or even if I would agree to come here."

"He knew that his blood ran in your veins. I tell you, daughter, he knew. Be at peace now. Try and learn to accept. Go to the valley; meet with Ramon. He is of the same world you came from. You cannot know your true feelings until you have first had a chance to find what they are, seeing both sides."

Again the shaman seemed to display an almost uncanny

power of reading my thoughts. "You are still angry at Lucas, are you not?"

"How can I help it? He has treated me despicably. There was a time when I tried to defend him to others. But when I was presented with proof…"

"The kind of proof you speak of has many sides, daughter. You heard this—proof from those who hate him. Have you asked him for the truth?"

"What truth?" I was too perturbed to be cautious. "I know that my father believed in him, but what of the things he did later? Shooting men from ambush, running away with Todd Shannon's stepdaughter, and then abandoning her. Selling her to another man! And all for revenge. She was killed at a barroom brawl afterwards. Does he know that?"

"Why don't you ask him?" The old man's voice was as soft as the rustling of dry leaves.

"Ask him?" I realized that my voice had risen, I tried to control it. "He would only lie, as he has done before. Or he would not answer my questions. Or he would grow angry with me."

"Is it justice that if a man has been accused by other men he should not be given a chance to answer these accusations?"

This old Indian might have been my own father—or my grandfather, who had first taught me of logic and justice.

My eyes dropped under his calm, steady gaze. "You think I should ask him?"

"It is what *you* think, my daughter. And what you must ask yourself. I can only tell you that Lucas is headstrong, and he is angry. But if you can put aside your hate and ask him what is in your mind, he will answer you. I have spoken to him, and he will show you the respect that he would show a sister. That is all." He sighed. "Peace can be achieved only if people will sit down together and speak of those things that trouble their minds. It is easy to be angry. Difficult to say, 'I would know what is troubling my brother—I will try to understand.'"

I sighed.

"You remind me of my grandfather. He was a stubborn, bull-headed old man with his own ideas. But he loved me, and he tried to teach me to use my mind. He told me that the fact that I was a woman didn't mean I could not think rationally. And I think you are trying to tell me the same thing."

"Did I not say that you had the mind of a clever man? You are your father's daughter. Seeing both sides of a coin."

I slept surprisingly well that night, perhaps because I had not yet seen Lucas. But all my feelings of resentment boiled up again the following morning, when we were supposed to set out.

I saw only two horses, already loaded down with supplies for our journey and stolen silver.

"But where are the *other* horses? You surely don't mean us to walk?"

"More horses would only slow us down, little sister." His voice was exaggeratedly polite, but I knew better. "You are an Apache now—walking will come easily to you, I'm sure."

I felt as if everyone else was watching us, as if I was being judged. The two women who were to accompany us were waiting, uncomplainingly, in spite of the heavy packs they carried on their backs. Julio stood beside his brother, his face, as usual, unreadable.

I shrugged lightly, hating myself for the gesture. At least *he* would understand sarcasm, if no one else did. "Of course. I should have guessed, shouldn't I?"

"When you see the kind of country we have to travel over, I think you'll understand better," he said quietly. I felt the words were a concession to his grandfather, who had risen early to see us off, and I turned away.

And so we traveled on foot, leading the horses more slowly than we had gone before, for we climbed upward.

The slopes of the Black Range became more thickly forested, the scent of piñon and alder sweet in the clear, cool air. The mountains seemed pristine, untouched; here were none of the ugly scars left by miners greedy for precious metals. It seemed as if nothing had ever dwelled here but the wild creatures whose natural habitat this was. I did not have to be told this was Apache country.

The men went ahead, their steps springy, easily breathing

the thinning air as we climbed. They carried rifles but when they shot game for our evening meal they used their ancient weapon, the bow and arrow.

Had I really walked all day? A week ago it would have seemed impossible. And yet we had only stopped a few times to rest the horses, and to snatch a quick meal of the pemmican-like paste that Little Bird had gone to such pains to show me how to prepare.

When we made camp for the night the sun had barely dropped behind the nearest ridge. The men found a small cave, scooped out in the side of a towering cliff, which would provide both shelter and protection from any predators. There were no brush shelters erected tonight; only a scooped out hollow for a small, smokeless fire, and blankets spread out against the rocky walls. I had begun to imagine that Apache women were merely slaves to their husbands, but seeing the shy looks that were exchanged, and the whispered talk between husbands and wives, I began to see another side of their lives. The two young women and their men were like young lovers anywhere—not quite used to each other yet, still embarrassed to show their feelings in front of others.

As for myself, I felt as if I was acting a part. Rowena Dangerfield—Apache virgin. Shy, modest, self-effacing. Blushing bride-to-be. The thought made me grimace. You're getting cynical, I warned myself; be careful! And indeed I would have to be careful if I ever wanted to be free again. I could dismiss Ramon Kordes easily. In spite of his bold Latin gallantry, he was a young man, and, I was sure, I could appeal to his sense of chivalry. No, it was not Ramon who made me frown thoughtfully into the darkness as I lay huddled in my blankets, trying to keep my teeth from chattering in the cold night air. It was the thought of his mother, the formidable Elena Kordes who had started a blood feud; the woman Todd Shannon hated and my father had loved. Ruthless, arrogant, designing; the kind of woman who had brought her sons up to hate as much as she did, and did not hesitate to use them as instruments of her revenge. What kind of a woman would I find when we arrived in the secret valley? Instinct told me that we would be adversaries, that I must not underestimate either her power or her determination. If Todd's story was to be believed this was the same woman who, when she was a young girl, had had her own cousin and her cousin's child killed so that *she* could take her cousin's husband. The woman of whom even her own father had said, "She was a strong-willed woman with a mind."

I turned uneasily, half-asleep. Tonight the men and the women slept separately, the men keeping watch in turns. The fire had been carefully extinguished, but I saw the dimly glowing red tip of a cigar, and smelled its odor, and knew which one of the men sat still and cross-legged just outside the small cave, his profile turned away from me.

Lucas Cord. The son who had made his mother's revenge his own. Was he too thinking of her? Half-remembered phrases flashed through my mind.

"He always did worship his mother... he adored her."

What kind of a man was he underneath all the savagery? What kind of woman was she to have produced such a son? I tried to imagine what she would look like after so many years. She would be older, of course, with wrinkles in her face, her black hair turned gray in streaks, no longer the young, passionately beautiful girl she had been. Imagination blended almost imperceptibly into half-dreamed images, and then everything vanished as I slid into a deep, dreamless sleep.

Twenty

As it turned out, Elena Kordes was not in the least as I had pictured her. But our first meeting did not take place at once. I had not expected the valley to be so large that it would take us almost four hours to cross it.

It took us a journey of almost five days after we had left the *ranchería* to reach a place of awesome grandeur, a mountaintop that seemed to jut out over another mountaintop. We had done nothing but climb to get here, and I felt myself ready to drop with weariness, although I knew better than to utter a murmur of protest. Lucas Cord had driven us all, and even his own brother had grumbled at him that there was no need for such haste.

"The hunting here is good—why hurry? We will get there in the end!"

Julio, when he spoke to me, had begun to address me with exaggerated politeness, always prefixing his requests with the word *nidee,* little sister. Still, when he thought I wasn't aware of it, I could feel his eyes upon me, making me feel vaguely uneasy.

Lucas, on the other hand, paid no attention to me unless he had to. He had dropped his old, sneering attitude, it was true, but this had been replaced by a kind of distance. He would thank me when I handed him his food, warn me when the terrain ahead of us became rough or perilous, but that was all. It was just as if the violent conflict between us had never been, and I found myself observing him, wondering what drove him.

All throughout our journey here he had seemed preoccupied. I noticed that he hardly spoke to anyone unless he was addressed, and he would sit by the fire when we made camp and stare away from the flame, into the distance. What was he thinking of?

Julio, sitting by me one night, followed the almost unconscious direction of my eyes and said softly, "My brother is a deep thinker, eh? Even for me, he is not an easy person to know." His voice had turned almost sly. "But in this case I can guess what he is thinking of. There is a woman who waits for him on my mother's rancho. She is young and lovely, the daughter of an old friend who died. I think she waits for Lucas to make up his mind."

"I'm sorry to say so," I said disdainfully, "but I cannot help feeling sorry for her!"

"You do not like my brother?" Was it my imagination, or did I fancy I heard a slight note of satisfaction in Julio's voice? The next moment he shrugged, as if the matter was unimportant. "Perhaps it is better so for your sake, *nidee*."

I did not ask him why he had said such a thing to me, not wanting the conversation to continue; and after a moment he stretched, yawning, and left me.

I stood with the others in the thin layer of snow that still lay on the ground here, and told myself vehemently that I could not possibly walk another step. What were we supposed to do now? Scale that unscalable cliff like mountain goats, and then think of a way to get around that jutting overhang that loomed menacingly over us?

Lucas Cord was looking upward also, and I thought I saw some strange blend of emotion in his face for the first time. There was the urgency I had sensed in him earlier, and something else. Despair? Frustration? It was hard to tell. Perhaps something had gone wrong; perhaps he couldn't find the way into the hidden valley, with the snow still lying on the ground.

I saw Lucas take a coiled length of rawhide from the saddle of one of the horses and put it around his neck. Then, without another word, he flattened himself against the sheer, rocky cliff face, and seemed to walk right off one edge. I think I must have gasped, for I saw Julio look towards me.

"There is a path, *nidee*. Not much, but the mountain goats made it long ago. That was how Lucas found the way into the valley. Wait, and you will see how we will all find our way there soon."

I thought we waited for an endless time, but it was probably no longer than fifteen minutes at the most. Julio and the three Apache braves talked together in casual tones. The women busied themselves with unpacking the horses, and in the end, feeling ashamed of my inactivity, I started to help them. The packs containing the silver were heavy. They reminded me of the way in which this same silver had been obtained. Stolen, and stained with the blood of those poor soldiers who had died trying to defend it.

I heard one of the women cry out and turned at almost the same time she did, to see the rope come snaking down.

There must have been some kind of cleft up there, between the huge, overhanging mountain edge and the rocky cliff I had dismissed as being unscalable.

I stared at it in dismay. Were we expected to crawl up that steep, rocky cliff face with nothing but a thin rope to support us?

I turned to Julio, intending to make some protest, but he had already seized the dangling end of the rope, and now, using his feet for leverage against the sheer wall of rock, he began to clamber up it with surprising agility.

No sooner had he disappeared into what, from here, seemed no more than a tiny, dark-shadowed cleft, than Lucas Cord came down, the rope sliding between his gloved hands.

Without a word to me he and the other men began immediately to loop the end of the rope around one of the saddlebags, which Julio then hauled up. I stood to one side with the two other women, trying to hide the fact that I was getting angrier and angrier by the minute.

I won't go up that ridiculous rope! If my hands were to slip… I shuddered inwardly, trying not to think of it. Already my palms had begun to feel damp with sweat, and although I despised myself for cowardice, I had never cared for great heights.

The silver was hauled up first, the heavy saddlebags bumping against the face of the mountain. Then our food and supplies, including the hides and meat of the deer and bear that the men had shot.

The men went up next, just as easily as Julio had done. The women motioned to me politely, indicating that I might go first, but I shook my head just as politely. I thought that Lucas Cord raised a sarcastic eyebrow, but he said nothing except to give the women what was obviously some advice, in Apache. I watched them both clamber up with amazing ease, giggling as if it was some kind of amusing game to them.

Why did I have to be left here with *him*? I thought he sensed my fear and gloated at it; even his next words seemed to carry an undertone of irony.

"It is your turn, little sister. You ain't afraid, are you?"

"Of course I'm not afraid!" I said sharply. "But what are you going to do about the horses? How do you intend to get *them* up there?"

I think he knew I was procrastinating. The cleft in his cheek deepened, and he narrowed his eyes at me thoughtfully.

"You worried about those two sorry-lookin' nags? Didn't think you'd be so softhearted."

Why did he always succeed in making me angry? I had the feeling he was taunting me.

"You're surely not going to…"

"Thought about butchering them for the meat." Catching my horrified look, he shrugged. "But if it upsets you, we could leave them right here. These are wild ponies. They'll find food for themselves until the others get ready to leave."

"How casual you are about life, whether it's animal or human! Those poor beasts…"

"Can look after themselves fine, like I just told you. An' if you don't get started I'm goin' to have to tie one end of that rope around your waist an' haul you up like one of them sacks!"

The threatening step he took towards me made me back away. Looking back, I think it was only my anger that gave me the courage to scale that cliff face, not daring to look down. Lucas offered me his gloves, but I would not accept them.

My palms carried rope burns for a few days afterwards, and I collected bruises on my knees and hips from bumping against sharp rocks as I pulled myself upward, trying to remember how the others had done it. I was never more relieved than when I felt Julio's strong hands close around my wrists as he lifted me up onto a rocky shelf that widened into a cave.

"Come, *nidee*. We go this way."

With my knees still shaking I followed Julio around a sharp bend, and saw light at the other end of what was not actually a cave, but a tunnellike fault in the mountain.

No wonder they called this the hidden valley! I could understand why it would be almost impossible to find, and how even one man, with enough ammunition, could hold off a whole army of attackers.

"My brother found this place when he came into the mountains alone to seek his medicine dream," Julio told me. "He saw a mountain goat seem to disappear and followed it, and that was how he came upon the valley. See, *nidee*? All around are the sides of the mountain, like walls. It is as if the mountains were split in the middle, to make this place."

I looked around wonderingly after we had emerged again into the daylight, and began to scramble down a rocky slope into a meadow with grama grass growing waist-high.

I thought I could see for miles ahead; the valley appeared narrow at this end, but I could see where it began to widen further on. The part I could see to my right was more rocky and mountainous, with enormous boulders scattered about as if they had rolled down the cliff many centuries ago, when perhaps a gigantic earthquake or some other upheaval of nature had created this natural valley. "It's beautiful!" I said to Julio, and he grunted with pride.

"But you have seen so little, yet. Wait until we travel farther, and then you will see! There is plenty of water here, and there are cattle and horses too. They do well here, and the herds grow, but I tell you it was a very difficult task to get them in here at the beginning!"

I thought of Lucas, who would not be troubled to bring those poor horses who had carried the silver all the way up here into the valley, and my lips tightened with indignation. And almost at the same time, he caught up with us.

The Apache warriors who had accompanied us here had disappeared, along with their women, and I was suddenly all too conscious of the fact that I was alone with my two adopted "brothers." I told myself angrily that I could almost see Julio in the role, perhaps, but certainly not Lucas.

"I suppose we have to walk again?" I said in a voice that had hardened instinctively, now that *he* had appeared.

I looked at Julio when I spoke, but it was Lucas who answered my question. "There are horses a few miles up ahead, in a small corral. Ramon always sees that they are kept here in case they should be needed."

"How thoughtful," I murmured coldly, and saw Julio's eyes go from one to the other of us, although he made no comment. He knew I had no fondness for his brother; why should I pretend?

We walked forward again, with Lucas in the lead this time, and Julio following closely behind me. He seemed considerate of me and it was his hand that closed around my arm when I stumbled. Lucas did not even turn his head to see if we followed or not.

I cannot remember how far we walked. The valley widened and seemed to stretch before us, like a miniature kingdom. The country to the left was flat and grassy for the most part, to the right, where the mountain peaks seemed to tower higher than they did anywhere else, the terrain seemed rougher, and split by deep, narrow gullies or arroyos, which, Julio explained, could become roaring watercourses in the summer, when the snow began to melt on the mountaintops.

The corral Lucas had spoken of was a rough, wooden enclosure nestled in grass taller than any I'd ever seen before. There were four or five horses in it: restless, high-stepping animals of Arab stock.

Apaches did not use saddles—only blankets thrown across a horse's back and bridles made of plaited horsehair or buckskin. Even these were provided in a small lean-to by the side of the corral.

"Would you like to choose which one you'd like to ride?" Surprising me, Lucas came to lean his elbows on the rough fence beside me.

I have always loved horses, and I couldn't pretend indifference.

"That one—the spotted stallion. The breed is unfamiliar, I think, although I believe I can detect Arab blood in him."

"You're a pretty good judge of horseflesh, *nidee*." Even the slightly sarcastic inflection of his voice when he called me sister could not detract from the fact that he had actually paid me a compliment. "He's half Appaloosa. Sired by the first horse I ever owned, off an Arabian mare. You sure you can handle him?"

Was he challenging me again? I gave him a level look, but I could detect no mockery in his face this time.

"May I ride him?"

He shrugged. "Mount him from the *right* side. An' remember he's used to bein' guided mostly by the pressure of your knees. Got a soft mouth, so don't saw back too hard on the reins. Best horse in the corral. You've chosen well."

In spite of my earlier forebodings I could not help feeling a thrill of anticipation at being able to ride again. Lucas, for a change, was being almost affable, and Julio, away from his responsibilities as a family man, seemed lighthearted.

After the horses had been "saddled" Apache fashion, we set out, and it was Julio who complimented me this time.

"I see that our little sister rides well," he commented to Lucas, who merely nodded, his eyes flickering over me without expression. He seemed to have relapsed into his usual mood of somber introspection, and as we rode forward I found myself studying him covertly. He looked like a man with something eating at him inside, but why? He was free; he had a girl waiting for him. I didn't think he was the kind of man who'd have a conscience that would bother him.

We skirted another deep, steep-sided canyon that seemed to climb to the mountain's edge, and Julio, riding close to me, said in a low voice, "My brother has a small cabin up there, a place he goes to when he wants to be alone. Even I have not been there. But then—" and he shrugged, "I do not come here often. I prefer the freedom of my people."

Every now and then I found myself forgetting that Julio was an Apache subchief, and the father of two young children. Like his brother, he was something of an enigma. But it was Lucas, in spite of everything I knew about him, who intrigued me most. A man like him—why would he want to be alone? I could better imagine him acting on sheer animal impulse. What had intrigued poor Flo so much that she would leave the security she had had to follow him? Above all, and the thought came to me like a blow, what was I doing here, in the midst of all this intrigue, playing the part of a helpless pawn?

We were descending, almost imperceptibly, into a part of the valley that was like a bowl, a green and brown depression within a depression. Even the climate seemed to have changed in some subtle way. There was no snow here, and the air seemed slightly warmer. The mountains that ringed us seemed to tower loftily and even more impenetrably. Craggy peaks brushed with snow, cloud-touched in some places.

Again I thought, what am I doing here? How did I come to be here? But strangely, the thought did not frighten me as it had done before. I could not help feeling exhilarated by the challenge that lay ahead of me, and the beauty of the land that lay around me. A tiny Eden. How long had this valley lain here, like a woman untouched, waiting to be taken? Even the thoughts that came into my mind were strange, not my usual, *practical* thoughts. I was here. The old shaman had talked of things that were meant to be; and I recalled now that I had heard so-called wise men in India speak of something they called *karma,* one's inescapable fate, shaped by all the events in the past. Strange, but ever since I had received that first communication from my father, I had been caught up in the past, moved and influenced by things that had taken place long before I was born. My being here too had something to do with the past, but I felt, quite suddenly, that for the first time since I had come to America I was completely on my own, with no one else to guide me, advise me. But I had my wits, my intelligence…

Julio, who had ridden ahead with Lucas for the last few

minutes, now dropped back, bringing his mount beside mine. "You like what you have seen so far?"

"How can I help it?" My response was honest. "It's beautiful. But—" and I spoke aloud the question that had been puzzling me for some time, "Where are all the people? I've seen cattle, and horses; who looks after them?"

He made a sound that might have passed for laughter in another man.

"You have sharp eyes, *nidee*. Yes, we have people who tend to the animals here—not many, but a few trusted men my mother brought with her from Mexico. But no doubt they are at the house now, having their evening meal. It is getting late, and the sun drops from view early here. There's no need to watch for intruders in this place, for who could find it?"

"But surely your people know of this place?"

"A few do. But we respect the dwelling places of our friends and families. Sometimes if a winter has been very hard, we come here. There is always food and game to be found if we want it. My brothers who came with us will stay here for a while, until the hides we took have been cured, and the meat smoked and packed away. And then they will return."

"Why don't they come with us?"

"The Apache does not like to live in a house. They will find their own place and the women will build a wickiup to shelter them."

"You left the silver too," I said a trifle sarcastically, but Julio was impervious to sarcasm.

"Who will touch it? Later, one of my mother's *vaqueros* will go and bring it back to the house."

"The house," I repeated slowly. "Won't you feel stifled within the walls and roof of a house?"

"I think that already you have come to understand my people, *nidee*. Yes, I do not like houses either. I will sleep outside, even though my mother will not like it."

I wanted to ask him why he had come. His voice held no inflection of affection when he spoke of his mother, although perhaps that was because he was an Apache, and not accustomed to any outward show of emotion. I said impulsively, "I wish Little Bird had come with us!" and he gave me a guarded look that might have held some pleasure.

"Little Bird does not like my mother. My mother does not like her. My wife is happier with her people. But I am glad you are fond of her, as she is of you. In the short time you lived with us you learned our ways very quickly, little sister."

I had the feeling that he might have said more if Lucas had not swung his horse around and ridden back to us.

As usual, I felt a surge of resentment at his flickering look that seemed to tell me how untidy and unkempt I must look, with strands of hair escaping from my braids.

"It ain't but a short distance now, but we'll stop for a while to rest the horses. You want to take a bath, change clothes, there's a small stream back there, behind those trees."

Unconsciously, my hand went up to brush tendrils of hair from my face, and his mouth tilted at the corner.

"Give you ten minutes on your own, sister. And then I'm comin' in too. Need to wash off some of the trail dirt."

Under his sardonic gaze I took the small pack containing my new clothes from the back of the horse I had chosen and walked, without a backward glance, in the direction at which he'd pointed. So I had to make myself more presentable before I met his mother, did I? I could almost have wished I had those ugly clothes I'd worn on my journey from Boston. Ramon would certainly not want to marry me if he had seen me then!

But in spite of the anger that Lucas could always arouse in me, the stream was cool and refreshing, and I *did* feel better for being clean again. Remembering my promise to the shaman, I put on the traditional Apache dress he had given me, and combed my wet hair so that it hung loosely down my back. Vanity, I chided myself, but I could not help staring at my reflection in the water and wondering what Elena Kordes would think when she saw me.

PART IV:

THE VALLEY OF HIDDEN DESIRES

Twenty-One

My first impression, as I saw Elena Kordes walk down the steps of the rambling Spanish-style adobe and wood house, was that she could not possibly be as young as she looked.

There was still light in the sky, but the lamps had been lit, and formed a background for the jewels that sparkled in the elaborate Spanish-style comb she wore in her high-piled black hair. They were rubies, like the stones she wore around her neck.

"My sons!"

Her voice was rich and musical, only slightly accented.

"*Si, madre*—your sons."

Was it my imagination, or was there a faintly sardonic note in Julio's voice?

I had the feeling that I was watching something carefully staged as Julio went forward to accept his mother's embrace with a casual one of his own.

"Lucas!" He had been standing at the bottom of the steps, his head tilted slightly to watch her, but now as he caught her against him I felt strangely awkward, as if I was watching some private performance I had no right to witness.

"You're more beautiful than ever, Elena!"

She laughed like a young girl, her hands going up to touch his face as he released her. "And you, what is your excuse for staying away so long this time? I've missed you. We have all missed you."

Again the words that my father had written flashed through my mind at that instant—"Lucas adores his mother…"

And certainly, as he looked down at her, his face looked suddenly young and unguarded. In the rapidly dimming light I could not decide what the expression he wore for just a moment could mean, and the next minute he was smiling at her teasingly.

"I think I stay away only to hear you say that when I return!" His tone was light, but it held an undercurrent of emotion I had never heard in his voice before. His hands touched her shoulders lightly, and close behind Julio said softly, "Is it not touching to see such devotion between mother and son?"

I thought he was jealous, and could not blame him. Those two…

And then, for the first time, Elena Kordes noticed me.

"But that is not Little Bird! Julio, have you taken another wife already?"

Lucas gave a smothered snort of laughter that made me throw my head back angrily. He had no right to place me in such an embarrassing position, and poor Julio as well.

But surprisingly Julio seemed equal to the occasion. "Not yet, *mamacita*, but it is not improbable that I may think about it soon."

Lucas stopped smiling and started to frown. I saw his eyes narrow at Julio.

I stepped forward boldly and stood at the bottom of the steps, looking up at this beautiful, proud-looking woman, who looked as young as I, and carried herself like a duchess.

"Since your sons have neglected to perform the common civilities, I suppose I must introduce myself," I said, keeping my voice even. "My name is Rowena Dangerfield. You knew my father."

If my rather blunt announcement had startled her, she hid it well. I noticed only the arching of her dark brows, and then, with a reproachful glance at Lucas, she hurried down to steps to me, both hands extended.

"*You* are Rowena? Guy's daughter? But how thoughtless

of my sons not to have sent ahead to tell me—they are both barbarians, I am afraid." She touched my hands, dropped them, and then, taking me by surprise, put one soft hand under my chin, tilting my face slightly to one side.

"Forgive me, but your eyes are so like your father's! Ah, yes—I should have noticed your eyes, in spite of the Apache ceremonial dress you wear." She laughed softly. "It was my father's idea, I suppose. So like him. But it was good of you to indulge him, all the same."

There was no trace in the woman who stood before me now of the half-wild Apache girl she had been. Except for her slight Spanish accent, Elena Kordes would have fit very well in any London drawing room.

"Your father was very kind to me. And the ceremonial dress of the Apache women is beautiful."

I heard Julio's grunt of approval behind me. "My little sister has adapted herself well to our ways. And she *is* Apache, now that the shaman our grandfather has adopted her as his other daughter."

I heard Elena's sharply drawn breath, and saw her turn her head to look at Lucas, who lounged negligently against one of the carved wooden posts that stood on either side of the stone steps.

His voice was noncommittal. "It is true. The shaman and Guy Dangerfield were blood brothers, remember? Seemed to take a liking to her."

"I'm sorry that I cannot say the same thing with regard to my feelings toward *you,* Lucas Cord!" I snapped.

"She's got a nasty temper, and the tongue of a shrew," he said to his mother over my head. "Still, perhaps Ramon can make something of her!"

I saw the bright glitter of Elena Kordes's eyes as her look went from one to the other of us.

When Julio, his voice heavy with significance, said suddenly, "You forget, brother, that I am also a Kordes by blood," it was Elena's sudden frown that held Lucas silent.

"That's enough! You will not begin your visit by squabbling like children! Rowena, please... Come with me. You are here, and I am happy. As for my sons, it is sometimes best to ignore them!"

I had had a biting retort on the tip of my tongue when Lucas had spoken. Now I bit it back, and went with Elena. I was *here,* with the mountains that ringed us reminding me that this valley could be a prison as well as a refuge. For the moment, protest would not only be pointless but foolish as well. "Know thine enemy…"

It seemed as if I was to be given both the time and the opportunity to know mine!

No whit perturbed by my tight-lipped silence. Elena Kordes continued to speak as she led me through the large entrance hall and up the shallow staircase that connected it with a kind of gallery, running along three sides of the room.

"This house is simply built, as you see, but I chose the Spanish style, which is so much better suited to our climate here. You like the idea of a gallery? It makes for coolness in the summer, and for a feeling. I think of—what is the word I seek? Spaciousness, yes, that is it. The bedrooms open off the gallery too." She moved her hand, and I saw the deep, rich gleam of an enormous pigeon's-blood ruby, embedded in an antique setting. "That wing is kept for my sons and their guests. On this side Luz and I have our rooms. You've heard of Luz?"

I shook my head, wondering why I felt that her expansive, friendly chattering was somehow at variance with the real nature of this woman. Was it only because my mind had already been prejudiced against her? She frowned slightly, pushing open a door that must surely lead into her own bedroom—large, and beautifully furnished, dominated by an enormous four-poster bed.

"They have neglected to tell you anything, I see! Luz is… the daughter of a very old friend. After her father died, Lucas brought her here, and she has lived here ever since. A sweet child, and I am glad of her companionship. When my son is ready to give up his wandering ways… well, I have always hoped they would marry some day. Luz imagines herself in love with him, I think." Again, I had the strange impression that I was being tested in some way; that Elena watched for my reaction.

I shrugged, moving farther into the room. "If they are to marry, I suppose it would help if she imagined herself in love with him. But if I am to be frank, I can only say I feel sorry for the poor girl. Does she know about Flo Jeffords, and what happened to *her*?"

I think it was at that moment that the pretense dropped between us. We faced each other fully, her hand on the door of a heavily carved armoire that stood in one corner of the room.

"You don't like Lucas. That is strange, for most women do. Perhaps you're only angry because he brought you here. Or is it because you really imagined yourself in love with Todd Shannon?"

It had been said, at last. Todd's name fell between us like a stone, and although I think she hoped to disconcert me, I was relieved that I could be myself again. "I don't know if I love Todd Shannon or not. I am engaged to marry him. It seemed the most practical thing to do. Why should love enter into it? I am more practical than sentimental, I'm afraid."

"And that is why you are here, is it not? Yes, you look like Guy, but you are not like him. Guy had too much sensibility, he felt too much."

"Perhaps I am more like *you*," I said softly. "I can bend, if I have to, but I will not break."

Amazingly, she clapped her hands together, the ruby ring sparkling in the lamplight. "I am almost sorry that you were not my daughter, now! I think you understand how much stronger than men a woman can be. I wondered, when I saw you in the Apache dress. Guy's daughter, I thought. Is she as meek as she looks? Will she be like Luz? And you are not. Luz is frightened of me. I think you have a mind of your own. There is a challenge here—for both of us. Will you marry one of my sons to please your dead father? Will you continue to be stubborn? In any case, I think your coming here will save me from boredom." She smiled, opening the armoire to reveal rows of dresses. "I think you will feel more comfortable in one of my gowns. We are almost of the same height and build, I believe. Will you choose?"

At least I was on familiar ground again. I smiled at her, and moved forward to study the variety of clothing she had offered me.

"You are very kind. And I *do* have a mind of my own, as well as being practical. Are you sure you will not mind my wearing one of these dresses?"

She laughed delightedly. "And why should I? No, I want you to look beautiful for my sons. And for me too, perhaps. For I think we will arrive at an understanding of each other in the end. It has been a long time since I've felt challenged."

"Or I..." I said softly, and we smiled at each other.

When we went down to dinner, we were almost allies. Beneath the surface we both knew the reasons for my being here, and my resentment of the fact. And yet, in some strange way, I think Elena enjoyed the thought that my presence might act as a catalyst. She helped me choose a gown of rich blue silk. Impatiently, seating me before her mirror, she helped me pin up my hair, so that it fell from a coiled knot at the back of my head to thick curls around my neck and shoulders.

"You have hair as black and as thick as mine... how is it that you did not take after your mother? She was an English blonde, Guy told me. You were not sorry to leave her?"

"My mother was not sorry to see me leave," I said shortly. "We had nothing in common."

"It's strange. I think that you and I have much in common after all," Elena said, and laughed softly.

I said bluntly, "I can't imagine why you would want me to marry your son. Would *you* do the same thing in my place?"

"Perhaps, if I had no other choice! Your father wished it, you know. And I have three sons. You may choose."

"And if I want none of them?" I had to ask it, but she only shook her head at me.

"I think, if you are sensible, and *practical,* as you say you are, you will choose one of them. It is the only way you will leave this valley. You see, I am not only practical, but determined as well. And after all, it is not such a hard choice, is it? My sons are young men. Todd Shannon is old—too old for you, I think. But we can talk about it later."

I recognized a certain note of implacability in her voice and shrugged my shoulders. We would talk. I was sure of it. And in the meantime, I felt sure that the meal we were about to partake of would prove an interesting experience.

The great, polished table could have held at least thirty guests without crowding them, and yet there were only six places laid.

I saw Ramon Kordes again, and answered his awkward bow with a slight inclination of my head. Luz was an attractive dark-haired girl of about nineteen, wearing the full, brightly colored skirt and low-cut blouse of a Mexican woman, her loosely flowing hair falling below her waist. Her pretty face looked rather sullen, and from the glances she threw in my direction I did not think she liked my being here. Her attention seemed to be centered on Lucas, who treated her with a casual indifference that set my teeth on edge. I noted that he had not bothered to change clothes, although he had shaved off his half-grown beard. And even Julio had made some effort to observe the niceties, although it was clear he felt uncomfortable seated at a table.

In spite of the formality of the place settings and the room we dined in, with its low-beamed ceiling and dark, Spanish furniture, I learned that we would have to serve ourselves. The food was of the highly spiced variety that Marta excelled in cooking; and the old woman who brought it in and left the covered dishes at one end of the table looked to be at least seventy years old.

It was Ramon, surprisingly enough, who began the argument after I had come down with his mother, and we had seated ourselves.

I had noticed that Luz jumped to her feet and began to pass the steaming dishes of food around, beginning with the men. It reminded me of the Apache *ranchería,* where the women always waited until the men had eaten first; and almost automatically, I started to help her.

Julio took my impulsive movement for granted. Lucas raised one eyebrow and looked towards his younger brother.

"You see how well-trained she is already? She has even learned how to cook; isn't that right, Julio?"

Ramon pushed back his chair with a crash that surprised us all, even I, with a retort on the tip of my tongue.

"Even for *you,* this is going too far!" He looked angrily at Lucas. "Have you forgotten the debt you owe to Rowena's father? She is a gently brought up lady, and not just another captive you've picked up on your travels! You have no right…"

"Little brother, I have every right to do as I please, an' you better start remembering that. Bought her for a perfectly good Henry rifle an' several rounds of ammunition, didn't I, Rowena? An' if I hadn't, she'd be in some crib in Mexico by now, or dead. Better be grateful I brought her here instead, brother, or I might just change my mind an' enter the goddamn sweepstakes myself!"

"If I am supposed to be the prize in the sweepstakes you talk about, you'd better forget it, Lucas Cord! You are the last man on earth I'd consider!"

"Rather have Shannon, wouldn't you? But as far as he's concerned you're dead—or worse. So you'd better start looking around for a substitute. Might do better with a younger man, even if he ain't half owner of the almighty SD!"

I heard my own sucked-in breath of rage in the silence that followed.

"*Man,* you say? Are we talking about *men*? Being hardly one yourself, how would you know? Taking a woman by force is more your style, isn't it?"

"You sorry that I didn't take you by force? Maybe that's what's turned you into a damned shrew."

Elena's voice cut across his angry speech like a knife blade.

"That is enough! Lucas, have you forgotten your manners?"

And then Ramon, his voice choked with anger. "It is always Lucas who forgets himself, as usual. He was insulting… it is clear he is not used to civilized company! I ask your forgiveness, Lady Rowena, for my brother's manners."

"Are you tryin' to tell me that being civilized means you've gotta act the hypocrite, little brother?" I hated the drawling, sarcastic manner in which Lucas addressed his own brother, leaning back in his chair with one eyebrow slightly arched. And if I had been Ramon, I would have hit him!

I thought, for a moment, that Ramon would do just that. He stood at the table, gripping its edge so hard that his knuckles looked white. "You dare call *me* the hypocrite, Lucas? You of all people!"

His voice was heavy with a significance that was lost on me, but for some reason I saw that Lucas had become angry, his narrowed eyes taking on the familiar cat-gleam I had learned to recognize.

It was only Elena's warning, "Lucas!" that stopped him from some violent, irresponsible action.

I saw him take a deep breath, and noticed that the corners of his mouth had whitened. There was a tension here that I did not understand, and as furious as I was, it made me curious.

"Ramon—you will sit down and try to remember that you, at least, were brought up as a gentleman!" Elena said sharply. She added in a more controlled voice, "I am sure that Rowena is quite able to fight her own battles. Is that not so?"

Since she had addressed me, I shrugged, putting a feigned lightness in my voice.

"So far I have been quite capable of doing so." I looked into Ramon's upset face and smiled. "It was kind of you to come to my defense, but unnecessary. I have become quite used to your brother's ill-mannered ways!"

"I apologize to you for him," Ramon said quietly, and for the moment the incident was ended. It had, however, made me aware that a kind of tension did exist between the three brothers, and that in some way my presence here had brought it out into the open. Had it always been there? Was it because both Julio and Ramon were jealous of Lucas, who was so obviously his mother's favorite?

I told myself that I would find out. For all that a polite pretense existed that I was a guest, all of us knew better. I had been brought here to this valley for a purpose, and furthermore, in a moment of weakness, I had promised an old man that I would try to keep an open mind while I heard the other side of the old story that had already affected so many lives, my own included.

My grandfather had taught me that there were always two sides to every argument. Surely there could be no harm in exercising some patience, in watching and listening? How long ago it seemed now since Mr. Bragg had given me that advice; and every time I thought of Mr. Bragg I felt my hatred and mistrust almost choke me. And Elena Kordes—how much did she know of her son's activities?

I suppose I must have looked thoughtful, for the next moment I heard Ramon, who was seated beside me, murmur in a low voice: "If you only knew how angry and unhappy it makes me to find what my brother has been up to *this* time! If he's treated you badly…"

I made an impatient movement of my shoulders. "Why speak of it? This is not the first time I've been forced to make the best of circumstances. Believe me, I'm not as weak as I may look!"

He said fervently, "You are magnificent! When I think of all that you must have undergone these past weeks…"

"Your brother Julio and his wife were very kind," I said pointedly. "And so was your grandfather." I hoped that Lucas Cord had overheard, but when I shot him a fleeting glance through the screen of my lashes, I found his attention fixed on his mother, who was laughing at something he had said.

Twenty-Two

~

Later that night, in my room, I finally had some time to collect my thoughts and impressions of the day.

Luz and I had connecting rooms which were separated by a low archway, instead of a door. She apologized in a small, rather sullen voice for the lack of privacy, but I could not help wondering if I had been deliberately put here so that she could watch me.

"If it grows too hot at night, you can step through the window here—you will see where the roof of the gallery below gives just enough room to stand and catch some coolness."

She made as if to close the shutters she had just opened, and it was at that moment that the smell of cigar smoke drifted up to us.

I heard Lucas Cord's husky voice, with an almost desperately yearning note in it.

"You know why I do not come more often! My God—do you think I'm made of steel? There are times…"

"And there are such times for me too! Do you think I enjoy feeling myself a prisoner here?"

"Jesus Montoya comes to see you. That ring on your finger is new, ain't it? He just give it to you for old times sake? *Christ*, Elena! I can't stay away, and every time I come back here I…"

"Remember when you promised to kill dragons for me? You were a child then, and more Apache than Julio is. And I saw your eyes on me… you did not want to like me, did you? And I did not want to like you. But I knew at that moment that we would ask you to come with us, and that you would come."

I have never heard such stark unhappiness in any man's voice, either before or since.

"Once I had seen you, you were my medicine dream. You were... but I haven't killed your dragon for you yet, have I?"

"I think you will, in the end. And then you will see..."

Elena's soft voice floated up to us, and I turned away at the same moment that Luz closed the shutters, very gently, but with a controlled kind of force.

Our eyes met, and her face was haggard, her lips compressed.

"So now you know why Lucas and I are not married. Why he will never marry any woman! Did you think that he brought you here for himself?"

"He brought me here for Ramon. Perhaps also out of some idea of revenge. I was engaged to marry Todd Shannon, or didn't anyone think to tell you?"

Luz's small face seemed to crumple. "They told me nothing! But they never do. I only thought... I *know* that Lucas has other women, but that is when he is away from the valley. Here... but what does it matter? He took me from Montoya, and said he wanted me as his woman, but he treats me as if I were a little sister! And *she*—she laughs, and encourages us to be together. 'Why don't you take Luz out riding with you? You and Luz...' she says. 'You are young, you ought to have fun... take her to Mexico with you...' She is so sure of him, you see! And then he brought *you*..."

Suddenly I wished that I hadn't heard that curiously revealing naked dialogue under the window nor Luz's unashamedly honest confession of the frustration that made her so wretched.

I had been so determined to remain a spectator; now I found myself angry, for her sake.

"If they have not told you anything else, at least you must have guessed that I am not exactly here of my own accord," I said dryly. I suddenly remembered Julio's sardonic, subtly sneering words. "Such devotion between mother and son!"

What we had heard could have been a conversation between lovers. Was that why there was so much tension in this house, and so many undercurrents?

I felt sorry for Luz, who had been foolish enough to fall in love with a man who loved his mother too much to have room in his affections for any other woman.

"Are you going to marry Ramon, then?"

Luz looked at me curiously, although I thought there was a trace of tears in her eyes.

"Quite frankly, I would rather choose the man I am to marry! But you may be sure I have no designs on Lucas Cord. I'm sorry, Luz, but I can neither like nor trust him. In fact, I think I have conceived a tremendous dislike for him! Even Julio is more of a gentleman."

Contrarily, she sprang to Lucas's defense. "You don't know Lucas then! I know what people say of him, but he is kind. It is not his fault that Elena has him bewitched. Julio is married, and Ramon—oh, Ramon is kind too, but he is not as much of a man as his brother is! It was Lucas who found this place and brought them all here. It is he who provides all that we need."

I faced her squarely.

"Well, then, if you are in love with him, why won't you do something about it? Why do you let him continue to walk all over you? And see you as a sister? Elena Kordes is an attractive woman, and she's strong, but *you* are not his mother, and if you set yourself to it…"

"You do not understand!" She turned away from me, and flung herself across her bed. "How could you? You have not been here long enough!"

"Perhaps *you* have been here too long," I answered her coolly. "Sometimes it takes an outsider to see things as they really are, you know! Do you expect to get what you want without making any attempt to achieve it? I've been only here a few hours, it's true, but already I've learned that you are infatuated with Lucas, that Ramon is already on the verge of becoming infatuated with *me*, and that Lucas Cord has eyes for nobody but his mother." She turned her head to look at me, her eyes startled, and I continued thoughtfully. "The only person here who remains something of an enigma is Julio, but I daresay I will come to understand him soon enough."

"How can you stand here and speak so calmly of all this?" Luz demanded, and I noticed that she was about to cry. "I watched you tonight, and I could not help noticing how easy you find it to talk, even if most of us are strangers to you! The only time you became angry was when Lucas said…" she bit her lip and continued in a quieter voice, "I thought that perhaps it was Lucas you might have preferred, and you were angry because he ignored you."

"I have many reasons for being angry with Lucas, but his *ignoring* me is not one of them! In fact, it would make my enforced stay here much more pleasant if I did not have to see him at all!" I bit back other words that sprang to my lips. There was no point in antagonizing Luz, after all. It might be much more convenient if I could persuade her to be my friend, or at least to confide in me. There might come a time when I would need help, for I was already determined that I would leave this valley without being forced into any marriage, no matter what devious methods I might be forced to resort to.

Luz had sat up, and continued to stare at me wonderingly. "You are so very different from the way I had imagined you would be. I think you have been used to doing as you please."

I shrugged. "I have always had an independent nature, I fear. A fact which many people have deplored. But I hope that I am also realistic. And so should you learn to be, if you mean to get what you want."

"All I want is to be married to Lucas! And to leave here with him. I would not care where he took me. Or even… well, there are times when I would not care if he married me or not, as long as I knew he wanted me!"

It was obvious that Luz needed someone to talk to, and I think she would have confided all her unhappiness to me at that moment, if I had let her. But I knew that I must be careful, and so I was evasive for the moment, yawning elaborately, as if the subject of Lucas bored me.

"Sometimes the best way to make a man notice you is

by changing. By being a little more reserved—or better still, making him jealous! But after all, it's none of my business, I suppose. I have always made it a point never to interfere in other people's affairs."

"Oh, well, I suppose you *are* sleepy!" Luz's voice was wistful as she watched me cross the room and begin to comb out my hair before the one mirror we were supposed to share. "Will you talk with me again tomorrow? I am usually up early, to help with the breakfast, but after that…". her voice brightened. "Perhaps they will let us go riding together, if you would enjoy that. I could show you the rest of the valley. It is quite beautiful, you know. And I would very much like it if you would tell me something of the big cities I have heard so much about, and the people who live in them. Ramon has told me a little, of course, but he is only a man; he does not understand what a woman would like to know."

I smiled at her in the mirror. "It's a bargain, then. And if you'll wake me early enough, I will even help you with the breakfast. Since I am here, I suppose I might as well make myself useful!"

I suppose I should have been ashamed of myself. I was planning to use Luz and Ramon too, if I had to. The two people who were the most friendly toward me. And yet I continued to rationalize as I lay in bed that night, and even afterwards, when I had been in the valley long enough to understand the reasons for the strange undercurrents I had sensed on that first night.

I reminded myself constantly that I was merely a disinterested observer. That the lives and loves and hates of these people here were not my concern. I had only one objective, and that was to regain my cherished independence and freedom. But why did I have to remind myself of this so often? Whether I liked it or not I was here, a virtual prisoner in a secret valley that was ringed by mountains that were all but unscalable. And whether I liked it or not, I was thrown too much into the company of those who lived here to be completely indifferent to the dark, secret emotions that swirled beneath a seemingly normal surface. Because this was no ordinary household, any more than Elena Kordes, who ruled it, was an ordinary woman.

I had sensed her strength from the beginning, and the power she wielded over her sons—even Julio, who always sounded sullen or sarcastic when he addressed her.

Luz was afraid of Elena but I was not. I think we had taken each other's measure when we had our first conversation. And yet, perhaps for that very reason, Elena seemed to make a point of seeking my company. We talked of books and plays and the opera—even of the latest fashions. Perhaps she meant to impress me with her education and her knowledge of the outside world, for indeed, she was an intelligent and well-informed woman. We talked of my father, and the kind of man he had been, and even, on a few occasions, of Todd Shannon. But here I would always become reticent, and shrug my shoulders, even when she suggested subtly that he had a way with women when it suited him, and was obsessed only with the thought of owning all of the land he considered rightfully his.

"Your father thought otherwise," she told me once. "He had a sense of justice. Men like Todd Shannon are pirates, taking what they want by any means. *My* husband had more right to those lands that Shannon now calls his, and yet the law of the Anglo saw only that he was a Spaniard, a member of a conquered race."

"And I am sure that the Spaniards took this same land from the Indians when they came to New Mexico," I responded evenly.

"You're clever with words, and with logic." I had half-expected her to get angry, but she only raised an arched eyebrow at me. "And still, this same logic must tell you that it is only right that one of *my* sons should inherit at least part of their father's inheritance. *Your* father realized that. And that is why we planned together that you would marry one of my sons." She smiled when I shrugged. "Surely you possess too much common sense to believe in *love*? I do not think you could have loved Todd Shannon; you have hardly the look or the manner of a heartbroken woman!"

"As you just pointed out, I am practical. But I cannot say that I like the idea of being forced into a choice of husband."

Our eyes met, and she smiled again. "But if you have no other *practical* choice? I have noticed that you spend a lot of time in Ramon's company. He is in love with you, and you will find him easy to manage, I think."

"Just as you find all of your sons easy to manage?" I saw her eyes narrow, and I stretched deliberately. "I don't know—perhaps I need a challenge. Like you, I have had things my way for most of my life. And there's no hurry, is there?"

"I think you are more like me than I care for you to be," she said softly, "but as you say, there is no hurry."

There was no hurry indeed. Ostensibly I was not even a prisoner. I went out riding whenever I pleased, and I had the use of Ramon's library and Elena's surprisingly extensive wardrobe. I was a guest, and yet this was almost a polite fiction, for I had soon discovered that in spite of the size of the *estancia* there were only two servants who lived in the house itself, and they were both old. Fernando was a sullen, crusty old man who was devoted to Elena and followed only her orders. Paquita was going deaf, and even older, with a habit of talking to herself as she moved slowly around the big kitchen. There was a man of about fifty and his wife, who grew vegetables and corn and helped, at the time of the roundup, with the cattle, and not more than about five *vaqueros*, who had their own quarters.

Luz, I discovered, did most of the dusting and bedmaking within the house itself, as well as helping with the cooking and serving of the only formal meal, which was dinner. Without my quite realizing what was happening, I found myself helping her, in spite of Ramon's protests.

The men usually ate breakfast before we did, and had their noon meal outdoors. To my relief, the only time I encountered Lucas was at dinner, and since that first night, we hardly spoke two words with each other, until the day that I encountered Julio in the kitchen.

I think it must have been about five days after I had arrived, and during that time he had ridden out with Lucas and the other men very early each morning, not to return until just before sunset. I had heard them talking of cattle that had to be branded, fences that needed mending. It reminded me of the short time when I had been *patrona* of the SD, when Todd lay wounded in Silver City... and when I thought about Todd I wondered what he thought now. Did he believe me dead? Was he searching for me? And Mark, who had turned out to be my true friend. At such times I felt my hate for Lucas Cord renewed, as well as my determination to leave here as soon as I could contrive it.

On this particular afternoon, however, I had persuaded Luz to take the noon meal out to the men and warned her not to pay too much attention to Lucas, if she saw him.

"The only way you will make him notice you is if he thinks you are becoming indifferent to him," I warned her. And I had even cajoled Ramon into accompanying her.

"Are you matchmaking?" he teased me. "You seem so cold and so unconcerned with all of us sometimes, and then..."

"I think you should pay some compliments to Luz in your brother's presence," I said primly. "For heaven's sake, it's high time you all began treating her as if she was a woman, instead of a slave!"

"And so you will slave instead, in the kitchen?" I know that he attributed my attitude to a soft heart instead of a designing mind, and I almost disliked myself for being so calculating. But Ramon, as Elena had already noticed, was well on the way to imagining himself in love with me, and it was not hard to persuade him to do whatever I asked of him.

He rode out with Luz and I found myself alone—a not unpleasant feeling, for I could think best when I was by myself.

Elena kept to the habit of taking a siesta every afternoon, and Paquita slept away most of the day. I did not know where Fernando was, but I guessed that he too was asleep somewhere. I enjoyed the feeling of solitude, while I soaked beans and chopped up meat for dinner. I would surprise Luz by showing her I could cook too, if I had to.

And then Julio found me. I had not heard him come in and

I turned around to see him leaning against the wall, watching me with the same closed, inscrutable look I remembered from so long ago, when I had first been brought as a prisoner to the Apache camp.

I suppose that I must have gasped and he gave that strange twist of his lips that would have passed for a smile on any other man.

"Surely I do not make you nervous? I saw Ramon and Luz ride out with food for the others, but since I had already decided to come back to the house for my meal, I hoped that you would not mind preparing it for me."

"I'm sorry that I did not hear you come in. It won't take long, the stove's still lighted, and all I need is more wood."

I had to pass him to go outside for more wood, and he reached out lazily to grasp my arm.

"Julio! I thought you were hungry."

"Not so much for food as for some talk with you, *nidee*."

I had to will myself to pull away.

"You can always talk with me. But if you wish to eat…"

"Surely you are not afraid of me?"

Somehow, I found that my back was against the wall, and he, still holding my arm, was leaning far too close.

"Julio."

"I think it is my turn now. I have seen you with my brother Ramon, and before that, it was Lucas who kept me from you. I saw the way your eyes caught mine that first night, when the warriors brought you into our camp. Yes, and afterwards too, little sister. I know what my mother plans, but she forgets that my father's name was Kordes too, and that I am her son. You saw how angry she became when I reminded her of this fact? It is not only for the reasons that she and your father thought of that I speak now. I am Apache—the land does matter as much to me as it does to the others, who value this staying in one place. It is you I desire, and I think you already know that too, but like the women of my people, you were modest, and cast your eyes down. And now your eyes look straight into mine."

All I could think of to say at that instant was, stupidly: "But you are married already! And I like Little Bird. If you think that I am the kind of woman who would…"

He shook my arm exasperatedly. "Did you think I meant anything less than marriage? You are a virgin, and since my grandfather adopted you into our tribe, I would not meddle with you if I had not intended an honorable offer of marriage. If you had lived with us longer, I would have tied the best ponies I had outside the shaman's lodge as a sign of my intentions. But as it is, I'm left with no other choice but to tell you what is in my mind. I have seen you accept calmly what my mother has told you, and I have seen that you do not love Ramon. So…"

I had regained my wits by this time, and although I was not foolish enough to attempt to twist out of his grasp I continued to look boldly into his eyes.

"Your grandfather told me that I would be allowed to make up my own mind, and although I have grown to respect you, I see you only as a brother, who is already married. It is true that I have learned to accept the ways and the wisdom of the Apache, Julio, but I am still a stubborn woman. When I choose a husband I will not be able to share him. I hope you can understand this, for I would not like to lose your friendship."

I tried to sound reasonable and calm, but I do not think that Julio, at the moment, was capable of either emotion.

I had borrowed some of Luz's clothes that afternoon—a full, ankle-length skirt and low-cut blouse, and my feet were bare for coolness. His eyes traveled over me.

"I hear your voice speaking to me, *nidee,* and it says one thing, but your eyes and the fast beating of your heart tell me another story. I think you are afraid of being possessed by a man, and your fear makes you seem cold. But I think that your senses call out for it. It was so with my grandmother, the Spanish woman captive that my grandfather made his third wife. In time…"

"No!" He held me against the wall, and the suddenly open look of desire I saw on his face, usually so expressionless, made me too angry for caution. "I tell you that when the time comes I will know it, and I will make my own choice! And is this how you keep your promise to the shaman of your tribe, to treat me as a sister?"

"It is not as a sister I see you, but as a woman! I wanted you when I first saw you standing there so proudly, with your head thrown back, meeting my eyes without fear, and I would have bought you…"

"But you did not. Your brother did. Have you asked his permission to approach me?"

I saw Julio's brown eyes, so like Ramon's, narrow into slits.

"My brother, eh? Perhaps he did more than lie beside you on all those nights! And is your dislike for him merely a pretense, or jealousy?" His laughter sounded harshly in my ears. "If it is Lucas you want, *nidee,* you will wait a long time—like Luz! Or haven't you noticed yet how things are with him? To my brother, all women but one are merely instruments of pleasure, to be used and thrown aside. You have sharp eyes, or have you deliberately tried to blind yourself to the truth in this instance? Perhaps you do not want to admit that my brother Lucas is in love with my mother!"

"I don't think you know what you are saying!" I stared into his dark, angry face, and felt that my lips had suddenly become stiff and cold.

"Do you not? Then I shall say it again, little sister, and try to make my meaning clearer. My brother and my mother are lovers."

I gasped in shock and Julio smiled cruelly.

"I have shocked you? But there is no need to be too shocked, after all. Lucas is my father's bastard, so they say. My mother was my father's wife. Do you see now?"

"But—she is so much older than he is!"

"Older, you say? But you have seen my mother, how beautiful she is, how young she looks. And in *his* presence she looks even younger, eh? I remember the day they rode into our camp, and we were told, Lucas and I, that our parents had come. Parents! I looked on my grandfather as my father, by then. They had abandoned us, and now at last they came, looking for their sons! I would not go with them. Lucas was older than I, and even more determined to stay, at first. And then he saw her, and she smiled, and her voice was soft and wheedling. I was watching his eyes, and I knew then that he would go, because of *her*. I saw, and my grandfather saw too, after a while. And there came a time when they could not hide the fact that they were lovers from my father... Do you want to know what happened then?"

Julio's fingers were still closed painfully around my arms, but I hardly noticed the discomfort any longer. I did not want to hear more, and yet I had to—and I think Julio read all this in my face, for he nodded slowly, as if satisfied.

"So you are curious. I was curious too, when one day Lucas came back to our camp, looking like a man in a daze. I was curious enough to sit outside the shaman's lodge and listen, while he told our grandfather of the quarrel he had had with his father. 'I cannot go back,' he said, and his voice held such anguish that I could hardly recognize it. But later that same night my mother, Elena, came herself; her hair flying behind her in the stormwind, and her face haggard—as haggard as *his* had been! 'He is dead!' How can I forget the way she cried it out? 'Shannon has killed him,' she cried, 'he or his men! And if there is not one who is man enough among you to revenge him, I will do it myself!'" Julio paused meaningfully, as if he expected me to say something, but I could only stare back at him silently. "You know the rest of it, I think," he said quietly. "He revenged my father's death, but was it the law of blood for blood or his own guilt that made him risk his life so carelessly?"

I felt a strange feeling of sickness in the pit of my stomach. An entry in my father's journal—the last one—that I had frowned over and then dismissed to be thought of later, came back to me then.

"I see the story of Oedipus enacted again," he had written in a scrawling hand that told only too clearly of his condition when he had written it. "And it is too late... too late to change the pattern of tragedy now. Must we forever be haunted by old crimes—old guilts?"

I remember that I wondered if he had been referring to

himself. How could I have understood then, knowing nothing of what I knew now?

With an effort I lifted my hands to Julio's wrists. "You are hurting my arms."

"Is that all you have to say?" But he released me, and stood glowering down at me.

"You were mistaken if you thought I turned your offer down because of some secret passion I cherish for your half brother. I do not think I am capable of loving any man strongly enough to give up everything for him and be content to be his slave and bear his children. In fact I would choose not to marry at all if I could, but if I must, then it will be only to a man who would not ask such things of *me*."

I managed a faint smile at his chagrined expression and added firmly: "You must not imagine that I am not appreciative of your concern for my future happiness, but when you think carefully about it I'm sure you'll realize what a disobedient wife I would make to any man!"

I could not be sure, for a few tense moments, whether Julio would accept my words or not. He stepped deliberately closer to me, until I could feel the heat of his body, and put a hand under my chin.

I refused to cringe, forcing myself to meet his darkly frowning gaze.

"It is true. I do not think you would be a submissive wife. You would make a better warrior, like the sister of Victorio, who fights as well as any of our young men." His lips stretched in an unwilling smile and he said gruffly, "So—it seems you will remain my sister after all. And I am not to be the brother who saves your life."

"Saves my life? What do you mean?" I frowned at him. He shook his head and moved casually to the great earthenware crock that was always kept full of cold, clear water for drinking.

"How fierce you can look, *nidee*. I can see that you have never learned proper respect in the presence of men!" His mood seemed to have changed like lightning from anger and resentment to light teasing, as he dipped up water and drank it.

"Julio!"

He shrugged carelessly. "It was only a dream my grandfather had. But the dreams of a shaman are never without some deeper significance. Perhaps it will be Ramon who saves your life someday, and you will marry him. He dreamed of a white bird pursued by hawks, who flew blindly into a hunter's net. Two of the hawks were clever enough to understand it was a trap and soared away, looking for other prey. But the other dropped down like an arrow from the sky and slashed at the hunter's face with his sharp beak and talons until he was blinded, and the white bird was free again and flew away under the shadow of the hawk's wings."

"What a horrible dream! And if I were a bird I'm sure I'd be a hawk instead of a silly, frightened dove."

But he only gave me a sardonic look, and went away as quietly as he had come, without another word to me. To tell the truth, the scene that had taken place between us had left me more shaken than I wanted to admit, and I was relieved to see Julio leave at last.

I went back to chopping meat into tiny cubes in a thoughtful frame of mind, still hearing the echo of Julio's voice beating against my ears.

"My mother... my bastard brother... they are lovers, or have you deliberately made yourself blind?"

This, then, was the reason for Luz's unhappiness, for the veiled resentment that both Julio and Ramon felt. And Elena herself, who was the center, the manipulator of all their lives. I thought I was beginning to know her, but I realized that I knew only as much as she permitted me to know. She exercised a subtle fascination, a subtle power and it seemed as if only Todd Shannon had been impervious to it.

Todd—his name came into my mind with a jolt. How long since I had thought of Todd? Had I deliberately tried to shut him out of my mind because I was afraid to think of him? If only I had listened to Todd, if only I had paid some attention to all of Mark's warnings! Unbidden came the memory of Todd crushing me in his arms until I was breathless, kissing my angry protests into silence. What was I doing here, in the middle of enough violence and dark intrigue to fill the pages of a volume of Greek or Roman tragedy?

Twenty-Three

IT WAS HOT IN THE KITCHEN, AND I COULD FEEL THE PERSPIRA-
tion pouring down my back and between my breasts. I pushed
a strand of damp hair off my forehead with the back of one
hand impatiently, wishing that my fingers were not so slippery
and my mind so active... and then it happened.

The knife slipped. All I can recall now is feeling a sharp,
stinging sensation, and then I heard the knife clatter down
onto the table, and I was staring down stupidly at my fingers
as if they did not belong to me, and at the blood that spurted
from the deep cut across two of them. I knew that I ought
to do something about it. I could not stand here bleeding all
over the meat I had been cutting up for dinner and the table
and the floor. I suppose it was a combination of shock and
annoyance at myself for having been so clumsy that held me
there as if I had been paralyzed, disinterestedly watching the
gushing of my own blood.

Suddenly the door was kicked open and I looked up in a
daze, and saw the one person I had least wanted or expected
to see.

"Luz? Where in hell is everyone?"

The doorway was low enough to make him duck his head
when he came in, narrow enough so that he seemed to block
out the bright sunlight that had streamed in for a moment,
almost blinding me with its sudden brilliance.

I was dressed as Luz usually dressed and I think that during those first few moments, until his eyes became used to the dimness, he mistook me for Luz. "There are times when I think everyone around here goes a little crazy! Where's Ramon? And what in hell did you say to Julio to make him look so grim? I had to shoot one of the horses." He turned away to the water crock and began to drink thirstily out of the dipper, grumbling all the while. "Of course it had to be the one *I* was riding, and then I had to walk all the way back here in the broiling sun. And Julio—you'd think he'd stop and give me a ride back, but no, he gave me a sullen answer instead and wouldn't stop. Why are you standin' there just staring at me, for God's sake?"

And then, over the rim of the tin dipper I saw his eyes widen very slightly, the green flecks coming alive in them when he recognized me at last as he turned back to face me.

"Rowena? To find *you* in the kitchen…"

I think I must already have been rather light-headed from loss of blood, for I began to back away from the look of surprise in his face, and felt suddenly weak, so that I almost fell and had to clutch at the table for support. I felt the sticky warmth of my own blood through the folds of my skirt, and then with an angry exclamation, *he* was there, clearing the room in a single stride.

He caught my wrist, and I cried out.

"Jesus Christ! What were you trying to do? Stand there and watch yourself bleed to death? If you can't chop meat without cutting your fingers off… come over here."

He dragged me across the room with him by the wrist. Sheer weakness made me fall against him when he stopped, tearing the red bandanna from around his neck and dipping it into the water crock with no regard for hygiene or cleanliness.

"Don't do that!" I protested faintly, but he ignored me, as he began to mop at the blood that kept dripping steadily onto the floor.

"Jesus!" He swore again, making me wince as much from pain as from the sheer anger in his voice. "How did even you manage to do a fool thing like that? You've cut almost as deep as the bone across two fingers. Lucky you didn't manage to slice 'em both off!" I found that it was easier to stay on my feet if I closed both eyes.

"You better sit down. Here... now just hold still..." I heard the scrape of wood across the floor and felt myself pushed unceremoniously into a sitting position.

"Put your head down between your knees," and he gave the back of my neck a shove. "Hold your hands—both hands—in front of you. Try holding your left wrist with your other hand if you can, an' for God's sake try not to fall out of the chair! I'll be right back. Where in hell is that darned Luz? And Ramon?"

"They—went out to take lunch to the rest of you—and you had no right to come back to the house so early! You never do!"

"Ah, Christ! Tryin' to argue with me already, an' you half-dead from losin' all that blood! I swear I never saw a more clumsy, stupid, stubborn female than you!"

"Oh!"

I tried to raise my head, but he pushed it down again... I gritted my teeth against the pain, and could not repress a shameful whimper when I felt him dab roughly at my wounded fingers again with a dripping wet cloth.

"You're bleedin' like a—" he bit the words off, swearing again, and then, in a harsh voice, "Only one thing to do, to stop that bleeding, and it's goin' to hurt like hell for a little while, so if you know how to faint, better do it now!"

"I never faint!"

But my voice sounded curiously weak and unsteady, even in my own ears.

"Well, grit your teeth then."

Before I was aware of what was happening he had picked me up—and dumped me on the floor.

"What..." I tried to sit up, my eyes opening to stare at him, and he was standing over me, with the knife in his hand, its tip glowing red-hot.

"Shut up and be still, or it'll be worse when I gotta do it over again."

And then, before I had quite realized what he intended, he

had grabbed my wrist, and I cried out as he drew the knife blade across my shrinking, agonized flesh.

He did it too quickly for me to have time to draw back, and the next moment he was wrapping the wet cloth around my fingers, working swiftly and efficiently.

I don't remember if I did faint then or not.

He had picked me up again and was carrying me somewhere... and I *do* remember that I tried to struggle and whispered angrily that I refused, I refused to let *him* be the one...

"What in hell are you muttering about, anyhow? And stop wiggling or I'll drop you, an' a broken neck won't be as easy to fix up as two cut fingers!"

"I don't see why *you* should be the one to be angry! And you didn't save my life. People don't die of a bleeding cut..."

"If that isn't just like a damned female! Listen, if I'd have thought stoppin' the bleedin' was saving your life, I'd have let you go on bleeding! Think I'd want to be saddled with a wife like you?"

"Of course not! It's Elena you want as your wife, isn't it?"

Before the words were out I regretted having said them. I felt the tightening of his arms and the sudden rigidity of his muscles against my cheek—and what was I doing, leaning my head against his shoulder so trustfully?

"Damned if I shouldn't throw you all the way down them stairs I just carried you up for that, you vicious-tongued little bitch!"

I opened my eyes and his were bleak and dangerous. His nostrils flared ever so slightly when he was angry, and at that moment I thought he might carry out his threat or strangle me. I don't know what else he might have said, or I might have said, but we were already upstairs, passing Elena's room, and at that moment, when he had stopped still and was glaring down at me, the door opened.

"Lucas? I thought I heard your voice."

And suddenly I felt that I could not bear to see her face, nor his either, with that naked, curiously revealing look that always came to it when he looked at her. So I closed my eyes and bit my lip and pretended to go limp, although I'm sure I did not deceive him.

"She cut her fingers pretty badly. There was no one there, and I had to cauterize the cuts."

"I suppose she fainted. Good heavens, Lucas, when I first saw you, I thought—"

He cut her off, and I know it was because he knew I was listening, and understood how things stood between them. He hated me for it; I could feel the hate emanating from him like a physical, tangible thing, in the way he held me.

"I am going to put her in her room, and then I will come back and tell you how it happened."

"Lucas."

I felt a kind of triumph when he walked past her without answering, but it did not last. I should not have said it—not yet. I should have had more sense than to blurt out aloud the thought that was uppermost in my mind, whether it was the truth or not.

He had pushed open the door to my room with a savage kick, and he roughly laid me down on my bed.

"Soon as Luz comes back, I'll send her up to you. And you—you learn to keep your mouth shut, an' to stop meddlin' in my life, askin' questions, or by God I'll…"

"You'll what? Kill me to get me out of the way? Sell me off to one of your friends as you did Flo? I said only what was true, and you know it! Why are you ashamed to admit it? You're in love with Elena. Do you think I'm blind? Do you think they are all blind, just because no one else has had the courage to speak the words aloud as I did?"

He was staring down at me, and his face had gone white under the sunburned skin. There was hate in it, and pain, and—was there guilt as well?

"I should never have brought you here," he said, in the same flat, cold voice he had used on me before, in the Apache camp. "Should have guessed after the first time I talked to you, what you'd be like."

I tried to sit up, but fell back again against the thin pillow. "You know nothing of what I really am, or how I feel. And you don't like the fact that I know *you* for what you are! Yes, you're right, you shouldn't have brought me here! I didn't want to come!"

"Yeah, I remember that, all right."

Suddenly, stupidly, I was staring at the closed door, feeling the reverberation of its slamming echoing in my ears. And for the second time in my life I felt the treacherous, hateful tears of sheer frustration and rage slipping down my face, until I turned it into the pillow.

I wanted to sleep, but pain kept me awake, and presently I heard the door open, and Luz was tiptoeing across the room to me, carrying a tray.

"Oh, Rowena! I am so sorry! And I have never seen Lucas so ornery, I think. Even Julio chooses to stay away from the house. Ramon wants to come up, but I told him to stay away until you feel better. Does it still hurt very much?"

I could hardly stand her kindness and her sympathy, nor the tenderness with which she untied the makeshift bandage that Lucas had put there before she began to place tiny poultices of some soothing, cooling stuff on my swollen, ugly-looking wounds.

"You might have bled to death, not knowing what to do to stop the bleeding, if Lucas had not come back." There was an unconscious note of pride in her voice when she spoke of him. I must have made some involuntary movement, for she reminded me quickly that I must hold still.

"These herbs will prevent any infection, and take away the pain in a while. You will have some scars, of course, but they will not matter. You can wear gloves, if you do not like to look at them! And you must drink this broth—it will prevent fever, and help you to sleep. You are to rest… and I will never, never leave you alone in the kitchen again! It was all my fault."

"Did *he* say that? It wasn't your fault. It was hot, and I was careless—clumsy."

I thought Luz's voice sounded deliberately cheerful. "Well, in any case you are to rest, and I will be back again soon to see if you need anything."

"I'm not an invalid! For heaven's sake! All I did was cut my fingers! It's no reason for my keeping to my bed."

"But Lucas said you were to stay in bed. And if you were to get up, they would all be angry with me."

"And I would be more angry than anyone!"

I had not heard Elena come in, but she was there, smiling at me, her expression impossible to read.

"Stay in bed—and rest. Later, if you feel up to it, you might want to come down to dinner. For the moment, in this heat, you might as well take a siesta."

I didn't know whether she was mocking me or commiserating with me, and it infuriated me.

Luz had left quietly, and I put on an innocent, rather confused tone of voice when I said: "I want to see Lucas. I did not thank him for what he did. I'm afraid I was rather rude."

She raised an eyebrow. "Lucas? And not Ramon?"

I looked her in the eye. "Lucas. Ramon was not here when I was—so stupid as to let the knife slip."

"And Julio had just left. You cannot imagine how concerned *he* is too. I think you have bewitched all three of my sons, Rowena."

"Oh, but I'm sure Lucas is by no means bewitched! He doesn't like me any more than I like him. But I do feel grateful toward him. I must have seemed ungrateful, I'm afraid. He hurt me, and at the time I did not realize that he did what he had to for my own good. I'm sure you understand how uncomfortable it makes me feel?"

She bent down to me, touching my hand lightly. "How much you remind me of myself, when I was younger! I always thought I wanted what I could not have. If Guy had been more like you… who knows? Everything might have been so different! But if it is Lucas you want to see, I will send him to you, at the risk of making my other sons angry."

"You're very sure of him, aren't you?"

I couldn't resist the question. Her smile put me in my place. "Why shouldn't I be? I think you understand that already. But as I have said before, you have a choice. Marry Julio, and you will be his second wife, accepting the Apache way of life. Marry Ramon, and you will have a husband you can control. You may marry Lucas, who knows? I think your open dislike of him intrigues him, for the moment. But if you are clever enough to maneuver such a thing, you will share him with me, and I will always have the greater share. No, I do not think you will be like my poor, pretty little Luz, who waits—and hopes. Like me, you will want to make things happen. So we will see, and I will tell Lucas you wish to speak with him."

"How good it is to feel indulged—and understood!"

My smile was just as deliberate as hers had been, and I thought her slight nod was an acknowledgment.

I lay back after she had left and closed my eyes. The throbbing in my hand was already less painful, and the broth I had drunk made me feel drowsy in spite of myself.

Why had I insisted that I must see Lucas? Until I had seen Elena, and watched her smile, there had been nothing further from my mind. But now it had become a challenge between us. I did not doubt that she would send him to me, and I would send him back, hating me more than ever. Or would I? As I had done so often before, I thought of a chess game. The black queen and the white. Who were the pawns? Or the kings, for that matter? Chess was a game of powerful women, and I would match Elena for the sake of matching her, if I had to.

I must have dozed off. The sound of the door banging back upon its hinges awakened me, and I could not help wincing. "Must you always be so noisy?"

"What in hell do you have to say to me that you haven't said before?"

"Your sense of—*duty* cannot fail to amaze me," I murmured in an exaggeratedly pained voice, and caught the wicked green gleam of his eyes through my shuttered lashes. I thought he controlled his anger with an effort, and it pleased me.

"Elena said you wanted to talk to me. Why me?"

"Elena said she'd send you to me. Why? Because I felt I had to thank you for your presence of mind, of course. That is what I told her, and she chose to believe me, I think. And I was rude. I must apologize for that too."

"You might fool me if the look in your eyes matched the words you say."

"I had no idea that my eyes betrayed me so."

Lucas stalked angrily past my bed to the window, and stood looking out.

"You want to play games, try Ramon. Maybe even Julio. That how you got even Shannon eatin' out of your hand?"

There was contempt in the look he turned on me then, but I faced it without flinching.

"Why do you so despise the same traits in me that you obviously admire in your—in Elena?"

He noticed my studied pause, as I had meant him to, and his eyes squinted at me dangerously.

"Why don't you come right out an' say whatever it was that was so urgent you couldn't rest?" His voice was carefully controlled, but the huskiness in it was even more apparent than usual, and I could sense his eagerness to leave. It made me even more determined to keep him here longer—long enough, perhaps, for Elena to wonder.

I made my voice deliberately innocent. "But I have already told you. I wanted to thank you. I must have seemed very ungracious, and I know now that you only did what needed to be done. I am not often so clumsy, and you know you *do* have a way of rubbing me the wrong way!"

"I can say the same thing about you, an' that's for sure!" Lucas said grimly, but I thought he gave me a rather puzzled, wary look, as if he wondered what I was up to this time.

I said softly, "I wanted to ask you not to be angry with Luz. It wasn't her fault. I insisted that she should have the chance to go riding… she's young and so pretty, it isn't fair that she should have to spend most of her time slaving in the kitchen!"

I thought I saw him flush with anger. "Luz is not a slave here! No one treats her as one. She does not think so."

"But then what *is* her position here? *Mine* is clear enough of course, but Luz? I understood at first that she was your… how do you say it in Spanish?… Yes, your *novia*. And she's in love with you—the poor child can hardly hide it. Are you going to marry her, Lucas? Or are you going to live this way forever, torn between your lust for Elena and your guilt because she was your father's wife?"

He looked as if I had struck him. His face whitened, and for an instant there was almost a stunned look in his eyes, as if he could not believe that I had said the words out loud.

"Christ!" he said at last, and his voice shook with the effort of controlling his anger. "This time you've damn well gone too far, you meddling…"

"Too far, you say? Because I've been honest enough to speak the truth? Don't you see that it needed to be said, just as what you did for me this afternoon, when you cauterized my knife cuts, needed to be done? Or are you such a coward that you will not even admit the facts to yourself?"

"Will you be quiet?" He took a threatening step towards me, but I sat up straight and faced him boldly.

"No! And why should I be? You've told me, too often, what you think of *me*. And there's Luz, whom I've grown fond of. Since you've seen fit to meddle in my life, Luke Cord, why should I not do the same with yours? As your concerned sister, of course."

He stood there and stared at me as if he could not trust himself to speak, and there was something in his face—a mixture of pain and frustration and rage—that suddenly made me ashamed of the game I had been playing. I had a weapon to use against him now that I knew where he was most vulnerable, but strangely enough I seemed to have lost the inclination to use it.

I forced myself to go on, keeping my eyes steadily on his. "Why, Lucas? If you love her, why won't you *do* something about it?"

"Do something, you say? Do what?" The words seemed torn from him, as if he could not help himself. "Do you think that we could ever marry? That they would let us? My God—how could *you* ever understand how it feels to want and yearn for something you know you'll never have?" I saw him turn away from me like a blind man and stand by the window, looking out, his fingers gripping the sill. "Elena's like—I think I fell in love with her the first moment I saw her. Ever since then she's been like a fever, like a sickness I can't shake off! And yet I don't want to shake it off either. Can you understand that? Can you understand how it happened? I thought, at first, that she really was my mother. That I was her son. It was natural for me to love her then, and I did without question.

And then one day she told me. I was old *enough* to hear the truth, she said. It must not make any difference to me, or to our relationship, for she loved me even more than she did her own sons, and I—God help me, all I could think of was that she was not my mother—that she was a woman, and I wanted her. Nothing else mattered, do you hear? I could think of nothing else but having her—holding her in my arms, kissing her mouth, and hadn't she told me that she loved me? 'Much more than if you had been my son,' she had said, and I read the meaning I wanted to read into her words. I… ah, *hell!*"

The sudden violence in his voice as he swung around suddenly to face me made me gasp.

"Why am I telling *you* all this? Why you? I've always known you judged me, an' hated me. And I don't even like you. But you know what? You *do* remind me of her in some way. The way your hair hangs so straight and heavy, and a certain look you get on your face sometimes when you get mad or stubborn. But you've got the damndest cold eyes I've ever seen, except when you're angry."

"Is that why you try to make me angry so often?" My voice came out as a mechanical whisper, and I had the strangest, light-headed feeling that I was on the brink of some frightening discovery that would change my life forever. I did not want to be changed, I did not want to feel helpless, to find myself completely incapable of either motion or protest as Lucas crossed the room to me.

He stood looking down at me with a baffled expression, as if he were really seeing me for the first time, and something in his eyes made me catch my breath.

"Why did you make me say those things out loud? What do any of our lives or our secrets matter to you? I think you play some game of your own, like the chess your father tried to teach me. If I love Elena, what is it to you? Marry my brother and leave this valley. Forget about the rest of us. For I do not think you care for anyone but yourself, Rowena Dangerfield."

He had spoken to me in Spanish, his voice oddly harsh, and it was in the same language that I replied to him.

"Did you kill your father?" I couldn't help myself, I didn't even understand why I asked the question. He flinched visibly; but surprisingly, he answered me.

"So you've thought that too? Yes—you see, I can admit to guilt when it is deserved. It might be said that I killed my father, but not in the way that you're thinking. I didn't fire the guns that put the bullets in him, but I was the cause of his being on SD land that day. You want to know how it happened? You haven't guessed?"

He gave a short laugh that wasn't a laugh at all, a muffled sound of self-contempt, and contempt for me as well.

"How innocent you can look! And I could almost swear your mouth is trembling. Why, Rowena? You want to hear the truth, don't you, so you can judge me for what I am?" With a lithe, violent movement he dropped his body onto the bed, holding me down against the pillow by the shoulders while his eyes looked narrowly into mine.

"Listen, then, and if you ever speak of this to me again, or tear at me with your questions, I swear I'll kill you!"

His voice was soft, but there was a threat in it that held me still and silent while he went on speaking. "He found us together. No, we weren't in bed, but I was kissing her, holding her in my arms, and her arms were about my neck. He walked in. Neither of us had expected him to return from Mexico that day so perhaps he came back so unexpectedly with a purpose. I'm only surprised that he was so calm. If I had been in his place I think I would have killed. As it was, he only walked up to her and struck her; and I would have killed him then, if she had not flung herself between us and told me to go. And he said—he said: 'Yes, you had better get yourself out of my sight, before I forget myself, and leave my wife to me. For I was responsible for the death of your mother, and would not have *your* blood on my hands as well.' And she kept screaming for me to go—to go quickly. Christ, I was so goddamn young then, I didn't know what in hell I should do! But I knew that I was guilty of a terrible crime, and he had every right to kill me if he wanted to. I think I would have preferred it if he had! But all he did, when I hesitated, was to strike at me contemptuously, as one would a dog, with the butt of the gun he wore. I still carry the scar—you see? Among others, but this one is the mark of Cain."

There was something so terrible, so despairing in his voice that I could not bear to hear more.

"But you left! You didn't kill him!" I cried out, and felt his fingers bite into my flesh.

"I should either have stayed, yes, and killed him myself, or taken her with me. He used the whip on her, and then he left. He blamed her for everything; he said he would find Shannon and tell him where to find her, so that the feud would be ended forever. But Shannon's men found him first, and they killed him from ambush, without giving him a chance to speak or even to defend himself. And if he had not been killed, I would have hated him forever for what he had done. As it was…"

"You killed the men who killed him. You revenged him! Even my father said it had been a fair fight, that you were justified."

"I didn't kill those two men for *him*. I killed them for *me*. You saw that at the very beginning, didn't you? I killed them, they didn't kill me—an' your father saved me from a hanging. He shouldn't have, should he? Because then you wouldn't be here."

"You *wanted* to die?" My voice was an accusing whisper.

"I don't know! Mebbe I did. I was so damned mixed up and confused I can't remember any longer. An' even after that…"

He didn't finish it. He didn't have to. I saw the look on his face and knew that he was thinking again of Elena. I don't know what madness took hold of me then, or if it was something in the broth that Luz had brought up to me. I hated Elena and I hated him. For there had been Flo, and there was Luz—and perhaps countless other women he'd played with and used, while all the time, all the time it was Elena he craved. I said in a voice I hardly recognized as my own:

"Perhaps all you need is something else to think about. Another woman who is just as unattainable, and just as calculating," and I put my uninjured hand up and touched the hair at the back of his neck, pulling his head down to mine.

I cannot remember now what it was I meant to prove. Did I mean to punish him for his earlier repudiation of me? Had I intended to show him that women too were capable of using their lips and their bodies to arouse a passion they intend only to use, never to fulfill? Or was it Elena's sureness of him that I challenged?

Whatever I had meant to prove or to achieve was all forgotten when Lucas kissed me. Even now, as I write the words, I can feel the emotions that erupted from nowhere, to take possession of me, draining away my will.

It was not as if I had never been kissed before, or responded to a man's lips. Todd Shannon's kisses had left me breathless and dizzy, forcing a response from me. He was a man used to getting his own way, a man who had decided he wanted me, and showed it.

But Lucas kissed me as if he hated me, as if he could not help himself, after that first instinctive movement of withdrawal I sensed in him—as if he was a man who had reached the depths of despair and had nowhere else to go.

I was there. I was a female and my lips were warm, and I had deliberately maneuvered him into this. He knew it and I knew it in those first few seconds when his hands moved from my shoulders and along my neck as if he longed to strangle me. And then he was holding my face with his palms against my temples, fingers tangling in my hair so that I could not escape his angry, hurtful kisses even if I had wanted to.

It was then that I realized I did not want to escape, and the discovery was frightening, as I felt myself swept across the threshold of feeling such as I had not dreamed existed within myself. It was like being possessed by a demon.

I moaned under the onslaught of his kisses. I forgot the pain in my hand and the bandages that Luz had so carefully wrapped round it as my fingers ripped at his shirt until I felt his bare, warm flesh under my hands. I wanted him, and it was a terrifying feeling, to realize I could feel such lust for a man.

What devil had seized us both, I know that *he* felt it too.

His body lay against mine, and I felt the heat and weight of his desire as he moved over me.

His lips moved from my mouth to my eyes, crushing them closed, and then to my earlobes. His whisper sounded like a curse.

"Bruja!" he called me. "Witch!" And yet I felt that it was I who was bewitched, until his lips took mine again and I went beyond thinking.

Twenty-Four

꙰

IT WAS LUCAS WHO PROVED TO BE THE STRONGER ONE OF US on that hot, sunlit afternoon when the Dangerfield devil, that "taint in the blood" made me forget everything else but the impulses of my body.

After he had pulled himself away from me abruptly, leaving me gasping with the shock of my return to reality, I heard Elena's cool, amused laughter drifting up through the open window. She was talking to someone, but I hardly heard what she said. The sound of my own breathing seemed far too loud, and I was bitterly, angrily ashamed of myself.

Lucas was staring down at me, but I couldn't read the expression in his eyes, for his back was to the window and the sunlight that streamed through it, yellowing the floor. I began to have some idea of how I must look to him—my lips swollen and bruised from the force of his kisses, my hair in tangles, my blouse slipping off my shoulders. I must have looked like a woman dazed with desire, and I hated myself for it and hated him most of all.

"Rowena…" There was a strange, almost apologetic note in his voice, but by now I was too angry, too humiliated to wonder at it.

"Well? Do you see how easy it is to find consolation in a woman's kisses? Did I make you forget *her* for a little while?"

My voice sounded high and forced, but I saw his lips tighten and knew that I had made him angry again, and I was glad! For now perhaps he would not recognize my shameful betrayal of myself for what it had been. Weakness. Wanting.

"You really enjoy playin' games with people, don't you?" His voice was hard, contemptuous. "Where'd you learn all the tricks of a teasin' whore? Was it from Shannon, or his Eastern nephew? An' what were you tryin' to prove, anyhow?"

My face burned, my whole body still felt hot and weak with reaction. But I forced a smile.

"Why are you angry? I was only trying to help you, you know. By proving that one woman is very much like another, given the right time and the right circumstances. You should marry Luz and make her happy."

"Christ almighty!" he exploded, his face dark with suppressed anger. "What kind of female are you? You look and act so cold sometimes, and yet you can feel so warm."

"Why must it surprise you that a woman can be just as devious and scheming as a man can be? Why does it always shock a man to find out that a woman can play his own game and beat him at it?"

"I haven't been playin' at any games, damn you!"

The bewildered frustration in his voice shook me for a moment, but I couldn't show it. "But then, what *were* you playing at? I know you wanted me, Lucas, but what else? Have you fallen in love with me? Would you want to marry me and control my fortune? Can you forget Elena so easily?"

His voice had quieted. Perhaps I had given myself away.

"No, I can't forget her. Don't you see that? She's as much a part of me as breathing. You wanted to know the truth, an' I gave it to you. Elena will always be a part of me, and of my life, as long as I stay alive. But I can want another woman, and I want you. Not your damn money, nor even your half of the SD. Is that enough for you? For God's sake, what do you want of me?"

"Nothing!" I flung the word at him. I had to hurt him in order to protect myself and my own vulnerability.

"What would I want with another woman's property? I'll never be content with second-best, Lucas Cord!"

"I don't think you know what loving is. You're the kind of

woman who would give a man enough to keep him crawlin' to you for more, and use him until he lost his use."

"Is Elena any different?"

"Elena is a *woman,* for God's sake! She's suffered. She feels. She's not like you, needin' to experiment with feelings."

"How blind you are!"

He said in a flat, hard voice: "I don't care to hear any more. An' you better listen good to what I'm saying. You've been nothing but a troublemaker since you've been here, and I'm warning you now to stop interfering! You've had enough time to choose, and you can damn well make your choice right now. Marry Ramon an' go away with him, or go away with Julio and live with him as his second wife."

"Are you leaving yourself out on purpose? Or just for the last?"

"Just for the last. You stay here, I'm goin' to do what I should have done a long time ago. Take you. But don't look for any marriage from me. Ain't been a woman yet I haven't tired of after I've had her. An' when I'm through with you, I'll let Shannon know where you are, an' make him pay a ransom for gettin' you back. Mebbe a trifle shopworn, but good enough for him!"

The slamming of the door hurt my ears. But I had time to compose myself before Ramon came upstairs to see me, his face drawn with anger and hurt

"Rowena! If you only knew how worried I've been! But my mother said it was Lucas you wanted to speak to, and I—" he had started to pace about the room, I had never seen him so tense and angry. "I didn't know what to think! Rowena, I must know. I'm sure you have sensed that I have come to care for you—more than that—to love you. And I have only held back because of the circumstances of your coming here. I did not want you to think... Oh, God! I don't even know what I am saying any longer. I had planned what I would say to you when the time was right, when I thought you were ready to listen. But now, I—what did he say to you? What has he done to you? If he's touched you, I swear that I'll kill him, brother or not!"

"There is no need for that. Lucas and I argued, as usual. And he gave me an ultimatum. A very difficult one, I'm afraid, because you haven't proposed to me yet, Ramon. Do you intend to?"

It was so easy because Ramon was in love with me. I had decided to be sensible. I would marry Ramon, if I had to, and leave the hidden valley. And after all, why not Ramon, if I must marry some man? Todd Shannon was too strong, too overbearing. Mark had never asked me to marry him. Ramon would do.

I did not even blush for myself at the time. And that night at dinner I accepted Elena's smiling toast and Julio's sullen good wishes. Lucas, I learned, had taken Luz with him and gone riding.

"But of course it's high time he paid some attention to the poor child," Elena said. Her voice was smooth, displaying nothing but pleasure. "Tomorrow we will all celebrate."

"Don't count on me!" Julio said in a surly voice, pushing his chair back. "I plan to return to my home and my people tomorrow."

It was Ramon who carried me up the shallow stairs to my room that night, in spite of my protests that I was quite capable of walking, that it was only my fingers that I had cut and not my feet.

Elena overruled me. While Ramon had left the room to fetch another bottle of wine she leaned across the table, still smiling.

"You must let the poor boy have his way. Surely you realize its just an excuse to hold you in his arms?" She sighed. "My Ramon has always been such a gentleman! Sometimes I have wondered if it wasn't a mistake to let the Jesuit fathers bring him up, but my husband insisted. You must not think that Ramon hasn't had his share of women, you understand? But he had always been too shy and too gentle, perhaps, with those he really respected."

"Oh?" I raised an eyebrow interrogatively, wondering what she was getting at. "You make me wonder if all your sons are not far too fond of women, after all."

"My sons are men, but when it comes to marriage there is a difference. Ramon was quite infatuated by your beauty from the very first time he set eyes on you. He could talk of nothing else. And since then, of course, you have made him fall in love with you."

"How very convenient for us both!" I could not help the slight note of sarcasm that crept into my voice, but it only seemed to amuse Elena.

"Of course! Ramon is an idealist. For all that he respected your father, and knew of *my* wishes, I don't think he would have agreed to marry you if he had not fallen in love with you."

"Heavens! Do you mean that that would have left me with a choice between Lucas and Julio? For I'm sure that *my* inclinations would not have been taken into account under any circumstances. Tell me, if I had not had the bad fortune to travel on that particular stagecoach, how would this—this marriage my father is supposed to have arranged for me have been contrived?"

Elena's look was mock-reproachful.

"But Rowena, surely you do not doubt my word, or that of *my* father the shaman of his people? If fate had not brought you here, it would have been arranged in some other fashion. But you would still have been given the choice to make up your own mind. You do not feel *forced* into a decision, do you?"

Her dark eyes fixed themselves on mine with an unreadable glow that made me wonder just how much she knew of the strange, tension-fraught interlude that had taken place between Lucas and myself.

I smiled faintly. "I'm sure that all women are forced into certain actions at some time or other in their lives—don't you agree? But in my case I have always been lucky enough to end up having my own way in the end."

Ramon came back at that moment, and our conversation turned smoothly from the intimate vein it had taken to more general matters. Elena said that she could see no reason why we should delay our marriage for too long. Ramon looked questioningly and rather diffidently at me, and I, determined that Elena must see I would not allow her to run *my* life, said primly that I thought we should discuss our marriage plans later.

"After all, we have just become engaged. I think we both need time to get used to *that* idea first!" I looked at Ramon, as if for support, and not at Elena, and he flushed with pleasure and pride as he agreed with me. I had the feeling that he would agree with almost anything I suggested to him, if I was tactful enough.

Ramon carried me up to bed in his arms, and kissed me gently but possessively on the lips before he left me there.

"Please, Rowena, you must believe that I do not wish you to feel forced into anything you do not desire. I love you, and I swear I will never be anything but gentle and patient with you, whatever you wish me to be."

Ramon was frank, open, and honest in his love for me. I knew that he believed me to be a virgin, and that this only added to his almost worshipful adoration of me. He was gentle, he was considerate, and he treated me as if I was fragile—something that not even Todd Shannon had done. I told myself that it might not be too uncomfortable an arrangement, especially since I had no other choice in the matter.

I told myself all this as I lay awake that night, watching the pale moonlight stream in through the windows, touching the blanket I had covered myself with, and casting barred shadows on Luz's empty bed in the other half of the room.

No, I told myself. I would not wonder where Lucas had taken her, or what they were doing out so late. And yet the moonlight made me restless enough to leave my bed and go to my window, and I saw the glow of a lamp in Elena's room as well. The thought that she too sat up and wondered gave me a spiteful satisfaction. I had already recognized her as a strong woman, and I could neither like nor trust her, for all her artful flattery of me, and her pretended consideration. Still, even she had her weakness, and it made me feel that my newly gained knowledge put me at a slight advantage.

I turned over in bed, feeling again the unpleasant sickness in the pit of my stomach that always came when I thought of the strangely incestuous relationship that existed between her and

Lucas. I blamed her most, but I blamed him too. His father's wife… and still he lusted after her without shame, using other women to satisfy his passing needs while he left her upon her pedestal. I hated myself for what I had done this afternoon, and above all, for my response to his kisses. And I hated him for his threat—the "ultimatum" he had given me. Desire— no, lust described it better—was an ugly thing to be feared and avoided. A thing that made slaves of men and women. Was that how my mother had ended up in Edgar Cardon's bed? "I love him!" she had told me. "It is something that *you* could never understand." Why had she called it love? What was love but lust dressed up in pretty words and phrases?

I was still awake when Luz came back, tiptoeing into the room with her shoes carried in her hand. I didn't know what time it was, but the moon had risen in the sky and no longer fell across our beds. I heard her fling herself down, and thought she sobbed softly.

In the morning, her face was sullen, and her eyes swollen.

"Luz? You look tired, and my hand doesn't hurt at all this morning. Why don't you stay in bed and let me help downstairs?"

"If I do not keep busy I think… oh, what is the use? You cannot possibly understand! I was so happy last night when he asked me to go riding with him in the moonlight, and then..,"

Her voice shook, and I knew I should leave her alone, but I could not forbear from prompting her.

"And then…?"

"Then—nothing! We rode, we talked, but it was I, as usual, who did most of the talking. He kissed me, after we had dismounted and lay side by side in the grass. And I thought this time, surely! This time he will go further than kisses, and I will let him, and later we will be married… but you know? Nothing! Sometimes I wonder why he took me from Montoya and brought me here! Sometimes I feel that *she* has taken all his manhood from him! I am a woman too, and more of a woman than she is, but he does not see me as one! At least—oh, God, at least Jesus Montoya saw me as one!"

I was alarmed at the high flush in her cheeks, and at the almost desperately angry note that had crept into her voice.

"You don't know what you're saying!" I said sharply. "I'm sure Lucas holds back because he respects you.'"

"Respects me!" Luz repeated the words in a voice that was high with hysteria. "Do you think that's enough for me? Must I remain a virgin, wanting to know a man, and how it feels to lie with one, forever? Lucas knows that I love him and that I want him! I forgot everything that you told me, I could not be cold under his kisses, I showed him that I wanted him, that I wanted him to—but he would not. And it was not because he respects me, but because he craves *her*. Do you think I don't know to whose room he went after he brought me back? When he went to put the horses away I went to his room. I took my clothes off, and I waited for him. Oh, God! Without shame I waited for him. I thought, when he sees me like this, he will not be able to stop himself, he will take me. But he did not come. And when at last I grew tired of waiting and started to come back here, I heard her laughter, and her voice, and *his*—in her room!"

We looked at each other, and I felt my own face flush with anger and disgust. "A man like that is not worth your love—he's not even worth spitting upon! Listen, Luz, when Ramon and I are married and leave here, you must come with us. There are other men in the world. Men who are kind, who treat a woman as a person, and not as a thing to be used."

I went to her, and held her by the shoulders. "Put some cold water on your eyes. Do you want him to see that you've been crying? For heaven's sake, have some pride! Ignore him. The next time he asks you to go riding, refuse to go!"

I do not know how much of my strong speech she comprehended, for in my anger I spoke in English, instead of the Spanish we usually conversed in. But at any rate she allowed me to bathe her eyes in cold water, and style her hair differently, pinned up on her head, with curls cascading down to her shoulders.

Like a child, Luz was immediately diverted by the sight of her own reflection in the mirror, and turned this way and that to admire herself.

"Oh, but you have made me look pretty! Like a fine lady—

oh, Rowena! Do you think he will notice me *now!* Aren't you jealous in case Ramon gives me a second glance? If only I had a beautiful gown, like the ones that Lucas brings *her...*"

I shrugged my shoulders in despair, but promised to see what I could do.

"Stay here."

Boldly, I went along the gallery to Elena's door and knocked on it.

"Come in."

Her voice sounded sleepy, but when she saw me her eyebrows lifted in surprise.

"You? But you should not be awake so early. Oh, dear!" She stretched and yawned, and I noticed, unwillingly, that even in the morning light she contrived to look young and quite attractive, with her hair hanging loosely about her shoulders. She was alone... had I really expected to find *him* still here?

"I'd meant to be up before anyone else to help Paquita with the breakfast. But I suppose the men have all left already. Is there anything wrong, Rowena?"

I apologized to her unwillingly. "I'm sorry if I disturbed you. But I wondered—you've been very kind to me, of course, letting me wear your clothes. There is the pink dress you gave me. Would you mind if I altered it for Luz?"

The way her eyebrow shot up told me that she had seen through my silly subterfuge, but her voice was indulgent, and even slightly amused.

"Of course you may! It is yours; you may do whatever you wish with it. And it's very kind of you to take such an interest in our little Luz. I'm afraid you must think I neglect her. Yes, really..."

Sitting up in bed, Elena frowned thoughtfully, as if she was really concerned, and yet I had the feeling that we still sparred with each other, as we had from the very beginning.

"I must tell that thoughtless son of mine to bring her some pretty gowns the next time he goes to Santa Fe or Mexico. And in the meantime, there are so many of mine that I hardly wear and might be altered for her." Our eyes met, and she smiled. "There, does that make you think a little better of me? You must not think that I'm not fond of Luz."

"I've never doubted it," I said noncommittally, and smiled when I thanked her for her generosity.

"If you need anything, you have only to ask, of course. You are my daughter." She paused for a moment and added mischievously, "Or my little sister, perhaps, since the shaman my father has adopted you!"

Elena Kordes and I understood each other well enough, and there were times when I almost enjoyed sharpening my wits against hers. This morning, I had the feeling that she was being deliberately, exaggeratedly kind—both to Luz and to me, as if we were children who must be indulged.

I went downstairs afterwards, leaving Luz admiring her new gown before the mirror, and had almost reached the kitchen when I heard Lucas's angry voice. He came striding through the archway before I had time to move past—almost barreling into me.

"What are *you* doing downstairs? You ought to be restin' up."

But his voice was distracted, and I think he would have brushed past me without any further ceremony if I had not deliberately stood in his way.

"Good morning, Lucas. Aren't you going to congratulate me? After all, you had so much to do with my decision to marry your brother!"

I thought he had to blink his eyes to focus them on me. And I noticed then that he was shirtless and bareheaded—beaded, Apache-style moccasins on his feet. I noticed too that he looked tired as well as angry.

"Congratulate you?" His husky voice echoed my words as if he hardly comprehended them, and I saw how his fingers riffled irritably through his hair, pushing it off his forehead.

"Of course—on my engagement to Ramon!" I repeated with mock-patience. "Do you intend to make a habit of coming back to the house this early every day, Lucas? If so I'll make an effort to stay out of your way."

"What in hell are you talkin' about? Where's Elena? We got company, seems like… Thought I'd better warn everybody."

I had a feeling he was thinking of something else, even though he had condescended to explain to me. There were tension lines in his face, and the sun wrinkles looked deeper.

"You mean that somebody's coming here? Somebody from outside?"

"Don't get your hopes up. No one *you* know."

"I suppose rudeness comes naturally to you!"

"An' you ask too damn many questions."

"I'm sure I can find out anything I wish to know without having to resort to asking *you* any questions!"

"Wait a minute!"

He grasped my arm roughly and swung me around to face him.

"Look—look, I'm sorry." His voice was as rough as the grip of his fingers around my arm, but sheer surprise held me still this time. "I'd no call to snap your head off the way I did. But there are some things you don't understand."

"I'm always being told that."

"Told what? Lucas, are you two quarreling again? I don't mean to intrude, of course, but when I heard your voice… is anything wrong?" Lucas dropped my arm as if it had suddenly burned his fingers, and I could have sworn he flushed guiltily when Elena's coolly amused voice sounded behind us.

I could not stop myself from watching his face. It changed as usual when he saw her, when he spoke to her—but this time taut anger came into it.

Perhaps he wouldn't have spoken so bluntly if I had not been present. "I came here to tell you that Montoya is on his way in. He gave the signal, and Julio went to meet him."

There was a slight pause, a fraction of an instant when Elena seemed to hesitate, and then she laughed softly.

"But that is wonderful! So, at last you two will meet again and settle your differences, as I have hoped for, for so long! It's high time, and you know it!"

"Don't be too sure of anything! Huh!" Lucas made a harsh sound. They both seemed to have forgotten me for the moment.

"Me and Montoya—you expect us to settle things and be friends again that easy, when you know damn well how it was when we last met? You *know* it, Elena. Why does he come here? Why do you encourage him to do so?"

Her head went back and I saw her eyes narrow. "And why shouldn't I? Just because you had a stupid quarrel with him is no reason why I should turn away from an old friend—and a friend of your father's too, must I remind you?"

He said savagely, "No, you don't have to remind me of that, an' you know it!"

The tension between them was a tangible thing. They looked at each other as if they were alone, and it was Elena who first remembered my presence.

"Lucas, please! Will you not try to act at least halfway civilized toward him? For my sake? Jesus is angry with you, yes, just as you are with him, but it was so long ago, and it is over now! He has been here, he accepts the fact that Luz stays here. Never has he tried to force himself on her."

"Or on you? Can you tell me that? Or why he never fails to bring you gifts? Like this…" he caught her hand and held it between them. The enormous ruby glistened with a dark fire of its own, and I did not know if it was my gasp or Elena's that echoed softly in my ears.

"Lucas!" Instead of pulling her hand away Elena brought her other hand up, touching his bare chest caressingly, almost tenderly. "You know that Jesus Montoya has been like a brother to me. We've known each other a long time, since you were no more than a child!" Her voice changed from softness to mock-severity. "Come now, who was it who made you a present of your first horse? And the first gun you ever owned? Before you two quarreled you were like father and son. Jesus always has been a generous man with his friends, and well you know it!"

I thought that he sighed, the expression in his eyes bleak. "And how well you know how to wheedle me out of my anger! But Montoya had better remember that I am no longer the niño he used to call me, and I warn you, if he…"

Elena turned to me with a teasing laugh. "Ah, Rowena! You see how fierce he is, this son of mine?"

I think Lucas felt himself driven past endurance at that

moment. "Not at all, *mamacita*. When you command me, I always become tame, do I not?"

It was the first time I had heard him call her "mother," and I saw her eyes widen; both at that, and the grim sarcasm that underlay his voice.

Before she could say anything else, he put his hand on my arm, drawing me with him.

"Will you excuse us? Rowena has reminded me that I have not congratulated her and Ramon yet, and I feel in the mood for a glass of wine."

Her indulgent smile put us both firmly in our places—as it was meant to, I suppose.

"But of course. You must find Ramon and you must all celebrate. And I have an even better idea—tonight we will have a fiesta!" With a rustling of her skirts, she walked toward the door leading into the kitchen, and Lucas dropped my arm to open it for her. I had noticed before that this was the kind of automatic courtesy he always showed her—and only her.

When he turned back to look at me I was armed against him, my eyes cold. "Why don't you go behind her and ask her forgiveness for having spoken like a jealous *boy!*" I could not prevent the venom from showing in my voice, nor the disgust, and his mouth tightened.

"Are you always so contemptuous of the feelings of others? Or is your damned indifferent air a cover-up for your own weakness?"

"Weakness!" I almost spat the word at him, even while I wondered at my own anger. "Why must those who are weak constantly look for the same infirmity in others?"

"I guess you'd call lovin' somebody weakness too, wouldn't you? What kind of a woman are you, for God's sake?"

"A woman who is none of your concern any longer!" I flashed back at him.

We were far too close, and in spite of my angry words I was afraid that he would touch me again, afraid of my own weakness.

I would have preferred him to show his anger in response to mine, but instead his green-flecked eyes had taken on almost a puzzled expression as he looked down at me. "What have I done to you to make you hate me as much as you do, Rowena? Oh, I know I've done things to make you mad, but it goes deeper than that with you, doesn't it?"

He was so close to me that I could see the faint scars, thin white lines against the brown of his bare chest. For an instant, I was seized with an almost overwhelming desire to reach my hand out and touch him as Elena had done, and the feeling shook me so much that I could not control the slight tremor in my voice.

"I don't hate you… that's ridiculous! For goodness' sake, what makes you think I'd feel so strongly about you, one way or the other? You have a way of making me lose my temper, that's all."

When I moved past him, walking far too quickly, I felt as if I was running away. He let me go without another word.

Twenty-Five

THE NIGHT THAT FOLLOWED WILL ALWAYS REMAIN "THE night of the fiesta" to me. No matter how far I travel or how much older I become, I think that I will always be able to close my eyes and see us all as we were on that particular night, with an enormous, slightly lopsided moon peering over the mountain ridges, and the tinier, flickering lights of the small fires that Elena had ordered built for warmth. There was a tree-shaded patio behind the house, with a wide half-wall surrounding it on three sides. Tonight, in addition to the small fires, there was torchlight and music. We were supposed to enjoy ourselves.

"You will have to get used to our Spanish ways, Rowena," Ramon had teased me earlier, when I protested that there was no need for such a *large* celebration of our engagement. "Any excuse to have a fiesta—to make merry and be happy. And tonight we will all be happy."

For Luz, it was the perfect occasion to wear her new gown, and to dazzle everyone with her high-piled, sophisticated hairstyle. Elena had given her pearls to wear, and they seemed to glow against her tawny skin. I wore white—like a bride, like a virgin, I thought to myself with a pang of self-derision, as I looked at myself in the mirror. A simple gown to make me appear young and innocent. Elena offered me jewelry to wear, but I refused it; and acting on a last-minute impulse I let my hair hang loose. Why not? It seemed that I had a role to play, and I would play it to the hilt. Elena would understand, if no one else did!

I was the last to go downstairs, for I had helped Luz to dress and pin her hair up in the elaborate style she had begged for. Outside, someone had started to play a guitar, a mournful Spanish air, and I could smell the spicy aroma of the food that Paquita was preparing in the kitchen; hear the murmured talk and laughter that floated through the widely opened doors.

Ramon waited for me at the foot of the stairs, handsome in his dark *charro* costume, with the white ruffle of his shirt forming a pleasing contrast to his olive-tinted skin. I saw a flare of desire spring into his eyes as he came forward to catch my wrists, pulling me against him for an instant to place a kiss at the corner of my mouth.

"You look so beautiful! Like a princess. Every time I set eyes on you, Rowena, I can hardly believe how lucky I am!"

We went outside, and there were more compliments. But of the three women there, I felt that I was the plainest, and the compliments merely kindness. Luz looked as if she sparkled from the inside out, and I saw Lucas at her side, a sullen expression on his face. His only concession to the celebration was the wearing of a red silk shirt, wide-sleeved and open down the front. I was reminded only too vividly of the scrap of red silk that had been his signal to Flo Jeffords and hers to him, and I felt my fixed smile falter for an instant. He did not move from his place to greet me, but I saw his eyes narrow slightly and his mouth go up at one corner as if he wished me to know that he was not to be taken in by my demure appearance.

"So Rowena has come outside to join us at last!"

Elena, silk and velvet skirts clinging to her body and swirling out behind her in a train that would have done credit to any duchess, came forward to greet me, just as if this had been some formal occasion, and I a shy guest.

Ramon stood back proudly as she linked her arm in mine and drew me forward.

"This is Rowena, of course, who is to be my daughter. Jesus, is she not as lovely as I told you she was?"

The tall, slender man who put aside the guitar he'd been

holding and came forward to greet me must be Jesus Montoya, then. The *comanchero*. The man whom Lucas had fought over Luz. I remembered everything that I had heard about these *comancheros*, and I suppose my eyes must have seemed guarded when I raised them to his, for I thought he smiled mockingly as he bent over my hand with true Spanish gallantry. He spoke to me in Spanish too.

"I have heard much about you, and you are no disappointment. I can only say that Ramon is an extremely lucky man!"

He straightened, and I met eyes so dark they seemed black. Streaks of white in his hair and moustache only seemed to emphasize the animal good looks of this man. He was neither as old as I had imagined, nor as brutish. And yet, I had sensed the scrutiny of his gaze, and some instinct told me that this was a man I should be very careful with.

I smiled at him in what I hoped was a guileless fashion. "You are a born courtier, señor! But what woman does not appreciate flattery?"

"With your beauty, señorita, you must be a connoisseur. You will let me flatter you again, I hope—later on? With Ramon's permission, of course!"

"Oh, but Rowena has eyes for no one but Ramon! She had three of my sons to choose from, but the other two she put in their places from the beginning, isn't that so?"

Elena's voice was as light as mine had been, and I matched her with my soft laugh.

"Oh, but to be fair you must admit I did not find it hard to choose! Your *other* sons are committed elsewhere, only Ramon was kind enough to fall in love with me!"

I wondered if we would all have to endure an evening filled with nothing but pretty, insincere speeches.

Ramon led me away, and the *vaqueros* smiled and nodded to me, each one in turn congratulating us. Jesus Montoya had brought one other man with him, an older man with swarthy, rather flat features, who gazed at me with no expression at all. But he took the guitar that Montoya flung at him laughingly after a while and played it until everyone forgot what he looked like.

"That is Chato," Ramon whispered to me. "He is the best guitar player I have ever heard. The only thing he does better, I think, is shoot."

"Well, I hope we do not have an exhibition of *that* particular skill!" I whispered back a trifle sharply.

I was beginning to wonder—and especially when I saw Elena go up to Lucas, and take his arm, with a laughing apology to Luz. Ramon had already swept me into the steps of a lively dance that I had some difficulty in following at first. Soon afterwards, Jesus Montoya walked over to where Luz sat perched on the low wall, and bowed to her, a trifle exaggeratedly. I expected her to turn away from him, but instead she smiled, and dimpled prettily at something he said as she took his arm with every evidence of enjoyment.

I stole a glance at Lucas, and his face looked grim. His head bent, he was engaged in some kind of low-voiced argument with Elena, whose smile never faltered.

I could not stop myself from glancing upward at Ramon.

"Do you think there will be trouble? There's Luz dancing quite unconcernedly with señor Montoya, and I thought she had to be rescued from him not too long ago!"

His fingers squeezed mine reassuringly.

"Do not worry, *querìda!* Do you not see that my mother has everything well in hand? Luz is taking your advice, I think, and making my brother jealous, which is good for him, you'll have to admit. And as for Montoya... well," he shrugged, half-humorously, "only Montoya knows what he thinks! But even he has too much respect for my mother to start any brawl here."

I told myself that he was right. How innocuous it all seemed on the surface! Even Lucas seemed on his best behavior, in spite of his sullen demeanor, and when he danced with Luz later I could read nothing in his manner that smacked of jealousy, or even anger. We were all so civilized... it was hard to believe that I was not somewhere else; and this not an evening like any other. I missed Julio. He, at least, had been honest, both in his feelings and his dealings with me, and with the others. But Ramon had already told me that Julio had left the valley after speaking with Jesus Montoya. Being all Apache in his thinking, he would not have believed farewells necessary. Still, I wondered what had made him leave so abruptly, and wondered, at the same time, if I would ever have an answer to all the questions that I found were in my mind.

I had some of those answers when, finally, Jesus Montoya asked me to dance with him.

I had already danced, one by one, with the *vaqueros,* who held me away from them as if I was something fragile, to be handled only with the greatest respect. I had drank at least three glasses of wine—and far too fast. They were all toasting Ramon and me, and I told myself that my flushed cheeks would be put down to the dancing.

"So, now at last it is my turn. Will you dance with me, señorita Rowena?"

He was formal, and I was just as formal, giving him a small curtsy in acceptance.

"You will have to guide me in the steps. I am just starting to learn them."

He lifted an eyebrow. "Shall I have Chato play a waltz? Yes, he can play even that. You have heard already, I think, how he can make the guitar come to life under his fingers."

And so I found myself dancing the waltz in the open, under a yellow moon, with only a guitar to give us music. But it was enough. Jesus Montoya was a born dancer, I have seldom danced with better.

"How light you are on your feet!" he murmured.

"How clever you are with your flattery."

He smiled, as if I had satisfied him in some way, showing white teeth.

"So you are Guy Dangerfield's daughter—and you are to marry Ramon. It is what your father would have wished, of course."

"And you too knew my father?"

"Not closely, alas. But I have met him. You have his eyes. But as for the rest… perhaps you have been told the same thing before, but it is of Elena that you remind me most. I think you are a strong woman, and not entirely the charmingly guileless girl you appear to be. Have I made you angry?"

"Why should honesty make me angry?"

"Ah! That is a good question. But it makes many people angry, as I'm sure you know. Shall I go even further, since you are a woman who appreciates directness, and tell you that *you* are one of the reasons for my coming here?"

I had to tilt my head back to look at him.

"I had no idea that news could travel so far, and from such an isolated spot."

"Ah, but I have my ways of obtaining such information that others do not. I am what others call a *comanchero*. I see from the flicker in your eyes that you try to hide that you have heard of us. And, no doubt, it has all been very bad. But I will not have you think that I am also guilty of evading the truth. I was curious, you see. Here is a young Englishwoman, lately come to this country. One would expect... what? Certainly not what I find here. A woman who survived capture by the Apaches. A woman who, I am told, captured even Todd Shannon's heart. Did you know that he has an enormous reward posted for any news of your whereabouts?"

His sudden question was abrupt, and yet I did not show him if it had startled me.

"Do you hope to claim it, señor?"

At last I had made him laugh. He threw his head back, but his laughter was strangely soft, almost soundless.

"And if I did, what would you tell me? You are to be married to Ramon Kordes, I find, and not to Todd Shannon. Frankly, I have no great love for your former fiancé, or his like! And, whether you choose to believe it or not, I do feel a certain loyalty toward my friends. So I will let you answer that question for yourself, señorita! And add one of my own. Do you wish to be rescued?"

His coal-dark eyes looked into mine, and I found that I could not answer him. But I refused to resort to subterfuge either.

"Perhaps, at the moment, I am not certain. And again... I'm not certain of your real motives either. Did you really come here to make sure that I was here? Or was it to settle old debts?"

I thought his arm around my waist tightened a trifle. "You

are indeed a clever woman, Rowena Dangerfield. You answer my question with questions of your own. You will give away nothing, eh? But you wish me to admit to… what? I think you have heard the whole story already, and as a tribute to your intelligence, I will not lie. Yes, my motives for coming here were many. And before my visit is ended, perhaps we will both find answers to our questions."

I thought I had the answers to everything that evening. I even thought that I could almost like Jesus Montoya, because he was honest with me. He was a clever man. He danced with me and acted the perfect gentleman. He danced with Elena, and I saw his head bending close to hers, his smile, faintly derisive, and hers in return. And he danced with Luz, and his manner was almost fatherly. I watched it all. The food was brought out—spiced roast beef, the inevitable beans. Steaming hot tortillas and chili; even a salad made of avocados, which tasted delicious. And there was wine, and tequila for those who wanted stronger. I tasted it, when Ramon, laughing, insisted, and it had no taste, but burned all the way down to my stomach. And all this time Lucas had not approached me; nor had I spoken to him.

I danced with him for the first time only after we had eaten, and after I had danced again with Jesus Montoya.

This time the wine made me bold enough to ask what was on my mind. "Have you made friends at last, you and Lucas?"

He smiled down at me in an amused fashion, but under his moustache I thought his mouth looked crooked. "Why should we be enemies? Always, it is a woman who can drive men apart. But women come and go, si? With Luz, her padre was my friend, an old friend. And I desired her, why should I lie about it? I spoke to him when he knew he was dying, he knew I wanted her, and it might have been arranged, if Lucas had not come back. Young—yes, he must have seemed so young to her! Young and hard and swaggering. She looked at him, and he looked at her. Soon it began to seem that she needed rescuing, and he was the one to do it. And there was the question of his proving something to me—a matter of manhood. Of a time when he was very young, and he went with us when we raided a certain village in Mexico. You are shocked? But I think you have heard of the *comancheros*. That we are worse than bandits, worse even than our Apache brothers whom the Anglos have learned to fear, and to respect. There was a woman, that time. A girl, you might call her. And Lucas, who was like my own son, had found her. He did not know what to do with her. It was a game of pursuit and capture. She expected to be raped... do I shock you? But he did not know how to go about it. And so—so I took her from him. 'When you are man enough to fight me for a woman we both want and win, then I will grant you the prize of war, niño,' I told him. And the time came when we fought again over Luz, and he won. It surprises you? It surprised me too. I would have killed him, if I could, but he had learned certain ways of fighting from the Chinese. Have you seen Lucas fight? He learned it in prison, and from the time he worked on the railroads in Kansas, and in Utah, working side by side with Chinamen. He does not use their style of fighting often, for he told me once that it was a secret, that he had sworn never to use his skill unless it was in self-defense. I was angry when we fought, and I had a knife—I suppose it gave him an excuse. Nevertheless, though it might surprise you, I too, in my way, am a man of honor. 'You owe me a woman, Montoya,' he said, and it was true. He left me lying senseless in the dust, when he might have killed me instead, and he took Luz with him when he left. Brought her here. By now, I would have thought he'd have married her. I could have forgiven him more easily if he had!"

"So you haven't forgiven him at all, have you?" I whispered. In spite of myself, his impassioned speech had caught my mind, making me wonder what else lay under the surface here. "And what of Elena?" I hadn't realized that I had put my thought into words, until I saw Montoya smile his crooked smile at me again.

"Ah, so you've noticed that too? Elena is like a distant star, the goddess all men crave for. I have always wanted her. Even when she was married to my closest friend. Even later, when I knew what killed him. And now... I do not know. Perhaps it is habit. Perhaps we are really friends at last, after all the years that have gone by, and the understanding we have gained of each other. I have a tremendous admiration for Elena. I respect her, as I have been able to respect no other woman. More than that, you will not get from me! I have told you more than I should. I wonder why."

He looked down at me thoughtfully. And it was at that moment that the music stopped for a few seconds, while Chato held a bottle of tequila to his mouth and drank thirstily from it.

When he turned back to his guitar again, one of the *vaqueros* accompanying him on the mouth-harp, it was Lucas who held me in his arms, while Elena, laughing, danced with Jesus Montoya.

How it had happened, I could never be quite sure. I had time to notice how well Luz and Ramon danced together, and then, because I became stiff, and my feet seemed to stumble of their own accord, he took me off into a corner of the patio, and lifted me up by the waist, so that I found myself sitting on the wide adobe wall.

I had had no time to struggle, nor even to protest. I remember that the moon was behind him, and I could not see his face clearly, only the bronze glints in his hair as he continued to hold me, his hands still on either side of my waist.

"You have a way of making men open their minds to you, without your feelin' a damn thing yourself, don't you, Rowena?"

I started to say furiously, "You have no right to question me…" when he cut me off, his husky voice curiously harsh.

"When will you stop playing games with me? And why only with me? I didn't drag you off here to start another argument with you, only to ask you something, for God's sake! I know how you feel about me, and maybe I've deserved most of it, but at least I've been honest with you Rowena. An' that's all I'm asking of you now."

It was to combat my own sudden breathlessness that I made my voice so icily cold. "I don't understand you, Lucas

Cord. At one moment you attack me, and the next you demand honest answers from me. Answers to what? And why from me?"

His voice quieted, but I felt the involuntary tightening of his hands about my waist and flinched.

"You and Montoya. I saw how long he talked to you, and I watched your face. He told you, didn't he?"

"What was there to tell? Or does your conscience bother you? One more example of your callousness... your selfishness! You did not want Luz, but you took her from a man who might have married her, and brought her here to this prison! And for what? Will *you* marry her? How long must she wait while you go off when you please and return if you please? Is there any feeling to *you* except for your ill-conceived lust for Elena and your hate for Todd Shannon? Why, you move everybody else around as if they were pawns, don't you? You brought me here to suit your own ends—because I was Todd Shannon's fiancée, and because my father left me a fortune. And if I had not promised to Ramon, what would you have done with me? Kept me here as a slave forever? Sold me across the border? Or would you kill me, as you tried to kill Elmer Bragg?"

My voice was shaking when I had finished. I had not meant to say so much, but suddenly, it was as if everything I had been holding inside me burst out, and I could not help myself. He had asked me for honesty and I had been honest with him.

He had dropped his hands from my waist and was staring at me, his head slightly tilted so that he could study my face. I thought I heard him suck in a deep breath and tensed myself for the angry tirade that must surely come. There was an aura of barely suppressed fury that I could feel emanating from him, and knowing his uncertain temper I should have been afraid. But there was such a welter of confused emotions within my mind by now that even if he had struck me I might almost have welcomed it as a release from the terrible tension that was between us at that moment.

But he had more control over his feelings, whatever they were, than I had shown tonight.

"Guess there's nothing more to be said between us now, is there? Come on, I'll take you back to Ramon now." His voice was flatly expressionless, and this time, instead of seizing me by the waist, he held his hand out to me.

I did not—could not—take it.

"I can manage quite well!" I said childishly, wondering why my voice still shook. My hands shook too, as I tried to lever myself off the wall, feeling the skirt of my gown catch on some slight protuberance as I did.

Afterwards, I blamed the cuts on my fingers, which had begun to sting and throb painfully again, and my misjudgment of the height of that wall, which seemed so low. Perhaps I had had too much wine to drink. But I felt myself pitch forward, and then his arms caught me. I was being held far too tightly and too closely, my face pressed against his shoulder, and I was too weak with shock and reaction to move.

I did not want to. I discovered that I was breathing far too fast, and that it made my head dizzy, so that I was forced to lean even more closely against him; and my most treacherous thought of all, I knew that I would not be able to bear it if he released me now.

There are certain times when certain actions seem natural and foreordained. Still holding me against him, Lucas put his hand in my hair, pulling my head back almost cruelly. Perhaps he read in my face what I could see in his: wonder. Even a kind of bitter anger. And hunger. Then he kissed me, with a violence and a passion that was like an explosion, stunning us both.

I felt the wall against my back, and his body against mine as I pressed myself closer to him with a shameless ardor I would not have believed myself capable of. I could no more have denied my longing for him than I could have commanded myself to stop breathing. We kissed, and kissing was not enough. With a passion I had been taught once, but now became natural and artless, I slipped my hands under his shirt, holding him with my palms against his skin, feeling the muscles in his back move.

I felt him wrench his lips away from mine and almost cried

out loud as my eyes flew open. His breathing was as uneven as mine—I noticed that, and wondered why he had stopped kissing me.

"Lucas…"

"*Don't,* for Christ's sake! What were you tryin' to prove this time? What a lecherous, dirty bastard I am? That I'm incapable of resisting any female who falls into my arms and presses her soft body against mine, even if she happens to be my father's wife or my brother's fiancée?"

I felt as if he had slapped me. I could feel the blood drain from my face and then flood back, leaving my cheeks burning. He had held me, kissed me, forced me into betraying myself a second time by using my own weapons against me. If I had had a gun with me, I think I could have killed him then.

"Is that how it happened with Elena too?" I said in a choked voice I could barely recognize as my own, and I raked my nails viciously across his back, wishing they had been knives. I felt—oh God, I felt the tearing of his skin and the warm stickiness of blood; then, with a grunt of pain and shock, he caught me by the shoulders, pushing me so hard against the wall I thought my back would break.

This time I would not close my eyes weakly when he brought his face close to mine. I glared into his eyes, and they looked dark and glittering, like the eyes of an Apache. I clawed at him again, and he slapped me; then before I could cry out he had leaned his body into mine and was kissing me again—so hard and so painfully that I felt I could not breathe, that I would forever feel the imprint of his lips on mine. My hands were pushing against his chest now, and I could hear my own helpless whimpering in my throat.

"Is *this* what it takes to keep you quiet?" He whispered it against my bruised, open mouth, and then, his hands moving from my shoulders to my breasts, "Whatever I am, whatever you are, I can't stop myself from wanting you."

I hit him, as hard as I could across the side of the face, using the back of my hand. "And I despise you, for the animal you are!"

My knuckles felt bruised and I almost sobbed with the

pain, but I had the satisfaction of knowing I had hurt him too. There was a livid welt across his cheekbone that he had begun to rub at absently while he stared down at me.

"Damned if you aren't the first woman ever slapped me that hard," he said quietly, almost wonderingly.

"But I'm sure you deserved it this time at least."

I gasped, and pressed my aching knuckles against my lips.

When had Ramon come up? And how long had he been standing here?

"You should have chosen a more isolated place for forcing your attentions upon my *novia... brother!*"

I had never known Ramon's usually easygoing, pleasant voice to sound so hard, nor seen his eyes so narrow and cold.

I felt as ashamed and humiliated, but his eyes had merely flickered over me, their expression unreadable, and now they were fastened upon Lucas, who turned slowly to face his brother.

"Well? Surely you have some explanation. You are not usually at a loss for one. Were you merely testing her true feelings for me? Or would you try and make me believe that she threw herself at you and deliberately enticed you into making love to her? Come, you must admit that I am patient! By now another man in my place would have shot you as you stand."

I noticed, for the first time, the awful, ominous stillness that surrounded us. There was no more music in the background. Here in this secluded, shaded corner even the torchlights were merely a faint glow somewhere behind us. And I saw, as he casually moved his hand upward, the gun that Ramon had carried against his thigh.

I opened my mouth to say something, but I could not make any sound emerge from my suddenly dry throat.

It was Lucas who spoke, his voice quiet. "I have nothing to say. No explanations."

"And you expect me to be content with that?"

The hammer clicked back on the gun. I felt as if I had been trapped in a nightmare.

"It seems as if you will be content with no less than to pull that trigger, Ramon. Why don't you do it quickly before your scruples get the better of you?"

Even in my half-dazed state I could not mistake the soft, deliberately taunting note in Lucas Cord's voice.

And it seemed to me in that tiny, suspended moment when they faced each other—Ramon with the gun in his hand, his face grim, and Lucas, standing so negligently, his arms at his side—that some men appear to court death deliberately, and that Lucas was one of these.

I know Ramon realized this too, and his handsome face twisted in a snarl of bitterness.

"I think you would like me to murder you and carry that guilt with me for the rest of my life. But I will not make it so easy for you. Where is your gun?"

"I saw no need to wear it this evening. And in any case, Ramon, I will not duel with you, if that is what you have in mind. For God's sake!" I saw Lucas's eyes narrow, and his voice turned harshly impatient, "Must we stand out here acting out some stupid drama? I kissed Rowena, and she slapped my face. Now… if you feel you ought to shoot me for that go ahead an' shoot. Or else I'm walking away."

"Must you be reminded that you are no longer dealing with a little brother, but a man you've insulted? I saw you strike my *novia,* and had I been close enough I would have killed you then!"

I saw, even in the darkness, the look on Ramon's face, and I managed to say faintly: "No, Ramon!" But Lucas, although he must have seen it too, merely raised an insolent eyebrow and started to walk past him. Perhaps he meant to take the gun from Ramon, perhaps he did not really believe that Ramon, the quiet-spoken gentleman who had been brought up by Jesuits, would actually shoot.

The gun went off with a blinding flash. I think I screamed, and the smell of powder was bitter in my nostrils. It is strange how the small details come soonest into one's mind afterward, when the recalling of violence is too frightening or too painful.

I remember that I leaned back against the wall, feeling my legs suddenly too weak to support me. I remember the warmth of the rough adobe bricks under my ice-cold hands.

Ramon had taken a step backwards, and now he took

another, the gun still steady. Lucas had seemed to stumble, but now he stood still, staring at Ramon. Very slowly he touched his right arm, and I saw him look down at fingers that were sticky with blood.

He looked back at Ramon then, and his voice sounded abstracted. "Either you're a very bad shot, *hermano,* or an excellent one. You've drawn blood. Does that satisfy your honor?"

"You have a poor idea of honor if you think so! Now, will you draw the knife that you carry in your boot, or will you stand there like a coward and let me use you as a target to prove that I am as good a shot as you are?"

"So it's to be knives, now?" Lucas's voice sounded faintly contemptuous. "Ramon, you're making a fool of yourself! Can't you see that?"

The gun boomed again.

This time the bullet had grazed his thigh, and already the blood was starting to drip down his pants leg, leaving an ugly, dark stain. I thought I saw a look of shock on Lucas's face as he looked from his wound and back at Ramon.

The moon had disappeared behind a cloud, but one of the torches suddenly flared in a rising wind, and I saw the cold determined look on Ramon's face. "Have I convinced you yet, Lucas?"

It was at that moment that Jesus Montoya, a cigar in his mouth, strolled casually to join us.

"So this is where you all are! Elena heard the shots, and asked me to find out what they were about. So—have you two been having a little target practice to impress the lady?"

"Montoya, you keep out of this!" Lucas said furiously, at the same time that Ramon gave a short, sneering laugh.

"I've been trying to persuade my usually reckless brother to fight like a man. But it seems he doesn't like having to face the consequences of his actions!"

Montoya took his cigar out of his mouth and studied it carefully. "So! This becomes interesting." He looked straight at Lucas then, and there was a knife edge of hardness underlying his smooth voice. "I am not so old that I do not have eyes, and ears. Did I not warn you once that women would be your downfall? I think you cannot make up your mind, Lucas *amigo*. I think you always want that which belongs to someone else… or is beyond your reach. Am I not right?"

Lucas said tightly, "This is an affair between Ramon and myself, Montoya. And you and I have not been friends for a long time. If you came here looking for a fight with me you can have it, but as for Ramon…" he looked at Ramon and said steadily, "I will not fight you, little brother. You will not make me, even if you go on shooting. So go on—finish it!"

"This is—I cannot believe this is really happening!" My voice sounded high and hysterical, but I managed to push myself away from the wall and stumble forward. I had the feeling that they had almost forgotten my presence until then, for all three turned to look at me. "Have you all gone completely mad? Do you expect me to stand here and watch slaughter? What's the matter with you all?"

"Rowena, you will please go back to the house." Ramon had never before spoken to me in such a harsh voice. "This is an affair between men."

"But it concerns *me,* does it not?" I was angry now, and still shaking from the reaction to fear. "Do you think I'll go away, just because I am *ordered* to! And I won't put up with being quarreled over!"

I would have said more, being both angry and over-wrought, but Jesus Montoya's fingers closed like steel over my arm, although his voice was deceptively mild.

"I think this quarrel has been a long time coming, señorita. And you have still a lot to learn about men. This has become a matter of honor."

"You want to see them fight! You'd sit back and enjoy watching them kill each other, wouldn't you?" I flung the accusation in his face, but he only chuckled.

"I would not stop them. But then, did you not just hear Lucas say he would not fight his brother?" His tone gave the words a lightly mocking contempt. "Here Ramon." I saw the long, wickedly pointed knife blade glitter as he tossed it, to stand quivering in the tree trunk behind Ramon. "Why don't you carve him up a little as a punishment, if you don't want to kill him? A knife is silent, at least. I have always thought guns far too noisy! As a matter of fact," he added thoughtfully, "it is something I should have done myself, and would have, if I had suspected how he would treat Luz."

"Damn you, Montoya, I've done nothing to Luz! And I warn you again to stay out of this, or by God I'll kill you this time!" There was a deadly note in Lucas's voice that made me catch my breath, but Montoya only laughed jeeringly.

"Without a weapon? And if we fight with our bare hands as we did before, how long before the blood you are losing makes you weak, eh?"

Lucas took a step toward him, but the knife blade, held against his chest, stopped him. Ramon, his face cold and set, had snatched the knife from the tree, holstering his gun as he did so.

"Before you try to kill him, you will first finish your business with me."

"Ramon, I've already told you that I have no quarrel with you. But my old friend Montoya and I have scores to settle. Get out of my way."

"The time is past when you can give me orders, my bastard half brother!"

The knife blade moved so fast it was like the flicker of lightning that lances through the clouds overhead.

Lucas Cord's carelessly unbuttoned shirt had a rent in it, and I saw the thin line of blood that suddenly sprang up across his bare brown chest

I think he put his hand up almost instinctively, and there was shock and anger on his face. But the knife moved too fast, and blood oozed from a cut across his palm.

"No," Ramon mocked, "you will not take the knife from me. Draw your own instead, if you dare. And then we will see."

"Ramon, you're crazy! You expect me to stand here and let you cut me up?"

I could not stop myself from crying out again when I saw the knife blade glimmer in another flash of lightning.

Lucas put his hand up to his face, staring at Ramon in disbelief.

"Damn you! Will you fight me now? How much does it take?"

This time the blade cut across his chest again. Two parallel lines, with the drops of blood already starting to run together.

I would have run between them, if Jesus Montoya's firm grip had not held me at his side.

"Let them be!" His voice was soft, and meant only for my ears, but I could sense the steeliness in it, and it made me shiver. "Do you have no understanding of pride? What you see before you now has been a long time coming. Either stand here with me and be quiet, or go back to the house, as you should have done before."

I stood there, not wanting to watch but unable to help myself. I saw Lucas move cautiously backwards, his eyes never leaving Ramon's face; saw the knife blade flicker like a serpent's tongue until his shirt was cut to ribbons and there were bloody cuts on his chest and arms. Why didn't he defend himself? I was reminded of gladiators in a Roman circus, and every time the knife slashed and cut viciously and I heard Lucas gasp softly with shock and pain, I gasped too.

Ramon too was panting now. I saw how his face gleamed with sweat and his nostrils flared with the effort of breathing.

"Why won't you fight? For God's sake, how much more will you take before you remember you're a man?" There was almost a sob of rage and frustration in his voice. "Shall I start to carve your face up too, so that no woman will care to look at you again?"

There was already a thin cut along Lucas's cheekbone, and now as Ramon slashed upward with the knife he moved his head instinctively sideways, bringing one arm up. The blade, dulled with blood now, left a wicked gash along his forearm.

It was then that his stubborn stoicism gave way to cold fury.

Once in India, I had watched a cobra and a mongoose fight. I remembered how the mongoose danced around its prey, darting in every now and then to bite, while the cobra, its hood spread, swayed back and forth, almost lethargically, waiting for the moment to strike. They had told me that a mongoose almost always won the contest, but on that particular occasion the mongoose must have been slow, or the cobra too wily. I shall never forget how quickly it struck...

And now, when Lucas moved, his whole body became as supple and as deadly as that of a coiled snake. He had seemed to sway backwards, his right arm shielding his face, but suddenly his body, whiplash-quick, swerved aside, and his left hand slashed upward. He used the heel of his hand against Ramon's wrist. I had time to notice that before the knife went spinning away in an arc. Ramon was holding his wrist, looking dazed, and it was Lucas now who held the knife, drawn from behind his neck.

I heard Jesus Montoya expel his breath in what sounded like a long sigh. "Ah!" And I could not tell whether he sounded relieved or disappointed.

It was only then that I noticed the cold breeze that had sprung up—the distant, intermittent flashes of lightning that would light everything for an instant in an eerie, steely glimmer; and even, in the background, the ominous growl of faraway thunder. How suddenly the moon had disappeared!

"Ramon..." Lucas said, and his voice was taut, husky with tension, "it is enough!"

But Ramon, I think, was past the point of reason, half-wild with rage and a sense of humiliation. "No!" he cried. "By Christ, it isn't over yet! You've got a weapon now, use it!" With a growing sense of horror I saw his hand move down towards his holstered gun. "Your knife—my gun. Throw it—and throw it fast, Lucas, because I will kill you anyway if you do not."

With an almost contemptuous ease and swiftness, Lucas threw the knife. It quivered, point down in the ground between Ramon's booted feet, a split second before Ramon drew his gun and fired.

Twenty-Six

REMEMBERING THAT NIGHT IS STILL NIGHTMARISH. I CAN SEE again the flash of lightning that made it all seem like a scene from Dante's *Inferno,* and I can hear my own despairing cry of agonized horror. I wake up drenched with sweat and see again how Lucas spun around, miraculously staying on his feet, to stagger against the adobe wall and slump over it, still on his feet.

His voice seemed to come from a long way off.

"Jesus God, Ramon! You're still a lousy shot when you get rattled!" And I was so relieved that he was still alive that I began to sob—dry, tearing sobs that came from the depth of my being.

What happened next is a blur, and part of the nightmare. I know I beat at Montoya's restraining arm, and cried out, "Let me go to him, let me go to him!" But he pushed me instead against Ramon, who stood there staring, with the smoking gun still held loosely in his hand.

I beat at him too, until he dropped the gun and held me by the wrists, some semblance of sanity, and of anger coming back into his face.

"Monster… animal!" I cried. "You are all animals, all the same! You… he… every one of you! I hate you all!"

"She is, after all, only a woman, and obviously not used to violence." It was Montoya's voice I heard, and it sounded deep and calm.

I twisted around in Ramon's grip and glared at him wildly. "He's dying! Isn't that what you wanted? Why don't you finish it?" I looked back at Ramon then, and my words were still wild, spilling out before I could control them. "You! You started it—aren't you going to kill him to prove you're a man? To avenge my honor? What are you waiting for?"

His grip on my wrists tightened until I almost screamed, but he looked over my head at Montoya, and his voice sounded flat and dead.

"I did not mean to go as far as I did! And yet I feel as if I had been urged to it for half of my life."

Lucas had turned, and the patch of blood was spreading on what remained of his shirt. He clung to the top of the wall with one arm, until he was able to lean his back against it. He did not speak, I don't think he was capable of speech at that moment, but his eyes caught the gleam of the lightning, and I thought they looked as green and pain-glazed as the eyes of a tiger I had shot once.

Jesus Montoya spoke, instead. "Take your *novia* back to the house, Ramon. There is a bad storm coming up, and I think we will have a cloudburst that will keep us all in the valley for some days to come. I will see to your brother."

"You mean that you will kill him. You will finish what *he* started, will you now?"

I could hardly recognize my own voice, it was so flat and drained of emotion.

Montoya's glittering black eyes looked into mine for a moment. "Once Lucas was closer to me than the son I never had. If I kill him, it will not be like this. Go now, you two. You are to marry and your place is with each other."

I went with Ramon. It seemed there was nothing else for me to do. His painful grip on my wrists did not slacken, and he almost dragged me for part of the way to the house.

Elena met us in the hallway, and she had changed her velvet dress for a silken wrapper; her cloud of dark hair was down over her shoulders, her face pale and haggard.

"For God's sake! What happened to you all? I heard shots, and I sent Jesus to find you... where is Lucas?"

"It was nothing, madre. We were having some target practice. And now Rowena and I have some things to talk about
with each other."

"Where is Lucas?" She almost screamed the words, and
Ramon gave a travesty of a smile, his lips pulling back from
his teeth.

"Lucas is with Montoya. I think that they have things to talk
about too. For once, my mother, will you go to bed and stop
interfering? Leave Lucas alone… leave *me* alone! When will a
mother learn to hold back when her sons are grown up?"

She paled as if she had been struck, but her back stiffened.
I had to admire the way she stood so straight, her voice
becoming stronger.

"And where are you taking Rowena? I want to talk with her."

Sensing an ally, I tried to pull away from Ramon, but he
held me fast. I was learning things I had not realized about the
Kordes males, it seemed.

"I am afraid you will have to put off your conversation
until tomorrow. Tonight Rowena will talk with me."

"Ramon! Do not forget that you aren't married yet!"
Elena's voice was sharp with anger.

"I forget nothing, *mamacita*. But I would advise you not to
come knocking at my door, filled with hypocritical morality!"
He tugged me forward by my wrists as if I had been bound,
so that I fell against him. "You have heard how Lucas bought
her, as a captive from the Apaches? Well, tonight, I took her
from him. And, as I have said, we have talking to do—perhaps
more than that."

"Ramon! If I did not know you better I'd say that you were
drunk. You forget yourself!"

He laughed. "Mother, if it is your *other* son, who is not
your son, that you are concerned about, I suggest you go
outdoors and find him!"

We left her staring after us as if she had been turned into
a statue of stone. I stumbled on the stairs, and Ramon lifted
me up in his arms, in spite of my feeble, half-dazed protests.

It was, I think, the way he kicked the door of his room shut
behind him that brought me back to my senses. That, and the

way he carefully bolted the door behind him, having flung me across his bed like an unwanted package. I watched him turn the lamp up slightly, and then turn back to me, casually unbuttoning his jacket.

"What's got into you?" I flung the words at him, but they sounded breathless and uncertain. He smiled, his mouth twisting mirthlessly under his neat moustache, and I realized that I did not know him at all. This was the man I had planned to play with, hoped to manage. The "gentleman of the family," and he turned out to be even worse than his brother.

"Nothing's got into me," he said calmly, and added, in the same tone of voice, "I would think that you'd be glad to see me turn into a man. It was the insult to you that did it, of course. And now, my sweet bride-to-be, I think that you should follow my example, and take your clothes off. Or would you prefer me to help you? Perhaps you're shy. I'm sure tonight must have been a shocking experience for you, and you must need some comfort." In the face of my stunned silence he raised an eyebrow. "Surely I don't shock you? After all, we are engaged to be married, what difference will it make if we are... how shall I put it... a trifle impatient? You will notice that my experienced brother did not let such small matters stand in his way. What surprises me is that having bought you, and had you to himself, he did not take advantage of such glorious bounty! Or did he?"

I drew what remnants of pride and aloofness I had left in me about myself like an invisible cloak, and looked coldly into his eyes.

"If you thought that, then you should not have acted the hypocrite, Ramon. I suggest that you let me go back to my room, and we can talk more calmly and reasonably in the morning."

He flung his jacket away from him, so that it landed on the floor. "In the morning, you say? My sweet, practical Rowena! Why should we wait until the morning? After all, we are engaged to be married, what difference will it make if I make you my bride tonight? I defended your honor... doesn't that make you feel differently towards me? I almost lolled my

brother over you—surely that must mean something? And
at least, *my* intentions are completely honest, and honorable.
You were Shannon's fiancée for a short time—surely you did
not hold back when *he* took you in his arms?"

He came to me, leaned over me, and I felt myself pressed
backward onto the bed. Suddenly, he had thrown his body
over mine, his hands gripping my wrists, pulling them over
my head.

"Did I coerce you into telling me you'd marry me? You
acted as if you were willing and eager. Was it all a game with
you? Rowena, tonight I'm going to have proof of your real
feelings. Are you capable of any real feelings? Kiss me then, as
if you love me, as if you meant what you said, and I will not
doubt you."

I let my lips part under his, and I suffered his searching,
encroaching tongue. Hadn't I learned from Edgar Cardon?
And yet even Edgar had always accused me of coldness, and
I had never been able to prevent a certain feeling of being
stifled—buried alive—when I felt his weight above me. I
felt the same way now. I let Ramon kiss me, but I could not
respond. I suffered his body on mine, his hands on my breasts,
and a voice in my mind kept telling me dully that this was
something I must get used to.

I was to marry Ramon. It was the only sensible, logical
way out of my dilemma. Not Lucas. Never Lucas, who loved
another woman, who hated me as much as I hated him—who
wanted me in the same way that I wanted him! Oh God, not
Lucas, who might be dying even now; who was the only man
who could kiss me past the point of thinking or of caring.

"Oh Rowena… Rowena!" Ramon was whispering. "You
kiss like a whore… like an angel! You're so cold, so unapproachable to look at, and yet, when a man holds you close
and your mouth opens under his, you're like one of the sirens
the Greeks wrote about, the taste of your mouth so sweet you
can drive a man out of his mind!"

I let Ramon kiss me, and I told myself that it didn't matter.
Once we were out of the valley I would be able to manage
him; he would be different, everything would be different.

Ramon's fingers were fumbling with the tiny buttons that held my gown together in front, opening it down to my waist. His lips moved against the skin of my neck, of my breasts. And I could feel—nothing. I lay there, unmoving, and I thought again of Sir Edgar Cardon, who had taken my cold, unresisting body so often, after that first time, and I wondered why it was that I had never been able to bring myself to pretend. With Todd I had come almost to the point of forgetfulness. Lucas had taken me beyond. Why did I have to think of Lucas?

I suddenly became aware that Ramon had raised himself up on his elbows and was staring down at me. He put his hand on one of my naked breasts, and I winced, not able to prevent my instinctive reaction.

"You'll let me take you, even if you obviously don't enjoy my touch?"

My voice sounded tired and unemotional. "I thought you said you wanted me. But if you've changed your mind, I could use some sleep."

His face changed. I thought for a moment that he would strike me, and I didn't care.

His voice was disturbingly quiet, however. "Were you thinking only of sleep when you pressed yourself against my brother like a woman in ecstasy, and put your arms around his body? Do you think I am a blind man, that cannot see what is before his eyes?"

I looked into his eyes, startled and angry, and they were like shiny brown stones, without feeling or expression.

"No, I am not blind, Rowena! But sometimes a man in love does not want to admit the truth. I loved you. I think I was infatuated from the first moment I set eyes on you. There was something in your very coldness, in your reserve, that excited me, intrigued me. I dreamed of you, and I thought that I would never be lucky enough to see you again, until Lucas brought you here. And you were still beautiful, still strong, still so cold and so arrogant in spite of everything I knew you must have gone through! I loved you all the more. I tried to show you respect and gentleness, all the things I thought you needed and were your due. And Lucas swore he had not touched you, and even Julio said that it was so. I thought you hated him, despised him! But was it that? Was it really that, or something else?"

He shook me, catching my shoulders with fingers that bit into my flesh like iron claws. "Answer me, damn you! Why did you say you would marry me? Was it only to make him jealous? Did you come here with me tonight only to make sure I would not finish the job of killing him?"

I whispered, "Did you *want* to kill him? You could have, and you didn't. And was it only because of me that you were so angry? I think you have always been jealous of Lucas, you have always resented him... and I provided a convenient excuse, didn't I?"

Outside I could hear the sound of the rising wind, and the thunder sounded louder. Or was it thunder? I thought I heard voices; the sound of horses' hooves, and something of my sudden apprehension must have shown in my face, for Ramon suddenly became still as he watched me narrowly.

He put his face close to mine, and I smelled the wine on his breath. This time I would not answer him; I made myself stare coldly up at him, and his laugh was an ugly sound.

"A short while ago you were hysterical. Do you realize that it was the first time you have ever showed any real emotion? But it was not for me, it was for my brother. Even when he slapped your face, and then took you in his arms... even when you struck him there was *feeling* there, was there not? And to me you have never showed more than a condescending tolerance. Even now. Why is it you have not struggled or screamed? Why did you pretend to kiss me back a few moments ago?"

I was stung into replying. "Why did you drag me in here? If it was only to hurl abuse at me, I wish that you would say whatever else you have to say, and let me go!"

"As easily as that, eh? And you think that everything will be all right in the morning. Would you still marry me after all that has happened?"

"That is up to you, isn't it?" I countered. "I think you are not yourself tonight, Ramon. In the morning..."

"In the morning! You think the rising of the sun will make things different? My God, how cold and how calm you are! You lie here in bed with me, and you speak of tomorrow. Do you think I cannot see the calculation in your eyes? 'Tomorrow Ramon will be himself again; he will apologize for his bad behavior, and things will go on as they were.' How easy to manipulate you must have thought me! You and my mother and Lucas! Well, I tell you that I am not finished with you yet. After the way you have behaved, I have a right to find out what I am getting. A block of ice, or a woman!"

Suddenly Ramon sat up, ripping my gown down the seam from waist to hem with one long, vicious movement. I made an involuntary gesture to cover myself, and he laughed.

"There's no need for modesty between us now! Tonight I fought for your honor and gained you as the prize. And what a prize!" His voice thickened as he gazed down at me. "A woman who does not need to wear those hideous corsets to improve her figure, a woman with a body as slender and beautiful as a dancer's. How lovely you looked, even when you were dressed as an Apache squaw. No wonder even Julio wanted you! You have a body and a mouth meant for passion and for pleasure. Perhaps it is only a matter of teaching you how to feel both."

He had already begun to undress, still watching me. The gown I had worn lay in pieces on the floor, along with my petticoats, and the thin chemise I had worn under it was ripped down the front, to the waist, hardly sufficient to hide anything from his hot, ardent gaze.

I forget what went through my mind during the next few moments. The last thing I remember thinking, as he turned down the lamp and came to me, was that I must not think of Lucas! All it had been was a physical, carnal attraction—an animalistic thing. Perhaps Ramon's possession of me would wipe it out. I could not help the stiffness of my limbs when Ramon pulled the chemise over my head, nor my instinctive shudder of revulsion when he began to caress me. I began to think of the promises I had made to myself when I left England, that I would be completely free, that I would

never allow any man to use my body again. And yet, it was
happening once more, and I had done nothing to prevent it.
This was my punishment for the ugly, uncontrollable feelings
that Lucas Cord's touch and kisses had aroused in me. Why
could it not have been Ramon instead who set my pulse
racing and my heart pounding so hard I thought it might burst
from my body? Why couldn't I *feel,* or at least pretend to feel?

Ramon tried to arouse some kind of response in me. He
kissed me, he was gentle with his caresses. But I could give
nothing in return. His body was warm, his flesh smooth to the
touch. His embrace, at first, had nothing of the roughness and
brutality I had experienced from his brother.

"Hold me, Rowena," he whispered. "Put your arms around
me, let yourself relax. I swear I will try not to hurt you."
And a little later, his voice roughened by passion, "For God's
sake! Do you find it so hard to kiss me back? Why do you lie
so still?"

I felt like a wooden puppet, and soon he lost his patience
and became cruelly rough.

"What does it take to turn your coldness into warmth? Is it
force you enjoy? Is it harshness?"

His kisses became hurtful, when I tried to twist my head
aside he wrapped his fingers in my hair to hold me still and
kissed me until I was breathless and gasping with pain and
anger. His kisses were like blows, leaving bruises down the
side of my neck and across my breasts. And in the end, when
I could not help struggling against him, he took me by force,
the pain of his entry making me cry out. And when it was
over at last, I felt bruised and empty and degraded as he had
meant me to feel, I think, when he had first brought me up
to his bedroom.

I tried to rise, when he finally rolled off my body, but he
pushed me back against the pillows. "In such a hurry to leave
already? No—I have not done with you yet!"

Dully, I watched him walk across the room, and the
lamplight became brighter, hurting my eyes. And now he was
watching me, his mouth twisted in a sneer.

"No blood on the sheets? I see now that your coldness was

all for me. Perhaps you showed another side of your nature to the man who took your virginity! Tell me, as a matter of curiosity, who was he, Rowena? Was it Shannon? Was it Lucas? Was that why you suddenly agreed to marry me? An available, gullible fool, eh? Were you looking for a convenient father for the child you may be carrying?"

I sat up, feeling bruised all over, forcing my eyes to meet his levelly.

"Oh, Ramon! What does it matter? You've had what you wanted from me, why can't we leave it at that? You don't have to marry me."

He walked toward me, and I think he expected me to shrink away from him in shame and fear, but I would not do so. I stood up and faced him, with no attempts at false coyness.

"Marry you? Do you think I want secondhand goods? No, not for all your money would I marry you now that I know you for what you are! A lying, cheating bitch!"

He slapped me, hard and unexpectedly, sending me floundering back against the bed. "You will tell me, damn you! Who was he? Or was there more than one man? God, when I think how pure and untouchable I thought you were, with your cool and haughty manners and your way of holding yourself aloof—but it was only for me, wasn't it? How did you intend to account for your slightly shopworn state? Answer me!"

He raised his hand to strike me again and I rolled away from him, kneeling on the bed to face him.

"You want answers when you no longer have a right to ask me questions? Why don't you use your knife on me too, Ramon? Or would you prefer to shoot me? You arrogant Spanish men with your stupid, empty talk of honor! You knew that I was brought here by force, and you closed your eyes to it. You took me by force, and now you're disappointed to find I was not a virgin! But if I had responded to you, if I had played the whore, it would have satisfied you better, wouldn't it?" I pushed the hair back from my face, past caution, past caring, and my eyes glared into his. "I'll tell you why I hate men, Ramon. And I'll tell you why my blood didn't stain your sheets tonight. My stepfather raped me, when I was only eighteen. And you're the only other man who has had me since. Not Todd, not Lucas. Yes, even *he,* in his way, was too much of a man to try to take me by force, even when he had me at his mercy in the Apache camp!"

Ramon's face had changed; he was staring at me with a strange look in his eyes: as if he did not want to believe me, for his own pride's sake. "And now perhaps you wish he *had* taken you. I saw the way you two were kissing, remember? And yesterday, after you had cut your fingers with the knife, it was Lucas you wanted to see. It is always Lucas! It is because of him that I am trapped here, as if I too had been a criminal. My mother—when Lucas is here she does not care for her own sons. And Luz—and now you. Well, at least I had you first! It is one thing he cannot take away from me." He caught my look and gave a strangely twisted smile. "You are thinking that I must hate him very much. You said so before. It is an odd thing. I do not hate him, but there are times when I do not like him either. And yet he is my brother; there is that bond between us. And you—for all your talk of hate, I think you feel the same way. I think that if it had been Lucas who brought you to his room tonight, your reactions might have been very different!"

I had no more answers for him. We looked at each other for a moment longer, and then I got up from the bed, and he made no move to stop me. I was naked, the torn remnants of my clothes not worth picking up. And I was past the point of caring. I walked to the door and unbolted it, and Ramon said behind me, his voice flat and without expression, "I suppose you are going to find him. Don't forget to try my mother's bedroom first."

I didn't look back as I left his room, closing the door gently behind me. I think that by then my mind was a blank. I acted purely by instinct. I walked boldly down the gallery and pushed open the door of Lucas's room. He wasn't there, of course, but had I really expected to find him? He was hurt, wounded, no doubt he would turn to Elena for comfort.

Would I really have gone to her door, knocked on it, and

demanded to see him? In the state of mind I was in at that time, I might have done so. All I knew was that I had to see Lucas, I had to find the answers to the strange yearning and weakness that consumed me whenever he touched me. I remembered the roughly efficient way in which he'd tended to my cut and blistered feet in the Apache camp; and later, the way he'd taken charge when I cut my fingers. Suddenly I remembered what my mind had been trying to shut out for the past hour, the way he had looked when I had let Ramon take me away. All that blood… Sudden panic took me. Perhaps he was badly hurt, perhaps he was dying, or dead by now.

I walked swiftly along the *galena*, my bare feet making no sound. Outside the thunder sounded much louder than before, and I thought I heard rain spattering against the roof in fitful spurts. Elena's door was open, and surprisingly she came out of her room as I drew level with it, just as if she had heard me, or had expected me to come. She looked at me. We looked at each other. And the only sign of surprise she showed at my unconventional appearance was the slight narrowing of her eyes.

I spoke first, forestalling anything she might have said.

"Where is Lucas?"

She threw back her head, and her face might have been a mask, except for the slight flaring of her nostrils. Her voice was a hard, cutting whisper.

"You dare to ask me that? *You,* coming naked from Ramon's bed? I should have listened to my instincts when you first came here! Your eyes were your father's, and that is what deceived me, but I should have known that your nature was not like his. I should have known that for all your talk of hate and dislike you wanted to take him from me. Did you plan everything that happened tonight, you and Ramon? Did you?"

All the smoothness and self-assurance had gone from her voice, and I could see that her fingers were like claws at her sides, longing to rake at my face.

I said contemptuously, "Did you plan, just so, to take Todd Shannon from his wife?" and I heard the hissing of her breath.

I looked beyond her into her room and saw only her empty bed, with rumpled sheets that told of her restlessness, and she saw my look.

"You thought he'd be here? Did you think that if he was I would let him come to you? I underestimated you, Rowena Dangerfield, but I do not underestimate the love that Lucas has for me. Yes. He loves me; neither you, nor any other woman will ever have more than his casual embraces!"

"In that case, it should not worry you if I want to see him, should it?" I said coldly. "Where is he?"

We measured each other again in that moment, and at last, she shrugged, although her eyes remained hard and cold.

"He's gone. That Montoya—he let him go, with a storm coming up, and he's wounded, with a bullet still in him. Do you think, if he was here, that he would not be with *me*!"

I turned from her without another word and went down the gallery to my room. Luz was not there, but even if she had been, I would not have cared. The windows had been left open, and the wind had put the lamp out, but the lightning that streaked across the sky gave its eerie, occasional light, and I found my clothes. A blouse, high-necked in the Apache style. A full, ankle-length skirt. Moccasins for my feet. I did not bother to wear anything else underneath.

Elena had followed me.

"What are you doing? Where are you going?"

"I think you know."

"You stupid fool! You'll never find him! He's probably out of the valley by now. Go out in this storm and you'll drown. And you're wasting your time, I tell you! Lucas hates you. Why don't you go back to the warmth and safety of Ramon's bed?"

"Is that what you would do in my place? You told me once that I was too much like you. Perhaps I'm just as unscrupulous. Does that make you less sure of yourself?"

She stood back to let me pass her, her mouth twisted. "Go then! And if the storm does not kill you, perhaps Lucas will."

"Perhaps," I said. "At least, you see, I am willing to take a chance."

I went down the stairs, not looking back to see if she followed me or not. I heard voices in the dining room. Montoya's deep, sardonic drawl and Luz's high, hysterical crying.

I pushed open the door, and they turned to face me. She was huddled in a chair, her hands over her face, and he had his back to the fireplace, facing her.

Luz raised her head, staring at me. Jesus Montoya's eyes narrowed speculatively.

"I thought you were with Ramon!" she cried accusingly. And then, when she saw how I was dressed, "What are you doing here? Don't you know what has happened?"

"Of course she knows. She was there when it all happened." He looked at me and his lips smiled, although his eyes remained opaque.

"Luz and I are to be married, as we should have been a long time ago. I will be taking her away as soon as the storm slackens. Don't you agree that it's a shame such beauty and youth should be wasted? I'm not much of a bargain, I'll admit, but I am better than some I could name."

"No—no! I am not a piece of merchandise, to be bargained for! You forced Lucas to say what he did when he was wounded and might have bled to death without a bandage. He *would* have married me in the end. I know it!"

"Do you really think so? I do not, and it was for your sake that I persuaded Lucas to speak the truth for once. You heard him say he felt nothing but a brotherly affection for you. That he would never marry you. Don't worry, *muchacha,* I will soon make you forget him. And the children I will give you will keep you too busy for regrets."

"Where is he?" I cut across their private quarrels, and while Luz only stared at me uncomprehendingly, Montoya nodded slightly as if he had heard something he expected.

"I could not persuade Lucas that it would be more sensible for him to remain here and have his hurts attended to. But I do not think he will attempt to go further than his cabin. You know where it is?" His eyes flickered over me consideringly. "I do not advise you to go out tonight. The storms here come up suddenly, and are all the more violent for that reason. The gullies become rushing watercourses. Perhaps you should wait."

He understood—Luz did not.

"What are you talking about? Rowena, where are you going? I thought that you and Ramon…"

"Ramon and I will not be married after all," I said baldly. "And I feel the need for fresh air."

"But it's raining!"

"Not too hard yet. Myself, I can understand that there are times when one needs to travel, feeling nothing but the wind and rain and motion. It is so with you tonight, eh? Chato is outside. He will saddle you a horse, if you tell him I said so."

I whirled and almost ran out of the room, hearing Luz's petulant voice behind me. "I do not understand! Where is Rowena going? What is the matter with everyone tonight?"

I felt driven. I let the door slam behind me, and as I crossed the hall I saw Elena looking down at me, but she said nothing, and neither did I. I went outside, and in the dark night the rain was merely a dampness. Chato moved forward from the shadows, and I found myself wondering if he ever slept.

"Montoya said you would saddle me a horse. A good one." His flat face betrayed no surprise. Perhaps my air of self-assurance convinced him that I was speaking the truth. He brought me a little, fleet-footed mare I had ridden before, and as if he knew where I was going, gave me directions. I wondered if he too had been watching from concealment when all the high drama had taken place earlier this same evening. And then I stopped wondering. I was riding, and although the mare tossed her head nervously at every flash of lightning and its answering rumble of thunder, she did not falter.

It was unbelievable, to think that only a few hours earlier there had been an orange moon in the sky, and the clouds, if there had been clouds, had blended with the shadowy outlines of mountain peaks, so that I had not known they were there. I remembered everything I had been told about the sudden, violent storms that could come up without warning in this country; the cloudbursts that could make every canyon or gully a watercourse, sweeping all before it. But at the moment I was not thinking of any danger to myself. Indeed, I hardly thought at all, or questioned why I was out here, with the rain beating against my face and drenching the few thin garments I wore.

Felice, my mare, seemed to know where she was going when I turned her towards the mountains that loomed forbiddingly ahead. The thunder seemed much louder here, reverberating against rocky walls; and the rain came down harder. But I had ridden this way before with Ramon, and all that Felice needed was a slight pressure of my knees, a light pull on the reins. We guided each other, and every now and then the lightning, like a giant torch, lit the countryside ahead of us.

I lost all sense of time, and sometimes, I thought, even of direction. But Lucas, I remembered, had ridden Felice before, and I had a feeling she knew where she was supposed to take me.

I do not know how long it took. I let the mare choose her own pace, and merely leaned over her neck, my hair clinging wetly to my face and shoulders. I must have been a little crazy, or suffering from shock, although I did not realize it then. There was a time when I didn't even know why I was out there in the rain and the wind, nor where I thought I was going. I would escape at last—if I did not find Lucas, or he did not find me, I would find my way out of the valley and be free. I had let myself become too involved with the twisted lives of the people here, I had to find myself again.

My thoughts were hardly coherent, I can see that now. And in the state I was in, I still wonder how I found my way to wherever I thought I was going. I remembered, even in my half-dazed state, what Julio had said to me on that day when I had first seen the valley.

"My brother has a cabin up there. A place he goes to when he wants to be alone." And I had wondered, at the time, why someone as brutish and unfeeling as Lucas Cord seemed to be would want to be alone. Then, I wanted nothing more than to be rid of his presence in my life. Now, I was running to him—or away from everything he had brought me to. I could not be sure which it was, until I found myself driving my horse up the narrow, steep-sided canyon that seemed to cut its way up into the highest mountain peak.

Twenty-Seven

꙳

I THOUGHT I SAW A DIM ORANGE GLOW HIGH ABOVE ME, BUT the lightning was too close and too fierce for me to judge properly, and the thunder, echoing against the narrow, rocky walls seemed to surround me and split my eardrums open.

"Lucas!" I screamed his name frantically and uselessly between cannonlike explosions of sound, and I thought I heard the noise of rushing water as my mare, as frantic and frightened now as I had become, seemed to stumble and then scramble for balance as she headed for the least steep portion of the rock-encrusted walls. I had lost the reins, and clung tenaciously to her mane, feeling how the suddenly ominous onslaught of the rain seemed to beat angrily against my face and body. I had never known such rain before. It was almost a solid sheet of water that attacked me viciously.

Felice stumbled, almost throwing me, and then her hoofs, frantically searching, found a foothold and started up a seemingly unscalable cliff. In a sudden flare of whitish light, I saw, for the first time, the water that swirled as high as my ankles, and kicked my feet from the stirrups as a wall of water roared down the wash towards us.

Only my most primitive instincts drove me on. Without conscious thought I jumped free of the struggling, terrified animal under me, and found myself clutching at an outcropping of rock, pulling myself upward; unmindful of the way my fingers were cut and scraped, I grasped and scrambled and pulled myself upwards, cursing the sodden wetness of my clothes.

I don't know how I managed it—clawing my way up the rock face of the canyon wall with my body clinging to it, using my hands and my feet, and feeling the rocks tear into my flesh and the water suck greedily at my ankles.

I heard myself cursing, using words I didn't realize that I knew, while the wind and the rain seemed to snatch away my breath, and the water, rushing like a riptide, came higher, pulling at me.

My grasping hands found a stunted tree that seemed to grow straight out of the side of the cliff. I found it and clung, and felt the water tug at me forcefully. And I screamed his name again.

"Lucas!" Lightning flooded everything with a blinding glow of white fire, and I screamed once more before the thunder came on its heels, making me cower, flattening myself against the cliff. I heard the high, whinnying scream of my mare from somewhere below me and did not dare look down, although my senses told me what had happened. She had been swept away by the water, and soon, when my hands were too cold and too numb to keep holding on, I too would be carried down the wash like a piece of debris... a floating log smashed against my thigh and I screamed again, despairingly, my hands still clinging, clinging with all the strength that was left in me.

And then just when I had lost hope, I thought I heard his voice from somewhere above me, and screamed his name again, with all the force and breath left in my lungs.

"Lucas! Oh, Luke—hurry, please!"

This time, I heard his voice clearly, almost disbelievingly, because it did not seem possible

"Rowena? Jesus Christ... what...?" And then, "Hang on, do you hear? Wait."

I began to sob helplessly, the breath rasping in my throat. I clung to the tiny tree, feeling the water whirling my skirts around me, tearing at me, and was only too conscious of the numbness that was creeping into my fingers. A rope—snaking down from above me somewhere, hit me in the face.

"Rowena! Can you hear me? Catch the rope. Can you hold onto it?"

"I... I can't!" I sobbed the words, and then strengthened my voice to scream my despair and fear up at him. "Lucas, I can't! My fingers..."

"Try to get it around you. Under your arms. It's a slipknot, hangman's noose. If you can get one hand loose..."

The rope dangled in front of my face, slapping wetly against my cheeks with every gust of wind. With an effort, I forced myself to loosen the fingers of my right hand, deliberately trying to close my mind to the sucking sound of the water that tried to drag me underneath. With one hand, I fumbled with the knot, pulling the loop wide.

I heard Lucas's voice above me, and wondered why it sounded so shaken and rough.

"Ro? For God's sake, try to hurry. You can do it. Just don't look down. Get the rope around you... tug on it when you're ready..."

My mind gave me commands that I obeyed by instinct, wriggling my head and shoulders through the loop. One hand, and then I knew I had to release my desperate, feverish grip on the tree I had clung to with my other hand and trust only in the rope. And now, if he wanted to, he could let me fall into the gushing torrent that seemed to get higher and higher every second, threatening to pull me under its swirling surface.

I heard myself gasp and moan, over the sound of thunder, and while the lightning flashed again I heard his voice. Was it possible that there was a note of anxiety, almost of desperation in it?

"Let go, Rowena! Hang onto the rope now, do you hear? Don't let go of the rope. I'm going to haul you up now."

Automatically I obeyed him, feeling the cold numbness creeping up to invade all of me, even my fingers. But I clung to the rope now, with as much tenacity as I had clutched onto the only handhold I had found earlier. I felt my body begin to slide upward—unbelievably, joyously. What did I care if the rocky face of the canyon wall scraped and bruised me? Even through my sodden garments I felt the pain as my knees, my breasts, and even my face were scraped raw.

My skirt caught on something and ripped... what did it matter? I was being dragged higher and higher, and I heard the water let go of me with an angry, sucking sound. It was below me now.

"Ro? Dear God, what are you doing out here in this storm? Didn't anybody warn you?"

Hands on me now, biting into my bruised flesh, almost as painful as the rope had been. And then I found myself lying face down in a puddle of water, hearing my own gasping breaths.

"Hold still. Don't move yet." The biting pressure of the rope eased as he tugged it off me, and he was a dark shape, silhouetted against a flash of lightning as he bent over me.

"Lucas?"

"Who the hell else did you expect to find up here?" His voice sounded harsh and uncompromising, and yet his hands were gentle enough as they pushed the hair off my face. "Can you get up? You're going to have to this time, because for sure I ain't in any shape to carry you."

His voice softened as he spoke to the horse that loomed over both of us, the rope that had dragged me up here still trailing from its saddle horn. Suddenly, I thought of Felice, the dainty, high-stepping little mare that had carried me here, and I began to sob bitterly, my shoulders heaving.

"For God's sake! This is hardly the time or place for you to start getting hysterical! We can't stay out here in the rain an' wind. Will you try to stand now? Hang onto me."

I clung to his outstretched arm, clambering laboriously to my feet, and wondered, vaguely, why he seemed to flinch away from me.

"Oh, damn!" he swore softly, and then, before I could say anything, "Come on. You can see the firelight from here, can't you? Pick your feet up—move! Want to be hit by lightning?"

We staggered the few feet to the small dugout, with its door flapping open, and the fire snapping and crackling inside. I dragged myself over the threshold, falling down clumsily on the dirt floor.

I heard the door slam shut behind me, and turning my head with an effort, saw him leaning against it, staring down at me, as if he could not believe what he saw.

"Rowena? What in hell are you doing here?"

The first thing I noticed was the blood soaking the make-shift bandage he wore, running down in rivulets. How could he lose so much blood and stay on his feet?

"You heard me…" I gasped out the words, and he frowned, but I thought he answered me with an effort.

"You crazy woman! Get over by that fire, and take them wet clothes off. I have to see to the horse."

"You're the crazy one. You're bleeding all over the place!" In spite of my wet, clinging garments I came to my feet. "I'll see to the horse, if you insist. But I think it is you who ought to lie down by the fire!"

"Why must you always argue with me?" He sounded angry, and when I reached him he swore at me, in English and Spanish and Apache. I was surprised at how calm my voice sounded.

"You're much worse off than I am. At least I'm not losing blood. I'll see to the horse, if you'll tell me what to do."

I went to him, and he flinched away from me. I caught his arm, and was tugging, half-dragging him with me, until he collapsed by the fire with a sigh that sounded like a groan.

"Listen—the horse has to be unsaddled, has to go in the lean-to. I can't pass out now, you can't…"

"Yes I can! I can do it. Do you think I've never unsaddled a horse before?"

I leaned over him, meaning only to tighten the bandage, and he turned white, his lips tightening with pain the moment I touched him. "I'll do whatever needs to be done, do you hear me? You're not to move until I come back."

A wry smile tugged at the corner of his mouth. "Yes, ma'am, I hear you. To tell the truth, I don't know if I can get up again or not."

"You're not to try," I repeated. I made my voice sound strong and self-assured, and tried to pretend that my knees weren't weak and trembling.

"You're bleeding too," he said in a strange voice.

"I'm only scratched. I'll do something about it when I come back inside."

I had to push against the door to get it open, and I heard it slam behind me as I staggered out into the rain and wind. His horse was well trained. He still stood there, sleek wet flesh quivering each time the lightning flashed. I led the animal—or it led me—around the side of the hut to the lean-to, which was a flimsy structure, open on two sides. My fingers were numb, making me clumsy and slow, but at last I managed to tug the saddle off the patient horse, and seizing handfuls of wet straw I did the best I could to rub him down. It took me longer to find his feed, but the lightning helped me to locate a box with a hinged lid. Now that I had done what I had come out here to do I began to shiver, feeling the water come sluicing down over me again as I stepped out of the slight shelter of the lean-to. The lightning was closer. I tried not to think about it as I fought my way to the door, clinging to the side of the house for guidance.

When I was back inside the small cabin again, leaning against the door with my eyes closed as I thankfully let my ice-cold body absorb some of the fire's heat, I found myself wondering what I was doing here? Why had I come?

"Ro? Are you all right?"

"Don't call me that!" I snapped, opening my eyes, and wondered why he didn't snap back at me, and why his voice had sounded so muffled until I saw him shiver under the blanket he had pulled over himself. "You're still bleeding!" I crossed the room to him, only realizing, when I bent over him, that I was dripping water everywhere.

The fire was hot, but I saw how he clenched his teeth together to keep them from chattering, his eyes half-closed. I pulled the blanket away and touched the soaked, bloody bandage and felt him wince.

"Oh, God, you're cold!" and then, still in the same, thick voice, "You'd better get them wet clothes off you… there's… another blanket, right there…"

"Don't talk!" He had a fever; I could feel the heat of his body, hear his rasping breathing.

I forced myself to retreat to the far end of the small room, and forgetting modesty, I turned my back and pulled off my soaking wet, clinging garments—or what was left of them. I snatched the blanket from the floor and wrapped it around myself, turning to face him.

"Stop staring!" I said angrily, and he narrowed his eyes at me, tilting the jug that sat on the floor beside him to his mouth.

"Better have some yourself."

Wondering why I felt so cross, I walked over to him and snatched up the jug, tilting it as he had done to let the fiery-warm liquid trickle down my throat. Almost tasteless, it burned me all the way down to my stomach, leaving me coughing and spluttering afterwards, so that I almost dropped the jug.

I looked down at him through the tears that were already forming in my eyes, and he was actually laughing, between chills that made his teeth clamped together.

"Oh! You!"

"Better save some."

"If I dropped it on you it would serve you right!"

He started to cough, grimacing, and I was immediately contrite, kneeling beside him.

"You have a fever. And that wet bandage isn't doing you any good. Let me look at that wound."

"Damn you, woman!" he gasped, "Keep your hands off... ugh!" He groaned with pain and closed his eyes as I ripped the bandage away ruthlessly.

I was glad, then, that he couldn't see my face. The knife cuts were bad enough, still oozing blood, but the bullet wound in his shoulder was an ugly cavity, with the flesh already red and mounded, almost closing it off.

"Oh God! Lucas... I've got to do *something*."

"Know anything... about gettin' a bullet out? It's still in there, someplace."

He spoke through his teeth, with his eyes still closed, and when I touched the wound gingerly I heard the hissing of his breath and thought, for a moment, that he had fainted.

"Lucas..." I could not control the shaking of my voice, and his eyes half-opened looking into mine.

"Stuck my... knife in the coals. Was going to do it myself, after I... got myself damn good and drunk... but now you're gonna have to... try. Hear me, Ro?"

"No!" I shook my head, even though I knew that there was no other way. I was going to have to get that bullet out or he would die... and if I didn't do it right he'd die anyway, and it was my fault, my fault!

The nightmare reached its climax during the next hour. The only light I had was the flickering, orange glow of the fire, and I needed another drink first. This time the liquor didn't burn quite as badly, and I think it even steadied me slightly as I tried to remember the thick medical books I had read. But reading textbooks in order to answer questions was one thing, and reality, was another. He told me between gasps what I would have to do, and I poured half the contents of that jug of tequila down his throat before I started.

I couldn't bring myself to use the knife because I was afraid that the shaking of my fingers would make it slip. So I poured some of the tequila over my fingers, and gritting my teeth against the sickness that threatened to engulf me, made myself probe for the bullet. Oh God—can I ever forget the feeling? My fingers, slippery with blood, knowing that I was hurting him almost past endurance, and the thought, more frightening than anything else—suppose the bullet had been deflected off bone and penetrated even deeper than we had thought? Suppose...

His eyes were closed, and I saw the beads of sweat standing out on his forehead, running down his pale face and over the livid cut that the knife had laid across his cheekbone.

My teeth bit down so deeply into my lower lip that I tasted blood. I wanted to cry out to him, to scream, "Lucas! I can't do it—I can't find it!" but mercifully he had lost consciousness, his body so still that I found myself wondering if he was dead. No... he couldn't be, I wouldn't let him be! And then, at last, I felt what I was looking for and extracted a flattened, ugly-looking piece of metal. I flung it away from me, and drops of blood spattered against my wet face as I did. I had to stop the bleeding now, and before that... I picked up the jug of tequila and poured some of the raw spirits into the wound, wincing as I did.

His body jerked involuntarily, and I thought I saw his eyelids flicker as he flailed out angrily with his other arm, knocking me backwards.

"Oh, *damn* you, Lucas! Will you hold still?"

I was sobbing. When I came back to him with the knife I leaned the weight of my body over his, remembering how swiftly he had cauterized the cuts on my fingers. It had to be done and I did it, gagging weakly when the smell of burning flesh assailed my nostrils.

By now the blanket had fallen away from me, and I had forgotten it. There was still more to be done. I boiled water in the battered, blackened coffeepot, dipping strips of cloth torn from my skirt in it, laying them over the wound and then bandaging it tightly again, passing the bandage around his neck, crossing it as I brought it back around his arm and shoulder. Only then was I aware that I was a mass of aching bruises, and that I was so tired I was shaking and limp with exhaustion.

I tugged at the blanket I'd allowed to drop, and felt even that effort almost too much for me. I leaned my face against his chest and heard, with relief, the quick, irregular beating of his heart. He was shivering, his skin cold, and he had begun to stir uneasily, his head moving. I had barely enough strength left to pull the blanket over us both, pressing my body against his, and feeling the long shuddering chills that shook him, willing some of the warmth of my body to find him. And then I must have slept, or fainted.

How much of the night had gone before I woke I do not know. Realization of where I was and what had taken place came slowly, as my eyes opened, blinking to focus on the fire, which had burned itself down to a bed of ashes.

Lucas was muttering something in a husky, incoherent voice, and his skin, no longer cold and clammy, was dry and burning to the touch. He kept trying to push the blanket away, to push my weight away.

"I'm not going to let you die, do you hear me, Lucas?" My voice sounded angry. He couldn't hear me, of course; I knew that, but I needed the sound of my own voice to give me reassurance as I crawled from under the blanket, shivering, and put more wood on the fire. Small, necessary things, to keep myself sane. Like filling the coffeepot, looking for coffee. It was there, in a canister on one of the shelves he had built along the wall, but I took some time to find it, discovering sugar and beans and flour first, and even a slab of bacon wrapped in several layers of newspaper.

I could still hear the rain beating down on the roof and against the door, the receding mutter of thunder, and underneath it all, like a sullen, ominous counterpoint, the rushing sound of water.

Suppose the whole hillside came crashing down on top of us, burying us under acres of mud and rock? Suppose…?

I had no idea whether it was still night or morning, but I no longer cared. Amid the leaping flames the coffee boiled quickly and I poured out a cup, taking it back to where Lucas had again pushed the blankets off himself. I poured some of the tequila into the cup and sipped at it, wincing when the fiery liquid scalded my lips. I managed to drink half of it before I became so tired again that I put the cup down and crawled under the blankets.

I was light-headed, and dozed fitfully, sometimes hot and sometimes feeling as if I was going to die of the cold. When I awoke—*consciously* awoke again, my head was aching, my eyes smarted, and my limbs felt as if they were strangely weighted down.

Rain still drummed on the roof, but pale glimmers of light seemed to have filtered inside. The fire had burned down to ashes, and the soot-blackened coffee pot still beside it.

I turned my head to find myself looking into Lucas Cord's drowsy, half-closed eyes.

"Thought I'd dreamed you!" he muttered huskily, and I felt his arm tighten around my shoulders. I had been lying on my side, my head resting on his unhurt shoulder, my body pressed far too closely against the length of his. "Warm—don't go yet, Ro."

Hardly aware of my own action I put my hand up, and

touched his beard-stubbled face, and then his mouth came down over mine—seeking, impatient, hungry. I remember sighing, as if I had been waiting a long time for just this to happen, and had been holding my breath in anticipation.

Twenty-Eight

❧

"DON'T GO! ROWENA..." HIS HUSKY, SHAKEN WHISPER sounded like a cry of reproach, but his arms had not enough strength to hold me, as they had done when we had kissed before. This time it had been I who had been the first to wrench myself away from the clinging, desperate pressure of his lips. I did it because I had to, and not because I had wanted to: I did it because the rush of violent emotion that seized me when his mouth first covered mine came close to making me lose all control of myself. We were like animals, pressing closely against each other for body heat until that heat was replaced by the force of our desire. Wanting more than kisses, I put my arms around his body, feeling him wince with pain.

Lucas's skin still felt too hot and dry, and when I rolled away from him, my breathing sounding more like sobbing. I could see that his eyes were bloodshot and fever-bright. He didn't want me to leave him. I stood up, belatedly remembering, when I saw the look in his eyes, that I wore nothing to cover myself.

"I'm not going far. I—I have to put some wood on the fire, don't you see? And you still have a fever."

I reached for the blanket, but he held it.

"No. Damn the fire! Come back to me." And then, as if the word had been forced from him, "*Please,* Rowena."

I heard myself babbling, to combat the weakness that flooded through me.

"We have to have something to drink—to eat. And I must find something to wear, don't you see? I—I'm so cold!" My teeth were chattering suddenly, and I heard him sigh.

"There's a shirt of mine. Hangin' on that peg to one side of the door. Do you have to put it on?"

"If I caught a chill it wouldn't help either of us, would it?" My voice sounded stronger, and I made myself avoid his eyes as I snatched it down, slipping my arms into sleeves that were far too long, my fingers fumbling with buttons.

I glanced at him once, over my shoulder, and his eyes had closed again. I threw chunks of wood from the untidy pile in one corner onto the almost-dead fire, blowing on it until I saw a red glow in the ashes.

The coffeepot was dry, and the canteen I had filled it from during the night was empty. I went to the door, opening it into a curtain of steady rain; shivering as the cold, wet air blew in. Water ran off the edge of the roof, and I held the pot under it. I could still hear the steady, roaring gush of water, the same torrential stream that had fought so hard to take me, as I would have been taken if Lucas had not heard my screams. And now, for the first time I became aware of our utter and complete isolation. I felt as if we were the last two people left in the world—as if the world had narrowed down to this tiny hut, and the rushing water and the steady beat of the rain. I remember sucking in deep breaths of the fresh, cold air, to clear my head of all the thoughts that scurried around in it, and behind me, I heard his voice, flat-sounding now.

"Better close that door pretty quick, or it'll be as wet in here as it is outside."

Stepping back, I let the door bang shut, and went quickly to the fire, which was just beginning to flare up again, sticking the coffeepot among the coals with an almost vicious gesture. I must have looked ridiculous, wearing a large, flapping shirt that reached to my knees, its sleeves rolled up; with my hair in snarls and tangles, and my scratched, bruised face. But surprisingly, I didn't care. Carefully avoiding Lucas's eyes, I measured out coffee, and finding a skillet left carelessly by the fireplace, I grabbed for the slab of bacon and the knife.

"Rowena. For God's sake. Can't breakfast wait?"

I resisted the pleading in his voice.

"Stop acting like a spoiled child! I'm hungry, and you should be too."

"Better watch it, or you'll cut your fingers again, the way you're usin' that knife."

I looked at him, startled, and he was sitting up, watching me, the bandage showing a stain of red already.

"Will you lie down?"

His voice held a half-angry note in it. "If I felt a mite stronger I'd come over there and make you lie down with me. Damn you, Ro! What is there about me that makes you shy away like a scared filly? An' what made you do a damnfool thing like coming up here in one of the worst storms I remember?"

I didn't answer him. Perhaps I was afraid to.

But, having made room for the skillet in the fireplace, I went back to him, pushing him down.

He put his hand up, catching my hair in his fingers, pulling my head down to his. I stiffened, but he only brushed my lips with his, surprisingly gently. It was enough to make me weak all over again.

"Don't, Lucas!"

"Why not? You know damned well I'm in no shape to force you to do anythin' you don't want to do. That was only to say thanks for what you did."

It was inevitable, I suppose. I knew it then, just as I think I must always have known it. Love or hate, there could never be indifference between us. Kneeling beside him, I bent my head to his and kissed him until the smell of burning bacon jerked us both back to reality.

"Why did you have to think about food?"

"You'll feel better when you have some inside you," I retorted. My voice sounded ridiculously happy, and I thought I saw his lips twitch in an unwilling smile. This time he let me go without protest. It was as if we had scaled some kind of invisible wall that had kept us separate, and now there was no need for impatience, no more misunderstanding. We were content to wait, knowing what would happen in the end, and by some unspoken mutual consent neither of us talked of anything that had taken place in the past.

The bacon was half-burned and the coffee too strong. Lucas told me he had never tasted better. He showed me where to find another jug of tequila, and I spiked the coffee liberally with it, drinking far too much, and hearing myself giggle with a lighthearted gayness I had not thought myself capable of.

"I feel so—so domestic! What would you like for supper?"

"Must you keep thinking only of food?"

I frowned at him in mock reproof.

"But I want you to feel strong again. Look, I found some beans. Would you like beans and bacon?"

"Better soak them in water first," he advised me solemnly, and this time I watched his eyes follow me as I moved around the cabin, and felt my heart beat faster.

I was happy. Even when, following his instructions, I mixed salt and water and dabbed the strong solution on his wounds with a piece of rag, I was happy doing it. Even though I winced every time he did.

There were no ghosts between us then. Not Todd's, not Ramon's, not even Elena's. We were alone, with the rain and the recurrent sound of thunder surrounding us. And we wanted each other, although we waited, because there was no urgency now. Time seemed to have stopped.

I swept the floor, and cleaned out the skillet with a wadded piece of newspaper, and filled the coffeepot again. Carefully taking off the shirt I had been wearing I braved the storm outside to see to the horse again, over Lucas's protests. By this time the tattered remnants of the clothes I had worn when I came here had dried out in the fire's heat, and I used them to rub myself dry.

Naked again, I went to him, and equally naked, he received me. We made love slowly and unhurriedly and inevitably. With Lucas, there was no holding back, no sense of violation. I wanted him, and he wanted me, and for the first time in my life I learned how it felt to be taken out of myself with longing, and to have that longing fulfilled.

Contentedly, our arms wrapped around each other, we slept. And awakened to make love again and sleep again.

I think that we had both lost track of time. We knew it was day when there was a gray light outside, and night when the light faded. I cooked the beans I had soaked with more slices of bacon and they tasted delicious. We got half-drunk on tequila, and explored each other's bodies. The rain came down as if it would never stop, sometimes gentle, sometimes loud and harshly, like the way Lucas made love to me. I wanted it to go on forever.

But with the same inevitability of the passion that had brought us together, we began to quarrel. It was my fault. I wanted to know more about him, and he told me roughly that he did not want to talk about the past.

"Would you prefer to talk of the future?" My eyes glared angrily into his. "What will we do when the rain stops, Lucas? Tell me; I must know!"

"Must know what? Isn't *now* enough for you?"

"Am I going to be just another one of the women you've used and then discarded? Is that it? Damn you, I have a right to know!"

"Rowena…" he expelled his breath in an impatient sigh that made me all the angrier.

"Don't! I'm not a child. I'm not as naive as Luz, nor as calculating as Elena. Why can't you treat me as a person?"

"And how have I been treating you? You're here—you came here of your own accord, didn't you? I asked you once why you came, and you wouldn't tell me. Now perhaps I don't want to know. You're here. I want you. Can't you take each moment as it comes?"

"No!" I almost screamed the words at him, hating him at that moment. "No I cannot. Is wanting all that's between us, Lucas? It's not enough for me."

"But what do you want of me? You haven't told me. What do you want me to say to you? I can only say what is in me now. I want you. I think I have always wanted you. And you held me off."

"You know why!"

"Why are you here? Tell me that, and perhaps I might have an answer for you."

His body was over mine, imprisoning me.

"I don't know. Yes—I do. I wanted you too. But Lucas, I'm a woman. There has to be more. I don't know anything about you…"

"And I don't know anything about you. For God's sake, can't you stop asking questions?"

I couldn't bring myself to ask the question that trembled on my tongue. "Do you love me? What do I mean to you?"

Instead I said bluntly: "Why haven't you asked me why I'm not a virgin? Ramon did. That night—he took me up into his bedroom, and he—he—"

"Oh, God! Rowena, it doesn't matter. Do you hear me? It's what I've been trying to tell you. I don't want to hear about your past, or whatever's done an' finished with. It's what's happening now, and what's between us now that counts."

"And Elena?" I do not know what drove me to ask that particular question, but I saw his face take on a closed, forbidding look.

"Why did you have to bring her up?"

With an abrupt, savage movement that took me by surprise he stood up, tossing the blanket aside.

"Lucas…!"

"I'm going outside. Going to see to Diablo. Get some air. I'm beginning to feel stifled in here."

I watched him snatch the yellow slicker down from its peg and throw it about his naked body. The door slammed behind him, and then there was only the sound of the rain and the rushing water and the crackling fire.

I remember that I lay there, on the crumpled blankets, and I told myself that I hated him, and myself as well. I had asked for this, I had come here after him, flinging myself at his head. What else did I expect? He loved Elena, and how sure of him she had been! She knew Lucas, much better than I ever did or could. I had merely made myself available, and he had taken me, just as he had taken Flo Jeffords, just as he must have taken countless other women. I shuddered with revulsion, remembering how I had almost pleaded with him for some avowal of love, or real feeling.

And then I told myself, stubbornly, that I was a Dangerfield, and I knew what I wanted. I would not give in! I wanted Lucas Cord, whatever he had been, whatever he was, whatever he had done. And I wouldn't let Elena have him. I was stronger than she was, and younger, and we were both trapped here for the moment.

I stood up, flinging the blankets away from me, and I went outside. The thunder growled menacingly, amidst the throaty roaring of the water and the ceaseless chatter of the rain. I gasped with shock and cold as gusts of wind drove the icy cold needles of water against my body, drenching me within a second. He was out here, with a wound that had barely begun to heal. I felt alone, and frightened. Suppose he had gone? Suppose he had some secret escape route known only to himself and he had decided to abandon me here? How long had he been gone? Where was he? I began to inch my way forward, feeling the driving rain like so many tiny icicles against my face and my unprotected body. I clung to the side of the house for support and for guidance in the pale gray light.

"Lucas! Lucas, where are you?" I heard a pounding in my ears like a drumbeat and wondered why I was suddenly so terrified. "Lucas!" I blundered around the corner of the hut, and suddenly, thankfully, I felt his arms go around my waist as I almost barreled into him.

"You! For Christ's sake, what are you doing out here?" But even while his angry voice slashed at me, he was dragging me with him, and we staggered together into the slight shelter of the lean-to, where Diablo was munching on his feed, wet coat quivering.

My teeth were chattering.

"I thought... you took so damned long!"

"Since when did you start swearing?"

"Since—since whenever I please! I'll swear when I feel like it! Damn you, damn you!"

He shoved me up against the wall, pushing his face close to mine, his brows drawn together in a black frown. "You swear just once more an' I'll belt you across the face! What in hell gets in you sometimes? One moment you're all soft and yielding, and the next you're a wolf-bitch, all claws."

"I can't help it! You make me that way! And you swear all the time…"

"That's different, I'm a man."

"Oh! Oh of all the… the…"

"Why don't you try shutting up?"

He was as wet as I was. Water dripped from his hair and ran down his face. Even his lips were wet and cold.

"Why did you come out here?" he whispered finally, raising his mouth a fraction from mine.

"I was afraid you wouldn't come back. You were so angry when you just stamped out, leaving me!"

"An' how far did you think I could go? Even if I'd wanted to? You crazy female!" He kissed my half-formed, angry protest into extinction, leaving me out of breath.

"There. Doesn't that tell you something?"

"Lucas…"

"No. Don't talk. Listen, I only stayed out here trying to fix up a better shelter for Diablo. Been meaning to do it before, only I kept putting it off. Even had the hammer an' nails out here, and the boards. See? Everything's wet, but that don't make too much difference."

"And you chose to come out here in the middle of a storm to do it?"

"You better get used to the fact that I aim to do as I please, anytime I damn well feel like it!"

It was the closest he had come to commitment, and I stared at him.

"Very well. And *you* had better accept the fact that I intend to be just as independent!"

"I accepted that the first time I talked with you. Remember how mad you got? An' then you came running after me like a fool, yelling out my name. Even then I didn't know what to make of you. Still don't. Look at you! Running out here in the rain, naked…"

"Don't you like me this way?" He was leaning over me, his

hands on the muddy wall on either side of me, still wearing that ridiculous yellow slicker. Laughing up into his frowning face, I put my arms around his damp body, pressing my face against his chest. "I love *your* body," I whispered. "And especially when you're not wearing any clothes."

"You're a shameless hussy!" I think he meant to sound angry, but his voice lacked conviction.

"And you can't hide the fact that you want me in spite of it!" I teased, and could almost have sworn that he reddened with embarrassment. He wasn't used to teasing, nor given to easy laughter unless it was cynical or bitter. I had already discovered this. Perhaps it was because he had never had the chance to feel young and carefree.

"I'll be goddamned if you ain't the boldest-tongued female I've ever come across!" he said threateningly, but when I slid my hand down his belly and touched him, I heard him catch his breath before he put his hands firmly on my shoulders and moved me aside.

"If you're goin' to stay out here you can help me finish what I started out to do, or else go back in the cabin an' stop distractin' me!" His voice was harsh, and his narrow-eyed look warned me to silence, but I obeyed him meekly enough when I saw him shrug out of the slicker and toss it aside. "Damn thing just keeps gettin' in the way, an' I ain't likely to get any wetter than I am now," he grumbled, adding, when he saw my smile, "an' I don't want any smart comments out of you, either!"

I picked up a board without speaking and held it for him to nail in place, knowing better than to offer to do the hammering myself, in spite of the grim-lipped, drawn look that came to his face when he had to use his right arm.

He was stubborn, almost as stubborn as I was myself. I remembered the time when I had thought of him only as a dark, brooding, and completely ruthless man—an outlaw and a murderer who deserved to be hunted down. I remembered the sickened feeling that had taken hold of me when I learned he was not Elena Kordes's true son, but her lover, and the anger and disgust I had felt afterward should have warned me of the inexplicable, unforeseen involvement of my emotions. But how could I have been prepared when I had never felt such emotions before? All I could be sure of was that Lucas had uncovered some need in me I had not known existed.

I watched him furtively as he worked with an angry concentration, blinking drops of water from my lashes whenever a gust of wind brought the rain slashing against my face. I had not thought a man's body could be beautiful until I had known his. But even the scars that my viciously raking nails and Ramon's knife had left, or the soaked, bloody bandage that showed whitely against his brown skin, could detract from the almost perfect symmetry of flesh and muscle and sinew. I was suddenly seized with a wild and unreasonable surge of jealousy. How could any woman not want such a man? How many women had *he* wanted, and taken?

He looked up suddenly, tawny-green eyes meeting mine, and something passed between us. He put down the hammer and the box of nails and took me by the arm.

"I think we're both crazy, stayin' out here in *this* when there's a fire in the cabin and warm blankets to lay on."

Water dripped from our bodies and made puddles on the cabin floor. My teeth chattered, and even my face felt numb. But when I made a move to take up the shirt I had discarded earlier, to dry my hair, he pulled me down with him onto the blanket by the fire.

"The blankets will be soaked through! Lucas… wait!"

"No!" he said it fiercely, savagely, his body already moving to claim mine. "I want you just the way you are now. Wet—your hair dripping. Cold outside and warm inside. Rain witch!"

Twenty-Nine

WITH THE STORM ENCLOSING US, OUR LOVING WAS ANOTHER kind of storm. I had never experienced such intensity of feeling, nor such a wanton abandonment to passion. Lucas possessed me, and I wanted to possess him. We gave each other, with our bodies, the commitment that neither of us dared put into words.

We mated. There is no other word for it. We were equal—man and woman; neither asking what we could not give. And later, when the fury of passion had died away into peace and we were content to lie together, still part of each other, I remember thinking that whatever happened later I would always have something that could not be taken from me or lost. An unchangeable moment, encapsulated in time.

We slept, with nothing but the hot, harsh glow of the fire to cover our naked bodies. And when I woke first, I lay still, not wanting to disturb his exhausted sleep; content to lie there and savor the pleasure and pressure of his hard-muscled body on mine. How well I had learned to know his body! I was as familiar with it now as I was with my own. Untaught, I had nevertheless learned how to excite it. I knew the feel and taste and touch of him; I had mapped every scar, every inch of his flesh with my hands and searching lips, as he had done mine. Was it really possible that I was the same woman they had called the marble goddess? With all my learning, and the rational, practical mind I had prided myself upon, how had I failed to recognize that such depths of passion and feeling existed? If, after our first joining, I had still had some stubborn, secret barriers left, they had disappeared now. Why had I kept trying to evade the truth? I was in love with Lucas Cord—shamelessly, recklessly in love, for the first time in my life; and the knowledge left me strangely weak and helpless. Why did it have to be Lucas, of all men? Why not Todd, whose very persistence and self-assurance had brought me close to a kind of loving; why not Mark, who would never hurt me... or even Ramon?

Lying there with my eyes staring into the orange glow of the fire and listening to Lucas's deep, even breathing against my heart, I wondered how it would all end. I had asked him that earlier and he had refused to answer me. There were too many unanswered questions that tugged at my brain when I allowed myself to think. The world outside, which must, inevitably, claim us both again. Elena... oh, God, why must I keep thinking about Elena? I should be more concerned by everything I had learned about Lucas himself. I should have remembered before I came here what he was and what he had done.

Deliberately, I thought of Elmer Bragg, shot from ambush and left to die. Todd Shannon, with the crimson patch of blood spreading, spreading on his white shirt as he lay in the dust. Flo, and what had happened to her. And all the others there must have been. I should have kept on hating and despising this same man in whose arms I now lay, but instead I found myself trapped by the call of my body and my senses, and I knew that against all reason I loved him and would continue to love him. I didn't care what crimes he had committed. If only I could stay with him, things would change, I would make them change! Lucas loved me—he *had* to love me. A man's body cannot lie...

He will not lie to me. I should have asked him before. So many questions, and yet I knew, without any pangs of shame, that no matter what answers he gave me, I was unalterably committed to him. Since we had quarreled our relationship had changed and I was more sure of myself, and of him. Start with the past, I told myself. I was still to afraid to question what the future might hold.

I suppose I must have stirred uneasily, for suddenly I found myself looking into Lucas's sleepy, half-closed eyes. "Are you always such a damn restless sleeper? What's the matter with you—hungry again?"

"Only curious. About something I should have asked before. Your grandfather told me to, but I..."

I felt the wary stiffening of his muscles and rushed on.

"Lucas—will you tell me about Elmer Bragg? The marshal in Silver City said..."

"I know what they all said. An' thought." I held my breath, releasing it only when I heard him give a long sigh. "All right, Ro. I guess you need to know. Been wonderin' if you'd ever get around to askin'—and then I figured that if your mind was already made up there was no point in my tryin' to change it. But no matter how it seemed, I didn't bushwhack him, Ro. Didn't even hear what had happened, until afterward."

I said nothing, taking comfort from the fact that his arms continued to hold me as he went on, in a quiet, voice: "I was in jail, a small town in the province of Sonora, when he found me, and God knows how he did that I'd gotten into some kind of trouble up there, and they said they were goin' to let me rot in jail until I could pay the fine they named, or work it off. Mexican jails ain't the healthiest in the world, and I had a hunch, besides, that they were just aimin' to keep me there until the damn *alcalde* got to checkin' across the border on how much reward money was bein' offered for my hide. An' then Bragg turned up. I hadn't seen him since my trial in Socorro; he was the last man I expected to see, and I thought, at first, that Shannon had hired him to find me. Until he started talking about you. About how you'd come all the way from England to claim your pa's share of the ranch, and had hired him to find out all he could. Said there were things he didn't know or wasn't certain of that I could tell you, that you needed all the help an' advice you could get, an' it was up to me to make sure you heard both sides of the story. An' all the time he was talkin' he had this kind of secret grin on his face, like he had somethin' up his sleeve. When he told me I'd probably find meetin' you a real nice surprise I remember he laughed out loud. It made me mad. I told him I didn't trust him, that I thought he was loco, but that old cuss was always the persistent kind. We argued back an' forth, an' he kept remindin' me I didn't have much choice. He'd arrange to bust me out of jail if I gave him a promise I'd go see you an' talk to you. An' to tell the truth…" Lucas grimaced ruefully, "by then I'd started to thinkin' of what would most likely happen to me when some of Shannon's bounty hunters found where I was, and I wasn't of no mind to find out. So Bragg and I made a bargain, and that same night I was loose. I guess he bribed a guard—never did find out, because he'd gone already. I was free, I had a horse and a gun, and I rode like hell until I'd crossed the border."

I believed him. God knows I had *wanted* to believe him in the first place, but now, meeting Lucas's steady expressionless eyes, all my instincts told me that he had spoken the truth.

"But Lucas, then who…"

"You think I haven't asked myself that too? Or why he kept callin' my name? Mebbe he was tryin' to warn me, mebbe it was just because I was the last one he talked to. Hell, mebbe he thought it *was* me, who knows? But it could have been anyone, Ro. That part of the world is the perfect hideout for outlaws, bandits—the thing that surprised me was that Bragg would have been careful, he *knew* the country, an' the risks."

We looked at each other, and suddenly, in spite of the fire's heat, I shivered.

"You think it was someone he knew?"

"Or *thought* he knew, maybe. I don't know! An' if half the Rurales an' lawmen on both sides of the border weren't lookin' for me, I'd have gone back to that convent where he was at an' done some checking on my own."

"*Was?* Oh Lucas, he's not…"

"Don't know that either. All I know is what Flo told me."

"Flo…"

He must have seen my face change, and sensed my instinctive movement of revulsion, for his arms tightened inexorably about me, holding me still.

"You knew damn well I was meeting Flo! An' I'm sure you guessed she was tellin' me things."

"You *used* her!" Why did he have to mention Flo?

"Yes, I did, an' I ain't goin' to make no excuses for it, Ro. I had a score to settle, and I went about settling it my way. Flo was unfinished business, an' when I came back an' heard she had left her rich husband an' was staying with her pa again, askin' questions about me—hell, all I could think of was the way she'd lied that time, sayin' I tried to rape her, when all the time she... all right, so she was only fifteen—that's what you were goin' to say, wasn't it? But she was a woman to look at, and she knew all of a woman's cheating, teasing tricks. Sure, I was goin' to use Flo if I had to. Give her back some of her own medicine, an' get back at Shannon too. You guessed that, didn't you? That first night I talked to you, you flung that at me."

"Why did you come? You were free, you need not have let your promise hold you when you had other things to do."

I tried to keep my voice even, but it shook traitorously. Oh, God, why did this man have such an effect on me? Even when he admitted how cold-bloodedly and calculatingly he'd taken advantage of Flo's weak nature, I could not escape my own longing for him.

"If I make a promise, I try to keep it if I can. Although there were times when you made me wish I'd told Bragg to go to hell. Do you realize that ever since I ran into you, you've brought me nothin' but trouble?"

"Oh! Of all the unfair... if *you* hadn't come to Silver City to kill Todd—"

"Wrong again. I came to Silver City to bring Ramon, so he could meet you. An' then all hell broke loose."

"But you had been with Flo! Oh, God... even now it makes me sick to think of it. After Todd was shot and I came up to find her, the bed was—and then she admitted it. She told me she'd been with you, that in spite of all the danger you couldn't stand to stay away from her." I would have pulled away from him then, if he had let me. The memory of Flo, the thought that they must have lain together, just like this were almost too much to bear thinking of.

"Damn you, Ro. You wanted answers from me, didn't you? I don't know what kind of story Flo made up—it sounds like the kind of thing she'd say, I guess. But if you're tryin' to say I went to bed with Flo, screwed her, and then walked over to the window and shot Shannon, you're... What kind of idiot do you take me for? Christ, Silver City was crawlin' with lawmen and Shannon's gunslingers, and no matter how I'd have liked to get a shot at Shannon, I wasn't aimin' to get shot by his men before I got close enough. I talked to Flo, sure, but I wasn't about to get myself trapped in bed in a hotel room with her. An' if you want the truth, I didn't even trust her that much. No, it wasn't me took that shot at Todd Shannon. I was headed out of town when it happened, an' I kept goin' when I heard. I wasn't the only one hated the bastard. Anyone could have done it, and then, if they knew I was in town, pinned it on me. If I hadn't have talked to Ramon and decided to get the hell out right then, they'd have had me trapped, an' no one, not even you, would have taken the time to ask me any questions."

He said it flatly and unemotionally, stating a fact, and I was suddenly shaken with horror at the thought of what might have happened.

"But then... you *knew* what everyone was thinking, and when Flo ran away to you, it only made it so much worse! Don't you see? They were certain then, that you and she..."

"What difference could that make? There was already a warrant sworn out against me, and when Flo turned up, it looked like a good way to get back at Shannon. But I didn't ask her to run off to me. Hell, I was running then, an' fast. Why would I want her in the way, slowin' me down? Only trouble was, I'd told her too much. She used to keep naggin' at me, asking where I was goin', what was I goin' to do about her. An' finally I told her one day I was planning to leave for Texas, getting in the freighting business again, and that if she wanted to get a message to me, there was a place she could send a letter. 'Bout a month or two later, a man I knew told me there was a woman lookin' for me, asking questions. He gave me the name of the hotel she was stayin' at, an' I went to see her. I was curious, I guess. And—" I heard a bitter, bleak note come into his voice. "She was *there,* Ro. Told me how she'd run off, tellin' everyone she was running away with me. Playin' right into my hands, the way I thought then. I took her. An' I think we got to hating each other long before we reached Kansas.

"I didn't lose her to that tinhorn gambler. She wasn't mine to stake. There'd been other men by that time. It seemed like she had to keep proving to every man she met how irresistible she was. She was like a leech, all greed: always wantin,' always graspin'. An' by then—hell, I didn't care what she did, or in how many beds she lay! It had gotten so I could hardly stand to touch her, or have her touch me. God knows why she stayed with me that long! An' then I got in that card game—mostly so I wouldn't have to spend another evening with her, I guess. An' I saw the way she looked at the gambler who was runnin' the game, and the way he looked at her. I guess she really wanted him; he said he was French, and he dressed real well and acted like he had lots of money. Anyhow, I lost a pot, and before I knew it, she was offering herself to him as the payoff. Well, he took her, and I thought I was shut of her until I heard later what had happened and what people were saying."

The fire crackled in the silence that followed, and I felt as battered and bruised as if I had been beaten. Why, why? A chain of events, all seemingly unrelated, and yet they had brought me here in the end. Who had tried to kill Elmer Bragg—and Todd? Had Flo's "accidental" death been an accident after all? Why? How? Something I had tried to push away flashed suddenly into my mind, and I moved my head, looking up into Lucas's flame-shadowed face.

"I've just remembered something. Lucas, did you know a man called Pardee?"

"Hmm?" He had been squinting into the flames, and seemed to drag his attention back to me with an effort. I saw his eyes narrow, and then focus on mine, the fire bringing out the strange, greenish lights in their depths. "You talking of Gil Pardee? That Texas gunslick that works for Shannon?"

"Used to work for him." I had to moisten my lips before I went on. "I killed him, Lucas. It was just before I left the ranch for Fort Selden. I was riding out alone, and he tried to stop me. He seemed to think…" My mind went back to that day, and I seemed to hear Gil Pardee's sneering insinuating voice in my ears all over again.

"Mebbe you think I don't know enough to please a lady. But that little Flo gal didn't think so! Came after me, askin' for more…"

Pardee had been outside the hotel when I left Flo on the morning Todd was shot. I hadn't noticed him afterwards. But if he had been Flo's lover, and he knew that both Mark and I had left and she was likely to be alone…

"Maybe it doesn't mean anything," I whispered. "Why should Pardee, of all people, want to kill Todd? But some man had been with Flo, in that room, on that bed! And she looked so guilty, she told so many lies, all contradicting each other."

Flo, running down the hotel corridor with her flimsy wrapper held carelessly under her breasts—Flo, her eyes shining peculiarly as she cried out to me: "Is he dead? Is Pa dead?" Flo, who knew that Lucas was in Silver City, and would be blamed. But why, why? It all came back to that.

Lucas's face had taken on a frowning, withdrawn look that seemed to shut me out. "That all of it?"

"I told you it probably doesn't mean anything!" I cried out defensively. "But if Flo thought I was going to marry Todd and she'd be cut out of his will, and *you'd* already told her you were going away…"

"Only trouble is, Flo's dead. And so is Pardee. An' even if they weren't, who'd believe that I wasn't the guilty one?" There was neither anger nor self-pity in his voice, but something in its inflection made me shiver. "Lucas…"

"Let it be, Ro. I didn't kill Bragg, an' I didn't shoot Shannon. But that don't mean I might not have, if things had been different. I've hired my gun out for pay too many times to start feelin' queasy about some of the things I've had to do. And as for Todd Shannon—I made myself *that* promise a long time ago. I mean to kill him, but not through any damn window, or from behind a clump of mesquite. I'm goin' to come face to face with him someday, and then…"

"No, no! Can't you see how pointless it would be? Todd's always surrounded by armed men, and even if you *did* kill him, you'd end up being killed yourself."

"Haven't I told you before that you talk too much, Ro?"

I opened my mouth, to cry out in protest, only to find my angry arguments stilled by his kiss. For a while, my mind went on protesting, but as his body moved over mine, reclaiming it, I found my senses taking over, leading me to passion, to need, and from there to oblivion.

In spite of all the questions that still went unanswered I could have stayed there forever, but for the gradual, inevitable diminishing of all the sounds that had surrounded us for so long. I half-woke when I felt Lucas pull one of the blankets over us; sleepily becoming aware that the fire that had burned so strongly had subsided into a red glow. The wind no longer seemed to push against the door with a frustrated rattle, and the rain had faded from an angry chattering to a muted whisper. Why must happiness always carry with it the burden of fear? The pleasure we had taken in each other suddenly seemed fragile, like a thin crystal—too easily shattered by the pain that must surely follow. My arms held my love, and I pressed closer to him, seeking comfort; but already, insidiously, I had started to feel within myself the beginnings of apprehension, and a kind of sadness. Without quite knowing how, I had already begun to suffer.

PART V:

THE BITTER SEASON

Thirty

THE STORM DIED, HISSING AND GRUMBLING INTO A SILENCE broken only by the slow, monotonous dripping of water from the edge of the roof. The outside world pushed its way obtrusively under the door with the first groping finger of pale sunlight. Where before time had seemed of no consequence, now it appeared we had not enough left.

There was tension between us that we both tried to pretend didn't exist. Lucas prowled restlessly about the cabin, pushing things around on shelves, opening boxes, and swearing when he couldn't immediately find what he was looking for. His beard-stubbled face wore a forbidding look that made me keep silent even when he began, clumsily, to pull on the bloodstained pair of pants he had worn on that evening of the fiesta, with a tear in it where Ramon's bullet had grazed his thigh. I could tell that the wound in his shoulder was still painful, from the stiff way in which he moved his arm, but I turned my back on him and made myself busy preparing a makeshift meal. Everything was running low, even the tequila with which we had fortified ourselves against the cold. Another reason why we must return… but to what?

I was determined that he should not see how I agonized inside myself, and I took refuge behind cool politeness, my mask of reserve slipping only for a moment when I saw that he had buckled on a gunbelt. He caught my eye at that moment, and I thought I detected a slight, sardonic twist of his lips.

He was deliberately reminding me, of course, of the argument that had kept us awake for most of the previous night—an argument ended in the usual way, with Lucas kissing me angrily and desperately into silence, making love to me as if it were the last time ever. When we had both fallen asleep, exhausted and drained, it had been dawn.

And now it was sometime in the afternoon, and the sun was shining again, and nothing had been resolved.

I gave him a cold, level look that I hoped would tell him nothing.

"I'm goin' outside for a while."

Well, this time at least I would not call him back. We both needed space—a short time to be alone, to think.

"All right," I said, and was surprised that my voice sounded cool and emotionless.

Our eyes clashed, and then he was gone, leaving the door open behind him so that the sunlight streamed in. Another reminder, I thought angrily, brushing tendrils of hair off my face. The world was back with us again, and last night it had been Lucas, and not I, who had talked of being practical. God, how I hated that word!

"For Christ's sake! Why isn't it in a woman to be sensible?" He had paced up and down the tiny space like a trapped mountain lion while he spoke to me. "Ro, you don't know what you're saying. I can't live in your world, and you can't live in mine. An' before the damned storm trapped us here together you saw that for yourself. I can't take you with me where I've got to go." His voice had hardened. "You'd slow me down, get in the way. What would I do with you?"

"What did you do with Flo? You told me you'd begun to hate her, and yet you..."

"Flo! My God, do you think she meant anything more to me than a woman to keep me warm in bed and a weapon against Shannon? Do you think I could risk the same thing happenin' to you that happened to her? Look, half the bounty hunters and lawmen in the territory are after me. Everywhere I go, there's always the chance someone will be shooting at me, and with you along..."

"We could go somewhere else, Lucas, listen to me! We could go away—anywhere you wanted to go. California, Mexico, even Europe, until things died down."

"No. It won't work. I ain't gonna run away, an' I ain't gonna be no kept man."

"But you're running now!"

"That's different."

"You said this was what my father wanted. To end the feud. You wanted me to marry Ramon."

"Ramon's not wanted by the law."

Stalemate.

The silence between us was like a sword, until I broke it.

"You didn't kill Elmer Bragg, and you didn't fire that shot at Todd. Don't you even care that everyone says you did? Don't you wonder who arranged so carefully for you to take the blame?"

"That's somethin' I mean to find out. But I still aim to kill Shannon. An' you don't like hearing that, do you?"

"No I don't. Because it's not for yourself you feel you have to do it, is it? It's for Elena—because of what happened years and years ago, before you were born, before I was born! And you don't like hearing that either, but I'll say it anyhow! Elena—Elena! Every time I say her name your face changes. How old were you when you first discovered you loved her? How long have you waited, and for what? How much does she love you? Or are there conditions you have to fulfill first, like killing Todd Shannon?"

"Don't say any more!" His voice was threatening, but I had gone too far to turn back now.

"If she loved you, nothing else would have mattered. She would have gone away with you, gone anywhere. And you would have done something about it! Why haven't you, Lucas? What have you been waiting for?"

His hands were on my shoulders, bruising, hurtful.

"That's enough!"

"No, it's not enough. It's time you faced the truth, and it's time you were honest with me. What do I mean to you, Lucas? Just another woman to keep you warm? Another weapon to use against Todd Shannon? Or am I substitute for *her*!"

I remembered that he had held me against him; his lips against my hair, I held that memory like a talisman against my doubts.

"Will you stop it, Ro? Stop tormenting yourself an' me." His voice had sounded muffled, as agonized as the beating of my own heart. "I'm not the kind of *man* you need. Remember you told me once you wanted all of a man? I can't give you anything like that. I can't make you any promises. You ask about Elena, and what you mean to me, an' all I can tell you is that lovin' can't be measured out. Think I've loved Elena about as long as I can remember—and I know that there's been no other woman I've wanted the way I want you. What do you need from me, Ro? You're the only woman I've been with who hasn't asked if I loved her. You've been like a nagging question in my mind I had to find an answer to. An' I don't have any answers for you—not the kind you need. I can't find the right words as easily as you can. I don't have the knack for taking feelings apart and weighing them."

It was all he had to offer me, and I took it, afraid to probe for more. When Lucas kissed me, when his arms held me and his body claimed mine fiercely and possessively, I told myself that it was enough.

But now, with the sunlight making the fire seem weak and ineffectual, I wondered.

Lucas had come as close to admitting that he loved me as he dared, without putting himself in a position where I might demand that he make a choice. But I wanted all of him, and he offered me nothing except the meager knowledge that he cared enough for me to send me away.

"I won't go!" I breathed the words out loud. "I'll use every weapon, every despicable wile and tactic I can think of—and I'll win. *She* shan't have him!"

But for all my brave words, I was afraid. And when I met Elena Kordes's dark, inscrutable eyes again for the first time since I had rushed so blindly from her house into the storm, I almost felt sick to my stomach. Elena, Jesus Montoya, and his silent man Chato had started out to find us, and seeing her, she was as immaculately beautiful as always, the velvet of her riding habit forming a richly glowing contrast to the high-piled dark hair. It was difficult to imagine that this was the same woman who had watched me from the gallery as I left the house, whose haggard face and angry voice had taunted me with her possession of the man I loved. Was it only because she was so completely sure of her hold over him that she had let me go? Had she come to look for him, or only because she hoped to find what remained of me?

I couldn't see the expression on Lucas's face as we rode up to them, and I was almost glad of it. He held me before him in the saddle, with one arm around my waist to hold me closely against him, and until I saw Elena's eyes upon me, I hadn't been aware of my disheveled appearance. I was wearing a shabby pair of pants that Lucas had given me, held around my waist with a red bandanna; a shirt that was far too large and I was soaking wet.

"Lucas! Thank God! If you only knew how worried we have all been! I would have sent someone, or come myself before, but the flood—"

"The water was down far enough to where Diablo could keep his footing." Lucas's voice was noncommittal, but he couldn't help the involuntary tightening of his arm around me, and I caught a small, triumphant flicker in Elena's eyes.

"But at least you're back, and you're safe—both of you." Her inclusion of me was a deliberate afterthought, and I lifted my head defiantly, but Jesus Montoya smoothed over the awkward moment; a sardonic smile lifted one corner of his mouth under the narrow black moustache.

"It is not for me to play the host in your own *hacienda,* of course, but since we have all found each other, and you two are very wet, would it not be more sensible to continue this happy reunion in the house?"

I felt like a prisoner being escorted back to a cell, with Montoya and Elena riding on either side of us and Chato behind. A slight breeze swept down the valley, and I shivered.

"You poor child! Why, you must be cold. How thoughtless

of me!" Elena's voice was all sweet consideration, but her eyes mocked me. "Here, you shall take my shawl. Lucas, what's the matter with you? You should have taken better care of her, she looks so pale and exhausted!"

I would gladly have flung the fleecy white shawl back at her, but Lucas had already taken it, and was putting it around my shoulders. All this time, he had said nothing, but when he bent his head to mine I thought I felt the brush of his lips against my hair. Was it to give me reassurance, or because he needed it himself? I was surrounded by Elena's faint, sweet perfume as she had meant me to be. It was as if she had subtly put her presence between us, for how could Lucas fail to be reminded of her, even though it was my body he held within the circle of his arms?

Jesus Montoya carried me upstairs, followed by a sullen, tight-faced Luz. No doubt Elena herself would see to Lucas. The exertion of the climb down the slippery, narrow trail that wound down the side of the canyon, and the battle against the muddy, still-fiercely flowing stream had tired and unnerved us both, and I had noticed that Lucas's wounds had begun to ooze blood again. When we had arrived at the house he had helped me down from the horse, and it was only then, when I felt him stagger slightly, that I noticed how pale he had become.

"Lucas!"

He shook his head almost angrily, as if in negation of my half-uttered cry of concern.

"I'll be all right, Ro. You go get some rest, an' I'll see you later."

I had ignored the others then. "We *have* to talk, don't you see that? I won't have you planning what's to be done with me without even..."

"You foolish, crazy children! Haven't you been reckless enough? You can quarrel later. Now I must insist that you both rest and change out of those wet clothes." Elena scolded like a mother, but the contempt in her eyes was meant for me. She wanted me to see myself through her eyes, a pitiful creature picked up in a storm.

I looked away from her, back at Lucas, and there were beads of sweat standing out on his forehead as he leaned against the gallery pillar, his eyes half-closed. But how much of his pain was from his wounds, and how much because of Elena? Another wound reopened.

"I am not too old to play the gallant yet, I hope! Come, señorita Rowena. To bed with you, and Luz will come with us to take care of the properties, eh?"

I could almost imagine that Lucas had whispered, his voice husky and tired, "Stay here, Ro…" but perhaps that was only because I wanted to hear him say it, as he had that night when we had shared a blanket for the first time.

Whatever he had said, or meant to say, it was too late. Montoya had already picked me up into his arms, firmly and purposefully, and I was taken upstairs like an errant child, to be laid gently in bed while Luz began to strip me of my borrowed garments, exclaiming at bruises and scrapes I had forgotten.

"You should have a nice warm bath. You're shivering!" And then, as I shook my head wearily, "You could very easily have been killed, you know! As it is, Ramon…" and then she compressed her lip as if she had said too much. "I'll fetch some hot water, and sponge you down. And a hot drink. Please do not try to get up."

"Ramon?" I remembered suddenly that he hadn't been downstairs to meet us. "Luz—what did you mean about Ramon?"

I had sat up in bed, and she turned at the door, her face suddenly carefully without expression.

"He went looking for you. There was guilt in him, I suppose. None of us knew, until the next day… oh, that was a terrible night, I can tell you! And the next day and night even worse. Elena was like a madwoman. She thought…"

"Luz!"

But I knew. "He had tried to cross the creek—you know how shallow and pretty it is. But Chato says it must have been a wall of water that came rushing down from the barracks—or perhaps a limb from the tree we found struck by lightning. I am sorry, Rowena, that I said anything. As usual, my tongue runs away with me. But I…"

She turned abruptly and went out of the room and I lay there, drained. Would Lucas blame me? And Elena—how could she have pretended so well? There had been no trace of grief in her face or her manner to betray the fact that she had lost a son, or did her love for Lucas, and her relief at finding him alive, blind her to everything else?

Suddenly I wanted to find Lucas again, to feel his arms close around me, and I half-sat up, then fell back again. Suppose his eyes looked at me in the same way Luz's had done? Suppose he had already begun to hate me? Elena would be with him, bending over him, and I felt I couldn't bear to see it. Perhaps his arms were around *her* at this very moment, comforting her, taking her back into that place in his mind that would always be hers. I was torturing myself, and I knew it. Oh, God, why had he brought me back here?

And then Luz was back, bearing a tray with a steaming hot mug of chocolate, her eyes still deliberately averted from mine.

"Drink this first, it will keep away a chill. I put some whiskey in it."

The whiskey made the chocolate taste bitter, but it was warming, spreading a burning glow all the way down to my stomach. I drank it down as quickly as I could, not caring if I burned my lips and tongue. I lay down again, suddenly feeling bone-weary.

"There, that's good. And now I will sponge you, and you will try not to think. Don't worry."

In spite of the almost impersonal kindness of her voice, Luz's hands were gentle. She was right, of course, I thought. Thinking, tormenting myself about something that had happened and could not be changed, would do me no good.

Tomorrow I would see Lucas again, and force an answer from him. I had been letting my imagination run riot. He cared for me; hadn't he shown me that much? Tomorrow, I thought, and then found myself too tired even to think.

Thirty-One

I SLEPT HAUNTED BY ONE NIGHTMARE AFTER THE OTHER. THERE was sound and motion and the orange glow of fire in my dreams. I felt myself picked up and held fast in the claws by a gigantic bird, then I was falling, from a tremendous distance, watching, paralyzed and powerless as the ground came up to meet me. For a while, there was nothing—a terrible, choking darkness—first heat, and then cold. And I was in a tumbril, being taken to the guillotine. I heard the creaking, felt the jolting—looked up to see the executioner waiting on the edge of the platform. Slowly, menacingly, he removed his mask, and the face was Ramon's. I heard myself scream, and someone held a cup of blood to my lips. "Drink…" they said, "drink! It will help you…"

And then, suddenly, I was awake again. I knew it, and yet my eyelids felt leaden, too heavy to open. I was still in the tumbril, the death cart, and my head ached with every jolt. I remember thinking that I must be dead, and I moved my hand to touch my neck. No, I was alive. I felt a breeze on my face, and motion under me—and then, with an effort, I forced my eyes open, and my nightmares had spilled over into reality.

"I am sorry, truly sorry it had to be this way." Luz's voice was small and hesitant with guilt, and her face looked drawn and pale. "But do you not see that it is only for the best? You would have become hysterical perhaps, you would not have understood."

"And so you drugged me." My voice sounded thick, and my head still ached, but I was beginning to think again, even though I did not want to.

"It was the only way!" Luz said again. "You have always been so sensible, surely you can understand? Did you want to be a prisoner forever in the valley? With Ramon gone..."

I interrupted her, my voice heavy and harsh.

"Does Lucas know?"

"Lucas? It was Lucas who suggested it."

I turned my face away from her and closed my eyes again, taking refuge in the headache that threatened to split my head in two. Not Lucas, not Lucas, my mind cried out, and then I remembered how adamant he had been. But without talking to me first? Without even telling me good-bye? Or had it been that as soon as he set eyes on Elena again he had known where his heart lay, and was anxious to put me out of his life?

Later, when the effects of the drug they had given me had completely worn off, some of the self-possession I had once prided myself upon came back to me, and I found myself thinking more rationally. That night Lucas had been close to unconsciousness himself. Suppose the drugged chocolate and my virtual abduction had all been Elena's idea? She had begun to hate me; she was jealous of me. Perhaps, after all, she was no longer as certain of Lucas's wholehearted adoration as she had appeared to be. Grasping at straws or not, I hugged that thought to me as I waited for Jesus Montoya to give me an answer to the questions that still remained to be answered.

The cart which I had imagined to be a tumbril was a small, crudely constructed, canvas-covered wagon. I learned that Luz slept beside me, and that I had been kept unconscious for two whole days. Luz seemed relieved that I hadn't tried to make a fuss, and appeared so calm.

"Jesus had to carry you most of the way. When we had to leave the valley he put the rope around his waist, and kept you in his arms. I was almost jealous, for a while!"

How soon she had got over her passionate infatuation for Lucas! Could I ever stop loving him? Cruelly I said, trying to hide my own emotions, "So now you're actually in love with the man you said you hated. Will you be married soon?"

She gave me a rather embarrassed look, and said defensively, "As soon as we reach Mexico. And Jesus is good to me. He makes me feel as if I am a woman. Do you know that of all the women he has taken, I am the only one he wishes to marry? It means something. And I will no longer be a slave to that bitch Elena Kordes. Jesus has promised that I will have a large house, and servants of my own."

"He's a man of ambition and far-reaching plans, it seems!" I murmured ironically. "Do you know what he plans to do with me?"

But she only said hastily that Jesus would tell me himself, as soon as he returned to the makeshift camp with the rest of his men. Warningly she added that Chato had remained here, to watch over us both, and I wondered why they thought I might want to escape. Where could I go, anyhow? We were still in the mountains, camped among thick timber. I had no idea where we were, or in which direction the valley lay. And I would not think of Lucas—alone there with Elena. I must not, for I needed all my wits about me now.

I shrugged, reassuring Luz, and she began to talk to me with a return of her old, friendly manner, although she still seemed wary.

It seems to me, even in retrospect, that I was far too calm. It was as if I had lived on the edge of an emotional pinnacle for so long that now I felt drained of feeling. I had lost Lucas. In my heart I knew that he would not do as I secretly hoped he would, and come looking for me. Even if he hadn't planned to get rid of me, he was bound to shrug his shoulders when he found out what had happened, and tell himself that it was for the best. And now I was alone again and forced to fend for myself, with only my wits to guide me. I thought all this without self-pity; in fact I was filled with an almost terrifying apathy soon after I had talked with Luz. I'll soon have my cherished independence back, I thought. For surely Montoya meant to claim that huge reward he'd told me Todd had offered for any news of my whereabouts. What did it matter?

Money had once provided my passport to freedom, and now I didn't care about it. I would pay Todd back, and I would never marry him now. And Lucas, to whom I had offered everything, including myself, had rejected me.

Jesus Montoya and the *comancheros* returned to camp that evening, and each man looked like a walking arsenal, with crossed bandoliers across his chests.

Luz and I retired inside the wagon until, sometime later, Montoya came up and politely asked me to accompany him. He was as suave and sardonic as I remembered him, and his black eyes seemed to glitter in the firelight. He had taken my arm, and now as he led me forward, there was a sudden cessation of the talk and laughter among his men.

My feeling of lethargy persisted, and I stood there passively, feeling the looks that were fastened upon me.

"This is the woman for whom Shannon is willing to pay so much money. She is not to be harmed. In fact"—his white teeth gleamed for an instant—"I will kill the first man who touches her. I only wish to make this matter clear: that she will not be treated like the other captives we take, but instead as a guest. *Comprende*?"

Apparently Montoya was sure of his control over his men. There were a few nods, a few muttered "si's" but the curiosity in their eyes was almost a palpable thing. I found myself wondering if they thought I was or had been one of Montoya's women, but what did that matter either?

Tonight Jesus Montoya was just as immaculately dressed as he had been on the occasion of the fiesta. When he led me into the darkness just beyond the fire's reach I could see the silver ornaments on his *charro* suit flash like stars.

"Was it necessary to put me on exhibit?"

"It was necessary to warn them. My men are impulsive at times. And as I've said before, I *do* have a great admiration for you, señorita Rowena."

"You certainly have a strange way of showing it!" I retorted. What was the man up to? It seemed to me he was playing a cat and mouse game with me, and I wished he would come to the point.

He chuckled softly. "Ah, but I think that you will understand, once you have had time to give the whole matter some thought. You do not mind if I smoke?"

I moved my head impatiently, and the tip of his glowing cigar lit his face for a moment as he puffed on it.

"I had the feeling, from the first time I talked to you, that you were a wise and intelligent young woman, and I am glad that you have taken all this so calmly. Of course I owe you an apology for the methods I was forced to use in order to... rescue you, shall we say? I see how angrily you lift your head, but believe me, it was all for the best!"

"Or because of the money you hope to get for returning me to Todd Shannon?"

"That too, of course! I am no philanthropist—only a poor man who must earn a living. And why not in this way? The señor Shannon can afford to give away some of his money. I am sure he will think it well worth it to get you back. And even my stubborn friend Elena Kordes had to agree that with poor Ramon gone, and Julio caring more about his little tribe than the regaining of his family's lands... well, what else could we do?"

"There was Lucas," I said defiantly. "She was so anxious to marry me off to one of her sons—why not Lucas?"

Montoya was shaking his head at me with exaggerated patience. "But Lucas is not Elena's son. Surely you will not pretend ignorance of the—er—rather unique relationship between them? Even so—yes, Elena did suggest that such a thing might be possible, but Lucas refused. He can be very stubborn, that one."

"But..."

"You must face facts, señorita. Come, you are strong enough for that! Lucas attracted you. In spite of his rude manners, he has a way with women. And he wanted you, especially when he learned you were to marry Ramon. But be realistic. You imagine yourself in love with him at the moment, perhaps, because you gave yourself to him. You see, I am being quite blunt. But Lucas? Lucas has always been in love with Elena, and he always will be. He wants other women, he takes them—and then, when he is finished with them, he goes back to Elena. If you had not been Shannon's fiancée, he would not have bothered himself with you in the first place."

"No!" I said, but the word sounded small and despairing. "You're lying to me; you and Elena arranged all of this, because she was jealous of me. She was afraid that Lucas—that Lucas and I…"

"And now you are speaking wildly of what you wish to believe!" Montoya said roughly. His cigar smoke stung my nostrils. "You deliberately try to blind yourself to the truth, but I think that you have always known that nothing could ever come of a relationship between you and Lucas except much unhappiness and hurt. What did you hope for? That he would marry you?" As if he had read an answer in my face Montoya gave a harsh laugh. "*Por Dios!* I did not think you so naive. A woman of your spirit and background—would you have been content to share him with another woman and receive the least part of his attentions? Would you have been prepared to live as a prisoner, just as my poor Luz was, and wait on Elena's whims? Elena is a very strong woman, much stronger than you are. And Lucas would do anything for her; do you take my meaning, my poor little one?"

I shook my head, refusing to accept what he was saying, kept shaking it until he seized my wrist with fingers that felt like steel.

"Must I make it even clearer before you will listen? You hate Elena and blame her, but although it is true she has no love for you, she still feels a strong sense of obligation to your father, and so she agreed to your going. Count yourself lucky! For if she had insisted that Lucas must marry you, he would have done so—for *her*, you understand? As for Lucas, he is a dead man. He is as good as dead right now. I am careful, but Lucas is reckless, even with bounty hunters snapping at his heels. He thinks he will kill Shannon, but it is Shannon who, in the end, will have him killed. It is—how do you say it? Inevitable. But as long as he is alive, he belongs to Elena." My earlier mood of apathy had disappeared, and I was sick with despair. Every one of Jesus Montoya's caustic words seemed to pierce me like an arrow.

I must have swayed, for immediately Montoya's arm went around my waist, and his voice softened. "I understand. You do not want to hear these things, but they had to be said, for your sake. I will take you back to the wagon now, and you will think about it and perhaps cry a little, no? It is good for a woman to cry. And then, if you are wise, you will try to forget Lucas. Forget everything that has happened to you, marry Shannon, and live like a queen. And perhaps you will one day remember me as a friend."

A friend, Montoya had called himself. But as more days dragged by and we traveled by "the smugglers' trail" into Mexico, I began to wonder why he offered me friendship—this strange and enigmatic man who was a self-confessed desperado with little or no scruples. What did he want from me?

He had advised me to put Lucas out of my mind, and yet it seemed as if he took a perverse pleasure in reminding me at every turn of how foolish I had been. I was not the first woman, after all, who had mistaken physical attraction for love. Perhaps the grief and hurt I had still not learned to cope with was a kind of punishment. If it was, I did not suffer it gladly. I tried to tell myself that I had been right to hate Lucas in the beginning, that I despised him now, and ended up despising my own weakness. For as the days passed I was shown more and more evidence of how little I had meant to him.

Montoya, I learned, had undertaken to dispose of the silver that had been taken to the valley on that first day.

"So you have become friends again?" I said acidly. "And I suppose you will also share the money that will be paid for my return."

He laughed softly, his black eyes speculative as they rested on me. "Ah, yes. That too. And why not, when it was Lucas's idea? Come, there is no need to look so stricken, surely you had guessed it already? And there is a saying that the love of money makes strange bedfellows, you know." His voice softened, becoming almost thoughtful. "Money, and love, and hate—these are the strongest emotions of all, si? And with hatred goes the desire for revenge. Lucas has all these motives; you must not blame him too much. He is what he is, just as I am what I am! You begin to understand, do you not?"

I felt the blood drain from my face. "You are trying to tell me that it was all for revenge?"

"Exactly. You have not thought of this before? Lucas loves Elena, whether he would like to admit it or not. And Elena has expensive tastes. And hate? You know he hates Shannon, who was your fiancé. What better revenge than to have Shannon pay a great deal of money to get you back, and then—to make sure that Shannon knows you have been... shall I use the word ravished, for want of a better?"

"He would not! He wouldn't go to such lengths—no, señor. You stretch my power of *understanding,* as you call it, too far!"

I had meant my words to sound firm and contemptuous, but they only sounded pitifully defiant.

"Ah, but you are a woman of such pride!" Montoya sighed as I stumbled to my feet and turned towards the wagon where Luz and I slept at night. His soft, pitying voice followed me. "That is one of the reasons why I have such admiration for you, and why I would have you regain your power of rational thinking again. One day, niña, I think you will thank me for being honest with you."

Even now, I can hardly bear to think of the endless days and long, sleepless nights that followed. For the first time in my life I experienced such anguish, such disillusion, that I almost wished for death. I think that I existed for a time in a daze of pain and hurt, not caring any longer what became of me.

Luz was sympathetic, but even she could not help reminding me of my own words of advice to her.

"Lucas has always been selfish—see that now. And you see how easy it is to forget when there is someone who really wants you? I am happy now, and you will be too, when you realize what a lucky escape you've had."

She spoke to me as sagely as if she had been a married woman already, and the next moment, her eyes sparkling, she had begun to describe the fine mansion to which Montoya was taking her, the clothes and jewels he had promised her.

Why did I keep tormenting myself with memories that were better forgotten? Why couldn't I accept the fact that I had been deceived? But Lucas had promised me nothing, given me no assurances beyond the fact that he wanted me. And his angry words, uttered on that afternoon when I had kissed him and forced him to kiss me back, now came back to haunt me.

"Ain't been a woman yet I haven't tired of, once I've had her... an' when I'm through with you I'll make Shannon pay a ransom to get you back. Mebbe a trifle shopworn, but good enough for him!"

Oh, yes, I had been warned. And bitterest thought of all, I had only myself to blame for everything.

Thirty-Two

❧

IT SEEMED RIDICULOUS TO ME THAT I SHOULD BE TAKEN ALL the way to Mexico, and then turn back again as soon as what Montoya referred to as "the transaction" had taken place. But he explained to me indulgently that such elaborate precautions were necessary because he didn't trust my partner.

"If we arrange a meeting in United States territory, what is to prevent Shannon from arriving with a deputy marshal, and a warrant for my arrest? No, as I have said before, I am a cautious man. In Mexico, we would meet on neutral territory? That is a good term?"

"As usual, you contrive to express yourself more than clearly," I said slowly. I was learning all over again to school my features into a mask of cool indifference, and I saw Montoya lift an appreciative eyebrow.

"We will cross the border tonight," he said soothingly, as if by questioning him I had revealed an impatience to return home, to safe and familiar surroundings. "Tomorrow, a message will be sent to Mr. Shannon, telling him that you are safe and well—and naturally anxious to be reunited with him. Perhaps you will prefer to send a note in your own handwriting, so that there can be no misunderstanding?"

I shrugged. Another week then, of waiting. But what difference would it make? A few more days in which to prepare myself, to armor myself...

The truth was that I had learned to mistrust my own

emotions. The truth was something I had refused to admit to myself earlier when I lay in my lover's arms. I had confused desire with love, and made love an excuse for desire. Love! A much misused word, and one I had always been contemptuous of before. A feeling of helplessness, of being swept away, an emotion that left one terribly vulnerable to hurt.

And yet, in spite of all my rationalization and stern self-admonishment, I couldn't stop myself from feeling pain that was like a knife twist in my heart every time I thought of him, or heard his name spoken. What good did it do me to be sensible, to blame myself and the Dangerfield devil in my blood, when I could not stop myself from *feeling*? Lucas— Lucas! Memories of his body claiming mine, his lips on my breasts and thighs while he murmured to me, his voice a husky whisper, that I was beautiful, that he wanted me. The rain and the fire. Cold and heat. Lucas kissing me; hungrily, desperately, as he told me: "There, doesn't that mean something to you?" But what had he meant to him beyond the slaking of his casual, momentary desire?

Whatever name I wanted to give an emotion that still had the power to wound and weaken me, it existed. I might make a frozen mask of my face, betraying no feelings on the surface; but inwardly I could no more force myself to feel indifference than I had before.

Jesus Montoya, I am sure, suspected what was beneath my coldly unconcerned exterior, for I had already betrayed myself to him, and he was not the kind of man who forgot.

I accused him once of deliberately trading on the weaknesses of others for his own gain. As I might have expected, he only smiled, his teeth gleaming whitely under his moustache.

"My dear señorita! And why not? One's enemy's weakness makes one strong—from strength, to power. As your partner, Shannon, discovered long ago. Of course," he shrugged deprecatingly, "much money can help. Ah, yes. You have been born to wealth and comfort. You take these things for granted, do you not? It is only the rich who can say honestly that money means nothing to them, and who are willing to give it up for some altruistic motive."

"You are a philosopher too," I said sharply, and his smile twisted.

"You are kind to call it that. I call myself a realist. I was born poor, the son of a peon who worked in the fields of a certain Don Emiliano—a proud man who boasted of his pure Spanish blood, his illustrious family. He had daughters—beautiful, delicately bred, and just as arrogant, as he was himself. Yes—it was nothing for one of the young dons to surprise some peasant girl in the fields, take his pleasure of her, and then go laughing back to his fine *estancia*. This, you understand was the common thing. But for a *vaquero* to look upon the daughter of a *hacendado* with bold eyes, even if the daughter herself encouraged such a thing, and indeed, made a point of—well, it does not matter. A simple *vaquero*, a peon's son—such are less important than the fine-blooded horses of a *hacendado*. Like dogs, they can be flogged for insolence. Some, like gelded steers, will bow even lower when the patron appears in the distance, will crawl to show their insignificance. But others, men with pride and ambition and a certain greed, what is meant to be a punishment can act instead as a spur, a goad. When you have been poor all your life, then truly you understand the significance of money, and what it can buy. And so, you see, today I own the *estancia* that once belonged to a Spanish don. Just as I had the use of all that once belonged to him, including his daughters and his fat wife. Alas, poor Don Emiliano had met with an unfortunate accident, and did not live long enough to see such unbelievable, impossible things take place." He broke off, watching my expression, and gave a sudden, almost soundless laugh. "I see you listen closely to my little parable. Has it taught you anything? Opened your eyes, perhaps? Alas for illusion, señorita, there are some people who would do anything for money, and all it can buy. Comfort—power—"

"It corrupts!"

"Yes, indeed. Even the incorruptible. Does this not tell you something?"

I looked him straight in the eye. "I think, señor, that you try either to instruct me or to warn me. You called yourself my friend—well then, I wish you would be frank. Which is it?"

"Are you sure you are ready for more honesty? I would not have you think that I deliberately drove you back to Shannon's arms."

My breathing quickened. I wanted to hear and yet I did not want to hear.

"Your meaning, señor? Will you persist in evasions and hints? For if you are truly my friend you will tell me the unvarnished truth."

I will never forget his look. Quizzical—half sly, half questioning.

"The truth, you say. You are ready to face it? Very well, then. Have you seen the codicil to your father's will? Has Lucas not told you of it? You look surprised. But I tell you that there was such a document. Part of it a letter, stating his wishes. When I was told that you were to marry Ramon, I thought you were aware of it. I would advise you to search more closely when you return. And to trust less easily. And apart from that—if you need help, you have only to send word to me."

"There would be a price attached, of course," I said bitterly, and he nodded.

"Of course. But what are a few dollars between friends? For I have this feeling, señorita—call it intuition, if you will—that once you have recognized your enemies, you will need friends."

"And…" I took a deep breath to steady my voice. "Is Lucas my enemy now?"

Montoya shrugged. "Lucas has always kept his thoughts to himself. I think he is his own worst enemy. But—if you were to actually marry Todd Shannon—I can well imagine that he would feel no scruples about making you a widow. And then— do you not see it? The ranch, everything would belong to *you*. What a fortunate man your *second* husband would be, eh?"

I felt as if I had been dealt a blow, although *this* time I would not let Montoya see what effect his words had had on me. *No,* I thought fiercely. What Montoya had suggested was too devious, too monstrous—or was it carefully calculated, like everything else? Had they decided to gamble, not for my fortune and my share of the SD alone, but for the whole of it? Had it been my openly declared passion for Lucas that had made them plan such a thing? *Them*—Elena and Lucas. The black queen and her knight. And in this game, played by experts, it seemed that I was only a pawn. But where did Montoya fit in? What was his role?

The man continued to puzzle me. He told me parables to illustrate the lengths to which revenge and ambition could drive a man. (I wondered, what had happened to the lovely daughters of Don Emiliano? But I dared not ask.) He was taking me back to Todd, but hinted that I would be unwise to marry him. He warned me against both Lucas and Elena, yet called himself their friend. And called himself *my* friend at the same time. What did he want?

"Money, of course!" he answered me blandly. "I am no longer a young man. I am taking a wife who will give me children. Why should I not think of settling down—of... retiring, shall we say? And I have conceived an admiration for you, señorita. Did I not sense at our very first meeting that you were no ordinary milksop female? You have all the advantages: intelligence, birth, beauty, and wealth. A shame to see it all wasted."

"You left out ambition," I said bitterly. "And the desire for power. What makes you think I want to be involved any further in such a sordid business? I came here because my father wished it. Because I wanted to find out more about him. I intended to rest, to think, and yes... to find out more about myself. And instead I found myself caught up in a feud that had nothing to do with me. In violence. I have discovered that what I want is impossible to achieve, even with all the advantages you speak of. And, oh, God, I am sick of being used and manipulated. Of being pushed this way and that to satisfy the ambitions of others! The SD means nothing to me; why should it? This is not my country; these are not my quarrels. If I continue to use the intelligence you say you admire, then I should leave as soon as I can and go back to a world of civilized people. Perhaps I might even go back to India, as I had planned to do, once."

"And do you say all these things to convince me, or yourself?" Montoya's voice sharpened to steel under his silky tones. "Will you continue to deceive yourself? You talk of running away from involvement because you *are* involved. And you have been, ever since you came here, escaping from a life of inexpressible boredom, I think! Is that what you would go back to?"

I stared at him, and he went on in a softer, insinuating voice: "And all these questions to which you have not yet found answers... are you not curious to know why your father suddenly decided to add a codicil to his will, a codicil of which, apparently, you know nothing. There was a letter, also—written just before he died... you have not seen that either? Do you not wonder why all these things were hidden from you, and to whose advantage? Or why your father died so suddenly, just before you were supposed to arrive, of an overdose of laudanum? He was in pain, yes, but he was used to pain, and he looked forward to seeing you... what made him a coward at the last moment? These are things which a certain Mr. Bragg was curious about too, and his curiosity led him to a murderer's ambush. Well? You grow pale and your eyes open wide with horror. Or is it fear? Are you afraid of what you might discover?"

There are certain segments in time, certain things that even now I find too painful to recall. I have to get up and walk around my safe, familiar room to remind myself that I live in the present. When I go back to my desk and take up my pen again, I feel an unwillingness to write of what happened. And yet, this is a task I have set myself, and I know I must continue to the end as I know it now. For on that day, when Jesus Montoya and I talked, I changed in some way. I made a choice, and in making it, faced the cruel harshness of reality. I acknowledged my weakness, and found the strength I thought I had lost. I see this now, but at the time I felt nothing but numbness that helped me to endure the days that followed.

Montoya was pleased with me. Luz was puzzled and jealous in turn. But as usual, she was easily distracted by the gifts he gave her—the thought that soon she would be mistress in a fine house, with servants to wait on her.

Among the wagons of the *comancheros* was one filled with tawdry finery, taken from God knows where, or at what price. Luz strutted as proudly as a peacock in her new clothes and her new sense of importance, and her manner towards me became faintly patronizing, even pitying.

For a short time, until Montoya found the priest who would marry them, I even acted as a *dueña*. Naturally, I did not tell Luz of a certain conversation I had with her *novio* on the day before I was to leave. He surprised me in the *sala* during the hour of the siesta, while Luz slept upstairs and asked me to join him in a glass of wine, and his black eyes held a strange, almost regretful look as they studied me over the rim of his glass.

"It is a pity that you have to go. You were turning my Luz into a lady, and I—I will miss our conversations." He went on slowly, still watching me. "If I had had the good fortune to meet you before, and in a different manner, I think I would have married you myself. What a challenge!"

"And think what a man of your ambition and talents could have achieved with all the wealth I possess," I retorted acidly.

We had taken each other's measure by now, and he gave his soundless laugh.

"Of course! That too. But to conquer a woman like you, to break through your defenses and your mask of coldness and distance—ah, that would be a challenge indeed!"

"Since you have removed whatever illusions I might have possessed, señor, I fear that even for you conquering me, as you call it, would prove an impossible task."

He gave a regretful, exaggerated sigh. "True. Perhaps it is better that we remain friends, si? As you have requested, I will find out what happened to your Mr. Bragg, who was so curious. And you will seek solutions to the rest of the puzzle. I shall look forward to the time when we will be able to compare notes."

I would not admit that I was afraid of such a time. I tried to think only of the immediate future—my meeting with Todd Shannon, *his* first reactions, and mine.

There was not much time left for anticipation in any

case. I lay in my bed that night and listened to the faint sounds of revelry that floated up from the village that nestled at the foot of the hill. Some of Montoya's men had come back from across the border with plunder—and captives, no doubt. I told myself that it was only the noise and the heat which kept me awake, for I had schooled myself during the time I had lived here not to wonder about the poor young woman in whose bed I now lay, and what her fate had been. It seemed there was violence everywhere here. Hidden behind a smile, lurking in the background of the most peaceful-seeming spring morning. And it appeared as if the course of action to which I was now committed could only lead to more violence.

I stirred, restless. How could Luz sleep, knowing that her betrothed was down there with the rest of his men? Just now, I could almost have sworn I heard a woman scream. And yet, earlier, Luz had shrugged carelessly, reminding me that her father too had been a *comanchero*.

"It is always so when they return. And why not? Men are men."

"And *your* man is there with them!" I could not help the sharpness of my voice, but she only shrugged again.

"He too is a man, and I am thankful for it. It makes no difference to me, as long as he climbs this hill and comes back to me every day."

Why couldn't I develop a similarly philosophic attitude? Why couldn't I forget those things that must be forgotten if I was ever to have any peace of mind again?

I slept in the end, and woke late, when the nervous-looking maid brought me coffee. And after that there was hardly time for thinking, as I prepared for what lay ahead. A short journey—of only a few hours, Montoya had told me, to an appointed meeting place.

I expected to see Todd, and had steeled myself to meet the question in his eyes, but instead it was Mark who came, accompanied by five SD men, carrying gold in his saddlebags as Montoya had stipulated.

Poor Mark! His face was drawn and pale with strain and

fatigue, and I couldn't mistake the look of anxiety and relief that came into his eyes when he first set eyes on me. How dear and familiar he looked—Mark, who had been my only real friend, the one person I could confide in.

He had pulled off his hat when he saw me, and his blond hair gleamed in the harsh sunlight. "Rowena! Thank God you're all right. If you only knew…"

"Yes, I have been quite a trial, haven't I?" I forced a note of lightness into my voice. "But the señor Montoya has been most kind, and as you can see, I am alive and quite unharmed."

With the innate tact and delicacy he had always displayed toward me, Mark did not attempt any further conversation until after the money had been counted, and Jesus Montoya, bowing over my hand with exaggerated gallantry, had waved us on our way.

It was I who spoke first, my words sounding more abrupt than I had meant them to. "How is it that Todd did not come himself?"

Mark stammered awkwardly, "I—he—there has been some trouble with rustlers recently, not to mention the Apaches. Fences cut, ranch houses burned. Victoria himself came close to overrunning Santa Rita not too long ago. So you see, someone had to stay behind at the ranch, Rowena. I persuaded my uncle to let me come in his place, because I—oh, God! You cannot imagine how I've blamed myself. If I had been strong enough to persuade you not to leave, if I had only insisted upon going with you myself…"

"And thank God you didn't!" I said sharply. "What happened to the men who survived the Indian attack was not—pretty. I counted myself fortunate, afterward, that I happened to be a female."

I saw the look in Mark's blue eyes and gave him an unwilling smile. "Oh, come, Mark! There's no need to be tactful any longer. Do I look as if I've been mistreated? Did you really expect to find me a miserable, groveling wretch, rendered almost mindless by my cruel captivity? I was lucky, you know, that the particular band of Indians who took me knew my father. In fact, their shaman called him blood brother. I was treated as a guest. No one harmed me…"

"Rowena, is that true?" Riding close beside me, Mark put out his hand and touched my arm almost pleadingly, his expression still worried. "You *look* unchanged, except that you have grown thinner. But there is something else. A difference I can only sense." He gave a half-bitter, half-angry laugh. "I have always been sensitive to your moods, remember? Even now I can feel your withdrawal. Am I pressing you, Rowena? Is it still too soon for you to bring yourself to talk about whatever it is has brought a guarded look to your eyes? You look at even me as if you don't trust me. I—"

"It *is* too soon, Mark." I interrupted him, frowning. "I'm sorry. Perhaps later we will be able to talk again, as if nothing had happened, and I have only returned from a short holiday, as I meant to have. Please, Mark."

He lifted his shoulders despairingly, sensitive lips tightening. "I'm sorry. Sometimes I'm a tactless idiot. But I only thought—" he lowered his voice, and I saw his eyes flicker warningly in the direction of the armed and taciturn SD men who rode closely behind us. "I thought," he went on determinedly, "that we should perhaps have a talk before you meet my uncle. There are certain things you *must* be made aware of, even though I'm aware that this is hardly the time or the proper place for such a conversation. You know my uncle's pride and his temper, and he…"

I had felt my body stiffen while Mark was speaking, and now I could hold my tongue no longer. "If there is something I should know, then you'd best come to the point and tell me what it is. I've had my fill of mysteries!"

It was to hide my own quickened heartbeat and the unpleasant memory of Jesus Montoya's sly hints that I spoke so coldly. Now, seeing Mark's hesitant, unhappy face, I tried to control my voice. "Is Todd not here because he cannot bear to face me? Did he really expect to find that I had been ravished by half the Apache nation? Is *that* what has stung his pride? I'm surprised that he should still have been willing to pay so much money to get me back. Or was that a matter of pride too?"

"Perhaps I shouldn't have spoken at all." Mark's voice sounded harassed. "You have never been afraid of him, and I know that once he sees you again you will soon be able to convince him of the utter falsehood of those rumors we heard. You must not think too badly of him, Rowena. You know his habit of flying into rages! If Flo's letter had not come so late, he would never have…"

"*Flo's* letter?" My eyes, squinted against the glare, flew wide open, and I could not prevent the look of shock that must have shown on my face. "Is she alive, then? But we heard…"

"No, no!" Mark shook his head distractedly. "I'm sorry that I did not make my meaning plainer. It was a letter she had written *before* she—well, I cannot understand why it took so long to arrive, and I would have hidden it from him, destroyed it, if I could only have known what she had written. She was deranged; I tried to tell my uncle that. *You* know how she was! She hated you, resented you even though you tried to help and understand her. You remember the letter she sent to me? This one was addressed to Uncle Todd, and in it she—oh, God, how does one explain the workings of a sick mind? It was full of vituperations, excuses for her own behavior. Accusations—"

"Accusations?" My lips felt stiff. "But what could she accuse me of?"

Mark gave me a miserable, distressed look as he answered me unwillingly. "Of—everything that she herself was guilty of. Yes, you must be told, no matter how ugly it all sounds. She said that she had run off to Luke Cord only to keep *you* from doing so. 'I did it for your sake, Pa.' Those were her very words. She accused you of—how can I force myself to say it? Of having an affair with Pardee, and then killing him to keep him quiet. Of carrying on with *me,* yes, even that. She knew that Cord had forced himself into your bedroom one night, and she made capital of it. She said that you and he were lovers. That you and he together had planned to kill my uncle that day, in Silver City, and you helped Cord get away afterward. There was no end to her filthy accusations!"

"And yet, it all hangs together very well, doesn't it?" It surprised me that my voice sounded so calm, and almost indifferent. "Her word against mine, and since she is dead, I cannot disprove it, can I? How clever of Flo. One would almost think that she..." I broke off quickly, for I had almost said what was in my mind at that moment. "One would almost think that she could see into the future." Instead, before Mark could speak, I said, "And the rumors—I suppose that they too were equally damning? Poor Mark, what a lot you have been through!"

"Don't say that, Rowena! Do you think that my feelings for you would permit me to tolerate such slander? I told my uncle everything! That it was Flo, and not you, who was the guilty one. He knew her, after all. I think that he had almost begun to believe me when—"

"Ah yes, those rumors," I murmured in the same coldly expressionless voice I had used before, and I thought Mark winced. "Rowena—"

"Tell me!" I said, strongly, and watched without pity as Mark stammered and stuttered over words.

"They started when a certain man—a *comanchero*, I believe—was arrested by the Rurales in Mexico. Trying to dispose of stolen silver, as I understand it. And the only reason they—there was a white woman with him, you see. Her name was Jewel Parrish, and she was quick to tell the Rurales that she was a captive, taken at the same time *you* had been captured. I went to Texas with my uncle, to the ranger headquarters in Austin, to hear her tell her story again." Mark paused, and I had to prompt him.

"And?"

"Oh, God, why did I start to tell you all this? Understand me, she made no accusations. She was full of admiration for your fortitude and your courage. She told us what happened at the Apache camp, and she even seemed glad for you that—the man who bought you was someone you knew, and seemed glad to go away with..."

Thirty-Three

✣

THE REST OF THE "RUMORS" THAT I FORCED MARK TO TELL ME were what I might have expected. Hadn't Montoya warned me? I felt myself growing numb and chilled, in spite of the intense heat, although my mind continued to function and to control the expression of the mixture of emotions that threatened to choke me.

I am sure that Mark attempted to spare me the worst. He still cared for me, in spite of everything, and he told me over and over that he believed in me, and that his uncle would too, once he had spoken with me.

"Who knows how this kind of talk gets started? A sly hint over a campfire. A stranger riding into town, frequenting the same bar as some of the SD cowboys. It was common knowledge that you had been taken captive by the Apaches, you were believed dead, at first. And then, when we suspected what might have happened and my uncle offered a reward for your safe return—don't you see how it all could have started? And of course it would be just the kind of thing that a swine like Luke Cord, who hates my uncle, would be capable of. Even if it meant vilifying *you*. To say that you were his mistress, to boast of the fact that he'd force my uncle to pay in order to get you back…"

"A trifle *used*, but in good enough condition for him?" I quoted the words with such bitterness that Mark looked startled.

"Rowena! How can you think such a thing? I never meant…"

"But I did, Mark. Why attempt to gloss over unpleasant facts? You say that I haven't changed—suppose I have? Suppose those rumors were true after all, would that make me a fallen woman in your uncle's eyes? Perhaps he would have preferred to hear that I had killed myself from shame and humiliation. *That* would have resolved the problem of what to do with poor Rowena, as well as saving you all a great deal of trouble, I'm sure!"

I laughed angrily at Mark's horrified expression.

"Poor Mark!" I said mockingly. "Now I've shocked even *you*."

His fingers closed about my wrist as he brought his horse closer to mine.

"Good God!" he said, in a low, almost harsh voice. "Do you really think so little of me as to imagine this would make a difference to my feelings for you? You were a prisoner—a helpless captive, and that brute, that animal took advantage of it... oh, my poor, dearest girl, what you must have been through!"

I hadn't expected such tender understanding, not even from Mark, and I was speechless. What a hypocrite you are, I thought bitterly. Why don't you tell him the truth? Tell him, and watch his face change. Tell Todd; you owe it to him too. Shout it from the rooftops! But whether it was pride, or whether it was cowardice, I kept silent.

Mark was almost overly solicitous of me during the rest of our journey. When I appeared wrapped in my own thoughts he left me alone, although I saw him glance worriedly at me from time to time. I had become so used to riding for long periods of time that I hardly felt the time go by and felt no sense of tiredness until late in the evening, when we arrived in Deming, having crossed the border some hours before.

Mark had already explained, apologetically, that we would spend the night here and start out early the next morning, and here we were met by more SD men, most of them gun-hung Texans.

What had Flo called them once? "Pa's own, unofficial army!" How well I remembered her sneering voice. I grimaced, and said to Mark, "I suppose I should be honored. Such a large escort!"

He gave me a quick look before he said noncommittally, "My uncle felt it was necessary. He didn't want to take any chances."

"Of having me carried off again after he paid such a large sum for my return? I wonder if he will think me worth the expense in the end."

"Rowena, don't! You're so cynical."

I could have told Mark that the cynicism he had accused me of was merely an armor against further disillusionment, but what would be the point? I merely shrugged instead and remarked that I was tired and wished to retire early. I had barely time to feel thankful that tonight I wouldn't lie awake staring at the ceiling before I fell asleep.

We left Deming in the gray light of dawn, and arrived at Fort Cummings just before noon. I remembered having met the major who was in command before. He was an acquaintance of Todd's, and all gallantry, although I could sense the curiosity he hid behind his smile and polite manners. I told myself that I must get used to this. By now there was not a person in the territory who did not know what had happened, or had not heard those rumors Mark had told me of. Mark and I dined in privacy with the major and his wife, and he offered us a small escort for the rest of our journey.

"Surely that's not necessary?" I said, before Mark could speak.

The major's wife, much younger than he, and less discreet, gave me a wide-eyed look. "Oh, but it *is*! I mean—it would be so much *safer*. You cannot imagine all the trouble we've had recently. Not only from the Indians, but from outlaws and renegades as well. I've not left the safety of the fort for weeks now, and Burton says..."

The major cleared his throat warningly.

"Ah—hrrm—yes. And I'm sure Mr. Shannon realizes this." He gave me one of his charming smiles. "But I can assure you, Lady Rowena, that we are not taking any *unusual* precautions. Some of my men will be going out on their regular patrol and it would be no trouble at all if they were to ride along with your party for some miles."

The major's lady, when she took me to her room to freshen
up before we resumed our journey, was less discreet. I thought
I saw pity mixed with curiosity in her eyes as she watched me
combing my hair.

"Will you be going to live back East now? I wish I had
never come out here. It's so lonely, and one always lives in
fear. I miss the changing of seasons in the Midwest, and even
the snow. We came here from Kansas, and it was very different
there." Her voice turned wistful. "I suppose you must miss
London, with all its gaiety. I have always longed to travel, and
Burton says we will one day—but on a major's pay…"

I could almost feel sorry for the poor, discontented woman,
and her husband who must risk his life for meager pay and
very little glory.

"London is no gayer than any other city," I answered her
casually. "It all depends on what one enjoys doing. I have
always liked the outdoors and the sunshine. I was brought
up in India, which is not very different from this part of the
world. No, I think I will continue to live in New Mexico. It
offers a challenge and adventure, which is sadly lacking in the
so-called *civilized* parts of this country."

I met her shocked eyes in the mirror and smiled. Why
did I suddenly feel so defiant? Was it only because everyone
expected me to be shamefaced and reticent?

I was in a strange mood, and it kept me silent and uncom-
municative for the rest of our journey that day, straining even
Mark's understanding.

He was upset when I insisted upon going directly to my
own house, instead of to the *palacio* where Todd waited
for me.

"But Rowena, why? Surely you realize that the sooner you
face him—you do not want him to think that you…"

"Are guilty? Is that what you meant to say, Mark?" I saw
his hurt, puzzled expression and moved my hand impatiently.
"I'm sorry. But I'm tired, and in no mood for either quarrels
or defending myself this evening. Since Todd was content
to wait until I was brought to him, he can wait a few hours
longer, until I am ready to receive him. You can tell him I

said so." I looked straight into Mark's eyes as I added, "I have nothing to apologize for. And if you are afraid for me, then don't be. Your uncle will find it no easier to browbeat me now than he did in the past."

I was being unreasonable, and I knew it. Todd would be angry, and vent his fury on Mark. But I had spoken the truth when I said I was tired, and Mark, after a long and searching look that seemed to take in more than I wanted him to, said nothing more to dissuade me from my purpose.

And so, at last, I returned to my inheritance. Home—the house standing square and strong against the backdrop of sky and mountains. This was *mine,* I had come back home.

With his usual tact, Mark stayed only long enough to make sure that I would be taken care of.

I remember that both Marta and Jules had tears in their eyes. It felt strange to be called patrona again, to see Marta crossing herself, muttering happily under her breath as she followed me from room to room, pointing out that nothing had been changed, everything was exactly as the patrona had left it.

"And we knew you would be back safe and unharmed, ma'am," Jules said in an unusual burst of volubility. "I told Marta—as soon as they find out she's Mr. Guy's daughter, they wouldn't harm a hair of her head."

I loved them both. As soon as Mark had left, refusing a glass of wine, I walked around the house, finding that everything was, indeed, unchanged. Here was my father's study, with the window open before his desk, and the locked drawer that still held his journals. And now, I thought, I would read them all. No more procrastination and lazing in the sun.

To take my mind off what lay ahead of me, I wandered back into the living room, finding the unfinished chess game that I had started with Mark so long ago, the ebony and ivory pieces in the same positions that they had been before.

The night, like other nights I remembered, had already started to fold down upon us with smoky wings, and I watched for a moment as Jules lit the lamps, whistling under his breath.

"I have made your bed every single day," Marta whispered to me. "The linens are fresh and aired."

Here, too, it seemed as if I had only left the day before. My bed made, with the covers turned back in readiness. My gowns hanging in neat rows in the carved armoire. Was it possible that I had really been away? That so much had happened to change me? Involuntarily I glanced upward, and found the trapdoor leading to the roof still bolted firmly shut.

Oh, God! Why must I remember *that*? I told myself later that I must have grown irrational from sheer weariness, but I heard myself call to Jules.

He looked puzzled when I told him what I wanted.

"Take the bolts off that trapdoor, ma'am? But..."

Marta, coming in close behind him, said softly, "Would you argue with the patrona? This is her house, to do with as she pleases."

And I pretended not to notice the long look that they exchanged; Marta frowning fiercely, and Jules's puzzlement smoothing out into a deliberately blank expression before he turned his face back to me. How much had they heard; how much did they suspect? And did it matter? There would be time to find out later—for the moment all I needed was a hot bath to take the travel-weariness from my body; a bowl of soup, and the haven of my own bed. I would think no further than that tonight.

I slept deeply and dreamlessly, until the heat of the sun outside and the sound of voices raised in argument forced me back to wakefulness.

Marta usually knocked softly before she entered my bedroom, but now she burst in precipitately, and had barely time to wail: "El patron—he is here, and insists..." when *he* filled the doorway behind her, pushing her roughly out of the way.

Todd Shannon. As big, blond, and invincible-looking as always, his bushy brows drawn together in an ominous frown. "An' what in hell was the meaning of that message you sent me? By God, woman, I ain't surprised that you'd want to hide yourself from me, but I see you've lost none of your high an' mighty ways either! Well, let me tell you something…"

I sat up angrily, wishing I did not need to rub the sleep from my eyes, and realized, belatedly, that I had been too tired last night to put on the prettily embroidered nightgown Marta had left out for me.

I saw his blue-green eyes narrow dangerously as I said pointedly: "I see that *you* have not changed at all! And surely whatever it was you came to tell me could have waited until I was dressed and ready to receive you?"

"You know damn well I'm not in the habit of being kept waiting, like I waited for you last night! No, and you'll find I won't be made a fool of either! So you get out of that damned bed you're hiding in an' come out here and face me if you dare. Because I'm warning you—you got a whole lot of explaining to do!"

In the face of his rage, I suddenly became calm.

"In that case," I said icily, "I must remind you that you are in *my* bedroom and in *my* house, and unless you recollect what few manners you used to possess, Mr. Shannon, you will be obliged to leave without these explanations you seem to crave. Is that clear?"

For a moment I thought he looked ready to murder me. His eyes, like shards of jagged glass, sent splinters into my skin. "Why, you—you—"

Like a brown shadow, Marta edged around his big body, her eyes round with terror.

"Your robe, patrona." Her subdued whisper brought some semblance of control to Todd Shannon's furiously red face.

His lips thinning, he swung on his heel, saying over his shoulder in a voice I hardly recognized as his: "I'll be waiting outside. Five minutes—or like it or not I'll be back in here, if I have to break the goddamn door down!"

I kept him cooling his heels for ten minutes while I put cold water on my face and chose a skirt and blouse to wear. He hated to see me dressed as a peasant. Let him find out he could no longer dictate to me! It was hard for me to imagine now that I had planned to marry him, that I had come close to being swept away by the sheer force of his personality. The Todd Shannon I rediscovered was an arrogant, blustering bully, far too used to getting his own way.

He greeted me, if it can be called that, with a sneer. "Damned if you don't look like some dirt farmer's gal in that getup. Is that how your half-breed boyfriend liked you to dress?"

"Why, no," I said sweetly. "*He* preferred me not to wear any clothes at all. Is that what you wanted to hear?"

"You're a brazen slut!"

"And you, Mr. Shannon, are a foul-mouthed, ill-tempered boor!"

We faced each other, and my eyes refused to give way before his. He was making a tremendous effort to keep his temper in check.

"So it's true. Well, is it?" His voice, deceptively soft at first, rose into a bellow of rage. "Damn you to hell! I have a right to know what kind of creature I asked to be my wife, an' don't pretend you don't know what I'm talking about! You and Pardee—you and Cord—God knows how many Apache braves in between. Will you tell me the truth, or am I going to have to beat it out of you?"

"Lay a hand on me, and you'll regret it!" I said sharply. "And before you threaten me again, Todd Shannon, you might control your temper long enough to remember that I still own half of the SD, and that I can afford to hire as many professional gunmen as you can. It's high time you remembered that you are not dealing with some poor, frightened female who cannot fight back—if a quarrel is what you came looking for."

I saw a stunned expression mingle with the rage in his face. "By God! Do you actually mean to stand there and threaten me?"

"I was merely replying to *your* threat," I reminded him coldly, and then, as his rage threatened to burst its bounds again, I added in a reasonable voice, "Surely you can see that we are getting nowhere as long as we continue to quarrel and hurl insults at each other? If you had asked me sensible questions instead of shouting accusations at me…"

"An' what in hell do you call sensible questions? Sensible—
when I've been made a laughingstock of—and that after I'd
been half out of my mind with wondering what those bastards
had done with you! What kind of man do you take me for, eh,
miss? A weak fool like my nephew, who'd believe anything
you tell him because he imagines himself in love with you?
Oh, yes—he's spent the morning and half last night trying to
explain, standing up for you. But, by Christ, I want to hear
those explanations for myself! Are you going to give them to
me or not?"

"I can give you the truth, although it may not be what you
want to hear. Must you stand there glowering at me?"

In the end he listened, his face set in harsh and uncompromising lines. And it was I who found it impossible to sit still,
so that I walked restlessly from one end of the room to the
other while I told him as much as I dared. Not everything—
there were some things I could not bear to talk about, much
less think about. Must I be made to feel guilty for having
loved? Todd would not understand, he would begin to shout
and bluster again, and so I left my own feelings out of my dry
and unemotional account

Except for a few blunt interruptions in the beginning,
Todd had fallen ominously silent, his tension showing only
in the way he chewed viciously on the end of his cigar. As
for myself, when I had finished I felt drained of all feeling. I
wished that Todd would go, and leave me to myself.

"An' that's all you're going to tell me?"

"That's all there is to tell! You may believe me or not, as
you wish."

He gave me a smile that was merely a thin curling of his
lips, while his eyes stayed as cold as bits of green glass.

"I'll let you know what I believe and what I don't
believe—when I've thought about it."

Then he surprised me by leaving without another word,
and his sudden quietness unnerved me more than his earlier
shouting and abuse had done. As he had perhaps meant it
to do. I turned back to the empty room, and the afternoon,
already heavy with heat, stretched before me. I had had my

first confrontation with Todd—what should I do next? My mind answered me. You came here with a purpose. Find the strength you thought you had lost, and find your answers. Face reality, as you once were capable of doing.

It was time, I told myself severely, for self-examination, and a methodical organizing of my time.

Thirty-Four

୬

By the time I had eaten the light breakfast that Marta prepared, the feeling of unease that Todd's visit had left with me had disappeared. I had decided that I would spend what remained of the afternoon reading my father's journals, as I should have done before.

But after Marta had cleared the table and vanished into the kitchen, I found myself staring curiously at my reflection in the mirror that hung over the mantelpiece.

Who was I? A dirt farmer's daughter, Todd Shannon had called me sneeringly. With my sunburned skin that made my eyes seem a darker blue than usual, and my black hair drawn into a careless knot at the back of my neck, I suppose I looked the part. The last time I studied my reflection so carefully, I had seen myself as an Apache squaw.

How had Lucas seen me? I caught back the forbidden thought quickly, angry with myself for my own weakness. Hadn't I promised myself that I would not look back? Over and done with—I must remember that. Never again would I let blind emotion rule me.

In spite of all my resolutions, it was almost with a sense of foreboding that I unlocked the drawer that held my father's journals—finding the one I was looking for pushed all the way to the back, where it could too easily be missed.

I forced myself to read from the beginning. No skipping and skimming over certain entries this time.

A man's whole life lay between the pages of these volumes, carefully numbered and bound in hand-tooled leather. His life—and part of some of the other lives that had touched his. How dared I treat the request he had made of me as lightly as I had done at the start? I had been far too lazy, and too full of the change in my own circumstances; now, for the first time I felt ashamed. He had given me everything he had, and made only a few requests in exchange. Not too much for a father to ask of his daughter, even one as self-centered as I had been. I had taken up a challenge, but for my own reasons. I had been too busy fulfilling my own ambitions and my own needs for *his* to seem of too much importance.

How strong I had felt myself to be! How contemptuous of what I had thought of as the weakness of others. But now that I had discovered my own weakness and my own failings, I could see my father as a man, instead of a kind of image—a human being who was human enough to acknowledge his own failings and accept the shortcomings of other people. A man capable of loving in the wrong place—of jealousy—yes, even of violence. But a *man* nevertheless. If only I could have known him!

I opened the book to the first entry, almost unwillingly, and a name leaped out at me.

"Tonight Lucas brought Ramon, a pleasant young man with impeccable Spanish manners. I found him well-bred and likable." His pen had sputtered ink, and then, in parentheses, my father had scribbled, "Would Rowena think so?" And had added, "I must start learning to be a father all over again. She must not be pushed and reminded of her duty as I was. But how convenient if she should find Ramon as easy to like as I do..." More splutters, and then—"I am afraid, though, that she might find Lucas less easy to read, and therefore more intriguing..."

I turned the page quickly. Afraid, he had written. Of what had he been afraid? Had he begun to have doubts, or was it because he had begun to suspect how things were between Lucas and Elena?

I forced myself to read further, and found pages and pages that were filled with hope and anticipation. Plans for my future and my happiness. Never a mention of his illness, and the pain he suffered constantly.

> *Braithwaite writes that she is considered one of the fashion-able beauties, and that in spite of all the adulation she has received, she remains cold and reserved. He says there are rumors that she has turned down the Prince of Wales himself... Beaconsfield has made her his protégé; it is said he has publicly stated that she is the most intelligent woman it has been his pleasure to meet...*

Had the woman my father wrote of so lovingly and proudly really been me? How faint the memory of *that* part of my life seemed now! My eyes blurred, and I had to blink them back to awareness as I continued to read.

Mr. Braithwaite had, apparently, been tactful. There was no mention in the closely written pages of any rumors concerning my relationship with my stepfather.

There were references to Todd Shannon, and to Mark.

> *Todd is too busy these days to bother with an old, dying man. Sometimes I think he imagines me dead already. Todd has always stayed so vital, so young. But Mark remains the personable young man I have always liked, very much like his mother, and with her air of breeding. He can even speak, with a rueful kind of amusement, of Corinne's elopement, and admits that she was too much like a sister to have made a perfect wife. One of those family arrangements—how can I expect Rowena to understand what I have arranged for her? But perhaps, once I have had a chance to talk to her and explain matters, she will not think me too much of a hypocrite... the feud must be ended...*

There were many blots and crossed out words. I thought, painfully, that there must have been occasions when my father had not known what he wanted to say. Interspersed with old memories and newly aroused hopes I read of everyday matters—how Jules had been sent to the store for

supplies—there had been a letter from Elmer Bragg—a visit
by Mark, a game of chess... Involuntarily I felt a quickening
of my pulse when I saw Lucas's name again.

> *I have tried to talk reason and caution to Lucas, but he does
> not hear me any longer. I feel that there is something eating
> at him, but he will not tell me what it is. Sometimes I feel
> that he would prefer to make a stranger of me, for all that
> he takes risks to visit me. What does Lucas want? I have
> offered him enough money with which to make a new life,
> but he only gives me a frowning, closed look. He says Elena
> needs him. He hates Todd, and I am afraid that his hate
> will warp his whole life...*

More trivialities, and then:

> *It is time, perhaps, that I should seek the advice, and the
> wisdom of my old friend who is the shaman of his tribe, and
> far wiser than I. I have been too long within these walls,
> with nothing but my own thoughts and impressions to guide
> me. How do I know that my daughter will feel the way I
> do? If she reads this, I beg her to forgive an old, sick man's
> doubts... there must be some way that I can ensure that the
> law of justice is fulfilled. A codicil to my will that Rowena
> can destroy if she sees fit? I will be able to think more clearly
> once I have breathed some of the clear mountain air, and
> have talked to my old friend...*

There was a gap, after that, and several torn-out pages. A
puzzling void before the last, and most confusing entry of
all—his writing almost an indecipherable scrawl, obviously
scratched across the page under great stress.

> *I have not been able to rest since my return from the
> mountains, where I went to seek, of all things, peace. It is my
> own fault for prying, for pressing, and now—I have given my
> word not to speak of what I have learned unless I must—but
> God, my God, when is must and how shall I recognize such*

a time? Why have I been blind, when the truth was always there for me to see? Do I have to judge now, when I still feel too strongly? I ask myself whether I have let myself be too much swayed by my emotions and my own desires.

Can I face the truth, even now? Was I deliberately lied to or did I close my mind against accepting what reason tried to tell me?

Oh, God, why do I have to keep imagining her as I first saw her? Must I love her still? Elena—a wild and primitive child, with the body of a woman; with the innocence of the wholly savage—naive and knowing, fierce and gentle—and what beauty! I was stricken and spellbound when I first saw her—am I equally bewitched now? Can I blame her? Or him? If any man knows how easy it is to love her and to be swayed by her, I do…

I do not think Lucas will listen to me, not even now. But I must speak with him, even if it turns him against me. He must see the nature of the unspeakable wrong he is committed to—he must be turned away—

There were more blots, and then, further down:

Oedipus—the tragedy come to life. I should have sensed it, recognized it, before. I am rambling. I must take hold of myself, for my daughter's sake. She must know the truth, and must be prepared. She must be warned against…

The next few lines he had written were so smudged and indecipherable, as if he had rested his hand on the page before the ink was dry. By straining my eyes, I thought I could make out a few words here and there, but nothing that brought me closer to understanding.

My own name, and then, almost certainly, making my heart beat faster: "Lucas is…"

Is what? What had my father found out that had upset him so? And then, farther down: "Hate corrodes… and in his case, how far he might go unless…" more blots, and then words that stood out clearly at last:

Whatever the consequences, I must act, for Rowena's sake; yes, even for Todd's. What I have learned changes everything. The letter I have written—yes, that must be destroyed. Later, I can write another that will explain, but I must wait until my mind has grown more clear. The first thing I must do, of course, is write a codicil to my will. I have put it off too long. There are certain matters that must be taken care of, and in doing so in this manner perhaps I might prevent—no, I will not accept it as inevitable. Lucas must be stopped…

I stared down at the page. It looked as if the inkwell had overturned and spilled, obliterating everything else that had been written—if, indeed, my father had been able to write more. The rest of the journal was blank. The pages that should have explained everything to me were so smudged and soaked through with black ink that the edges of the paper had begun to curl, and were hardly readable.

And I was left with a greater, and in some ways more frightening, mystery than I had started out with. The torn and ink-splattered pages, the letter to me that my father himself had destroyed, and the fact that his diary had ended so abruptly, on that last, ominous note, "Lucas must be stopped…"

Here were my facts, if I could piece them together to make some sense. What was the truth that my father had been afraid to face? He had learned about Lucas and Elena, that much was apparent, but I was left with the impression that his grief and disillusion went deeper than that. And now it was I who did not want to face the evidence I was confronted with, and an even worse thought that crept insidiously into my mind and would not go away.

I rose so abruptly to my feet that the chair I had been sitting on overturned and went crashing on the floor, bringing Marta running to me—a startled question in her eyes. I did not know and did not care what she must have seen in my face that made her start twisting her hands together, her plump face creasing with concern.

"Patrona! You are ill?"

I shook my head impatiently. "No, not ill. Only... Marta, would you ask Jules to come in for a moment? There are some questions that I must ask."

I could tell that they were both uneasy. Jules's face was a guarded, impassive mask, but Marta looked frightened and began to shake her head as if to ward off more questions.

I had asked bluntly for details of my father's death. Had it been expected... was there a doctor with him? Did he die of his wasting illness, or—I could not help hesitating, the memory of Jesus Montoya's sly hints coming back to me with a new significance.

"Jules—was it sudden? Had he been... upset in any way before?"

I thought I saw Jules's eyes flicker, although he answered me straightforwardly enough. "Mr. Guy had not been his usual self since he returned from his trip into the mountains, ma'am. It worried me to see how pale he looked, and the way he'd pace around this very room, from one end to the other. Sometimes I thought he hadn't slept at all all night—I'd leave him sitting here when I retired, and find him sitting with his head in his hands in the morning, with—begging your pardon, ma'am—the bottle of brandy empty beside him."

"But didn't he *say* anything? Didn't he..."

"I took the liberty of speaking to Mr. Mark myself, ma'am. About the advisability of asking the doctor to visit. Mr. Shannon was away on a business trip at the time, but Mr. Mark came over that very evening, and they sat talking for a long time. And afterwards, for a little while, Mr. Guy seemed calmer. But that same night..." Jules paused, and his face had grayed, as if the memory was still painful to him.

I said softly, "Go on. *Please*. It is not morbid curiosity that makes me ask all this, but—perhaps I will be able to explain later. There is a reason why I must learn as much as possible."

"Yes, ma'am." Jules's tone was wooden, and I wondered how much he really *did* understand.

He went on slowly. "He was sitting at his desk, writing in his book, when I came to ask him if there was anything else he'd need before I retired. And I brought him his drops too, in the coffee he always had just at that time. I remember he looked up, but his eyes were—well, like he was looking somewhere else and didn't see me. He looked very tired, and he said something about the pain being worse, and he needed the drops tonight. And then he asked me to bring along another bottle of brandy and leave it by him, for he and Mr. Mark had finished half the bottle that was out already. And that was all, ma'am. Except..."

"Except what? Jules, I must know. All the little details, even if they do not seem important now."

I heard Marta muttering to herself in Spanish, and did I only imagine that Jules sighed before he gave me his reluctant answer?

"He asked me to leave the door open, ma'am. It was seldom locked anyhow, for Mr. Guy—he was a man who trusted people. He was expecting Mr. Bragg early in the morning, he said, and..."

This time I did not imagine the hesitation in Jules's voice, the almost imploring look in his eyes. But before I could prompt him again, Marta burst out in a torrent of voluble Spanish, her mouth working.

"But he did not come! We *know* this, Jules—he did not come. If he had, he would have spoken to us, he would have said: 'Marta, won't you give me some of your good tortillas to take with me on my journey?' You know this is what he always did—there was never a time when he visited the patron that he did not come into the kitchen to taste what I had in the pot, and to tease me..."

I looked from her to Jules, and felt a dryness in my mouth.

"Who..." She was talking of Mr. Bragg of course. Please, God, let it be Mr. Bragg. Not...

"It was Mr. Lucas he was expecting, ma'am." Jules's voice sounded as dry as mine must have been, and he went on quickly, seeing, I suppose, the sudden lack of color in my face. "But he didn't come, ma'am. Like Marta said. It was Mr. Bragg who found Mr. Guy, and woke us up. It was still dark, not quite five in the morning. He looked... it was just as if he had fallen asleep over his writing, his head on the desk and the ink spilled all over."

I found that now that I had heard the final indictment—the last piece of evidence I had both dreaded and expected to hear—I could be amazingly calm and clear-headed. It was just as if all emotion had drained out of me, leaving only a cold hardness in its place.

There were only a few more questions to be asked, a few more facts to be ascertained. *Facts,* I called them, for neither Marta nor Jules had any reason to lie to me. They had both been unwilling to speak at all. I had begun to think that they were the only two people in the world that I could trust any longer.

I was thinking this while I composedly ordered a light supper, pretending I didn't notice Marta's tear-stained cheeks and pushed-out lower lip. She did not like the turn my questions had taken, but I was the patrona, and she bobbed her head when I had finished speaking. Yes, in spite of everything I could count on her loyalty... and then, suddenly, I thought of Mark. Perhaps it was because my eyes had fallen casually on the chessboard, and that made me remember the last game I had played on it—so long ago, it seemed.

Mark, my patient friend, whose steadiness and common sense had helped me before. Mark, who loved me. How unnecessarily cruel I had been towards him yesterday! Why hadn't I thought of Mark before? And if I needed an excuse, he had been one of the last persons to speak with my father before he died. Mark would help me decide what must be done; Mark would listen, and help me find an objective point of view.

And so I said to Jules, who still hovered uncertainly by the door, "Would you mind waiting for a few moments, until I write a note to Mr. Mark? You might ask one of the cowboys to deliver it to him. And ask Marta if she will lay an extra place for supper, if you please."

I thought Jules was on the verge of saying something, but when he met my eyes he seemed to purse his lips, and only inclined his head courteously instead.

It did not take me long to scribble a short and carefully

worded note, and when Jules had taken it and left I went back to my room to plan what I would wear. For a change, I found it easy to keep my mind a deliberate blank. I spent an endless amount of time on trivialities, a bath in warm, scented water. One of my pretty, Paris-bought dresses to wear. And my hair piled high upon my head, with ringlets falling to my shoulders. To my reflection in the glass I said aloud: "There, and now you look more like yourself, my girl. You should never have allowed yourself to forget what you've been taught."

Thirty-Five

꒰

MARK CAME EARLY, AND I WAS GLAD TO SEE HIM COME. I HELD
out my hands to him, and as he took them I thought I saw a
quickly veiled spark in his eye, a look I had seen in other men's
eyes before. But now I needed it, as I needed the reassurance
that only Mark could give me. I needed to be reminded who
I was, and that I, like Mark, came from a civilized world of
elegance and beauty and subtle wit, where birth and breeding
and education counted for something.

As usual, Mark was carefully, impeccably dressed; his neatly
trimmed blond hair gleaming in the lamplight. As usual he seemed
to understand my mood; and he didn't press me about the urgent
message, but complimented me on my appearance instead. We
said all the polite things, as Jules brought out the decanter of
wine and two thin-stemmed crystal glasses. We watched the
light fading through the open windows, and talked casually of
New York and London. Mark's mother, the same Mrs. Shannon
who had been so kind to me in Boston, sent him copies of all
the newspapers—even, several months late—the *London Times*.
He told me what was playing at all the large theaters and opera
houses and related clever anecdotes that made me smile.

"My mother says that Corinne has been dragging her to
all the concerts. Jack is becoming quite famous now, you
know. And Corinne, of course, basks in his glory and tells
everyone who will listen how clever she was to choose such
a talented husband!"

Mark's wry, comical expression reminded me that *he* had been her family's choice at first, until my father had persuaded them to let Corinne have her way and marry her orchestra leader. But he seemed to have no regrets.

He held his glass up against the light, smiling at me.

"A toast, Rowena?"

"To the misfits, then!" I said it lightly, speaking my thoughts aloud, but his face had suddenly become serious as he studied me over the rim of the glass.

"So *you* feel it too?" he said quietly. "I have never felt you belonged here, Rowena. Anymore than I do. And yet here we are, trapped by circumstances…" with a deliberate attempt at recovering his former lightness of tone he added banteringly: "There is *one* thing that I will never regret, however, and that is the privilege of having known you."

I sipped my wine too quickly, and felt it rush to my face, leaving it uncomfortably warm. It was more to avert the sudden constraint that had risen between us that I murmured offhandedly, "I'm afraid your uncle doesn't feel the same way any longer. I hope he did not give you too difficult a time? I would not have asked you to come this evening if I had not…"

"I was already on my way here when I met Bill Klein," Mark broke in, his voice hardening. "Did you think I could force myself to stay away, invitation or no? Oh, God, Rowena! I'm well aware of the kind of man Uncle Todd is and I think his arrogance blinds him to everything but his own feelings! He has no sympathy, no delicacy. I would have given anything to have spared you such an ugly scene as he must have forced on you this morning, but it was hardly my place to interfere in a matter that concerned the two of you."

I put my glass down on the inlaid table with such force that I felt the thin crystal vibrate.

"Did he tell you that whatever might have existed between us before is over? I think he's my enemy now, Mark."

I thought there was an odd hesitancy in Mark's voice before he said quickly, "But I hope you will count *me* your friend, as I have always felt myself to be. As for my uncle, he has always been a man of extreme moods. He flies into a rage too quickly and shouts and blusters, but later, when he's had time to think… well, I did not come here to defend my uncle, but to ask if there was anything I could do for *you*."

Without asking, he leaned forward and filled my glass again, his eyes not leaving my face as he said quietly, "There *is* something wrong, isn't there? I have felt it all along, in spite of your brave attempt at gayness and insouciance. Are you ready to talk about it now, or shall we wait until after dinner? I have no wish to disturb you, or to bring that sad, preoccupied look back to your face."

"Oh, *Mark*!" I said, as I had said so many times in the past, "What on earth would I do without you?" And caught his rather wry smile.

"Why, I hope you will never come to think yourself so self-contained that you cannot turn to me!" Mark said lightly, and then, with unwonted firmness, "Drink your wine, Rowena. And then we will speak of whatever is troubling you."

Once I had begun, Mark made it easier for me to continue. He was silent when my words tumbled over each other in my eagerness to have them said and over with; and when I hesitated and stumbled in my recital, he prompted me gently.

This time, I held nothing back, as I had with Todd; not even that part of the blame which attached to myself. I had been a fool. In the face of everything I had heard and been warned of, going against all reason, I had loved, and had thought myself strong enough to overcome all obstacles… this was one of the few times that Mark interrupted me. His agitation visible, he stood up and began to pace about while he spoke to me, until I begged him to sit down again.

"Good God, Rowena! Why do you continue to blame yourself? You—a gently brought up young woman who had never been exposed to such treachery and such miserable, unhappy circumstances before. You were a helpless victim of a twisted, perverted group of people who… but don't you see *now* how it happened? You had had one shock after another, and he played upon your sympathy. You must open your eyes and realize for yourself how you came to imagine yourself in love with this unscrupulous scoundrel! You were violated by his brother, the so-called *gentleman* who wished to marry you. In a state of shock, you ran away. And found yourself isolated for days on end with a man who would stop at nothing to gain his own ends, who knows no law but that of the jungle. You gave yourself to him because you had no choice; he would have taken you by force otherwise, and I think you knew this subconsciously. And afterwards, you felt forced to rationalize, to find excuses that would enable you to live with your own conscience."

"Mark, no!"

"That is *all* it was, Rowena," he said adamantly. "Face the truth. A few stolen hours on a mountaintop with a man you hardly knew, who discarded you soon afterwards as callously as he had taken you. You cannot go on thinking that was love. Love needs something on which to sustain itself, a foundation on which to grow. Use your mind, as you were always capable of doing before! Why, that was one of the very reasons I admired you and why I still continue to love and respect you. And now"—he released my hands abruptly and went back to sit down across from me—"now you must tell me the rest—and quickly, before you lose your courage."

To this day, I don't know how I found the strength to go on. I heard myself speak, in a coldly distant voice, and I hardly remember what I said, for my mind was in such a state of turmoil. I pictured myself in a court of law, and Mark as my attorney, who wanted to help me. And as I repeated what I had learned, I saw all over again how damning it all was. Evidence—each piece fitting so neatly into the other that there could be no other solution than that which I had been afraid and unwilling to face earlier.

And Mark, very much the lawyer now, with all the cold logic of his training at his disposal, tore away even the last thread of hope to which I had clung so stubbornly all this time.

"You say he *explained* away his part in the attempted murders of Mr. Bragg and my uncle, and even his virtual abduction of Flo? But Rowena, surely you can see why he bothered to give you an explanation at all, and at *that* late stage? It was because he had already planned what he was going to do with you. Perhaps he hoped that after you were freed you would continue to believe in his innocence, and proclaim it. Perhaps he meant to make use of you again, if he had to."

Mark's words were like hammer blows in my head, and I pressed my fingers against my temples, wanting to shut them out.

"No..." I whispered, but he was inexorable, his voice firm with conviction.

"If he was capable of killing your own father, who had done so much for him, do you think he would stop at anything else? Your father had learned something damning—had become disillusioned enough to destroy his letter to you requesting you marry one of Elena Kordes's sons. You were expected any day, and you must not find out he had changed his mind. Don't you see now how carefully calculated Luke Cord's every action has been? I should have asked more questions of the servants myself, but we were all so upset at the time, and of course there was the possibility it was an accident—that he had forgotten he had already taken his medicine and taken more. Perhaps Mr. Bragg suspected, and that is why... but I need not go on. My dearest, bravest girl—you have had quite enough for one evening, have you not?"

I said weakly, "But the codicil to my father's will... why..." and braced myself for the final demolishing of everything that remained.

Mark's face changed. There had been tenderness and even pity to be read in his expression a moment before, and now it seemed as if it became guarded, slightly wary. I heard him sigh.

"I should have known that you would remember that. I had hoped that later, when you were in a calmer frame of mind... well, I see that it is my turn to make a clean breast of things, and to beg your understanding. You see, I promised my uncle..." Mark's eyes looked steadily into mine as he told me the rest of it, and his closing of the gap in my knowledge proved just as damning a piece of evidence as the rest.

It had to do with the mysterious letter my father had written to me and then destroyed. Todd had known of it, for my father, with his usual honesty, had given him a copy.

"You see, Rowena, it was not exactly a letter. As a lawyer, I was the one to warn my uncle that as the last request of a dying man, such a document could be upheld in a court of law, as a further stipulation... and *you* at the time were an unknown quality. He even had Jules and Marta witness it—this *letter* could be regarded as a codicil of sorts itself!"

"But..."

"I know what questions you must have, and I intend to answer them. As for *my* part in it, I'm ashamed to say that I let my uncle coerce me into keeping silent, and then when I met *you,* I could not bear the thought that you might feel yourself obliged to... oh, God! To marry one of *them*? To let them steal part of your inheritance from you as an alternative? It was unthinkable—in this one instance I agreed with my uncle that your father was carrying his sense of justice too far."

The letter that Todd had concealed had given reasons for my father's wishes. And then had stated baldly that if I chose *not* to marry one of Alejandro Kordes's issue, either land, or a lump sum of money be gifted to each of them, and to Elena herself. If I did marry one of the brothers, he stipulated that I should give the others a reasonable amount of money each.

"And then, Rowena, on that night—he would not tell me his reasons, but he told me he had changed his mind and had burned the letter. I was overjoyed! You see now why I did not feel it necessary to even mention the existence of such a document? It was no longer valid—and he told me he intended to draw up a codicil that would make everything clear. You were no longer to be forced into an objection-able marriage, although he still intended to see that Ramon Kordes, and Julio, if he wished it, should be provided for. He would pay for Ramon's education and travel abroad, he would deed to Julio fertile land where he and his people might be encouraged to settle down as farmers before they were all killed off or herded onto a reservation. You understand, I am only repeating what he told me he intended to do. Whether he had the time to draw up such a document I do not know; certainly, I never saw it. But this time, as he told it to me, there was a glaring omission—Luke Cord."

I looked at Mark, and he returned my look. In the background I could hear the ticking of the big grandfather clock that stood in a corner of the room, a popping noise in the fireplace as one of the logs that Jules had placed there burst into flame. I could almost imagine I heard the beating of my own heart.

Mark had been right earlier. I had had enough for one night—for one day—for a lifetime.

There was nothing more to be said for now except the usual things. Jules came back in to clear off the table and bring us coffee. Mark refused the brandy I offered him and said he must leave soon. I asked him to spend the night, and to my surprise he accepted, after a short hesitation, saying that he would have to leave very early in the morning and I must on no account disturb myself to see him off, for he would visit me again tomorrow.

"And your uncle?" I said with an attempt at lightness. Again, his answer surprised me. "I'm past the point of caring what my uncle thinks, or has to say!" he said in a tight voice. We had both stood up, and I had my hand outstretched to bid him good night when he suddenly took me in his arms. Not with force, but gently, tenderly. And for a few moments I took comfort in being there, with his lips pressed against my forehead.

With a ragged exclamation that sounded almost like an oath, he suddenly put me away from him. "You make it too easy for me to forget myself! But if you were not engaged to my uncle…"

"Mark, didn't you hear me say earlier that *that* piece of nonsense is all over with?"

"I didn't mean to burden you with any further problems tonight, Rowena." Nevertheless, I caught a warning note in Mark's voice. "But you would be wise to remember that my uncle is not only proud and arrogant but as stubborn as the devil as well. In spite of all his raging, I do not think he intends to release you from your promise to marry him yet. Not only because he still wants you as a woman but because of the SD and all it means to him. To own the whole of it has become an obsession with him, I'm afraid. I only thought I should mention it, and—yes, I'll be honest enough to say it, whether you continue to frown at me or not—especially in view of *my* feelings towards you."

Poor Mark—torn between his loyalty to his uncle and his feelings for me! And as for Todd's ridiculous assumption that he could hold me to a promise made under stress, a promise I had often had second thoughts about; well, I could soon clear *that* up with Todd himself.

I caught back the angry words I had been about to utter and kissed Mark on the cheek instead. "That is to thank you for everything, dear Mark," I said softly. I could tell he was pleased by the slight flush that rose in his face, and before we went our separate ways to bed the slight feeling of constraint between us had passed.

Mark told me later that he had slept well, and if he was surprised to see me up early enough to join him for breakfast, at least he was tactful enough not to say so, nor to make any attempts at serious conversation. He looked preoccupied, and I found myself concentrating on forcing down at least a part of the food that Marta set before us.

After Mark had taken a hurried leave of me, promising to come back in the evening for a game of chess, I wandered aimlessly into the study taking books at random from the shelves. I told myself that my father might have concealed the codicil to his will in one of his books; I can see now that it was an excuse to keep myself occupied.

I had found some of the answers I had been looking for—what would I do with them? What was I going to do with myself?

The sun was climbing, and it was already hot. I told myself that I should go riding, and take an interest in the running of the ranch. I must not let this sudden, letdown feeling of lethargy overcome my strength of purpose, not *now*.

And yet the truth was that I was tired. I had risen early because I could not sleep, except in fitful snatches. I had

had frightening dreams which I could not remember upon waking, and every time I closed my eyes I could hear Mark's firm and pitilessly logical words repeating themselves in my mind, superimposed upon memory-pictures I had not yet shut out. I had seen myself lying naked and content in Lucas's arms, the way the sun wrinkles deepened when he squinted his eyes against the glare and the leaping green flames in their depths when he looked at me. The almost tormented note in his voice when he had told me, "I've wanted no other woman in the world the way I want you…" Had that, too, been another one of his lies? I could no longer trust him nor believe in anything he had told me—but how could I stop myself from loving him? This was the private hell that I had to learn to adjust to, and to live with, if I could. That in spite of everything I continued to feel this unnatural, irrational yearning for a man who had never denied his love for another woman, a man who was ready to cheat and steal and even kill for her, and who had in all likelihood caused my father's death.

I put the books I had taken down away and called for Jules to saddle a horse for me. I had no clear idea of where I intended to go, or for how long I meant to ride. But the constriction of walls around me, pressing in on me like my memories, was too much to bear in my present mood of self-hatred.

And it was in that frame of mind that I met Todd Shannon again.

Thirty-Six

❧

In spite of Jules's protests I had insisted upon riding alone. I was already too familiar with the terrain that lay between my house and Todd Shannon's *palacio,* and this time I rode north, towards the mountains. The strange thing was what I was no longer afraid of riding alone and unescorted. I felt as if I had already faced everything, and did not particularly care what might happen to me next.

I rode out of the shelter of a grove of trees, and found myself looking down the barrels of five carbines. I reined up, and met Todd Shannon's narrowed eyes and thin smile.

"Told you boys an Injun wouldn't make that much noise!" His sarcastic drawl scraped along my nerve ends, but I retained my composure.

"Were you expecting to see anyone else?"

"Nobody tell you about the troubles we've been havin'?"

The carbines had been lowered, and I looked beyond Shannon and his men at a dilapidated wooden building that seemed to lean to one side, the door gaping open on broken hinges.

As if he had read my mind, Todd's lips curled mockingly downward.

"You met your lady boss yet, boys?" And to me, in a lowered voice as he kneed his mount forward, "The way you ride around by yourself makes me wonder…"

The four cowboys with him seemed slightly embarrassed as

they lowered their carbines and touched their bats awkwardly. I nodded slightly and looked back at Todd.

"This is my land, is it not? And I happen to enjoy riding by myself."

"Just like Flo, in the old days. This is where *she* used to come."

I should have known, from the narrow-eyed look he bent on me. And yet curiosity made me glance again at the building, as I remembered what I had been told. I tried to imagine Lucas as a young man, hardly more than a boy, coming here to meet Flo. Had he cared for her at all, even then? And the killing that had taken place here—Flo's hysterical screams, and Lucas himself—what had he thought, how had he felt?

Ignoring Todd, I slipped off my horse and walked forward.

"I didn't know," I said over my shoulder. "But I've heard what happened here."

His men rode away quietly and I found myself alone with him. I felt his presence close behind me as I paused at the doorway; not wanting to go inside, but fascinated by what had once taken place in this very spot.

"So you've heard. Did *he* tell you?"

I became aware of Todd, of his pent-up anger.

"Does it matter?"

"Hell, yes, it does! I don't want you traipsing around on your own anymore, and I won't have any secrets between us. You hear me?" He put his hands on my shoulders, and I stiffened coldly. "You told me some of what happened, mebbe I'm ready to believe part of it. But if we're going to be married there are a few things we're goin' to get straight."

I twisted away from his grasp.

"We're not going to be married! After what you've thought, and the things you said... oh, really, Todd! Why keep on with a farce?"

"And I tell you that you ain't going to make a fool of me! Maybe you don't realize it, miss, but out here, when you give your word you better be ready to keep it. We'll settle our differences after we're married. I tell you, I'm willing to forgive and forget what's happened, maybe all of it wasn't your fault after all. But from now on, you start changing those independent ways of yours, you understand? And…" his voice rose into a bellow that made me wince involuntarily, "you stop asking Mark to spend the night! I won't have any more talk about you than there is already."

"Will you get it through your head that I have no intention of marrying you?" Without my realizing it, my voice had risen, and I felt my own anger rising to match his. "It was a mistake—we would never have suited each other. And now, especially now—I would think you'd be glad to be rid of whatever obligation you may have felt towards me."

His voice was a low growl that should have warned me. "How is it you still have that high and mighty, touch-me-not air about you after all the fornicating you've done? Or is it only an act? Maybe you're one of those women who has to be forced to enjoy it. Yeah, I can remember some times when I've held you in my arms an' you were almost begging for it, only I held back. She's a lady, I told myself. She's Guy's daughter. But maybe none of us knew you, and you've always been a bitch in your heart, like that mother of yours."

I had forgotten how strong he was, how quickly he could move. He caught me in his arms and I felt the boards crack behind my back as he pressed me against the side of the shack.

"*Now*—" he whispered triumphantly and somehow cruelly. "Now let's see if you've forgotten how it was with us."

I felt his lips claim mine. No matter how I moved my head to avoid his kiss I was helpless. It had been this way before, I remembered, but this time there was a difference. This time, no matter how long and how fiercely he kissed me, I remained unmoved.

I had stopped struggling against him, and when at last he lifted his head to look down into my eyes with his face mirroring both frustration and anger, I whispered, "And now you see that I do not enjoy having kisses forced upon me, nor anything else! And you, Todd, you do not want me for myself any longer. Why don't you admit it? You want the SD, and you think you will still get it through me, even though you have begun to hate me. Don't bother to deny it! I can see it in your eyes. Why won't you admit that whatever was between us once is finished?"

I pulled away from his slackened grasp and began to walk to where my horse stood with its ears pricked. His voice followed me, making me pause momentarily, with my hand on the saddle horn.

"I'll be tellin' you something, and you'd better listen. Hate you or not, we're going to be married in a month's time, and like any filly, you're going to be bridle-broke, and learn your proper place. You don't like that idea, you can run back East—or back to England, for all I care. But the SD is mine! I've fought for it and bled for it, an' there ain't no one going to take what's mine from me—you understand that?"

He stayed where he was, feet astraddle, his brows drawn together in a threatening, lowering look, that followed me while I mounted my horse unaided and rode away from him without another word being said between us.

Todd had given me his ultimatum. It only remained to be seen what I would do about it. At least Todd knew what he wanted and would fight for it.

Could I say the same for myself?

During the week that followed, it was made clear to me that Todd had meant what he had said. He did not attempt to force his presence on me again; in that alone he was subtle. But I was reminded in countless other ways of my rather ambiguous position here, and his power.

For instance, I became suddenly aware that I was being followed wherever I went, and watched. When I went out riding now, there were always two or three men who seemed to appear from nowhere, and trailed me at a distance. If I protested angrily, they would tug at their hat-brims and apologize—and tell me that Mr. Shannon had given orders I was to be escorted wherever I wished to go. When I ordered them to stop following me, they would disappear from sight for a while, but I knew, nevertheless, that they were some-where about—lurking behind trees or stumps of mesquite, no doubt, I would think maliciously; watching me through field glasses.

Even when I went to Santa Rita, accompanied by both Jules and Marta, to visit the post office there, I saw the familiar faces of SD men, the familiar brand on several of the horses that lined the hitching posts. And it was Jules who told me that Todd had actually posted a guard on the house at night— all this for my "protection," of course!

I protested furiously to Mark, whom I seldom saw these days. He admitted that Todd kept him busy with various errands and business trips. Legal matters that conveniently cropped up just at this time. And *he* was as unhappy at the situation as I was, although he tried to be fair.

"I know how you must hate it, but after all it *is* for your own good in a way, Rowena. The Apaches have been getting more daring in their raids of late. They overran a small homestead less than fifty miles from here just the other day! And there seems to be a well-organized gang of rustlers operating in this area as well; didn't Uncle Todd tell you? The SD alone has lost over a hundred head during the past two weeks. There's been talk of all the ranchers banding together to form a vigilante committee; the soldiers are too busy chasing Indians to be of much help. So you see…"

I could not control the telltale leaping of my pulse at the mention of rustlers, and Mark's penetrating look made me feel I had given myself away, so that I said quickly, "But I won't put up with it! And if Todd thinks he can *force* me to marry him by using these tactics…"

"He cannot force you to marry him, of course," Mark said soothingly, but I thought he frowned slightly.

"And he cannot force me to keep his men on my land." I went on recklessly, "Suppose I hired my own cowboys? Men who would take orders from *me*. I'm tired of being watched over like a prisoner."

"Rowena, please be sensible, face facts. How many men in this part of the country would take orders from a woman? Oh, I suppose that with sufficient money you could hire professional gunfighters, but remember that such men are born predators and how long do you think you'd be able to control them alone? Surely you can't mean to start a range war, with all its attendant bloodshed, merely because my uncle insists that you must have protection? Woman or not, there won't be a soul in the territory who would condone such an action on your part. I hate to sound so severe and uncompromising, but you must realize that for the moment, my uncle has the advantage of you. If you'll only be patient..."

"Patient! When your uncle thinks he can wear down my resistance or drive me away? There are times when I feel I might go mad—either with rage or with boredom. What am I waiting for? Why hasn't Montoya contacted me yet? And *you* for all your protestations of friendship—you let yourself be sent away like a... a..."

I stopped suddenly, my fingers pressed against my mouth; appalled at what I had almost said.

But Mark, his face white with suppressed emotion, finished my sentence for me. "Like a lackey, you mean? One day, I will prove to you that I..."

"Mark, don't be angry with me—I'm sorry! I didn't even know what I was saying. It's not like me to get so emotional." I tried to laugh, and the sound I made was more like a sob.

"It's this heat, I suppose. And everything else. If only I knew if Mr. Bragg is really alive, and where he is—if only there was something I could do to prove I was of some use, that my coming here had some purpose!"

"But it had! Never think otherwise." His own hurt forgotten, Mark put his hands on my shoulders and looked seriously into my face. "Listen, since it means so much to you, I'll do what I can to contact this man Montoya again. I have to go to Las Cruces tomorrow, and I'll spend an extra day there if I have to. I'll talk to him myself, if I can. If Mr. Bragg is alive, we'll find him. And if necessary, when I return to Boston I'll hire another Pinkerton man to discover what happened to him."

"When you go back to Boston?" Dismayed, I stared into Mark's face. "But you never mentioned... surely you're not going to leave me here alone?"

I sounded like a spoiled, selfish child. I realized it soon after I had spoken, and tried to make amends.

"I'm sorry. I should have realized that this is not yet your home, and you have a law practice which you love. How self-centered you must think me!"

"Rowena." Mark's fingers tightened, pressing into my flesh. "I have wanted to say this to you for a long time, but I wasn't certain. You sounded as if you might miss me. Is it possible? Listen to me, and don't interrupt me until I have finished, or I will never find the courage to say it again. You know I love you—you don't know yet how much. Let me prove it to you. Come back East with me, please! This is no place for you—or for me either. Remember when you called us both misfits? Marry me, Rowena. Let my uncle keep his empire, what does it matter? You can have nothing but unpleasant memories of this place; you need to put them behind you. You know how your father died, and you know what his last wishes were. You can see to everything without having to be here yourself, and to suffer any longer. Even if you will not marry me, at least agree to come back with me to Boston. Call it a holiday if you will. My mother would love to have you live with her until you make up your mind. Rowena! Can't you see how impossible it has become for you to live here any longer?"

I looked into Mark's pleading face, and I could think of nothing to say except, feebly: "But your uncle! He would never forgive you."

"And if I have *you* my uncle can go hang, and so can the inheritance he holds over my head!" Mark's voice was impassioned. "My God! Sometimes it's more like a yoke about my neck! If not for you, I wouldn't have stayed here this long. Rowena, before I go, and I must leave you soon, will you promise that you'll think about what I have said? I don't want an answer now. I want you to be sure in your own mind."

And that was how things stood until the day before Mark was due to return from Las Cruces... and Lucas came back into my life.

Thirty-Seven

❧

I HAD HAD TIME TO THINK, SINCE MARK HAD BEEN GONE. HE was later than he had estimated he would be in getting back from Las Cruces, and while I wondered whether his delay had any significance, I was glad to have some time to myself. I realized that I had begun to cling to Mark, and to depend on the strength and comfort he offered me.

I had too many things on my mind. There was Mark, and the answer he would expect from me when he returned. What could I tell him? And there was Todd, who in a twisted way both hated and desired me; he had given me a month's grace in which to make up my mind whether I would marry him or run away. Whenever I thought of Todd I felt angry. Did he really think he could compel me to marry him? I tried to tell myself that Todd was an egotist, too much obsessed with a sense of his own power, too used to trampling over the feelings of others. And yet I persisted in feeling uneasy. It was strange that he should continue to stay away from me, especially with Mark gone. I was positive he knew of every movement I made; his men continued to follow me everywhere. What did he hope to achieve?

I attempted to set a pattern to my days, a certain routine that I could follow automatically. I went riding as usual, pretending to ignore my distant escorts. In the afternoon, when it grew too hot to stay outdoors, I read my father's journals, hoping to understand him better.

There was another reason why I tried to keep myself busy, and so tired that I would fall into bed every night, almost too exhausted to think. A reason I was not yet ready to face—a nagging suspicion I tried to avoid I had always resented certain inescapable physical proofs that I was a woman, and subject to all the weaknesses and infirmity of my sex. There were times when I wished fiercely that I had been born a man. But now it was too late for wishing. I had learned to avoid Marta's worried eyes when she insisted upon bringing me my hot chocolate each morning, and I shook my head just as stubbornly, or pushed my cup away after taking a single sip. No, I told myself. It was the heat, nothing else. And the fact that I slept only fitfully and uneasily of late, tossing and turning; waking from strange, haunted nightmares to thoughts that were even more painful.

Since Mark had left, all days seemed the same. Until that particular day that I began to write of earlier, and still recall in every detail.

It had been unusually hot, and I woke up drenched with sweat, the covers sticking to my flesh. It was the sun that roused me, shooting golden arrows of light into my bedroom as if to remind me of the molten-hot, pitiless hours that lay ahead.

I got out of bed and splashed cold water over my face and body, and with its mild, pleasant shock, the uneasiness I had felt upon waking vanished.

I ate two slices of toast and a glassful of freshly squeezed lime juice for breakfast, conquered the slight feeling of queasiness afterwards, and went riding, as was my custom. My usual escort fell in behind me, and I wondered what they would do if I kept on riding, as far as my horse could take me. The mountains shimmered in a slight haze, and I remembered how cool and green the thickly forested upper slopes had been. Suppose I went back there, of my own accord this time? Just as my father had gone, when he needed to find peace—except for the very last time, when he had learned something that brought him death, in the end. It was this thought that turned me around and took me back to the house at last. To the comparative coolness of my bedroom where Marta awaited me, her usually smiling mouth turned down at the corners to show her disapproval of my crazy behavior. I was dripping with perspiration, my thin silk blouse clinging to my back, my face unnaturally flushed. She muttered to herself as she helped me change.

"Such madness! To go riding in this heat, under such a fierce sun. And for what? You will make yourself ill, and the Señor Mark will blame us for not taking better care of you."

It was partly to mollify her and partly because I suddenly felt limp and drained of all energy that I agreed to take a siesta.

"Just this once, mind you," I murmured drowsily as she pulled the covers of my bed back. "I will not make a habit of such laziness."

And then, before I knew it, I had fallen into an exhausted sleep. I must have slept until after nightfall, for when I opened my eyes again the lamp on my dressing table had been lit, and Lucas was leaning up against the wall as he had been the very first time I set eyes on him, watching me with a wary, brooding look on his face.

At first I thought I was dreaming again. I had conjured him up out of my imagination. It *was* Lucas, and yet it wasn't. He was dressed as an Apache warrior, naked except for a breech-clout and knee-high moccasins, a medicine pouch suspended around his neck by a thin strip of rawhide.

I could feel my eyes widen, and then I met his narrowing, green-fired eyes, and my heart began to thud so loud and painfully I thought I was going to faint, and he would disappear again.

"Lucas?"

I know that my lips moved, forming his name, but no sound escaped my suddenly constricting throat. I could only watch him cross the room to me, his face shadowed now, moving with the same long, almost angry stride I remembered so well.

Even his voice was the same—still with that husky note to it, tinged by some emotion I had no time to fathom, as shaken as I was by my own feelings.

"You were sleepin' so sound I didn't want to wake you right away. Ro, I..." I never learned what he had been about to say. I sat up, the covers falling away from my naked breasts like the memory of everything I had heard and thought during the past few weeks, and all my firm resolutions. It is a frightening thing, and especially for a woman, to discover that she is capable of desire so strong that it can blind her to everything else. But that thought came later.

It was sheer, primitive instinct that made me hold my arms out, tugging his head down to mine, returning his kisses greedily, almost savagely. Not thinking.

I felt myself pulled off the bed and onto my bare feet; my knees were so weak that I could only lean helplessly against the familiar length of his body, my arms still locked around his neck. I rediscovered the feeling of losing my identity, of being carried beyond myself to some distant place where nothing mattered but wanting and fulfillment. This was what I had craved for, hungered for, yearned for, without shame or reason. This was lust, desire, love—how does one put a label on feeling?

I only knew that I was held fast in a net of my own making and could not have broken loose if Lucas himself had not shattered the spell that held me trapped and helpless.

He released me so suddenly that I felt myself flounder back against the bed. It was only pride, and the anger that came from rejection that kept me on my feet and facing him.

I did not know then that the harshness of his voice was meant to cover up his own indecision and frustration. I could only feel the pain and humiliation of what I took to be another form of rejection, as cold and as calculated to bring me to my senses as a slap in the face.

"What's this I hear about you marrying Shannon next week? Have you gone crazy?"

"Is *that* why you came?" My head was spinning, and yet I heard myself laugh. "Really, Lucas, I'm surprised you wasted your time—not to mention the risks you are taking by being here at all. Did you think you could stop me from doing whatever I wanted to do? Just because..." My voice almost broke to betray me, but I managed to steady it, taking a deep breath before I added with calculated scorn, "Just because of a casual physical attraction between us?"

He made a movement towards me and stopped, his face going bleak and hard. "Was all that your way of tellin' me you're going to marry Shannon after all?"

"After all *what*, Lucas Cord?" I walked away from him then, knowing that if I let him touch me again I would be lost. I walked to my dressing table and swung around, forcing him to turn too, to face me. The light from the lamp made his eyes look tawny green, narrow like those of a mountain cat about to spring, and I spoke quickly, before I had time to weaken, my voice sounding curiously strident for all that I spoke softly.

"Do you think that what happened between us gives you the right to question me? It filled some hours that would have been unbearably dreary otherwise—and then, since you no longer had a brother to marry me off to, you sent me back here for your share of the ransom money—or did your friend Montoya forget to give it to you? Is that why you came here? Well, if it was, then you have taken the trouble for nothing! You see, I know all about that letter my father wrote *now!* I also know that he destroyed it, and why. And I know... I know..."

This time, for all my efforts, my voice shook. Everything that I had read in my fathers journals, everything that Mark had so patiently tried to explain to me came back, filling my mind with revulsion.

"I don't know what in hell you're talking about!" Lucas's voice was taut, his brows drawn together in a frown. "Rowena..."

"No—don't! Don't make it worse by saying anything, by lying any more than you already have done! You see, I've learned such a lot about you! Did you think to fool me and to use me as you've done all the other women you've wanted and had? I think you tried to kill Elmer Bragg because he knew too much—about the letter that was destroyed by my father's own hand, about the codicil to his will that vanished on the night he was... *did* you kill him, Lucas? Did you put more laudanum in his glass when he wasn't looking? Oh,

God. He *trusted* you. And to think that I had actually begun to trust you too, that I could have thought I…"

"That's enough!" He had crossed the room in two long, angry strides, to catch me by the shoulders. I tried to twist away, but he held me fast, his fingers tightening cruelly until I gasped with pain and shock. I felt the table edge cutting into the naked flesh of my thighs, and in spite of everything I was all too aware of his closeness, the slight, angry flare of his nostrils, the white tension lines around his mouth.

"Listen to me…" he said, and his voice was flat—colder than I had ever heard it. "I still don't know what you're driving at, but I think you're trying to say I killed your father. And I think that something, or the lies someone's been feeding you, has twisted your mind up so bad you won't see the truth even if it's put under your nose!"

"How dare you…"

"I dare anything I damn well please, or ain't you learned that yet?" He shook me slightly, and the blazing anger in his eyes made me flinch. "You don't like what I'm sayin' you can always open your mouth and scream, and the guards Shannon's got posted outside will come running. Why don't you do that? Or are you scared in case they tell Shannon they found his woman naked in her bedroom with a half-breed murderer?"

"Stop it!" I was sobbing now, tears of rage and humiliation almost blinding me. "I don't want to hear anything else. I don't ever want to see you again. I hate you, do you understand? I hate you, I despise you! Why don't you go back to Elena and wallow in your filthy, incestuous lust for her?" I started to beat at him with my clenched fists until his hands slid down my arms, pinioning them.

His voice was dangerously soft. "Not yet. Not until I prove something to myself—and to you."

This time I did open my mouth to scream, and the scream died into a whimper in my throat as his mouth covered mine savagely. Useless to struggle and try to break free. And just as useless, I discovered a moment later, to fight against the treacherous response of my own senses.

When Lucas lifted me in his arms I was too weak to do

anything more than let my head fall limply back against his shoulder. When he put me on the bed I could hardly stand the few seconds of waiting until he came to me, now as naked as I was.

What followed was an act of violence; of raw, undiluted passion that needed no words, no preliminaries. This was need and its response. Desire and its culmination. And the only questions and answers given were with our bodies.

When it ended I suppose I was still in a kind of daze. I could not understand, at first, why instead of continuing to hold me close, as he used to do, Lucas disengaged my clinging arms and legs from around his body and moved away from me without a word. He did so gently, but dispassionately, and when he sat on the edge of the bed, calmly pulling on his moccasins I felt a dryness in my mouth that presaged fear.

"Lucas…" it came out as a whisper, softer than the pounding of my own heart.

He turned his head to look at me, and I could read no expression on his face. I had to moisten my lips with my tongue before I could speak again.

"Lucas, you're not…" because he wouldn't help me I had to force the words out. "You're not going yet?" I hated to hear the abject pleading in my voice, and I thought I detected the slightest narrowing of his eyes.

He stood up and began to put on the breechclout he had worn. "Why not? There's nothing to keep me here now, is there?" And then, as if he regretted the cruelty of his words he added, in the same toneless voice, "I thought that was what you wanted. Besides, Shannon might not like it if he came by to visit you in the morning and found me here. Might change his mind about wantin' to marry you."

I felt the blood ebb from my face, leaving me with a cold, empty feeling. "*That* should please you!" I said in a low, bitter voice. "I suppose you'll make sure he finds out in any case, just as you did before!" I saw green flame leap in his eyes for a moment, and then he said in the same calm voice he had used before, "Guess that's another of the evil deeds I'm supposed to have committed? Well, I'm sorry I ain't got the time to stay here and defend myself, not that there would be any point in that, since you seem to have had your mind all made up before I was a damn fool enough to come here."

"If none of it is true, then tell me so! If you can explain..."

He cut me off coldly. "Explain what? All those crazy accusations you been throwing at me this evening or what happened just now? No, I'm damned if I will. Ever since the first time we met, you've been judging me, judging everyone else. It's time you did some figuring out for yourself, Ro. An' while you're doing that, better take a good look at yourself too. There ain't a human being in this world who's perfect, an' at least I never asked that or expected it from you. But you set yourself above everybody, make your own conclusions... what gives you that right?"

I stared at him, one hand pressed against my throat to fight off the sick, cold feeling that had been rising in me with every word he had spoken. Was it true? Was that how he really saw me?

I shook my head as if to refute my own thoughts. "No... that's not true, you're not being fair..."

"Like you've been?" His voice was just as cold, just as merciless and I shrank from it. And still I couldn't keep silent.

"All I wanted was some answers! That's not being unreasonable, is it? Is it?" To my mortification, I felt tears start to slip down my face.

"Ro..." his voice sounded tired, "I gave you some answers once. But it didn't do no good, did it? No matter what I tell you, you'd start doubting me again as soon as I'm gone. Seems to me the best thing for us both is for me to get the hell out of your life an' stay out of it from now on. An' that's just what I aim to do."

The tears had turned into silent, gulping sobs that seemed to be wrenched out of me. I set my teeth in my lower lip, biting down so hard that I tasted blood.

"But why did you come here tonight? *Why?*"

Lucas was already at the door, but he turned to give me a long look before he shrugged.

"That ain't important now. Call it a crazy notion I had."

What I had really wanted to say was "Don't leave me!" but now it was too late. I had asked my question and he had chosen not to answer it. Perhaps he felt I didn't deserve an answer.

I thought I heard him say in a low voice, "I'm sorry, Ro."

And then the door closed behind him and on a part of my life, and I was lying back in bed with the sobs choking me, wishing I could die.

I was so wrapped up in my own misery that I did not wonder why Lucas had chosen to go through the house instead of using the trapdoor, until Marta came to me, her face creased with worry.

I could only look at her, incapable of speech, seeing her as a blur through tear-swollen eyes, and then, as if I had been a child needing comfort she put her arms around me, rocking me against her.

I heard her murmuring in Spanish: "Cry, cry, it is good for you... ah, *pobrecita!* I know how hard it is to be a woman, it hurts, no?" Her soothing voice hardened slightly as she said: "Men! They are without understanding, they are all selfish! I told him so. I said, 'Why did you come here like a *ladron,* like an Apache who must hide in the night, if it was only to leave her again? She has been troubled enough, with the patron coming here to shout and threaten and try to frighten her, and Mr. Mark making her cry with the ideas he puts in her head.' Si, I have never been one to mince words with him, and Lucas knows this."

I twisted my head around to look up at her, wondering why I was not surprised at her words. Of course Marta and Jules must have suspected the truth right along! They too must have heard the rumors, and no doubt my manner since I had returned had confirmed everything.

With no more need for pretense I asked, in a voice so hoarse I could hardly recognize it as my own, "He's... really gone?"

She began to smooth my hair awkwardly, her head nodding.

"Si, he has gone. Jules called to the men who guard outside, offering them coffee. He could not sleep, he told them. And while they were busy, *he* left. As quietly as if he had been Apache himself. Don't worry; he knows how to take care of

himself, that one. He asked me to look after you," she added
in a slightly softened tone. "'Go to her, Marta,' he said, and
only shook his head when I scolded him for upsetting you.
'She may feel unhappy for a little while, perhaps, but later she
will understand that it was for the best.' *Madre de Dios,* there
are times when I think that it is men who understand nothing!"

Thirty-Eight

❧

I CANNOT REMEMBER IF I SLEPT AGAIN THAT NIGHT OR NOT. I cried myself into a semistupor, in spite of all Marta's attempts to comfort me. And the next morning, when I managed to drag myself out of bed at last, to study my tear-swollen, almost unrecognizable face in the mirror, I was suddenly swept with such waves of nausea that I could only clutch at the edge of my dressing table and moan like a sick animal.

Marta, who had gone to fetch a basin of cold water with which to bathe my eyes, came running to me; holding my head, smoothing the tangled hair back from my brow while I retched violently, unable to help myself. I did not need to meet her eyes afterward to read there, in her pitying look, the confirmation of something I had suspected already.

"I'm pregnant."

I saw Mark's face whiten with shock at the uncompromising bluntness of my statement. He had come to see me straight after his return from Las Cruces, and the first thing he had noticed was the redness of my eyes, my rather distracted manner. When he asked me directly what was wrong, I saw no point in evasion.

"My God! Rowena, are you sure?"

I had looked down, for a moment, at my clasped hands. Only the whiteness of my knuckles showing my inner agitation. And when I looked up I thought I had imagined the strange, fleeting look in Mark's blue eyes. His face showed nothing but concern for me as he leaned forward. "Are you sure?" he repeated, and then when I nodded his voice grew firmer and harder than I had ever heard it before.

"Then there's only one thing to be done. Surely you can see that for yourself?"

"Mark…" the mood of apathy into which I had relapsed had dulled my senses, and I could not think what he meant until he had taken my hands and was saying strongly:

"We shall be married. As soon as possible. No, Rowena, you must not argue with me. It is the only solution—for your own sake, and the sake of… of the child you are carrying. For your protection."

I did argue with him, of course. But he demolished every argument I could offer. I must think of my future and the future of my unborn child. I did not want to think about Lucas, who had given me no answers and no explanations, and who, in his way, had been much more pitiless before he walked so casually out of my life. And, worst thought of all, suppose the child I was carrying was Ramon's? Lucas had turned his back on me, but Mark had not. Mark loved me enough to accept me as I was, with all my shortcomings, and in spite of my embarrassing condition.

He was right, there *was* no other way. I had to accept the fact that I lived in a man's world, and a pregnant woman without a husband, even if she was enormously rich and titled, would be ostracized wherever she went. This was something I could not run away from, and I had brought it on myself.

I was grateful to Mark, during the days that followed, both for his surprising strength of character, which I had not realized before, and for his kindness and tact. Once I had bowed to the inevitable, I found it easier to let Mark make the decisions for us both.

We would be married in three days' time, and go to Boston for our honeymoon. And then we would return to New Mexico. Mark was adamant that I should lose no part of my inheritance.

"It's what your father would have wanted, Rowena," he said gently, and I could not find the strength nor the words to argue with him, especially when he added that he had, in fact, made contact with Jesus Montoya who had promised to have news for us by the time we returned.

"Of course he demands far too much money for whatever information he can give us," Mark said grimly, "but I did not think you would mind." No, I did not mind. I let Mark take charge of everything, and moved through the time I had left in a kind of daze, as if I was dreaming everything that happened. It was this state of mind that helped me to a short, but extremely unpleasant interview, with Todd Shannon.

He was furious, disbelieving, and contemptuous in turn. And in spite of my mood of cold remoteness I could not help but be proud of the way Mark stood up to his wrath.

"Rowena is going to marry me, and that's that. You might as well get used to the fact, for we are going to be neighbors—and partners, Uncle Todd, whether you like the thought or not. I won't allow you to intimidate her any longer. She has the right to make her own decisions."

"She's nothing but a…" Todd did not choose to mince his words, in spite of Mark's angry protests. I was unmoved, even when his ugly, narrowed eyes bored into me. "You're a damn fool, an' a weakling, Mark! If she's been carrying on with you behind my back, what's to prevent her doing it again? You going to take that Injun's leavings? Or…" and his voice sharpened, "is it that you've got her breeding? You sure you know whose brat she's carrying?"

It was only for Mark's sake that I did not blurt out the truth. But perhaps there was something showing in my eyes which made Todd Shannon throw back his head and laugh—an ugly, mocking sound.

"That's it, I'll bet! My noble nephew. Or mebbe you're just smarter than I gave you credit for. This way you'll get half of the ranch without waiting for me to die, an' you can run for governor with all that money she'll be bringing you. Ain't that what you always planned on?" His raucous laughter jarred on my ears again. "By God—maybe you're more of a Shannon than I thought, after all!"

His laughter followed us as Mark hurried me outside.

"Rowena!"

I shook my head at him. "No, Mark. There's no need to say anything. Do you think I don't know what he's like? It doesn't matter... he had to say something, don't you see?"

But it was only my earlier training, under Edgar Cardon's tutelage, that enabled me to make some pretense of responding when Mark took me in his arms and showered kisses on my face and throat

"Wait—*por Dios,* if you will only wait—a few weeks, a few days..." Marta pleaded with me. Her manner since that night had become almost motherly, and she had stopped her infuriating habit of referring to me as la patrona. "He will come back. I know he loves you; how can he help it? Men are stubborn sometimes." But I couldn't wait, any more than I could bear to disillusion her.

Lucas wouldn't come back. He was with Elena, back where he had always belonged, and I knew this, although I did not tell Marta so. And in one thing, at least, Lucas had been right. We belonged in different worlds, he and I, and in spite of the fact that I could not help loving him and yearning for him I had, at the same time, to accept the fact that I could never trust in him again. There was too much evidence that pointed at him, too many unexplained incidents that taken together added up to damning proof. I had to put him out of my mind, and that was all there was to it. As for the child I carried within me, it was not yet a reality, nothing more than another uncomfortable, unpleasant fact that I had to face.

The days passed far too fast. Marta helped me to pack, in spite of her constant, muttered protests, and before I had time to get used to the idea, Mark and I were married by a justice of the peace in Kingston, with strangers as our witnesses, and had begun our journey back to civilization.

It seemed strange, to be retracing the journey I had made with such anticipation only months ago. Even stranger to realize that I was married, a gold band on my finger marking my changed station in life. There were changes in me too, and in Mark, although looking back now I find it difficult to fix on a particular time, a particular day when I first noticed these changes. Perhaps this was because I was too busy with trying to keep my mind free of unpleasant and hurtful thoughts. I remember that once or twice Mark mentioned laughingly that once we had stopped traveling he would have to tear down the wall I had erected about myself. On my part, I preferred not to look too far into the future, not back at the past. To live one day at a time was enough for me. Or so I thought then.

When, on our wedding night, Mark only kissed me tenderly at the door to our room and told me I must get the rest I needed, for we would be leaving early in the morning, I put it down to a further example of his consideration and love for me. I even felt a pang of guilt that my first reaction was a feeling of relief. Mark and I had been friends for too long for either of us to be able to adjust easily to the fact that he now had all the rights of a husband. But as I lay in bed that night, willing myself to fall asleep quickly, I remember telling myself firmly I must make an effort to be a good wife to Mark—to feign my responses when he finally took me, if that would make him happy.

However, it was not until we had reached Socorro that Mark made any attempt to claim his conjugal privileges, and it was on that same night that I realized I had married a man with depths to his character I had not even suspected.

I am getting ahead of myself. Even now I wonder why I did not see certain things that were before my eyes, and why, during the painfully slow days of traveling it took us to arrive in Socorro, I did not question the fact that my husband of only a few days had not yet frequented my bed, but seemed content with a few kisses and almost absentminded caresses. Consideration for my condition and the sickness that plagued me almost constantly? Or infinite patience? Easy to ask myself that later. At the time I was only grateful, when I was not too ill to care. I had always prided myself on my strong constitution and excellent health. Like most people who are not used to sickness I began to despise what I looked upon as weakness, in between bouts of acute misery. I even wished, fiercely, that I might miscarry. Anything would be better than the embarrassment of this constant reminder of a time in my life that I was trying to forget. Why couldn't I be like the peasant women in India, who never had a day's sickness in their lives, and would go back into the fields to work the day after they had given birth?

"It's because you're not a peasant but a lady," Mark said. He had entered my bedroom from the adjoining room where he had spent our wedding night, to find me only half-dressed, and trying to fight back the nausea that threatened to choke me.

When I protested that I would be all right in a little while and refused to be the cause of delaying our journey he shook his head at me, a slight smile on his lips.

"That's nonsense, of course. You must realize, my dearest, that we have all the time in the world. Now go back to bed and lie down, and I will make some other arrangements." He had never taken such a decisive tone with me before, and I surprised myself by obeying him weakly.

It was almost noon when we set out, and the "arrangements" Mark had made were to hire our own coach and round up an escort of hard-bitten men who looked eminently capable of using the guns they wore.

I was feeling better by then, if a trifle limp. I roused myself to ask Mark, "But how did you manage to do all this in such a short time?"

He smiled at me. "One of the advantages of all the traveling around my uncle forced me to do. I met a lot of people, some of them useful. In fact, it was the owner of the saloon where they gave me a bachelor party last night who arranged everything for me." He gave me an apologetic look. "You don't mind? I could see how tired you seemed and did not want to disturb you, so I played some poker with friends, and when they found out I had just been married, well…" he spread his hands, "they insisted there must be a celebration."

I accepted what he told me, just as I learned to accept the fact that the man who drove our coach swore constantly and spat long streams of tobacco juice that splattered the sides of the vehicle as it swerved and swayed around bends and jounced over every rock on the trail.

"Must he drive so fast and so recklessly?" I said once, and

Mark patted my hand, looking at me a trifle reproachfully. "He's one of the best, they told me. And this is the way they all drive here. You'll learn not to notice it, after a while."

After that I made no more protests. In fact, I became too tired and sleepy after a while to care. And that night too, I slept alone in a hastily procured hotel room, while Mark said he would go downstairs and "join the boys" for awhile.

I told myself it was my fault that the journey to Socorro took almost four days instead of two. My fault that we were so late starting out every day. And I continued to be grateful to Mark for his forbearance.

We always took adjoining rooms, and since I had begun to sleep heavily and exhaustedly, I had no idea what time he came up to bed at night. But he had taken to coming in in the mornings, to watch me dress, and although this habit of his made me feel strangely ill at ease, I said nothing. He was, after all, my husband, and the sooner I got used to the idea the better. I learned not to flinch when he came up behind me in the mirror and ran his fingers caressingly over the bare flesh of my shoulders and arms.

"You're beautiful, Rowena. If you only knew what it means to know that you are mine at last. My wife."

Mark's hands were always cool, with no rough calluses to burn my skin. Sometimes I felt that he caressed me quite impersonally, as one would a statue, or a prized possession. Once, as if he had read my mind, he smiled at me in the mirror, bending to kiss my neck as he said softly, "Is it a sin to admire perfection? You have the perfect body, my darling. So slim. So firm. I would like to have a statue done of you, in the finest marble. In the nude of course—does that shock you? A body like yours needs no coy draperies." And while he talked he slid the robe I had been wearing off my shoulders and began to stroke my breasts, very gently.

I think what made me vaguely uncomfortable was the way he kept watching me in the mirror—first my eyes, and then his hands on my breasts, stroking across each nipple until they stood upright. I broke away with a smothered cry, wondering why I had done so.

"Mark, I..."

"You're too modest, Rowena. Surely there's nothing wrong with a husband admiring his wife's nakedness?"

But he stood back, smiling, and let me dress, and I was angry at myself for being so foolish. For at least the hundredth time I had to remind myself that I was now Mark's wife, and fortunate that he was so patient with me.

That was the day before we arrived in Socorro. I had no way of realizing, as I dozed through most of the journey with my head on Mark's shoulder, how everything would begin to change after we got there.

PART VI:

THE TANGLED WEB

Thirty-Nine

꙾

FROM THE SMALL VILLAGE OF MAGDALENA, WHERE WE HAD spent the night, it was only some twenty-seven miles to Socorro—that ancient town by the Rio Grande that seemed to slumber wrapped in dreams of its past glories. Today Socorro was still a large town, as Mark pointed out. A meeting place for ranchers and farmers and businessmen from all over the county.

The two-story hotel where we would be staying was larger and more imposing than any we had stayed in so far, and Mark told me with a smile that he had already reserved the very best rooms for us.

"The honeymoon suite," he said teasingly, and added that we would be staying here for three or four days in order to give me time to recover from the strain of traveling.

"I think you will enjoy this part of the country, Rowena. And I have a friend, John Kingman, who owns a large ranch across the river. I would like to take you to visit him. His wife is a charming woman, a French Creole from New Orleans."

"You never mentioned this to me before," I said a trifle sharply.

"I wanted it to be a pleasant surprise. And besides," Mark added thoughtfully, "I'm afraid I've been too selfish, rushing you off your feet in this fashion. We've hardly had time to get to know each other, have we? And I want our marriage to start out right, Rowena." His charming smile flashed out at me, disarming me. "Come now, admit it! Aren't you glad at the prospect of a few days' rest?" I had to admit that I was. What heaven it would be to lie abed late without a feeling of guilt, and to spend leisurely days just *walking* instead of being cooped up in the swaying interior of a coach.

Mark put his arm around my waist and squeezed it. "I am going to enjoy showing you the town—and showing you off, of course. Later this evening, when the sun is lower, you might care for a stroll around the plaza. It's an old Spanish custom. Everyone comes out, lovers exchange secret glances, and the young men and women like to display their finest clothes." He looked at me consideringly as he added in a lower voice, "I would like to see you wear a high comb and a white mantilla over your dark hair, like the Spanish women. And after our promenade, we'll have a champagne supper in the private dining room. I'll be the envy of every man who sees you."

I looked at him in some surprise, unused to such flowery speeches from him. "You're becoming as gallant as a Spaniard yourself."

"Why not? I am only just becoming used to the fact that you're mine, and that I have the right, at last, to tell you all the things I've had to hold back for so long. You're everything I've ever looked for or wanted in a woman, Rowena."

But in spite of the ardent note in his voice, that uneasy feeling crept over me again, and it was all I could do to force a smile. I was being ridiculous, I told myself. Mark was my husband. Why shouldn't he give me that long, slow look, as if he was undressing me with his eyes? He had that right too, and I had given it to him.

Mark left me to take a siesta while he made arrangements for the stabling of our coach and horses and accommodations for our escort. He had insisted on unhooking the back of my gown himself, and I could still feel the warmth of his kiss on the back of my neck.

"I don't think I shall ever permit you to hire a lady's maid," he had teased. "I enjoy dressing and undressing you far too much to let anyone else usurp my privileges."

To please him, I had slipped on a flimsy wrapper while

he pulled the heavy, fringed drapes together to shut out the sunlight. He had even turned back the covers on the large bed for me, and fluffed up the pillows. How solicitous of me he was, and I should really sleep, if only to please him. This was what I told myself, but the moment he left the room I found myself far too restless and hot to stay in bed.

I did not like the opulence of this room, with its turkey-red carpet and gilt-framed mirrors. The crimson and gold wall-paper made me feel as if the walls were closing in on me. The room was too dark, too gloomy; even the enormous four-poster bed with its heavily embroidered brocade bedspread and red-tasseled canopy made me feel stifled.

I felt the perspiration beading on my body and the slight, nauseous feeling that I had learned to dread seemed to curl like a fist in the pit of my stomach. I told myself I was being fanciful. If I didn't look out I would end up a hypochondriac, like my mother. All I needed was some fresh air.

And so I made excuses to myself, swinging my bare legs off the edge of the bed and feeling the soft plush of the carpet under my feet as I went to the window, which was closed. I had a slight struggle opening it, wondering crossly as I did so, if people in this town were all afraid of fresh air. But with that much achieved I stood there for a while, studying the people on the street. I thought I recognized Mark, standing hatless, his fair hair burnished by the sun as he talked with a group of men. One of them, a portly gentleman wearing a dark suit and stovepipe hat, shook Mark's hand as he clapped him heartily on the back.

Another acquaintance? I frowned slightly. Strange that I should have had no idea before that Mark knew so many people. He had never spoken to me of his friends in the territory; only of people he knew in Boston and New York. A misfit, he had called himself, and yet he seemed perfectly at ease down there. I saw him throw back his head and laugh at something the older man had said—a mannerism that reminded me strangely of Todd, and which I had never observed in Mark before. He had always seemed so restrained, so reserved. But ever since we had been married I had noticed an air of self-assurance, even of firmness about him that had seemed lacking.

And now, I scolded myself, I was being fanciful again. I had only known Mark in the shadow of his uncle. And now he was free—we both were. Perhaps I was only just discovering the real Mark, the promising young attorney who was so highly spoken of in Boston, the gay young man-about-town who had all the eligible young females there setting their caps at him. I was lucky, I repeated that to myself as I saw Mark and the portly man detach themselves from the others and walk down the street together, talking earnestly. They went into a building that adjoined the town marshal's office, with a boldly painted sign that proclaimed it to be the Bank of Socorro. And why shouldn't Mark visit the bank? No doubt he needed money to take care of all our expenses and pay the wages of the men who had escorted us here.

And then I forgot Mark, for my eyes were drawn with morbid curiosity to the white-painted structure on the other side of the marshal's office, with a covered walkway connecting the two. The courthouse. I remembered the story I had heard so long ago, when none of the protagonists were familiar to me. Had my father occupied a room in this very hotel while he waited for Lucas to come to trial? And Lucas himself... what had he been like then? I imagined him standing at the window of his cell, staring out at the mountains which had been his home. Perhaps he had wondered if he would ever see them again... And then I thought, oh, God, must everything I see remind me of Lucas? When would I come to accept that *that* part of my life was finished and done with?

But in spite of everything I could tell myself, it was difficult *not* to remember, especially when Mark himself brought the subject up.

As he had promised, we went walking in the plaza that evening. It was getting dark, the mountains a dark purple, like enormous shadows splashed against the fading blue and crimson sky. Mark named these ranges for me, the names Spanish and musical. "Magdalena, Galinas, Los Piños..." He had surprised me with gifts when he returned to our rooms. A ruby and diamond-studded comb for my hair, a white mantilla made of the sheerest lace to wear over it, and even a white silk shawl to put around my shoulders. He had insisted upon choosing the gown I would wear—a burgundy red silk with deep blue and green threads woven into the material, giving a shot effect when it caught the light. I had never worn this particular gown before, thinking it a trifle too flashy for my taste, and cut too low in front, but Mark liked it. It made me look Spanish, he said, and I had given in to his wishes with a shrug.

Mark was very attentive to me, keeping his arm around my waist and whispering to me that every man on the street envied him, and all the other women paled to insignificance beside me. I wished that he had not fallen into the habit of flattering me so excessively; it had begun to embarrass me. I was almost glad of the crowds that surrounded us and the bustle of activity on the street.

The lamps had been lit everywhere, cowboys dressed in their Sunday best with slicked down hair rode into town whistling and whooping. And in the plaza where, following the Spanish custom, people paraded slowly around and around from one end to the other, a mariachi band played lively music.

We received many curious glances, Mark and I; perhaps because of the contrast we formed—I with my black hair and he so blond.

"You see, my love? You're so beautiful that no one can help staring at you."

"I don't enjoy being stared at." I retorted more sharply than I had intended. "Mark, can't we sit down for a while? All this walking round and round is making me feel quite dizzy."

Somehow he managed to find a stone bench under some trees, apologizing for his thoughtlessness. We sat there in silence for a while, alone and yet not alone. Anyone who noticed us would have taken us for lovers, choosing this quiet corner to whisper to each other,

Mark's arm had been around my waist, now he moved, drawing me closer to him. I felt his hand slide up my back under the shawl I wore; and then his fingers, moving lightly over my skin, were caressing my shoulder and the curve of my breast. I could not help stiffening. I turned my head, and he was watching me intently, a slight smile curving his lips. I repeated the thought that was on my mind aloud.

"Sometimes I feel as if I do not really know you, Mark."

"And I feel as if I have always known you. But not enough. All human beings are strangers to each other, I think. Marriage can be a dull affair of a contract between two persons, or a voyage of discovery—shall we spend the next few days discovering each other, my darling wife?"

I could not help widening my eyes. "I've never heard you speak that way before. I think you are quite a complex person, Mark."

"Does that frighten you or intrigue you? My dearest Rowena, if you only knew how puzzled you look!" His tone became almost teasing. "At least I've managed to take that lost and distant look from your face and to make you see me as a man. My poor girl, has it really been so bad? Is forgetting him so hard to do?"

I caught my breath, but I did not pretend not to know what he meant. "Has it been so obvious? I've tried…"

"Perhaps you try too hard. Sooner or later, you will see Lucas Cord for what he is—a conscienceless, predatory killer, not far removed from the level of a beast. And then you will stop romanticizing what happened to you, and go back to being your true self."

"Mark," I began, "I don't—"

"You must not stop thinking of me as your friend, just because we are now husband and wife," he said gently. "And that is all the more reason why we should be completely frank with each other. It does not pain me to hear you speak of him, Rowena, because you see, I have you; he does not. And the day will come when you will make your own choice, of your own accord, and turn your back on the past forever."

An impassioned speech, but a slightly puzzling one, unless Mark meant that he was wooing me with gentleness, where Lucas had taken me by force. What would he think if he knew the truth? Dare I tell it to him? I might have been tempted to make a clean breast of everything, including the last visit Lucas had paid me, if Mark had not kissed me at that moment, his arms holding me possessively. And this time his kisses held a passion and ardency he had not shown me before as he forced my lips apart with his.

I felt myself thrown off balance, a feeling I did not altogether enjoy. And I found myself wondering, as we walked slowly back to the hotel, what other surprises Mark might have in store for me this evening.

There were none, at first. Mark had reserved a table for us in the corner of one of the smaller dining rooms, where we could eat in privacy. The food was tolerable, and the champagne was iced. Under Mark's amused eyes, I drank far too much of it. Perhaps I was preparing myself for the test of the night that lay ahead of us—Mark had made no mention of his joining his friends later.

He drank more champagne than I did, and I noticed that his face became slightly flushed, but he made no attempts to draw me into an intimate conversation again, limiting his remarks to the kind of thing we used to talk about before. Books and music and the theater, some of his experiences in the law courts.

And then... "The law has always fascinated me; I suppose it comes from being born into a family of lawyers." He spoke casually, twirling the stem of his glass between his fingers. "Even when I was not directly involved, I would make a point of visiting the courts whenever I could, particularly when a case that was exceptionally interesting or controversial was being heard. The territorial courts fascinate me; the atmosphere here is so much less formal than it is in the more civilized parts of the country. As a matter of fact," he went on in the same casual tone, "I traveled up here to Socorro with my uncle for Luke Cord's trial, but more to hear Jim Jennings, the attorney from San Francisco your father retained, than from morbid curiosity." He looked up at me. "You've heard about it?"

"Mr. Bragg told me the whole story before I ever came here," I said through stiff lips. "He—his descriptions were very vivid."

"Cord was guilty, of course. He should have been hanged in the interests of justice—it would have saved so much trouble and unhappiness if he had! Did he tell you he was innocent? My poor Rowena!" My expression must have given me away, for Mark shook his head slightly. "I talked to Flo afterwards, at your father's urging. He imagined—well, the poor girl had always been a flirt—you saw how she was. He thought that perhaps it was her fear of my uncle that made her cry rape. But she swore to me that that was what actually happened, and if you could have seen the state she was in, with her clothes ripped and bruises on her body, you would have had no choice but to believe her too."

"But, my father…"

"Your father did not want to believe that his protégé, the son of the woman he loved, would lie to him. And Cord, of course, had his own motives for going to your father, instead of running away. We know what those were, don't we? That letter, the money he hoped to inherit. I think he believed your father's influence would get him off scot-free; you should have seen the stunned look on his face when the judge handed down his sentence!"

"Must we talk of these things *now*? It's all in the past, Mark."

"But to understand the future you must understand the past as well. Don't you see that, Rowena? This is not an unjustly treated, put-upon man we are talking of, but a cold-blooded, calculating one. 'And the truth shall set ye free'… remember?" Mark quoted.

"Very well!" I raised my chin defiantly. "I accept the truth. You were all right and I was wrong, gullible, foolish! But is it foolish of me to ask that we change the subject of our conversation to… something more pleasant?"

"Of course!" Mark said equably. "I didn't mean to upset you. One day, you know, we will be able to mention his name and you will do no more than give a casual shrug… Well, shall we talk about Paris and London now, or shall we go upstairs to bed?"

"To bed, please," I said a trifle unsteadily. "I think I have had a little too much champagne to drink."

Mark carried me across the threshold to our room because, he said, this was our *real* wedding night. And although I did not realize it at the time, another threshold had been crossed as well—this time, in our relationship. For at last I was to begin understanding the real nature of the man I had married.

"I am a sensualist," Mark said to me, as he turned up the lamps, one by one. "Does it surprise you?" I stood with one hand on the back of a chair to support myself, watching him, and made no answer. He smiled at me and went on, "You see, I am being honest with you. I want you to understand *me,* Rowena, just as I mean to understand every little thing about you. Your likes and dislikes, your desires, your—needs. Our marriage is going to be perfect. We shall be partners, lovers, friends, achieving all our goals together. Why do you think I have waited so long to be married? I was looking for the perfect woman, you see, and I think I have found her in you. Beauty—and I love beautiful things around me, had you guessed that? Intelligence and wit, strength and ambition; the ability to rise above all obstacles and setbacks…"

"Mark, you flatter me!" I said a trifle desperately. "But I don't think I can ever live up to the perfection you demand. I'm *not* perfect, surely you of all people must realize that?"

"I realize that you are the only woman I have ever wanted," he said seriously, coming to me and tilting my chin up with his fingers. "Your being here with me as my wife is an example of what I have just been speaking of. You see, from the first moment I saw you I was determined to have you; just as I am determined now that you shall love me and admire me too—just as much as I do you."

"Mark!"

"Hush," he said, turning me around as if I had been a doll. "It's time I made love to you, worshiped your body as it deserves to be worshiped."

Somehow I found myself in front of the mirror again, almost too dizzy to move or do anything more than grip the edge of the dresser with both hands as my husband began to take the pins from my hair.

One by one, just as slowly as he had turned up the lamps

so that the whole room glowed with their light like the center of a giant ruby. And then the tiny hooks that held my gown together at the back. I would not look at Mark's eyes in the mirror. Mirrors reminded me of Edgar Cardon, of myself, naked except for the diamonds sparkling about my throat.

The silk gown fell rustling to the floor around my ankles, trapping me where I stood, trapping me like the gold circle on my finger. Mark was a blur behind me as he began to slip the thin silk chemise I wore down my shoulders, his fingers lingering against my skin. Mark—or Edgar? I saw only my own eyes in the mirror, and they were the eyes of a stranger, staring back at me, wide and startled and shining with an unusual, glittering brilliance.

"Sapphires to match your eyes," Edgar had whispered once, and I was a marble statue with jewels for eyes.

I felt Mark's body move against mine—the rough texture of his clothes, the softness of his hands as they stroked my cringing flesh.

"Watch…" he was whispering, or did I only imagine it? "Watch, Rowena! See how beautiful you are? All this loveliness—mine."

I felt myself begin to shiver. Lucas… Lucas… oh, God, where are you? Roughness of his hands, hardness of his mouth… hardness… I closed my eyes against the memory, feeling my head spin as I leaned back passively against Mark.

Even my thoughts had become disjointed now. Too much champagne… I was dreaming all this…

"I think I forgot to mention one other thing I searched for in the perfect woman," Mark said softly, his hands moving lower. "She must be the perfect lady in public, ice-cold and reserved. But in our bedroom… my mistress and my whore…"

Forty

❧

I CANNOT, LIKE SOME POPULAR NOVELISTS OF MY DAY, DRAW A
discreet veil over all that is unpleasant to recall. I write in these
journals for myself, only my eyes and the eyes of my children
will read what I have written. And it has become a compulsion with me to write everything down exactly as it happened.
I have learned that nothing can be gained from running away
from the truth. And so I will be exact, and detailed in my
account of all the events that have taken place.

I am full of good intentions, and what is past is past. But
even now I feel a certain reluctance to remember certain
things. And that morning in Socorro, when I woke up with
a headache that was like a thousand hammer blows in my
temples, threatening to split my skull open, is one of these.

At first I could not even remember where I was, could
hardly recall *who* I was. There was the pain in my head that
seemed almost to blind me—and then, surge after surge of
sickness so acute that I must have cried out weakly. I say I
must have, because I was suddenly aware that someone was
supporting my head, holding a basin for me while I gasped and
retched and was disgusted with myself all the while for being
subject to such weakness.

A strange voice spoke soothingly to me—in French of
all things.

"*Pauvre petite!* There, there, it is just one of these things that
all women must bear, *hein*? So—you will be all right soon, no

need to feel ashamed. It is that husband of yours who needs a talking to, yes?" I was lying against the pillows, limp and exhausted, too drained of strength to open my eyes. And I felt my lips and forehead sponged gently with water so cold it made me gasp.

"You feel better now?"

Something—I did not yet understand what—made me imagine for a moment that I was still in London, lying in my bedroom at Cardon House.

"Martine?" I could not manage more than a faint whisper, but I heard a gurgle of amused laughter underlying the voice that answered me.

"Non, non! You are thinking of someone else, *pauvre cherie*. I am Monique, and we have not yet met... formally. But that is all right, for I had already heard so much about you."

I forced my eyes open at last, and saw a smiling yet sympathetic face bent over me. Strange how much I noticed, even in my semi stupor. She was attractive, with a piquant face and masses of auburn hair that contrasted sharply with her milky white skin. Her eyes were green—large, and slightly slanted, and she wore a pale green gown that formed a pleasing contrast to her vivid coloring. Everything about Monique Kingman, I was to discover later, was vivid, exciting. Some might even have called her flamboyant. Certainly she seemed out of place here, in the dull red hotel room.

Seeing me open my eyes, she waved a hand at me, as if to tell me not to make the effort of speaking again.

"Don't exert yourself yet. I will send your husband to you, and after that, when you feel well enough, we will let him perform the proper introductions, *oui*?"

She was gone, with a rustling of her long skirts, before I could protest, and then Mark was bending over me, his face concerned.

"Rowena! I had no idea... why, my poor girl, how you must be suffering. Lie still. Are you sure you will be all right now?"

I tried to sit up, and he put his hand on my shoulder, gently, but firmly.

I was frowning with the effort of trying to remember. "What happened to me? I've had more champagne than I had last night, and never felt so unwell. Mark—I cannot remember..."

But I did—it was beginning to come back in snatches. The mirror... Mark undressing me, caressing me... the dizzy feeling that had made everything whirl around me and seem unreal...

"It was not a very good champagne, I'm afraid, and I should have remembered your delicate condition." Mark laughed suddenly and boyishly, "I'm afraid you were quite drunk, my love! And it's a pity you cannot remember, for *I* can—every detail, I must confess." He leaned close to me and whispered, "Never have I known a woman so passionate, so abandoned! My darling, you were everything I imagined you would be."

Was it possible? How was it I could not remember? But then, the whole evening seemed rather vague to me. There was only a slight soreness between my thighs to remind me that I was now Mark's wife in every way. I told myself that it would all come back later, but I must have seemed unusually quiet for the rest of the afternoon, while we journeyed to the Kingman Ranch, which was some thirty or forty miles distant from Socorro.

My silence was put down to the fact that I had been so ill this morning. They were all very patient with me, and from time to time Mark would give my hand a reassuring squeeze. He seemed so confident, so sure of himself! I watched him, and listened to him talk, and wondered how it was possible that I had once accused him of being nothing more than his uncle's lackey.

We were riding in the Kingmans' own light carriage—custom-made by Abbot & Downing, I had noticed. John Kingman was a still-handsome, graying man of about forty-five or so. Monique, his wife, must have been at least ten years younger. And yet, there was an air of easy comradeship and affection between them. She spoke vivaciously, gesturing with her hands; I could not help noticing that she had long and slender fingers that were accentuated by the rings she wore.

Later that day, soon after the lamps had been lit, I was to hear Monique play on the grand piano that her husband had ordered snipped from Europe, especially for her. To this day, I cannot hear a piece by Chopin without remembering Monique, her auburn hair catching the light as she bent her head over the keyboard.

She wore black that first evening. Stark and unaccentuated, and her skin seemed to take on a pearly sheen under the lights. She was beautiful, and she played like an angel. No wonder John Kingman seemed so proud of her!

The ranch house was large and rambling, built Texas-style, Mr. Kineman explained. It was by no means a palace, such as Todd had built for himself, but far larger than my own small house, although it was built of stone and adobe, with a shingle roof.

"It's just a typical ranch house, nothing very grand," Monique said with a deprecating shrug when she showed me through it. But it was comfortable inside, and the guest room where Mark and I would sleep was spacious and airy, with a polished wooden floor that had colorful rugs scattered over it.

I assured Monique that I would be very comfortable here, and she smiled, showing white, slightly pointed teeth. "Oh, but I hope so! For I have already told Mark that you must stay longer than just a few days. I think it is a ridiculous idea, to take you all the way to Boston, traveling all those miles when you are *enceinte*—only to turn right around and come back. Why should you not spend your honeymoon here? Me, I would not trust that uncle, that fierce Monsieur Shannon. He is—what is the word?—a very unscrupulous man. I think he would not want you to keep what is yours."

I felt that Monique was the kind of woman who would always speak her mind. She knew of my condition; she knew how short a time Mark and I had been married. And yet she showed no signs of condemning me, but seemed slightly amused instead.

It was growing more and more obvious to me that Mark's friends knew more about me than I knew of them, in fact, and this was borne out later on that same night, as we sat around the supper table while a smiling Mexican maid cleared away the dishes.

John Kingman, who was a man of few words, was leaning back in his chair puffing on a cigar, a glass of bourbon before him. The rest of us sipped some excellent cognac, which Monique confided had come all the way from France.

"Mark brought it back for us—two cases. Wasn't that nice of him? All I want from Paris is some really good cognac, I told him. And you see? He kept his promise. Mark always keeps his promises, do you not, *mon cher*?"

"I did not know you had been to Paris!" I looked from Mark to Monique. "Why, we've spoken often of Europe, and never once did he mention…"

"Did he not? Mark, you are a wicked man! Yes, of course he has been to Paris—it was about two years ago, I think, and when he came back—ah, he could talk of nothing but you. Remember I told you that Mark always keeps his promises? This was one that he made then. He told me, 'Monique, I have seen the woman that I am going to marry someday.' And he has done so…"

Before I could speak, Mark leaned forward and took my hand. As it had been last night, his face was rather flushed. "I was going to tell you last night, dearest, but—I'm afraid you made me forget everything but yourself."

His low, intimate tone made me embarrassed as well as angry. "*You* spoke of honesty between us!"

"So I did—on both sides, remember? Tonight we will tell each other all our secrets."

Monique broke into the awkward moment with a bright laugh. "Look at them, John! They are still lovers. And perhaps we should be tactful, you and I, and allow them to go to bed, yes?"

It was all I could do to maintain an air of politeness as we said our good nights. I had been deceived too often, and to think that Mark, of all people, whom I thought the only man I could trust, and had married…

"How could you?" I stormed at him as soon as the door had closed behind us. "All these months, when you pretended to be my friend, encouraged me to confide in you—"

"Rowena!" He caught my shoulders, forcing me to face

him. "This is not like you, to be so quick to condemn. I remember that you defended Luke Cord almost to the end, even after he had deceived you in the worst possible way."

"Oh!" I felt as if he had struck me. "How long will you throw *that* in my face in order to cover up your own perfidy?"

"Until I have proved to you that he is not worth your regrets! Until you are able to dismiss his memory with a grimace of distaste! Can't you see that everything I do and have done is all for *you*, Rowena?" He did not give me a chance to reply, but went on heatedly. "Yes, I saw you in Paris. A glimpse of you at the theater once, with your mother and stepfather. And—other times. I tried to get myself invited to all the balls and intimate parties where *you* would be invited. I saw your picture in the newspapers, the glorious portrait that was painted of you and now hangs in the Prince D'Orsini's private collection in Venice. I heard what they called you—'the marble goddess,' was it not? And I guessed, no, I *knew*, even then, that you were not made of cold marble, that underneath that withdrawn and icy look there was a real woman. Warm and passionate and vibrant..."

I tried to twist away from him, but he held me fast.

"You have not explained anything!" I said coldly at last. "Why you deceived me, why you pretended..."

"I did not even recognize you at first, in that ugly disguise! Don't you remember? And after that—well, you wanted to be left alone. And then, when you showed some slight warmth toward me, I didn't want to spoil anything, in case you might think me like all the other men you seemed to despise. So I waited. Why do you think I remained so long at the ranch? I waited, Rowena, and we became friends. I began to hope, but I warned myself to go slowly, to be careful. I knew that you had been hurt and disillusioned, that for all your poise and beauty you were frightened of me underneath."

"This is ridiculous!"

"No—it is not! Admit it, you distrusted men. And then— oh, God, can you imagine my feelings when my uncle told me bluntly that he wanted you, and meant to have you? That he had kissed you, and you had responded? He warned me that you were his property, and after a time I began to feel that this was really so. You quarreled with him, stood up to him, swore you would never marry him, and yet—do you think, loving you as I did, that I could not see how flushed and breathless you seemed after you had been alone with him? I knew he had been kissing you, I had seen that triumphant gleam in his eyes before. I tried to warn you…"

"Yes," I said in a dull voice. "Yes, I know you did. Just as you tried to warn me about Lucas. But that still does not explain…"

"I am coming to that." Mark's voice became serious. "Come here, sit down beside me on the bed, Rowena. No, I will not do more than put my arm around you—yet. But you must listen."

It sounded almost too simple, the way Mark explained it. He had seen me in Paris and had fallen in love with me. He had tried in vain to get an introduction to me, had haunted my favorite theaters and art galleries. But I had never noticed him.

"Why should you? You moved in another sphere, another plane. Lady Rowena Dangerfield—and I was only a middle-class American, on his Grand Tour in Europe. How could I ever manage to meet you?"

But Mark had, in the end, contrived it. Having found out who I was, it was *he* who had informed my father of the fact that my grandfather was dead, and I was no longer living in India, but was under the care of my mother and her husband.

"*You* did that? All that—on the slender chance that I might agree to come to America?"

"I would have taken any chance at all! And of course, just to see your father's face when I told him made it all worthwhile, even if you had not wanted to come. He used to talk about you by the hour, Rowena!"

"But why didn't you tell me all this before? Surely, once I had agreed to marry you…"

"For this very reason that we are sitting here now, instead of lying in each other's arms. I was afraid you would be angry and turn against me. I wanted to wait, until I was more sure of you—until I had had the time to win your love. And last night…"

I did not want to think about last night. I still had an indefinable feeling of repugnance, thinking that I could have abandoned myself so wantonly, without even knowing what I was doing. Was that the kind of woman I really was? Was lust my own particular devil?

Mark did not give me time for more introspection. His manner becoming firm and self-confident again, he insisted that we would finish our talk tomorrow.

"I wonder how many more secrets you are keeping from me," I said tiredly, and he smiled, drawing me to my feet.

"No secrets. Only surprises—and pleasant ones, I hope. And you, my love?"

"It has become obvious that you know much more about me than I do of you!" I returned sharply. "And as for the rest, perhaps you will discover that too—tomorrow!"

The truth was that I no longer knew how to deal with Mark, or what I could expect of him. I was relieved that he was too patient—or too clever?—to press me further tonight, but contented himself with unhooking my gown, telling me that he was going outside to smoke a cigar and talk over some business with John Kingman.

If he returned to our room, it was long after I had fallen asleep. I did not wake up, although I was troubled by strange dreams, that made me move about restlessly. In the morning the covers trailed onto the floor and the bed linens were all rumpled, and still damp with sweat. I was alone, and the only dream I could remember vividly was that I had been lying with Lucas, and he had been making love to me…

I found myself left alone with Monique for most of that day, Mark having ridden out early in the morning with Mr. Kingman. She wore a thin blouse of pale orange silk, which in some strange fashion seemed to complement the rich color of her hair, instead of clashing with it. Under the blouse Monique wore nothing—the outline of her breasts and nipples clearly visible. Beside her vivid, bright beauty and vivacity of manner, I felt myself to be dull and insignificant. How could any man think *me* beautiful when Monique was present?

"You feel better this morning, eh?" Her slanted green eyes

swept over me and she nodded with satisfaction. "Oui—the dark rings are gone from your eyes. You look more as Mark described you. You do not take offense, I hope, that I am frank? I have always been so. Sometimes it makes John angry, that I must always speak what is on my mind. But I tell him... 'You knew how I was when we married. If you cannot take me as I am now, well, I will go away.'" Monique stretched with unself-conscious, sensuous grace. "And you know what? This he does not want. He needs me. I am a... how do I say it? I am a clever thinker, me. As you are, Mark tells us."

The morning passed, with Monique alternately yawning and gossiping. She was lonely, she told me, but she struck me as being a very self-sufficient woman, as well as one used to having her own way. She did not exactly *say* so, but I received the impression that she and John Kingman enjoyed a rather unique relationship. She spoke of trips to New Orleans and San Antonio and even to San Francisco—but always separately. "Someone has to stay here and look after things, yes?" And once she mentioned that jealousy had no part in a perfect marriage.

"Is there any such thing?" I could not help sounding rather bitter, and Monique, after a sidewise glance, gave a gurgle of laughter.

"Wait," she said wisely. "You have a lot to learn yet!"

And then, jumping to her feet as if she could not bear to sit still for too long, she asked if I would care to go riding with her. "Just a little way, I don't want to tire you."

I noticed, for the first time, the unusual lack of activity around the ranch house. The maids were Mexican, buxom and giggling, and the cook a wizened old Frenchman who had accompanied Monique from Louisiana. But the few men who lounged outside looked more like gunmen than cowboys, and did not seem to have any particular duties to perform. I was struck, too, by the strange isolation of the house itself. Nestled in the foothills, it was built on a small plateau that commanded a view of the rolling Estancia Valley. Behind, the layered peaks of the Los Piños mountain range towered thickly forested; and in the distance to the left the Manzano Mountains.

As we followed the narrow and winding trail that led us downwards, Monique said laughingly, "And now you see why we so seldom have visitors! This place is too difficult to find, and the trail too rough to get here easily—you remember how sick you felt yesterday?"

Yesterday, I reflected grimly, I had been too ill to remember very much, nor to notice much either. But today my mind seemed to have cleared and I observed too many things that puzzled me.

A clearing guarded by heavily armed men who put up their rifles only when they recognized Monique. Far too many cattle milled around in this one spot, and some of them wore unfamiliar brands, although a certain amount of branding was going on at the moment we passed through. Monique stopped only to ask a few questions, her voice clear and businesslike, and then we rode on through a thickly growing stand of trees, splashing through a shallow stream to come out into another small cleared space.

"One of the bunkhouses," Monique said airily. "Some of our men stay here too, but we keep this place mostly for... certain friends who may be passing through, or wish a safe place to stay for a few weeks."

Safe? My look must have been questioning, for she laughed.

"I can see that Mark has not told you anything. Perhaps he preferred that I should do so. I believe that Mark is still a little bit shy of you; isn't that silly?"

I agreed that it was. I was suddenly very cold, very clear-minded. And as we turned our horses back towards the house and Monique continued to talk, I began to understand everything. It would be left to Mark, when he returned late in the afternoon, to tell me the rest.

Forty-One

WAS THIS REALLY THE MAN I HAD THOUGHT OF AS "POOR Mark," and even, sometimes, "dear Mark"? I had begun to notice in him a certain resemblance to Todd. Mark was almost as tall; they had the same coloring. And he had thrown off his diffident air to become almost as arrogant, just as self-assured. The difference was that Mark was much more intelligent than Todd. He had reason and logic behind every action, whereas Todd had been more given to shouting and bluster.

Suddenly there was a rational explanation for all that puzzled me.

"Why did you have to pretend?" I asked Mark, and he gave me a twisted smile.

"Did I have a choice? You know what Uncle Todd is like. 'Overbearing' is the kindest way to describe him. I was his 'lawyer nephew' and he was contemptuous of that. After all, what had my father achieved besides being appointed a judge before he died? Todd Shannon—the illiterate rough-and-tumble fighter from Ireland—he had everything. Land. Money. Position. Power. Yes, you were right. I was supposed to be his lackey. Grateful for the fact that he had chosen me to be his heir, because there was no one else. I must give up my career, my friends, the civilized way of life. And all to come here and run his errands. Follow his orders. 'Yes, Uncle Todd' and 'No, Uncle Todd.' Do as you're told, Mark, even if it means staying away from the woman you love. As long as I had no choice, Rowena, I did as I was ordered to. And I learned. Just as you did once."

"As I did?"

We were in our bedroom, and Mark, with a sudden violence that took me by surprise, put his hands on my shoulders, his fingers gripping so hard that I heard the thin lawn of my sleeves rip.

"Yes! Did you think I didn't know what you were to Sir Edgar Cardon? I was in Paris, remember? He wasn't so discreet there. I knew you were his mistress. There was a certain very exclusive, very expensive house, on the outskirts of Paris—do you recall it? He took you there one night. I recognized you, in spite of the heavy veil that covered your face. I was there. I followed—just another curious guest. I saw everything that you saw. I couldn't see your reactions, but I could guess them! And I was more fascinated than I had been. More under your spell. Do you understand? A woman who can hide her emotions, who can still appear to be made of marble, who can use her head to her best advantage—do you wonder why I admired you so? Why I wanted you? You and I, Rowena. We will have everything. Remember when you said that we would be the builders? We will build our own empire."

"And Todd?" I was amazed that my voice sounded so matter of fact.

"You don't love him!" Mark laughed, drawing me closer to him. "And I think that by now you have reason to hate him, just as I have. He's trampled on other people too long, had his own way too long. He'll learn."

"Mark—I can hardly believe all this. Or the change in you. Do I really know you?"

"You will. And you're going to help me, just as Monique helps John."

"John Kingman is not an ordinary rancher, is he?"

I felt Mark's hands slide down my arm.

"You *know* that by now. Monique told you. John was run out of Texas. He fought for the South, and came back to find his ranch confiscated by carpetbaggers for nonpayment of taxes. It was an excuse that was used very often in those days. Can you blame him for being bitter?"

"So he became an outlaw."

"You can call it that. Until he met Monique. She was the brains behind this idea. An isolated ranch. A place where men on the run could hide out."

"Where stolen cattle can be driven, and rebranded, and sold in the big cow towns, where nobody asks many questions. Yes, I know. Monique told me. But you and I, Mark. Where do we enter into this?"

"You said 'we.'" Mark's eyes looked searchingly into mine and I returned his look with an unblinking, level glance of my own.

"I'm married to you. I think I have a right to know what we're involved in."

If I could not discern any emotion in my voice, then Mark could not either. I remember thinking, distantly, that it was easy to use my intelligence and to be *practical*—hated word!—when my emotions were not involved.

"You have every right, and you shall know! Rowena—my dearest wife—I knew that you would understand!"

I suffered Mark's crushing embrace, I made no protest when, his fingers shaking, he began to undo the buttons that ran down the front of my gown.

"I must tell you," I said to Mark as I stepped out of my dress and kicked it aside, "that I am not easy to arouse. I am your wife, and I will submit when you want to take me. But I'm not a whore, and I will not feign response if I feel none. Do you understand, Mark?"

In the dimness of the room his eyes looked fever-bright. "And Cord, whose name you cried out last night while I caressed your sleeping body. Did he arouse your slumbering passions?" I realized that I would have to tread very carefully as I looked into Mark's face, narrowing my eyes slightly.

"Are you jealous, Mark?"

"Answer me!"

"Well, then—" I chose my words deliberately. "At the beginning, yes. I didn't think we would live through the fury of that storm. I was so frightened that it was easy to be abandoned. And afterward... well, you know what happened. I think I was too cold to suit him."

"But you continued to want him—to dream about him. I must know the truth, Rowena!"

Mark's face was flushed as he pulled the chemise from my body with unusual roughness.

For the first time, since we had come here to talk, I let some emotion come into my voice. "Yes! Why not? No woman likes to feel rejected. It would have been different if I had been the one. If he came crawling to my feet then I would not want him. If you want a passionate creature as your wife, Mark, then you'll have to get used to the fact that I might someday desire another man." I saw the look on his face and forced a laugh. "My goodness! How Monique would laugh if she thought you were capable of jealousy! She's told me how understanding John is and how she loves him all the more for it. Must our marriage be governed by bourgeois morality?"

The one weapon I had against Mark was rationality. He prided himself upon his logic and his intellectual outlook.

Now I saw a baffled look come into his eyes as he gazed down at me. "You—expect me to allow you to take lovers?"

"I would be very discreet of course. And I would expect the same of you. Really, Mark, you've been begging me to understand, and now that I have accepted your philosophy, you don't seem too happy about it. Are we to be partners or not? If you wanted a meek, conventional wife, you should not have chosen me, especially since you know me so well."

"Suddenly you've changed, Rowena. You're no longer the lost, unhappy girl who turned to me for comfort."

"It was the shock to my system. I'm not used to being pregnant! But now I've had time to think and adjust myself, and I'm back to being the woman you fell in love with. Or was that a pretense on your part?"

"Don't say that, Rowena! You know how I've always admired your strength of character."

"Then you'll take me as I am?"

He was looking at my body, his hands reaching out to

touch me. "On any terms, my darling. Just as long as you're all mine in our bedroom. Just as long as you remember you're my wife, mine!"

There would be time later for self-hate. For disgust and revulsion at what I had submitted to. I think that only another woman would understand what I am speaking of. From the moment that Mark put his hands on me, drawing me before the mirror, I closed my mind to what was happening to me, seeing my body as someone else's, willing myself not to feel, not to think. I almost wished I had had an excess of champagne again, to dull my senses. The French have a word for a man like my husband. *Voyeur.*

I heard him whisper, "When we build our own home, there will be mirrors everywhere in our bedroom to reflect the perfection of your body. Silk sheets on the bed. And rose-shaded lamps. You will learn—I will teach you to surrender yourself to the pure pleasure of sensuality…"

I learned instead to dissemble. Mark's caresses did not arouse me, but I learned to accept them passively. Apparently satisfied with my complaisance, he grew more expansive regarding his plans—*ours* he called them—for the future.

I listened, frowning slightly. "But, Mark, why is the SD so important to you? I thought you missed your law practice in Boston, and civilization. You once talked of traveling in Europe."

"We can go to Europe later. And as for Boston—what could I ever hope to be but a lawyer, just another one of many? To be appointed a judge, perhaps, when I am old, just as my father was? Rowena, *this* is where the future of this country lies, this is the time to start building. Nowhere else in the world is there so much opportunity—acres and acres of land to be had for almost nothing. The SD is only the beginning, our foothold here. The nucleus around which we can build an empire as vast as that of Charlemagne. Do you think that certain other far-sighted men have not already recognized this? The old world is growing cramped. Why do you think that men like the Marquis of Mora, John Tunstall, yes, even your own father, have torn up their roots to plant new ones here? We will be the new aristocracy: It's time for men like my uncle who only know the use of fists and guns and think to keep what they have seized by brute force alone, to move aside."

"And how will you contrive to make them do so except by the use of guns and violence?" I retorted sharply. "You've often talked of respect for the law, Mark. How can you justify your own disregard for it?"

"My dearest, I do not disregard the law. I know the law. Believe me, everything we do will be perfectly legal! There will be no violence unless it is forced upon us—and in the end, we'll bring law and order into the territory, preparing it for statehood."

"And you, I suppose, will be our first senator."

"With you beside me as my wife." My sarcasm had no effect on Mark. He squeezed my hand lightly. "Trust me, Rowena."

Suddenly, I was remembering something that Jesus Montoya had once said. Something about ambition and money and power. And being able to corrupt the incorruptible with enough money... Money! Mark intended to buy his dreams with money. The thought that frightened me was that he might succeed.

I had become too clever to let him see how completely I opposed him. I sat with the others every evening and listened, with growing amazement and disbelief, to their carefully laid plans. John and Monique Kingman were very much involved too; Monique even more enthusiastic than her husband. I began to think of a well-thought-out military campaign.

Get rid of the "robber barons" first. Men like Shannon, who would hold back progress. Organize vigilance committees to keep the lawless elements out of the territory.

I raised an eyebrow at that, and Monique shook her head at me playfully. "I know what you are thinking! But we will all be respectable, law-abiding citizens by then."

"And until then?"

They expected me to ask questions. Mark was pleased that I had begun to take interest in his schemes. "A legal revolution," he called it.

And for all their talk of getting rid of the lawless element, it was this same element they planned to use in order to achieve their ends.

"But only the elite—the very best," Monique said, her eyes shining. "Professional gunmen who have been clever enough to stay on the right side of the law."

"An army of mercenaries?"

"Under disciplined leadership, of course," Mark put in. "And there are a few men we know of who already have their own, well-organized bands of men who will follow them and take orders—for a certain share of the profits, of course. We're not concerned with the fools, the criminals who kill for the sake of killing, or in the heat of rage. We want men who are self-disciplined, and who look ahead into the future."

Even John Kingman leaned forward in his chair to look at me, a slightly bitter note underlying his soft Texas drawl. "Every man dreams of being able to settle down some day. To have something of his own, to stop running. The constant taking of risks begins to pall, after a while."

Monique broke in: "Surely you can see it, Rowena? We will be offering those who throw in their lot with us the chance to begin a new life. To become respectable, yet with enough money to lead a good life."

"Rowena, you shall be our devil's advocate," Mark said teasingly. "What objections can you see now?"

"I seem to recall a Chinese proverb about riding a tiger," I said slowly.

"Give such men weapons and the license to kill—how do you know that when it's over they will stop, or that you will be able to continue to control them?"

It was Monique who shrugged airily.

"But who says there will be any killing? Only if it's necessary—and there will be enough for all. Why should we have to quarrel among each other like dogs?"

"I think the men we choose will have too much intelligence not to consider the advantages they are being offered against the disadvantages of attempting to be too greedy," Mark said, and I put forward no more arguments for the moment.

Days passed. I realized, without having to be told, that we

were not, after all, going to Boston. Another of Mark's clever ruses. He had meant to come here all along, but his uncle would believe that we were still journeying slowly across the continent. Clever, clever Mark. I was constantly discovering new facets to his nature. Difficult, now, to believe that I had ever dismissed him lightly as his uncle's errand boy; a weak, but good-natured young man, nothing out of the ordinary. I had seen only what he had meant me to see, of course. No, I must never underestimate Mark again, nor his infinite patience.

The strange thing was that I believed he actually loved me. I had become as much of an obsession with him as his dreams of power. It was not only the money that I had brought him; he really wanted me, and my approval of his plans.

Nevertheless I was careful. There were times when I was almost frightened, although I never let Mark see this. I was his wife, I submitted to his peculiar way of making love, and yet I held myself aloof. As I had warned him, I made no pretended response, but there were times when I wondered if my very coldness did not excite him more, as it had Sir Edgar.

"My lovely statue," he whispered. "Someday I will bring you to life!" But in the meantime he seemed content with the nightly proof that I was indeed his possession, to be touched and handled as he wished.

I began to feel myself sinking deeper and deeper into the depths of a nightmare from which there was no escape. For all the solicitude I was shown I was a prisoner here. I was never alone. If Mark and John Kingman left the ranch house together, as they often did, there was always Monique, the perfect hostess to keep me company. And in spite of all my outward calm and resolution, I had begun to feel that I was living on my nerve ends.

This, then was the state of affairs when, late one afternoon, I heard Monique call out that we had visitors.

Forty-Two

⤳

I HAD FALLEN INTO THE HABIT OF RESTING EACH AFTERNOON, just as Monique did. It provided me with an excuse to be alone for a little while, for Mark, if he was not out somewhere, would usually sit out on the trellised back porch with John Kingman, discussing business.

But on this particular afternoon Mark surprised me by coming quietly into the room, waking me out of the light doze I had fallen into. I must have sensed his presence. I opened my eyes to find him staring intently down at me.

"Why do you have to wear anything in bed? Only my eyes will ever see you here. Let me take it off for you, my darling."

He bent over me, already beginning to slip off the thin chemise I wore. With a sinking heart, I recognized the telltale flush on his face, the ardent note in his voice.

A little later he whispered, "I cannot imagine a pleasanter way to spend a long afternoon than making love to my beautiful wife."

I closed my eyes and willed the time to pass quickly, wondering how I could stand much more of this. And as if he meant to force me back to awareness, Mark began to kiss me.

It was with a feeling of reprieve that I heard Monique's voice; and then, a few minutes later, her tap at the door.

"Do hurry, you two lovebirds!"

Over my protests, Mark tossed aside my crumpled chemise

and began to hook me into the thin cotton gown I had worn that morning.

"Darling, you don't need to feel ashamed of your magnificent body! Why must you be so modest? Look at the way Monique dresses. Besides, these are old friends. There's no need to stand on ceremony."

I caught a glimpse of myself in the mirror as he hurried me outside. My face unnaturally flushed, my hair tumbled, my lips still bruised and slightly swollen from Mark's passionate kisses.

I told myself bitterly later on that I should have been warned by the strange, barely suppressed note of triumph in Mark's voice when he spoke of "old friends." For when we went out onto the porch, Mark's arm around my waist, the first person I saw was Lucas—and behind him Jesus Montoya, one eyebrow lifted as he surveyed my disheveled state, his mouth twisting in the same sardonic smile I remembered so well.

I couldn't say a word. And after that first glance I couldn't look in Lucas's direction again—not then. I was only too conscious of how I must look, standing there with Mark's arm holding me so possessively against his side. A pair of lovers, fresh out of bed. I think I might have fallen if Mark hadn't held me so tightly.

"It's a pleasure to see you again, of course," Montoya was saying in his smooth, silky-soft voice. "My congratulations to you both."

Lucas said nothing. And I—I wished that the earth would open up and swallow me.

I became aware that Montoya was staring at me curiously through heavy-lidded eyes.

"Thank you, señor. My wife and I are happy to see you," I heard Mark say, and my own voice, repeating through lips that seemed numb: "Thank you..."

As if we had all been posing stiffly for a photograph before, there was suddenly the bustle of movement all around me. I heard John Kingman's bluff drawl, Monique's prettily accented voice; and Mark was helping me into a chair, his fingers lingering possessively on my shoulders.

I remember thinking: I must be calm, I must be calm! This is some new trick of Mark's to make me give myself away... and I took a deep breath, trying to still the wild beating of my heart. "You see? I came as soon as I received your message. Jesus Montoya does not forget his old friends."

Did I imagine it, or had Montoya's coal-dark eyes flickered in my direction for just an instant?

"And we're sure glad to see you. I think you'll find your journey worthwhile after we've talked." John Kingman's voice held a significance I could not miss.

"Ah, that is what I had hoped! And Madame—" Montoya let his eyes linger openly on Monique, his gallantry as exaggerated as usual. "You grow lovelier each time I see you."

Monique's tinkling laugh had suddenly become jarring to my ears. Recklessly I glanced again at Lucas, and he was looking at her.

"What a flatterer you are, señor!" And then, her voice becoming almost caressing, "Lucas, you've hardly said a word yet. Surely you're not still angry with me?"

I felt as if I were watching a performance staged solely for my benefit, where everyone was aware of the plot except I.

Lucas shrugged, his eyes not leaving her flushed, laughing face. "Hard to stay angry with someone as pretty as you are. But don't pull no more tricks like you did the last time."

She pouted. "No, no—I promise! But you made such a magnificent gladiator! Such a fight!"

Kingman's laugh was almost complacent. "Monique should have been born in ancient Roman times. As Messalina! But she did promise me that she would try to behave."

So he knew her—he knew her! And from the looks they exchanged—hers a pouting moue meant to convey apology and his a half-smile that showed he forgave her—it was obvious they had known each other very well. I hated him; I hated her. I hated them all. And most of all, I was angry at myself for having shown all too clearly how shaken I was.

"So—" Montoya said suddenly, his voice almost a purr, "now that we are all here, and we all know each other..."

"Business after supper!" Monique said quickly, and John

added: "And drinks before, while we all get reacquainted. What do you say, Mark?"

I could not see Mark's face, for he stood behind me; but I felt his fingers tighten on my shoulders. It was the only sign he gave of whatever emotion was contained within him, for his voice sounded perfectly amiable.

"I think that's an excellent idea, although I seem to be the only person here who is not formally acquainted with—señor Montoya's friend."

Montoya said smoothly, "But there is no need to be formal among ourselves, is there? Lucas, amigo—you know Mr. Mark Shannon?"

I thought that Lucas took his eyes from Monique with an effort. His voice was curt. "We've seen each other. A long time ago."

"In Socorro, I believe. But as you say, that was a long time ago."

I would ask myself the questions afterward. I watched Lucas as if I had been starved for the sight of him and had only just recognized my hunger. He had let his whisker stubble grow out into a beard that somehow made him look older—and harder. But his eyes, and the easy grace with which he moved, were the same. And he had not yet looked at me fully and directly. Was it because he could no longer bear the sight of me?

It seemed as if everyone had started to speak at once. Monique was calling to one of the maids, patting the arm of the chair on which she sat invitingly. Jesus Montoya had already seated himself, and was talking to John Kingman.

Suddenly I rose to my feet. A trifle unsteadily, for Mark's hand caught my arm.

"I think I'll just go back to my room and freshen up before dinner. You'll excuse me?"

Every head was turned in my direction. If I wanted Lucas's attention I had it now. His narrowed eyes touched me for a moment, long enough for me to see the greenness in their depths. And then he had turned back to Monique, who was saying with false concern in her voice: "Rowena

hasn't been feeling well since she's been here. *Pauvre petite!*
It was all that traveling."

"I'll come with you, sweetheart," Mark said, his voice
overly solicitous. And I couldn't wait to turn my back on all
of them.

"Rowena, until you have faced him, and discovered what
he is, he would always remain a question in your mind. A raw
spot. Don't you understand why I had to do it? Montoya was
one of the men we'd had in mind in any case—I merely asked
that he bring Luke Cord with him."

"And what were you hoping for? That he would refuse?
That Montoya would bring him as a prisoner?"

Mark shrugged, but his blue eyes were very bright.

"That might have been a better way. But since he's
obviously here of his own accord, it only means one thing.
He's interested in the plunder. Or perhaps it's the thought
of revenge. Rowena," his voice sighed, "surely you can see
for yourself? Since he learned you are now my wife he's lost
interest in you. Monique is more his type. He could hardly
take his eyes off her."

"You said you hated him!" I couldn't leave it alone. My
voice accused Mark. "You know what happened. How can
you stand to talk business with him? Why him?"

"I'm a civilized man, Rowena, and he's a savage, but
perhaps he can be useful to us. And there's another reason I
wanted him here. You see, I love you. And I don't want Luke
Cord between us. I'm hoping that at last you'll have the opportunity to see him for what he is. A mercenary. An uncivilized
killer who would do anything for pay. And if I did not trust
in your good judgment in the end," Mark's voice hardened
almost unrecognizably, "I would have had him killed."

I turned away from him to the mirror, forcing myself
to concentrate on pinning my hair up. As if I had been a
cornered animal, with no other place to hide, my wits began
to come to my rescue at last.

"Well, it's done now." I lifted one bare shoulder as if I did
not particularly care. "It's just that I don't like to feel tricked,
Mark. And particularly by my husband."

I saw his blond head bend in the mirror, and felt the warm pressure of his lips on my neck. "My darling! Don't you understand?"

I pretended to consider this, and shrugged. "I suppose so. You're jealous. But you should have remembered what I told you before. The only reason why Lucas Cord continues to—intrigue me, if you will, is because he seemed to tire of me first. But if it were the other way around…"

"What are you trying to tell me?"

It was my turn to laugh teasingly. The laugh of a woman who is sure of herself and her charms.

"Since you have appointed yourself my lady's maid, Mark, why don't you help me choose one of my prettiest, most seductive gowns? Perhaps Monique will have some competition tonight… if you can be as understanding as John, that is!"

So now I found myself playing a dangerous game of pretense again. Like the spangle-costumed woman in a circus I had once watched, who walked a tightrope. It was almost a relief to find myself seated next to Montoya at supper that night, and listen to his flowery compliments.

There were only five of us, though, who sat down at the flower-decked table. When Montoya, immaculate in his silver-embroidered *charro* suit, had entered to bow gallantly over the ladies' hands he had said apologetically, "Lucas asked to be excused. He met an old friend, in the bunkhouse—one of your guests who is passing through. He said he would join us afterward."

Mark's quizzical glance met mine, and I could almost read his thoughts. "Obviously he's the kind of man who would be embarrassed at a formal meal such as this." But I was determined to make up for my earlier breach of the control I normally had over my reactions, and merely observed laughingly that I could not possibly miss anyone else when I had such a gallant cavalier at my side.

"No amount of gallantry could do justice to the beauty of the two ladies present. I find myself overwhelmed."

Monique and I exchanged glances, both faintly appraising. She had decided to dress for dinner too, in a low-cut green silk gown that showed her figure off and exposed her gleaming, milky-white arms and shoulders. The emerald eardrops she wore flashed each time she turned her head, or laughed, and her auburn hair shone with a rich fire of its own in the candlelight.

I wore the midnight blue velvet I had not worn since the night of Todd Shannon's grand party, and I couldn't help wondering if Mark had chosen that particular gown on purpose, to remind me… of what? How mistaken I had been in my reading of his character that night?

"You are the loveliest creature in the world," he had whispered as he helped to pin the diamond stars in my hair. But I had wanted Lucas to see me—I had wanted him to realize what he had lost. Never mind, I told myself; he will be here later. And then we'll see. I was in a strange mood, my nerves like fine-strung wires that might snap at any moment. I would not be anybody's "poor Rowena" tonight! Mark could not deal me any worse surprises than he had already, and no—not even the coldness of Lucas's eyes when he looked at me could shake my poise.

I was like a gambler who had nothing left to lose and could afford to laugh recklessly as the wheel spun for the last time. I was the same woman who had been her stepfather's mistress and Todd Shannon's betrothed. The marble goddess with no heart. As cold and as calculating as I had ever been accused of being. For sometime during the past two hours I had made up my mind.

It was strange that I had thought of myself as a gambler. For after the dishes had been cleared away and Lucas had joined us, with a cursory apology for his lateness, that is exactly what we did.

It was Monique's idea. She had sat at the piano for a while, until Lucas made his appearance, and then she got up, clapping her hands together.

"Oh, but we're far too stiff! The night is young, and the brandy, thanks to Mark, is excellent. You men shall not leave us to smoke your cigars outside. We shall play cards. Poker, I think. It's my favorite game, next to roulette. Rowena… do you know it?"

I caught her mood and smiled. Lucas had paid no attention to me, but he would, he would! I would make sure of it.

"It was one of my grandfather's few vices, although he would only indulge in a game with his few close cronies. Even while he taught it to me he didn't fail to remind me of one of our ancestors, a Regency rake, who lost the family fortune on the turn of a card."

"But how exciting! This ancestor—he sounds like a man after my heart. And you, Rowena, are you fond of gambling too?"

I thought her words had a hidden meaning, which I pretended not to notice for the moment.

"Occasionally. Isn't everybody who is in the least bit adventurous?"

"It seems as if these females have us outnumbered," John Kingman grumbled as he rose to get the deck of cards. I saw Mark look at me thoughtfully, and Montoya's eyes, hidden behind a thin veil of cigar smoke, looked opaque and shiny.

For the first time that evening I spoke directly to Lucas, my voice challenging. "And you—you haven't said anything. Perhaps you're a poor loser?"

"Everybody loses some time or other. But I've never been afraid of taking a chance." His eyes, meeting mine for an instant, told me nothing. But his words—had they been meant to convey something to me?

Before I had time to ponder, Monique was declaring delightedly that this was going to be such fun. And the men could talk business while we played.

"But first we shall create an atmosphere that is deliciously sordid, just like the saloons you men like to frequent." She flung a green baize cloth across the table, and lowered all the lamps in the room but the one directly above. "There! Is that not more like it?"

"We'd hardly be sitting down in some gambling saloon with two grand ladies like Rowena and yourself, my love," John Kingman said mildly. I thought his eyes asked a question of his wife, but she, smiling wickedly, shook her head so that the long eardrops danced above her shoulders.

"Ah non! But do you forget so easily? In New Orleans, where you met me, there were always pretty women at the tables, to encourage the men to bet high. Remember the Silver Slipper?"

I saw their eyes meet, and it was almost as if, for a moment, they were alone in the room.

"It's not something I can forget…" John Kingman said quietly. "You lost to me—everything, you remember? Down to your own silver slippers. And you left with me that night."

"I always pay my gambling debts!" She laughed, shuffling the cards expertly so that they seemed to flow through her long, be ringed fingers. "And I have never regretted losing that night. But tonight…" and her voice became light, teasing, "what shall be the stakes we play for tonight?"

"Why not… ourselves?" Jesus Montoya's voice was deceptively soft; he shrugged as our eyes turned to him. "Why not?" he repeated, and leaned forward across the table as he looked at Monique. "You want us to play a game, si? And this is why we are all here tonight, to make plans for another kind of game, just as much of a gamble. So I suggest to you that the only reason for taking risks is if the stakes are high enough to make it—shall we say—interesting?" He gave his short, almost soundless laugh. "It is not as if we were strangers to each other—but if we are to be partners in an enterprise where both the risks and the rewards are great, what better way to find out how much we are prepared to risk—who are the daring, and who are the cowards? I propose that we play this game, each against the other, and for whatever we have on our persons, including our services, of course."

I tried to keep all expression from my face as I looked around at the other faces in the short silence that followed.

Monique's eyes gleamed with a strangely lambent fire, and she breathed more quickly. Her husband looked thoughtful, but in no way dismayed. Mark, his face more than usually flushed, drained his glass at a gulp, as if it had been water and not brandy he was drinking.

Lucas was frowning, and I thought for a moment that he was going to protest, but the next moment, catching

Montoya's slightly amused stare, his lips tightened and he
kept silent.

It was Monique to whom Montoya had directed his
suggestion, and Monique who answered for us all, her voice
strangely breathless.

"Yes! I say yes! I may be a woman, but I have never been
a coward. And if you lose, Jesus, you will work with us
for nothing?"

"That would depend on how heavily I lose—if I lose—
wouldn't it?" His lips smiled thinly under his dark moustache.
"And if I win—more than you have to offer as you sit there—
then, of course, my fee would be doubled." His hooded eyes
looked around the table. "It is agreed? In this game, there are
no husbands and wives, or friends. We play for ourselves, each
one of us, and the winner names his or her price."

Forty-Three

❧

Perhaps it was the brandy I had consumed so recklessly that evening, but I remember having the oddest feeling that this had all happened before. The French call it déjà vu. Everything seemed familiar, and in some way foreordained.

The polished brass chandelier cast a bright glow over the green baize that covered the table, and the intent faces of the players seemed shadowed. I remembered that my father had killed a man over a game of poker, and that my reckless ancestor, the Black Earl, as they had called him, had shot himself later after realizing the extent of his losses. And did Lucas remember what had happened with Flo, or was his mind too occupied with Monique's nearness?

I was surprisingly clear-headed as I studied my cards, and the faces of the others. It was one of the things my grandfather had taught me. I could almost hear his voice.

"Always watch their faces, granddaughter. Tell you everything. There isn't a poker player in the world that doesn't show some kind of sign, even a too-blank look."

But in this case, there was nothing that I could read in any of the varying expressions around the table. Not yet…

With a little laugh that betrayed her barely suppressed excitement, Monique dropped one of her rings onto the table.

"There—" she said. "That's for openers."

The game that had seemed a kind of joke only a little while before had begun in earnest. Time passed, the atmosphere grew heavy with cigar smoke and tension. I was able, at last, to recognize a kind of pattern in the way each person played, although at first the cards seemed evenly divided.

Lucas was overly cautious, while Monique played recklessly. John Kingman never bluffed. Montoya was completely unpredictable. It was Mark, sitting next to me, who seemed nervous. A few times, I saw his hands actually shake. But it was Lucas I watched most closely, from behind the convenient screen of my lashes.

He had deliberately avoided glancing in my direction all evening, but now, as all talk of "business" had become more desultory and finally died away into the silence of concentration, I forced him to notice me at last.

When I saw that the cards were running in my favor I began to play with luck quite ruthlessly. Montoya saw what I was doing and knew why—once or twice I caught his black eyes on me, bright with a half-hidden gleam of mockery. As for the others, I saw them begin to look at me with expressions that mirrored varying degrees of surprise and respect. The diamond stars I wore in my hair gave me an advantage over them all, and I wasn't afraid to use it. As I began to win consistently I forced the bidding up higher, and even Monique began to frown over her cards.

"Your wife's quite a poker player," John Kingman said to Mark as he threw in his hand.

"So I have discovered." Mark's voice was deliberately expressionless, making me wonder whether he suspected what I was about. I said lightly, "It's only beginner's luck. I feel that I cannot lose tonight!" and he followed Mr. Kingman's example, tossing his cards onto the center of the table with a shrug.

Monique was biting her lip, looking from my face to the cards she held. Her hand went up unconsciously to touch her one remaining eardrop. And then, saying petulantly, "You're too lucky this evening!" she too threw in her hand. I looked at Montoya, who lifted his shoulder expressively. "As Monique says, you are too lucky. And me, I have always been a cautious man." But I thought I saw a half-smile lift the corner of his mouth, as if he wished to convey to me silently that he knew very well what I planned.

For now, only Lucas and I remained in the game, and because he had played carefully and conservatively his pile of winnings almost equaled mine. But I had lost only one diamond star, and that to him—and there were nine more pinned among the coils of my hair.

"And you?"

This time he met my eyes, and I saw the green lights flicker in his.

"I think you're bluffing."

I laughed, and pushed everything I had won into the center.

"Then prove it—if you dare."

He saw how I had trapped him, and his face grew stony.

"Don't have anything more to bet."

They were all silent now, watching us. I thought I heard Mark's indrawn breath beside me, but I did not take my eyes from Lucas's face.

"Your gun. That must be worth something."

His lips tightened, but he drew it from his holster and put it on the table before him.

I pretended to consider it thoughtfully, and Mark said tightly, "You're still about five hundred dollars short. Why, those emeralds and that diamond ring alone are worth more than a thousand dollars!"

"But Mark's right, of course," I said sweetly. "Let me see—I hate to be unfair, especially when I have been challenged." I looked appealingly at Montoya, who sat regarding me with his twisted, sardonic smile. "What do you think, señor? You set the rules for this game. And you did say 'services,' did you not?" He inclined his head, and I turned back to Lucas, who was watching me narrowly. "Then I will name the stakes, and if you are not afraid of having your bluff called you may accent my proposal—or lose everything you have won this evening."

I thought that Monique clapped her hands together softly as she murmured "Bravo, Rowena!" The sun wrinkles deepened about Lucas's eyes and he said tightly: "Name them!"

"Well," I said softly, "if you win I will throw in another

one of my diamonds. You heard my husband say how much they are worth. But if you lose—you came here to listen to a business proposition, did you not? If you lose, you will work for me and follow my orders. You've already staked your gun. I'll buy it. At top wages, until you've paid off your debt."

It was Mark, I think, who tipped the scales when he laughed. "By God! Rowena, I'm proud of you!"

I looked questioningly at Lucas, and he said, his voice almost savage, "Done! All right—I'm calling you."

Smiling, I put down three aces, and then, after a pause, two queens.

I thought his face whitened with fury, but I couldn't be sure. There was a concerted sigh as he put his hand face up on the table almost indifferently.

"Three kings!" Jesus Montoya murmured. "A pity. But you should never bet against a woman who is sure of herself, amigo. I could have told you that before."

"Then why the hell didn't you? Before you dealt that hand?"

"Amigo!" Montoya's voice was reproachful. "If I didn't know you better I might think you were accusing me of cheating."

"I think your friend is a bad loser. Perhaps he does not care to have the tables turned."

It was the first time that Mark had referred openly to the past, and seeing the dangerous look in Lucas's narrowed eyes I said quickly: "Why do men always hate losing to women? I just felt lucky this evening."

Careless of my low-cut gown, I leaned forward, pulling my winnings toward me. The gun I pushed back at Lucas.

"If you're to work for me, you'll need that."

For an instant when our eyes met, I felt myself swept back in time. And then, as if the tension had been too much to bear, everyone began to speak at once.

I didn't realize I had been holding my breath, until I released it in a long sigh that, fortunately, went unnoticed.

Without looking at me again Lucas picked up the gun. John Kingman was pouring more brandy into our glasses, and Monique said softly, her green eyes glittering, "I have not decided yet, Rowena, if you are very lucky or very clever."

"My dear," John Kingman raised his glass, toasting me, "I think Mrs. Shannon possesses both advantages."

The cigar smoke had begun to sting my eyes; and perhaps the brandy, combined with the headier wine of success, had gone to my head slightly.

"Thank you," I said to Mr. Kingman, and then, draining my glass defiantly, I rose to my feet. "Perhaps I'm of a mind to find out if you are right."

Mark had also risen automatically, pulling back my chair, and I smiled at him sweetly. "May I have my shawl, please? Suddenly I find it very close in here, and if you'll excuse me, I think I would like to take a walk outside." I turned abruptly to Lucas. "Would you act as my escort? I'm sure the others would like to continue playing—or perhaps discuss the business that we've so sadly neglected."

The surprising thing was that no one, not even Mark, whom I had taken by surprise, raised a voice to stop me. I heard Monique's high, tinkling laugh behind me as she said poutingly, "Lucky Rowena! Now she had a bodyguard to escort her wherever she pleases to go!"

And Montoya's smooth voice murmuring, "There's no need to look so angry, amigo! It was a fair contest, and the lady won. You will not embarrass your old friends by appearing ungallant, would you?"

I did not expect Mark to follow me. The laughing comments of the others and his own pride would not allow him to do so. And I did not deign to turn my head, as I walked outside, to see if Lucas followed me or not. I only knew he had done so when I heard the outer door slam shut behind him. Still without looking around I walked to the edge of the porch, leaning my elbows on the wooden railing that ran its length. "I do hope you're not so poor-spirited a loser as to continue acting so sullen and fierce, especially when it was all your fault for accusing me of bluffing."

In spite of the somewhat sarcastic tone I had adopted, I could not repress the nervous shiver that ran up my spine when Lucas came up silently beside me, casually leaning his back against the railing. I told myself that this time I would remain calm. I would show him that his nearness could not affect me any longer.

"I should have guessed it. You're real good at playing games—always were."

His husky voice was deceptively soft, but I could sense the bitter anger behind his words as I turned my head to look at him directly.

"As I recall..." and this time I could not prevent my voice from shaking slightly, "you are the one who excels at—playing games, as you call it!" I went on recklessly, determined to have my say before my newly found self-confidence faltered: "Why did you come here after promising to stay out of my life? Was it the thought of the profits you think to gain from this crazy scheme? Or was it the notion that you will at last have the chance to be revenged on Todd Shannon? But I forget—you don't like to give explanations for your actions, do you? Perhaps you have none that will not incriminate you!"

"You've always thought the worst of me, so what the hell difference does it make? You're giving the orders now, Mrs. Shannon. Maybe you should tell me what you had in mind."

It was impossible to read any expression in his hard, beard-shadowed face. Against my will, I found myself wondering, does he hate me? Do I really mean nothing at all to him? And then—is there always to be a wall of lies and pretense between us?

I hardly knew what I said, or why. Perhaps I only put my thoughts into words. I heard myself say, in a clear, cold voice, "To begin with, I think you ought to kiss me."

"You comparin' notes already, Mrs. Shannon? On your honeymoon? From what I could see this afternoon, your husband takes damn good care of you. Or did you want to find out if he's capable of feelin' jealous?"

"Is that what you're afraid of? You shouldn't be. Mark's a very understanding husband, and after all, if I could understand your feelings for Elena..."

I put my arms around his neck, and it was like that afternoon when we had kissed for the first time, and only Elena was between us. I could almost feel my fingers throbbing with pain again as they touched the soft thickness of his hair. I remembered how he had called me a witch, even while his lips were claiming mine; unwillingly, almost despairingly.

And suddenly, I felt time fall away. Like the breaking of an iron band that had kept all my real feelings locked within myself, like a river bursting its banks in flood. How could I have forgotten? How could I have pretended to myself for so long?

There are times when words are unnecessary, when the body knows truer than the mind. And Lucas, when he kissed me now, was no more capable of holding back than I. If they had all come out onto the porch at that moment, we could not have broken away from each other. I had forgotten that they existed—had forgotten Mark, had forgotten all the doubts that had tortured me for so long.

"For God's sake, Ro… Why?" His whisper was both angry and agonized. "You and Mark Shannon! When Marta told me I was crazy-mad enough to kill you both! That damned interfering old woman—she had it in her mind it was all my fault. An' maybe it was, for not tellin' you straight off why I'd come. But damn you, Ro, when you started flinging all those crazy words at me…"

"You went back? To see me?"

"Oh, Christ! A woman always knows when she's got a man so mixed up in his mind he can't even think straight! You knew that, and you… how long did you think I could stay away from you?" He put his hand at the back of my neck, forcing me to look up at him, and his voice held a bitter accusation that made me flinch. "You couldn't even bring yourself to tell me you were carrying my child, and yet you found it easy to turn to him!"

"Lucas, don't! Please! If you only knew…"

"All I know is what you've told me! Damn it—what do you expect me to think? Seeing you with him, watching the way you acted tonight. Ro, I don't know what kind of game you're playing this time, but I ain't good at pretending, not the way you are."

I couldn't bear to hear any more. I set my mouth against his, standing on tiptoe, and heard him make a half-smothered sound that was almost a groan as his fingers closed painfully on my arms, pulling me up against him with a violence that drove the breath from my body.

"Do you still think I'm pretending?" I asked at last in a shaky whisper.

Lucas dropped his hands from my arms, moving a little distance away, as if he didn't trust himself too close to me. I thought I heard him sigh.

"Christ, I don't know! You're such a damned unpredictable woman, Ro. I never have known what to make of you, or what you wanted of me." He had begun to roll a cigarette, each movement swift and impatient. For a moment, as the match flared, I saw the familiar green fires come to life in his eyes. "An' I still ain't certain..." he went on in the same deliberately expressionless voice, just as if he had not paused.

In the sudden silence between us I heard Monique's high laugh from inside the house.

"Then that makes two of us." I couldn't keep the slight breathlessness from my voice. "Lucas, don't you see?"

"I can see that it's time you went back inside, before your husband starts wondering what you're doin' out here for so long, with the hired help."

Why did he have to remind me of Mark? I bit my lip, trying to keep my voice as even as his.

"But we have to talk. Please, Lucas!"

He shrugged. "Sure. You're the boss." In the faint glow of his cigarette his face looked bleak and withdrawn. It was almost as if he was determined, after what had just taken place, to put a distance between us. And I was equally determined not to let it happen again.

"When?" I persisted, and saw his brows draw together.

"Tomorrow maybe. I'll think of something."

Something in his voice warned me not to press him any further, and yet I was not content to leave things as they were. I wanted reassurance. Before I was forced to go back indoors to the man who was my husband, I wanted, once more, to feel of my lover's kiss on my lips.

I saw him send the half-smoked cigarette arcing away into the darkness and put my hand up, tracing the outline of his mouth with my fingers.

"Lucas."

With a fury that startled me he caught my wrist, forcing it down.

"Don't!" I had the impression he spoke through clenched teeth. "Go back in the house now, Rowena. I've had just about all I can take for one night—what the hell are you trying to do?"

He was still holding my wrist, fingers gripping it so hard I thought it must surely snap. But I almost welcomed the pain, because he was inflicting it, and I knew why.

"Do you think I want to go back in there? Oh, God, Lucas, will we ever stop hurting each other? I'm not pretending—I never have, with you. It's only been my pride that's made me try to hate you. Even to hurt you, if I could, because you hurt me. You see, I haven't loved a man before, I haven't been prepared."

"Don't, Ro." But this time his voice was a husky whisper, no longer harsh as it had been a moment ago. "You didn't have to tell me that, I guess I always knew it, and yet I— Christ, if you only knew how mixed up I've been! But tomorrow…" He kissed me then, without another word, his kiss at once gentle and angry, tender and cruel. And when he released me, he said roughly, "There! Take that back with you to your bedroom tonight!"

It seemed that it was only seconds later, as I still stood there with one hand on the railing to support myself, that I found myself listening to the sound of retreating hoofbeats; Lucas's words still echoing in my ears.

I had to go inside.

Straightening my shoulders, I pulled the shawl closely about myself as if to ward off the chill I felt gathering in me like a cold hand closing about my heart. Without giving myself any more time to think, I pushed open the door and the heat and the cigar smoke hit me like a blow in the face. And I told myself that if I had never acted before, I would act now, and deceive them all.

Four pairs of eyes turned to watch me as I walked slowly into the center of the room. Monique's slanted green gaze—amused, and somehow knowing at the same time. Montoya's dark, glittering stare, over his twisted, cynical smile. John Kingman's eyes told me nothing. Mark…

I let the shawl slip to the floor with a careless shrug of my shoulders, smiling at them all.

"My goodness! Are you still talking business?" I sat down in the chair that Mark held stiffly for me and picked up the fan I had left on the table, beginning to fan myself languidly. "It's so hot in here, after the cool air outside."

"Did you walk far?" Mark sounded as if the words had been forced from his throat. I met his eyes, and they seemed unusually bright.

I raised my shoulders negligently, almost glad that the role I had chosen to play kept my thoughts occupied and concentrated. "Oh, we stayed on the porch in the end, and talked. I didn't care to ruin my slippers in the dust."

I looked around at them all, my eyebrows raised. "Why is everyone so silent? Mark…" and this time I looked directly into his eyes, noticing his flushed, almost sullen face. "You didn't mind, did you? After what we had talked about, I knew that you would understand."

Montoya interposed smoothly, "I think we were all rather worried because my headstrong friend does not take kindly to following orders. And especially those given by a woman. But I was sure, señora Rowena, that you would not find it difficult to persuade him otherwise."

I shrugged, as if I had dismissed an unpleasant subject "We argued a great deal, of course. But at least I made him admit that he had lost fairly. I believe that when he is over feeling angry he will keep his word."

Monique's laugh broke the slight tension that had seized us all. "There! Didn't I tell you? 'Rowena is quite capable of holding her own,' I told these silly men. And you see,

I was right." Her eyes caught mine in what was almost a conspiratorial look. "And now that you are back, *cherie,* and quite unharmed, shall we retire? I think we will have a long day ahead of us."

Forty-Four

❧

I DO NOT CHOOSE TO DWELL TOO CLOSELY ON THE REST OF that night. Once we had left the others, Mark's indifferent attitude changed to one of anger and jealousy. The only way I could calm him was to affect an air of arrogance.

"For heaven's sake Mark! Don't act so—so middle class. Surely you remember that I married you of my own free will?"

He had drunk too much brandy, and swayed slightly on his feet, the flush on his face more apparent than ever.

"Yes, by God! I remember that. But do you? Does he?"

"You brought him here, Mark. Pray, do not spoil the effect of your clever idea with a display of jealousy." I pouted deliberately. "Surely you trust me? I am already beginning to see him through your eyes, now you must allow me the opportunity you promised—of bringing him to heel. Perhaps I might even be able to persuade him to admit to a few of the crimes he has committed."

"Rowena, Rowena! If I thought…"

Mark's hands tightened on my shoulders, but I continued to remove the diamond stars from my hair, wrapping each one carefully in tissue paper before I put them away in the chamois leather bag I kept them in.

"If you're afraid of him, Mark, then why don't you send him away? Tell him we've changed our minds, that his services are no longer needed."

My purposely indifferent tone had the effect wanted.

"Damnation! Of course I'm not afraid of him! An illiterate, half-breed gunman, with barely enough intelligence to follow orders… and you'll see that for yourself too, soon enough!" Mark began unhooking my gown, and his voice became almost feverish. "Yes—we'll use him, and the blind hate he has for my uncle—his own killer instincts. And he won't even guess it! When Lucas Cord is the one to kill Todd Shannon there won't be a person in the whole territory who won't think it was done out of revenge. And in his turn, he'll die for it! There'll be no more reminders, nothing left to come between us. And it will happen soon—very soon, my darling." Mark laughed triumphantly. He went on, his words slightly slurred, "I think that you must be the one to suggest it to him. After all, he gave his word that he would follow your orders. And I will arrange for just the right opportunity. Nothing will go wrong this time! Don't you see the subtle irony of it all?"

This time, Mark had said. What had he meant? Was it possible that… but no, I must not start thinking along those lines yet. I still had a part to play. It was all I could do to control my expression, to force a faint smile as I met his bloodshot eyes in the mirror.

"You're even cleverer than I had already suspected, Mark. But when is all this to happen?"

"Soon." He mumbled the word, and I realized, with a feeling of relief, that he was more inebriated than I had thought. He swayed against me as he bent his head to kiss my bare shoulder, and it was all I could do not to shudder.

"Soon," he repeated, his hands cupping my breasts. "There's no reason to wait any longer! We'll leave here very early in the morning, the day after tomorrow. You're well enough now to travel, aren't you?"

Fortunately for my state of mind, the most I had to suffer that night was a few drunken caresses. It was not difficult to persuade Mark that it was my turn to undress him tonight, if he would only help me by lying down, and no sooner had he done so than he fell into a drunken stupor. I took off his boots, and let him continue to sleep as he was, lying as far away from him as possible when I finally went to bed myself. But before

I turned out the lamp, I could not help turning to look at Mark's sleeping face. How handsome and almost boyish he looked, in spite of his flushed cheeks and slack mouth. Was it possible that this was the same man I had once thought of as my dearest friend? Had I really pitied him, and blamed myself for using him?

But how clever Mark had been, how infinitely patient! I had begun to trust him completely, until one by one his lies and deceptions had been revealed—with a logical explanation for each one. And my mind had accepted what was presented to me as evidence. I had despised my instincts, disdained the pull of my emotions. Oh, God, why? Because Lucas was no lawyer, and had been too stubborn to answer to my accusations with excuses and "reasonable" explanations? How easy and how convenient to blame a man already branded an outlaw and a murderer with other crimes. And Mark—it came to me suddenly that all along it had been Mark who had subtly, certainly pointed out to me all the evidence that supposedly showed Lucas's guilt. Yes, and it had been Mark too, in just as subtle a way, who had contrived to make me see his uncle as a selfish, domineering man, even while he pretended to defend him. How could I have been so blind? Why had I let myself be trapped?

I didn't have to feign the headache I used as an excuse to lie abed late the next morning. I had only to study my face in the mirror later to see how pale it looked, with the dark smudges under my eyes testifying to the sleepless night I had spent. I grimaced at my reflection as I began to pin my hair up with slow, lethargic movements. I was becoming an accomplished actress. This morning I had put off Mark's expressed concern by snapping irritably that he had kept me awake half the night with his tossing and turning, and he had left me with an apology, announcing that he had promised to ride out with John Kingman to see to arrangements for our journey the next day.

No, I had not felt ready to face Mark yet; I was relieved that I would be spared his presence until later in the afternoon. I was beginning, slowly and painfully, to realize the full extent of the folly I had committed in marrying Mark. I was Mrs. Mark Shannon. I had given up not only my name, but my freedom as well. And what on earth are you going to do now? My pale reflection gave me back no answers. I might almost have been looking at a stranger's face that was far too thin, a haunted expression in the eyes.

The cheerful maid who was dusting the living room told me that Monique was out on the sun porch, where she could usually be found at this time of the day, a pitcher of iced tea beside her. "I'm lazy!" Monique admitted cheerfully. "I would like nothing better than to lie out here all day and sleep…"

But this morning, in spite of the oppressive heat, she was certainly not sleeping. I heard her gay laughter as I pushed open the door and stepped out onto the porch, my eyes blinking as they accustomed themselves to the sunlight.

Monique was not alone; clad in a cream silk shirt and a tightly fitting pair of leather riding breeches, she was perched on the wooden railing, one leg swinging as she smiled into the face of her companion. And he—did he have to be sitting so close to her that their shoulders touched? Before they noticed me I had time to observe that Lucas had shaved off his beard and trimmed his hair, leaving thick sideburns that came almost to his jawline. I could see the cleft in his cheek deepen as he smiled at something Monique had said. He looked younger and more carefree than I had ever seen him, his checked cotton shirt open at the neck to reveal a carelessly knotted blue bandanna, and I was shaken by a rush of love and desire that left me weak.

The next moment, when Monique put her hand on his arm, I was ragingly jealous. Now I understood how some women could threaten to scratch a rival's eyes out. I would dearly have liked to rake my nails down the smooth skin of Monique's face!

I deliberately let the door bang shut behind me, and was glad that the sound made Monique start. "Oh, Rowena! I didn't think you'd be awake so early! Have you eaten anything yet? Would you care for a glass of iced tea?"

Lucas, his eyes crinkling at the corners, had come to his

feet with an easy, casual movement, and the angry thought flashed through my mind, as he put his hands on either side of Monique's waist to help her down, that he had learned some manners somewhere after all, even if he had never bothered to show me such consideration!

He had been smiling at Monique. Why did his eyes have to take on such a guarded look as soon as he looked at me? Even his husky voice held a slight trace of mockery as he acknowledged my presence. "Mornin'... ma'am."

"Good morning," I said coldly, and saw Monique's eyes flash from one to the other of us with a wickedly amused expression.

"Lucas, *mon cher,* will you bring a chair for Rowena? Oui, that one, by the door. Sitting on that railing would ruin her pretty gown." The subtly caressing tone in which she spoke irritated me almost as much as Lucas's exaggerated politeness did. I found myself gritting my teeth when Lucas obeyed her without a murmur, without even offering to lift me up to sit on the wide railing as they had done.

Just as if she had not noticed my silence, Monique continued chattering unconcernedly.

"We have already been riding, Lucas and I. But it became far too hot, and I have so much to do, to prepare for our journey tomorrow." She gave me an inquiring look. "Did Mark tell you?"

I tried not to notice that Lucas had resumed his original seat on the railing, his back against one of the wooden roof supports, one foot on the floor for balance.

"Only that we will be leaving tomorrow." I wanted suddenly to go to Lucas and run my fingers through his thick, dark hair—making him notice me, making him want me. He was bareheaded, the sun turning his hair bronze and gold. And when his face did not look sullen or angry, and he smiled, I could understand why so many other women, even Monique, had wanted him. With an effort, I took my mind back to what Monique was saying.

"...but how like a man! They never tell us anything. Of course I am *desolée* that John will have to stay behind, but perhaps such a long journey might have its consolations too, do you not agree?" She looked directly at Lucas, the glow in her green eyes almost predatory. How could any man not keep his eyes on her vivid, openly inviting beauty? Her auburn hair glowed richly, with a fire of its own; and as usual, it was obvious she had worn nothing under the thin blouse, with far too many buttons undone.

I said abruptly, "Where are we going?" and they both looked at me.

Again it was Monique who answered. "We should make camp just outside San Antonio tomorrow night. A very small and dusty town, not far from Socorro." Did I only imagine it, or did she glance obliquely and somehow significantly at Lucas again? "And after that," she went on, "we will have to cross the desert for a while, until we arrive at a certain place, close to Carizozo, where Montoya will meet us with the rest of his men. From there... but you know the rest, Rowena. You've listened to all our plans." With a laugh, she stretched her arms over her head. "Rowena doesn't think we will succeed. Perhaps, Lucas, you can convince her that we cannot fail!"

I could hardly believe that she intended to leave me alone with Lucas, after the bold way she had been flirting with him, but she did.

"I have much packing to do. And if I leave you two alone for a short time, you would not mind too much, I think?"

Meeting Lucas's eyes, I was hardly aware when the door closed behind her, or which of us moved first. I forgot that only minutes before I had been jealous. His arms held me, I felt his lips against my temple, and I no longer resisted the instincts I had once decried as wanton. I slipped my hands under his shirt, and felt the muscles of his back move under my fingers. I heard myself say, "I wanted to kill Monique. And you too. I must be going mad."

"How do you think I felt last night, knowin' you were going to lie with him?"

I tilted my head back, looking into his face.

"Lucas—what are we going to do?"

His arms tightened, almost cutting my breath off.

"If you're sure, woman, you know I ain't got nothing to

offer you. You know what I am, an' how it's going to be. Running and hiding, maybe for all our lives. But, God, I want you, Ro. I've tried to fight it, I've tried to tell myself you're better off this way."

"And I—do you think a woman is not capable of wanting as hard and as strongly as a man? I've always known I've wanted you. If I have nothing else, it's you I need. I want to be where you are, lie in your arms at night, bear your children—do you think anything else matters to me?"

He laughed softly, but this time it was not the bitter, cynical laughter of a man who had learned to trust in nothing and no one.

"I think you're crazy. Just like I am for even askin' you to leave everything and run off with me. Maybe you'll change your mind, once you've found out how it feels. But if you come, I don't think I'm goin' to let you go again." His face suddenly hard, he looked down at me. "Ro—you're sure? Sure you trust me enough?"

"I love you. Isn't that enough?"

"Then sit up here an' stop distracting me. There's a few things you have to know first."

The railing was sun-warm beneath me, and wide. But Lucas kept his arm around my waist while he spoke, his voice carefully emotionless.

"You might change your mind," Lucas said again. "After you talk with Bragg." He must have felt my stiffening, for I thought I felt the muscles in his arm become taut. "He's going to be at Fort Selden. He wanted me to bring you there, so he could explain things. That's what he said, anyhow. You know how he is, Ro, as well as I. Won't tell any more than he has to. Wasted part of the time I did hunting him up. You put questions in my mind, darn you! And Ro—you better know this—before I talked to him I had it all set in my mind I was goin' to leave you be; that you'd done what you always wanted to do, marry one of your own kind. But then he started hinting about Mark Shannon. 'There are some men who are clever enough to plant seeds… and wait for them to take root,' he said. 'The patient ones are the most dangerous.' But right up until the time I saw your eyes an' the sleep-walkin' look on your face, I wasn't sure. Ain't rightly sure now."

"And I—I've been sure for a long time. I've had time to learn... a lot of things."

Even now, I could not bring myself to talk about Mark. I had married him, and the reasons I had used to convince myself seemed weak and senseless now. But Lucas had looked for Elmer Bragg—had found him. But why, of all places, Fort Selden?

It was a question I was to ask myself many times during the long journey to San Antonio. Lucas knew no more than I of Mr. Bragg's motives. He was only able to tell me that Elmer Bragg had recovered from his coma after he had been left for dead, and that the use of his legs had been impaired, so that he was obliged to use a wheelchair, or two canes. But his infirmity had impaired neither his curiosity nor his determination to search out facts. And now he wanted to see me, but I must come to him—and at Fort Selden.

I had tried to protest that it was too dangerous; that there would be time later to get in touch with Elmer Bragg. I was relieved that he was alive, after all; but at the same time I wanted only to go as far away from New Mexico Territory as I could—with Lucas. For him to attempt to take me to Fort Selden was far too dangerous.

I suppose that I had forgotten how stubborn Lucas could be. There was not enough time in which to argue with him that hot morning—and we were too busy rediscovering ourselves. Later I would have to face Monique with as much insouciance as she would have faced me after meeting a lover. Later, I would have to face Mark too, and this was easier than I imagined, with Monique as my incongruous ally.

"Tell him you are tired—that you stayed in bed all day with a headache. A woman who is *enceinte* has all kinds of excuses to use—if she needs them. *Pauvre* Rowena..." she smiled at me teasingly. "Did you imagine I would not understand? Every woman with a husband needs a lover as well. A pity Mark is not as tolerant as my John. But you—I think you are a *femme du monde,* just as I am."

Monique was far more practical than I could ever be. I began to know her better as we sat side by side in the canvas-topped buggy that we were to travel in until we reached San Antonio. As amoral as a cat, she enjoyed thinking that I was the same way too. Mark, it seemed, had confided in her one night, when they had both had too much to drink.

"Your story intrigued me, *p'tite*. And especially after I had met you. I suppose it is because you are English that you appear to be so cold—on the surface. No wonder you are so good at playing poker!" She laughed, and looked at me sideways. "One gets tired of being made love to before a mirror. All preliminaries, and not enough after. You see, I spent a weekend with your husband in San Francisco once, and I can understand that you might become bored, even if you are on your honeymoon still. Now Lucas—ah, he is still close to being a savage, *n'est-ce pas?* And a woman needs variety, just as men do."

I had learned, before we reached our destination that night, that Monique had worked "upstairs," as she put it, at the Silver Slipper in New Orleans, before she met her husband. That she was in the habit of going after any man she desired, just as a man might do with a woman. I think she enjoyed the chance to speak frankly to another woman, and I had schooled myself well enough not to let my jealousy show when she made it obvious that she still wanted Lucas.

"It is going to be a long, long journey, after all," she said slyly. "But you and I, if we help each other, can keep from becoming too bored!"

Forty-Five

So Monique made her plans, and I made mine. She was not the kind of woman that I could pity, for she meant to use me, just as I intended to use her sudden alliance. I think it amused her to help arrange matters so that I could spend some stolen moments with a lover, besides putting us both on the same footing. Each time I met her knowing eyes they seemed to say, "So we are not so very different after all, you and I—the English Lady and the girl from the Silver Slipper."

The heat shimmered like a golden haze over dusty plains, growing even more intolerable as the sun climbed higher. Mark, his fair, flushed face wearing a slightly sulky expression, rode beside us for part of the way, and it was not hard, in his presence, for me to feign illness.

"I thought you said yesterday that you were ready to travel—that you had quite got over your feelings of sickness in the morning."

"It's this heat, Mark! Of course Rowena is strong enough to travel. Let her have a good night's sleep tonight—she shall sleep with me in the wagon, honeymoon or not—and she'll be fine by morning."

Yes, I could not help but feel grateful towards Monique for the clever way in which she had maneuvered matters; and even when, a short time later, she began to flirt quite outrageously with Lucas, who had just ridden up, I gave a creditable impression of being completely unconcerned.

I had become so accustomed to the feeling of blank despair that I had carried with me for so long, like a stone over my heart, that I could not help being afraid that things were going too smoothly now.

We made camp a few miles east of San Antonio, just before sundown. A barren spot, I thought, in spite of a small clump of trees some distance away that concealed a small stream—one of the many tiny tributaries of the Rio Grande. And here, with Mark offering to stand guard for us, Monique and I washed some of the trail dust off our bodies.

I remember that only a faint light filtered down through the leaves of closely growing trees that leaned thirstily over the shallow water. Monique was quicker at undressing than I, removing all her clothes, flinging them carelessly on the bank.

"Come on, hurry—before it gets dark. Don't you want to get clean all over?"

Her light, teasing words held a hidden significance that was not lost on me.

Following Monique's example, I put my head under the water and came up with my hair dripping, clinging to my face and shoulders so that I had to push it out of the way. It was then that I looked up and saw Mark. He stood between the trees only a few feet away, watching. The flush I had learned to recognize and to dread was on his face, his eyes were glazed.

"So beautiful... the bright and the dark, together."

"No!" I cried out involuntarily. I think I took a step backward, almost slipping into the water.

"Be careful, cherie!" Monique put her arm around my waist; it was all I could do not to flinch away from her touch. No, I was not naive. I knew this had been planned—I even knew what he wanted.

"Since you've been too tired for my caresses, why don't you let Monique arouse you? Two lovely women—don't you want to touch her, Rowena? Haven't you ever wondered what it would be like?"

"Don't push her, Mark. It's too sudden, can't you see she's not ready yet? Perhaps later..."

I had grown so stiff that I was incapable of moving. I looked at Mark, and even my lips were stiff. "Please—go away."

He blinked his eyes, as if he was coming out of a trance. "Rowena…"

And again it was Monique who spoke, her tone both amused and tolerant.

"I told you, Mark. She is not ready. Give her time." Her arms slipped from about my waist, and she patted my cheek consolingly.

"There, cherie! But after all, he is your husband. There's nothing wrong with his watching you take a bath, is there? And me, I do not mind. I am proud of my body, and so should you be of yours."

When I looked back at the bank again, Mark had gone, and Monique, completely at ease, began to dry her hair, still naked.

After a while, because there was nothing else I could do, I followed her example.

"Never mind," Monique whispered to me later as we scrambled up the steep bank. "Tonight, you will be consoled, yes?" She shook her head as if torn between amusement and anger. "That Mark! I knew he would watch us, of course—didn't you? But to expect that we would put on an exhibition for him, like two *poules*… when such things happen between people it must be in their own time and setting, don't you think so?"

Again it was my desire not to appear ingenuous that made me shrug and agree that she was right. How much had Mark told her of me—and how much else had he implied?

That night, as we took our meal some distance apart from the rest of our party, Mark acted as though nothing had happened. He had discarded his usual dark jacket as a concession to the heat, but his white linen shirt was immaculate—his manner towards me as devoted and attentive as ever.

"I ordered some wine chilled in the stream—I thought you might care for some, my love." He filled our glasses and toasted us both. "To two beautiful and elegant women!" He put his arm around me, drawing me close so that I was forced to lean against him. "And my compliments to your chef,

Monique. It's hard to believe that he contrived such an excellent dinner over an open fire."

"Oh, Henri can cook anywhere—and over anything. He's a Cajun, from Louisiana." She smiled, and added, "Like myself."

I listened quietly while Monique and Mark began to discuss our 'arrangements' for the night and for the real journey which would begin tomorrow.

"I doubt if there's a chance of an Indian attack tonight, and especially with Fort Craig close by. But in any case the men will be taking turns as sentries. I have them posted around the entire perimeter of our camp tonight, so that you ladies will be able to get a good night's sleep without any apprehensions." Mark's manner sounded completely self-assured and almost arrogant, just as if he had been used to giving orders all his life. And again I found myself thinking how much like his uncle he seemed at times.

"You're not nervous, are you, my darling?" He smiled down at me, and under the shawl I had thrown about my shoulders to keep off the night chill his fingers began to caress my breast, slowly and intimately, as if he wished to remind me I was his possession now, and subject to his wishes. It was all I could do not to flinch away, but I could feel the color rise in my face, and Monique's amused look told me that she knew very well what was happening.

"Oh, you two lovebirds!" she said teasingly, and then, frowning inquiringly, "but where is my gladiator tonight? I was thinking that while you two are saying your goodnights he might take me for a short stroll before it's time for bed."

For an instant, I felt Mark's fingers press into my flesh, and then he gave a contemptuous laugh.

"Oh, you mean my wife's half-breed bodyguard? I sent him into San Antonio with some of the other men, to see what information they could pick up. I hope you don't mind, my love? He seemed glad to go—I've heard there's a cantina there that boasts of very bad liquor and extremely pretty girls." With hardly a change in his voice he went on softly,

"Rowena has such lovely breasts—they are perfectly formed, you know—and so quickly excited…"

"And now you will make me jealous—especially since you've seen to it that I'll have no cavalier to tell me the same thing tonight!" Monique pouted, and then shrugged. "But there will be other nights, I'm sure."

I kept my mind closed—my face blank. If I had looked into a mirror now I knew that my eyes would have showed no expression at all—they would be wide, staring, the eyes of the stranger I had seen so often in the mirror.

He held me against the wheel of the wagon in which Monique and I were to sleep afterwards, and his ardent kisses covered my face and bosom.

"How shy you are, Rowena! It never fails to surprise me. But we are in the shadows now, sweetheart, and no one can see us." I had to suffer his fingers against my skin, as they unfastened my gown and then roamed at will. His whispers, that told me of the nights we were to share later. I sensed that in some strange way he enjoyed the thought that only the wagon separated us from the campfire and the men who still sat around it, their voices carrying to us clearly.

Even when, finally, he let me go, and I climbed back into the wagon still shaking with reaction, his words kept echoing in my mind.

"You're mine, Rowena, mine at last. No one else shall have you, do you understand me?"

"So, you're back at last." Monique's voice sounded drowsy. "There's nothing like putting a man off, is there? It makes them all the more eager and appreciative later."

I felt, rather than saw, her stretch as she turned on her back.

"Wear your prettiest shift, Rowena. Or better still, wear nothing at all. I do not think it will take your husband long to fall asleep tonight. I had Henri mix a little sleeping draught with that last glass of wine."

I felt that my nerves had turned into taut wires that would snap far too easily. Monique appeared to be my friend and ally, but how far could I trust her? It amused her to play procuress at the moment, but I had already learned how her moods could change. "My gladiator," she had called Lucas. I had heard the story, on our journey here, of how she had deliberately arranged for two other men who also wanted her to become angry enough to fight him—and all because he had refused to demonstrate the Chinese style of unarmed combat he had learned.

"Joe and Magruder were both such big dirty-fighting Irishmen. But Lucas... ah, I have never seen anything so exciting in my life. Yes, John was right—it was like a Roman circus that day. I have never seen anything like it—so primitive, so fierce... and I made myself the prize..." I had not asked her if the victor had claimed his spoils or not. But now I wondered if Monique's love of intrigue and excitement might not lead her to betray us—merely to see what would happen.

Tonight, I deliberately feigned indifference.

"Well... perhaps he'll find those señoritas in San Antonio far more enticing than another man's wife..."

Turning my back on Monique, I stripped off my clothes, pulling a plain cotton chemise over my head. I heard her chuckle lazily.

"Oh, he'll be here. I do not think Lucas is as disinterested as he seems. Perhaps you are a challenge to him, for the moment."

"And for the moment, perhaps I find myself challenged by him," I answered perfunctorily, turning on my side.

I could not sleep, of course. I stayed awake, listening to the sounds of the camp die down, until there was only silence, broken by the faint sounds of coyotes howling in the distant mountains, and closer by, the stamping and whickering of horses. I even imagined that I could hear the angry noises that the fire made, as it subsided sullenly into itself, to leave only a glowing bed of coals.

Where was Mark—where was Lucas? Perhaps, learning of the guards that had been posted, he had decided that it was too risky to attempt a clandestine meeting with me.

I started when I felt a sudden draft of cold air fan my face. I should have remembered that Lucas could be as silent as an Apache when he wanted to be.

I snatched up a blanket to wrap around myself, and heard

Monique whisper, "Try to get back before it's light, you two. And enjoy yourselves!"

And then I found myself embarked on a journey that was to change my life forever, although I couldn't have known it at the time—and would not have turned back, even if I had. For I had learned, by then, that happiness must be paid for, and the price is often pain, but I was ready to risk anything for happiness with Lucas.

What I remember most about that night, though, is the feeling of relief I experienced when I realized that Lucas had come for me after all: the sensation of being swept up into his arms and carried, my face against the curve of his neck and shoulder. He knew, of course, where each of the guards were posted, and even with my weight in his arms he was able to travel on foot further and faster and more quietly than he would have done if he had set me down.

We came, at last, to the place where he had left the horses, and a pack mule.

"The ponies are desert-bred—an' that old mule once belonged to the army. It'll make for faster traveling, at the beginning, and we can pack supplies. Water an' food..." an infinitesimal pause and then he went on in the same expressionless voice, "an' a rifle and some extra ammunition."

We would be followed, of course. Mark might have my money, but he wanted me too. The runaway wife... and because of me, we would both be in danger—Lucas more so than I, for I felt that Mark would want to get me back alive.

I remember that all these thoughts ran through my mind as I stood there, straining my eyes to see the expression on Lucas's face. A premonitory shiver ran up my spine, and the blanket slipped from about my shoulders.

"Jesus, Ro!" His voice was half-amused, half-exasperated. "Seems like you're always half-naked when you start runnin' off somewhere. A good thing I thought to bring some clothes with me." It was as if, in silence, there had been an exchange of some kind between us. There was no more asking each other if we were sure, if we trusted. Words like 'do you love me? How much? Will you love me and take care of me always?' no longer needed to be said, for at some point, without words, we had progressed beyond such preliminaries, and everything had been decided.

I had crossed the Jornado del Muerto before, and that on foot, but this time there was an urgency that was missing before, when we had chosen our own pace.

We traveled on without stopping for the rest of that first night. The miles we put between ourselves and the camp, and the fact that Lucas knew this desolate country as well as any Apache, would be our only advantage during the long and grueling hours that lay ahead. I realized this as well as he did, and I vowed to myself that I would show myself to be as stoical as an Apache woman. Lucas would not find me a burden, slowing him down in our headlong flight.

For flight it was—and we were the hunted, although we were not certain until sometime in the morning of the second day we spent traveling across the desert.

My mind prefers to dwell on the time before that, when it seemed as if we were completely alone in a vast, primeval wasteland, and I felt like an explorer on a voyage of discovery. It was not only the desert that I began to understand better—it had its own life cycle, I found, and long ago the Apaches had discovered how to survive here, living only on what the desert itself provided. More important, now that the barriers were down between us, Lucas and I learned more about each other.

"I felt I knew you even before I had met you. Only then it was a story, something I might have read about. Mr. Bragg tried to warn me about the feud, but it did not seem real."

We had stopped to rest in the shade of some gigantic boulders, and he turned, running his finger from my temple to my jaw, as if he traced the outline of my face.

"You didn't seem quite real either. I couldn't believe that you'd come all the way out here, fresh from England, knowing nothing, caring nothing about any of us. An' when you did come, I didn't think you'd stay. Rowena—even your name sounded grand, and different."

"And when you met me?"

His laugh sounded free, and young and open—no longer the bitter laughter I remembered so well.

"I was of half a mind to rape you. Is that what you wanted to hear?"

"Lucas!"

He mimicked me teasingly, rolling his body over mine.

"Lucas! I kinda like the way you say my name, all cut off short at the end. If I'd known you were a witch-woman, I'd have kept my Henry rifle and let Julio buy you that night."

His lips, coming down hard over mine, muffled my angry retort, and after that, for a long time, we didn't talk at all.

During that first day and a half we didn't speak about Mark, and there was still some secret fear, buried deep in my mind, that kept Elena's name from my tongue. It was enough that Lucas and I were together. We would go to Fort Selden first, since he insisted upon it; and I would speak to Mr. Bragg and learn the truth that I had already begun to suspect. Because it had to be Mark all along. Only Mark was clever enough, devious enough, patient enough. Lucas had a temper, and he was capable of violence, but not of the kind of guile that Mark had shown. And after I had spoken to Mr. Bragg? I had already resolved that Todd had to be warned. As much as I disliked the man, he deserved that much at least. Mr. Bragg would see to it. And then—I didn't know, I had not asked where Lucas intended to take me. But my finest and most expensive jewels hung from my neck in the chamois leather bag that was stamped with my initials in gold leaf.

Lucas had only raised an eyebrow and said: "Your medicine pouch?" I found that he was more curious about me than what I wore.

And I looked like an Apache woman again, in the skirt and high-necked blouse that Lucas had found for me—moccasins on my feet and my hair braided and tucked under a wide-brimmed hat. What did it matter? I told myself that I could turn my back on civilization, on everything I had known before without a qualm, as long as Lucas continued to want me. This was the kind of peace I had been seeking in the *ashram* I had run away to after my grandfather had died. A small hut, open on four sides, in the mountains of India. A place where I had been told, gently, that it was necessary to detach oneself from worldly possessions in order to find the freedom of the mind I looked for. Even then I had not been sure what I wanted from life, or what I searched for. And then, on another mountaintop, I had found it and turned my back on it. It seemed to me now that I had been trying to escape from the fact that I was born a woman.

My concentration on all these things is an excuse to postpone the inevitable, of course. We had formed the habit of traveling fastest and farthest at night, and resting during the hottest part of the day. That particular morning, when we first discovered that we were being followed, and by whom, is one I would forget if I could. But my mind keeps returning to it.

That morning. After the coolness of the night, the renewed heat each day seemed even more unbearable. The sun reflected off the stones and the dust and even the boulders.

Last night we had traveled more slowly than we should have, for Lucas said safer to cross the dreaded malpais, or lava flow, in the daylight, and the land that lay ahead of us now was truly a desolation. A river of liquid fire, it must have been once, and now, hardened, the fire had turned to rock, twisted into weird shapes and formations, its surface a mass of knife-sharp pebbles and smaller rocks. And beyond, the towering bulk of the Fra Cristobal mountains. I saw Lucas look up at those jagged peaks, frowning.

"It'll be faster going around, but I ain't certain." I thought that he spoke almost to himself, eyes still squinted against the reflected sunlight. "I have a real funny feelin'…" in that moment he was all Apache, acting on his instincts alone.

He said sharply, when I made some movement, "Stay here, Ro. Undercover. I'm going up there to check on our back trail."

I had learned not to ask questions, so I did as I was told, while he took the field glasses and went easily up a slope formed by an ancient rockfall. I had dismounted, and I waited as quietly as I could, resting while I could, trying not to think that he had been gone a long time—almost too long.

I held the gun that Lucas had given me across my knees and tried to stay alert, but even so I did not hear his return until he was almost on top of me.

"Lucas! I had begun to—" and then, seeing his face I broke off sharply. "Something's wrong. Isn't it?"

"You're beginning to read me as easy as a book, seems like!" He hunkered down beside me, eyes narrow and bleak. "Listen, Ro—it's worse than I thought it might be, or maybe your husband's just a darn sight smarter than I had him figured, which makes me plain stupid, I guess."

"We're being followed? But you were expecting that we would be…"

"Not by them. Damn! It don't make sense, or else he was just plain lucky. Apache scouts—White Mountain, from the look of them. An' if anyone can pick up our back trail, they can." Lucas rolled a cigarette, something I had not seen him do since we had started out together, and each movement was almost vicious. "Your husband's with them," he added conversationally. "Didn't expect that either, but I guess he figures a woman like you is worth riding through hell for. An' that's somethin' I can hardly blame him for."

"Scouts? You mean army scouts?" My mind was still trying to register the shock of his first statement.

"Apache scouts," Lucas said patiently. "They work for the army, sure—General Crook had a bunch of them working for him. But it ain't normal to find them up this far north, an' as far as I'd heard, they didn't have any working out of Fort Craig. Only thing I can think of is that some of them were sent up here on some special mission—maybe there was trouble on the Warm Springs Reservation. An' if they were gettin' ready to head back at just about the time your husband rode into Fort Craig all wild-eyed an' upset."

I remembered Mark's boasting of all the important people he knew, and I could almost see it happening, just as Lucas had described.

"He'd have told them that you took me away by force," I said slowly. Yes—that was exactly what Mark's pride would have made him say. Unthinkable to have anyone know that his bride of only a few weeks would run away from him with a lover. "And he probably told them that these were part of the reason." I touched the pouch that hung so heavily between my breasts. "My jewels. I thought they might come in useful."

"Your—" and then the corner of Lucas' mouth twitched in an unwilling grin. "Trust a woman to think of everything."

Looking back, it seems incredible that we could sit there so calmly, talking of what might have happened, with our pursuers coming closer every minute. I think now that Lucas deliberately gave me time to digest the news he had just given me, and to become calm.

"Well—" he said at last, "I guess that leaves us with no choice. We head for the mountains." But he still frowned.

Forty-Six

꙳

IN HOW MANY WAYS IS IT POSSIBLE TO RELIVE HORROR? LUCAS told me later that he should have heeded the faint, uneasy feeling that persisted as we began the slow and tortuous ascent of the mountain that loomed almost directly in front of us. But he had me to worry about now, and the San Andres Mountains, where he would have preferred to hide out, if it came to that, lay across a stretch of comparatively flat desert that afforded little cover and no water at all. The Fra Cristobal Range was almost upon us, and if we could cross it, the Black Range, which Lucas called home, would soon loom up to the west.

There would be no time to rest today, except for very short periods. I knew that without having to be told. And our pursuers, although more than half a day's journey behind us, would not rest either. Neither of us, unfortunately, could have guessed that an even worse danger lay ahead.

It was late evening when it happened, and I was almost dropping from sheer weariness. I remember glancing upward, at serrated peaks that had turned crimson in the last fierce rays of the sun, the shadows dark between them. Here, in the narrow gorge up which we rode, following some centuries-old Indian trail, it was already gloomy and menacing-looking. Lucas was riding a little ahead of me when I thought I noticed a sudden rigidity in the way he held himself.

I kneed my horse forward, and without turning his head he

said quietly, "Don't stop to argue with me. Get off your horse, quickly. Slip off its right side and stay still." At the same time he brought up the rifle he held across his saddle horn with incredible speed.

Everything seemed to happen too fast—one detail merging into another. Rifle shots, deafening in the stillness, bouncing off rocky walls to assault the eardrums. I almost fell off the horse, barely remembering to hang onto its reins, and hardly felt the stinging, burning sensation in my arm as I did. A dark shape came tumbling down from some rocks to the left and above us, but I was too occupied with my plunging, rearing horse to even question what was happening yet.

I heard a wild, fearful yell, and a horse, riderless, went headlong up the canyon, drawing more fire from above. Suddenly, before I could scream his name, Lucas was beside me, pushing me back against the rocky wall so that I went stumbling to my knees. A shot ricocheted screamingly from just above my head. The horse I was still holding shuddered, and seemed to sink very slowly, folding into itself like a cardboard animal. And I was lying flat on my belly beside it, suddenly aware of a warm trickling down my arm, a gun thrust into my hand, while Lucas whispered urgently, "Lie just the way you are, an' don't move. But I want you to keep firing, up at those rocks. Take your time, but just keep firing often enough to keep him off guard. I'm goin' up there after him."

My mind was too numb with shock and disbelief for me to be able to utter a word, much less protest. It was suddenly darker than I had remembered only a few minutes earlier, and Lucas fired twice in quick succession, disappearing from my side while the acrid powersmoke still hung in the air.

I heard another, somehow perfunctory shot from somewhere above, and then, remembering what I had been told, my mind began to function mechanically. I must keep firing to give Lucas the cover he needed. I held the carbine balanced across the carcass of the dead horse, and keeping my head down, began to shoot, very carefully, at the place where I could see white puffs of smoke. I remember hoping that I wouldn't have to reload. Already my arm, where a bullet had grazed me, was beginning to feel numb. I tried not to wonder where Lucas was—if he had reached cover before one of those shots had found him. Thank God for the fact that darkness falls so quickly here in the mountains… and remember to keep firing, Rowena, you can bandage your arm later, it's only a scratch…

The carbine bucked against my shoulder, and the smell of burned powder was acrid in my nostrils. I tried to space out my shots, aiming carefully enough at that notch in the rocks above where I could see flashes so that he or they would think that Lucas was shooting. I had the advantage of being in deep shadow, but twice at least I heard bullets buzz within a few inches of my head like angry bees, ricocheting off the wall of rock at my back.

I hadn't yet had time to feel frightened. It was only when, from somewhere above me, I heard a choking scream of terror, suddenly cut off short, that I suddenly began to tremble with sheer reaction, hardly realizing I was sobbing aloud until I felt the wetness of tears on my dust-streaked cheeks. What had happened up there? Who had screamed? There was no more firing now, and the silence seemed to press heavily against my ears and was all the more unnerving because it had followed on that terrible scream.

I think I almost screamed myself when, after what seemed like hours, I heard Lucas call softly from somewhere up ahead.

"Ro? Hold your fire. It's all right now."

And then he was holding me in his arms; and I was clinging to him as if I had to reassure myself of the reality of his presence, trying to fight back the shameful sobs that threatened to choke me.

"It all happened so suddenly that I still can't believe— Lucas, no, I'm not crying because I am afraid! Only because— because I'm so happy you're back and you're safe!"

He tilted my chin up with one finger. "Who else but a fool woman would cry from gladness?" But in spite of the pretended harshness of his words, his voice was tender.

It was only later, after Lucas had washed out and bandaged the ugly bullet groove in my arm, that he told me what he had learned.

"There were only three of them, luckily for us. I got the first one, you saw him fall. An' wounded the second bad enough so he was barely breathin' by the time I got up there. But he talked before he died."

As Lucas continued to talk, my mind became filled with a different kind of horror.

"Mark Shannon's no fool, an' so far, he's been lucky as well. He sent some of his best men up ahead, while he followed our trail with Burris and Sonora an' three Apache scouts he met up with at Fort Craig. Seems like they'd been visiting relatives at Warm Springs, an' the colonel there suggested they might be glad to help track down an abducted wife—if he offered them enough money."

Lucas's voice was expressionless, but I drew my breath in sharply. "There's more," he said before I could speak. "Half the cavalry is out lookin' for us too, but your husband's given the men in his pay orders to stay one jump ahead of the soldiers—an' to shoot first."

It was dark by now. A clear, cool night with a scattering of stars spangling the velvety midnight blue of the sky. Lucas and I looked at each other, and he got up and began methodically to strip the horse of the gear it had carried. I think he wanted to give me time to digest the thought that Mark wanted me dead too.

And once I had realized this, I wondered why I hadn't seen it before. Not only did I know far too much about Mark's plans, but worse, from his point of view, I had betrayed and publicly humiliated him. So now he had begun to hate me, I was sure, with the same unrelenting single-mindedness with which he had once loved and pursued me.

I put some of these thoughts into words later, when Lucas and I had started off again, slowed down by the fact that the bullet wound in my arm had weakened me.

"An' there's your money too," he said quietly, and I was almost surprised that I had not thought of that first. The money, of course. If Mark couldn't have me he'd have enough wealth to buy him the power he craved. And it was my money he was offering as the price for my death!

The thought seemed unreal. Everything seemed unreal during those hours when we seemed to walk endlessly, both of us strangely calm. The horses were gone, and the mule would only slow us down now. I knew, without having to be told, how far sounds could carry in the clear desert air. The shots would have been heard, of course, and now they would all be racing to cut us off. I must have been slightly light-headed from loss of blood and nervous reaction, for I remember thinking with a kind of cynical amusement that it was a change to be the hunted instead of the hunter. Strange, that all those times in India, when I had gone on tiger shoots with my grandfather and his friend the maharajah, I had never once stopped to think of how the tiger might feel.

I tried to concentrate on putting one foot in front of the other as I had done once, so long ago. I carried only a water canteen, and as much beef jerky as I could carry, stuffed into the pocket of my shirt. Lucas carried a rifle, two handguns and bandoliers crossed over his chest with all the ammunition he could find. I took comfort from the fact that we were together.

Even if... I found myself thinking, *even if the worst happens, I wouldn't care. We love each other.* And yet, even the thought of death seemed unreal. I could not imagine dying, I would not think of the possibility that we might be trapped after all.

I cannot recall how many miles we had covered before we rested, and this, I know, only because of me. Every breath I took seemed to rasp in my throat, and in spite of the coldness of the night I was soaked with sweat. Lucas put his arm around my waist and made me lean against him, while my breathing slowed.

"Where..."

He seemed to know what I had been going to ask.

"Fort Thorn. It's the closest now, an' the one place they won't expect us to be headed for. An' you'll be safe. Make sure you get the colonel there to send off a telegraph to Fort Selden." Lucas cut himself off to swear softly and bitterly. "Damn! That's somethin' I didn't think off. The telegraph. That's how he got the cavalry from Fort McCrae out lookin' for us too. Now if only they sent a message on to Colonel Poynter at Selden…"

"You mean that he might come out to look for us as well? Oh, Lucas!"

"Ro, don't hope too hard. Fort Thorn's still the closest. But if I can get you there safely…"

"And you? I'm not going anywhere without you! And how do you know it'll be safe for you?"

"Stop arguin' and start walking." He wouldn't answer me, and soon afterward I had almost lost my breath again, and time seemed unending and meaningless.

It seemed impossible that the sun could be rising again, turning the sky faintly pink. Had we really walked all night?

In the shelter of a nest of boulders I waited, conscious only of the relief I felt to be resting again. Leaving one of the handguns with me, Lucas had taken the field glasses and disappeared. I think that in spite of all my resolutions I must have dozed off through sheer exhaustion, for the next thing I knew was that I was being shaken awake.

"Ro? Are you all right?"

"Yes." I heard myself mumble, and then I was being pulled to my feet again, and I had barely time to wonder why Lucas looked so strange when he told me, his husky voice dispassionate.

"I couldn't see how close or how far away your husband is. My guess is he an' his men are right behind us—in the mountains already. But you got friends comin' to the rescue from the direction of Fort Thorn. Todd Shannon… wonder what in hell he was doing there?"

"Todd?" I couldn't keep the dismay from my voice. I looked up at Lucas, and he was staring down at me through narrowed, thoughtful eyes.

"Lucas—what are we going to do?"

"Fort Thorn's still the safest place for you. An' for all that I hate Shannon's guts, I doubt if he'll shoot you down in cold blood. So—we're still goin' south."

"It's all my fault. If I hadn't…" Almost unwillingly, his arms went around me. "It's no one's fault. Or mine, for not seeing earlier that I'd come to need you. Rowena… crazy name. Crazy woman…"

I had the terrible, horrifying feeling that we were saying good-bye as our lips met. I suppose we wasted precious time as we held each other closely, bodies molding together. How can I remember now what thoughts went through my head, if, indeed, I was capable of coherent thought by then? What I remember most vividly is exactly what I do not care to recall—a nightmare without end.

I remember too that I would not do as I was told, so that what happened later was my fault, my guilt to bear.

The mountains were no longer a haven and a refuge but danger, because of the cover they gave to those who followed too closely behind us. And if I had not been along, as a liability and a burden, that Lucas could have escaped them all. But he had accepted me, and taken me as his woman, in much the same way that an Apache warrior would take a wife. And having taken the responsibility for me, Lucas also accepted the risks.

I want to digress here—if only to postpone the inevitable. I want to tell of what I did not know then but know now.

Todd Shannon had been supposed to meet Mr. Bragg at Fort Selden, but as luck would have it, he was still at Fort Thorn, being entertained in style by the commanding officer there, when the telegraph message had arrived.

And at Fort Selden, which was much further off, the same message had also been received, but with very different reactions from Colonel Poynter and Mr. Bragg. They had set out too, but several hours behind the rest. And closest of all was the man that I had chosen to be my husband—or who had chosen me. I had never felt closer to the Apache, whose very name meant "enemy," than I did then. I was with my lover, my man, and I would not leave him. I would die with him if I had to, but I would not be separated from him again.

I didn't try to explain these emotions to myself, nor to Lucas either. But when the shooting started, and we were in a place sheltered on three sides but not from behind, I disregarded Lucas's angry order that I should stay beside him until there was a lull in the firing, and he could send me down to whatever safety I could find with Todd Shannon and his Texan gunslingers.

I said very calmly, "If we're going to die, Lucas, then we'll die together. Did you really imagine that I would agree to leave you?"

I took one of the handguns and a cartridge belt, and crawled up the unprotected slope at our back. I suppose now, looking back, that the first man I encountered, hearing the shots, had not imagined he would meet anyone as he crept silently up from the rear. But he met me, and I shot him, without pausing to think, and all I remember now is the surprised look on his face as he tumbled backwards among the rocks.

"Ro—come back here, damn you!"

I heard Lucas call to me, and I must have turned my head. The next thing I knew an arm had clamped around my waist, and a voice, gloatingly triumphant, said: "Better throw down that gun, Cord, or she gets a hole blown in her pretty body." And at just about the same time I heard Mark's voice, with a cold ugliness to it I had never noticed before.

"The only chance I'll give you is if you'll turn around and shoot that gun at my uncle. Maybe I'll let Rowena live then…"

Almost without thinking I made myself go limp, kicking backwards only when I felt the man who held me let his grip slacken. I fell to the ground, hearing the now-familiar sound of a bullet wing past my ear and the man who had held me fell also, a grunting, burbling sound coming from his throat.

When I looked, Lucas was lying on his side, where he had flung himself, and he had just fired his gun. Mark was dead—and a second bullet, fired while I watched, made sure of it.

I was glad that I couldn't see his face. Mark had fallen some distance, and the sunlight reflected off his blond hair, turning crimson in the slowly widening pool of blood that seeped from under his prone body. The gun that had been in his hand had fallen somewhere as he fell; but at least his face was turned away from me…

I had time to notice all this as I ran back down the slope

toward Lucas, wondering why he stood so stiffly—but only until I saw all the rifles.

"You murderin' bitch!" Todd Shannon's harsh voice rang out. "I suppose this was what you planned on all along!"

Forty-Seven

※

"WHY WON'T YOU LISTEN TO ME? ARE YOU AFRAID OF hearing the truth, afraid that for once in your life you might be proven wrong?"

"Shut up, an' stop wastin' your breath. I wouldn't want you to miss it when that half-breed lover of yours starts screaming—if he don't choke to death first."

There was no mercy in Todd Shannon's voice—none in his face. And I think that I would have tried to kill him myself if he hadn't tied my wrists to his saddle horn.

"It was Mark, for God's sake, I can prove it! Todd—if you'll only take us to Fort Selden! I tell you that's where we were going. Mr. Bragg—"

"Bragg can tell me whatever it is was so damn urgent after I've done what I should have done a long time ago. Look up, missy. That sun's getting hotter now, ain't it? Hot enough to shrink that green rawhide real fast." I began to shudder weakly, and Shannon laughed. "Tell you what—I don't want him to die too fast—not before he's had a chance to suffer. So why don't you take that canteen an' go wet down that piece of hide he's got wrapped round his neck? Mebbe you two can exchange some last words—while he can still talk, that is!"

Had it been an hour yet? Or longer? I had begun to wish that Todd, in his blind anger, had killed me or even beaten me unconscious as he had threatened to at first. Instead he had contented himself with forcing me to stand roped to his saddle, to watch...

I couldn't believe my ears when I heard Todd describe—his voice tight with rage and grief, of sorrow as he looked down at his nephew—what he intended to do.

"You murdering, woman-stealing 'breed. Your dying ain't gonna be easy as his was, I promise you that. Because you're gonna die real slow, Apache fashion. Boys, you see that cactus down there, just about the height of a man? You know what to do. An' make sure you use green hides when you're tyin' him up."

I had never been closer to madness than I was then. I must have screamed. The next thing I remembered clearly was reeling backward, the side of my face throbbing where Todd had struck me.

"Only cure for a hysterical bitch," I heard him snarl, and then Lucas, who had remained impassive, up until then said: "Send her back. She's got nothing to do with the hate that's between us, Shannon, and you know it."

"Is that why you run off with her—an' had to kill my nephew to make her a widow?"

No—even now I don't want to remember. I don't want to and I must, Lucas and I. Each of us suffered a different form of agony, on that hot afternoon, when we all waited.

My hysteria and grief had turned into a kind of numbness. I had talked until my throat ached; trying to explain to Todd what Mark had really been like and what he had planned to do, but Todd would not listen. So now, when he handed me the canteen and untied my wrists, I said nothing more, merely looking at him with hatred in my eyes. He seemed to find this amusing.

"Go ahead! Mebbe you should rightly be the one who makes the choice whether your lover dies from strangulation or them cactus spines pushing their way into his flesh. Get up close an' watch him suffer—I want you to carry that picture with you for the rest of your days, you treacherous, murdering bitch!" I said nothing—I told myself that if Lucas could be silent and stoical, then I could too. And I promised myself that I would kill Todd Shannon. Yes—suddenly I could understand why blood feuds could come into being!

They had stripped off his shirt to crucify him against that giant cactus, and beads of sweat stood out on his brown torso. His arms were tied above his head, and blood from the rawhide that had already cut into his wrists slowly trickled down them.

His eyes were closed, and I could see the corded muscles stand out as he fought for breath against the strip of rawhide that was tightening around his neck. I couldn't help whispering his name. His eyes opened and looked into mine, but he didn't know me.

I remembered Todd Shannon's jeering voice when he had told me that I could make the choice—a slow, agonizing death, or one slightly less slow and almost as painful. God, God, how strong was I? How much could I stand? I heard a gasping noise escape from Lucas's throat, and I couldn't bear it. Not yet, I thought. Not like *this,* his life choked away with agonizing slowness while I was forced to watch.

I lifted the canteen, careful not to lean against his taut, strained body and poured most of the water on his neck, saturating the strip of hide that was strangling him with the life-giving fluid. Only a deferment...

I suddenly felt my arm seized and the canteen snatched away as Todd Shannon, coming up silently behind me, said harshly: "That's enough! I don't want to make it easy on him." He began to drag me with him, laughing when I made a grab for his gun.

"Still got some fight in you, huh? I must say I didn't figure on you having this much guts." And then, his voice hardening, "Did he tame you? Too bad he ain't gonna last long enough to see how tame you get when I'm through with you."

He held my wrists in a cruel grip, obviously enjoying my struggles to get free.

"Ever seen such a wildcat, boys? Half-Apache herself, seems like—it comes from associating too much with Injuns, I guess. We'll have to teach her how to act halfway civilized again, won't we?" One of his men laughed, but the others, all standing by their horses watching, seemed unusually silent. I think they were remembering that I was after all a white woman, and still half owner of the SD, now that Mark was dead. Perhaps they were thinking of what might happen afterward.

I was never to know exactly what they thought, for at that moment, putting his face close to mine, Todd growled: "Only regret I got is that Elena Kordes ain't here to watch her oldest cub die!" And the import of his words hit me like a blow, making my face stiffen and my struggles cease so suddenly that I fell against him.

"Lucas is not Elena's son!" I think I whispered the words at first, and then I almost screamed them at him. "He's not her son, do you hear me? Is that why you're killing him, to punish her?"

His eyes, like green glass, bored into my face as he shook me violently.

"What the hell kind of story you got thought up this time?"

"But it's true—it's true! Even my father knew it, at the end—it's all written down in his journals for you to read, unless you don't want to accept the truth!" I looked wildly into his face, bending over mine, his red blond hair bright in the sun, and suddenly I felt a strange, terrifying sense of premonition as the numbness in my mind seemed to fall away.

"He—he doesn't even look like her!" I gasped. "He doesn't look like any of them! His hair has blond streaks in it, and his eyes... Lucas was adopted by the Indians—he isn't one himself! He looks—he looks..."

I thought I was dreaming when another voice, familiar and yet unfamiliar, finished my half-formed sentence, and put the incredible, stupefying thought that had suddenly come to me into words.

"Strikes me that we've all been blind. He looks a lot like Alma did, Todd—and a little like you in the eyes an' jaw."

Todd flung me away from him and I would have fallen if a pair of blue-clad arms, appearing from nowhere, hadn't caught me. And I was looking into a face I hadn't expected to see again. Elmer Bragg's—looking grayer, and just as enigmatic as always.

But he wasn't looking at me, he was looking at Todd—and Todd had whirled around and gone to Lucas, and there was a knife in his hand.

Colonel Poynter, sitting stiffly on his horse, seemed frozen, as did Todd's own men and the troopers who had appeared so suddenly.

"Bragg—you've always been a nosy, interferin' bastard! But this time justice is going to be done. Any of you make a move, an' I'm goin' to slit his throat, you hear? That you dare use Alma's name…" Todd's voice was hoarse, I had never heard it shake with rage before. Even his eyes had a wild look to them.

Of us all, only Elmer Bragg seemed completely unconcerned. He shrugged.

"Always did think you were a blind, pig-headed fool, Todd Shannon. Just don't want to admit you're wrong, do you? Well—go ahead, if you must. Play right into her hands. It's what she always intended, you know. Brought the boy up to hate you—she hoped that one day he'd kill you or you'd kill him—and then she'd have the ultimate pleasure of telling you you'd killed your own son."

"You're lying! You're trying to trick me, all of you! Trying to save a murderer who just killed my own brother's son!"

"Just as your own brother's son planned to have you killed, and even—I'm sorry, Lady Rowena—made sure your own partner died conveniently of an overdose of his sleeping medicine? No, Todd—no one's lying except you, to yourself."

Todd had his fingers in Lucas's hair, the knife edge against his throat. But he hesitated. I remember praying, although I cannot remember the words I used.

Remarkably calm, remarkably controlled, Elmer Bragg's voice cut again through the silence that had seized us all.

"If he killed Mark, he'll have to stand trial for it in any case. And if they find him guilty of murder, he'll hang. But are you going to take the chance of never knowing, for sure? Or finding out the truth too late? Use your brains, man! Think! Did you ever find Alma's body—or the boy's? No—you were told that her brother had taken them both for burial. An old, dying man told you he saw your wife fall with an arrow through her breast, still carrying her child. That Alejandro ran forward with a cry of grief. Think, I tell you! What happened after that? Suppose the child lived? You remember when Elena came, to offer you your son—did you let her finish what she had begun to say? Didn't you jump to the conclusion that it was the child she was carrying that she was talking of? But how could she have known her child would be a son? And another thing I learned from the shaman of that particular band of Apaches, who is Elena's grandfather—why did Alejandro Kordes himself tell Lucas that he had been responsible for his mother's death? Evidence, Todd Shannon. This is what the shaman told Guy, and this was one of the reasons that Guy had to die before his appointed time—before he could warn both you and Lucas. And if you need more evidence I suggest that before you cut your son's throat you look in the medicine pouch he carries about his neck. In it you'll find the silver medal he was wearing when the Apaches took him, the medal you had given to his mother."

There was such a terrible uncertainty in Todd Shannon's eyes and in his voice when he spoke that I could almost feel sorry for him. But he remained unconvinced of the truth—or seemed to be. I think for the first time in his life Todd Shannon was afraid; that he had found himself backed into a corner, faced with one shocking fact after another, and didn't know what to do.

He cut open the medicine pouch, and the battered silver medal fell into the palm of his hand. He looked from the medal to the face of the son he had denied all his life, and had almost killed, and wept.

How dispassionately I can write all this down as I come near the end as I know it. I say "as I know it" because it is not yet finished, and I must wait, with uncertainty gnawing at my brain and only my writing to keep me busy and take my mind off what may be. The trial must be almost over now. There were reporters there, I was told, from as far east as Boston and as far west as San Francisco. And for that matter the whole of the Territory has. Everyone in Sante Fe heard or read the story. I have been praised and vilified—my pregnancy (which can no longer be hidden) and the parentage of my unborn child—the circumstances under which the man who had been my husband died—all these have been discussed and speculated upon for weeks now.

Todd is at the trial, and so is Mr. Bragg. I have been told that even Elena Kordes left her secluded valley to travel to Santa Fe. Lucas and I were quietly married by Colonel Poynter only a week before he had to leave for Santa Fe, but as usual, when I hear Elena's name, I am afraid. What will they say to each other? He told me only that they quarreled when he learned of the trick that she and Montoya had played. That he left the valley in anger. But that, as Montoya himself had reminded me before, was not the first time they had quarreled. "Always, he goes back…" Why do I have to think of that now?

Just as I wrote those words, I felt the stirring of my child within me. Mine—I am almost afraid to call it ours, in case… why must I think of that night with Ramon?

Lucas will not let me talk about it. "The child you have will be our child," he said firmly on the last occasion we were together, and stopped any further protesting on my part with his kiss.

Too many doubts, too many fears when he is not here, especially when Elena is where he is and I am not.

Marta comes in, looking worried—tears coming to her eyes when she sees them in mine. How easily I cry these days. It's my condition—God, I'm tired of hearing them all say that!

What will we do after the trial—if there is any afterward? Lucas will not speak to Todd—he told me, sullenly, that it isn't easy to get rid of a hate that has lived with you for years. But Todd has—hasn't he? Todd wants an heir, of course; he wants a son to inherit the SD, his kingdom that so many have lusted after. But Lucas won't have it. "After it's over—if they decide not to hang me after all—you can choose between staying here or coming with me—wherever I might feel like going." When Lucas said that, he sounded like the suspicious, hard-faced stranger I had first known. What am I going to do? Oh God, I'm so tired of journeying!

That is where I ended my journal yesterday, just before

I decided that in order to keep myself busy I must change everything around, dust and polish the furniture, sort out all my father's journals and papers.

Today—today I have found the missing codicil to his will, fallen behind the drawer where he kept his journals. This is what Mark looked for, knowing what was to be in it. Perhaps it is another one of the reasons why he put the overdose of laudanum in the half-empty bottle of brandy that always sat at my father's elbow... and paid a hired killer to murder Mr. Bragg in case he had found it. Just as he paid Pardee to kill Todd—

But instead, it was I, tugging angrily at the drawer which was stuck, who found the folded piece of paper that my father must have carelessly pushed into it—perhaps when he felt himself becoming sleepy.

I have read it over and over again. How much agony and heartbreak would have been saved if only I had discovered it earlier! My father had indeed learned from the shaman that Lucas was Todd Shannon's son—but he had been sworn to secrecy. I could easily guess who had spilled ink all over the vital parts of his journals, even tearing out some pages—leaving only those entries which sounded particularly damning where Lucas was concerned.

Of course he must be stopped from killing his own father! And there was Elena, whom my father still loved, in spite of all the disillusionment of learning what she had done.

He spent some time explaining his motives in changing his will—for my benefit, of course. He begged my understanding. For I was not to inherit half of the SD after all; but this share would go to my husband if I married either Lucas or Ramon—with a large bequest of money to the one I did not choose. If I decided to marry neither one, then my father's half of the ranch was to have been divided equally between Ramon and Lucas—his way of righting old wrongs, I supposed!

And Elena—yes, my father knew Elena! Perhaps he had tried to end what he saw happening between her and Lucas.

"To Elena Kordes, with my undying love and devotion—fifty thousand dollars and a reasonable income for life (I leave this to my daughter's discretion) on condition that she leave New Mexico Territory forever..." He had added—for her I think—"A jewel needs a setting worthy of it. I think you will take Europe by storm..."

There were other, smaller bequests. A deed to some fertile land in the mountains, for Julio—money to buy horses and cattle. Legacies to Jules and Marta, and one to his old friend Elmer Bragg.

So this—and I felt I had rediscovered him—was the man who had been my father! The man I was cheated of seeing, but who I have come to know through his writings as my children some day might want to know me.

I fold the codicil away and wait. It's time. Marta, standing by me, follows the direction of my eyes to the clock, and puts my half-frightened thoughts into words.

"The trial, it must be over now. Have faith, patrona. You will have your husband back soon." And the silver medal of St. Christopher that Todd once gave to Alma and Lucas gave to me hangs coldly between my breasts—as cold as the hours that must still pass before I will know.

EPILOGUE

SILVER CITY—1878

THEY MIGHT HAVE BEEN ANY PROSPEROUS RANCHER AND HIS wife—their blond-headed son sitting between them in the buckboard, hardly able to keep still for excitement. And yet the sight of them together, and in town, was always enough to set the gossips' tongues wagging.

Madame Fleur, standing talking with a customer in the doorway of her small establishment, gave a gasp as she saw them pass on their way to the State Depot.

"Oh my! Did you see them? And he, the other one, is already at the Depot!"

"You mean Mr. Shannon? Mr. Todd Shannon?" Mrs. Vickery, whose husband owned the local dry-goods store, echoed the plump milliner's gasp. "My goodness—" her voice dropped. "Is it true…?"

"All true, all of it! Ah, such a scandal it was! I remember her—she has not changed much. There was always an air of—such haughtiness in her. And she has it still."

"But—"

Madame Fleur was determined not to have her story spoiled by interruptions.

"All you have heard is the truth," she repeated. "One of my customers went all the way to Santa Fe for the trial, and she told me everything. They acquitted him in the end, and everyone expected him to come back and live on that ranch—but instead he went off into the mountains, and his

wife, she followed him. I've heard they own a small ranch
there, but just where nobody knows for sure. Of course…"
and Madame's voice became a whisper, "he was brought up
by the Indians, you know. And it is true that he has been in
prison, and was an outlaw."

It still felt strange to be riding into a town quite openly like
this. And towns, especially bustling, brawling ones like this,
always had given him a closed-in feeling.

Lucas met his wife's raised eyebrow and grimaced.

"I still ain't sure how in hell you talked me into this. I don't
even know these friends of yours."

"Corinne and Jack are nice people," Rowena said evenly.
And then, smiling faintly: "Besides I'm proud of you. What's
wrong with a woman wanting to show her husband off to
her friends?"

He looked into violet blue eyes, shadowed by the longest,
blackest lashes he had ever seen, and suddenly he was remembering her at other times—sitting up in bed, staring at him—
brown-faced, with braided hair, eyes spitting hate at him. And
still later, her warm, sweet lips; her voice calling his name…

It was the last thing he could remember before the pain,
and the terrible choking as the breath was slowly, very slowly
strangled in his throat. And after that there had been more,
worse pain, making him clamp his jaws together so that he
wouldn't cry out—and crying out anyway and finding his
voice only a whisper. And Rowena's tears falling on his face,
her voice saying his name again, over and over.

He couldn't talk above a whisper for weeks afterward.
Lucas thought later, wryly, that it was just as well, maybe.
Else he would have done a lot more arguing, and a lot more
swearing. And there had been times when he didn't want to
talk to anyone at all, not even to Rowena, until the day she
came storming into his room, calling him a selfish bastard,
reaching out to claw at him before he grabbed her wrists.

The colonel had married them two days later, and two
weeks after that they took him to Santa Fe to be tried for
murdering Mark Shannon.

It was strange, Lucas thought, how suddenly some little

thing could bring back a whole flood of memories, flashing across the mind in just the short time it took to maneuver the buckboard around a wagon that almost blocked off the street.

A hat in a window, and two women, turning to stare. The hat reminded him of Elena—and that thought was still pain, although it was fading. Elena, the dream every man has and clings to. Smiling, beckoning, giving just enough to make him keep wanting her, and in the strangest way, hating her at the same time. But Elena was over and gone forever, and in her place Ro, who was flesh rather than substance: strength and sweetness and giving. Following him into loneliness in the mountains and facing the ghosts in the house in the valley. Having her child there, with only him and an old midwife to help her—and in the end he'd sent the old woman out of the room and done everything that needed to be done himself, remembering everything she had told him before. Hot water, clean sheets, everything boiled that would touch her or the baby, even the knife.

He had been truly horrified. "My God, Ro! I didn't know what women have to go through, havin' a child." And she, smiling, eyes like purple bruises in the whiteness of her face, saying: "I didn't either. But I'd go through it again, if you will." And as a matter of fact he had felt almost faint himself, when it was all over, although he'd never have admitted it to her. But it had made his son all the more his—had brought Rowena closer, and sent the memory of Elena even further away.

Elena—strange that he should think of her today. Perhaps it was seeing the jail across the street that had brought her back as she had stood there in the dark, windowless cell under the courthouse in Sante Fe, filling it with her particular fragrance; the hat he bought her in El Paso worn forward over her forehead.

"So you couldn't do it after all! You let him almost kill you instead—and all because of that white-faced bitch you married. Married!" Her laughter had been sharp as thrown knives, making him wince. "Was it to give that brat she's carrying a name? Were you being noble, Lucas *mio*? Or has she really made you as weak as her own father was? I had to see for myself, you see."

"And now you have seen."

Her high heels clicked on the stone floor as she walked impatiently up and down before the barred door.

"Is that really your voice, sounding so cold? What are you trying to hide behind it?" And then, her voice dropping, becoming low and slightly husky: "Do you really think you will ever forget me? You'll get over her, just as you got over all the others—she'll begin to bore you."

"Elena—why are you really here?" Lucas's voice sounded tired.

"Why isn't she here? No—I came to see for myself. And I wanted to see his face. It will be the first time, you know, since..." For the first time he heard some agitation under the smooth, cutting voice, and meeting her eyes, wide and shining with a liquid brilliance, he could almost see her as she had been then. Young, and uncertain of herself. Lovely, even then.

"So he's decided to accept you as his son, has he? I am almost surprised..."

"Am I his son?"

Brows arching, she shrugged. "I suppose so. Alejandro said so. But it was only for Alma's sake, and because of his guilt, that he saved you. He could never love you, for all his talk of duty—but you knew that, didn't you? My poor Lucas, you were starved for love, until we found each other, you and I. And now—" again her laugh, "even now I think that you long to take me in your arms, isn't that right? There is that between us, *mio,* that no other woman can change or take away. Remember that."

Elena's exotic, perfumed presence in the courtroom had only added another touch of drama into an event that had already been magnified out of proportion. Lucas had not been able to decide if he felt more like an audience of one or a freak on exhibition. Certainly, he had seemed to be the only person who had not come out of curiosity, or to play some role to the hilt. There had been times when, either lying in his cell or sitting in that overcrowded room beside his attorney, he had begun to wonder who he was. All his life before there had been two things. His love for Elena and his hate for Todd Shannon. And then, suddenly, he was adrift. Not even knowing himself.

When he came back from Santa Fe to tell Ro what he planned to do he had half-expected that she would stay where she was and wait for him to come back to her later. This was what Elena would have done.

"I just don't know where I'm goin' yet. Or what I'm going to do or even who the hell I am an' what I want. Do you understand that, Ro? I've got to find my own answers—mine."

"All right, Lucas. When do you want to leave? I can be ready whenever you are."

He had argued with her, tried threatening, even tried picking a quarrel with her. But she had followed, gently rounding belly and all. And stayed.

"There they are."

Back in the present Lucas's sun-squinted eyes went from the laughing young man and woman who stood in front of the Depot, to the older man, towering above them both. He swore softly.

"I should have guessed."

"Well? Did you expect to keep avoiding him for the rest of our lives? What are you afraid of, Lucas?"

He looked at her angrily, fingers going up involuntarily to tug at the black neckerchief that concealed a thin, red scar, circling his neck.

"Sometimes, woman, you push me a mite too far!"

He was annoyed at her, and more annoyed at himself. Did Shannon really think he'd been avoiding him for some damnfool reason like that? Strange, that he could never think about the man as his father. Just Shannon. Hated name he refused to bear.

The boy was standing up, eyes big with excitement.

"Mama...?"

Rowena looked over his head at Lucas, and after a second in which his mouth stayed taut and hard she saw one corner lift in a sheepish grin.

He hitched the buggy to the rail, ducking under it, and

came around to lift her down. First her, and then the child. The usual knot of hangers-on had been enlarged, although all kept their distance, trying to keep their stares unobtrusive.

"Damned if that isn't Todd Shannon and his son—they say they ain't spoken a word to each other since the trial some years back."

"His wife—wasn't she engaged to the old man hisself once?"

It was bubbly Corinne, who hadn't changed at all since Rowena had seen her last, except to become slightly plump, who first broke the awkward silence that followed introductions.

"My goodness, Rowena, it's still hard for me to imagine that you're a mother. Uncle Todd, little Guy Ramon looks exactly like you. He has your eyes, except they're not so flinty-hard... oh!"

Jack Davidson reddened as Corinne clapped a hand before her mouth, eyes wide.

"Oh! Oh I'm sorry! I did promise I wouldn't let my tongue run away with me, didn't I? But it just seems so strange, somehow. Like something in a storybook, except that it couldn't have been very pleasant for all of you, could it? I mean..."

"Corinne!"

"Let her be, Jack. At least she speaks her feeling, which is more than most of us have learned to do."

Shannon's voice was gruff—he was looking from under his beetling brows at his grandson, who stared back curiously, apparently unafraid.

"You understand English, boy?"

"And Spanish and Apache," Rowena put in quickly. "Would you care to be introduced, Todd?"

She probably planned all this, Lucas was thinking, from behind his frowning expression. She, and that friend of hers. Damn all scheming women anyhow! He caught Corinne's half-laughing, half-apologetic glance at that moment, and smiled back at her unwillingly. She was honest, at any rate. Shannon had been right about that much.

"Well! Now that we've been introduced I may as well tell you that you don't look at all as I used to imagine." Corinne tilted her head consideringly. "You remind me of—yes, of Heathcliff, in Miss Bronte's book, *Wuthering Heights*. Although, of course, Rowena has far too much character to be a meek and mild Cathy, don't you think so?"

"I have never met a woman who talked as much and from whom I actually felt I needed rescuing!" Lucas said wrathfully later.

"Did you really think so? I thought you liked Corinne. The way you kept staring at her with that look on your face...!"

He looked down rather grimly at Rowena, who merely smiled back at him demurely.

"She fascinated me, all right! And you—suppose you tell me what the look on your face means, ma'am? Are you satisfied with your trickery? My God, I never thought I'd actually feel relieved to have him suggest we go someplace more private to get acquainted. And I'm warning you right now, I don't aim to sit by her all through dinner either! How in hell did I let you talk me into this?"

"Are you really ready to listen? I think it's because, like me, you suddenly saw Todd today as—a lonely old man. And because he is Guy's grandfather, and you and I don't have the right to deprive him of that very special relationship. Oh, Lucas!" Rowena turned suddenly, putting her arms around him, and the movement of her body against his was supple, and still exciting. "Think of all the years that were wasted in feuds and misunderstandings! And think of what your adopted grandfather, the shaman, said once, about seeing both sides of a coin. Is there any reason why, now that time has passed, you and Todd cannot greet each other in a civilized fashion?" Sensing his indecision, she added slyly: "When Montoya brought Luz and their children to visit us this spring you were perfectly willing to forget everything he'd done to try and keep us apart!"

"Didn't notice that you acted too mad, either."

"Well?"

"If you don't want to get seduced before dinner and keep everyone waiting, I guess we'd better go on downstairs." A bar of crimson light, like a sullen parting shot from the setting sun, pushed its way through the partially drawn drapes of the hotel window, making the lamplight seem suddenly insignificant.

They looked into each other's faces; searching, renewing, re-evaluating. It was as if, without words, Rowena was saying: "I love you, and I have chosen you. There is room in our lives for other people too, now that we are sure of each other."

In the corridor outside a child laughed, and Lucas lifted her chin up with his finger, brushing his lips gently against hers.

"There, ma'am. That's to hold you until later. Let's go rescue that boy of ours and get him to bed before he's spoiled rotten with all the attention he's been getting."

The distant ghosts receded, and were gone. Arm in arm, laughing, they left the room.

About the Author

ॐ

New York Times bestselling author Rosemary Rogers has been called the "reigning queen of romance," "the princess of passion," and "the bestselling novelist in America," with over 60 million copies of her books sold. She has written twenty-four bestselling romances, nineteen of which have been *New York Times* bestsellers. She was born in Ceylon (now Sri Lanka).

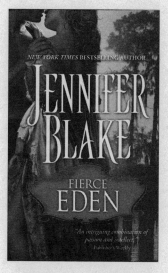

Fierce Eden

Jennifer Blake

⚬⚬

SHE WAS LIVING IN FEAR...

Beautiful, young widow Elise Laffont embraces her freedom during the daylight hours, running the farm she loves so dearly, but the night brings with it painful reminders of the torment she endured at the hands of her abusive husband. Fate may have taken her husband, but it hasn't erased the scars he left, and Elise wonders if she will ever be able to bear the touch of a man again.

HE WAS A MAN TORN BY DESIRE...

From the moment he laid eyes on the beautiful widow, Reynaud Chevalier wanted her. When disaster offers him the chance to claim her as his own, Reynaud seizes the opportunity to bind Elise to him, unaware that behind her determined bravado lays a heart shattered by the past.

"Blake's style is as steamy as a still July night on the bayou, as overwhelmingly hot as Cajun spice." —Chicago Tribune

978-1-4022-3848-2 ~ $9.99 U.S./$11.99 CAN

Uncertain Magic

Laura Kinsale

New York Times bestselling author

∽

A MAN DAMNED BY SUSPICION AND INNUENDO...

Dreadful rumors swirl around the impoverished Irish lord known as "The Devil Earl." But Faelan Savigar hides a dark secret, for even he doesn't know what dark deeds he may be capable of.

Roderica Delamore, cursed by the gift of "sight," fears no man will ever want a wife who can read his every thought and emotion, until she encounters Faelan. Roddy becomes determined to save Faelan from his terrifying and mysterious ailment, but will their love end up saving him... or destroying her?

"Laura Kinsale creates magic." —Lisa Kleypas, *New York Times* bestselling author of *Seduce me at Sunrise*

"Magic and beauty flow from Laura Kinsale's pen." —*RT Book Reviews*

978-1-4022-3702-7 ~ $9.99 U.S./$11.99 CAN

My Love, My Enemy
Jan Cox Speas

∽

A PASSION FOR ADVENTURE...

Beautiful, naïve, and impulsive, Page Bradley inadvertently rescues English spy Lord Hazard in Baltimore during the tumultuous War of 1812. Now she must put herself at the mercy of her enemy.

AN APTITUDE FOR DECEPTION...

Lord Hazard is no stranger to the atrocities of war, but he never imagined the beauty that could come of it until he meets the fiery and irresistible Page. Now he finds himself questioning every loyalty he's ever felt for King and Country.

Amidst the turmoil of war and the peril of the high seas, these two sworn enemies are destined to discover that denying love may be worse than treason.

"Irresistible... This novel of high romance moves on wings from Annapolis to Bermuda to London and back to Washington..." —**Library Journal**

"Appealing and refreshing... a lovely romance told in a delightful swashbuckling manner." —**Memphis Sunday Commercial Appeal**

978-1-4022-5577-9 ~ $9.99 U.S./$11.99 CAN

Legacy
Jeanette Baker

A DREAM COME TRUE...

Christina Murray is elated to inherit her family's ancestral Scottish home, especially when she meets her gorgeous neighbor Ian Douglas, full of Scottish charm and intriguing knowledge of the house's secrets...

TURNS INTO A NIGHTMARE...

But at night, Christina is visited by haunting dreams from ghostly ancestors who lead her through the terrifying labyrinth of her family's bloody history. As much as Ian longs to help her, there's nothing he can do to alleviate Christina's terrors...

Clinging to her sanity, and to her newfound love for Ian, Christina discovers the family curse that threatens to bring them both to a terrifying end...

"A vibrant tapestry pulsating with the fiery code and honor of the Highlands."
—*RT Book Reviews*

978-1-4022-5583-0 ~ $9.99 U.S./$11.99 CAN